STEPHEN JONES is the winner of two World Fantasy Awards, two Horror Writers Association Bram Stoker Awards and The International Horror Critics Guild Award as well as being a ten-time recipient of the British Fantasy Award and a Hugo Award nominee. A full-time columnist, television producer/director and genre movie publicist and consultant (the first three *Hellraiser* movies, *Night Life, Nightbreed, Split Second, Mind Ripper, Last Gasp* etc.), he is the co-editor of *Horror: 100 Best Books, The Best Horror from Fantasy Tales, Gaslight & Ghosts, Now We Are Sick, H.P. Lovecraft's Book of Horror, The Anthology of Fantasy & the Supernatural* and the *Best New Horror, Dark Terrors, Dark Voices* and *Fantasy Tales* series. He has written *The Illustrated Vampire Movie Guide, The Illustrated Dinosaur Movie Guide, The Illustrated Frankenstein Movie Guide* and *The Illustrated Werewolf Movie Guide,* and compiled *The Mammoth Book of Terror, The Mammoth Book of Vampires, The Mammoth Book of Zombies, The Mammoth Book of Werewolves, The Mammoth Book of Frankenstein, The Mammoth Book of Dracula, Shadows Over Innsmouth, Dancing With the Dark, Exorcisms and Ecstasies* by Karl Edward Wagner, *Looking for Something to Suck: The Vampire Stories of R. Chetwynd-Hayes, James Herbert: By Horror Haunted, Clive Barker's A–Z of Horror, Clive Barker's Shadows in Eden, Clive Barker's The Nightbreed Chronicles* and *The Hellraiser Chronicles.*

THE MAMMOTH BOOK OF

Dracula

Vampire Tales for the New Millennium

Edited by
STEPHEN JONES

Carroll & Graf Publishers, Inc.
NEW YORK

Carroll & Graf Publishers, Inc.
260 Fifth Avenue
New York
NY 10001

First published in the UK by Robinson Publishing 1997

First Carroll & Graf edition 1997

ISBN 0–7867–0428–4

Printed and bound in the United Kingdom
10 9 8 7 6 5 4 3 2 1

CONTENTS

CONTENTS

ACKNOWLEDGEMENTS

Special thanks to Sylvia Starshine, Mandy Slater and Kim Newman for all their help and support.

'Introduction: I Bid You Welcome' copyright © 1997 by Stephen Jones.

'Foreword: Great Uncle Bram and Vampires' copyright © 1997 by Daniel Farson.

'Dracula: or The Un-Dead: Prologue' by Bram Stoker. Reprinted from the Lord Chamberlain's Play List 1897, courtesy of The British Library Department of Manuscripts and Sylvia Starshine.

'Dracula's Library' copyright © 1997 by Christopher Fowler.

'The Heart of Count Dracula, Descendant of Attila, Scourge of God' copyright © 1985 by Thomas Ligotti. Originally published in *Songs of a Dead Dreamer*. Reprinted by permission of the author.

'Daddy's Little Girl' copyright © 1997 by Mandy Slater.

'Conversion' copyright © 1977 by Ramsey Campbell. Originally published in *The Rivals of Dracula*. Reprinted by permission of the author.

'The Devil is Not Mocked' copyright © 1943 by Street and Smith Publications, Inc. Originally published in *Unknown Worlds*, June © 1943. Reprinted by permission of the author's estate.

'Teaserama' copyright © 1997 by Nancy Kilpatrick.

'Blood Freak' copyright © 1997 by Nancy Holder.

'Zack Phalanx *is* Vlad the Impaler' copyright © 1977 by Brian Lumley. Originally published in *Weirdbook* No.11, © 1977. Reprinted by permission of the author and the author's agent.

'When Greek Meets Greek' copyright © 1997 by Basil Copper.

'Coppola's Dracula' copyright © 1997 by Kim Newman.

'The Second Time Around' copyright © 1997 by Hugh B. Cave.

'Endangered Species' copyright © 1997 by Brian Mooney.

'Melancholia' copyright © 1997 by Roberta Lannes.

'Children of the Long Night' copyright © 1997 by Lisa Morton.

This one is for the Chicago gang:
Sara and Randy, Lou and Sue,
Bob and Nancy, Jay, and Frank
– fangs for the memories!

But first on earth, as Vampyre sent,
Thy corpse shall from its tomb be rent;
Then ghastly haunt thy native place,
And suck the blood of all thy race;
There from thy daughter, sister, wife,
At midnight drain the stream of life;
Yet loathe the banquet, which perforce
Must feed thy livid, living corpse,
Thy victims, ere they yet expire,
Shall know the demon for their sire;
As cursing thee, thou cursing them,
Thy flowers are withered on the stem.

– from *The Giaour* (1813)
by Lord Byron

Introduction

I BID YOU WELCOME

Do we really need another collection of vampire stories? That is the question I had to ask myself before compiling this present volume. In the past few years, the bookshelves have been groaning under the weight of new vampire fiction. There have been countless novels, collections and anthologies published about every conceivable permutation of the Undead and, truth to tell, most of it has been quickly forgettable. However, as we approach the new millennium, vampires have never been more popular, almost becoming a sub-genre in themselves. As my colleague Kim Newman has cleverly remarked elsewhere, vampire fiction has become the *Star Trek* of horror.

When my publisher and I began discussing a follow-up volume to our very successful 1992 anthology, *The Mammoth Book of Vampires*, we agreed that we didn't want to produce just a second collection of stories. So after careful deliberation, I decided that it might be interesting to see if I could compile a loosely-constructed, "fictionalized history" of the most memorable vampire of them all – Count Dracula. You hold the result in your hands.

Of all the fictional vampires ever created, Dracula continues to endure a century after he was created by Bram (Abraham) Stoker. Born in Dublin, Ireland, in 1847, Stoker was a sickly child until he discovered books at around school age. A qualified barrister, his first love was always the theatre, and while working as a civil servant he was introduced to the greatest actor-producer of his time, Henry Irving. The two became friends, and in December 1878 Stoker assumed the acting managership of Irving's Royal Lyceum Theatre in London, much to the dismay of his family. The same year Stoker married Oscar Wilde's ex-sweetheart, the Irish-born Florence Anne Lemon Balcombe (whom George du Maurier, author of *Trilby*, described as one of the three most beautiful women he had ever seen).

Although he had written the occasional short story, it was during this period that Stoker really began to concentrate on his fiction. Possibly inspired by J. Sheridan Le Fanu's vampire novella, 'Carmilla' (1871), he began working on a novel manuscript entitled *The Un-Dead*. It was finally published in an edition of 3,000 copies as *Dracula* in June 1897, the year of Queen Victoria's Diamond Jubilee. The book received mixed reviews ("appalling in its gloomy fascination") and although it sold steadily, Stoker never earned much money from it. Unfortunately, Stoker's subsequent novels – *The Mystery of the Sea*, *The Jewel of the Seven Stars*, *The Lady of the Shroud* and *The Lair of the White Worm* – failed to achieve even comparable success.

The author loosely based his character on the mid-fifteenth century Wallachian prince, Vlad Tepes IV, known as Vlad the Impaler because of his predilection for impaling live victims on sharpened wooden stakes while he dined. For the Count's physical form, Stoker took his hero and employer Henry Irving as his inspiration.

Following Irving's death in 1905, Stoker suffered a stroke which left him weakened and partially-sighted for the rest of his life. Also suffering from a degenerative kidney disease, possibly complicated by tertiary syphilis, Bram Stoker died on April 20th, 1912, the same week that the Titantic hit an iceberg and sank in the Atlantic.

The following year, Florence Stoker offered her husband's working notes for *Dracula* at auction. They were sold for little more than two pounds. In 1914 she published *Dracula's Guest*, a collection of her husband's short stories, including the self-contained chapter of the title, which was originally omitted from Stoker's novel because of length.

Since its author's death, *Dracula* has gone on to influence countless imitators and formed the basis of a worldwide entertainment industry created around the character.

Dracula has been immortalized in plays, movies and on television by Max Schreck, Raymond Huntley, Bela Lugosi, John Carradine, Christopher Lee, Jack Palance, Louis Jourdan, Frank Langella and numerous other, less memorable, actors. In fiction he has met everyone from Sherlock Holmes to Batman. He has appeared in cartoons and comic books, and his image has been used to sell everything from jigsaw puzzles to breakfast cereals. Like Mickey Mouse, James Dean and Marilyn Monroe, Dracula has become a twentieth century icon. He is also very big business.

In his excellent 1990 study *Hollywood Gothic*, author David Skal has pointed out that the "appeal of Dracula is decidedly ambiguous. Most monsters take and trample. Dracula alone seduces, courting before he kills. Unlike other monsters, he is not always recognizable as such. Dracula looks too much like one of us." In the literature of the vampire, the monster could be someone we know or, even worse, *ourselves*.

As with my other *Mammoth* volumes, I have collected together several reprints which are particular favourites of mine, plus original stories by established writers and a few newer names. I believe that only in this way can the horror genre, particularly the anthology, hope to survive and grow.

I trust you will enjoy this volume as it asks how the King of the Vampires would adapt to the social and technological changes that are already shaping the beginning of the twenty-first century. Is it possible that the Count's undead condition could be cured by modern medicine? How would the mythology perpetuated by literature and movies have affected the existence of a real bloodsucker? And what if Dracula found himself ruler of a world controlled by vampires? Or perhaps poverty, crime, political instability and ecological disaster will result in the Count's *final* destruction . . . ?

Of course you can dip in and out of the book if you prefer – as the reader that is your prerogative. However, I have designed this volume to be read from the beginning through to the end, thereby creating an historical chronicle of Count Dracula, stretching from the Victorian era through to the new millennium and beyond. As an added bonus, I have also included the long-lost Prologue to a theatrical version of *Dracula* by the Count's original creator, Bram Stoker, presented here for the very first time since its only performance in 1897.

So, I bid you welcome to this special centenary celebration of the World's Greatest Vampire. Enter freely and of your own will. Come freely, go safely, and leave some of the happiness you bring! But most of all, have fun . . .

Stephen Jones
London, 1997

Foreword

Great Uncle Bram and Vampires

One of my proudest boasts is my relationship to Bram Stoker. The more I have researched his life, the closer I feel to this strange man who was taken for granted in his lifetime and receives begrudging recognition even now, though the centenary of Dracula's publication in 1897 and the 150th anniversary of his birth should bring him belated honour, especially in Dublin where he was born.

As Stoker's great-nephew I have been asked to a Dracula convention in Los Angeles, a celebration in Dublin of the Bram Stoker Society, and have signed a hundred envelopes for 'first day covers' of the horror stamps to be issued by the Royal Mail.

Though I bask vicariously in the fame of Dracula I realize that Stoker himself remains the least known author of one of the best known books ever written. People ask me constantly what sort of a man he was and why was he obsessed with the occult, and vampires in particular. It's a rum story.

When he was a child Bram was stricken by an illness which has never been explained satisfactorily. Spending several years virtually confined to his room, unable to stand upright, his mother did her best to keep him amused with nightly bed-time stories which centred around the cholera epidemic that reached Sligo in 1832. Her family barricaded themselves inside their fumigated house while neighbours were carried away, looters robbed their empty homes, and coffin-makers battered on doors touting for custom. My grandmother, Enid Stoker, remembered her mother-in-law, Charlotte, as a formidable woman who saw a hand creeping through a skylight on one of the last terrible days. Seizing an axe she hacked it off with one tremendous blow – she was just twenty-four years old. Even if this family legend became distorted over the years it shows how her family stood in awe of her, and she always demanded the highest standards from her sons, yet her bedtime stories could hardly have been less suitable for a sensitive child. Either she encouraged Bram's fascination with the macabre or she appealed to an instinct already there. Bram was greedy for horror and she supplied it. Crucially, she gave first-hand examples of premature burial, the most likely and logical explanation for vampirism.

One incident concerned a Sergeant Callan who died from cholera and was so tall they needed to break his legs to fit him into the coffin. At the first blow he rose, shrieking, and presumably walked with a slight limp afterwards. Another significant story described a man who brought his wife to the hospital, to be told when he returned that she was dead. In the panic to overcome the epidemic, corpses were being thrown into trenches covered with lime, as many as thirty at a time. Searching for his wife to give her a private burial, he glimpsed her red handkerchief under a pile of corpses and found she was still alive – 'He carried her home and she lived for many years.' When you consider that in the 1990s there have been at least two cases of women who were certified as dead and saved just in time, it is easy to imagine how rumours spread in Transylvania where peasants were superstitious and there was no electric light to dispel the shadows. Dennis Wheatley explained to me that beggars were so destitute they broke into mausoleums emerging at night to steal for food. If they were seen they could have been mistaken for the Undead. Ignorance explains a lot about vampires.

In 1732 a deputation was sent from Belgrade to investigate reports of a vampire who was attacking his family in a remote village, draining three nieces and a nephew of their blood. The officials opened the coffin to find a man who might have been asleep, his hair and nails exceptionally long, his eyes half-open. When they pierced his heart with the obligatory iron stake white fluid and blood gushed out, though they out off his head and buried the remains to make sure. Other corpses looked healthy, though puffed up like balloons, only to decompose when pierced.

In most of these cases, if not all of them, people were ignorant of the many changes affecting bodies differently after death, and mistakes were commonplace. As recently as 1974 I spoke to a handsome gipsy woman in the valley of Curtea de Arges in Romania, who remembered that when they dressed her dead father they found the body was soft. The frightened villagers plunged a wooden stake through his heart unaware that the stiffness of rigor mortis is a temporary state.

Equally there have been so many cases of people buried alive that the writer Wilkie Collins famously instructed his family to take every precaution. Another man fixed up an eleborate series of bells inside his prospective coffin so he could ring for help if he woke up to find he was incarcerated.

The impression made on Bram by his mother's alarming reminiscences can be clearly seen in his own equally unsuitable collection of stories written for his son Noel and other children, *Under the Sunset.* One story told of an orphan girl who warns the town of impending plague – 'Presently she saw far off the great shadowy Giant Plague moving away to the border of the Land,' echoing his mother's relief when her family opened their doors – 'There we found the streets grass-grown and five-eights of the population dead. We had great reason to thank God who had spared us.'

Bram had been blooded. His illness was cured miraculously, he grew into a huge red-bearded athlete by the time he entered Trinity College, Dublin. It is unwise to attach labels when you do not know the truth, but it does seem that Bram Stoker was a split personality. On the one hand he was brave and bluff, diving into the Thames to save a drowning man who was attempting to commit suicide. Dragging the soaking man into the hall of his home nearby, he received no thanks from the man, and a rebuke from his fastidious wife, but was awarded the Royal Humane Society's medal for gallantry. When two 'ruffians' tried to rob him in Edinburgh, he knocked them down and delivered them to the nearest police station. Conversely, he was a man of unusual sensitivity, the champion of Walt Whitman whose work was condemned by the Trinity College hearties as 'morally offensive'. Bram's affinity with Whitman was passionate; reading the poems under a tree, Bram recorded – 'From that hour I became a lover of Walt Whitman' and wrote him a long letter, never posted, in which he declared a sympathy for everything the American poet stood for, including the special rapport between men. In this, I believe that Bram reflected an ideal that was spiritual, far removed from any physical relationship. My father, Negley Farson, felt the same way about Whitman, the same intense love for the masculinity of the poems. And the ease with which Bram described his infatuation shows that he thought there was nothing to conceal.

Obedient to the wishes of his parents, Bram followed his father Abraham, after whom he was named, into the Irish Civil Service. Finding the need to escape from the clerical tedium, he found relief in the novella *Carmilla*, written by his fellow Dubliner, Sheridan Le Fanu, about a Styrian Countess who was really a vampire, and contributed a horror story of his own to the *Shamrock* magazine about a character called the Phantom Fiend. However, the turning point in Stoker's life came with his job an unpaid critic for the Dublin *Daily Mail* which led to an invitation to dinner from the young, mesmeric actor Henry Irving, who was flattered by the praise for his performance as Hamlet – 'In his fits of passion there is a realism that no one but a genius can ever effect.' With none of today's hype, it is hard to conceive of the impact Irving made, which spread by word of mouth, and made him as idolized as any contemporary pop star but with greater justification. After the dinner in Irving's private rooms, the actor recited the melodramatic poem *The Dream of Eugene Aram* with such power that Bram was close to hysterics while Irving staggered into his bedroom emerging with a photograph signed 'My dear friend Stoker. God Bless You! God Bless you! Henry Irving, Dublin, December 3 1876'. Bram had found his new hero. Years later he recorded, 'In those moments of our mutual emotion, he too had found a friend and knew it. Soul had looked into soul! From that hour began a friendship as profound, as close, as lasting as can be between two men.'

Today such a friendship would be highly suspect and fodder for the tabloids, yet I remain convinced that the two men would have been appalled by any hint of homosexuality. Victorian males enjoyed relationships which were as close if not closer than with their wives – Charles Dickens and Wilkie Collins were another example. There is a nice irony here: around this time Bram became engaged to my great-aunt Florence Balcombe, whose former suitor was Oscar Wilde. Though possibly in love with the idea of love, Oscar's admiration seems to have been genuine: 'We telegraph each other twice a day and do all the foolish things that wise lovers do.' He drew an excellent portrait of her, revealing an unexpected talent, and gave her a small gold cross for Christmas, confiding to a friend that he was bringing 'an exquisitely pretty girl. She is just seventeen with the most perfectly beautiful face I ever saw and not a sixpence of money.' Why did she reject Oscar from Bram three years later? By then she was twenty, Oscar twenty-four, and Bram thirty-one (Irving was forty-one). Perhaps she preferred the security of the older man to the flamboyant poseur, but there was a steely personality behind her porcelaine facade and when Oscar asked for the return of his gold cross, she refused. Oscar wrote indignantly: 'Worthless though that trinket be, it serves as a memory of two sweet years – the sweetest of all the years of my life. Though you have not thought it worthwhile to let me know of your marriage, still I shall always remember you at prayer.' Bram married Florence on 4 December 1878. Five days later they sailed for England to join Henry Irving who had bought the Lyceum Theatre and asked Bram to be his acting manager. Bram had accepted instantly, to the dismay of his mother. When she learnt he had forfeited his pension, she made the chilling remark – 'I see you have become the manager of a strolling player.' But Bram knew he was embarking on one of the greatest theatrical partnerships in history.

It is claimed that Irving was the inspiration for Count Dracula. One memorable night in Paris when I was twenty-one, Orson Welles told me that when he was in Dublin at much the same age he met Stoker who confided 'an extraordinary story – that he had written a play about a vampire especially for his friend Henry Irving, who threw it aside contemptuously. But, you know' – Orson's voice deepened dramatically – 'Stoker had his revenge. He turned the play into a novel and the description of the Count is *identical* to Irving!'

A nice story: only two things wrong with it – Stoker died three years before Orson Welles was born; and the Count in the book has a big white moustache. Yet there are elements of truth in the association of Irving with Count Dracula. The sardonic actor was an honorary vampire himself, draining the life out of those around him, Stoker in particular. The actress Ellen Terry noted: 'For years Irving has accepted favours, obligations through Bram Stoker. Never will he acknowledge them himself.' He took Stoker for granted and frequently made fun of him in front of the company though Stoker was loyalty personified. Yet few actors could have played Count Dracula to such melodramatic effect, and a portrait of Irving exists which fits our concept of the vampire exactly, even though it is different from the book. *But* – and I feel this passionately – it is too glib, as 'experts' do so easily today, to state categorically that Count Dracula was based on Irving. This denies Stoker's vivid imagination which made Dracula his masterpiece, and though the actor treated him unkindly at times, he was Stoker's lifeline to a world he would not otherwise have known. On their American tours, Stoker met his idol, Walt Whitman, and neither man was disappointed: 'What a broth of a boy he is!' Whitman remarked afterwards, 'Like a breath of good healthy, breezy sea air,' though he

wished that Bram was still called Abraham – 'because of manhood.'
Stoker responded by describing him as 'A man amongst men!'

Irving's contribution to *Dracula* stemmed inadvertently from the
Beefsteak Room at the back of the Lyceum which they used as a
private club entertaining the lions of the day after the performance.
One was Professor Arminius Vambéry, an intrepid adventurer who
played The Great Game by penetrating to remote parts of the Middle
East in heavy, if unlikely disguise, to learn how the Russians were
proceeding in their plan to march on India. This was a British
obsession and his information was regarded as priceless, he was
rewarded with honours and presentation to Queen Victoria as 'a
constant friend'. Coming from Hungary, I am certain that it was
Vambéry who told Stoker of the superstitions surrounding vampires
that were so rife in Transylvania, and that he was the model for Van
Helsing, the vampire hunter in the novel. In his *Personal Reminiscences
of Henry Irving*, Stoker singles out the Professor at the University of
Buda-Pesth as one of their most interesting visitors after he saw the
play *The Dead Heart* on 30 April 1890 and remained to supper. When
asked if he never felt fear, Vambery replied – 'Fear of death – no;
but I am afraid of torture. I always had a poison pill fastened here,
where the lappet of my coat now is. This I could always reach with
my mouth in case my hands were tied, and then I did not care!'

I believe it was Vambéry who told Stoker of Vlad the Impaler,
also known as Dracula, son of Dracul, meaning either dragon or
devil. I can imagine the relish with which Stoker rolled this name
around his tongue, his only novel with a one-word title – *Dracula*.
Perfect!

Vlad was bloodthirsty and extraordinarily cruel even for his own
time. He invited the beggars to a feast in Brasov, locked the doors
and set fire to the place in an early example of ethnic cleansing.
He gained his nickname from eating his lunch while his Turkish
prisoners were impaled on wooden spikes, slithering down to a
slow and appalling death as they were gradually split asunder. But
he was not a vampire. Indeed, he was a national hero and after one
victory over the infidel Turk the bells rang out in Christendom as
far as Rhodes.

When I arrived in Bucharest in 1972 the Minister for Propaganda
was decidedly unhappy as he explained that few Hungarians knew of
Count Dracula and it was vital not to confuse him with one of their
few, respected heroes. This is exactly what has happened. Today
bemused tourists shuffle across the wooden floors of Bran Castle
assured by their guides that this was Castle Dracula. Just as Jack
the Ripper has assumed the proportions of a myth, Count Dracula
is thought of increasingly as a real person.

There is no Castle Dracula though Romanian tourism have thought of building one, a horror Disneyland with the manager greeting the coachloads – 'I am Dracula, welcome to my house', with blood-red wine served at dinner to the accompaniment of howling wolves on tape. There is no doubt, as Stephen Jones indicates in his introduction to this amazing and original collection, that Stoker was influenced by 'the mid-fifteenth century Wallachian prince' and this is acknowledged in the novel when the Count tells Harker that the land was 'fought over for centuries by the Wallachians, the Saxons and the Turks. Why, there is hardly a foot of soil in all this region that has not been enriched by the blood of men, patriots or invaders.' Boasting of his ancestor who avenged the shame of defeat by the Turks – 'One of my own race who as Viovode crossed the Danube and beat the Turk on his own ground. This was a Dracula indeed!'

However, and I feel this so wholeheartedly I shall state it again, Stoker used *every* source available – that was part of his skill in *Dracula*. To deny him his vaulting imagination if only in this one book is dreadfully unfair. It is now being claimed that the Castle is based on Slains Castle near Cruden Bay, north of Aberdeen, where he wrote so much of *Dracula*. Though Slains is perched on a cliff above the north sea – hardly the land beyond the forest – Stoker gained ideas there, but it is too glib to label his sources so neatly. On my first morning in Bistrita (Bistritz in the novel, where Jonathan Harker is warned by the landlady that it was Walpurgis Nacht, 'When all the evil things in the world will have full sway'), I was woken by the sound of hammering and looked out to see a carpenter assembling a coffin in the courtyard – a good beginning! Later that day I crossed the Borgo Pass as Harker did, to find it just the same, mists, pinewoods and all. Yet Stoker never set foot there, gleaning his information from an old Baedeker and an exhibition on Transylvania he visited in London. It is not overstating the case to say that Stoker was inspired. The relationship with Irving ended miserably when the actor went behind Stoker's back, betraying him by accepting an offer from another company. With no business acumen, the project failed but Irving could not admit his part in it. Ellen Terry lent him several thousand pounds – I have seen the IOUs – but they were so hard up on Irving's farewell tour that Stoker stayed in cheaper lodgings in Bradford, called to Irving's hotel to find his friend dead in the foyer. After carrying him upstairs, he did his duty as he had done for twenty-five years and sent out the telegrams to inform the world that the first actor to be knighted had died.

His son Noel detested Irving as the man who had devoured his father's life, yet in a sack of Bram's letters which he gave me when I was very young, I found an envelope with a message scrawled in indelible pencil by Irving's seismographic hand – 'You above all men whom I hold dear.' Stoker himself was devastated by the death, suffering a slight stroke which left him with a limp and failing eyesight. Back at Cruden Bay he could no longer afford the Kilmarnock Avins Hotel but rented a simple fisherman's cottage instead. I like to think that as he limped across the sands with his stout stick that he remembered Dracula's snarling words as he turns on his pursuers in Piccadilly: 'My revenge is just begun. I spread it over centuries and time is on my side.' But he had no inkling that he had created one of the myths of the twentieth century and an industry which made fortunes for others though not for himself. When the novel was published a hundred years ago it had a mixed reception, hailed by the *Daily Mail* as a 'weird, powerful and horrible story', while the *Atheneum* was mocking: 'It reads like a mere series of grotesquely incredible events.' Appealing to her own sense of the macabre, the most prophetic comment came from his mother: 'No book since Mrs Shelley's *Frankenstein* has come near yours in orginality or terror. In its terrible excitement it should make a widespread reputation and much money for you.' But she was wrong about the money. The first edition was only 3,000 copies and it was not the instant, never-out-of-print best-seller that some 'experts' claim. His widow Florence was paid nothing for the silent film *Nosferatu* and sued, prompting Universal to pay her a handsome $40,000 which enabled her to end her days in comfort. It was that film with Bela Lugosi that stamped Count Dracula on the public mind though the image is so powerful he would have survived even without Hollywood. Hamilton Deane had presented a version on stage, with a curtain speech in his role as Van Helsing: 'When you get home tonight, and the lights have been turned down and you dread to see a face at the window, why, just pull yourself together and remember that after all – *there are such things*!'

To the end, Stoker applauded others. Trinity College gave a degree to Irving and even to Professor Vambéry, with Stoker writing admiringly, 'He soared above all the other speakers', but awarded nothing to Stoker himself though a Dubliner. When I suggested they should do so in 1997, I received the curt reply – 'It is not possible to mark the occasion of the centenary of *Dracula* with the award of a posthumous degree: such degrees are not awarded.' Neglected even now which gives this enthralling collection of stories a special importance. How proud my great-uncle would have been if he had glimpsed the future of his creation and read this worthy tribute.

Daniel Farson, 1997

Bram Stoker

Dracula: or
The Un-Dead: Prologue

At 10.15 a.m. on Tuesday May 18th, 1897, a few weeks prior to the first publication of Bram Stoker's Dracula, *the author himself produced a single performance of his novel at the Royal Lyceum Theatre in London's West End.*

As Sir Henry Irving's acting manager, he was in an ideal position to produce what amounted to little more than a marathon read-through of the book, which was done solely for the purpose of copyright protection and to file the play with the Lord Chamberlain's office.

The script was compiled in obvious haste, partially in Stoker's handwriting and partly by pasting in portions of a proof copy of the book. It consisted of more than one hundred pages containing five acts and no less than forty-seven scenes and took more than four hours to "perform".

According to Stoker's biographer and great-nephew, Daniel Farson, when asked what he thought of the reading, Irving, who had listened to a few minutes, loudly responded, "Dreadful!"

The play is uneven: care has been taken with some scenes, while others waste large amounts of time on Van Helsing's pontifications. The final scene describing Dracula's pursuit back to his castle and subsequent death takes up only half a page!

Sardou's Madame Sans-Genet, *starring Henry Irving as Napoleon and*

Ellen Terry in the title role, was currently playing during the week and in Saturday matinees at the Lyceum. The King and Miller *and* The Bells *were performed on Saturday evenings. Props and scenery from any of these plays could have been used to support the action in* Dracula.

Stoker used mainly supporting and touring members of the company for his cast. Overtime payments would have been unthinkable, with cast and crew obliged to comply with Stoker's wishes. The first actor to portray Count Dracula was, in the manner of the day, listed simply as "Mr. Jones". The most likely candidate was probably T. Arthur Jones, who could be seen in the role of "Jardin" in Madame Sans-Genet *and who appeared in the payroll accounts under that name and earned the sum of £2.10s per week (compared to Irving's £70.00). Among the other leading roles, Herbert Passmore played Jonathan Harker and Thomas Reynolds portrayed Professor Van Helsing. Mary Foster took the role of Lucy Westenra and Ellen Terry's daughter Edith (Ailsa) Craig played Mina Harker.*

It is unlikely that Dracula: or The Un-Dead *played to anywhere near a full house, with probably only the general staff, friends of the cast and a few curious onlookers in the audience. The additional cost of mounting the performance ran to £1.7s.8d, with total returns of £2.2s. This compares to the theatre's total running costs of the week of £1,896.13s.3d and returns of £2,128.13s.7d!*

Following this single performance, no one undertook the task of bringing Dracula *to the stage again until 1924, when Hamilton Deane, with the permission of Stoker's widow Florence, produced what was to become the basis of most future interpretations.*

Presented here for the first time, with a few minor corrections, is the Prologue *to Stoker's version of the play. The complete text has been published to coincide with the Centenary.*

In his creator's own words, this is how the horror of Dracula begins . . .

Scene 1

OUTSIDE CASTLE DRACULA.

ENTER JONATHAN HARKER FOLLOWED BY DRIVER OF CALECHE CARRYING HIS HAND PORTEMANTEAU AND BAG. LATTER LEAVES LUGGAGE CLOSE TO DOOR AND EXITS HURRIEDLY.

HARKER: Hi! Hi! Where are you off to! Gone already! (*Knocks at door*) Well this is a pretty nice state of things! After a drive through solid darkness with an unknown man whose face I have not seen and who has in his hand the strength of twenty men and who can drive back a pack of wolves by holding up his hand; who visits mysterious blue flames and who wouldn't speak a word that he could help, to be left here in the dark before a – a ruin. Upon my life I'm beginning my professional experience in a romantic way! Only passed my Exam at Lincoln's Inn before I left London, and here I am conducting my business – or rather my employer Mr. Hawkins' business with an accompaniment of wolves and mystery. (*Knocks*) If this Count Dracula were a little more attentive to a guest when he does arrive he needn't have been so effusive in his letters to Mr. Hawkins regarding my having the best of everything on the journey. (*Knocks*) I wondered why the people in the hotel at Bistritz were so frightened and why the old lady hung the Crucifix round my neck and why the people on the coach made signs against the evil eye! By Jove, if any of them had this kind of experience, no wonder at anything they did – or thought. (*Knocks*) This is becoming more than a joke. If it were my own affair I should go straight back to Exeter; but as I act for another and have the papers of the Count's purchase of the London estate I suppose I must go on and do my duty – thank God there is a light, someone is coming.

SOUNDS OF BOLTS BEING DRAWN, AND A KEY TURNED. DOOR OPENS. WITHIN IS SEEN COUNT DRACULA HOLDING AN ANTIQUE SILVER LAMP.

COUNT DRACULA: Welcome to my house! Enter freely and of your own will!

STANDS IMMOVABLE TILL HARKER ENTERS, WHEN ADVANCES AND SHAKES HANDS.

DRACULA: Welcome to my house! Come freely! Go safely! and leave something of the happiness you bring!
HARKER: Count Dracula?
DRACULA: I am Dracula, and you are I take it, Mr. Jonathan Harker, agent of Mr. Peter Hawkins? I bid you welcome Mr. Harker to my house. Come in, the night air is chill and you must need to eat and rest.

PLACES LAMP ON BRACKET AND STEPPING OUT CARRIES IN LUGGAGE.

HARKER: (*Trying to take luggage*) Nay sir, I protest–

DRACULA: Nay sir, the protest is mine. You are my guest. It is late, and my people are not available. Let me see to your comfort myself.

DOOR CLOSED AND BOLTED ETC.

Scene 2

THE COUNT'S ROOM.

LARGE ROOM — OLD FURNITURE — ONE TABLE WITH BOOKS ETC., ANOTHER WITH SUPPER LAID OUT. GREAT FIRE OF LOGS IN HUGE FIREPLACE.

ENTER DRACULA.

DRACULA: (*Calling through open door at side*) When you have refreshed yourself after your journey by making your toilet – you will, I trust, find all ready – come and you will find your supper here.

DRACULA LEANS AGAINTS MANTLE. ENTER HARKER.

DRACULA: (*Pointing to table*) I pray you be seated and sup how you will. Excuse me that I do not join you, but I have dined already, need I do not sup.

HARKER HANDS LETTER TO COUNT WHO OPENS IT AND READS AS HARKER SITS AT TABLE AND EATS.

DRACULA: Ah! from my friend Mr. Peter Hawkins. This will, I am sure, please you to hear:

(*Reads*) "I much regret that an attack of gout from which malady I am a constant sufferer, forbids absolutely any travelling on my part for some time to come, but I am happy to say I can send a sufficient substitute, one in whom I have every possible confidence. He is a young man, full of energy and talent in his own way, and of a very faithful disposition. He is discreet and silent, and has grown to manhood in my service. He shall be ready to attend on you when you will during his stay, and shall take your instructions in all matters."

Well Mr. Harker Jonathan – forgive me if in my ignorance I place, as by the habit of my country, your patronymic first – Mr. Jonathan Harker we shall, I trust, be friends.

FIRST STREAK OF DAWN — THE HOWLING OF MANY WOLVES.

DRACULA: Listen to them – the children of the night. What music they make! Ah, sir, you dwellers in the city cannot enter into the feelings of the hunter. But you must be tired. Your bedroom is all ready, and to-morrow you shall sleep as late as you will. I have to be away till the afternoon; so sleep well and dream well.

EXEUNT.

Scene 3

THE SAME.
ENTER HARKER WHO TAKES CARD FROM TABLE AND READS.

HARKER: (*Reads*) "I have to be absent for a while. Do not wait for me. Dracula."
Strange! The whole thing is unaccountable. I have seen not a soul as yet except the Count. No servant; no sound or sign of life. If no servant, then who was that mysterious muffled coachman with the strength of twenty men and who commanded the wolves? Why the Count too, has the strength of twenty in that hairy palmed hand of his. Surely it cannot be? – No! No!

RUNS SUDDENLY TO DOOR AND TRIES LOCK.

HARKER: Locked from without! What does it mean?

DRACULA SUDDENLY APPEARS BEHIND HIM.

DRACULA: I am glad you have found your way in here, for I am sure there is much that will interest you. These friends – (*Indicates books*) have been good friends to me, and for some years past, ever since I had the idea of going to London, have given me many, many hours of pleasure. Through them I have come to know your great England, and to know her is to love her. I long to go through the crowded streets of your mighty London, to be in the midst of the whirl and rush of humanity, to share its life, its change, its death, and all that makes it what it is. But alas! as yet I only know your tongue through books. To you, my friend, I look that I know him to speak.
HARKER: But, Count, you know and speak English thoroughly!
DRACULA: (*He bows gravely*) I thank you, my friend, for your all too

flattering estimate, but yet I fear that I am but a little way on the road I would travel. True, I know the grammar and the words, but yet I know not how to speak them.

HARKER: Indeed, you speak excellently.

DRACULA: Not so. Well I know that, did I move and speak in your London, none there are who would not know me for a stranger. That is not enough for me. Here I am noble; I am *boyar*; the common people know me, and I am master. But a stranger in a strange land, he is no one; men know him not, and to know not is to care not for. I am content if I am like the rest, so that no man stops if he see me or pause in his speaking if he hear my words to say, "Ha, ha! a stranger!" I have been so long master that I would be master still, or at least that none other should be master of me. You come to me not alone as agent of my friend Peter Hawkins, of Exeter, to tell me all about my new estate in London.

You shall, I trust, rest here with me a while, so that by our talking I may learn the English intonation; and I would that you tell me when I make error, even of the smallest, in my speaking. I am sorry that I had to be away so long to-day; but you will, I know, forgive one who has so many important affairs in hand.

HARKER: I am quite at your service. When you are away may I come into this room?

DRACULA: You may go anywhere you wish in the castle, except where the doors are locked, where of course you will not wish to go. There is reason that all things are as they are, and did you see with my eyes and know with my knowledge, you would perhaps better understand. We are in Transylvania, and Transylvania is not England. Our ways are not your ways, and there shall be to you many strange things. Nay, from what you have told me of your experiences already, you know something of how strange things here may be.

HARKER: May I ask you about some things which have puzzled me?

DRACULA: (*Bowing*) Go on, I shall try to answer.

HARKER: Last night your coachman several times got down to look at places where blue flames rose from the ground, though there were wolves about and the horses were left uncontrolled. Why did he act thus?

DRACULA: Those flames show where gold has been hidden. I see you do not comprehend. I shall then, explain. It is commonly believed that on a certain night, Saint George's, or last night, in fact, when all evil spirits are supposed to have unchecked sway

– a blue flame is seen over any place where treasure has been hidden. That treasure has been hidden in the region through which you came last night, there can be but little doubt; for it was the ground fought over for centuries by the Wallachian, the Saxon, and the Turk. Why, there is hardly a foot of soil in all this region that has not been enriched by the blood of men, patriots or invaders. In old days there were stirring times, when the Austrian and the Hungarian came up in hordes, and the patriots went out to meet them, men and women, the aged and the children too, and waited their coming on the rocks above the passes, that they might sweep destruction on them with their artificial avalanches. When the invader was triumphant he found but little, for whatever there was had been sheltered in the friendly soil.

HARKER: But how can it have remained so long undiscovered, when there is a sure index to it if men will but take the trouble to look?

DRACULA: Because your peasant is at heart a coward and a fool. Those flames only appear on one night, and on that night no man of this land will, if he can help it, stir without his doors. And, dear sir, even if he did he would not know what to do. Why, even the peasant that you tell me of who marked the place of the flame would not know where to look in daylight, even for his own work. You would not, I dare be sworn, be able to find these places again.

HARKER: There you are right, I know no more than the dead where even to look for them.

DRACULA: But come, tell me of London and of the house which you have procured for me.

HARKER: Pardon my remissness.

GETS PAPERS FROM HIS BAG. WHILST HIS BACK IS TURNED DRACULA REMOVES FOOD ETC. AND LIGHTS LAMP. DRACULA TAKES PAPERS AND REFERS TO MAP. JONATHAN WATCHING HIM.

HARKER: I really believe that you know more about the place than I do.

DRACULA: Well, but, my sir, is it not needful that I should? When I go there I shall be all alone, and my friend Jonathan Harker will not be by my side to correct and aid me. He will be in Exeter, miles away, probably working at papers of the law with my other friend, Peter Hawkins.

So! But tell me how you came across so suitable a place.

HARKER: I think I had better read you my notes made at the time.

(*Reads*) "At Purfleet, on a by-road, I came across just such a place as seemed to be required, and where was displayed a dilapidated notice that the place was for sale. It is surrounded by a high wall, of ancient structure, built of heavy stones, and has not been repaired for a large number of years. The closed gates were of heavy old oak and iron, all eaten with rust.

The estate is called Carfax, no doubt a corruption of the old Roman *Quatre Face*, as the house is four-sided, agreeing with the cardinal points of the compass. It contains in all some twenty acres, quite surrounded by the solid stone wall above mentioned. There are many trees on it, which make it in places gloomy, and there is a deep, dark-looking pond or small lake, evidently fed by some springs, as the water is clear and flows away in a fair-sized stream. The house is very large and of all periods back, I should say, to mediaeval times, for one part is of stone immensely thick, with only a few windows high up and heavily barred with iron. It looks like part of a keep, and is close to an old chapel or church. I could not enter it, as I had not the key of the door leading to it from the house, but I have taken with my kodak views of it from various points. The house has been added to, but in a very straggling way, and I can only guess at the amount of ground it covers, which must be very great. There are but few houses close at hand, one being a very large house only recently added to and formed into a private lunatic asylum. It is not, however, visible from the grounds."

DRACULA: I am glad that it is old and big. I myself am of an old family, and to live in a new house would kill me. A house cannot be made habitable in a day; and, after all, how few days go to make up a century. I rejoice also that there is a chapel of old times. We Transylvanian nobles love not to think that our bones may be amongst the common dead. I seek not gaiety nor mirth, not the bright voluptuousness of much sunshine and sparkling waters which please the young and gay. I am no longer young; and my heart, through weary years of mourning over the dead, is not attuned to mirth. Moreover, the walls of my castle are broken; the shadows are many, and the wind breathes cold through the broken battlements and casements. I love the shade and the shadow, and would be alone with my thoughts when I may.

DRACULA POURS OVER PAPERS AND HARKER LOOKS AT ATLAS.

HARKER: (*Aside*) I wonder what these rings mean drawn round particular places. There are only three, I notice, that one is near London on the east side, manifestly where his new estate is situated; the other two are Exeter, and Whitby, on the Yorkshire coast.

COUNT PUTS DOWN PAPERS ON TABLE.

HARKER: (*Aloud*) I notice Count that when you speak of your race you do so as if they were present.

DRACULA: To a *boyar* the pride of his House and Name is his own pride; their glory is his glory; their fate is his fate.

We Szekelys have a right to be proud, for in our veins flows the blood of many brave races who fought as the lion fights for lordship. Here, in the whirlpool of European races, the Ugric tribe bore down from Iceland the fighting spirit which Thor and Wodin gave them, which their Berserkers displayed to such fell extent on the seaboards of Europe, ay, and of Asia and Africa too, till the peoples thought that the were-wolves themselves had come. Here, too, when they came, they found the Huns, whose warlike fury had swept the earth like a living flame, till the dying peoples held that in their veins ran the blood of those old witches that had been expelled from Scythia, who had mated with the devils in the desert. Fools, fools! What devil or what witch was ever so great as Attila, whose blood is in these veins?

HE HOLDS UP HIS ARMS.

Is it a wonder that we were a conquering race; that we were proud; that when the Magyar, the Lombard, the Avar, the Bulgar, or the Turk poured his thousands on our frontiers, we drove them back? Is it strange that when Arpad and his legions swept through the Hungarian fatherland he found us here when he reached the frontier; that the Honfoglalas was completed there? And when the Hungarian flood swept eastward, the Szekelys were claimed as kindred by the victorious Magyars, and to us for centuries was trusted the guarding of the frontier of Turkey-land, ay, and more than that, endless duty of the frontier guard, for, as the Turks say, "water sleeps, and enemy is sleepless." Who more gladly than us throughout the four nations received the "bloody sword," or at its warlike call flocked quicker to the standard of the King? When was redeemed that great shame of my nation, the shame of Cassova, when the flags of the Wallach and the Magyar went down beneath the Crescent? Who was it but one of my own race who as Voivode crossed the Danube and beat the Turk on his own ground? This was a Dracula indeed! Woe was it that his own unworthy brother when he had fallen sold his people to the Turk and brought the shame of slavery on them! Was it not this Dracula indeed who inspired that other of his race who in a later age again and again brought his forces over the great river into Turkey-land, who when he was beaten back came again, and again, and again, though he had to come alone from the bloody field where his troops were being slaughtered, since he knew that he alone could ultimately triumph? They said that he thought only of himself. Bah! What good are peasants without a leader? Where ends the war without a brain and a heart to conduct it? Again, when, after the battle of Mohaes, we threw off the Hungarian yoke, we of the Dracula blood were amongst their leaders, for our spirit would not brook that we were not free. Ah, young sir, the Szekelys and the Dracula as their heart's blood, their brains, and their swords, can boast a record that mushroom growths like the Hapsburgs and the Romanoffs can never reach. The warlike days are over. Blood is too precious a thing in these days of dishonourable peace, and the glories of the great races are as a tale that is told. But now – I want to ask you questions on legal matters and of the doing of Actuari Kinds of business.

HARKER: I hope I may be able to meet your wishes, and especially as I see so many law books here.

DRACULA: First. In England may one have two solicitors, or more than two?

HARKER: You can have a dozen if you wished, but that it would not be wise to have more than one solicitor engaged in one transaction, as the court would only hear one at a time, and that to change would be certain to militate against your interest.

DRACULA: Would there be any practical difficulty in having one man to attend, say, to banking, and another to shipping, as if local help were needed in a place far from the home of the banking solicitor. I shall illustrate. Your friend and mine, Mr. Peter Hawkins, from under the shadow of your beautiful cathedral at Exeter, which is far from London, buys for me through your good self my place at London. Good! Now here let me say frankly, lest you should think it strange that I have sought the services of one so far off from London instead of some one resident there, that my motive was that no local interest might be served save my wish only; and as one of London resident might, perhaps, have some purpose of himself or friend to serve, I went thus afield to seek my agent, whose labours should be to my interest only. Now, suppose I, who have much of affairs, wish to ship goods, say, to Newcastle, or Durham, or Harwich, or Dover, might it not be that it could with more ease be done by consigning to one in these ports?

HARKER: Certainly it would be most easy, but we solicitors have a system of agency one for the other. Local work can be done locally on instruction from any solicitor, so that the *client* simply placing himself in the hands of one man, can have his wishes carried out by him without further trouble.

DRACULA: But could I be at liberty to direct myself. Is it not so?

HARKER: Of course. Such is often done by men of business, who do not like the whole of their affairs to be known by any one person.

DRACULA: Good! Now I must ask about the means of consigning goods and the forms to be gone through, and of all sorts of difficulties which may arise and which by forethought can be guarded against.

HARKER: You would have made a wonderful solicitor, for there is nothing that you do not think of or foresee. For a man who was never in the country, and who does not evidently do much in the way of business your knowledge is wonderful.

DRACULA: Have you written since you arrived to our friend Mr. Peter Hawkins, or to any other?

HARKER: Well, as yet I have not seen any opportunity of sending letters to anybody.

DRACULA: Then write now, my young friend, write to our friend and to any other and say, if it will please you, that you shall stay with me until a month from now.

HARKER: Do you wish me to stay so long?

DRACULA: I desire it much; nay, I will take no refusal. When your master, employer, what you will, engaged that some one should come on his behalf, it was understood that my needs only were to be consulted. I have not stinted. Is it not so?

HARKER: (*Aside*) After all, it is Mr. Hawkins's interest, not mine, and I have to think of him, not myself.

DRACULA: I pray you, my good young friend, that you will not discourse of things other than business in your letters. It will doubtless please your friends to know that you are well, and that you look forward to getting home to them. Is it not so?

DRACULA AND HARKER EACH WRITE NOTES. COUNT GOES AWAY FOR A MOMENT AND HARKER READS ENVELOPES OF HIS LETTERS LEFT ON TABLE.

HARKER: (*Reads*) "Samuel F. Billington, No. 7, The Crescent, Whitby; to Herr Leutner, Varna; Coutts & Co., London; Herren Klopstock & Billreuth, bankers, Buda-Pesth."

ENTER DRACULA.

DRACULA: I trust you will forgive me, but I have much work to
do in private this evening. You will, I hope, find all things as
you wish.

   Let me advise you, my dear young friend, nay, let me warn
you with all seriousness, that should you leave these rooms you
will not by any chance go to sleep in any other part of the castle.
It is old, and has many memories, and there are bad dreams for
those who sleep unwisely. Be warned! Should sleep now or ever
overcome you, or be *like* to do, then haste to your own chamber
or to these rooms, for your rest will then be safe. But if you be
not careful in this respect, then –

HE MOTIONS WITH HIS HANDS AS IF HE IS WASHING THEM.
EXIT COUNT.

HARKER: The castle is a veritable prison and I am a prisoner. I
shall try to watch him to-night.

Scene 4

THE CASTLE WALL.
   HARKER IS SEEN LOOKING OUT OF AN UPPER NARROW WINDOW.
COUNT'S HEAD IS SEEN COMING OUT OF LOWER WINDOW. GRADUALLY
THE WHOLE MAN EMERGES AND CLIMBS DOWN THE WALL FACE DOWN
AND DISAPPEARS GOING SIDEWAYS.

HARKER: What manner of man is this, or what manner of creature
is it in the semblance of man? I feel the dread of this horrible
place overpowering me; I am in fear, in awful fear, and there
is no escape for me; I am encompassed about with terrors that
I dare not think of . . .

Scene 5

THE LADIES HALL.
   A LARGE ROOM WITH BIG WINDOWS THROUGH WHICH MOONLIGHT
STREAMS — SPLENDID OLD FURNITURE ALL IN RAGS AND COVERED
WITH DUST. HARKER LIES ON SOFA.

HARKER: Here I can rest. It was lucky that the door to this wing
was not really locked but only appeared to be.

DOZES.

FIGURES OF THREE YOUNG WOMEN MATERIALIZE FROM THE
MOONLIGHT AND SURROUND HIM.

FIRST WOMAN: Go on! You are first, and we shall follow; yours is
    the right to begin.
SECOND WOMAN: He is young and strong; there are kisses for us
    all.

COUNT SUDDENLY APPEARS BESIDE THEM, AND TAKING WOMAN WHO
IS JUST FASTENING HER LIPS ON HARKER'S THROAT, BY THE NECK
HURLS HER AWAY.

DRACULA: How dare you touch him, any of you? How dare you
    cast eyes on him when I had forbidden it? Back, I tell you all!
    This man belongs to me. Beware how you meddle with him, or
    you'll have to deal with me.
THIRD WOMAN: You yourself never loved; you never love!
DRACULA: Yes, I too can love; you yourselves can tell it from the
    past. Is it not so? Well, now I promise you when I am done with
    him you shall kiss him at your will. Now go! Go! I must awaken
    him, for there is work to be done.
FIRST WOMAN: Are we to have nothing to-night?

COUNT POINTS TO BAG WHICH HE HAS THROWN ON FLOOR AND
WHICH MOVES AND A CHILD'S WAIL IS HEARD. WOMEN SEIZE BAG
AND DISAPPEAR ALL AT ONCE. COUNT LIFTS UP HARKER WHO HAS
FAINTED AND CARRIES HIM OFF. DARKNESS.

Scene 6

THE LIBRARY — HARKER DISCOVERED.

HARKER: Last night the Count told me to write three letters, one
    saying that my work here was nearly done, and that I should
    start for home within a few days; another that I was starting on
    the next morning from the time of the letter, and the third that
    I had left the castle and arrived at Bistritz. In the present state
    of things it would be madness to openly quarrel with the Count
    whilst I am so absolutely in his power, and to refuse would be
    to excite his suspicion and to arouse his anger. He knows that I
    know too much, and that I must not live, lest I be dangerous to

him; my only chance is to prolong my opportunities. Something
may occur which will give me a chance to escape.

ENTER DRACULA.

DRACULA: Posts are few and uncertain, and your writing now would
ensure ease of mind to your friends. Your letters will be held
over at Bistritz until due time in case chance would admit of
your prolonging your stay.

HARKER: (*Aside*) To oppose him would be to create new suspicion.
(*Aloud*) What dates shall I put on the letters?

DRACULA: The first should be June 12, the second June 19, and
the third June 29.

EXIT DRACULA.

HARKER: (*Aside*) I know now the span of my life, God help me!
There is a chance of escape, or at any rate of being able to
send word home. A band of Szagany have come to the castle,
and are encamped in the courtyard.

I shall write some letters home, and shall try to get them to
have them posted. I have already spoken to them through my
window to begin an acquaintanceship. They take their hats off
and make obeisance and many signs, which, however, I cannot
understand any more than I can their spoken language ... I
have written the letters. Mina's is in shorthand, and I simply ask
Mr. Hawkins to communicate with her. To her I have explained
my situation, but without the horrors which I may only surmise.
It would shock and frighten her to death were I to expose my
heart to her. Should the letters not carry, then the Count shall
not yet know my secret or the extent of my knowledge ... I give
the letters; I throw them through the bars of my window with a
gold piece, and make what signs I can to have them posted. The
man who takes them puts them to his heart and bows, and then
presses them in his cap. I can do no more.

ENTER DRACULA.

HARKER: Steady, the Count has come.

DRACULA: The Szagany has given me two letters, of which, though
I know not whence they come, I shall, of course, take care. See!
– One is from you, and to my friend Peter Hawkins; the other
– (*Sees shorthand – anger*) other is a vile thing, an outrage upon
friendship and hospitality! It is not named. Well! so it cannot

matter to us. The letter to Hawkins – that I shall, of course, send on, since it is yours. Your letters are sacred to me. Your pardon, my friend, that unknowingly I did break the seal. Will you not cover it again?

HARKER WRITES ENVELOPE.

DRACULA: So, my friend, you are tired? Get to bed. There is the surest rest. I may not have the pleasure to talk to-night, since there are many labours to me; but you will sleep!

EXIT DRACULA.

HARKER: I hear without, a cracking of whips and pounding and scraping of horses' feet up the rocky path beyond the courtyard. I must hurry to the window. I see drive into the yard two great leiter-wagons, each drawn by eight sturdy horses, and at the head of each pair a Slovak. I shall go to them. (*Tries door*).

My door is fastened on the outside. I run to the window and cry to them. They look up at me stupidly and point, but the "hetman" of the Szagany comes out and seeing them pointing to my window, says something, at which they laugh. They turn away. The leiter-wagons contained great, square boxes, with handles of thick rope; these are evidently empty by the ease with which the Slovaks handle them and by their resonance as they are roughly moved. They are all unloaded and packed in a great heap in one corner of the yard; the Slovaks are given some money by the Szagany, and spitting on it for luck, lazily go each to his horse's head. The cracking of their whips die away in the distance. The Szagany are quartered somewhere in the castle, and are doing work of some kind. I know it, for now and then I hear a far-away, muffled sound as of mattock and spade, and, whatever it is, it must be to the end of some ruthless villainy.

I see something coming out of the Count's window. He has on the suit of clothes which I had worn whilst travelling here and slung over his shoulder the terrible bag which I had seen the women take away. There can be no doubt as to his quest, and in my garb, too! This, then, is his new scheme of evil: he will allow others to see me, as they think, so that he may both leave evidence that I have been seen in the towns or villages posting my own letters, and that any wickedness which he may do shall by the local people be attributed to me.

I shall watch for the Count's return. What are these quaint little flecks floating in the rays of the moonlight? They are like the tiniest grains of dust, and they whirl round and gather in clusters in a nebulous sort of way. I watch them with a sense of soothing, and a sort of calm steals over me.

Hark. What is that low, piteous howling of dogs somewhere far below in the valley? Thank God I did not fall asleep. There is something stirring in the Count's room, and a sound like a sharp wail quickly supressed:

(*Runs to window*) A woman with dishevelled hair, holding her hands over heart as one distressed with running. She leans against a corner of the gateway. When she sees my face at the window she throws herself forward and shouts in a voice laden with menace:– "Monster, give me my child!"

She throws herself on her knees, and raising up her hands, cries the same again and again.

I can hear the beating of her naked hands against the door. High overhead, probably on the tower, I hear the voice of the Count calling in his harsh, metallic whisper. His call seemed to be answered from far and wide by the howling of wolves.

A pack of them pour like a pent-up dam when liberated through the wide entrance into the courtyard.

There is no cry from the woman, and the howling of the wolves stops. Before long they stream away singly, licking their lips.

I can not pity her, for I know what has become of her child, and she is better dead!

What shall I do? What can I do? How can I escape from this dreadful thrall of night and gloom and fear? To-night goes to post, the first of that fatal series which is to blot out the very traces of my existence from the earth.

Let me not think of it. Action! If I could only get into his room! But there is no possible way. The door is always locked, no way for me.

Yes, there is a way, if one dares to take it. Where his body has gone why may not another body go? I have seen him myself crawl from his window; why should not I imitate him, and go in by his window? The chances are desperate, but my need is more desperate still. I shall risk it. At the worse it can only be death; and a man's death is not a calf's, and the dreaded hereafter may still be open to me. God help me in my task! Good-bye, Mina, if I fail; good-bye, my faithful friend and second father; good-bye, all, and last of all Mina!

Scene 7

SAME SCENE.

HARKER: (*Writing*) I have made the effort, and, God helping me, have come safely back to this room. I must put down every detail in order. I went whilst my courage was fresh straight to the window on the south side, and at once got outside on the narrow ledge of stone which runs round the building on this side. The stones were big and roughly cut, and the mortar had by process of time been washed away between them. I took off my boots, and ventured out on the desperate way. I looked down once, so as to make sure that a sudden glimpse of the awful depth would not overcome me, but after that kept my eyes away from it. I know pretty well the direction and distance of the Count's window, and made for it as well I could, having regard for the opportunities available. I did not feel dizzy – I suppose I was too excited – and the time seemed ridiculously short till I found myself standing on the window-sill and trying to raise up the sash. I was filled with agitation, however, when I bent down and slid feet foremost in through the window. Then I looked around for the Count, but, with surprise and gladness, made a discovery. The room was empty! It was barely furnished with odd things, which seemed to have never been used; the furniture was something the same style as that in the south rooms, and was covered with dust. I looked for the key, but it was not in the lock, and I could not find it anywhere. The only thing I found was a great heap of gold in one corner, gold of all kinds, Roman, and British, and Austrian, and Hungarian, Greek and Turkish money, covered with a film of dust, as though it had lain long in the ground. None of it that I noticed was less than three hundred years old. There were also chains and ornaments, some jewelled, but all of them old and stained.

At one corner of the room was a heavy door. I tried it, for, since I could not find the key of the room or the key of the outer door, which was the main object of my search, I must make furthur examination, or all my efforts would be in vain. It was open, and led through a stone passage to a circular stairway, which went steeply down. I descended, minding carefully where I went, for the stairs were dark, being only lit by loopholes in the heavy masonry. At the bottom there was a dark, tunnel-like passage, through which came a deathly, sick odour, the odour of old earth newly turned. As I passed through the passage the smell grew closer and heavier. At last I pulled open a heavy door

which stood ajar, and found myself in an old, ruined chapel, which
had evidently been used as a graveyard. The roof was broken,
and in two places were steps leading to vaults, but the place had
recently been dug over, and the earth placed in great wooden
boxes, manifestly those which had been brought by the Slovaks.
There was nobody about the place, and I made search for any
further outlet, but there was none. Then I went over every inch
of the ground, so as not to lose a chance. I went down even into
the vaults, where the dim light struggled, although to do so was
a dread to my very soul. Into these I went, but now nothing but
fragments of old coffins and piles of dust; but in the third I made
a discovery.

There in one of the great boxes, of which there were fifty in
all, on a pile of newly dug earth, lay the Count! He was either
dead or asleep, I could not say which – for the eyes were open
and stony, but without the glassiness of death – and the cheeks
had the warmth of life through all their pallor, and the lips
were as red as ever. But there was no sign of movement, no
pulse, no breath, no beating of the heart. I bent over him, and
tried to find any sign of life, but in vain. He could not have lain
there long, for the earthy smell would have passed away in a few
hours. By the side of the box was its cover, pierced with holes
here and there. I thought he might have the keys on him, but
when I went to search I saw the dead eyes, and in them, dead
though they were, such a look of hate, though unconscious of
me or my presence, that I fled from the place, and leaving the
Count's room by the window, crawled again up the castle wall,
and regaining my own chamber, threw myself panting upon the
bed and tried to think . . .

To-day is the date of my last letter, and the Count has taken steps
to prove that it was genuine, for again I saw him leave the castle
by the same window, and in my clothes. As he went down the wall,
lizard fashion, I wished I had a gun or some lethal weapon, that
I might destroy him, but I fear that no weapon wrought alone
by man's hand would have any effect on him. I dared not wait
to see him return, for I feared to see those weird sisters. I came
back to the library, and read there till I fell asleep.

DRACULA APPEARS.

DRACULA: To-morrow, my friend, we must part. You return to your
beautiful England, I to some work which may have such an end
that we may never meet. Your letter home has been despatched;
to-morrow I shall not be here, but all shall be ready for your

journey. In the morning come the Szagany, who have some labours of their own here, and also come some Slovaks. When they have gone, my carriage shall come for you, and shall bear you to the Borgo Pass to meet the diligence from Bukovina to Bistritz. But I am in hopes that I shall see more of you at Castle Dracula.

HARKER: Why may I not go to-night?

DRACULA: Because, dear sir, my coachman and horses are away on a mission.

HARKER: But I would walk with pleasure. I want to get away at once.

DRACULA: And your baggage?

HARKER: I do not care about it. I can send for it some other time.

DRACULA: You English have a saying which is close to my heart, for its spirit is that which rules our *boyars*: "Welcome the coming, speed the parting guest." Come with me, my dear young friend. Not an hour shall you wait in my house against your will, though sad am I at your going, and that you so suddenly desire it. Come. – Hark!

HOWLING OF WOLVES HEARD AS THE COUNT RAISES HIS HAND.

HARKER: I shall wait till morning.

EXIT DRACULA.
SOUND OF VOICES AND WOMEN LAUGHING OUTSIDE DOOR.

DRACULA: (*Outside*) Back, back, to your own place! Your time is not yet come. Wait. Have patience. To-morrow night, to-morrow night, is yours!

HARKER: To-morrow! To-morrow! Lord, help me and those to whom I am dear!

I shall scale the wall again and gain the Count's room. He may kill me, but death now seems the happier choice of evils.

Scene 8

THE CHAPEL VAULT.
HARKER DESCENDS BY WALL AND PEERS ROUND.

HARKER: The great box is in the same place, close against the wall. The lid laid on it; not fastened down, the nails ready in their

places to be hammered home. I must search the body for the
key. (*Raises lid and lays it back against wall*)

Ah! Something which filled my very soul with horror. The
Count, looking as if his youth had been half renewed, for the
white hair and moustache are changed to dark iron-grey; the
cheeks are fuller, and the white skin seems ruby-red underneath;
the mouth is redder than ever, for on the lips are gouts of fresh
blood, which trickle from the corners of the mouth and run over
the chin and neck. Even the deep, burning eyes seem set amongst
swollen flesh, for the lids and pouches underneath are bloated.
It seems as if the whole awful creature were simply gorged with
blood like a filthy leech. I must search, or I am lost. The coming
night may see my own body a banquet in a similar way to those
horrid three.

This was the being I am helping to transfer to London,
where, perhaps, for centuries to come he may amongst its
teeming millions satiate his lust for blood, and create a new
and ever-widening circle of semi-demons to fatten on the helpless.
The very thought drives me mad. I shall rid the world of such a
monster. There is no lethal weapon at hand, but with this . . .
(*Seizes shovel and strikes at Count, head turns and he sees eyes. Shovel
strikes wide and gashes forehead and, as he pulls it away flange catches
lid and pulls it over chest. Distant roll of wheels and cracking of whips*)
I shall rush out when they open the hall door.

CLIMBS WALL AND DISAPPEARS.

Scene 9

THE LIBRARY.
AS HARKER ENTERS BY WINDOW DOOR SLAMS AND SHUTS.

HARKER: I am still a prisoner, and the net of doom is closing round
me more closely.

I hear the sound of many tramping feet and the sound of
weights being set down heavily, doubtless the boxes, with their
freight of earth. There is a sound of hammering; it is the box
being nailed down. Now I can hear the heavy feet tramping again
along the hall, with many other idle feet coming behind them.

The door is shut, and the chains rattle; there is a grinding of
the key in the lock; I can hear the key withdrawn: then another
door opens and shuts; I hear the creaking of lock and bolt.

Hark! In the courtyard and down the rocky way the roll of

heavy wheels, the crack of whips, and the chorus of the Szagany as they pass into the distance.

I am alone in the castle with those awful women. Faugh! Mina is a woman, and there is nought in common. They are devils of the pit.

I shall not remain alone with them; I shall try to scale the castle farther than I have yet attempted. (*Takes gold from table*)

I may find a way from this dreadful place. And then away for home! Away to the quickest and nearest train! Away from this cursed spot, from this cursed land where the devil and his children still walk with earthly feet!

At least God's mercy is better than that of these monsters, and the precipice is steep and high. At its foot a man may sleep – as a man. Good-bye, all! Mina!

CLIMBS OUT BY WINDOW.

Christopher Fowler

Dracula's Library

Christopher Fowler lives and works in central London, where for half of each day he runs the Soho movie marketing company The Creative Partnership, producing TV and radio scripts, documentaries, trailers and promotional shorts. For the remainder of the day he writes short stories and novels.

His books include Roofworld, Rune, Red Bride, Darkest Day, Spanky, Psychoville, Disturbia, *and the collections* City Jitters, City Jitters Two, The Bureau of Lost Souls, Sharper Knives, *and* Flesh Wounds. *Several of his books are in various stages of development as movies, while his story "The Master Builder" was filmed by CBS-TV as* Through the Eyes of a Killer *(1992) starring Tippi Hedren, and* Left Hand Drive, *based on his first short story, won Best British Short Film in 1993.*

Jonathan Harker stays on at Dracula's castle, but at what cost to his immortal soul . . . ?

Being a diary chronicle of the true and hitherto unrevealed fate of Jonathan Harker, discovered within the pages of an ancient book.

From The Journal of Jonathan Harker, 2 July —.

I HAVE ALWAYS believed that a building can be imbued with the personality of its owner, but never have I felt such a dread ache of melancholy as I experienced upon entering that terrible, desolate place. The castle itself – less a chateau than a fortress, much like the one that dominates the skyline of Salzburg – is very old, thirteenth century by my reckoning, and a veritable masterpiece of unadorned ugliness. Little has been added across the years to make the interior more bearable for human habitation. There is now glass in many of the windows and mouldering tapestries adorn the walls, but at night the noise of their flapping reveals the structure's inadequate protection from the elements. The ramparts are unchanged from times when hot oil was poured on disgruntled villagers who came to complain about their murderous taxes. There is one entrance only, sealed by a portcullis and a pair of enormous studded doors. Water is drawn up from a great central well by a complicated wooden pump-contraption. Gargoyles sprout like toadstools in every exposed corner. The battlements turn back the bitter gales that forever sweep the Carpathian mountains, creating a chill oasis within, so that one may cross the bailey – that is, the central courtyard of the castle – without being blasted away into the sky.

But it is the character of the Count himself that provides the castle with its most singular feature, a pervading sense of loss and loneliness that would penetrate the bravest heart and break it if admitted. The wind moans like a dying child, and even the weak sunlight that passes into the great hall is drained of life and hope by the cyanic stained glass through which it is filtered.

I was advised not to become too well-acquainted with my client. Those in London who have had dealings with him remark that he is "too European" for English tastes. They appreciate the extreme nobility of his family heritage, his superior manners and cultivation, but they cannot understand his motives, and I fear his lack of sociability will stand him in poor stead in London, where men prefer to discuss fluctuations of stock and the nature of horses above their own feelings. For his part, the Count certainly does not encourage social intercourse. Why, he has not even shaken my hand, and on the few occasions that we have eaten together he has left me alone at the table before ten minutes have passed. It is almost as if he cannot bear the presence of a stranger such as myself.

I have been here for over a month now. My host departed in the middle of June, complaining that the summer air was "too thin and bright" for him. He has promised to return by the first week of September, when he will release me from my task, and I am to return home to Mina before the mountain paths become impassable for the winter. This would be an unbearable place to spend even one night were it not for the library. The castle is either cold or hot; most of it is bitter even at noon, but the library has the grandest fireplace I have ever seen. True, it is smaller than the one in the Great Hall, where hams were smoked and cauldrons of soup were boiled in happier times, and which now stands cold and lifeless as a tomb, but it carries the family crest of Vlad Drakul at its mantel, and the fire is kept stoked so high by day that it never entirely dies through the night. It is here that I feel safest.

Of course, such heat is bad for the books and would dry out their pages if continued through the years, but as I labour within this chamber six days out of every seven, it has proven necessary to provide a habitable temperature for me. The servant brings my meals to the Great Hall at seven, twelve and eight, thus I am able to keep "civilized" hours. Although I came here to arrange the Count's estate, it is the library that has provided me with the greatest challenge of my life, and I often work late into the night, there being little else to do inside the castle, and certainly no one to do it with. I travelled here with only two books in my possession; the leather-bound Bible I keep on my bedside table, and the Baedeker provided for my journey by Mina, so for me the library is an enchanted place. Never before, I'll wager, has such a collection of volumes been assembled beyond London. Indeed, not even that great city can boast such esoteric tastes as those displayed by the Count and his forefathers, for here are books that exist in but a single copy, histories of forgotten battles, biographies of disgraced warriors, scandalous romances of distant civilizations, accounts of deeds too shameful to be recorded elsewhere, books of magic, books of mystery, books that detail the events of impossible pasts and many possible futures!

Oh, this is no ordinary library.

In truth, I must confess I am surprised that he has allowed me such free access to a collection that I feel provides a very private insight into the life and tastes of its owner. Tall iron ladders, their base rungs connected to a central rail, shift along the book-clad walls. Certain shelves nearest the great vaulted ceiling have gold-leafed bars locked over them to keep their contents away from prying eyes, but the Count has provided me with keys to them all. When I asked him if, for the sake of privacy, he would care to sort the books before I cast my gaze upon them (after all, he is a member of the Carpathian aristocracy, and who knows what family secrets hide here) he demurred, insisting that I should have full run of the place. He is a charming man, strange and distant in his thoughts, and altogether too much of an Easterner for me to ever fully gain his confidence, for I act as the representative of an Empire far too domesticated for his tastes, and I suspect, too diminished in his mind. Yes, diminished, for there is little doubt he regards the British intellect as soft and sated, even though there is much in it that he admires. He comes from a long line of bloodletting lords, who ruled with the sword-blade and despised any show of compassion, dismissing it as frailty. He is proud of his heritage, of course, yet learning to be ashamed, contrition being the only civilised response to the sins of the past.

I think perhaps he regards this vast library, with its impossible mythologies and ghastly depictions of events that may never happen, as part of that bloody legacy he is keen to put behind him. He is, after all, the last of his line. I suspect he is allowing me to catalogue these books with a view to placing the contents up for auction. The problem, though, is that it is almost impossible for me to judge how I should place a price on such objects. Regardless of what is contained within, the bindings themselves are frequently studied with precious and semi-precious jewels, bound in gold-leaf and green leather, and in one case what suspiciously appears to be human skin. There is no precedent to them, and therefore there can be no accurate estimate of value.

How, then, am I to proceed?

From The Journal of Jonathan Harker, 15 July —.
Regarding the library: I have devised a system that allows me to create a table of approximate values, and that for now must suffice. First, I examine the binding of the book, noting the use of valuable ornamentation and pigments. Then I make note of the author and the subject, gauging their popularity and stature; how many copies have been printed (if indicated) and where; how many editions; the age of the work and its length; and finally, content, whether scandalous and likely to cause offence, whether of general interest, usefulness and the like. To this end I find myself making odd decisions, putting a history of Romanian road-mapping before the *Life and Times of Vladimir the Terrible* because the former may be of more utility in charting this neglected territory. Thus the banal triumphs over the lurid, the ordinary over the outrageous, the obvious over the obscure. A fanciful mind might imagine that I was somehow robbing the library of its power by reclassifying these

tomes in such a manner, that by quantifying them I am reducing the spell they cast. Fancies grow within these walls. The castle is conducive to them.

In my tenth week I started upon the high barred shelves, and what I find there surprises, delights and occasionally revolts me. Little histories, human fables set in years yet to be, that reveal how little our basest nature changes with the passing decades. These books interest me the most.

I had not intended to begin reading any of the volumes, you understand, for the simple reason that it would slow my rate of progress to a crawl, and there are still so many shelves to document. Many books require handling with the utmost care, for their condition is so delicate that their gossamer pages crumble in the heat of a human hand. However, I now permit myself to read in the evenings, in order that I might put from my mind the worsening weather and my poor, pining Mina.

The light in the library is good, there being a proliferation of candles lit for me, and the great brocaded armchair I had brought down from my bedroom is pulled as close to the fire as I dare, deep and comfortable. Klove leaves his master's guest a nightly brandy, setting down a crystal bowl before me in the white kid gloves he always wears for duties in this room. Outside I hear the wind loping around the battlements like a wounded wolf, and in the distant hills I hear some of those very creatures lifting their heads to the sky. The fire shifts, popping and crackling. I open the book I have chosen for the evening and begin to read.

From The Journal of Jonathan Harker, 30 August 30 —.
I have the strangest feeling that I am not alone.

Oh, I know there are servants, four, I think; a raw-looking woman who cooks and cleans, her husband the groom, an addle-pate under-servant born without wits who is only fit for washing and sweeping (he might be the son of the cook; there is a resemblance), and Klove, an unsmiling German butler whom I take to be the Count's manservant. I mean to say that there is someone else here. I sense his presence late at night, when the fire has banked down to an amber glow and the library is at its gloomiest. I can feel him standing silently at the windows (an impossibility, since they overlook a sheer drop of several hundred yards) but when I turn to catch a glimpse of this imagined figure it is gone.

Last night the feeling came again. I had just finished cataloguing the top shelves of the library's west wall, and was setting the iron ladders back in their place when I became aware of someone staring at my back. A sensation of panic seized me as the hairs stood on my neck, prickling as though charged with electricity, but I forced myself to continue with my task, finally turning in the natural course of my duty and raising my gaze to where I felt this mysterious watcher to be standing.

Of course, there was nothing corporeal to see – yet this time the feeling persisted. Slowly, I made my way across the great room, passing the glowing red escarpment of the fire, until I reached the bank of mullioned windows set in the room's north side. Through the rain that was tickering against the glass I looked out on the most forsaken landscape imaginable, grey pines and burned black rock. I could still feel him, somewhere outside the windows, as if he had passed by on the wall itself, and yet how was this possible? I am a man who prides himself on his sensitivity, and fancied that this baleful presence belonged to none other than my host. Yet the Count was still away and was not due to return for a further fourteen days, (I had been informed by Klove) having extended his trip to conclude certain business affairs.

This presents me with a new problem, for I am told that winter quickly settles in the mountains, and is slow to release the province from its numbing grip. Once the blizzards begin the roads will quickly become inundated, making it virtually impossible for me to leave the castle until the end of spring, a full seven months away. I would truly be a prisoner here in Castle Dracula. With that thought weighing heavily on my mind I returned to my seat beside the fire, fought down the urge to panic, opened a book and once more began to read.

I must have dozed, for I can only think what I saw next was a hallucination resulting from a poorly digested piece of mutton. The Count was standing in the corner of the library, still dressed in his heavy-weather oilskin. He seemed agitated and ill-at-ease, as if conducting an argument with himself on some point. At length he reached a decision and approached me, gliding across the room like a tall ship in still seas. Flowing behind him was a rippling wave of fur, as hundreds of rats poured over the chairs and tables in a fanned brown shadow. The rodents watched me with eyes like ebony beads. They cascaded over the Count's shoes and formed a great circle around my chair, as if awaiting a signal. But the signal did not come, so they fell upon one another, the strongest tearing into the soft fat bellies of the weakest, and the library carpet turned black with blood as the chamber filled with screams . . .

I awoke to find my shirt as wet as if it had been dropped into a lake. The book I had been reading lay on the floor at my feet, its spine split. The gold crucifix I always wear at my neck was hung on the arm of my chair, its clasp broken beyond repair. I resolved to eat earlier from that night on.

From The Journal of Jonathan Harker, 22 September —.
The weather has begun to worsen, and there is still no sign of the Count. Klove has heard nothing of his master, and as the days grow shorter a forlorn darkness descends upon the castle. The skies are troubled, the clouds heavier now, ebbing to the west with their bellies full of rain. The library occupies my waking hours. It is like an origami model of Chinese paper, ever-unfolding into new configurations. Just when I think I have its measure, new delights and degradations present themselves. Yesterday, I started on a further set of shelves housing nautical chart-books and maps, and while reaching across the ladder to pull one stubborn tome free, triggered the opening of a mahogany flap built in the rear of the shelf that folded down to reveal a hundred further volumes.

I carefully cleared a space and set these books in stacks according to their coordinated bindings, and only once they all stood free of their secret home did I start to examine them.

I find delicacy escapes me at this point; they were lexicons of erotica, frankly illustrated, alarmingly detailed, outlining practices above, below and altogether beyond the boundaries of human nature in such an overt and lascivious manner that I was forced to return them to their hiding place before Klove brought me my nightly brandy, for no gentleman would wish such volumes to fall into the hands of servants.

After he had departed the room I took time to examine the single edition I had left out. It was much like the others, designed more to arouse the senses than to provide practical advice concerning the physical side of matrimony. The room grew hot about me as I turned the pages, and I was forced to move back from the fireplace. The drawings were shameless, representing actions one would scarcely countenance in the darkest woods, here presented in brightest daylight. Still more shocking was my discovery that the book was English, produced in London, presumably for foreign purchasers.

While I was examining this, I began to sense the presence once more, and this time as it grew I became aware of a smell, a sweet perfume akin to Atar of Roses – a scented water my own Mina would often dab at her swan-pale neck. The perfume, filled as it was with memories of home, quite overpowered me and I grew faint, for I fancied I saw a lady – no, a *woman* – standing on the staircase nearest the windows.

She was tall and handsome rather than beautiful, with a knowing

look, her auburn hair swept back and down across a dress of sheer
green gossamer, with jewels at her throat, and nothing at all on her
feet. She stood with her left side turned to me, so that I could not
help but notice the exaggerated posture of her breasts. It was as
though she intended them to incite my admiration. The effect was
indecent, but nothing to the effect produced when she turned to
face me directly, for the front panel of the dress was cut away below
her waist to reveal - well, her entire personal anatomy. Stupified by
her brazenness, wondering if she was perhaps ill, I found myself
unable to move as she approached. Upon reaching my chair she
slid the outstretched fingers of her right hand inside my shirt,
shearing off each of the buttons with her nails. I was acutely aware
that the naked part of her was very close to me. Then, reaching
inside the waistband of my trousers, she grasped at the very root of
my reluctantly extended manhood and brought it forward, bursting
through the garment's fly-buttons. When I saw that she intended
to lower her lips to this core of my being, every fibre of my body
strained to resist her brazen advances.

Here, though, my mind clouds with indistinct but disagreeable
impressions. A distant cry of anger is heard, the woman retreats
in fear and fury, and I awake, ashamed to discover my clothing in
considerable disarray, the victim of some delirious carphology.

From The Journal of Jonathan Harker, 7 October —.
The snow has started falling. During these increasingly frequent
squalls, all sights and sounds are obscured by a deadening white
veil that seals us in the sky. From my bedroom window I can
see that the road to the castle is becoming obscured. If the
Count does not return soon, I really do not see how I shall
be able to leave. I suppose I could demand that a carriage
be fetched from the nearest village, but I fear such an action
would offend my absent host, who must surely reappear any
day now.

I am worried about my Mina. I have not heard from her inside a
month, and yet if I am truthful part of me is glad to be imprisoned
here within the castle, for the library continues to reveal paths I
feel no Englishman has ever explored.

I do not mean to sound so mysterious, but truly something weighs
upon my mind. It is this; by day I follow the same routine, logging
the books and entering them into the great ledgers my host provided
for the purpose, but each night, after I have supped and read my
customary pages before the fire, I allow myself to fall into a light
sleep, and then –
   – then my freedom begins as I either dream or awaken to

such unholy horrors and delights I can barely bring myself to describe them.

Some nights bring swarms of bats, musty-smelling airborne rodents with leathery wings, needle teeth and blind eyes. Sometimes the ancestors of Vlad Drakul appear at the windows in bloody tableaux, frozen in the act of hacking off the howling heads of their enemies. Men appear skewered on tempered spikes, thrusting themselves deeper onto the razor-poles in the throes of an obscene pleasure. Even the Count himself pays his respects, his bony alabaster face peering at me through a wintry mist as though trying to bridge the chasm between our two civilizations. And sometimes the women come.

Ah, the women.

These females are like none we have in England. They do not accompany themselves on the pianoforte, they do not sew demurely by the fire. Their prowess is focussed in an entirely different area. They kneel and disrobe each other before me, and caress themselves, and turn their rumps toward me in expectation. I would like to tell you that I resist, that I think of my fiancee waiting patiently at home, and recite psalms from my Bible to strengthen my will, but I do not, and so am damned by the actions taken to slake my venomous desires.

Who are these people who come to me in nightly fever-dreams? Why do they suit my every morbid mood so? It is as if the Count knows my innermost thoughts and caters for them accordingly. Yet I know for a fact that he has not returned to the castle. When I look from the window I can see that there are no cart-tracks on the road outside. The snow remains entirely unbroken.

There are times now when I do not wish to leave this terrible place, for to do so would mean forsaking the library. And yet, presumably, it is to be packed up and shipped to London, and this gives me hope, that I might travel with the volumes and protect them from division. For the strength of a library exists in the sum of its books. Only by studying it – indeed, only by reading every single edition contained within – can one hope to divine the true nature of its owner.

From The Journal of Jonathan Harker, 15 November —.
Somewhere between dreams and wakefulness, I now know that there is another state. A limbo-life more imagined than real. A land of phantoms and sensations. It is a place I visit each night after darkness falls. Sometimes it is sensuous, sometimes painful, sometimes exhilarating, sometimes foul beyond redemption. It extends only to the borders of the library, and its inhabitants, mostly

in states of undressed arousal, are perfumed with excrement. These loathsome creatures insult, entice, distract, disgrace, shame and seduce me, clutching at my clothes until I am drawn amongst them, indistinguishable from them, enthralled by their touch, degraded by my own eagerness.

I think I am ill.

By day, my high stone world is once more quiet and rational. Would that it were not, for there is no comfort to be had from the news it brings me. The road leading to and from the castle is now quite impassable. It would take a team of mountaineers to scale the sharp gradient of the rock face beneath us. The Count has failed to return, and of his impending plans there is no word. My task in the library is nearly over. The books – all save one single final shelf – have been quantified and, in many cases, explored.

I begin to understand the strangely parasitic nature of my host. His thirst for knowledge and his choice of literature betray his true desires. There are volumes in many languages here, but of the ones I can read, first editions of Nodier's *Infernalia*, d'Argen's *Lettres Juives* and Viatte's *Sources Occultes du Romantisme* are most familiar. Certain medical periodicals and pertinent copies of *The London Journal* add subtler shades to my mental portrait of the Count. Of course I knew the folk-tales about his ancestry. They are bound within the history of his people. How could one travel through this country and not hear them? In their native language they do not seem so fanciful, and here in the castle, confabulations take on substantiality. I have heard and read how the Count's forefathers slaughtered the offspring of their enemies and drank their blood for strength – who has not? Why, tales of Eastern barbarism have reached the heart of London society. But I had not considered the more lurid legends; how the royal descendents lived on beyond death, how they needed no earthly sustenance, how their senses were so finely attuned that they could divine bad fortune in advance. Nor had I considered the consequence of such fables; that, should their veracity be proven, they might in the Count's case suggest an inherited illness of the kind suffered by royal albinos, a dropsical disease of the blood that keeps him from the light, an anaemia that blanches his eyes and dries his veins, that causes meat to stick in his throat, that drives him from the noisy heat of humanity to the cool dark sanctum of his sick-chamber.

But if it is merely a medical condition, why am I beset with bestial fantasies? What power could the Count possess to hold me in his thrall? I find it harder each day to recall his appearance, for the forbidden revelations of the night have all but overpowered my sense of reality. And yet his essence is here in the library, imbued within each page of his collection. Perhaps I am not ill, but mad. I fear my senses have awoken too sharply, and my rational mind is reeling with their weight.

I have lost much of my girth in the last six weeks. I have always been thin, but the gaunt image that glares back at me in the glass must surely belong to a sickly, aged relation. I appear as a bundle of blanched sticks by day. I have no strength. I live only for the nights. Beneath the welcoming winter moon my flesh fills, my spirit becomes engorged with an unwholesome strength, and I am sound once more.

I really must try to get away from here.

From The Journal of Jonathan Harker, 18 December —.
The Count has finally returned, paradoxically bringing fresh spirits into the castle. For the life of me I cannot see how he arrived here, as one section of the pathway below has clearly fallen away into the valley. Last night he came down to dinner, and was in most excellent health. His melancholy mood had lifted, and he was eager to converse. He seemed physically taller, his posture more erect. His travels had taken him on many adventures, so he informed me as he poured himself a goblet of heavy claret, but now he was properly restored to his ancestral home, and would be in attendance for the conclusion of my work.

I had not told him I was almost done, although I supposed he might have intuited as much from a visit to the library. He asked that we might finish the work together, before the next sunrise. I was very tired – indeed, at the end of the meal I required Klove's helping hand to rise from my chair – but agreed to his demand, knowing that there were but a handful of books left for me to classify.

Soon we were seated in the great library, warming ourselves before the fire, where Klove had set bowls of brandy out for us.

It was when I studied his travelling clothes that I realised the truth. His boots and oil-cloth cape lay across the back of the chair where he had supposedly deposited them on his return. As soon as I saw that the boots were new, the soles polished and unworn, I instinctively intuited that the Count had not been away, and that he had spent the last six months here in the castle with me. I knew I had not imagined what I had seen and done. We sat across from each other in two great armchairs, cradling our brandies, and I nervously pondered my next move, for it was clear to me that the Count could sense my unease.

"I could not approach you, Jonathan," he explained, divining my thoughts as precisely as an entymologist skewers a wasp. "You were simply too English, too Christian, too filled with pious platitudes. The reek of your pride was quite overpowering. I saw the prayerbook by your bed, the cross around your neck, the dowdy little virgin in your locket. I knew it would be simpler to sacrifice you upon the completion of your task." His eyes watched mine intently. "To suck your blood and throw your drained carcass over the battlements to the wolves." I stared back, refusing to flinch, not daring to move a single nerve-end.

"But," he continued with a heartfelt sigh, "I did so need a good man to tend my library. In London I will easily find loyal emissaries to do my bidding and manage my affairs, but the library needs a keeper. Klove has no feeling for language. To be the custodian of such a rare repository of ideas requires tact and intellect. I decided instead to let you discover me, and in doing so, discover yourself. That was the purpose of the library." He raised his arm, fanning it over the shelves. "The library made you understand. You see, the pages of the books are poisoned. They just need warm hands to activate them, the hands of the living. The inks leaked into your skin and brought your inner self to life. That is why Klove always wears gloves in this room. You are the only other *living* person here."

I looked down at my stained and fragrant fingers, noticing for the first time how their skin had withered into purple blotches.

"The books are dangerous to the Christian soul, malignant in their print and in their ideas. Now you have read my various histories, shared my experiences, and know I am corrupt, yet incorruptible. Perhaps you see that we are not so far apart. There is but one barrier left to fall between us." He had risen from his chair without my noticing, and circled behind me. His icy tapered fingers came to rest on my neck, loosening the stiff white collar of my shirt. I heard a collar stud rattle onto the floor beneath my chair.

"After tonight you will no longer need to use my library for the fulfilment of your fantasies," he said, his steel-cold mouth descending to my throat, "for your fantasies are to be made flesh, just as the nights will replace your days." I felt the first hot stab of pain as his teeth met in my skin. Through a haze I saw the Count wipe his lips with the back of a crimson hand. "You will make a very loyal custodian, little Englishman," he said, descending again.

Here the account ends. The library did not accompany Count Dracula on his voyage to England, but remained behind in his castle, where it continued to be tended by Mr Harker until his eventual demise many, many years later.

Thomas Ligotti

The Heart of Count Dracula, Descendant of Attila, Scourge of God

Thomas Ligotti has been called "one of the few consistently original voices in contemporary horror fiction," by Ramsey Campbell. He is the author of three acclaimed volumes of horror stories: Songs of a Dead Dreamer, Grimscribe: His Lives and Works *and* Noctuary, *as well as a collection of short short stories entitled* The Agonizing Resurrection of Victor Frankenstein and Other Gothic Tales. *His most recent book is* The Nightmare Factory, *a compilation of previously collected and new stories.*

Another recent project is a collaboration with British group Current 93 in a recording of a new novella with musical accompaniment. It will be simultaneously published as a compact disc with a limited edition hardcover in Britain.

Count Dracula travels to England, where he is about to lose his heart . . .

COUNT DRACULA RECALLS how he was irresistibly drawn to Mina Harker (née Murray), the wife of a London real estate agent. Her husband had sold him a place called Carfax. This was a dilapidated structure next door to a noisy institution for the insane. Their incessant racket was not undisturbing to one who was, among other things, seeking peace. An inmate name Renfield was the worst offender.

One time the Harkers had Count Dracula over for the evening, and Jonathan (his agency's top man) asked him how he liked Carfax with regard to location, condition of the house and property, and just all around. "Ah, such architecture," said Count Dracula while gazing uncontrollably at Mina, "is truly frozen music."

Count Dracula is descended from the noble race of the Szekelys, a people of many bloodlines, all of them fierce and warlike. He fought for his country against the invading Turks. He survived wars, plagues, the hardships of an isolated dwelling in the Carpathian Mountains. And for centuries, at least five and maybe more, he has managed to perpetuate, with the aid of supernatural powers, his existence as a vampire. This existence came to an end in the late 1800s. "Why *her?*" Count Dracula often asked himself.

Why the entire ritual, when one really thinks about it. What does a being who can transform himself into a bat, a wolf, a wisp of smoke, anything at all, and who knows the secrets of the dead (perhaps of death itself) want with this oily and overheated nourishment? Who would make such a stipulation for immortality! And, in the end, where did it get him? Lucy Westenra's soul was saved, Renfield's soul was never in any real danger . . . but Count Dracula, one of the true children of the night from which all things are born, has no soul. Now he has only this same insatiable thirst, though he is no longer free to alleviate it. ("Why her? There were no others such as her.") Now he has only this painful, perpetual awareness that he is doomed to wriggle beneath this infernal stake which those fools – "Harker, Seward, Van Helsing, and the others – have stuck in his trembling heart. ("Her fault, her fault.") And now he hears voices, common voices, peasants from the countryside.

"Over here," one of them shouts, "in this broken down convent or whatever it is. I think I've found something we can give to those damned *dogs*. Good thing, too. Christ, I'm sick of their endless whining."

Mandy Slater

Daddy's Little Girl

Mandy Slater's short stories have been published in Dark Terrors, Sex Macabre *and* 365 Scary Stories. *She recently dialogue scripted* The Animals of Farthing Wood *CD-ROM for BBC Multimedia, and is a contributor to* SFX Magazine *and* Science Fiction Chronicle.

The decades pass, and Dracula travels widely, never staying for more than three or four years in one place. But now his past is about to come back to haunt him . . .

THE CALL OF the night beckoned, but I ignored it and hailed a taxi instead.

The streets were empty tonight. Only the sound of a few motor cars, and the occasional *clip-clop* of a horse-drawn carriage interrupted the silence. Although I was tempted to book a room at The Grand and ignore my problems, I had to leave the city. The dank smell of the metropolis left a foul, acrid taste in my mouth, which was a further blow to what was rapidly becoming the worst week of my existence.

The previous night's excursion had left me mentally drained.

That despicable man Crowley had stared at me all evening. There was something about him that I couldn't quite put my finger on. He spouted nonsense about magic and religion – obviously a self-deluded crackpot. It was no wonder that his last mistress had committed suicide. I should have known better than to frequent such an establishment as the Gargoyle Club. Places like that always brought out the worst dregs of society. Nowadays, nightclubs like the Kit-Cat were more to my taste.

The taxi dropped me off at the train station and I could barely see the driver speed away in the rapidly descending gloom. I hastily purchased my ticket, and found my train quickly, climbing into the comfort of the first class carriage with a sense of relief. Moments after I closed the door with a hollow *thump*, the train began to move forward.

I couldn't stop thinking about *him*. And at the end of my journey he would be waiting. He was tangled in my thoughts like a spider in a web. Why here? Why now?

Our disagreement had been a stupid one; they always were. I hadn't seen him in years. He said he'd contact me, but he never did. I wrote a few cards, posted a letter or two, but there was never any reply, never so much as a hastily written scribble or a wispy voice on the other end of a telephone line.

I'd tried to justify his behaviour in my mind. I kept telling myself that I moved a great deal – perhaps the mail was never forwarded? He was always busy, ruling his empire with an iron fist, manipulating the masses, commanding the multitudes. The powerful ones never had time – or so they said.

I guess you could say I gave up on him after a while. Or maybe, just maybe, he gave up on me. Perhaps I never really lived up to his expectations. Following in his footsteps had always been a nightmare. There was such a mystique surrounding him.

The adopted ones always exceeded me in their achievements. I often heard their accounts, read about their adventures in the newspapers. Following the headlines had become a daily ritual. Perhaps I hoped to catch a fleeting reference to him. I thought I did once, just after the war. The name was wrong, but then he rarely used the real one nowadays. Legends had myriad titles.

He had wealth now, and he had it in abundance. I wondered if it made him happy. The endless parade of women never did. I'd watched them too. I was good at watching. Perhaps observation was my only real talent on this earth, although I never seemed to learn from it.

My anxiety about the forthcoming appointment was interrupted by a hesitant knock on the door of my compartment. I quickly switched on the reading light. It might look suspicious if someone found me staring out into the darkness.

"I was wondering if I could come in?" a male voice asked from the other side of the doorway.

I opened the door cautiously, expecting the ticket inspector on his rounds. But it was that man Crowley again.

"Oh, excuse me," he said, acting surprised. "I was looking for an associate of mine, and I thought she was in this compartment."

"I'm afraid not sir. Excuse me, but I really *must* get back to my book," I added, hoping he would disappear to whence he came, and quickly.

"Yes, of course. I hope you don't mind me asking, but have we met before?" He suddenly smiled. "Yes, I remember now, you were at the Gargoyle Club last night. What a small world . . ."

"No, I'm afraid I don't remember," I lied, my teeth clenching as I tried to close the door on his fingers.

It was then that he brushed past me and sat down. I was so surprised by his brusque manner, that words escaped me.

"Well, if I can't find my associate, perhaps you'd honour me with a conversation? I have a least an hour before I reach my destination. Assuming of course you don't mind?" He smiled again. My skin crawled.

I wanted to tell him to get out and let me be. The note that I had received the previous evening had left me drained. Somehow I no longer felt in control of my own actions.

"I've not encountered someone with such beauty as yours in a long time," he purred. "And you have a touch of the True Power, although I doubt you know that . . ."

"Really sir," I said firmly, "I must ask you to leave at once."

Then he scowled. "Don't play the proper little miss with me. What's that expression everyone's using? 'You can do anything you like so long as you don't do it in the streets and frighten the horses.' I don't see any horses here, madam. After all, most women who frequent the Gargoyle Club are after one thing and one thing only." He licked his lips in anticipation.

At that moment, there was another knock at the compartment door. I could hear a tiny voice squeaking from the other side. "Are you there Aleister? I've been looking for you everywhere."

"Ah, my companion, what perfect timing. Let her in my dear, let her in," he demanded.

Without hesitation I opened the carriage door. Crowley had a certain presence, I'd acknowledge that. A tipsy red-head stared back at me. Then she brushed past and collapsed into the lap of her lover.

"Come my dear," he said while struggling with the woman's clothing. "Why don't you join us? I have delights to show you beyond your imagination . . ."

The woman laughed, a shrill screech that threatened to overpower the din of the steam engine. The situation was quickly getting out of control. I sighed, realizing there was no other way. "If that's what you really desire . . ." I said simply.

This disgusting man was beginning to become a nuisance – a potentially dangerous one at that. I leaned down and grasped his shoulders, pulling him closer to my red lips. Then my instincts took over. As my fangs pierced his flesh, the hot blood spurted down my throat, sending the first rich waves deep into my soul. All I could hear was the *clacking* of the wheels on the tracks. The sound roared in my ears, drowning out his gasps.

I could sense strange thoughts swirling within my mind. He was fighting me, but not in a physical sense. As he lapsed into unconsciousness, I turned towards his cowering companion. It was over very quickly. I drained her dry.

My dear, sweet father, would you be proud of me now? See what your gift has wrought? I glanced out of the carriage window; we were nearly there. I would be very glad when this journey came to an end.

Before the train came to a complete stop, I stepped off onto the platform. No one followed. The deserted station was mute witness to the train's arrival and departure. It was a characterless structure, a concrete edifice that even the pigeons would avoid.

"Angelica," a voice called softly from the night's gloom. The darkness seemed to part as a figure strode purposely towards me. I recognized his scent instantly – it was my father.

I took a deep breath and tasted the cool night air. He stood watching me. His crimson eyes betrayed nothing.

"What are you doing here?" I managed to say, hoping he would not smell the fresh blood on my breath.

As always, he seemed to take control of the situation. "I thought I would meet you after your long journey," he said simply. "I have a car waiting for us." My father pointed towards a magnificent, black Rolls Royce. He always liked to travel in style.

He was more conservatively dressed than at our last encounter. I had not seen him in person for more than twenty-five years and outwardly, at least, he had changed since then. Now he wore a black, perfectly-cut business suit, with gold cufflinks that shone with an unearthly gleam. His dark hair was trimmed neatly above the collar, swept back in a widow's peak from his forehead. The polished shoes reflected the dim glow of the moon. They probably cost enough to feed a whole village for a year in the old country.

"Come," he commanded. "It will be dawn soon."

I walked beside him towards the car. A uniformed chauffeur jumped out, and swiftly opened the back door of the vehicle. He was dressed all in black as well. I climbed in, acutely aware of my father's breath on the back of my neck.

We sat there in silence. The Rolls Royce cruised through the winding, country roads for nearly an hour. I couldn't tell whether it was getting light or not. The car windows had obviously been blacked out.

"A good journey then?" he asked, finally breaking the silence between us.

"No . . . there was a small problem," I said.

"I trust you handled it with your usual degree of tact and style?" He smiled and his teeth were very white.

I did not reply. He was baiting me. Not this time, I thought to myself. *Not this time.*

Eventually the car pulled into a long driveway, the sound of gravel crunching beneath the tyres.

"We must hurry into the house," he warned. "The first light of dawn approaches."

I fumbled with the door handle and finally slid out of the car. The driver was nowhere in sight. The house in front of me was typical of the country homes you would normally see in the society pages. I hated it on sight.

A Szgany woman greeted us at the doorway and quickly beckoned us in. My father was a few paces behind me. I could hear his shoes against the marble flooring, but I refused to turn around and look at him. I didn't want to be transformed into a pillar of salt.

"Are you hungry?" the servant asked me with a hint of fear in her dark eyes.

"No thank you, I've already . . . eaten," I replied quietly.

She looked relieved. From the bruises on her neck, her role was obviously a simple one.

"Come my daughter. We can talk in the study."

It was not a request. Few lived who crossed my father's wishes. The people of Transylvania were witness to that. So I followed him, praying to whichever gods protect such as I that this time he had reconciliation in his thoughts, not destruction. But perhaps secretly I still craved the latter.

He sat in a large leather chair. It reminded me of a throne, with its high back and ornate carvings on the legs and arm rests. I chose a simpler piece of furniture, more suited to my nature.

"It has been too long," he said.

For the first time I saw weariness in his eyes.

"I am very alone Angelica," he continued. "The years have been long."

He looked old. I could imagine grey strands in his thick dark hair. Of course I knew that he would never age. It was just an impression of what might have been . . . or was yet to come.

"I have made some mistakes. I expect you know that. But you are my only true daughter of this century. A miracle in more ways than one." He let his statement hang in the air, waiting for me to bring it down to earth.

I wasn't sure if I believed him, but I had heard enough. The question that sprang from my lips had been trapped inside me for far too long. "Do you really expect me to forgive you? I know what *you* are. I know what *I* am. Haven't you done enough?"

For a moment he said nothing. The silence in the room felt like an eternity. Finally he said: "I need you. You are the only one, there is no other like you."

"No father, I've grieved enough. This has been a waste of time. You haven't changed, you'll never change." I was gripping the arms of the chair so tightly, that I left indentations in the wood with my nails. "I'll be leaving tomorrow, once the sun has set."

"You fed today, didn't you?" he asked.

"Yes, you know that. Some self-styled mystic and his companion." The image of Crowley's face immediately surfaced again in my mind.

My father rose from the chair. "You think you are so *different* Angelica. But you still take life. You see, my daughter, we are . . . one and the same."

"But it was in self-defence," I tried to explain. "They were dangerous. There was something about that man . . . something unusual. I had to protect myself, protect what *we* are." His growing anger was piercing me like sharp knives. "However, I did spare the man . . ." I added quietly.

"What? Then perhaps you are not the one I had hoped for after all . . ."

Deep down I knew he was right. That's why I hated him so much. That's why the years had been such long ones. I'd been the one to push *him* away. I couldn't deny that any longer. He was a part of me and I of him. The connection was of blood *and* flesh.

I could feel the tears rolling down my cheeks. They were tears of blood. He moved towards me then, not quite touching the floor. His eyes were warm, and I stared into them as he wrapped me in his strong embrace.

I felt safe and secure in the knowledge that he would protect me from anyone or anything. As he held me closer, I didn't need to breathe, let alone utter a whisper. That might break the spell – shatter it into thousands of pieces that could never again be reformed. He was of course my dear father, and I would always be Daddy's little girl . . .

I gazed into his eyes. Once again they were like cold steel. At that moment I gasped as his teeth pricked my skin, sending my body into a spasm of delight. It was better than any earthly pleasure.

"It has been *too* long daughter," he finally said, as he pulled back from my throat, smearing the blood from his red lips with the back of his hand.

"You've missed me then?" I asked, once again falling into his embrace.

His throat was like ice, and he let out a small gasp of surprise as my teeth pierced his cold flesh. I drew the warmth deep inside, not tasting, just desperately feeding upon his life force.

"Enough," he demanded, trying to withdraw from my grip.

"No," I said. My hands were firmly grasped around his throat, my whole body trembling. But he was too strong, even for me.

I barely saw the blow as he struck me. The force threw me backwards across the room. I heard dry bones crack, and suddenly I couldn't move my body.

"You left me no choice, daughter," he said. "I will not accept failure, even from you. That man you allowed to survive will cause us trouble in the future, mark my words, and *you* are to blame." He looked so tall standing over me, so powerful, so cold. "I am afraid your neck is broken daughter. That is fatal – even for such as us."

His features were becoming blurry now. A single tear of blood ran down his cheek. At least he grieved, but as the final blackness swept over me, I wondered did he grieve for me . . . or for the future?

Ramsey Campbell

Conversion

*Ramsey Campbell has won the World Fantasy Award four times, the British
Fantasy Award eight times, and the Bram Stoker Award twice.*

His first book, a collection of stories entitled The Inhabitant of the
Lake and Less Welcome Tenants, *appeared from August Derleth's
legendary Arkham House imprint in 1964. Since then he has published
such acclaimed novels as* The Doll Who Ate His Mother, The Face That
Must Die, The Parasite, The Nameless, Incarnate, The Claw *(aka*
Night of the Claw*),* Obsession, The Hungry Moon, The Influence,
Ancient Images, Midnight Sun, The Count of Eleven, The Long
Lost, The One Safe Place *and* The House on Nazareth Hill. *His
short fiction has been collected in* Demons by Daylight, The Height of
the Scream, Dark Companions, Scared Stiff, Waking Nightmares,
Alone With the Horrors *and* Strange Things and Stranger Places,
and he has edited a number of anthologies including Superhorror, New
Terrors, Uncanny Banquet *and the first five volumes of* The Best New
Horror *series (with Stephen Jones).*

*He is a film reviewer for BBC Radio Merseyside since 1969 and
President of both the British Fantasy Society and the Society of Fantastic Films.*

Dracula returns to the Carpathians, but continues to take a great interest in world events and politics. However, some things never change . . .

YOU'RE IN SIGHT of home when you know something's wrong. Moonlight shivers gently on the stream beyond the cottage, and trees stand around you like intricate spikes of the darkness mounting within the forest. The cottage is dark, but it isn't that. You emerge into the glade, trying to sense what's troubling you.

You know you shouldn't have stayed out so late, talking to your friend. Your wife must have been worried, perhaps frightened by the night as well. You've never left her alone at night before. But his talk was so engrossing: you feel that in less than a night you've changed from being wary of him to understanding him completely. And his wine was so good, and his open-throated brightly streaming fire so warming, that you can now remember little except a timeless sense of comfortable companionship, of communion that no longer needed words. But you shouldn't have left your wife alone in the forest at night, even behind a barred door. The wood-cutter's cottage is nearby; at least you could have had his wife stay with yours. You feel disloyal.

Perhaps that's what has been disturbing you. Always before when you've returned home light has been pouring from the windows, mellowing the surrounding trunks and including them like a wall around your cottage. Now the cottage reminds you of winter nights long ago in your childhood, when you lay listening to a wolf's cry like the slow plummeting of ice into a gorge, and felt the mountains and forests huge around you, raked by the wind. The cottage feels like that: cold and hollow and unwelcoming. For a moment you wonder if you're simply anticipating your wife's blame, but you're sure it's more than that.

In any case you'll have to knock and awaken her. First you go to the window and look in. She's lying in bed, her face open as if to the sky. Moonlight eases darkness from her face, but leaves her throat and the rest of her in shadow. Tears have gathered in her eyes, sparkling. No doubt she has been crying in memory of her sister, a sketch of whom gazes across the bed from beside a glass of water. As you look in you're reminded of your childhood fancy that angels watched over you at night, not at the end of the bed but outside the window; for a second you feel like your wife's angel. But as you gaze in discomfort grows in your throat and stomach. You remember how your fancy somehow turned into a terror of glimpsing a white face peering in. You draw back quickly in case you should frighten her.

But you have to knock. You don't understand why you've been delaying. You stride to the door and your fist halts in mid-air, as if impaled by lightning. Suddenly the vague threats and unease you've been feeling seem to rush together and gather on the other side of the door. You know that beyond the door something is waiting for you, ready to pounce.

You feel as if terror has pinned you through your stomach, helpless. You're almost ready to flee into the woods, to free yourself from the skewer of your panic. Sweat pricks you like red-hot ash scattered on your skin. But you can't leave your wife in there with it, whatever nightmare it is rising out of the tales you've heard told of the forest. You force yourself to be still if not calm, and listen for some hint of what it might be.

All you can hear is the slow sleepy breathing of the wind in the trees. Your panic rises, for you can feel it beyond the door, perfectly poised and waiting easily for you to betray yourself. You hurry back to the window, but it's impossible for you to squeeze yourself in far enough to make out anything within the door. This time a stench rises from the room to meet you, trickling into your nostrils. It's so thickly unpleasant that you refuse to think what it might resemble. You edge back, terrified now of awakening your wife, for it can only be her immobility that's protecting her from whatever's in the room.

But you can't coax yourself back to the door. You've allowed your panic to spread out from it, warding you further from the cottage. Your mind fills with your wife, lying unaware of her plight. Furious with yourself, you compel your body forward against the gale of your panic. You reach the door and struggle to touch it. If you can't do that, you tell yourself, you're a coward, a soft scrabbling thing afraid of the light. Your hand presses against the door as if proving itself against a live coal, and the door swings inwards.

You should have realized that your foe might have entered the cottage through the doorway. You flinch back instinctively, but as the swift fear fades the panic seeps back. You can feel it hanging like a spider just inside the doorway, waiting for you to pass beneath: a huge heavy black spider, ready to plump on your face. You try to shake your panic out of you with the knowledge that it's probably nothing like that, that you're giving in to fancy. But whatever it is, it's oozing a stench that claws its way into your throat and begins to squeeze out your stomach. You fall back, weakened and baffled.

Then you see the rake. It's resting against the corner of the cottage, where you left it after trying to clear a space for a garden. You carry it to the door, thinking. It could be more than a weapon, even though you don't know what you're fighting. If your wife doesn't awaken and draw its attention to her, if your foe isn't intelligent enough to see what you're planning, if your absolute conviction of where it's lurking above the door isn't false – You almost throw away the rake, but you can't bear the sense of your wife's peril any longer. You inch the door open. You're sure you have only one chance.

You reach stealthily into the space above the door with the teeth of the rake, then you grind them into your prey and drag it out into the open. It's a dark tangled mass, but you hurl it away into the forest without looking closer, for some of it has fallen into the doorway and lies dimly there, its stench welling up. You pin it with the teeth and fling it into the trees.

Then you realize there's more, hanging and skulking around the side of the door-frame. You grab it with the rake and hurl it against a trunk. Then you let your breath roar out. You're weak and dizzy, but you stagger through the doorway. There are smears of the thing around the frame and you sway back, retching. You close your mouth and nostrils and you're past, safe.

You lean on the rake and gaze down at your wife. There's a faint stench clinging to the rake, and you push it away from you, against the wall. She's still asleep, no doubt because you were mourning her sister all last night. Your memory's blurring; you must be exhausted too, because you can remember hardly anything before the battle you've just fought. You're limply grateful that no harm has befallen her. If she'd come with you to visit your friend none of this would have happened. You hope you can recapture the sense of communion you had with him, to pass on to your wife. Through your blurring consciousness you feel an enormous yearning for her.

Then you jerk alert, for there's still something in the room. You glance about wildly and see beneath the window more of what you destroyed, lying like a tattered snake. You manage to scoop it up in one piece this time, and you throw the rake out with it. Then you turn back to your wife. You've disturbed her; she has moved in her sleep. And fear advances on you from the bed like a spreading stain pumped out by a heart, because now you can see what's nestling at her throat.

You don't know what it is; your terror blurs it and crowds out your memories until it looks like nothing you've ever seen. It rests in the hollow of her throat like a dormant bat, and indeed it seems to have stubby protruding wings. Its shape expands within your head until it is a slow explosion of pure hostility, growing and erasing you. You turn away, blinded.

It's far worse than what you threw into the forest. Even then, if you hadn't been fighting for your wife you would have been paralysed by superstition. Now you can hardly turn your head back to look. The stain of the thing is crawling over your wife, blotting out her face and all your sense of her. But you open your eyes an agonized slit and see it couched in her throat as if it lives there. Your rage floods up, and you start forward.

But even with your eyes closed you can't gain on it, because a great cold inhuman power closes about you, crushing you like a moth in a fist. You mustn't cry out, because if your wife awakens it may turn on her. But the struggle crushes a wordless roar from you, and you hear her awake.

Your seared eyes make out her face, dimmed by the force of the thing at her neck. Perhaps her gathered tears are dislodged, or perhaps these are new, wrung out by the terror in her eyes. Your head is a shell full of fire, your eyes feel as though turning to wash, but you battle forward. Then you realize she's shrinking back. She isn't terrified of the thing at her throat at all, she's terrified of you. She's completely in its power.

You're still straining against the force, wondering whether it must divert some of its power from you in order to control her, when she grabs the glass from beside the bed. For a moment you can't imagine what she wants with a glass of water. But it isn't water. It's vitriol, and she throws it in your face.

Your face bursts into pain. Howling, you rush to the mirror.

You're still searching for yourself in the mirror when the woodcutter appears in the doorway, grim-faced. At once, like an eye in the whirlwind of your confusion and pain, you remember that you asked his wife to stay with yours, yesterday afternoon when he wasn't home to dissuade you from what you had to do. And you know why you can't see yourself, only the room and the doorway through which you threw the garlic, your sobbing wife clutching the cross at her throat, the glass empty now of the holy water you brought home before setting out to avenge her sister's death at Castle Dracula.

Manly Wade Wellman

The Devil is Not Mocked

Manly Wade Wellman (1903–1986) twice won the World Fantasy Award. He was born in the village of Kamundongo in Portuguese West Africa, and settled in the United States where he worked as a reporter before quitting his job in 1930 to write fiction full-time.

He was one of the most prolific contributors to the pulp magazines of the 1930s and '40s, and some of his best stories are collected in Who Fears the Devil?, Worse Things Waiting, Lonely Vigils *and* The Valley So Low. *He wrote more than seventy-five books in all genres, including horror, fantasy, science fiction, crime and adventure, and had over two hundred short stories and numerous comic books and articles to his credit.*

As the Nazi hordes sweep across Europe, the Count's warrior soul admires the new German spirit of patriotism and discipline. But when Hitler's forces begin to overrun his homeland, Dracula feels the hatred rise within him . . .

Do you not know that tonight, when the clock strikes midnight, all the evil things in the world hold sway? Do you know where you are going, and what you are going to?

– Bram Stoker

BALKAN WEATHER, EVEN Balkan spring weather, was not pleasant to General von Grunn, leaning heavily back behind the bulletproof glass of his car. May 4th – the English would call it St George's Day, after their saint who was helping them so little. The date would mean something to Heinrich Himmler, too, that weak-chinned pet of the Führer would hold some sort of garbled druidic ritual with his Schutzstaffel on the Brockenburg. Von Grunn grimaced fatly at the thought of Himmler, and leaned forward to look out into the night. An armed car ahead, an armed car behind – all was well.

"Forward!" he growled to his orderly, Kranz, who trod on the accelerator. The car moved, and the car ahead took the lead, into the Borgo Pass.

Von Grunn glanced backward once, to the lights of Bistritz. This country had been Romanian not so long ago. Now it was Hungarian, which meant that it was German.

What was it that the mayor of Bistritz had said, when he had demanded a semiremote headquarters? The castle along this pass, empty – ready for him? The dolt had seemed eager to help, to please. Von Grunn produced a long cigarette. Young Captain Plesser, sitting beside him, at once kindled a lighter. Slim, quiet, the young aid had faded from von Grunn's consciousness.

"What's the name of that castle again?" inquired the general, and made a grimace when Plesser replied in barbarous Slavic syllables. "What's the meaning in a civilized tongue?"

"Devil's Castle, I should think," hazarded the captain's respectful voice.

"*Ach*, so – Transylvania is supposed to be overrun with devils," nodded von Grunn, puffing. "Let them defer to us, or we'll devil them." He smiled, for his was a great gift for appreciating his own epigrams. "Meanwhile, let the castle be called its German name. *Teufelstoss* – Devil's Castle."

"Of course," agreed Plesser.

Silence for a while, as the cars purred powerfully up the rough slope of the pass trail. Von Grunn lost himself in his favourite meditation – his own assured future. He was to establish an unostentatious command post for – what? A move against Russia? The Black Sea? He would know soon enough. In any case, an army would be his, action and glory. There was glory enough for all. Von Grunn remembered Wilhelm II saying that, in the last war.

"The last war," he said aloud. "I was, a simple *oberlieutenant* then. And the Führer – a corporal. What were you, captain?"

"A child."

"You remember?"

"Nothing." Plesser screwed up his courage to a question. "General von Grunn, does it not seem strange that the folk at Bistritz were so anxious for you to come to the castle – *Teufelstoss* – tonight?"

Von Grunn nodded, like a big, fierce owl. "You smell a trap, *nicht wahr*? That is why I bring two carloads of men, my trusted bodyguard. For that very chance. But I doubt if any in Transylvania dare set traps for me, or any other German."

The cars were slowing down. General and captain leaned forward. The car ahead was passing through the great open gate-way of a courtyard. Against the spattered stars rose the silhouette of a vast black building, with a broken tower. "We seem to be here," ventured Captain Plesser.

"Good. Go to the forward car. When the other arrives, form the guard."

It was done swiftly. Sixteen stark infantrymen were marshalled, with rifles, bombs, and submachine guns. Von Grunn emerged into the cold night, and Kranz, the orderly, began to bring out the luggage.

"A natural fort, withdrawn and good for any defense except against aircraft," pronounced the general, peering through his monocle at the battlements above. "We will make a thorough examination.

"*Unteroffizer*!" he barked, and the noncom in charge of the escort came forward woodenly, stiffening to attention. "Six of the men will accompany me inside. You will bivouac the others in this courtyard, maintaining a guard all night. *Heil Hitler.*"

"*Heil Hitler,*" responded the man briskly. Von Grunn smiled as the *unteroffizer* strode away to obey. For all the soldierly alacrity, that order to sleep outdoors was no welcome one. So much the better; von Grunn believed in toughening experiences for field soldiers, and his escort had lived too softly since the Battle of Flanders.

He walked to where a sort of vestibule of massive, rough stone projected from the castle wall. Plesser already stood there, staring at the heavy nail-studded planks of the door. "It is locked, *Herr General*," he reported. "No knob or latch, bell or knocker – "

But as he spoke, the door swung creakingly inward, and yellow light gushed out.

On the threshold stood a figure in black, as tall as von Grunn himself but thinner than even Plesser. A pale, sharp face and brilliant eyes turned upon them, in the light of a chimneyless oil lamp of silver.

"Welcome, General von Grunn," said the lamp holder. "You are expected."

His German was good, his manner respectful. Von Grunn's broad hand slid into a greatcoat pocket, where he always carried a big automatic pistol.

"Who told you to expect us?" he demanded.

The lamplight struck blue radiance from smooth, sparse black hair as the thin man bowed. "Who could mistake General von Grunn, or doubt that he would want this spacious, withdrawn structure for his new headquarters position?"

The mayor of Bistritz, officious ass, must have sent this fellow ahead to make fawning preparations – but even as von Grunn thought that, the man himself gave other information.

"I am in charge here, have been in charge for many years. We are so honoured to have company. Will the general enter?"

He stepped back. Plesser entered, then von Grunn. The vestibule was warm. "This way, excellency," said the man with the lamp – the steward, von Grunn decided to classify him. He led the way along a stone-paved passage, von Grunn's escort tramping authoritatively after him. Then up a great winding stair, and into a room, a big hall of a place, with a fire of logs and a table set for supper.

All told, very inviting; but it was not von Grunn's way to say as much. He only nodded, and allowed Captain Plesser to help him out of his great-coat. Meanwhile, the steward was showing the luggage-laden Kranz into an octagonal bedroom beyond.

"Take these six men," said von Grunn to Plesser, indicating the soldiers of the escort. "Tour the castle. Make a plan of each floor. Then come back and report. *Heil Hitler.*"

"*Heil Hitler,*" and Plesser led the party away. Von Grunn turned his broad back to the fire. Kranz was busy within the bedroom, arranging things. The steward returned. "May I serve the *Herr General?*" he asked silkily.

Von Grunn looked at the table, and with difficulty forebore to lick his fat lips. There were great slices of roast beef, a fowl, cheese, salad, and two bottles of wine – Kranz himself could not have guessed better what would be good. Von Grunn almost started forward to the table, then paused. This was Transylvania. The natives, for all their supple courtesy, disliked and feared soldiers of the Reich. Might these good things not be poisoned?

"Remove these things," he said bleakly. "I have brought my own provisions. You may eat that supper yourself."

Another bow. "The *Herr General* is too good, but I will sup at midnight – it is not long. Now, I will clear the things away. Your man will fetch what you want."

He began to gather up dishes. Watching him stoop over the table, von Grunn thought that he had seldom seen anyone so narrow in the shoulders – they were humped high, like the shoulders of a hyena, suggesting a power that crouched and lurked. Von Grunn was obliged to tell himself that he was not repelled or nervous. The steward was a stranger, a Slav of some kind. It was von Grunn's business to be scornful of all such.

"Now," he said, when all was cleared, "go to the bedroom and tell my orderly – " He broke off. "What was that?"

The other listened. Von Grunn could have sworn that the man's ears – pale and pointed – lifted voluntarily, like the ears of a cat or a fox. The sound came again, a prolonged howl in the distance.

"The wolves," came the quiet reply. "They speak to the full moon."

"Wolves?" The general was intrigued at once. He was a sportsman – that is, he liked to corner and kill beasts almost as much as he liked to corner and kill men. As a guest of Hermann Goering he had shot two very expensive wild bulls, and he yearned for the day when the Führer would graciously invite him to the Black Forest for pigsticking. "Are there many?" he asked. "It sounds like many. If they were not so far – "

"They come nearer," his companion said, and indeed the howl was repeated more strongly and clearly. "But you gave an order, general?"

"Oh, yes." Von Grunn remembered his hunger. "My man will bring me supper from among the things we have with us."

A bow, and the slender black figure moved noiselessly into the bedroom. Von Grunn crossed the floor and seated himself in an armchair before the table. The steward returned, and stood at his elbow.

"Pardon. Your orderly helped me carry the other food to the castle kitchen. He has not returned, and so I took the liberty of serving you."

He had a tray. Upon it were delicacies from von Grunn's mess chest – slices of smoked turkey, buttered bread, preserved fruits, bottled beer. The fellow had arranged them himself, had had every opportunity to . . . to –

Von Grunn scowled and took the monocle from his eye. The danger of poison again stirred in his mind, and he had difficulty scorning it. He must eat and drink, in defiance of fear.

Poison or no poison, the food was splendid, and the steward an excellent waiter. The general drank beer, and deigned to say, "You are an experienced servant?"

The pale, sharp face twitched sidewise in negation. "I serve very few guests. The last was years ago – Jonathan Harker, an Englishman – "

Von Grunn snorted away mention of that unwelcome people, and finished his repast. Then he rose, and stared around. The wolves howled again, in several directions and close to the castle.

"I seem to be deserted," he said grimly. "The captain is late, my orderly late. My men make no report." He stepped to the door, opened it. "Plesser!" he called. "Captain Plesser!"

No reply.

"Shall I bring you to him?" asked the steward gently. Once again, he had come up close. Von Grunn started violently, and wheeled.

The eyes of the steward were on a level with his, and very close. For the first time von Grunn saw that they were filled with green light. The steward was smiling, too, and von Grunn saw his teeth – white, spaced widely, pointed –

As if signalled by the thought, the howling of the beasts outside broke out afresh. It was deafeningly close. To von Grunn it sounded like hundreds. Then, in reply, came a shout, the voice of the *unteroffizer* uttering a quick, startled command.

At once a shot. Several shots.

The men he had encamped in the courtyard were shooting at something.

With ponderous haste, von Grunn hurried from the room, down the stairs. As he reached the passageway below, he heard more shots, and a wild air-rending chorus of howls, growls, spitting scuffles. Von Grunn gained the door by which he had entered. Something moved in the gloom at his very feet.

A chalky face turned up, the face of Captain Plesser. A hand lifted shakily to clutch at the general's boot top.

"Back in there, the dark rooms – " It was half a choke, half a sigh. "They're devils – hungry – they got the others, got me – I could come no farther than this – "

Plesser collapsed. Light came from behind von Grunn, and he could see the captain's head sagging backward on the stone. The side of the slender neck had been torn open, but blood did not come. For there was no blood left in Captain Plesser's body.

Outside, there was sudden silence. Stepping across Plesser's body, the general seized the latch and pushed the door open.

The courtyard was full of wolves, feeding. One glance was enough to show what they fed on. As von Grunn stared, the wolves lifted their heads and stared back. He saw many green-glowing eyes, level, hard, hungry, many grinning mouths with pointed teeth – the eyes and the teeth of the steward.

He got the door shut again, and sagged upon it, breathing hard.

"I am sorry, general," came a soft, teasing apology. "Sorry – my servants were too eager within and without. Wolves and vampires are hard to restrain. After all, it is midnight – our moment of all moments."

"What are you raving about?" gasped von Grunn, feeling his jaw sag.

"I do not rave. I tell simple truth. My castle has vampires within, wolves without, all my followers and friends – "

Von Grunn felt for a weapon. His great-coat was upstairs, the pistol in its pocket.

"Who are you?" he screamed.

"I am Count Dracula of Transylvania," replied the gaunt man in black.

He set down the lamp carefully before moving forward.

Nancy Kilpatrick

Teaserama

*Nancy Kilpatrick has been a finalist for the Bram Stoker Award and the
Aurora Award, and she is a winner of Canada's Arthur Ellis Award for
best mystery story.*

*She was born in Philadelphia, Pennsylvania, but is now a resident of
Montreal, Canada. Her books include the* Darker Passions *series of erotic
reworkings of classic horror themes (under the pseudonym 'Amarantha
Knight') and the vampire novels* Child of the Night, Near Death *and*
As One Dead, *the latter a collaboration with Don Bassingthwaite. Her
short fiction has appeared in numerous anthologies and magazines,* Sex
& the Single Vampire *and* The Vampire Stories of Nancy Kilpatrick
are collections of her stories, Endorphins *contains two vampire novellas,
ar.d she has also edited a number of erotic horror anthologies, including*
Love Bites, Flesh Fantastic *and* Sex Macabre.

*"All the events in this story surrounding Bettie Page and Irving Claw
are true," she explains. "Except Dracula, of course."*

*Dracula's financial fortunes have multiplied, and he finally foresakes
his homeland for the New World. But he is about to be smitten by
the charms of an aspiring showgirl who poses provocatively to pay the
rent . . .*

THE LEGGY BEAUTY wearing impossibly high stilettos pranced across the silver screen. Tall, raven haired with bangs, midnight undergarments gracing her slim yet curvaceous pale figure, she seemed to be the only star of these unusual movies able to do anything more than hobble in the patent-leather shoes. She undulated with a frolicsome grace that ignited him, and his ashes had been long cold.

Much to his amazement, humanity was changing. Five centuries he had walked the earth, nightly supping from the veins of these crass mortals. What he had imbibed contained not just vital nourishment for him, but the sum total of his cretinous victims' values. He had come to see humans as less than insectoid, with nothing to offer him but the blood. But now, oddly, he felt an infusion of life where he had expected none.

Vlad rewound the film around the reel and re-played the short black and white story for the tenth time. *Varietease* was one of his favourites, featuring Lili St. Cyr, and, more to his taste, Miss Betty Page! This Betty was a marvel, the woman of his dreams, were he still able to dream. Fetching, attractive, and most of all playful in her sensuality. Females in his youth had expressed either violence towards him, or had proven passive enough to retain his interest. Early on, when natural life had bubbled hot in his veins, when he had been full of passion, a warlord, fighting the Turks to retain his territory, and his own countrymen for power, he demanded his women be subdued. Life had been brutal enough back then – his mortal death verified that fact. Why fight with a woman in the boudoir? Oddly, immortality proved far easier, not particularly violent, yet he found himself less than enthralled with the 'humanizing' global changes. He was alone. Always. Stalking vapid prey through the streets of European and North American urban forests, destined to find none in sympathy, no empathy from the living, none in the progressively dispassionate centuries to inspire his appetites... This turn of the tide had left him depleted. Existence in a bland world produced ennui in one such as himself, one of immense substance. And he knew the cause: humanity. They were worse than peasants. Worse than the insects that crawled from the earth's graves. They viewed his state of ungrace far too simplistically, as they viewed their own pathetic lives. And that was the problem. They were neither terrified of him – hell bent on destroying him as those in the past had been – nor utterly enamoured. He lost interest in his snivelling soul-pale victims before he had drained the last drops of their vitae.

He watched the two lovelies cavort on screen, focusing mostly on Betty. She was young, winsome. She forced him to feel himself an anachronism, and that he could not, would not tolerate! He was Vlad Tepesh! Prince of Transylvania! King of the Living Dead! Lord of the Darkest Night! And he would have more than banality. He would have *love*.

As if out of a mist his celluloid vision turned towards the camera, towards him. He watched his pristine darling glide with the grace of a she-wolf. She played with the other, revelling in her role, whether as the giver or the receiver. Miss Page enjoyed herself to her naughty fullest. He longed for a woman who could enjoy herself. Who could appear so sweet and alluring and yet obviously kindle his intense passions. He deserved to enjoy himself as well. And, as always, he would have what he wanted.

The dark-haired beauty, who reminded him so much of his second wife, flirted with the camera lens. She seemed to stare right at him, a brazen, teasing look, one that he felt moved to tame. The other on screen punished her mildly – he would be more firm, that was certain. But even mild chastizement titillated him. This decade was truly a turning point in history, and like nothing else he had experienced. Oh, there had been French postcards, and those mild Victorian moving pictures at the turn of the last century. And he'd encountered a sufficient share of ladies of the night during his nocturnal wanderings. But never in several centuries had he witnessed such verve, such panache, such . . . full-blown erotic expression on a woman as fresh as the one he saw before him now.

Beside him lay an assortment of publications and film canisters, all featuring Miss Page: girlie magazines with cheesecake shots; *Cartoon and Model Parade* No. 53; various calendars; *Playboy Magazine*, January 1955, featuring Betty as the centrefold, photographed by Bunny Yeager . . .

Ah, Bunny Yeager. He remembered with pain spiking his heart the events of but one year ago. It had taken some time to find Betty, but when he did he acted at once. He discovered that Miss Page had gone to Florida, to be photographed by Yeager. Travel arrangements were made, and he arrived in Miami at the end of an arduous journey which spanned several days of riding by night on a train, only to discover after much searching that she had gone that day to a remote tourist attraction called Rural Africa, some seventy miles north of the city, and had not yet returned.

He discovered the location of her apartment – information in this less-congested city was not difficult to obtain with his powers – and there he awaited her return. She did return, but rather than retire, she proceeded to a main building. He watched her through a window, talking animatedly with several others, dining, relaxing, sewing a small leopard-skin garment out on the verandah while she chatted, one of the adorable outfits she wore. And all the while, his ardour grew. She was as effervescent in the flesh as on the screen. He determined that this night she would be his! Finally, just after 1.00 a.m., she left the main building for her cottage close by. This was the first time he had found her alone. He watched her walk along the path, as stunned as a novice lover, unable to approach her, fearful of rejection. She entered her residence and bolted the door. He rebuked himself. How had he been reduced to this! He, a *vivode*, Prince of Wallachia! Destroyer of the Ottoman invaders, and the betrayers who called themselves countrymen! His childish hesitation now meant that she was inaccessible. He could not gain admittance without an invitation, and without contact with Miss Page, he would not receive one.

The frustration drove him to her window, in the alley at the back, where he peered inside through a break in the Venetian blinds. He watched her undress for bed. He held his breath; the sight of her sublime physique stunned him to silence. Such beauty felt unearthly, as if a cloud had parted and this angel had fallen from heaven – did they know she was missing? Unawares, his fingernails clawed the screen over the window. Only when she turned, a delicious look of terror streaking her features, did he realize what he had done.

Quick to remedy the situation, he decided that when she came to the window, he would instil the thought in her mind, through the glass, to open the window, to admit him. He pulled the screen away, for a better contact, and watched her snatch an article of clothing with which to cover herself and hurry toward him until she was so close he could only see her waist. He paused, waiting for the blind to lift.

"I'll give you two seconds to get away from this window or I'll blow your brains out!"

Startled by her booming voice, he had no idea she possessed a weapon. The pistol would not harm him, of course, but the noise would draw others. His sense returned, and he retreated, biding his time, until the following night, when he would find a way to meet her outdoors, to look into her eyes, to capture her will and make her his own.

But the following evening she was gone. Inquiries let him know that the photo shoot had been completed and Miss Page had returned to New York. He felt devastated. Thwarted like a mere schoolboy. Unable to grasp this failure. There had seemed nothing to do but return to New York himself, and plot out a further opportunity.

Varietease finished and the end of the film spun off the feeder reel. It was one of his favourites, but he liked the others as well, the ones with the girls play-spanking each other. The one where Miss Page helped tie another to an oak. Miss Page was a woman of unusual thespian talents. She excelled as both the discipliner and the disciplined, and that he found exceptional. He especially enjoyed that odd contraption, so like a medieval instrument of torture, on which a woman tied Miss Page, spread-eagled, upright, only to pull on both ends of the rope and lift the enchanting Betty off the ground. Four centuries of seduction of increasingly insipid mortals had left him a tad jaded; his libido had grown as quiet as had his once-beating heart. And now, at this juncture in history, in this metropolis of New York City, he was revived. Had he been capable of tears, he would have cried them – tears of joy.

A glance out the window and he could see how the night quivered. He felt youthful, driven by something other than pure bloodlust. This city was the hub of the universe. The dawn, as it were, of a proverbial new day. It also teemed with human beings. Finding blood was never a problem. Finding Miss Page alone had been. She was popular, always busy, always accompanied. Two years of effort on his part had resulted in constant frustration. But he sensed that time, though eternal, held an urgency he had not experienced for centuries, and he valued that tension.

He snapped off the projector and grabbed up his cane to begin the search for Miss Betty Page.

Irving Klaw's studios, he had only recently learned, lay close by, in a warehouse. Rumour had it, Klaw was shooting *Teaserama*, and Vlad hastened to make his way there before the filming was completed.

Enroute, he stopped at a kiosk to flip through a new publication, with still photos from *Strip-o-Rama*, one of her films. There was the sparkling Miss Page, in all her titillating glory! This era was indeed marvellous. Nothing left to the imagination. He felt he had finally come home in a sense, returning full-circle to the core of life. Finally society was opening, like the wounds of pierced flesh, and the lifeblood poured forth for all to drink at will. And at the centre, Miss Page, a woman into whom he seriously wanted to sink his fangs.

"She's a doll, alright. Have a gander at that, bub." The rat-like man who ran the kiosk nodded at a calendar hanging from the back wall.

Miss Page on a beach, in the sunshine – oh how she caused him to long for the sun! – wearing a sparse swimsuit. Smiling her engaging, teasing smile, her lithe body with the come-hither tilt of her hips . . .

"You buyin'?"

He turned toward the rat of a man. One glance at those rodent eyes and the creature was made nearly dumb, only murmuring, "Go ahead. Take it, mister."

Vlad threw the photoplay volume at the vendor. He did not need these cheap imitations. By sunrise, he would possess the flesh and blood woman of his desires.

Klaw's studio lay hidden in the warehouse district, protected by meat packing plants and dry goods wholesalers. Vlad had been here before, many times, searching for Betty. But as dumb luck would have it, either she was elsewhere, or else accompanied by a gaggle of friends. Even when he'd staked out this premises nightly when they first began to shoot *Teaserama*, he could not find her alone. Tonight, though, he was determined. Tonight he would gain admittance to the building, then to the studio. And finally to Miss Page herself.

He waited until he saw someone head towards the entrance. No sooner had they entered the main door than he was behind, catching the door as it closed, calling out.

A young man delivering sandwiches from a delicatessen turned, a startled look denting his freckly face. It took no time for Vlad to embed the proper words in his brain, and the youth soon repeated the magic phrase, "Sure, come on in."

Once inside, the warehouse was a maze of doors. Some sported signs: Friedman's Fruitcakes; The Button Hole; Crown Cork and Can . . . He wandered the twenty stories, disregarding the doors which obviously did not house a film studio on the other side, pressing his ear to the ones that gave little or no indication of what lay within. Finally, after much searching, he heard voices:

"Don't worry, honey, just gimme a big smile. It's gonna be alright." This accompanied by the sound of what might have been a crank.

It was do or die the true death. He knocked and heard a "Damn!"

The man who appeared at the crack the door opened was of ordinary height, with a dark moustache and intense, red-rimmed eyes. "Yeah?" he said suspiciously.

"I am searching for Betty Page."

"You and a two thousand other guys," he said. "What's your business with her?"

It took only seconds to mesmerize this man and to gain admittance.

Within lay a film studio in one large space, or what remained of it. The area was almost barren. Boxes had been packed and stacked near the door. Tripods were propped against the wall, and cameras and film canisters had been gathered together. A woman in midlife, the only other person in the room, wanted to know, "Irving, who's this guy?"

The man named Irving shook his head, as if waking from sleep.

"You a fed?" she asked.

"Nah. He don't look the type," Irving said.

"I am searching for Miss Page. Where may I find her?" Vlad said.

"That's anybody's guess. She took off last week, like all the others, God knows where. Just after they started in on us."

"Make yourself clear!" Vlad demanded, impatience rising alongside the fear gnawing up his spine.

"The House of Representatives. You know, the federal government? Don't you read the papers?"

The woman moved closer. "The House Unamerican Activities Committee. They figure we film smut and that ain't exactly American or something."

"Meaning?" Vlad asked, but after five centuries walking the earth, he already understood.

"Meaning," the man said, "they shut us down. That there's all that's left. A copy."

Vlad walked to the canister the man pointed at and picked it up. *Teaserama* the label read. All that remained of Betty Page.

"Hey! You can't take that!" the man shouted, as Vlad turned towards the door, cradling the canister against his stone-cold heart.

One look from the Price of Darkness, a look not intended to mesmerize, a look that conveyed a depth of pain no mortal could bear to see for long, caused Irving Klaw to say softly – and Vlad knew it was not out of terror but out of empathy – "I got the original anyways, or Friedman does. Take it. You need her."

And he did.

Nancy Holder

Blood Freak

Nancy Holder is the winner of four Horror Writers Association Bram Stoker Awards, three for short stories and one for novel. She has written fifteen romance novels under a variety of bylines, the mainstream thriller Rough Cut, *the tie-in volume* Highlander: Measure of a Man, *the horror novels* Dead in the Water, Making Love *and* Witch-Light *(the latter two in collaboration with Melanie Tem), and she is currently working on a science fiction trilogy. Her short fiction has appeared in a wide range of magazines and anthologies, including* Love in Vein, The Mammoth Book of Vampires, Dark Voices 6 *and* Narrow Houses.

It is the Swinging Sixties and Dracula feels reborn. Always a natural leader, he now finds himself surrounded by young people who regard him as a figure of mystery and great power . . .

CAPTAIN BLOOD. The Bat Man. He lived in a real castle, that is to say, someone built it to live in, not to film it, in the middle of the Borrego Desert. That is to say, east of San Diego, that Republican bastion of the Military Industrial Complex of Amerika, north of the Mexican border, where you could score lids of grass for five bucks a pop. His craggy, Scottish castle had been in some John Carradine movie, which some people found more trippy than the rumour that the current owner was a vampire.

Blood was his freak. No surprise, Pranksters: because if you travelled the rippling sidewinder dessication to that *Shock!* Theater on the mesa, you had to have resources, interior (that is to, say, grey matter) and exterior (that is to say, eyes and ears) that the average headfeeder either did not have or use very well. So you synthesized; that is to say, you took things in. You figured things out.

You were observant. You grokked the fullness of the situation.

Going to the castle was the Great Bloodfreak Trek, the GBT, and you did it straight enough to drive, stoned enough to take the edge off, beating on the dashboard to the arhythmic spasms of your carotid artery and the great good muscle that pumped it all together now. You and whatever merry band you had banded with could not help but hear the stories at the gas stations where you copped a pee and the bars where you guzzled whatever was cheapest ("We don't serve no hippies"; "Right on, man, we don't eat 'em"). The bourgeoisie crossing themselves like flipped-out movie extras, and cops warning you off the rumble-crunching dirtrock road. Go back, go back, go back, you stupid kids; he really is a fuckin' bloodsucker.

So are mosquitoes, baby. It's all one big mandala. He was out front with it, *he liked to suck people's blood*, and if you pretended not to grok his trip and showed up on his doorstep anyway, that was your bullshit, not his.

Vlad Dracula was no longer certain if he was mesmerized or bored to tears by the antic dances of the counterculture. In the fifties – Kerouac and the beats, bongos and a fascination with Italy – he had moved from San Francisco with his servants and his Brides and sought refuge in the desert. In San Francisco there had been too much scrutiny, too many questions, and then a woman he had entertained a number of times began writing poetry that she read in coffee shops:

> *He is my biterman, Daddy-o,*
> *he ramthroats my red trickle*
> *down.*

Thus identified, he had fled.

In the desert, he had hibernated for a time, missing the chill and the rain of San Francisco, the cold and the snow of Europe. But he had existed undetected, and kept himself fed, enjoying his homesickness as only someone who is very old can enjoy the sublime delicacy of emotions less intense than grief or despair – wistfulness, nostalgia, the watercolour washes of faint regret. But for him this was a game; he could leave any time he wanted.

Then came the changeling children, with their psychedelia and their excesses that reminded him of the oldest of his old days. The pageantry and drama of his Transylvanian court, the blood baths and virgins and the joy of opulence and extremity. Somehow one confused flower child stumbled to his castle, and then another, and another, until he was the source of a pilgrimage.

His servants begged him to leave, or at least to halt the flow of half-baked mortality. But he found he enjoyed the little hippies not so much for the quality of their company as the fact that they sought him out. They capered and gyrated for his amusement; ate his banquets; made up terrible, overwrought poetry which they loved to recite to him after dinner; and dared one another, in hushed tones, to bare their necks for him, even though he never asked them to. Was he or wasn't he? He never revealed himself, keeping his own counsel and instructing the Brides and the servants to do likewise.

Gradually he came to trust his admirers as he had once trusted his Gypsies. They proved worthy of that trust, if only because no one who could do anything about him listened to their conjectures about the Court of the Crimson King. His most ardent groupies were ineffectual and inarticulate, and therefore, harmless.

For that harmlessness, Dracula pitied them. In their beaded costumes and banshee hair, they whirled and swirled and postured. *I'm so . . . so much, man!* He wondered if they were actually more controlled and controlling than their middle-class comrades who had gotten Beatle cuts and stayed home with their families. Among the scruffy little vagabonds, each stunt, each pronouncement, each thought was scrutinized, analyzed, compared against an unfathomable standard of intellectual prowess they didn't possess and karmic serendipity that did not exist:

I said "red," man, and the Captain walked into the room!

Whoa, heavy! Check it out! You just told me that and he left the room!

He was sorry that there was no such thing as karmic serendipity. It would have made his long life more interesting. So, like the hundreds of thousands of this time, he turned to drugs. The children took an astonishing variety of drugs: hashish, marijuana, Thai sticks, peyote, mushrooms, and pills of all shapes and sizes. They popped the pills as one might vitamins; they smoked their hemp and hashish like cigarettes, and the rest they cooked with butter and honey and nibbled like Turkish Delight.

But none of it worked on Dracula. He tried everything, smoking and popping and even shooting up as well as sucking the blood of some child who was high or tripping or strung out. Nothing worked.

Nor could they explain to him what it felt like. Mostly they lay on the cold castle floors with the same vacant delirium that accompanied one of his feedings, making trails with their hands and quoting song lyrics. It was a terrible waste to him that the expansion of these inarticulate, unformed minds yielded nothing more than an increased capacity for vacuousness. Whereas he, with his supernatural lifespan and deep connection to the very mythos of this race, possessed a mind worth expanding, and he couldn't do it.

He kept hoping one of them would rise like cream to the top, someone with whom he could explore and converse, that from this one he would learn the secrets of the drug-taker's universe. He continued to encourage their pilgrimages to his castle, their whisperings and invasions of his privacy. (Is he or isn't he? It's so trippy, the man's so *white*!) The young men all wanted to have sexual intercourse with the Brides, and the young girls wanted to have sexual intercourse with him. That was all right; he was into their scene of promiscuity. Breasts and thighs and hips and sex organs, so much writhing flesh brimming with ramthroat red; it was groovy, as they said.

But after a while, it was all only a series of repeat performances, endlessly repeatable. There was not a one among them he would considering Changing. He had not Changed anyone in almost a century. The hippie children became tiresome and he considered impaling them all. But someone on the outside was bound to find out and then there would be hell to pay. The authorities in America were currently as repressive and autocratic as he had been in his prime. They didn't torture their victims physically, as he had; instead they lied about them to the press and threw them in prisons on trumped-up charges. Had he possessed the same means of mass communication in his day back in Carpathia, he might have done the same thing. It certainly was effective.

He reverted to old, secret habits. In the cold desert night, he swooped down on coyotes, rabbits, soared upward and tore owls to shreds. But depressed and listless as he had become, even the atavistic joy of the hunt proved muted and fleeting.

Then his lieutenant, Alexsandru, came to him one day with excellent news: Dr Timothy Leary wanted to pay him a visit. The famous Dr Leary, father of this entire movement of tuning in and turning on, of dropping acid and exploring alternate realities.

The standard bearer of the deeper life.

Dracula didn't realize at the time that Dr Leary had just broken out of jail in San Luis Obispo, a town up the coast. He hadn't known Dr Leary was in jail in the first place. But word of his imminent arrival swept through the castle like the sharp wail of a wolf.

Tim Leary, Dr Leary. The mortal's name was a mantra among the hippie children. Despite his anxiety about the local authorities, Captain Blood found it within himself to chuckle at his own jealousy of their anticipation of the visit. He was used to being the princely topic of discussion. Perhaps a legend should never try to compete with an icon.

He only hoped that Dr. Leary would bring rain to the desert.

He waited like a school girl for the visit, laying in food – the hippies were happy with brown rice and *miso* soup, but one noble must entertain another suitably. He went over his wardrobe – fringed jacket and tie-dyed T-shirt? Black turtleneck sweater and sports jacket? He presided over the castle preparations – rooms cleaned, linens washed and pressed – until one sunset, Alexsandru rapped soundly on the door of Dracula's inner sanctum and announced, "They've arrived!"

Dracula finally decided on a Nehru jacket and black trousers – he was not a hippie child; he was a grown man – and descended the staircase with an unhurried air although his unbeating heart contracted once or twice.

Leary came to him with both arms extended and took Dracula's hands in his. Dracula looked into his large, deep eyes and knew that at last he had found his mortal counterpart: a man who had lived the depth and breadth of experience. Hopeful, Dracula embraced him.

"Ah," said the mass of counterculture lounging in the great hall. The cavernous room was thick with scented marijuana smoke, clove cigarettes, astringic red wine and sweat. The yeast of sex.

"Welcome," Dracula said.

Leary winked at him and presented his wife. Dracula gaped. She was astonishingly beautiful. His attraction to her was immediate and intense, and to mask it he ignored her.

"We'll dine," he added, and sounded to himself old-fashioned and silly, a movie version of himself. Lugosi the Drug Addict, not Vlad the Impaler, in whose presence the fathers of daughters trembled and the daughters fainted. In those days, his favour was like a comet tail: either a beautiful radiance or a harbinger of disaster.

How he had fallen in the New World! Plummeted!

The servants prepared an exquisite table, which the hippie children devoured with no hesitation or delicacy whatsoever while

Leary spoke of the movements toward universal truth and inner peace. He revealed to Dracula that many prominent psychiatrists in Los Angeles were using LSD in their practices. They were giving LSD to movie stars like Cary Grant and Jack Nicholson. Cary Grant had wanted to make a movie about LSD. So had Otto Preminger. He spoke of all the brilliant thinkers who had moved to Los Angeles, attracted by the climate of intellectual freedom: Thomas Mann, Aldous Huxley. As he talked, his wife listened as if she had never heard any of this before. Excellent woman! Intriguing man! Dracula was overjoyed that they had come.

So were the flower children, who sprang up in the castle hothouse like so many celestial poppies. In microvans and magic buses, caravans and myriad groups of simpleton singletons. Across the Great Desert on the GBT, to sit at the feet of the great and mysterious Leary.

Who talked faster than a speeding bullet.

Who leaped thought chasms in a single bound.

"If we charged admission, you'd be rich," Leary told Dracula one night, as they kicked back with some Panama Red. Rosemary was nowhere to be found, but a few addled braless girls lounged about, perhaps angling to become Brides. Dracula contented himself with caressing them idly, if only to feel the heat of the pulses beneath their skin. It was was a pleasant habit, like biting one's nails.

He was more interested in discovering what pulsed inside Leary's brain. The stories the man told! The adventures he had had, inspired by the drugs he had taken! Taking psilocybin in Tangier with William S. Burroughs! Discussing with Allen Ginsberg and the politics of ecstasy. Arguing with Jack Kerouac, who disdained him. Leary's life was one vast experimental, highly responsive moment in the now. Dracula came to look upon him as a counterculture Scheherazade, a mortal who could tempt him to stay up all night and look upon the fatal sun.

"Let's go in the hot tub," Leary said suddenly one night, shedding his clothes. The girls threw theirs off as well.

Dracula had once been warned that he couldn't immerse himself in water, but he had found that to be untrue. The hot tub almost warmed his cold flesh. So he took off his clothes – the king of the undead! – and joined Leary and the young virgins in the water.

"Admission, " Leary said. "We'd make enough money to fund the film."

"I'm a nobleman," Dracula replied. "I have obligations of hospitality."

"Vladimir, you've got to shed these outmoded thought patterns," Leary chided him. Though the girls bobbed and grinned, Leary ignored them, talking only to Dracula. It was apparent that the man was faithful to his wife and would continue to be so. Dracula found that admirable, if somewhat stifling. He would like very much for Leary's wife to have a reason to retaliate against ill treatment. She was that stunning.

The girls got tired and left. Leary leaned forward and whispered, "Bite me. I want to know what it feels like."

"So, you believe I'm really a vampire?" Dracula asked. "I'm not just another acid trip for the little kiddies?"

Leary looked surprised. "I believed in you before I got here, man. Why do you think I came?"

Dracula was momentarily embarrassed. He had assumed the sophisticated Leary believed that he, Dracula, was simply another guru of the times, a charismatic leader who attracted rootless, searching kids. Dracula had taken pride in the notion that there was something intrinsically fascinating about him besides the fact that he was a supernatural being.

But over the course of the days and weeks, it became apparent that that was the only thing Leary found fascinating about him. Leary interrupted Dracula's musings, both when they were alone and in front of his hippie children of the night. He debated him, and handily won, as Dracula didn't have many facts and figures to pull from his head, while the well-read, well-connected Leary did.

He revitalized many of the young hippies who came to the castle, as a decent guru should. In their quest for coolness, they had become radicalized; they were leftist, cynical, and unhappy.

But Leary lambasted them: "You can't do good unless you feel good," he told them. It became the phrase of the day on the GBT.

The goal became to be happy, to feel good, to grow and learn. And it became obvious to Dracula that his groupies believed Leary could teach them how.

Leary, and not he.

They ate his food and slept in his rooms and barns and outbuildings and bothered his horses and hit on his servants, all the while discussing What Tim Said, What Tim Meant, What Tim Did. They lost sight of the fact that they were guests and became squatters; that they were visitors and became denizens. They stopped cleaning up after themselves, because Leary didn't. They stopped saying thank you, because Leary never did.

But worst of all, they stopped being afraid of Dracula. Was he or wasn't he? No one cared. Their minds dwelled now on all the confounding possibilities Leary presented with so much charm and enthusiasm that they didn't appear to realize he was casting pearls before swine. At least, that was how Dracula saw it all.

One day Alexsandru came to him, bowed deeply, and told him with all deference that the great lord must reassert his position, and that His Grace the Count must tell Leary to leave. Dracula promised to do both.

But it was difficult. In this modern country, he possessed no authority to compel the hippie children to do anything, least of all respect him because he once had been more ruthless than any of the leaders they distrusted. And he didn't want Leary to leave, because as dominating as Leary was, he was the most interesting person Dracula had ever met.

"I sense you have cognitive dissonance about something," Leary ventured one night in the hot tub. "How about this?"

Then he suggested a wild plan: that on the next full moon, when the forces of night were strongest, he, Leary, would ingest terrific quantities of LSD and other drugs, and then he would hypnotize Dracula into a receptive state, and then *he* would bite Dracula.

"It will Change you," Dracula told him.

Leary smiled. "It'll Change you, too."

So, Leary tempted Dracula into making him a vampire by promising him an acid trip. That was what it boiled down to, when Dracula examined the offer from all sides. Was it worth it? He imagined Leary moving through the centuries, gathering acolytes, spreading the word. Not about vampirism, surely. Either he would agree to silence on that score, or Dracula would refuse him. The moon moved through her courses. Dracula watched its progress and Leary watched him, eager to die.

Finally Dracula decided that as much as he wanted the gift of great consciousness, he could not share his powers with Leary. The man was already too strong. His powers of persuasion were admirable and awe-inspiring. If ever one day they found themselves in disagreement, Dracula would have created his own worst enemy.

He put off telling the charismatic mortal, hoping Leary would understand his reticence and give up on the idea himself.

Then Alexsandru informed them that the FBI were coming. They had been pursuing Leary, a fugitive from justice, ever since his jail break, and they had just picked up the scent.

Dracula was alarmed. This did not bode well for a blood freak. The *blood* freak of all time.

He told Leary, who apologized profusely.

"The best thing you can do now," Dracula told him, "is to leave as soon as possible."

"Yes," Leary agreed, and Dracula was relieved. He ordered his servants to prepare a marvellous feast for the great man's last night among them. Rosemary dressed for the occasion in a stunning black velvet dress with jet bead decorations, a costume Dracula's mother might have worn. He wanted her more than ever, and he was sorry he would never have her.

There was wine, and revelry, and though neither Leary nor Dracula had told the hippie children that Leary was leaving, they appeared to know. Some were packing with the idea of following him wherever he went. At dinner he rose and begged them not to, pointing out that the FBI would surely find him with so many little bloodhounds trailing after. Dracula, jealous, wished the disloyal ones would leave: he would cull his herd that way, swooping down in the dead of night as they made their way across the vast expanses of Leary's flight to Egypt.

"One last glass together?" Leary asked after they finished the magnificent dinner.

"Yes," Dracula agreed.

Dracula led him to the turret room where the already-bubbling hot tub was. They got in, sighing with the heat, and Leary poured two glasses of deep, rich Hungarian wine from a bottle on the deck. He handed one to Dracula, who *could* drink it, contrary to folk myth, and they toasted.

"To the incredible possibilities of existence," Leary said, and Dracula found tears in his eyes for that which was not to be, a long and enduring friendship with this extraordinary man.

They drank. Above them, in the skylight, the full moon glowed. Dracula leaned back in the hot water, to discover the beautiful hands of Rosemary kneading his shoulders. He smiled at her and closed his eyes while Leary spoke of something; of what he was not sure, the religion Leary had founded or the beauty of LSD or any of a number of topics. His muscles relaxed, releasing the tension of centuries. He drank more wine, unable, as mortals were, to get drunk.

Words in Leary's soft voice spoke of change and optimism for the future, and the unfolding of mankind, and the need to fly out of oneself
>   and change
>   and Rosemary melted the furrows out of Dracula's brow
>   and change
and the next thing Dracula was aware of was a sharp, deep penetration in his neck, and sucking. Slowly he opened his eyes and said, "You tricked me," but he didn't know how.

Yet, as the blood seeped out of him, the room melted down itself and became a stunning, incandescent forest. Beatific women smiled down on him like the Madonnas of Russian Orthodox icons. His muscles were completely gone, his veins, his arteries, his princely blood. That was okay, that was, as they said, groovy.

He saw the melodies of his homeland – blood red, crimson, scarlet, vermilion; he heard the colours of his life – Gothic chants and Gregorian chants, the keening of lonely wolves and the sweet, ethereal voices of his Brides. The sweeping gales of the children of the night. The laughter of the bat; the plaintive whispers of rodents.

Beautiful, beautiful; chimes in the back portion of his mind, promising him midnight, one, two, three, in the depths of the black night in Carpathia. The splendour that he was, more magnificent than ever he had remembered. The miracle that he was, and the endless possibilities for expression given to him.

"I can catch my soul," he whispered. "It's so beautiful."

Leary said, "You made it, Vladimir. You're tripping."

And Dracula immediately crashed.

No longer tripping, no longer mesmerized, no longer relaxed. His eyes flew open and he said, "Bastard. Out of my sight. Betrayer. Thief."

"But, Vlad," Leary began.

Dracula flung himself at him, teeth bared, preparing for the kill, when Leary flew out of reach.

Flew.

Rosemary looked frightened, and backed away from them both.

"I've been Changed," Leary said. He opened his mouth and showed Dracula his teeth.

"There's only one way to settle this," Dracula said, rising from the dripping water in all his majesty. He was the King of the Vampires; he would not let this usurper survive another minute.

"Settle it?" Leary asked, perplexed.

"Yes, you idiot." Dracula advanced, sneering at him. The King of Peace and Love. He had no idea what violence he would commit as a vampire.

Leary backed away, ran up against the side of the tub, and crawled out. "What a minute. Wait." Perhaps he was beginning to understand he had made a terrible miscalculation.

Then Alexsandru rushed in. "The FBI! They're at the gates!"

Suddenly everyone was scrambling. Into clothes and coats, passports and money stuffed into hands, the fugitives sneaking through the dungeon to the unguarded rear of the castle. The

flower children, rising to the occasion, harassing and teasing the
authorities.

The Learys took flight, and were safe.

The FBI were too stupid to see what Dracula was, and left after
stern warnings about harbouring criminals.

Dracula was alone with his motley crew, and as he looked up at
the setting moon, he wept.

Years later, after the flowers and the pharmacopoeia and the
dog-eared copies of the *Tibetan Book of the Dead* were locked in
attic trunks, it was said that Leary died. It was said that his head
was severed from his body and frozen. It was said that he had
requested this action in the hope that he could be revived in a
more advanced time and brought back to life.

When Alexsandru told Dracula of this, Captain Blood laughed. No
one knew exactly why. Some claimed it was because he remembered
Leary so fondly. Others, that he found Leary's hope for a second
chance as a disembodied head typically Leary, and very amusing.

And still others, that he had ordered the beheading, because
that was one way to kill a vampire.

But everyone agreed that of a night, he took the hand of his
best beloved Bride, who looked very much like Rosemary Leary,
and they flew together over the rippling sidewinder dessication,
shadows like condors against the full and glowing desert moon.

For Alan Scrivener, dear and respected friend.

Brian Lumley

Zack Phalanx is
Vlad the Impaler

Brian Lumley's vampiric 'Necroscope' series has made him a bestseller on both sides of the Atlantic with such titles as Necroscope, Wamphyri!, The Source, Deadspeak *and* Deadspawn; *a follow-up 'Vampire World' trilogy:* Blood Brothers, The Last Aerie *and* Bloodwars, *plus the two-volume* Necroscope: The Lost Years. *His other novels include* Beneath the Moors, The Burrowers Beneath, The Transition of Titus Crow, Spawn of the Winds, The Clock of Dreams, In the Moons of Borea, Elysia, The Compleat Crow, Hero of Dreams, Ship of Dreams *and* Mad Moon of Dreams, Khai of Ancient Khem, Psychomech, Psychosphere *and* Psychamok, The House of Doors *and* Demogorgon. Ghoul Warning and Other Omens *is a slim volume of poetry, and his short fiction is collected in* The Caller of the Black, The Horror at Oakdene, The House of Cthulhu and Other Tales of the Primal Land, The Last Rite, Fruiting Bodies and Other Fungi *(which includes the British Fantasy Award-winning title story),* Dagon's Bell and Other Discords, Return of the Deep Ones and Other Mythos Tales *and* The Second Wish and Other Exhalations.

Back in Transylvania, a Hollywood film crew is about to discover that old legends never die . . .

HARRY S. SKATSMAN, Jr., was livid. He was a tiny, fat, cigar-chewing, fire-eating, primadonna-taming, scene-shooting ball of absolutely *livid* livid. Of all things: an accident! And on his birthday, too! Zack Phalanx, superstar, "King of the Bad Guys", had been involved in some minor accident back in Beverly Hills; an accident which, however temporarily, had curtailed his appearance on location.

Skatsman groaned, his scarlet jowls drooping and much of the anger rushing out of him in one vast sigh. What if the accident was worse than he'd been told? What if Zack was out of the film (horrible thought) permanently? All that *so*-expensive advance publicity – all the bother over visas and work permits, and the trouble with the local villagers – all for nothing. Of course, they could always get someone to fill Zack's place (Kurt Douglash, perhaps?) but it wouldn't be the same. In his mind's eye Skatsman could see the headlines in the film rags already: "*Zack Phalanx WAS Vlad the Impaler*!"

The little fat man groaned again at this mental picture, then leaned forward in his plush leather seat and snarled (he never spoke to anyone, always snarled) at his driver: "Joe, you sure the message said Zack was only *slightly* hurt? He didn't *stick* himself on his steering wheel or something?"

"Yeah, slightly hurt," Joe grunted. "Minor accident." Joe had been driving his boss now for so many years, on location in so many parts of the world, that Skatsman's snarls no longer fazed him –

– But they fazed most everyone else.

Even as the big car ploughed steadily through mid-afternoon mist as it rose up out of the valleys on old, winding roads that were often only just third class, high above in the village-sized huddle of caravans, huts and shacks, up in the glowering Carpathian Mountains, Harry S. Skatsman's colleagues prepared themselves for all hell let loose when the florid, fiery little director returned.

They all knew now that Zack Phalanx had been injured, that his arrival at Jlaskavya airport had been "unavoidably delayed". And they knew moreover just exactly what that meant where Skatsman was concerned. The little fat man would be utterly unapproachable, poisonous, raging one minute and sobbing the next in unashamed frustration, until "Old Grim-Grin" (as Phalanx was fondly known in movie circles) showed up. Then they could shoot his all-important scenes.

This dread of the director in dire mood was shared by all and sundry, from the producer, Jerry Sollinger (a man of no mean status himself), right down to Sam "Sugar" Sweeney, the coffee-boy – who was in fact a man of sixty-three – and including sloe-eyed Shani Silarno, the heroine of this, Skatsman's fourteenth epic.

Oh, there was going to be a fuss, all right, but what – they all asked among themselves – would the fuss really be all about? For in all truth Zack Phalanx's scenes were not to be many. His magic box-office name on the billboards, starred as Vlad the Impaler himself, was simply to be a draw, a "name" to pull the crowds. For the same reason Shani Silarno was cheesecake, though certainly she had far more footage than the grim, scarfaced, sardonic, ugly, friendly "star" of the picture.

And most of that picture, filmed already, had been dashed off to Hollywood for the usual pre-release publicity screenings – except for the Phalanx scenes, which, now that the star was known to be out of it, however temporarily, Jerry Solinger had explained away in a hastily drummed-up, fabulously expensive telephone call as being simply too terrific, too fantastically *good* to be shown in any detail before the actual premier. Of course, the gossip columnists would know better, but hopefully before they got their wicked little claws into the story Phalanx would be out here in Romania and all would be well . . .

But meanwhile the important battle scenes, all ketchup and zenf though they were, would have to wait on the arrival of Old Grim-Grin, injured in some minor traffic accident.

Producer Jerry Sollinger was beginning to wish he'd never heard of Vlad the Impaler; or rather, that Harry S. Skatsman had never heard of him. Sollinger could still remember when first the fat little director had snarled into his office to slam down upon his desk a file composed of bits and pieces of collected facts and lore concerning one Vlad Dracula. This Vlad – Vlad being a title of some sort, possibly "Prince" – had been a fifteenth-century warlord, a Wallach of incredible cruelty. Like his ancestors before him, he had led his people against wave after wave of invading Turks, Magyars, Bulgars, Lombards and others equally barbaric, to beat them back from his princedom aerie in the foreboding mountains of Carpathia.

He was, in short, the original Dracula; but whichever historian appended the words "the Impaler" to his name had in mind a different sort of impaling than did Bram Stoker when he wrote his popular novel. Vlad V Tsepeth Dracula of Wallachia had earned his name by sticking the captured hundreds of his enemies vertically on rank after rank of upright stakes, where they might sit and scream out the mercifully short remainder of their lives in hideous agony while he and other nobles laughed and cantered their warhorses up and down amidst the blood and gore.

The vampire legend in connection with Vlad V probably sprang up not only from this monstrous method of execution, but also from the fact that a Wallachian curse has it (despite his lying dead for over five hundred years) that Vlad the Impaler "will return from the grave with his warriors of old to protect his lands if ever again invaders penetrate his boundaries."

This, roughly, was the information Skatsman's file contained, and to its cover he had stapled a single sheet of paper bearing the following story-line, his synoptic "plan" of the epic-to-be:

"Vlad Drac, (Zack Phalanx), scorned by his subjects and the sovereigns of neighbouring kingdoms and princedoms alike for his chicken, pacifist ways, finally loses his cool and takes up the sword against the invader (something like *Friendly Persuasion* but with mountains and battle-axes). This only after his castle has been burned right off the edge of its precipice by the advancing Turks, and after his niece, the young Princess Minerna, (Shani Silarno), has been raped by the Turk barbarian boss, (Tony Kwinn?). To conclude, we'll have Vlad V suicide after his boys mistakenly stick his mistress, (Glory Graeme?), who has dressed like a Turk camp-follower to escape the invaders, not realizing that Vlad has already whupped them? Robert Black can whip this up into something good." To this brief, almost cryptic outline, Skatsman had appended his signature.

And from that simple seed the idea had blossomed, mushrooming into a giant project, an epic; by which time it had been too late for Sollinger to back out. Truth of the matter was that the producer was a little fearful of these so-called "epic" productions: just such a project had almost ruined him many years ago. But with such a story – with the awesome, disquieting grandeur of the Carpathian Mountains as background, with a list of stars literally type-cast into the very parts for which they were acclaimed and which they played best, with Skatsman as director (and he was a very *good* director, despite his tantrums) – well, what *could* go wrong?

Much could go wrong . . .

And yet at first it had seemed like plain sailing. The new peace-pact with the Eastern-bloc countries had helped them in the end to get the necessary visas; that and the promise of recruitment as extras of hundreds of the poor, local villagers into bit parts. And this latter of course had saved much on costumary, for the dress and costumes of these people had not much changed in five centuries. On the other hand, there had been little of the filmstar in them. When they were used, each fragment of each and every scene had to be directed with the most minute attention to detail, always through an interpreter and invariably with the end result that Skatsman, before he could be satisfied, would have the set in uproar. The stars would be threatening to walk out, the local "actors" themselves gibbering in fear of the little man's temper, as though the director were the great Vlad V himself resurrected!

Indeed, when finally those locals – all two hundred eighty of them – *had* walked off the set, flatly refusing to work any longer on the giant production, Skatsman had been blamed. Not to his face, of course not, but behind his back the cast and technicians had "known" that he was the spanner in the works. This did not explain, though, the fact that when Philar Jontz the PR man went after the runaways, in fact to pay them their last wages, he discovered two empty villages! Not only had the rather primitive "actors" deserted the film – not that it mattered greatly, for all of their important scenes were already in the can – but they had taken their families, friends, indeed the entire populations of their home villages with them. Stranger still, the quaint old town into which they had all moved *en masse* was only a mile or so further down the mountain road. Whatever they were running away from, well, they had not bothered to run very far!

Ever the PR man, Jontz had followed them, only to discover that in the now badly overcrowded town no one would have anything to do with him, neither refugees nor regular inhabitants. Mystified, he had returned to his colleagues.

Within a day or so, however, rumours had found their way back to the mobile town in the mountains. The whispers were vague and inconclusive and no one really bothered much to listen to them, but in essence they gave the lie to anyone who might try to attach the blame to Skatsman. No (the rumours said), the villagers had not been frightened off by the little boss; and no, they had not found the work distasteful – the money had been more than welcome and they were very grateful.

But did the rich American bosses not know that there had been strange rumblings in the mountains? And were they not aware that in Recjaviscjorska a priest had foretold queer horror in the highlands? Why! – wasn't it common knowledge that an ancient burial place in the grounds of certain crumbling and massive ruins high in the rocky passes was suddenly most – unquiet? No, better that the Americans be given a wide berth until, one way or the other, they were gone and the mountains were peaceful again.

Though of course he had his ear to the ground, still it was all far beyond Philar Jontz's understanding, and even had he thought or bothered himself to look at a map of the region (though there was no reason why he should) it is doubtful that he would have noticed anything at all out of the ordinary. Maps being what they are in that country, in all probability the ancient boundaries would not be marked, and so Jontz would not have seen that the two deserted villages lay within the perimeter of what once had been the princedom of Vlad V Tsepeth Dracula of Wallachia, or that the now bulging town lower down the mountain slopes lay *outside* the centuried prince's domain . . .

Now all this had happened before the latest crisis, but even then Phalanx had been overdue on location, delayed for first one reason and then another in Hollywood. And so a number of restless, wasted days had gone by, until finally came that great morning when the poisonous little director received the telephone message everyone had been waiting and praying for. Old Grim-Grin was on his way at last; he would be on the mid-afternoon flight into Jlaskavya; could someone meet him and his retinue at the airport to escort them to location?

Could someone meet them, indeed! Skatsman *himself* would meet them; and without further ado the delighted director had set out in his huge car with Joe, his driver, down the steep mountain roads to distant Jlaskavya.

For once in his life Skatsman had been truly happy. He had known (he told Joe) that it was all going to be okay. Nothing ever went wrong on his birthday – nothing *dared* go wrong on his birthday! And thus he had snarled cheerfully to Joe all the way to the dismal airport . . . where finally he had been informed of his superstar's latest and most serious delay.

Having picked up a smattering of the local language, it was Joe who first received the news, and when Skatsman had recovered from his initial convulsions it was Joe who phoned the facts through to Philar Jontz in the overcrowded town where the PR man had not yet given up trying to solve the mystery of the runaway extras. Jontz, in turn, had taken the dread message back to his film friends in the mountains.

Later, it also fell to the PR man to spot the horde of extras – all costumed for a battle scene, helmeted and leather-sandaled, with a variety of shields, swords, maces and lances – as they came creeping down out of the higher passes, flanked by riders astride great warhorses. The PR man had been astounded, but only for a moment, and then he had given a *whoop* of understanding.

Why, Skatsman, the old fraud! They might have expected something like this of him. Wasn't it his birthday? This explained everything. The runaway extras, the alleged "accident" of Zack

Phalanx: it had all been a build-up to the Big Surprise. And surely that great, grim-faced, leading rider *was* Zack Phalanx?

Dusk was settling over the mountains like a great grey mantle by that time, and the actors and technicians and all were already settling in their caravans and tents, preparing for the next day's work or bedding down for the night. Philar Jontz's cry went up for all of them to hear:

"Well, I'll be damned! Zack! Zack Phalanx! Where's that old rogue Skatsman hiding?" Then they heard his quavering, querying exclamation of disbelief, and finally his awful, rising scream, cut off by a thick sound not unlike a meat cleaver sinking into a side of beef . . .

Something less than an hour later, Harry S. Skatsman's big car came round the last bend in the winding mountain road and turned off onto the fringe of the flat, cleared area that housed the sprawling units of the vast, mobile film town. The headlights cut a swathe of light between the shadowed ranks of shacks, trailers, trucks, caravans and tents – illuminating a scene that caused Joe to slam on his brakes so hard that Skatsman almost shot headlong over into the front of the car. Twin rows of stakes stretched away towards a bleak background of dark and sullen mountains, and atop each stake sat the motionless form of a dressed dummy, head down and arms bound.

"What in hell – ?" Skatsman snarled, leaping from the car with an agility all out of character with his shape and size. A hundred torches suddenly flared in the dark behind the shacks, trucks and tents, and their bearers came forward out of the shadows to form a circle about Skatsman and the car.

And suddenly the director knew, just as Philar Jontz had "known", what it was all about. Why, this was one of Zack's scenes! The stakes, torches, the grimly-helmeted warriors . . .

"Where is he?" Skatsman roared, slapping his thigh and doing a little jig. "Where's that bastard Zack Phalanx? I might have known he wouldn't forget my birthday!"

The silent torch-bearers closed in, tightening the circle. Down the path of stakes horses came clopping, the lead horse carrying a huge figure clad in the cape and apparel of a warrior prince.

"Zack! Zack!" cried Skatsman, pushing forward – to be grabbed and held tight between two of the encircling torch-bearers. And then he smelled a smell that was not greasepaint, and beneath the nearest helmet he saw –

"*Zack!*" he uselessly croaked once more.

At the same time Joe, too, noticed something very wrong –

namely, the skeletal claw that held a torch close to his driver's window. He convulsively gunned the car's big motor, twisting the wheel, spinning the car on madly screaming tyres. A hurled lance crashed through the windscreen and pinned him like a fly to the upholstery of his seat. His arms flew wide in a last spasm and the car turned on its side, splintering the nearest stake and flinging the grisly corpse it supported in a welter of entrails at the director's feet. No dummy this but a dumb blonde! – Shani Silarno, naked but for a torn and bloodstained dressing-gown, eyes glazed and bulging.

Skatsman swayed and would have fallen, but he was flanked now by two great horses. Their riders reached down to lift him bodily from the ground. He kicked feebly at thin air as they cantered with him down between the ranks of stakes to where the caped Vlad V now waited.

Before the director's unbelieving eyes there passed a bobbing procession of mutilated forms, some of them still writhing weakly on the cruel stakes. Jerry Sollinger, Glory Graeme, Sam "Sugar" Sweeney, they were all there. Even Philar Jontz, though only his head decorated its stake.

As the horses drew level with the bony horror in the cape, Skatsman was lifted higher still and he saw the waiting, needle-sharp point of the last, empty stake. He might perhaps have screamed but only knew how to snarl. He did neither but threw back his head and laughed – albeit hysterically, insanely – laughed right into the fleshless, helmeted face whose black eye-sockets so keenly regarded him.

He was Harry S. Skatsman, wasn't he? And this was his epic, wasn't it? This was *his* big scene!

What else could he do?

"Action! Camera!" he snarled – as they rammed him down onto that last terrible fang of Vlad the Impaler.

Basil Copper

When Greek Meets Greek

Basil Copper published his first story in the horror field in The Fifth Pan Book of Horror Stories (1964). *Since then his short fiction has appeared in numerous anthologies, been extensively adapted for radio and television, and collected in* Not After Nightfall, Here Be Daemons, And Afterward the Dark, From Evil's Pillow, Voices of Doom, When Footsteps Echo *and* Whispers in the Night. *Besides publishing two non-fiction studies of the vampire and werewolf legends, his other books include the novels* The Great White Space, The Curse of the Fleers, Necropolis, House of the Wolf *and* The Black Death. *He has also continued the adventures of August Derleth's Holmes-like consulting detective in several volumes, the most recent being* The Exploits of Solar Pons *and* The Recollections of Solar Pons, *both published by Fedogan & Bremer.*

Dracula wanders across the world, often spending long periods observing humanity . . .

I

FROM WHERE THOMPSON sat at the high terrace, the sea was a blinding incandescence below him, the sun stippling the wavetops to points of fire. Across it crawled black shadows like beetles: fishing boats returning from their afternoon catches. Thompson had been involved in a bad motor smash some weeks before and had come down to the Cote d'Azur for a month's rest to complete his recovery. For this reason and because he had come so close to death, the beauty of the world and the merest minutia of everyday life arrested his attention as never before.

He had chosen the Magnolia because it was high up and far from the coast road and also because close friends had stayed there some while before. He had escaped the roar of traffic and the resultant fumes, but the shrill *chirring* of the cicadas at their day-long worship of the sun, and the occasional whine of a jet belonging to the French Air Force making white scratches across the blue, did not disturb him and after three days he did not even notice them.

Below him, on the lower terrace, he could see the Greek pacing with long athletic strides, his shadow stencilled on the dusty tiles as a hard, black silhouette. A tall commanding figure in an impeccable white drill suit and collar and tie, despite the heat. He had deep black hair brushed back from his broad forehead, and a sensitive, highly intelligent face, which, however, often wore an expression of intense melancholy. Thompson had first noticed him two mornings before, when he was crossing the hotel lobby to set out on one of his solitary walks.

The Greek, whose name was Karolides, was accompanied by a dazzlingly beautiful girl. The Englishman was so taken by her strange, almost ethereal beauty, that he had questioned the proprietor of the Magnolia, who had told him she was the guest's daughter. The couple came there for a month every year and Thompson's informant had added that the Greek was reputed to be fabulously wealthy but unlike many people who gave that impression when they came to stay, was actually a millionaire. But the girl was in delicate health and needed sunshine and sea air.

Perhaps that was the reason for his melancholy, Thompson thought. Now, as he sat on with the early dusk beginning to slant across the sea, he saw that the Greek had been joined by his daughter. Darkness comes early on that side of the Mediterranean as the sun descends behind the mountains, so that the solitary watcher was unable to make out the details of her features at this distance.

That she was beautiful, he had no doubt. Although he had only momentarily glimpsed her in the hotel lobby, she had the sort of striking looks that made men's heads turn to stare after her. Some, possibly older men, would retain the memory of her until the end of their lives.

The hotel was not overfull, even though it was the height of the season, and the sprinkling of elderly diners who assembled for the evening meal would not distract him from the contemplation of the Greek financier and his daughter, Thompson thought. For he understood from the proprietor that the couple often stayed in for the evening meal, though they were sometimes out on various expeditions during the day.

Thompson did not really know why he was taking such an interest in this couple. That they were striking and sophisticated people, used to wealth and wide travel was obvious, but there was something beyond mere idle curiosity in Thompson's case. Perhaps it was an invalid's preoccupation with events from a distant and contemplative viewpoint. For Thompson's gruelling background of medical research had given him little opportunity for leisure until now. Time seemed to stretch endlessly before him and he was beginning to enjoy his enforced idleness, now that more interesting people were starting to swim within his vision.

Now, their muffled conversation drifted up to him in snatches from time to time, blended with the soft susurrance of the sea, so that he was unable to make out anything other than fragmentary phrases in Greek and English. The forms of the pair, who had drawn close together, were dark now, blended into the gloom of the encroaching night, the only distinct thing about the tableau being the red glow of a cigar which Karolides had lit, which carried to the silent watcher an even richer aroma than the suffocating perfume of tropical plants.

A purple dusk was hovering in the gulf below, somewhere between sea and sky and a solitary bird was trilling his own version of "The Last Post" before relapsing into silence. Presently, the pair went in and the night seemed cold and chilly, now that it was no longer warmed by their presence. There was a steely glint to the hazy sea and far out, the dim lights of vessels passing and re-passing on their mysterious errands. Thompson shivered suddenly, though it had nothing to do with the slight breeze which had suddenly sprung up. Presently he too went in to his solitary dinner.

II

Thompson saw nothing of his fellow guests the following morning, for he breakfasted late and it was past ten o'clock before he quit the table. He took the hotel bus the short trip into town and did various errands. He called in at the post office, where there were several letters awaiting him, none of any importance; went to Thomas Cook; and drank an aperitif at a cafe terrace, in a shady corner overlooking the sea, where he never ceased to marvel at the passing parade of grotesque human beings that aimlessly meandered to and fro along the Grand Corniche.

Later in the afternoon he would swim, but for the moment he was content to idle away an hour or two in such trivial pursuits. He passed the interval before lunch in investigating the cool interiors of two elegant bookshops and then walked back up the dusty road that wound among luxurious villas, until he reached the hotel. Guy, the dark-haired waiter who usually served his lunch, brought Thompson a Cinzano with ice and lemon on the lower terrace before he went to his room to freshen up.

He ate lunch in his usual corner of the dining room, oblivious of the animated hubbub about him, and after a reasonable interval strolled back down the hill to the town, where he changed into bathing trunks and enjoyed a leisurely swim out to a tethered raft about half a mile from shore. The freshness of the sea and the salt air did his tired limbs good and he lay spread-eagled on the raft for what must have been two or three hours. No one came near him, for most of the other swimmers, who included many young children, kept to the shallows close in shore.

Once or twice sailing boats and larger yachts passed quite close to him, and just before he quit the raft for his return swim, a blonde girl, who was sunning herself on the stern of a rather palatial vessel, switched on her portable radio, and the nostalgic voice of Charles Trenet singing "La Mer" came drifting across the water, making an appropriate background to his return to the beach.

He took the bus back this time, as he was feeling rather tired after his exertions and once again climbed up to the high terrace for the tranquil hour before dinner which he had come to enjoy. But on this occasion there were some loud-mouthed English tourists at an adjoining table so he came down early. As he was passing into the dining room he was faintly surprised to be accosted by the tall, commanding figure of Karolides.

"Mr Thompson, is it not?"

The Greek, once more immaculate in white tropical drill, paused with amusement, noting the faint flicker that passed across his fellow guest's face.

"Oh, I admit I looked you up in the hotel register. You seemed rather lonely in your corner by yourself last night, so I wondered whether you would care to join us for dinner this evening."

"That is extremely kind of you", Thompson stammered. "If you're sure I wouldn't be an intrusion . . ."

The other put a hand on his shoulder in a sudden intimate gesture.

"Not at all. We'd love to have you. Ravenna is easily bored, I'm afraid, and there are so few guests here of a suitable age."

He indicated the elderly diners in the background with a wry gesture, and the amusement in his eyes prompted a hesitant laugh from Thompson.

"Of course. It's very kind of you. If you're sure . . ."

"Certainly, Mr Thompson. Come along."

The Greek glided effortlessly between the restaurant tables so that Thompson had difficulty in keeping up with him. As they approached the corner where the girl was sitting he saw that she was even more beautiful than he had imagined. Her face was a perfectly round oval and she had the most extraordinary eyes he had ever seen; a deep emerald green which seemed to have unclouded depths in them, so that Thompson felt almost embarrassed to look into them. But he noticed also that though she could not have been more than twenty-six or twenty-eight, and her complexion was smooth and perfect, yet there was a pallor which should not have been there.

"This is Ravenna."

The girl acknowledged the Englishman's presence with a slight inclination of the head. Her dark hair was cut short and immaculately coiffed, and she wore gold earrings of a conch-like shell pattern which set off her beauty in a way the guest had not seen on any other woman. The table was in a railed-off enclosure that was banked with flowers. The maitre d'hotel and a wine waiter were hovering in attendance and the latter hurried forward to draw out the chair for the Greek. Thompson's speculations were cut short by Karolides indicating to him the vacant chair which one of the waiters had immediately pulled up and, almost before he was seated, an extra dinner service was being put in position on the white linen tablecloth.

He had hardly time to settle himself, when Karolides announced, "You will be our guest, of course."

He waved away the Englishman's protests.

"Think nothing of it. A great pleasure to have you with us."

He spoke perfect English, and Thompson guessed that he had mastered a number of languages, which would obviously be necessary in his dealings with the international world of commerce.

"Mr Thompson is a distinguished man of science, my dear. But now he is recuperating from a bad motor accident. It is up to us to help entertain him and rescue him from the boredom endemic to the lot of one who is passing a solitary sojourn in a Riviera hotel. Is it not so, Mr Thompson?"

Karolides smiled and the distinction of his countenance and the beauty of his daughter erased the momentary irritation Thompson had again felt at being introduced in such a manner. He wondered how his host had got the information. But his slight embarrassment passed as the girl again inclined her head and said in a low, musical voice, "I am so sorry to hear that. I do hope you will soon be better."

Thompson mumbled some banal expression of thanks and was relieved when Karolides started studying the menu and there was a sudden flurry of waiters around the table. During the transmission of the orders and the decanting of the wine, the guest again had the opportunity of studying the couple. His first impression of the girl was reinforced rather than diminished as the meal progressed. As might have been expected the food and the wine were of the finest quality and, perhaps slightly under the influence of the latter, Thompson found his stiffness relaxing and soon he was completely under the spell of the pair. Karolides spoke eruditely and entertainingly about a wide variety of topics; firstly regarding his world-wide business interests and particularly his Greek shipping fleet.

From there he advanced to literature and the arts in general and Thompson then realised that the reason his host's name was familiar was because he had donated wings to hospitals in Greece, Great Britain and America and had also given prodigious sums to art foundations and a great many charities.

Ravenna too was well-read and steeped in the classics as well as modern authors; and she seemed equally informed on a wide range of interests in the arts, including painting, ballet and music. As the meal progressed, Thompson lost his reserve and started to open his heart a little more freely. As a scientist he had never had enough time for the gentler pursuits which occupied much of the leisure hours of the wider world, and when he was able to converse on an equal level with Karolides on some obscure literary point he felt his spirits lifting and the Greek seemed equally appreciative of his guest's background and taste.

When the evening was over Thompson felt as though he had

known this couple all his life. A naturally reserved man, he was drawn out by the brilliant conversation of this pair and especially through Karolides, was led into another world; one where money was no object. But this was no mere vulgar matter of acquisition but the accumulation of funds for specific purposes; although he was too courteous and tactful to mention it, his host had done much to alleviate suffering and poverty in the world with the great outpouring of his wealth; this Thompson already knew from a quick study of the financial pages of national newspapers.

The girl too, with her own interest in art and culture made a deep impression on him, as might have been expected. He did wonder why, with all the assets at their disposal, the couple did not stay at one of the big international hotels that were scattered along the coast, but assumed that natural modesty and the discretion already displayed by the couple were the reasons behind it. After all, it was fairly obvious that they would be recognised at one of the great palaces and would probably run into friends in the international set. He remembered too, that the girl's health had not been good. Then he dismissed the question from his mind; after all, it was none of his business.

When they parted at the entrance to the dining room, Karolides laid his smooth, manicured hand on his guest's shoulder in a discreet gesture of affection.

"Consider us your friends", he said in a deep, resonant voice.

Thompson saw that the girl's eyes were fixed on him with a particular brilliance and he could not resist their appeal. He mumbled his thanks and made his way somewhat awkwardly up the fine marble staircase with the wrought iron balustrade that led to the guests' rooms, instead of taking the small, creaky lift. When he sought his bed he lay awake for a long time, listening to the distant murmur of the sea. He felt a little feverish, but his somewhat overheated state owed nothing to the wine.

III

Thompson was up early the next morning, bathing and shaving himself quickly and was downstairs for breakfast by half-past eight. When he entered the dining room he felt slight disappointment, mingled with relief, to find it occupied merely by a sprinkling of middle-aged ladies toying with their coffee and croissants. Disappointment at not seeing Ravenna; relief that he might not have to make small talk in the presence of her father, when he wanted to take a walk with her alone and find out more about her.

The illness of which he had heard also intrigued him; as a scientist as well as a medical man, for he had several doctorates, he was professionally concerned as well as in a friendly capacity. But there had been a pallor in her features which he had noted and which was not normal in such a young and vicacious woman, though it had not been obvious the night before. Possibly the wine and the warmth of the summer night had temporarily dispelled it.

He was just going out when he saw, through the wide windows facing the sea, Karolides and Ravenna passing along the front of the building where they got into a big open touring car parked in the driveway. As they disappeared down the steep, winding road that led to the Corniche and the open sea, he had a sudden stab of disappointment. It was absurd, of course, as he barely knew the couple, but there was something about the girl that captivated him. He had been too busy in his career ever to contemplate marriage and now that he was approaching forty, and had narrowly escaped death a short time before, he was conscious that there were a great many things in life that he had missed. A wife, for one thing.

Most men regarded matrimony or at least, carnal love, as one of the most important things in life, if not the most important, and he had smiled rather superciliously when listening to colleagues' stories of frustrated hopes or amorous adventures. Now things were different, and he had a glimmer of hope that Ravenna might find him attractive. It was utterly absurd, of course, because she and her father lived a jet-set life; travelling the world in great luxury; and obviously the girl would attract many men. In fact, she might already be engaged to be married. He had never thought of that. He bit his lip with frustration, mumbled some banality to the restaurant manager and went out into the blinding sunlight and set off to walk down to the town, which was slowly composing itself from out of the morning haze.

He wandered idly about the shops, keeping mostly in the shade, avoiding the tourists and holidaymakers who thronged the beaches fringeing the Corniche. He ate a frugal lunch at a small restaurant in a side street where fans in the ceiling distributed cooled air from small vents. As he went out and back toward the beach, he was arrested by the sight of Karolides' big green touring car, parked outside a bar. As he approached, the couple came out of a gown shop a little farther down, the girl laden with expensive-looking parcels. Their smiles were open and welcoming.

"Just the person we wanted to see," said the Greek, after they had shaken hands.

"I have to attend to business here in town, but Ravenna wants to go swimming. Would you be kind enough to accompany her?"

Thompson was caught unawares.

"Certainly," he said hesitantly. "But I have no costume."

Karolides smiled again.

"That can soon be taken care of. I own a small club out on the point there. They will supply you with a costume and towels. Ravenna is a member, of course, so you will have no difficulty. And I will come by with the car and pick you up at six o'clock, yes."

Thompson felt the girl's hand on his elbow and he joined her in the back seat, while Karolides drove swiftly but well along the Corniche. Presently they came to a place where a *calanque*, a sort of creek, joined the sea. Here, on the headland was a dazzling white building, flanked by ornamental trees and bushes that threw welcome shade. There were terraces, striped parasols, men and girls engaged in idle chatter and, somewhere an orchestra was playing, or, Thompson mused, perhaps it was a radio.

There were waves and shouted invitations from the people on the terrace as Karolides drew the big machine to a halt, but he smilingly shook his head. Thompson and the girl got out, their shadows dark and clear-etched in the dust.

"Until six o'clock, then," and Karolides expertly reversed and drove smoothly away along the coast road. Thompson followed the girl, who had not uttered a word during the drive, waiting while she spoke to one or two people at tables and then they were in the cool interior of the club where a discreet manager summoned a white-coated attendant who led them to locker rooms for men and women and left them.

"Ten minutes," Ravenna said in a low voice.

"I'll be on the terrace," Thompson said.

He was turning toward the door labelled HOMMES when he found the attendant at his elbow. He thrust a plastic case in his hand which bore the printed figure 6 on its cover. Once inside the cubicle, Thompson found scarlet trunks, toilet things, a comb, soap and brush, and three huge towels. When he had hung his clothes in a grey steel locker and fixed the key by its cord on to the elasticised waistband of his trunks, he surveyed himself in the mirror.

He felt the sight he presented would probably not disgrace the girl, but he was a little worried about the scars on his legs – souvenirs of his accident – although he knew they would fade to thin white lines within a few weeks. He went outside into the blinding sunshine and sat down in a cane chair to await Ravenna. The sea looked green and cool and inviting, and there were metal steps with cork inserts that led

down from the promenade into the gentle undulations of the
water.

He turned as a shadow fell across the tiling. He was prepared
for the sight of an exceptional woman, but he was so struck by
the bronzed apparition that bent over his chair that he let out an
involuntary gasp of admiration. The white bikini made a striking
contrast to her brown skin which, however, gradually faded out
toward the throat, leaving her face clear and free from the ravages
of the southern sun. But the pallor he had previously noted had
receded, and the smiling young woman pretended not to see his
embarrassment and laughingly told him to follow her.

She made a perfect dive from the swimming club promenade
into deep water and was already creaming her way to a distant
moored raft before Thompson had even put his somewhat hesitant
feet upon the ladder. The water was cold and stinging at the first
shock, as it always was in this part of the Mediterranean, but
the warmth returned to his limbs as he ploughed doggedly on
behind the sparkling wake the girl was leaving. She swam with
beautiful flowing strokes, and he guessed that she had been an
expert swimmer from a very early age.

Now Thompson felt a sense of well-being that he had not had for
some time and he realised that his complete recovery could only be
a matter of weeks. It was not only his medical expertise that told
him this, but it was reinforced by the beauty of his surroundings
and the presence of the new friends he had made. That they were
friends he had no doubt; with their wealth and background the
couple had no reason to befriend an obscure scientist other than
on purely social grounds.

The girl was laughing down at him as she drew herself up on to
the raft with lithe supple movements. He trod water, then rested
his forearms on the warm surface of the inlay that rocked gently in
the swell. Once again he noticed that Ravenna had very beautiful
teeth. Like everything else about her; for the rich, he thought with
inward amusement, everything was perfect.

"I am so sorry, Mr Thompson," she was saying in her very precise
English.

"I don't know what you mean."

She shook her head, sending a fine spray of water from the dark
tangle of her hair.

"Merely that I was thoughtless. I had forgotten that you were
recovering from a severe accident and thought to race you to the
raft. But you kept up well. I do hope I have not hindered your
recovery."

Thompson laughed.

"Hardly."

But as he drew himself up to sit beside her, there were tingling pains in his legs which warned him that he must not over-exert himself at this stage in his convalescence.

"You are sure?"

She was serious again now.

He nodded.

"Quite sure. But thank you for your concern."

The goodness of salt air and the gentle murmur of the sea, combined with the healing rays of the sun, made him even more conscious of the importance of good health. Without it life was practically meaningless. He had a quick flash of the oncoming car and closed his eyes quickly to blot out the impact.

Ravenna was very close to him now.

"Is everything all right? You turned quite pale."

He was touched by her concern.

"It was really nothing. Just a momentary recollection of my accident. The contrast between then and now was quite over-whelming."

"That is good then. Let us enjoy the sun."

She lay back on the raft, stretching out long legs, closing her eyes against the brilliant light. Thompson did the same. Rarely had he felt so contented as time slipped by. Presently he slept. Later, he turned over. Somehow his flank brushed against the girl's side. In an instant she was upon him, her mouth on his in a fierce, primitive kiss. Almost without any awareness of what he was doing, he had undressed. The girl was already naked and they made love in the blazing sun, oblivious to their surroundings. Once an elderly man swam close and gave them a disbelieving stare before splashing loudly away in the direction of the shore. When they had exhausted their lust, they drew apart, Ravenna laughing into his face.

"I hope I didn't hurt your leg!"

Thompson laughed in turn.

"Hardly."

They quickly resumed their costumes and plunged into the sea, holding on to the ropes at the side of the raft, staring intently into one another's eyes.

"I do not know how that happened," he began hesitantly.

Ravenna gave him another of her secret smiles.

"Does it matter?"

"Perhaps not."

On the raft Thompson had noticed that the girl had a small, triangular tattoo high up on her right thigh, which seemed to contain a minuscule heraldic symbol within it. Now, as they trod water at the edge of the raft, face to face, he discovered for the first time that she had a similar, but smaller symbol in the deep valley between her breasts. She intercepted his gaze.

"It is a fancy within our family. We are very numerous and widespread. All the women wear this crest. By that way we can know one another."

Thompson was somewhat taken aback. He hoped it did not show on his face.

"I do not understand. Isn't that rather an intimate form of identification?"

Ravenna laughed once more, showing very white teeth.

"You do not understand, certainly. We live mostly in tropical climates. The women wear low-cut dresses and are often in bathing suits."

"You are extraordinarily like your father," Thompson said.

Ravenna looked at him with a serious expression on her face.

"He would be very amused – or annoyed – to hear you say that."

Before he could ask what she meant the girl went on, "Let us return to the shore. I see that the car has arrived."

She must have had extraordinary eyesight because, as they swam slowly back toward the beach, it was some while before he could pick out Karolides' opulent vehicle in the bathing club car-park. Thompson felt embarrassed and ill at ease, but the Greek was in good spirits.

"I trust you have had a pleasant afternoon?"

"Wonderful!" Thompson had blurted out, but the dark-haired man did not seem to notice anything amiss.

Later, after the couple had showered and dressed, they drove back to the hotel, the girl chattering away in Greek and Karolides listening intently as he steered the big machine skilfully and safely between what Thompson regarded as dangerously narrow gaps in the traffic, something he would never have attempted himself. Perhaps it was the residue of his accident, but he still felt nervous over motor vehicles.

Despite his protests, he was again the guest of the pair at dinner that evening, though he was disappointed when the girl left the table early, saying she had an appointment to meet friends at the Casino. After the two men had lingered over coffee and liquers in a side salon, they parted amicably and Thompson went back to his room. He spent half the night lying awake, consumed alternately with happiness and guilt.

IV

It was with mingled relief and disappointment that Thompson saw that there was no sign of his hosts in the Magnolia dining room when he came down late to breakfast the next morning. He later learned from the hotel proprietor that Karolides and Ravenna had gone up the coast to visit friends for two or three days. Left to himself, Thompson went for solitary walks on the heights above the hotel, but neither the sun nor the romantic vistas of sea and sky held his attention any more. He wandered aimlessly and at last sprawled in the shade of a great cypress tree and tried to clarify his whirling thoughts.

He had never been in love before. Somehow, the experiences so commonplace to the majority of mankind had eluded him. It was true he had not sought it; he had been too absorbed in his scientific work. He had been an only child, and his parents had died years before and he had few surviving relatives. Yet something disturbed him about Ravenna's attitude. A beautiful, wealthy and obviously sought-after girl who moved in the international set, why had she chosen him of all people? Or was he merely a passing fancy to a woman to whom having sex with an almost complete stranger was as commonplace and meant no more than if another woman accepted a cup of coffee from a friend?

Yet the more he mulled it over, he could not accept that. He did not wish to, of course, and a small hope was growing within him, as a flame ignited in dry undergrowth slowly blossoms into a roaring furnace. But he could not afford to get too carried away or he might be in for a terrible disappointment. So he busied himself in mundane matters as the day slowly passed; he wrote letters to friends in the North of England and in London; and to colleagues in his laboratory. Or rather, letters to the former and exotic cards to the latter.

He still had several weeks of his convalescence to run, and he would take things slowly and see what developed on Ravenna's return. Then, on the third morning, a sudden thought struck him and he sought out the proprietor of the Magnolia to ask if the couple had quit the hotel. That suave gentleman smiled and said they were due back that afternoon. Reassured, he ate a leisurely lunch at a restaurant in the town and later in the day again swam out into the bay and then sun-bathed on the rocks, hoping that Karolides and his daughter would have reappeared when he got back to the hotel.

He saw the big green touring car was parked in the concourse and a hotel employee was carrying in luggage. He hurried into the lobby with a beating heart. He met Karolides on the staircase coming down, immaculate in a white tropical suit and a scarlet tie. He started to ask if the couple had had a pleasant visit with friends but something stamped on Karolides' face stopped him. There was an ineffable sadness about the mouth and eyes. He took the Englishman familiarly by the arm and they went down the stairs together. He anticipated Thompson's next question.

"Ravenna is resting," he said. "She is very ill, I am afraid. Our trip was not a social occasion, unfortunately."

Thompson felt a tightening of the heart and expressed his concern. The two men were at the bottom of the staircase now and Karolides looked at him gravely.

"Shall we go into the lounge? It is always deserted at this hour. If you could spare a few minutes I should be grateful. It is most important."

Thompson readily agreed, and soon the two men were seated on gilt chairs with a marble table between them, in the empty silence of the vast room, where rococo mirrors gave back their pale images, illuminated by the misty light that filtered through the drawn blinds. Karolides began without preamble.

"You may think what I am going to tell you is an impertinence and my request an imposition, but I would be grateful if you would hear me out."

Thompson found he could not speak, but gave the merest of nods. Had he found out something about him and Ravenna? Surely she would not have told him? But he need not have worried. It was nothing like that. Karolides leaned forward until his hypnotic eyes were boring into the other's.

"As I noted before, Mr Thompson, you are a blood specialist and a very distinguished one. I might say, in fact, one of the two leading specialists in the world. Ravenna is extremely ill, I am afraid. She suffers from a rare blood deficiency. So rare is her group that only a handful of people in the world have the same."

Amid his alarm at the state of Ravenna's health, Thompson felt a quickening of interest but he kept silent as the other went on.

"We have travelled the world to find a cure but without result. She has remissions when we are able to get occasional transfusions, but that is not the answer. I happen to own a rather celebrated clinic along the coast here. We have run your particulars through our computer and have obtained a fascinating CV."

He held up his hand as the other started forward.

"Please hear me out, Mr Thompson, and forgive my presumption. You must know that such details are readily available to the medical fraternity on a world-wide basis."

He smiled thinly.

"In fact, to the non-medical fraternity also; such is the spread of these electronic marvels. You are one of that small select band of people who have this extremely rare group. As I have said, I am not a medical man and I forget its actual designation."

He lowered his voice and leaned forward again, his pale, distinguished face bearing a supplicating expression.

"I know you are on holiday; I know you have had a bad accident. And I am asking a great deal. What I am attempting to say is this. I suspect you have a growing fondness for Ravenna. It really is a matter of life and death. I implore you to help us by giving some of your blood. In other words to undergo a transfusion at my clinic under the expert supervision of Professor Kogon, whose name may not be unknown to you."

He paused, his eyes never leaving the other's face, and Thompson felt a little rivulet of perspiration trickle down his forehead. He mopped it away with his handkerchief to conceal his confusion. And Karolides had been right. He was more than fond of the girl and alarmed and dismayed by this threat to her safety. He did know Professor Kogon's work well. He was also a blood specialist, but in a different area, and he had written some fascinating papers which explored hitherto unknown forms of research.

Instead of answering the millionaire directly he said something very strange, that appeared to have come unbidden to his mind.

"My great grandfather was of Greek extraction . . ." he began haltingly.

Karolides gave him a brilliant smile.

"Ah! So Greek meets Greek! I knew there was a rapport between us as soon as we first met. It is a million to one chance that you and Ravenna have the same blood typing. As I have already said, I know little or nothing of medical matters, but the Professor and his colleagues are working on a synthetic compound which may, if perfected, save her. But that will take time, obviously. In the short term, you are our only hope. I can assure you that the earth is yours if you will agree to my suggestion."

Thompson gathered himself together.

"You realize this can only be temporary . . ." he began.

Karolides put a hand on his arm.

"That is all we ask. We have found, in fact, that with care the remission can last as long as six months. Anything can happen after that."

Thompson hid his surprise as best he could.

"But," he answered, "I will do everything I can."

Karolides' face was transformed.

"Then you agree!"

"Certainly! Anything to help Ravenna."

V

Thompson sat back in his cane chair and looked out toward a clear blue horizon. He still felt a little weak, even after a day, but he relished the sight of Ravenna's smiling face. Karolides' gleaming clinic had been everything he had said, and Thompson and Professor Kogon had had interesting conversations on their specialities and had compared notes on their individual research. The actual transfusion procedure had rather puzzled him and he did not recognize the equipment in use, which Kogon had assured him was the latest technology and embodied a machine which he and his colleagues had themselves designed.

In fact its workings were unlike anything in his own experience, and Thompson had actually fainted during the minor operation. When he came to himself he was lying on a bed in another room, with one of Kogon's colleagues raising a small glass of cognac to his lips. As soon as he was fit to travel, Karolides had driven him back to the Magnolia, saying that Revenna was staying on at the clinic overnight as the Professor wanted to keep her under observation.

In his euphoric mood, the Greek had suggested a fee so munificent that it had taken Thompson's breath away, but he had smilingly declined all his host's offers. Karolides had finally given up with good grace, but had insisted that Thompson should be his guest for the remainder of his holiday and that he would pay all his bills at the hotel. In the end Thompson had graciously given way, but he had privately resolved to buy Ravenna some extravagant piece of jewellery to express his feelings toward her and also to repay Karolides' own generosity.

Ravenna had only just come back from the clinic that morning and the Greek had told him that she was resting. She had come to his bedside after the operation, and before he had quite recovered had expressed her gratitude in a most touching manner, impulsively seizing his hand and kissing it, much to his embarrassment. Just before lunch, Karolides had met him in the lounge by appointment and had brought him a sheaf of computer print-outs relating both to the transfusion and to the components of both Ravenna's blood and his own. They were identical, as Thompson had expected, but there was a curious symbol which occurred again and again throughout the calculations; vaguely, it reminded him of the curious tattoos on Ravenna's thigh and breast.

"Greek, is it not? But my knowledge of Greek is very hazy at this distance in time."

Karolides gave him a smile in which sweetness was mingled with melancholy.

"It is our own private notation, which you will not find in any textbook or lexico. It refers to *agape*, which, as you must know, is the word for 'love' in the Greek language."

Somehow, Thompson felt a little uneasy at this and wished to turn the conversation in another direction. As though sensing his thoughts, his companion added, "You will be quite yourself in a day or two, Mr Thompson. Professor Kogon tells me that he had to extract a little more blood than usual to restore Ravenna, but I am sure you will not regret being so generous."

"No, of course not," Thompson had replied.

Karolides had then become brisk. "Ravenna will be sleeping this afternoon but will join us at dinner. In the meantime I would suggest a little expedition. I have something interesting to show you. We will go by car, of course, but may I suggest four o'clock, as it will not be quite so hot at that time of day?"

Thompson had readily agreed and now he was waiting for Karolides' call. It was still only half-past three, and he had put down his novel as much out of boredom as tiredness. He found his white-coated waiter at his elbow.

"Monsieur would like iced *limonade*?"

Monsieur would, and he passed the remaining half-hour in pleasant contemplation of the scenery, all the time his mind revolving the enigma of Ravenna and whether the incident on the raft had happened or not – it had now assumed such a dream-like quality in his mind. Presently he heard the imperative salvo on the horn of Karolides' car and descended to the hotel concourse to find the Greek already at the wheel, a blue silk scarf at the open vee of his expensive scarlet sports shirt, which he wore beneath one of his white tropical suits.

"A perfect afternoon for our little expedition, Mr Thompson," he observed, as his guest slid into the seat alongside him.

"Where are we going?"

Karolides shot him a mysterious smile.

"All in good time, Mr Thompson," he said softly. "A little way along the coast, actually. It's rather a curiosity and connected with my own family at a great distance in time."

Thompson was intrigued.

"Would you care to tell me a little more about it?"

Karolides glided expertly around a group of motor-cyclists who were swerving too close, turned off the Corniche at the next junction and set the car's long bonnet snaking up into the foothills.

"What would you say to the discovery of a Greek temple hereabouts along this coast?"

"I should say it would be extremely unlikely."

Karolides gave a throaty chuckle.

"And you would be perfectly correct, my dear Mr Thompson. This is by way of being a folly, but I thought you might be interested."

Thompson felt his curiosity quickening.

"Seeing that we both have Greek connections, Mr Thompson. It is of no great antiquity I might say. Only about a hundred and sixty years old, but an interesting curiosity just the same".

And he said nothing further as the car effortlessly ate up the miles, guided by his skilful hand, and they climbed the corkscrew bends until the sea was a mere blue haze on the horizon. Once they traversed a dusty village square where locals dozed in the shade of a great tree outside a small bar, and a somnolent dog dragged himself lazily out of the way.

"We're almost there," Karolides said after they had driven a mile or two further and the road had narrowed to a tiny lane that bisected the parched terrain like a sinuous thread.

"Here we are."

Karolides stopped the car and got out, slamming the door behind him. As Thompson joined him, the air hit him like a furnace and for a moment he regretted that he had come. Then they were in under the welcome shade of Spanish oaks, following a path that was barely visible beneath the tangled weeds that fringed the lane. A short distance more and they came to a rusty gate, which Karolides entered without a backward glance. The scream of its corroded hinges was like the drilling of a nerve in a tooth, the Englishman thought. He stopped to wipe the perspiration off his forehead with his handkerchief and in a flash Karolides had turned and was at his side.

"Are you all right?"

"Yes, thank you. It is nothing."

"We will be at the top of the rise in a few moments and there you will find a cooling wind."

Sure enough, as they got to the rocky ridge, a breeze swept the hillside and through rusty railings Thompson could see broken columns and blanched pillars standing all awry. The place was bleached with the harsh sunlight and sparse grass grew, white as an old woman's hair, that made a sharp rustling sound as the breeze caught the stems. Thompson could make out the far sea now, with the faint curve of the horizon. He followed the Greek along a path that wound among withered trees and stunted bushes. Then he saw the pediment of the temple, a stark white, though much mottled with age, some of the pillars beneath the vast portico split and seamed with long years of rain and sun. The paving around it was all cracked too and lizards ran in and out of the long grass that surrounded it.

"My ancestor's folly," said Karolides softly. "Interesting, is it not? It must have cost him a fortune, even in those days. Forty workmen and two years' work. Circa 1810, I believe."

Thompson went closer, lost in wonder, while the Greek looked at him with pleasure. The Englishman was suddenly conscious of a strange element in the atmosphere of the place. That is, even beyond the oddness of such a structure in a remote spot like that. Conscious too of the sun beating on his bare head, now that he was in the open. Then he became aware of something else, and he stared about him with dawning recognition.

"Why, this is a cemetery!"

Karolides nodded, smiling. "Long disused."

Thompson took another step forward, came closer to the temple, his manner a little wild and disturbed.

"Then this must be a tomb!"

"Yes, that is perfectly correct."

Thompson was up close now, felt dryness in his throat and a slight giddiness. He was overtaken by faintness. Somehow, he did not quite know how, he found himself on the ground. There was a Greek inscription on the base of the temple. As he had told his host his Greek was extremely rusty. He could only make out one word: DRAKULA. It meant little to him, other than the misspelt title of a lurid Victorian novel, which he had never read. Then he lost consciousness.

VI

When he awoke he was surrounded by a sea of faces. There was a gendarme, a man in a white uniform with a red cross on the chest, and a crowd of gaping onlookers. Then Karolides came shouldering his way imperiously through the crowd, followed by two men with a stretcher.

"My dear Mr Thompson: What with the sun and your weakened state following your illness. I should never have brought you. A thousand pardons."

Thompson tried to struggle up, was pushed back by the gentle hands of the attendants.

"Don't try to move. You are in good hands."

He could taste blood now, could see scarlet on his white shirt. Had he cut himself on the unyielding stone as he fell? As his vision cleared he saw Ravenna striding through the gravestones, her white dress torn and creased by the thorny plants. He felt feeble and unable to move. He did not stir when he was lifted on to the stretcher and must have lost consciousness for the second time, because when he again awoke he was in an ambulance with the anxious face of Karolides above him.

There was blood on the lapel of his white suit, Thompson noticed. He must have picked it up when he bent over Thompson on the ground to help him on to the stretcher. Absurdly, he thought that this trivial matter was assuming vast proportions in his mind. Should he not pay for Karolides' cleaning bill? And what was the extent of the damage to his own body? The Greek leaned over him with a reassuring smile.

"Ravenna is following on behind with my car. She will stay with you in the hospital tonight. It is only a routine check. You must have slightly gashed your throat when you fell on those flinty stones. A touch of the sun, I suppose. It is all my fault. Again, a thousand apologies. The doctor who came with the ambulance team told me your injury was superficial and that they will keep you only a few hours for rest and an overhaul."

He smiled bleakly.

"Can you ever forgive me, my dear Mr Thompson?"

Suddenly, Thompson felt as though he were about to cry. He seized the Greek's extended hand and clung to it convulsively all the way to the hospital.

Contrary to expectations he was not discharged until three days later, still feeling a little weak, but as Karolides and Ravenna drove him back along the Corniche in the big open coupé, he felt his spirits reviving. The punctures in his neck had been cauterised and were now covered by a thin gauze bandage. He understood that his host had found him lying by the side of the mausoleum and had hurried back to the car to use his mobile telephone, which had brought the ambulance team, the gendarmerie and Ravenna out from the town.

Thompson thought she looked ravishing this morning as she sat close to him in the back seat of the car, squeezing his hand affectionately. That Karolides could see them in the rear mirror was obvious, as he gave the couple a subtle, approving smile, but

Thompson no longer felt embarrassment and returned the smile in the same manner.

Back at the Magnolia he thanked his hosts again and went to his room to lie down. He woke more than two hours later to find a slip of paper had been pushed beneath his door. It was a message from Karolides, asking him to call at his suite if he felt up to it. It was Suite 44. Thompson made a quick toilet and took the lift to the fifth floor as he still felt a little weak. He found No. 44 without any trouble and tapped at the door but received no reply. He knocked again, but still there was no response so he turned the handle. The room was unlocked and he went in, closing the door softly behind him.

It was a magnificent panelled room, and the afternoon sun on the blinds made mellow patterns on the cream-painted walls. He called out Karolides' name but there was still no response. He thought that perhaps the Greek had stepped out for a minute or two, so he decided to wait. He sat down on a gilt chaise-longue beneath an oil painting of a sumptuous nude and let his eyes glance idly around the room.

There was a rosewood desk some eight or nine feet away and he saw a scattered tumble of books, some with ancient bindings. He got up and went over to look at them. Curiously enough, they were in English. There was *Chiromancy* by Flud; *Heaven and Hell* by Swedenborg; and a curious volume which lay open. It was called *Vampires By Daylight*. Thompson was inwardly amused. Certainly the Greek's tastes were esoteric, to say the least.

The latter volume was written by a man named Bjornson and had been translated from the Danish. He read a paragraph with mounting amusement: *The modern vampire is a creature who walks about in daylight. No Fustian superstitions about being destroyed by the rays of the sun or stakes driven through the heart at the crossroads. He or she is often a sophisticated, cultured man or woman, who mixes unobtrusively in high society, behaves impeccably with great charm and suavity, and who is able to blend perfectly into the background of other people's lives as he or she searches out victims.*

Thompson put the book down with a smile when he was suddenly arrested by a thin volume which lay on the blotting pad. It had a wine-red cover, was sumptuously bound, and had been privately printed by an expensive and exotic London press; in fact Thompson had a number of their volumes in his own library. He opened the title page and saw: *Poems* by Ravenna Karolides. Fascinated, he took it up. The book fell open at page 14 and he read:

WALKING PAPERS

All times are bad times now
Now that the drear, sad tide of winter flows
Cheerless through the empty vaults of the heart.
Mute mockery of the peaceful summer days
The "ifs" and "might have beens"
The promise in bright eyes, the sheen of light brown hair.
Are all men thus?
Is it always the same?
When a lover is given his walking papers?

When the surge of emotion flings the heart
Forward, bursting in white spray
Like cherry blossom on the May hedgerow
And the hot, dry ebb in the throat
Burns into the slow ache of loneliness.
Bitter now are the remembrances of the lovely, far-off times.
Are all men thus?
Is it always the same?
When a lover is given his walking papers?

Or should one laugh and drink with the forgetful throng?
Drowning the sound of distant laughter
The heart-stopping loveliness of a glance
As soft, as fleeting, as ephemeral as mist
Rent by the wind after the time of storm?
It is hard to forget such things
Are all men thus?
Is it always the same?
When a lover is given his walking papers?

One remembers when the bright lilies of love burnt
Strong, sure to outride the tempests of life.
When the touch of a hand on the shoulder was enough.
When lip to lip, limb to limb, love throbbed
In white ecstasy and then to blissful sleep.
One remembers too much, life is too long.
Are all men thus?
Is it always the same?
When a lover is given his walking papers?

All times are bad times now
Now that the rain taps the window's frosted pane

The empty chair mocks, bright were the glances
That flickered each to each
When love was at the peak in that happy, long-lost time.
It will be a bad winter.
One wonders idly, all hope gone
Are all men thus?
Is it always the same?
When a lover is given his walking papers?

Thompson put the book down slowly and carefully, deeply moved, despite himself. He was roused to a consciousness of his surroundings by a slight noise. He turned to see the tall, silent figure of Karolides, dressed in a quilted white silk dressing gown, one hand on the doorknob of an adjoining room, his eyes fixed sorrowfully on his visitor. Thompson fell back from the desk.

"Please forgive me. I had no right to look at those books. I can assure you that I did knock and call out when I arrived."

Karolides smiled a sad smile, coming forward into the room.

"There is no need to apologise, Mr Thompson. I heard you come in."

The Englishman was surprised.

"Then I was meant to see those books?" he surmised.

Karolides shrugged.

"Perhaps," he said softly. What did you think of the poems?"

"Interesting," the visitor replied. "But . . ."

The Greek broke into a broad smile.

"You found some of the wording obscure and the similes inapposite, perhaps? It has been translated from the Greek, of course."

"But what does it mean? The poem about Walking Papers?"

Karolides came closer.

"It happened to her," he said simply. "But she changed the gender. She was to have been married. Some ten years ago."

"What happened?"

"The man died," Karolides said abruptly. "It took her years to get over it. Our wanderings became even more frequent, as I hoped to take her mind off things. So she transposed the piece into a lament by a man for a lost woman."

"I see."

The two men stood deep in thought for a few moments more.

"There are some beautiful things in it," Thompson said awkwardly, feeling that he had been less than enthusiastic about the piece.

"Thank you, Mr Thompson. I just thought I would warn you

about this matter, as I note that you and she are becoming good friends. It was a long time ago, of course. But such memories run deep and I would not wish her to be hurt again."

"I understand."

Then Karolides came forward and put his hand on Thompson's shoulder in what was becoming a familiar gesture.

"What I really wanted to tell you was that Ravenna would like to take you to a very entertaining little restaurant in town."

He glanced at his watch.

"Shall we say an hour's time? In the lobby downstairs?"

VII

The tzigane orchestra was low and pleasing and the food excellent, even if Thompson found the bizarre decor a little garish. But he had no time for the blurred background to their meal, as he was concentrating entirely on the girl.

She looked extremely beautiful in a dark low-cut gown with just a simple gold pendant around her neck. He noticed that somehow – perhaps with a type of white makeup – she had obscured the tattoo marks, for which he was thankful, as he was conscious that the two of them were the centre of attention.

"You look wonderful," was all he could manage as they waited for the dessert to be brought to the table.

And it was true. The recent transfusion she had undergone had worked a remarkable transformation in her. Her eyes were sparkling, her cheeks flushed, her whole manner animated and vivacious. The melancholy had gone from her expression and she smiled frequently, exposing the beautiful white teeth.

"This is all due to you, Mr Thompson," she said in a low voice.

Thompson shrugged deprecatingly. Ravenna smiled again.

"Your blood now runs in my veins. That means a great deal in our country."

Thompson felt uneasiness, not for the first time.

"It was the least I could do," he stammered. "What would the alternative have been?"

"Ah!"

She drew in her breath with a long, hissing sigh.

"That does not bear thinking about."

She cast her eyes down toward the snow-white tablecloth.

"Tonight you will get your reward."

Again a great flash of unease passed through Thompson. He

pretended to have misheard. And he was so unused to the ways of women that he was afraid he might misinterpret the meaning.

"I already have that in the joy of your company."

They had finished the dessert and were on coffee and cognac when Thompson found the manager at his side, deferential and suave.

"Mr Karolides' guests," he said to Thompson, but looking across at Ravenna. Thompson felt a flicker of amusement; perhaps Karolides owned the restaurant too? They drove back to the Magnolia in the big coupé, the warm Mediterranean air ruffling the girl's dark hair. The pair rode up in the lift in silence. He saw her to the door of her own suite, next to her father's, No. 46.

"Will you not come in for a nightcap?"

The invitation could not be refused; it was more of a command than a question, and she had already opened the door and switched on the light. He followed her in to find a replica of Karolides' suite next door. He glanced at a gold-framed photograph of Ravenna and a young man of striking beauty, with clear-minted features and bronze curls. The girl intercepted his glance.

"None of these things will ever come back and all we can do is cry and beat our wings against the encroaching darkness."

An oppressive silence had descended on the room and Thompson answered hurriedly, "That is the poetess in you speaking again."

She brightened.

"Oh, yes. I heard you had been reading my work."

"I hope you don't mind."

She shook her head.

"You certainly have esoteric tastes," Thompson went on. "Chiromancy, witchcraft and all those things."

"I find them fascinating. Can I offer you a goblet of our very special wine?"

Thompson assented and went to sit on a rococo divan so huge that it took up one third of the room's length. She handed him the gold-rimmed crystal goblet and they drank a silent toast. The time passed in a hazy dream. Thompson awoke to find himself sprawled on the divan. The room was in darkness, with only a pale light shining through the blinds. Ravenna's cool, nude body was beside him. She helped him to undress. Then they made love fiercely for what seemed like hours. It was past three a.m. before he let himself out into the corridor. He sought his room, showered and fell on to the bed. He had never felt so happy in his life.

VIII

Next morning he was down early, but Ravenna was earlier still. There was no one else in the dining room except for a solitary waiter, who stood yawning in the far corner near the coffee percolator. The couple's hands met beneath the tablecloth.

"Did you sleep well?"

Thompson laughed.

"Fragmentarily," he conceded. "I hope we didn't wake your father in the next suite.

It was the girl's turn to express amusement.

"Do you not recall what I told you on the raft? That he would laugh if he heard you say that."

Thompson was bewildered.

"I don't understand."

Ravenna gave him a level glance.

"He is not my father. He is my husband!"

"Your husband!"

Thompson felt a great wave of shock and nausea well up inside him. He felt betrayed and looked around the room like some animal at bay. She put a cool hand on his own as though he were a child who needed to be soothed.

"I had such great hopes . . ." he began wildly.

"Do not abandon them," she said softly.

Thompson half-got to his feet, caught the waiter's surprised glance across the room and sat down again hurriedly.

"What am I to say to him?" he said bitterly. "This betrayal . . ."

She laughed again.

"You do not understand us. He and I do not have proprietory rights in one another."

"What do you mean?"

"She means just what she says."

A shadow had fallen across the tablecloth and Karolides' tall figure was behind him. He gently pressed the Englishman back into his seat. He sat down opposite, his hypnotic eyes boring into Thompson's own.

"Let me explain, Mr Thompson. We had to get your help to save Ravenna. Let that be agreed between us. It is true we deceived you but that was for a good cause. And nothing has changed in the relationship."

Anger was stirring in Thompson now.

"But how can you condone such a thing!"

Ravenna looked at him pleadingly but Thompson ignored her.

"Just listen," Karolides went on in such a very low, even tone that Thompson lapsed into silence.

"In our philosophy of *agape*, women are not property to be bought and sold. I thought all that old sense of morality and fidelity had long since disappeared. Ravenna and I enjoy an open marriage. Beautiful women have a duty to spread their charms about in as wide a sphere as possible, so long as they are not doing harm to others. Think nothing of it."

All manner of resentful thoughts were boiling in Thompson's brain, but he remained silent beneath Karolides' imperious gaze. The Greek went on in an even lower voice.

"Do not look so shocked, my dear Mr Thompson. It means nothing to us. Women are not mere possessions as in many Anglo-Saxon societies. They have minds and bodies that belong to themselves only. A beautiful woman has a duty to share her charms with others and give them joy also."

Thompson noticed his napkin had dropped to the floor. To cover his confusion and anger he bent down to pick it up. As he straightened, he saw a small stain on the underside of the cuff of Karolides' white jacket.

"There's a spot of blood there," he mumbled.

His host glanced at it casually.

"Oh, yes," he said awkwardly. "I cut myself shaving. Thank you."

He dipped his handkerchief in his water glass and rubbed the stain away. Thompson did not miss the strange glance that passed between husband and wife.

Karolides resumed his monologue as though nothing had happened.

"Such beauty should be shared, is it not? Not hidden away for one man's selfish delectation. Let us be friends again."

He returned Ravenna's smile good-naturedly.

"You will see it our way, in time . . . Come, let us commence our breakfast."

But Thompson staggered from the room, disgusted to his soul. His anguish was indescribable – his brain on fire and chaotic thoughts inhabiting his fevered imagination as he walked like a drunken man along the Corniche, not knowing or caring where he was going. It was only the blare of motor horns that warned him of his danger, and he ran across the road to the promenade and sought the beach.

Dusk found him there, staring sightlessly out at a sea which had grown cold and turned a gun-metal grey. It was there that Ravenna and Karolides found him, after a long search, and sat with him for a while. When it was dark they took his insensible form, placed it in the back of the car, and the Greek drove swiftly to Professor Kogon's clinic, Ravenna cradling her lover's head as the miles slipped by beneath the whirring tyres.

When Thompson woke he was in a white bed with metal trolleys alongside and a bright light beating from the ceiling. He vaguely made out the anxious faces of Karolides and Ravenna. He could remember nothing of the intervening hours. His thoughts were jumbled; like dreams, hallucinatory and chaotic with images that made no sense. As a medical student he had read in a textbook that ants used greenfly as milch cows. In a brief interval of sanity he realised that he had been Ravenna's milch cow. He mumbled something unintelligible before relapsing into unconsciousness. When he was again aware of his surroundings he saw that Professor Kogon had a serious face as he conversed with Karolides in low, urgent tones.

"He is dying," the Professor was saying. "I cannot understand it. He is almost completely drained of blood. And as you know, his type is so rare that we are unable to give him a transfusion."

He shook his head despairingly. Ravenna looked radiant. Thompson thought she had never looked so beautiful or desirable. His consciousness was fading but he could just see that Ravenna and Karolides were giving him welcoming smiles as he went down to *Eternal Life*.

Kim Newman

Coppola's Dracula

Kim Newman's epic historical vampire novel, Anno Dracula, *has won* The Children of the Night Award, *presented by the Dracula Society; the Fiction Award of the Lord Ruthven Assembly, and the International Horror Critics' Guild Award. His other novels include a sequel to* Anno Dracula, The Bloody Red Baron, *plus* The Night Mayor, Bad Dreams, Jago *and* The Quorum, *while under his 'Jack Yeovil' pseudonym there are a string of gaming novels:* Drachenfels, Demon Download, Krokodil Tears, Comeback Tour, Beasts in Velvet, Genevieve Undead, Route 666 *plus* Orgy of the Blood Parasites. *His short fiction is collected in* The Original Dr. Shade and Other Stories *(which includes the British Science Fiction Award-winning title story) and* Famous Monsters. *Among his non-fiction books are* Nightmare Movies, Ghastly Beyond Belief: The Science Fiction & Fantasy Book of Quotations *(with Neil Gaiman),* Horror: 100 Best Books *(edited with Stephen Jones, and winner of the Bram Stoker Award) and* The BFI Companion to Horror.

"It's pretty obvious that the premise of this story is what it would have been like if Francis Ford Coppola had made Dracula as one of his good films," explains the author. "Originally I was going to write it as a parodic skit consisting of the film itself, but it became more substantial as I thought of the process of the making of Apocalypse Now. Of course, I owe a debt to Eleanor Coppola's book Notes and the documentary Hearts of Darkness."

Having considered what Coppola might have made of Dracula, *I'm struck with the thought of the other filmmakers who at various times promised but didn't deliver versions of the story – Orson Welles, Ingmar Bergman, Ken Russell – or by those who made* Draculas *that don't quite fit their filmographies – what if John Badham's* Dracula *had been the* Saturday Night Fever *follow-up, with John Travolta as a disco Dracula . . . ?"*

"Coppola's Dracula" takes place in the same world as Kim Newman's ongoing Vampire series, and Kate Reed – a character invented by Bram Stoker but deleted from Dracula *– has previously appeared in* Anno Dracula *and* The Bloody Red Baron . . .

A TREELINE AT DUSK. **Tall, straight, Carpathian pines. The red of sunset bleeds into the dark of night. Great flapping sounds. Huge, dark shapes flit languidly between the trees, sinister, dangerous. A vast batwing brushes the treetops.**

Jim Morrison's voice wails in despair. "People Are Strange".

Fire blossoms. Blue flame, pure as candle light. Black trees are consumed . . .

Fade to a face, hanging upside-down in the roiling fire.

Harker's Voice: *Wallachia . . . shit!*

Jonathan Harker, a solicitor's clerk, lies uneasy on his bed, upstairs in the inn at Bistritz, waiting. His eyes are empty.

With great effort, he gets up and goes to the full-length mirror. He avoids his own gaze and takes a swig from a squat bottle of plum brandy. He wears only long drawers. Bite-marks, almost healed, scab his shoulders. His arms and chest are sinewy, but his belly is white and soft. He staggers into a program of isometric exercises, vigorously Christian, ineptly executed.

Harker's Voice: *I could only think of the forests, the mountains . . . the inn was just a waiting room. Whenever I was in the forests, I could only think of home, of Exeter. Whenever I was home, I could only think of getting back to the mountains.*

The blind crucifix above the mirror, hung with cloves of garlic, looks down on Harker. He misses his footing and falls on the bed, then gets up, reaches, and takes down the garlic.

He bites into a clove as if it were an apple, and washes the pulp down with more brandy.

Harker's Voice: *All the time I stayed here in the inn, waiting for a commission, I was growing older, losing precious life. And all*

the time the Count sat on top of his mountain, leeching off the
land, he grew younger, thirstier.

Harker scoops a locket from a bedside table and opens it to
look at a portrait of his wife, Mina. Without malice or curiosity, he
dangles the cameo in a candle flame. The face browns, the silver
setting blackens.

Harker's Voice: *I was waiting for the call from Seward. Eventually,*
it came.

There is a knock on the door.

"It's all right for you, Katharine Reed," Francis whined as he picked
over the unappetizing craft services table. "You're dead, you don't
have to eat this shit."

Kate showed teeth, hissing a little. She knew that despite her
coke-bottle glasses and freckles, she could look unnervingly feral
when she smiled. Francis didn't shrink: deep down, the director
thought of her as a special effect, not a real vampire.

In the makeshift canteen, deep in the production bunker, the
Americans wittered nostalgia about McDonald's. The Brits – the
warm ones, anyway – rhapsodized about Pinewood breakfasts of
kippers and fried bread. Romanian location catering was not what
they were used to.

Francis finally found an apple less than half brown and took
it away. His weight had dropped visibly since their first meeting,
months ago in pre-production. Since he had come to Eastern
Europe, the insurance doctor diagnosed him as suffering from
malnutrition and put him on vitamin shots. *Dracula* was running
true to form, sucking him dry.

A production this size was like a swarm of vampire bats – some
large, many tiny – battening tenaciously onto the host, making
insistent, never-ending demands. Kate had watched Francis –
bespectacled, bearded and hyperactive – lose substance under
the draining siege, as he made and justified decisions, yielded
the visions to be translated to celluloid, rewrote the script to suit
locations or new casting. How could one man throw out so many
ideas, only a fraction of which would be acted on? In his position,
Kate's mind would bleed empty in a week.

A big budget film shot in a backward country was an insane
proposition, like taking a touring three-ring circus into a war zone.
Who will survive, she thought, and what will be left of them?

The craft table for vampires was as poorly stocked as the one
for the warm. Unhealthy rats in chickenwire cages. Kate watched
one of the floor effects men, a new-born with a padded waistcoat
and a toolbelt, select a writhing specimen and bite off its head.

He spat it on the concrete floor, face stretched into a mask of disgust.

'Ringworm,' he snarled. 'The commie gits are trying to kill us off with diseased vermin.'

'I could murder a bacon sarnie,' the effects man's mate sighed.

'I could murder a Romanian caterer,' said the new-born.

Kate decided to go thirsty. There were enough Yanks around to make coming by human blood in this traditionally superstitious backwater not a problem. Ninety years after Dracula spread vampirism to the Western world, America was still sparsely populated by the blood-drinking undead. For a lot of Americans, being bled by a genuine olde worlde creature of the night was something of a thrill.

That would wear off.

Outside the bunker, in a shrinking patch of natural sunlight between a stand of real pines and the skeletons of fake trees, Francis shouted at Harvey Keitel. The actor, cast as Jonathan Harker, was stoic, inexpressive, grumpy. He refused to be drawn into argument, invariably driving Francis to shrieking hysteria.

'I'm not Martin Fucking Scorsese, man,' he screamed. 'I'm not going to slather on some lousy voice-over to compensate for what you're not giving me. Without Harker, I don't have a picture.'

Keitel made fists but his body language was casual. Francis had been riding his star hard all week. Scuttlebutt was that he had wanted Pacino or McQueen but neither wanted to spend three months behind the Iron Curtain.

Kate could understand that. This featureless WWII bunker, turned over to the production as a command centre, stood in ancient mountains, dwarfed by the tall trees. As an outpost of civilization in a savage land, it was ugly and ineffective.

When approached to act as a technical advisor to Coppola's *Dracula*, she had thought it might be interesting to see where it all started: the Changes, the Terror, the Transformation. No one seriously believed vampirism began here, but it was where Dracula came from. This land had nurtured him through centuries before he decided to spread his wings and extend his bloodline around the world.

Three months had already been revised as six months. This production didn't have a schedule, it had a sentence. A few were already demanding parole.

Some vampires felt Transylvania should be the undead Israel, a new state carved out of the much-redrawn map of Central Europe, a geographical and political homeland. As soon as it grew from an inkling to a notion, Nicolae Ceausescu vigorously vetoed the proposition. Holding up in one hand a silver-edged sickle, an iron-headed hammer and a sharpened oak spar, the Premier reminded the world that "in Romania, we know how to treat leeches – a stake through the heart and off with their filthy heads." But the Transylvania Movement – back to the forests, back to the mountains – gathered momentum: some elders, after a ninety years of the chaos of the larger world, wished to withdraw to their former legendary status. Many of Kate's generation, turned in the 1880s, Victorians stranded in this mechanistic century, were sympathetic.

"You're the Irish vampire lady," Harrison Ford, flown in for two days to play Dr Seward as a favour, had said. "Where's your castle?"

"I have a flat in Clerkenwell," she admitted. "Over an off-licence."

In the promised Transylvania, all elders would have castles, fiefdoms, slaves, human cattle. Everyone would wear evening dress. All vampires would have treasures of ancient gold, like leprechauns. There would be a silk-lined coffin in every crypt, and every night would be a full moon. Unlife eternal and luxury without end, bottomless wells of blood and Paris label shrouds.

Kate thought the Movement lunatic. Never mind cooked breakfasts and (the other crew complaint) proper toilet paper, this was an intellectual desert, a country without conversation, without (and she recognized the irony) life.

She understood Dracula had left Transylvania in the first place not merely because he – the great dark sponge – had sucked it dry, but because even he was bored with ruling over gypsies, wolves and mountain streams. That did not prevent the elders of the Transylvania Movement from claiming the Count as their inspiration and using his seal as their symbol. An Arthurian whisper had it that once vampires returned to Transylvania, Dracula would rise again to assume his rightful throne as their ruler.

Dracula meant so much to so many. She wondered if there was anything left inside so many meanings, anything concrete and inarguable and true. Or was he now just a phantom, a slave to anyone who cared to invoke his name? So many causes and crusades and rebellions and atrocities. One man, one monster, could never have kept track of them all, could never have encompassed so much mutually exclusive argument.

There was the Dracula of the histories, the Dracula of Stoker's book, the Dracula of this film, the Dracula of the Transylvania Movement. Dracula, the vampire and the idea, was vast. But not so vast that he could cast his cloak of protection around all who claimed to be his followers. Out here in the mountains where the Count had passed centuries in petty predation, Kate understood that he must in himself have felt tiny, a lizard crawling down a rock.

Nature was overwhelming. At night, the stars were laser-points in the deep velvet black of the sky. She could hear, taste and smell a thousand flora and fauna. If ever there was a call of the wild, this forest exerted it. But there was nothing she considered intelligent life.

She tied tight under her chin the yellow scarf, shot through with golden traceries, she had bought at Biba in 1969. It was a flimsy, delicate thing, but to her it meant civilization, a coloured moment of frivolity in a life too often preoccupied with monochrome momentousness.

Francis jumped up and down and threw script pages to the winds. His arms flapped like wings. Clouds of profanity enveloped the uncaring Keitel.

"Don't you realize I've put up my own fucking money for this fucking picture," he shouted, not just at Keitel but at the whole company. "I could lose my house, my vineyard, everything. I can't afford a fucking honourable failure. This has abso-goddamn-lutely got to outgross *Jaws* or I'm personally impaled up the ass with a sharpened telegraph pole."

Effects men sat slumped against the exterior wall of the bunker – there were few chairs on location – and watched their director rail at the heavens, demanding of God answers that were not forthcoming. Script pages swirled upwards in a spiral, spreading out in a cloud, whipping against the upper trunks of the trees, soaring out over the valley.

"He was worse on *Godfather*," one said.

Servants usher Harker into a well-appointed drawing room. A table is set with an informal feast of bread, cheese and meat. Dr Jack Seward, in a white coat with a stethoscope hung around his neck, warmly shakes Harker's hand and leads him to the table. Quincey P. Morris sits to one side, tossing and catching a spade-sized bowie knife.

Lord Godalming, well-dressed, napkin tucked into his starched collar, sits at the table, forking down a double helping of paprika chicken. Harker's eyes meet Godalming's, the nobleman looks away.

Seward: Harker, help yourself to the fare, Jon. It's uncommonly decent for foreign muck.

Harker: Thank you, no. I took repast at the inn.

Seward: How is the inn? Natives bothering you? Superstitious babushkas, what?

Harker: I am well in myself.

Seward: Splendid . . . the vampire, Countess Marya Dolingen of Graz. In 1883, you cut off her head and drove a hawthorne stake through her heart, destroying her utterly.

Harker: I'm not disposed just now to discuss such affairs.

Morris: Come on, Jonny-Boy. You have a commendation from the church, a papal decoration. The frothing she-bitch is dead at last. Take the credit.

Harker: I have no direct knowledge of the individual you mention. And if I did, I reiterate that I would not be disposed to discuss such affairs.

Seward and Morris exchange a look as Harker stands impassive. They know they have the right man. Godalming, obviously in command, nods.

Seward clears plates of cold meat from a strong-box that stands on the table. Godalming hands the doctor a key, with which he opens the box. He takes out a woodcut and hands it over to Harker.

The picture is of a knife-nosed mediaeval warrior prince.

Seward: That's Vlad Tepes, called 'the Impaler'. A good Christian, defender of the faith. Killed a million Turks. Son of the Dragon, they called him. Dracula.

Harker is impressed.

Morris: Prince Vlad had Orthodox Church decorations out the ass. Coulda made Metropolitan. But he converted, went over to Rome, turned Candle.

Harker: Candle?

Seward: Roman Catholic.

Harker looks again at the woodcut. In a certain light, it resembles the young Marlon Brando.

Seward walks to a side-table, where an antique dictaphone is set up. He fits a wax cylinder and adjusts the needle-horn.

Seward: This is Dracula's voice. It's been authenticated.

Seward cranks the dictaphone.

Dracula's Voice: Cheeldren of the naight, leesten to them. What museek they maike!

There is a strange distortion in the recording.

Harker: What's that noise in the background?

Seward: Wolves, my boy. Dire wolves, to be precise.

Dracula's Voice: To die, to be reallllly dead, that must be . . . glorioussssss!

Morris: Vlad's well beyond Rome now. He's up there, in his

impenetrable castle, continuing the crusade on his own. He's got
this army of Szekeley Gypsies, fanatically loyal fucks. They follow
his orders, no matter how atrocious, no matter how appalling. You
know the score, Jon. Dead babies, drained cattle, defenestrated
peasants, impaled grandmothers. He's god-damned Un-Dead. A
fuckin' monster, boy.

Harker is shocked. He looks again at the woodcut.

Seward: The firm would like you to proceed up into the
mountains, beyond the Borgo Pass . . .

Harker: But that's Transylvania. We're not supposed to be in
Transylvania.

Godalming looks to the heavens, but continues eating.

Seward: . . . beyond the Borgo Pass, to Castle Dracula. There,
you are to ingratiate yourself by whatever means come to hand
into Dracula's coterie. Then you are to disperse the Count's
household.

Harker: Disperse?

Godalming puts down his knife and fork.

Godalming: Disperse with ultimate devotion.

"What can I say, we made a mistake," Francis said, shrugging
nervously, trying to seem confident. He had shaved off his beard,
superstitiously hoping that would attract more attention than his
announcement. "I think this is the courageous thing to do, shut
down and recast, rather than continue with a frankly unsatisfactory
situation."

Kate did not usually cover showbiz, but the specialist press –
Variety, Screen International, Positif – were dumbstruck enough to
convince her it was not standard procedure to fire one's leading
man after two weeks' work, scrap the footage and get someone
else. When Keitel was sent home, the whole carnival ground to
a halt and everyone had to sit around while Francis flew back to
the States to find a new star.

Someone asked how far over budget *Dracula* was, and Francis
smiled and waffled about budgets being provisional.

"No one ever asked how much the Sistine Chapel cost," he
said, waving a chubby hand. Kate would have bet that while
Michaelangelo was on his back with the brushes, Pope Julius II
never stopped asking how much it cost and when would it be
finished.

During the break in shooting, money was spiralling down a drain.
Fred Roos, the co-producer, had explained to her just how expensive
it was to keep a whole company standing by. It was almost more costly
than having them work.

Next to Francis at the impromptu press conference in the Bucharest Town Hall was Martin Sheen, the new Jonathan Harker. In his mid-thirties, he looked much younger, like the lost boy he played in *Badlands*. The actor mumbled generously about the opportunity he was grateful for. Francis beamed like a shorn Santa Claus on a forced diet and opened a bottle of his own wine to toast his new star.

The man from *Variety* asked who would be playing Dracula, and Francis froze in mid-pour, sloshing red all over Sheen's wrist. Kate knew the title role – actually fairly small, thanks to Bram Stoker and screenwriter John Milius – was still on offer to various possibles – Klaus Kinski, Jack Nicholson, Christopher Lee.

"I can confirm Bobby Duvall will play Van Helsing," Francis said. "And we have Dennis Hopper as Renfield. He's the one who eats flies."

"But who is Dracula?"

Francis swallowed some wine, attempted a cherubic look, and wagged a finger.

"I think I'll let that be a surprise. Now, ladies and gentlemen, if you'll excuse me, I have motion picture history to make."

As Kate took her room-key from the desk, the night manager nagged her in Romanian. When she had first checked in, the door of her room fell off as she opened it. The hotel maintained she did not know her own vampire strength and should pay exorbitantly to have the door replaced. Apparently, the materials were available only at great cost and had to be shipped from Moldavia. She assumed it was a scam they worked on foreigners, especially vampires. The door was made of paper stretched over a straw frame, the hinges were cardboard fixed with drawing pins.

She was pretending not to understand any language in which they tried to ask her for money, but eventually they would hit on English and she'd have to make a scene. Francis, light-hearted as a child at the moment, thought it rather funny and had taken to teasing her about the damn door.

Not tired, but glad to be off the streets after nightfall, she climbed the winding stairs to her room, a cramped triangular space in the roof. Though she was barely an inch over five feet, she could only stand up straight in the dead centre of the room. A crucifix hung ostentatiously over the bed, a looking glass was propped up on the basin. She thought about taking them down but it was best to let insults pass. In many ways, she preferred the camp-site conditions in the mountains. She only needed to sleep every two weeks, and when she was out she was literally dead and didn't care about clean sheets.

They were all in Bucharest for the moment, as Francis supervised script-readings to ease Sheen into the Harker role. His fellow coach-passengers – Fredric Forrest (Westenra), Sam Bottoms (Murray) and Albert Hall (Swales) – had all been on the project for over a year, and had been through all this before in San Francisco as Francis developed John Milius's script through improvisation and happy accident. Kate didn't think she would have liked being a screenwriter. Nothing was ever finished.

She wondered who would end up playing Dracula. Since his marriage to Queen Victoria made him officially if embarrassingly a satellite of the British Royal Family, he had rarely been represented in films. However, Lon Chaney had taken the role in the silent *London After Midnight*, which dealt with the court intrigues of the 1880s, and Anton Walbrook played Vlad opposite Anna Neagle in *Victoria the Great* in 1937. Kate, a lifelong theatregoer who had never quite got used to the cinema, remembered Vincent Price opposite Helen Hayes in *Victoria Regina* in the 1930s.

Aside from a couple of cheap British pictures which didn't count, Bram Stoker's *Dracula* – the singular mix of documentation and wish-fulfilment that inspired a revolution by showing how Dracula could have been defeated in the early days before his rise to power – had never been made as a film. Orson Welles produced it on radio in the 1930s and announced it as his first picture, casting himself as Harker *and* the Count, using first-person camera throughout. RKO thought it too expensive and convinced him to make *Citizen Kane* instead. Nearly ten years ago, Francis had lured John Milius into writing the first pass at the script by telling him nobody, not even Orson Welles, had ever been able to lick the book.

Francis was still writing and rewriting, stitching together scenes from Milius's script with new stuff of his own and pages torn straight from the book. Nobody had seen a complete script, and Kate thought one didn't exist.

She wondered how many times Dracula had to die for her to be rid of him. Her whole life had been a dance with Dracula, and he haunted her still. When Francis killed the Count at the end of the movie – if that was the ending he went with – maybe it would be for the last time. You weren't truly dead until you'd died in a motion picture. Or at the box office.

The latest word was that the role was on offer to Marlon Brando. She couldn't see it: Stanley Kowalski and Vito Corleone as Count Dracula. One of the best actors in the world, he'd been one of the worst Napoleons in the movies. Historical characters brought out the ham in him. He was terrible as Fletcher Christian too.

Officially, Kate was still just a technical adviser – though she had never actually met Dracula during his time in London, she had lived through the period. She had known Stoker, Jonathan Harker, Godalming and the rest. Once, as a warm girl, she had been terrified by Van Helsing's rages. When Stoker wrote his book and smuggled it out of prison, she had helped with its underground circulation, printing copies on the presses of the *Pall Mall Gazette* and ensuring its distribution despite all attempts at suppression. She wrote the introduction for the 1912 edition that was the first official publication.

Actually, she found herself impressed into a multitude of duties. Francis treated a $20,000,000 (and climbing) movie like a college play and expected everyone to pitch in, despite union rules designed to prevent the crew being treated as slave labour. She found the odd afternoon of sewing costumes or night of set-building welcome distraction.

At first, Francis asked her thousands of questions about points of detail; now he was shooting, he was too wrapped up in his own vision to take advice. If she didn't find something to do, she'd sit idle. As an employee of American Zoetrope, she couldn't even write articles about the shoot. For once, she was on the inside, knowing but not telling.

She had wanted to write about Romania for the *New Statesman*, but was under orders not to do anything that might jeopardize the cooperation the production needed from the Ceausecus. So far, she had avoided all the official receptions Nicolae and Elena hosted for the production. The Premier was known to be an extreme vampire-hater, especially since the stirrings of the Transylvania Movement, and occasionally ordered not-so-discreet purges of the undead.

Kate knew she, like the few other vampires with the *Dracula* crew, was subject to regular checks by the *Securitate*. Men in black leather coats loitered in the corner of her eye.

"For God's sake," Francis had told her, "don't *take* anybody local."

Like most Americans, he didn't understand. Though he could *see* she was a tiny woman with red hair and glasses, the mind of an aged aunt in the body of an awkward cousin, Francis could not rid himself of the impression that vampire women were ravening predators with unnatural powers of bewitchment, lusting after the pounding blood of any warm youth who happens along. She was sure he hung his door with garlic and wolfsbane, but half-hoped for a whispered solicitation.

After a few uncomfortable nights in Communist-approved beer-halls, she had learned to stay in her hotel room while in Bucharest. People here had memories as long as her lifetime. They crossed themselves and muttered prayers as she walked by. Children threw stones.

She stood at her window and looked out at the square. A patch of devastation, where the ancient quarter of the capital had been, marked the site of the palace Ceausecu was building for himself. A three-storey poster of the Saviour of Romania stood amid the ruins. Dressed like an orthodox priest, he held up Dracula's severed head as if he had personally killed the Count.

Ceausecu harped at length about the dark, terrible days of the past when Dracula and his kind preyed on the warm of Romania to prevent his loyal subjects from considering the dark, terrible days of the present when he and his wife lorded over the country like especially corrupt Roman Emperors. Impersonating the supplicant baker in *The Godfather*, Francis had abased himself to the dictator to secure official co-operation.

She turned on the radio and heard tinny martial music. She turned it off, lay on the narrow, lumpy bed – as a joke, Fred Forrest and Francis had put a coffin in her room one night – and listened to the city at night. Like the forest, Bucharest was alive with noises, and smells.

It was ground under, but there was life here. Even in this grim city, someone was laughing, someone was in love. Somebody was allowed to be a happy fool.

She heard winds in telephone wires, bootsteps on cobbles, a drink being poured in another room, someone snoring, a violinist sawing scales. And someone outside her door. Someone who didn't breathe, who had no heartbeat, but whose clothes creaked as he moved, whose saliva rattled in his throat.

She sat up, confident she was elder enough to be silent, and looked at the door.

"Come in," she said, "it's not locked. But be careful. I can't afford more breakages."

His name was Ion Popescu and he looked about thirteen, with big, olive-shiny orphan eyes and thick, black, unruly hair. He wore an adult's clothes, much distressed and frayed, stained with long-dried blood and earth. His teeth were too large for his skull, his cheeks stretched tight over his jaws, drawing his whole face to the point of his tiny chin.

Once in her room, he crouched down in a corner, away from a window. He talked only in a whisper, in a mix of English and

German she had to strain to follow. His mouth wouldn't open properly. He was alone in the city, without community. Now he was tired and wanted to leave his homeland. He begged her to hear him out and whispered his story.

He claimed to be fifty-two, turned in 1937. He didn't know, or didn't care to talk about, his father- or mother-in-darkness. There were blanks burned in his memory, whole years missing. She had come across that before. For most of his vampire life, he had lived underground, under the Nazis and then the Communists. He was the sole survivor of several resistance movements. His warm comrades had never really trusted him, but his capabilities were useful for a while.

She was reminded of her first days after turning. When she knew nothing, when her condition seemed a disease, a trap. That Ion could be a vampire for forty years and never pass beyond the new-born stage was incredible. She truly realized, at last, just how backward this country was.

'Then I hear of the American film, and of the sweet vampire lady who is with the company. Many times, I try to get near you, but you are watched. *Securitate*. You, I think, are my saviour, my true mother-in-the-dark.'

Fifty-two, she reminded herself.

Ion was exhausted after days trying to get close to the hotel, to "the sweet vampire lady", and hadn't fed in weeks. His body was icy cold. Though she knew her own strength was low, she nipped her wrist and dribbled a little of her precious blood onto his white lips, enough to put a spark in his dull eyes.

There was a deep gash on his arm, which festered as it tried to heal. She bound it with her scarf, wrapping his thin limb tight.

He hugged her and slept like a baby. She arranged his hair away from his eyes and imagined his life. It was like the old days, when vampires were hunted down and destroyed by the few who believed. Before Dracula.

The Count had changed nothing for Ion Popescu.

Bistritz, a bustling township in the foothills of the Carpathian Alps. Harker, carrying a Gladstone Bag, weaves through crowds towards a waiting coach and six. Peasants try to sell him crucifixes, garlic and other lucky charms. Women cross themselves and mutter prayers.

A wildly-gesticulating photographer tries to stop him slowing his pace to examine a complicated camera. An infernal burst of flash-powder spills purple smoke across the square. People choke on it.

Corpses hang from a four-man gibbet, dogs leaping up to chew on their naked feet. Children squabble over mismatched boots filched from the executed men. Harker looks up at the twisted, mouldy faces.

He reaches the coach and tosses his bag up. Swales, the coachman, secures it with the other luggage and growls at the late passenger. Harker pulls open the door and swings himself into the velvet-lined interior of the carriage.

There are two other passengers. Westenra, heavily moustached and cradling a basket of food. And Murray, a young man who smiles as he looks up from his Bible.

Harker exchanges curt nods of greeting as the coach lurches into motion.

Harker's Voice: *I quickly formed opinions of my travelling companions. Swales was at the reins. It was my commission but sure as shooting it was his coach. Westenra, the one they called "Cook", was from Whitby. He was ratcheted several notches too tight for Wallachia. Probably too tight for Whitby, come to that. Murray, the fresh-faced youth with the Good Book, was a rowing blue from Oxford. To look at him, you'd think the only use he'd have for a sharpened stake would be as a stump in a knock-up match.*

Later, after dark but under a full moon, Harker sits up top with Swales. A wind-up phonograph crackles out a tune through a sizable trumpet.

Mick Jagger sings "Ta-Ra-Ra-BOOM-De-Ay".

Westenra and Murray have jumped from the coach and ride the lead horses, whooping it up like a nursery Charge of the Light Brigade.

Harker, a few years past such antics, watches neutrally. Swales is indulgent of his passengers.

The mountain roads are narrow, precipitous. The lead horses, spurred by their riders, gallop faster. Harker looks down and sees a sheer drop of a thousand feet, and is more concerned by the foolhardiness of his companions.

Hooves strike the edge of the road, narrowly missing disaster.

Westenra and Murray chant along with the song, letting go of their mounts' manes and doing hand-gestures to the lyrics. Harker gasps but Swales chuckles. He has the reins and the world is safe.

Harker's Voice: *I think the dark and the pines of Romania spooked them badly, but they whistled merrily on into the night, infernal cake-walkers with Death as a dancing partner.*

In the rehearsal hall, usually a people's ceramics collective, she introduced Ion to Francis.

The vampire youth was sharper now. In a pair of her jeans –
which fit him perfectly – and a *Godfather II* T-shirt, he looked less
the waif, more like a survivor. Her Biba scarf, now his talisman,
was tied around his neck.

"I said we could find work for him with the extras. The
gypsies."

"I am no gypsy," Ion said, vehemently.

"He speaks English, Romanian, German, Magyar and Romany.
He can coordinate all of them."

"He's a kid."

"He's older than you are."

Francis thought it over. She didn't mention Ion's problems with
the authorities. Francis couldn't harbour an avowed dissident.
The relationship between the production and the government was
already strained. Francis thought – correctly – that he was being bled
of funds by corrupt officials, but could afford to lodge no complaint.
Without the Romanian army, he didn't have a cavalry, didn't have
a horde. And without the location permits that still hadn't come
through, he couldn't shoot the story beyond Borgo Pass.

"I can keep the rabble in line, maestro," Ion said, smiling.

Somehow, he had learned how to work his jaws and lips into a
smile. With her blood in him, he had more control. She noticed
him chameleoning a little. His smile, she thought, might be a little
like hers.

Francis chuckled. He liked being called "maestro". Ion was good
at getting on the right side of people. After all, he had certainly
got on the right side of her.

"Okay, but keep out of the way if you see anyone in a suit."

Ion was effusively grateful. Again, he acted the age he looked,
hugging Francis, then her, saluting like a toy soldier. Martin Sheen,
noticing, raised an eyebrow.

Francis took Ion off to meet his own children – Roman, Gio and
Sofia – and Sheen's sons Emilio and Charley. It had not sunk in
that this wiry kid, obviously keen to learn baseball and chew gum,
was in warm terms middle-aged.

Then again, Kate never knew whether to be twenty-five, the age
at which she turned, or 116. And how was a 116-year-old supposed
to behave anyway?

Since she had let him bleed her, she was having flashes of his past:
scurrying through back-streets and sewers, like a rat; the stabbing
pains of betrayal; eye-searing flashes of firelight; constant cold and
red thirst and filth.

Ion had never had the time to grow up. Or even to be a proper
child. He was a waif and a stray. She couldn't help but love him

a little. She had chosen not to pass on the Dark Kiss, though she had once – during the Great War – come close and regretted it.

Her bloodline, she thought, was not good for a new-born. There was too much Dracula in it, maybe too much Kate Reed.

To Ion, she was a teacher not a mother. Before she insisted on becoming a journalist, her whole family seemed to feel she was predestined to be a governess. Now, at last, she thought she saw what they meant.

Ion was admiring six-year-old Sofia's dress, eyes bright with what Kate hoped was not hunger. The little girl laughed, plainly taken with her new friend. The boys, heads full of the vampires of the film, were less sure about him. He would have to earn their friendship.

Later, Kate would deal with Part Two of the Ion Popescu Problem. After the film was over, which would not be until the 1980s at the current rate of progress, he wanted to leave the country, hidden in among the rest of the production crew. He was tired of skulking and dodging the political police, and didn't think he could manage it much longer. In the West, he said, he would be free from persecution.

She knew he would be disappointed. The warm didn't really *like* vampires in London or Rome or Dublin any more than they did in Timisoara or Bucharest or Cluj. It was just more difficult legally to have them destroyed.

Back in the mountains, there was the usual chaos. A sudden thunderstorm, whipped up out of nowhere like a djinn, had torn up real and fake trees and scattered them throughout the valley, demolishing the gypsy encampment production designer Dean Tavoularis had been building. About half a million dollars' worth of set was irrevocably lost, and the bunker itself had been struck by lightning and split open like a pumpkin. The steady rain poured in and streamed out of the structure, washing away props, documents, equipment and costumes. Crews foraged in the valley for stuff that could be reclaimed and used.

Francis acted as if God were personally out to destroy him.

"Doesn't anybody else notice what a disaster this film is?" he shouted. "I haven't got a script, I haven't got an actor, I'm running out of money, I'm all out of time. This is the goddamned Unfinished Symphony, man."

Nobody wanted to talk to the director when he was in this mood. Francis squatted on the bare earth of the mountainside, surrounded by smashed balsawood pine-trees, hugging his knees. He wore a stetson hat, filched from Quincey Morris's wardrobe, and drizzle was running from its brim in a tiny stream. Eleanor, his wife, concentrated on keeping the children out of the way.

"This is the worst fucking film of my career. The worst I'll ever make. The *last* movie."

The first person to tell Francis to cheer up and that things weren't so bad would get fired and be sent home. At this point, crowded under a leaky lean-to with other surplus persons, Kate was tempted.

"I don't want to be Orson Welles," Francis shouted at the slate-grey skies, rain on his face, "I don't want to be David Lean. I just want to make an Irwin Allen movie, with violence, action, sex, destruction in every frame. This isn't Art, this is atrocity."

Just before the crew left Bucharest, as the storm was beginning, Marlon Brando had consented to be Dracula. Francis personally wired him a million-dollar down-payment against two weeks' work. Nobody dared remind Francis that if he wasn't ready to shoot Brando's scenes by the end of the year, he would lose the money and his star.

The six months was up, and barely a quarter of the film was in the can. The production schedule had been extended and reworked so many times that all forecasts of the end of shooting were treated like forecasts of the end of the War. Everyone said it would be over by Christmas, but knew it would stretch until the last trump.

"I could just stop, you know," Francis said, deflated. "I could just shut it down and go back to San Francisco and a hot bath and decent pasta and forget everything. I can still get work shooting commercials, nudie movies, series TV. I could make little films, shot on video with a four-man crew, and show them to my friends. All this D.W. Griffith-David O. Selznick shit just isn't fucking necessary."

He stretched out his arms and water poured from his sleeves. Over a hundred people, huddled in various shelters or wrapped in orange plastic ponchos, looked at their lord and master and didn't know what to say or do.

"What does this cost, people? Does anybody know? Does anybody care? Is it worth all this? A movie? A painted ceiling? A symphony? Is anything worth all this shit?"

The rain stopped as if a tap were turned off. Sun shone through clouds. Kate screwed her eyes tight shut and fumbled under her poncho for the heavy sunglasses-clip she always carried. She might be the kind of vampire who could go about in all but the strongest sunlight, but her eyes could still be burned out by too much light.

She fixed clip-on shades to her glasses and blinked.

People emerged from their shelters, rainwater pouring from hats and ponchos.

"We can shoot around it," a co-associate assistant producer said. Francis fired him on the spot.

Kate saw Ion creep out of the forests and straighten up. He had a wooden staff, newly-trimmed. He presented it to his maestro.

"To lean on," he said, demonstrating. Then, he fetched it up and held it like a weapon, showing a whittled point. "And to fight with."

Francis accepted the gift, made a few passes in the air, liking the feel of it in his hands. Then he leaned on the staff, easing his weight onto the strong wood.

"It's good," he said.

Ion grinned and saluted.

"All doubt is passing," Francis announced. "Money doesn't matter, time doesn't matter, we don't matter. This film, this *Dracula*, that is what matters. It's taken the smallest of you," he laid his hand on Ion's curls, "to show me that. When we are gone, *Dracula* will remain."

Francis kissed the top of Ion's head.

"Now," he shouted, inspired, "to work, to work."

The coach trundles up the mountainside, winding between the tall trees. A blaze of blue light shoots up.

Westenra: Treasure!

Harker's Voice: They said the blue flames marked the sites of long-lost troves of bandit silver and gold. They also said no good ever came of finding it.

Westenra: Coachman, stop! Treasure.

Swales pulls up the reins, and the team halt. The clatter of hooves and reins dies. The night is quiet.

The blue flame still burns.

Westenra jumps out and runs to the edge of the forest, trying to see between the trees, to locate the source of the light.

Harker: I'll go with him.

Warily, Harker takes a rifle down from the coach, and breeches a bullet.

Westenra runs ahead into the forest, excited. Harker carefully follows up, placing each step carefully.

Westenra: Treasure, man. Treasure.

Harker hears a noise, and signals Westenra to hold back. Both men freeze and listen.

The blue light flickers on their faces and fades out. Westenra is disgusted and disappointed.

Something moves in the undergrowth. Red eyes glow.

A dire wolf leaps up at Westenra, claws brushing his face,

enormously furred body heavy as a felled tree. Harker fires. A red flash briefly spotlights the beast's twisted snout.

The wolf's teeth clash, just missing Westenra's face. The huge animal, startled if not wounded, turns and disappears into the forest.

Westenra and Harker run away as fast as they can, vaulting over prominent tree-roots, bumping low branches.

Westenra: *Never get out of the coach . . . never get out of the coach.*

They get back to the road. Swales looks stern, not wanting to know about the trouble they're in.

Harker's Voice: *Words of wisdom. Never get out of the coach, never go into the woods . . . unless you're prepared to become the compleat animal, to stay forever in the forests. Like him, Dracula.*

At the party celebrating the 100th Day of Shooting, the crew brought in a coffin bearing a brass plate that read simply DRACULA. Its lid creaked open and a girl in a bikini leaped out, nestling in Francis's lap. She had plastic fangs, which she spit out to kiss him.

The crew cheered. Even Eleanor laughed.

The fangs wound up in the punch-bowl. Kate fished them out as she got drinks for Marty Sheen and Robert Duvall.

Duvall, lean and intense, asked her about Ireland. She admitted she hadn't been there in decades. Sheen, whom everyone thought was Irish, was Hispanic, born Ramon Estevez. He was drinking heavily and losing weight, travelling deep into his role. Having surrendered entirely to Francis's "vision", Sheen was talking with Harker's accent and developing the character's hollow-eyed look and panicky glance.

The real Jonathan, Kate remembered, was a decent but dull sort, perpetually 'umble around brighter people, deeply suburban. Mina, his fiancée and her friend, kept saying that at least he was real, a worker ant not a butterfly like Art or Lucy. A hundred years later, Kate could hardly remember Jonathan's face. From now on, she would always think of Sheen when anyone mentioned Jonathan Harker. The original was eclipsed.

Or erased. Bram Stoker had intended to write about Kate in his book, but left her out. Her few poor braveries during the Terror tended to be ascribed to Mina in most histories. That was probably a blessing.

"What it must have been like for Jonathan," Sheen said. "Not even knowing there were such things as vampires. Imagine, confronted with Dracula himself. His whole world was shredded, torn away. All he had was himself, and it wasn't enough."

"He had family, friends," Kate said.

Sheen's eyes glowed. "Not in Transylvania. *Nobody* has family and friends in Transylvania."

Kate shivered and looked around. Francis was showing off martial arts moves with Ion's staff. Fred Forrest was rolling a cigar-sized joint. Vittorio Storaro, the cinematographer, doled out his special spaghetti, smuggled into the country inside film cans, to appreciative patrons. A Romanian official in an ill-fitting shiny suit, liaison with the state studios, staunchly resisted offers of drinks he either assumed were laced with LSD or didn't want other Romanians to see him sampling. She wondered which of the native hangers-on was the *Securitate* spy, and giggled at the thought that they all might be spies and still not know the others were watching them.

Punch, which she was sipping for politeness's sake, squirted out of her nose as she laughed. Duvall patted her back and she recovered. She was not used to social drinking.

Ion, in a baseball cap given to him by one of Francis's kids, was joking with the girl in the bikini, a dancer who played one of the gypsies, his eyes reddening with thirst. Kate decided to leave them be. Ion would control himself with the crew. Besides, the girl might like a nip from the handsome lad.

With a handkerchief, she wiped her face. Her specs had gone crooked with her spluttering and she rearranged them.

"You're not what I expected of a vampire lady," Duvall said.

Kate slipped the plastic fangs into her mouth and snarled like a kitten.

Duvall and Sheen laughed.

For two weeks, Francis had been shooting the "Brides of Dracula" sequence. The mountainside was as crowded as Oxford Street, extras borrowed from the Romanian army salted with English faces recruited from youth hostels and student exchanges. Storaro was up on a dinosaur-necked camera crane, swooping through the skies, getting shots of rapt faces.

The three girls, two warm and one real vampire, had only showed up tonight, guaranteeing genuine crowd excitement in long-shot or blurry background rather than the flatly faked enthusiasm radiated for their own close-ups.

Kate was supposed to be available for the Brides, but they didn't need advice. It struck her as absurd that she should be asked to tell the actresses how to be alluring. The vampire Marlene, cast as the blonde bride, had been an actress since the silent days and wandered about nearly naked, exposing herself to the winds. Her warm sisters needed to be swathed in furs between shots.

In a shack-like temporary dressing room, the brides were transformed. Bunty, a sensible Englishwoman, was in charge of their make-up. The living girls, twins from Malta who had appeared in a *Playboy* layout, submitted to all-over pancake that gave their flesh an unhealthy shimmer and opened their mouths like dental patients as fangs – a hundred times more expensive if hardly more convincing than the joke shop set Kate had kept after the party – were fitted.

Francis, with Ion in his wake carrying a script, dropped by to cast an eye over the brides. He asked Marlene to open her mouth and examined her dainty pointy teeth.

"We thought we'd leave them as they were," said Bunty.

Francis shook his head.

"They need to be bigger, more obvious."

Bunty took a set of dagger-like eye-teeth from her kit and approached Marlene, who waved them away.

"I'm sorry, dear," the make-up woman apologized.

Marlene laughed musically and hissed, making Francis jump. Her mouth opened wide like a cobra's, and her fangs extended a full two inches.

Francis grinned.

"Perfect."

The vampire lady took a little curtsey.

Kate mingled with the crew, keeping out of camera-shot. She was used to the tedious pace of film-making now. Everything took forever and there was rarely anything to see. Only Francis, almost thin now, was constantly on the move, popping up everywhere – with Ion, nick-named "Son of Dracula" by the crew, at his heels – to solve or be frustrated by any one of a thousand problems.

The stands erected for the extras, made by local labour in the months before shooting, kept collapsing. It seemed the construction people, whom she assumed also had the door contract at the Bucharest hotel, had substituted inferior wood, presumably pocketing the difference in leis, and the whole set was close to useless. Francis had taken to having his people work at night, after the Romanians contractually obliged to do the job had gone home, to shore up the shoddy work. It was, of course, ruinously expensive and amazingly inefficient.

The permits to film at Borgo Pass had still not come through. An associate producer was spending all her time at the Bucharest equivalent of the Circumlocution Office, trying to get the tri-lingual documentation out of the Ministry of Film. Francis would have to hire an entire local film crew and pay them to stand idle while his Hollywood people did the work. That was the expected harassment.

The official in the shiny suit, who had come to represent for everyone the forces hindering the production, stood on one side, eagerly watching the actresses. He didn't permit himself a smile.

Kate assumed the man dutifully hated the whole idea of *Dracula*. He certainly did all he could to get in the way. He could only speak English when the time came to announce a fresh snag, conveniently forgetting the language if he was standing on the spot where Francis wanted camera track laid and he was being told politely to get out of the way.

"Give me more teeth," Francis shouted through a bull-horn. The actresses responded.

"All of you," the director addressed the extras, "look horny as hell."

Ion repeated the instruction in three languages. In each one, the sentence expanded to a paragraph. Different segments of the crowd were enthused as each announcement clued them in.

Arcs, brighter and whiter than the sun, cast merciless, bleaching patches of light on the crowd, making faces look like skulls. Kate was blinking, her eyes watering. She took off and cleaned her glasses.

Like everybody, she could do with a shower and a rest. And, in her case, a decent feed.

Rumours were circulating of other reasons they were being kept away from Borgo Pass. The twins, flying in a few days ago, had brought along copies of the *Guardian* and *Time Magazine*. They were passed around the whole company, offering precious news from home. She was surprised how little seemed to have happened while she was out of touch.

However, there was a tiny story in the *Guardian* about the Transylvania Movement. Apparently, Baron Meinster, some obscure disciple of Dracula, was being sought by the Romanian authorities for terrorist outrages. The newspaper reported that he had picked up a band of vampire followers and was out in the forests somewhere, fighting bloody engagements with Ceausescu's men. The Baron favoured young get; he would find lost children, and turn them. The average age of his army was fourteen. Kate knew the type: red-eyed, lithe brats with sharp teeth and no compunctions about anything. Rumour had it that Meinster's Kids would descend on villages and murder entire populations, gorging themselves on blood, killing whole families, whole communities, down to the animals.

That explained the nervousness of some of the extras borrowed from the army. They expected to be sent into the woods to fight the devils. Few of them would come near Kate or any other vampire, so any gossip that filtered through was third-hand and had been translated into and out of several languages.

There were quite a few civilian observers around, keeping an eye on everything, waving incomprehensible but official documentation at anyone who queried their presence. Shiny Suit knew all about them and was their unofficial boss. Ion kept well away from them. She must ask the lad if he knew anything of Meinster. It was a wonder he had not become one of Meinster's Child Warriors. Maybe he had, and was trying to get away from that. Growing up.

The crowd rioted on cue but the camera-crane jammed, dumping the operator out of his perch. Francis yelled at the grips to protect the equipment, and Ion translated but not swiftly enough to get them into action.

The camera came loose and fell thirty feet, crunching onto rough stone, spilling film and fragments.

Francis looked at the mess, uncomprehending, a child so shocked by the breaking of a favourite toy that he can't even throw a fit. Then, red fury exploded.

Kate wouldn't want to be the one who told Francis that there might be fighting at Borgo Pass.

In the coach, late afternoon, Harker goes through the documents he has been given. He examines letters sealed with a red wax "D", old scrolls gone to parchment, annotated maps, a writ of excommunication. There are pictures of Vlad, woodcuts of the Christian Prince in a forest of impaled infidels, portraits of a dead-looking old man with a white moustache, a blurry photograph of a murk-faced youth in an unsuitable straw hat.

Harker's Voice: *Vlad was one of the Chosen, favoured of God. But somewhere in those acres of slaughtered foemen, he found something that changed his mind, that changed his soul. He wrote letters to the Pope, recommending the rededication of the Vatican to the Devil. He had two cardinals, sent by Rome to reason with him, hot-collared – red-hot pokers slid through their back passages into their innards. He died, was buried, and came back . . .*

Harker looks out of the coach at the violent sunset. Rainbows dance around the tree-tops.

Westenra cringes but Murray is fascinated.

Murray: *It's beautiful, the light . . .*

Up ahead is a clearing. Coaches are gathered. A natural

stone amphitheatre has been kitted out with limelights which fizz and flare.

Crowds of Englishmen take seats.

Harker is confused, but the others are excited.

Murray: *A musical evening. Here, so far from Piccadilly . . .*

The coach slows and stops. Westenra and Murray leap out to join the crowds.

Warily, Harker follows. He sits with Westenra and Murray. They pass a hip-flask between them.

Harker takes a cautious pull, stings his throat.

Into the amphitheatre trundles a magnificent carriage, pulled by a single, black stallion. The beast is twelve hands high. The carriage is black as the night, with an embossed gold and scarlet crest on the door. A red-eyed dragon entwines around a letter "D".

The driver is a tall man, draped entirely in black, only his red eyes showing.

There is mild applause.

The driver leaps down from his seat, crouches like a big cat and stands taller than ever. His cloak swells with the night breeze.

Loud music comes from a small orchestra.

"Take a Pair of Crimson Eyes", by Gilbert and Sullivan.

The driver opens the carriage door.

A slim white limb, clad only in a transparent veil, snakes around the door. Tiny bells tinkle on a delicate ankle. The toe-nails are scarlet and curl like claws.

The audience whoops appreciation. Murray burbles babyish delight. Harker is wary.

The foot touches the carpet of pine needles and a woman swings out of the carriage, shroud-like dress fluttering around her slender form. She has a cloud of black hair and eyes that glow like hot coals.

She hisses, tasting the night, exposing needle-sharp eye-teeth. Writhing, she presses her snake-supple body to the air, as if sucking in the essences of all the men present.

Murray: *The bloofer lady . . .*

The other carriage door is kicked open and the first woman's twin leaps out. She is less languid, more sinuous, more animal-like. She claws and rends the ground and climbs up the carriage wheel like a lizard, long red tongue darting. Her hair is wild, a tangle of twigs and leaves.

The audience, on their feet, applaud and whistle vigorously. Some of the men rip away their ties and burst their collar-studs, exposing their throats.

First Woman: *Kisses, sister, kisses for us all . . .*

The hood of the carriage opens, folding back like an oyster to disclose a third woman, as fair as they are dark, as voluptuous as they are slender. She is sprawled in abandon on a plush mountain of red cushions. She writhes, crawling through pillows, her scent stinging the nostrils of the rapt audience.

The driver stands to one side as the three women dance. Some of the men are shirtless now, clawing at their own necks until the blood trickles.

The women are contorted with expectant pleasure, licking their ruby lips, fangs already moist, shrouds in casual disarray, exposing lovely limbs, swan-white pale skin, velvet-sheathed muscle.

Men crawl at their feet, piling atop each other, reaching out just to touch the ankles of these women, these monstrous, desirable creatures.

Murray is out of his seat, hypnotised, pulled towards the vampires, eyes mad. Harker tries to hold him back, but is wrenched forward in his wake, dragged like an anchor.

Murray steps over his fallen fellows, but trips and goes down under them.

Harker scrambles to his feet and finds himself among the women. Six hands entwine around his face. Lips brush his cheek, razor-edged teeth drawing scarlet lines on his face and neck.

He tries to resist but is bedazzled.

A million points of light shine in the womens' eyes, on their teeth, on their earrings, necklaces, nose-stones, bracelets, veils, navel-jewels, lacquered nails. The lights close around Harker.

Teeth touch his throat.

A strong hand, sparsely bristled, reaches out and hauls one of the women away.

The driver steps in and tosses another vampire bodily into the carriage. She lands face-down and seems to be drowning in cushions, bare legs kicking.

Only the blonde remains, caressing Harker, eight inches of tongue scraping the underside of his chin. Fire burns in her eyes as the driver pulls her away.

Blonde Woman: *You never love, you have never loved . . .*

The driver slaps her, dislocating her face. She scrambles away from Harker, who lies sprawled on the ground.

The women are back in the carriage, which does a circuit of the amphitheatre and slips into the forests. There is a massed howl of frustration, and the audience falls upon each other.

Harker, slowly recovering, sits up. Swales is there. He hauls Harker out of the mêlée and back to the coach. Harker, unsteady, is pulled into the coach.

Westenra and Murray are dejected, gloomy. Harker is still groggy.

Harker's Voice: *A vampire's idea of a half-holiday is a third share in a juicy peasant baby. It has no other needs, no other desires, no other yearnings. It is mere appetite, unencumbered by morality, philosophy, religion, convention, emotion. There's a dangerous strength in that. A strength we can hardly hope to equal.*

Shooting in a studio should have given more control, but Francis was constantly frustrated by Romanians. The inn set, perhaps the simplest element of the film, was still not right, though the carpenters and dressers had had almost a year to get it together. First, they took an office at the studio and turned it into Harker's bedroom. It was too small to fit in a camera as well as an actor and the scenery. Then, they reconstructed the whole thing in the middle of a sound stage, but still bolted together the walls so they couldn't be moved. The only shot Storaro could take was from the ceiling looking down. Now the walls were fly-away enough to allow camera movement, but Francis wasn't happy with the set dressing.

Prominent over the bed, where Francis wanted a crucifix, was an idealised portrait of Ceausecu. Through Ion, Francis tried to explain to Shiny Suit, the studio manager, that his film took place before the President-for-Life came to power and that, therefore, it was highly unlikely that a picture of him would be decorating a wall anywhere.

Shiny Suit seemed unwilling to admit there had ever been a time when Ceausecu didn't rule the country. He kept looking around nervously, as if expecting to be caught in treason and hustled out to summary execution.

"Get me a crucifix," Francis yelled.

Kate sat meekly in a director's chair – a rare luxury – while the argument continued. Marty Sheen, in character as Harker, sat cross-legged on his bed, taking pulls at a hip-flask of potent brandy. She could smell the liquor across the studio. The actor's face was florid and his movements slow. He had been more and more Harker and less and less Marty the last few days, and Francis was driving him hard, directing with an emotional scalpel that peeled his star like an onion.

Francis told Ion to bring the offending item over so he could show Shiny Suit what was wrong. Grinning cheerfully, Ion squeezed past Marty and reached for the picture, dextrously dropping it onto a bed-post which shattered the glass and speared through the middle of the frame, punching a hole in the Premier's face.

Ion shrugged in fake apology.

Francis looked almost happy. Shiny Suit, stricken in the heart, scurried away in defeat, afraid that his part in the vandalism of the sacred image would be noticed.

A crucifix was found from stock and put up on the wall.

"Marty," Francis said, "open yourself up, show us your beating heart, then tear it from your chest, squeeze it in your fist and drop it on the floor."

Kate wondered if he meant it literally.

Marty Sheen tried to focus his eyes, and saluted in slow motion.

"Quiet on set, everybody," Francis shouted.

Kate was crying, silently, uncontrollably. Everyone on set, except Francis and perhaps Ion, was also in tears. She felt as if she was watching the torture of a political prisoner, and just wanted it to stop.

There was no script for this scene.

Francis was pushing Marty into a corner, breaking him down, trying to get to Jonathan Harker.

This would come at the beginning of the picture. The idea was to show the real Jonathan, to get the audience involved with him. Without this scene, the hero would seem just an observer, wandering between other people's set-pieces.

"You, Reed," Francis said, "you're a writer. Scribble me a voice-over. Internal monologue. Stream-of-consciousness. Give me the real Harker."

Through tear-blurred spectacles, she looked at the pad she was scrawling on. Her first attempt had been at the Jonathan she remembered, who would have been embarrassed to have been thought capable of stream-of-consciousness. Francis had torn that into confetti and poured it over Marty's head, making the actor cross his eyes and fall backwards, completely drunk, onto the bed.

Marty was hugging his pillow and bawling for Mina.

All for Hecuba, Kate thought. Mina wasn't even in this movie except as a locket. God knows what Mrs Harker would think when and if she saw *Dracula*.

Francis told the crew to ignore Marty's complaints. He was an actor, and just whining.

Ion translated.

She remembered what Francis had said after the storm, "what does this cost, people?" Was anything worth what this seemed to cost? "I don't just have to make *Dracula*," Francis had told an interviewer, "I have to *be* Dracula."

Kate tried to write the Harker that was emerging between Marty and Francis. She went into the worst places of her own past and realised they still burned in her memory like smouldering coals.

Her pad was spotted with red. There was blood in her tears. That didn't happen often.

The camera was close to Marty's face. Francis was intent, bent close over the bed, teeth bared, hands clawed. Marty mumbled, trying to wave the lens away.

"Don't look at the camera, Jonathan," Francis said.

Marty buried his face in the bed and was sick, choking. Kate wanted to protest but couldn't bring herself to. She was worried Martin Sheen would never forgive her for interrupting his Academy Award scene. He was an actor. He'd go on to other roles, casting off poor Jon like an old coat.

He rolled off his vomit and looked up, where the ceiling should have been but wasn't.

The camera ran on. And on.

Marty lay still.

Finally, the camera operator reported "I think he's stopped breathing."

For an eternal second, Francis let the scene run.

In the end, rather than stop filming, the director elbowed the camera aside and threw himself on his star, putting an ear close to Marty's sunken bare chest.

Kate dropped her pad and rushed into the set. A wall swayed and fell with a crash.

"His heart's still beating," Francis said.

She could hear it, thumping irregularly.

Marty spluttered, fluid leaking from his mouth. His face was almost scarlet.

His heart slowed.

"I think he's having a heart attack," she said.

"He's only thirty-five," Francis said. "No, thirty-six. It's his birthday today."

A doctor was called for. Kate thumped Marty's chest, wishing she knew more first aid.

The camera rolled on, forgotten.

"If this gets out," Francis said, "I'm finished. The film is over."

Francis grabbed Marty's hand tight, and prayed.

"Don't die, man."

Martin Sheen's heart wasn't listening. The beat stopped. Seconds passed. Another beat. Nothing.

Ion was at Francis's side. His fang-teeth were fully extended and his eyes were red. It was the closeness of death, triggering his instincts.

Kate, hating herself, felt it too.

The blood of the dead was spoiled, undrinkable. But the blood of the dying was sweet, as if invested with the life that was being spilled.

She felt her own teeth sharp against her lower lip.

Drops of her blood fell from her eyes and mouth, spattering Marty's chin.

She pounded his chest again. Another beat. Nothing.

Ion crawled on the bed, reaching for Marty.

"I can make him live," he whispered, mouth agape, nearing a pulseless neck.

"My God," said Francis, madness in his eyes. "You can bring him back. Even if he dies, he can finish the picture."

"Yesssss," hissed the old child.

Marty's eyes sprang open. He was still conscious in his stalling body. There was a flood of fear and panic. Kate felt his death grasp her own heart.

Ion's teeth touched the actor's throat.

A cold clarity struck her. This undead youth of unknown bloodline must not pass on the Dark Kiss. He was not yet ready to be a father-in-darkness.

She took him by the scruff of his neck and tore him away. He fought her, but she was older, stronger.

With love, she punctured Marty's throat, feeling the death ecstasy convulse through her. She swooned as the blood, laced heavily with brandy, welled into her mouth, but fought to stay in control. The lizard part of her brain would have sucked him dry.

But Katharine Reed was not a monster.

She broke the contact, smearing blood across her chin and his chest hair. She ripped open her blouse, scattering tiny buttons, and sliced herself with a sharpening thumbnail, drawing an incision across her ribs.

She raised Marty's head and pressed his mouth to the wound.

As the dying man suckled, she looked through fogged glasses at Francis, at Ion, at the camera operator, at twenty studio staff. A doctor was arriving, too late.

She looked at the blank round eye of the camera.

"Turn that bloody thing off," she said.

The principles were assembled in an office at the studio. Kate, still drained, had to be there. Marty was in a clinic with a drip-feed, awaiting more transfusions. His entire bloodstream would have to be flushed out several times over. With luck, he wouldn't even turn. He would just have some of her life in him, some of her in him, forever. This had happened before and Kate wasn't exactly happy about it. But she had no other choice. Ion would have killed the actor and brought him back to life as a new-born vampire.

"There have been stories in the trades," Francis said, holding up a copy of *Daily Variety*. It was the only newspaper that regularly got through to the company. "About Marty. We have to sit tight on this, to keep a lid on panic. I can't afford even the rumour that we're in trouble. Don't you understand, we're in the twilight zone here. Anything approaching a shooting schedule or a budget was left behind a long time ago. We can film around Marty until he's ready to do close-ups. His brother is coming over from the States to double him from the back. We can weather this on the ground, but maybe not in the press. The vultures from the trades want us dead. Ever since *Finian's Rainbow*, they've hated me. I'm a smart kid and nobody likes smart kids. From now on, if anybody *dies* they aren't dead until I say so. Nobody is to tell anyone anything until it's gone through me. People, we're in trouble here and we may have to lie our way out of it. I know you think the Ceausecu regime is fascist but it's nothing compared to the Coppola regime. You don't know anything until I confirm it. You don't do anything until I say so. This is a war, people, and we're losing."

Marty's family was with him. His wife didn't quite know whether to be grateful to Kate or despise her.

He would live. Really live.

She was getting snatches of his past life, mostly from films he had been in. He would be having the same thing, coping with scrambled impressions of her. That must be a nightmare all of its own.

They let her into the room. It was sunny, filled with flowers.

The actor was sitting up, neatly groomed, eyes bright.

"Now I know," he told her. "Now I really know. I can use that in the part. Thank you."

"I'm sorry," she said, not knowing what for.

At a way-station, Swales is picking up fresh horses. The old ones, lathered with foamy sweat, are watered and rested.

Westenra barters with a peasant for a basket of apples. Murray smiles and looks up at the tops of the trees. The moon shines down on his face, making him look like a child.

Harker quietly smokes a pipe.

Harker's Voice: *This was where we were to join forces with Van Helsing. This stone-crazy double Dutchman had spent his whole life fighting evil.*

Van Helsing strides out of the mountain mists. He wears a scarlet army tunic and a curly-brimmed top hat, and carries a cavalry sabre. His face is covered with old scars. Crosses of all kinds are pinned to his clothes.

Harker's Voice: *Van Helsing put the fear of God into the Devil. And he terrified me.*

Van Helsing is accompanied by a band of rough-riders. Of all races and in wildly different uniforms, they are his personal army of the righteous. In addition to mounted troops, Van Helsing has command of a couple of man-lifting kites and a supply wagon.

Van Helsing: *You are Harker?*

Harker: *Dr Van Helsing of Amsterdam?*

Van Helsing: *The same. You wish to go to Borgo Pass, Young Jonathan?*

Harker: *That's the plan.*

Van Helsing: *Better you should wish to go to Hades itself, foolish Englishman.*

Van Helsing's Aide: *I say, Prof, did you know Murray was in Harker's crew. The stroke of '84.*

Van Helsing: *Hah! Beat Cambridge by three lengths. Masterful.*

Van Helsing's Aide: *They say the river's at its most level around Borgo Pass. You know these mountain streams, Prof. Tricky for the oarsman.*

Van Helsing: *Why didn't you say that before, damfool? Harker, we go at once, to take Borgo Pass. Such a stretch of river should be held for the Lord. The Un-Dead, they appreciate it not. Nosferatu don't scull.*

Van Helsing rallies his men into mounting up. Harker dashes back to the coach and climbs in. Westenra looks appalled as Van Helsing waves his sabre, coming close to fetching off his own Aide's head.

Westenra: *That man's completely mad.*

Harker: *In Wallachia, that just makes him normal. To fight what we have to face, one has to be a little mad.*

Van Helsing's sabre shines with moonfire.

Van Helsing: *To Borgo Pass, my angels . . . charge!*

Van Helsing leads his troop at a fast gallop. The coach is swept along in the wake of the uphill cavalry advance. Man-lifting box-kites carry observers into the night air.

Wolves howl in the distance.

Between the kites is slung a phonograph horn.

Music pours forth. The overture to *Swan Lake*.

Van Helsing: *Music. Tchaikowsky. It upsets the devils. Stirs in them memories of things that they have lost. Makes them feel dead. Then we kill them good. Kill them forever.*

As he charges, Van Helsing waves his sword from side to side. Dark, low shapes dash out of the trees and slip among the horses' ankles. Van Helsing slashes downwards, decapitating a wolf. The head bounces against a tree, becoming that of a gypsy boy, and rolls down the mountainside.

Van Helsing's cavalry weave expertly through the pines. They carry flaming torches. The music soars. Fire and smoke whip between the trees.

In the coach, Westenra puts his fingers in his ears. Murray smiles as if on a pleasure ride across Brighton Beach. Harker sorts through crucifixes.

At Borgo Pass, a small gypsy encampment is quiet. Elders gather around the fire. A girl hears the Tchaikowsky whining among the winds and alerts the tribe.

The gypsies bustle. Some begin to transform into wolves.

The man-lifting kites hang against the moon, casting vast bat-shadows on the mountainside.

The pounding of hooves, amplified a thousandfold by the trees, thunders. The ground shakes. The forests tremble.

Van Helsing's cavalry explode out of the woods and fall upon the camp, riding around and through the place, knocking over wagons, dragging through fires. A dozen flaming torches are thrown. Shrieking werewolves, pelts aflame, leap up at the riders.

Silver swords flash, red with blood.

Van Helsing dismounts and strides through the carnage, making head shots with his pistol. Silver balls explode in wolf-skulls.

A young girl approaches Van Helsing's aide, smiling in welcome. She opens her mouth, hissing, and sinks fangs into the man's throat.

Three cavalrymen pull the girl off and stretch her out face-down on the ground, rending her bodice to bare her back. Van Helsing drives a five-foot lance through her ribs from behind, skewering her to the bloodied earth.

Van Helsing: Vampire bitch!

The cavalrymen congratulate each other and cringe as a barrel of gunpowder explodes nearby. Van Helsing does not flinch.

Harker's Voice: Van Helsing was protected by God. Whatever he did, he would survive. He was blessed.

Van Helsing kneels by his wounded Aide and pours holy water onto the man's ravaged neck. The wound hisses and steams, and the Aide shrieks.

Van Helsing: Too late, we are too late. I'm sorry, my son.

With a kukri knife, Van Helsing slices off his aide's head. Blood gushes over his trousers.

The overture concludes and the battle is over.

The gypsy encampment is a ruin. Fires still burn. Everyone is dead or dying, impaled or decapitated or silver-shot. Van Helsing distributes consecrated wafers, dropping crumbs on all the corpses, muttering prayers for saved souls.

Harker sits, exhausted, bloody earth on his boots.

Harker's Voice: *If this was how Van Helsing served God, I was beginning to wonder what the firm had against Dracula.*

The sun pinks the skies over the mountains. Pale light falls on the encampment.

Van Helsing stands tall in the early morning mists.

Several badly-wounded vampires begin to shrivel and scream as the sunlight burns them to man-shaped cinders.

Van Helsing: *I love that smell . . . spontaneous combustion at daybreak. It smells like . . . salvation.*

Like a small boy whose toys have been taken away, Francis stood on the rock, orange cagoul vivid against the mist-shrouded pines, and watched the cavalry ride away in the wrong direction. Gypsy extras, puzzled at this reversal, milled around their camp set. Storaro found something technical to check and absorbed himself in lenses.

No one wanted to tell Francis what was going on.

They had spent two hours setting up the attack, laying camera track, planting charges, rigging decapitation effects, mixing kensington gore in plastic buckets. Van Helsing's troop of ferocious cavalry were uniformed and readied.

Then Shiny Suit whispered in the ear of the captain who was in command of the army-provided horsemen. The cavalry stopped being actors and became soldiers again, getting into formation and riding out.

Kate had never seen anything like it.

Ion nagged Shiny Suit for an explanation. Reluctantly, the official told the little vampire what was going on.

"There is fighting in the next valley," Ion said. "Baron Meinster has come out of the forests and taken a keep that stands over a strategic pass. Many are dead or dying. Ceausescu is laying siege to the Transylvanians."

"We have an agreement," Francis said, weakly. "These are my men."

"Only as long as they aren't needed for fighting, this man says," reported Ion, standing aside to let the director get a good look at the Romanian official. Shiny Suit almost smiled, a certain smug attitude suggesting that this would even the score for that dropped picture of the Premier.

142 KIM NEWMAN

"I'm trying to make a fucking movie here. If people don't keep their word, maybe they deserve to be overthrown."

The few bilingual Romanians in the crew cringed at such sacrilege. Kate could think of dozens of stronger reasons for pulling down the Ceausecu regime.

"There might be danger," Ion said. "If the fighting spreads."

"This Meinster, Ion. Can he get us the cavalry? Can we do a deal with him?"

"An arrogant elder, maestro. And doubtless preoccupied with his own projects."

"You're probably right, fuck it."

"We're losing the light," Storaro announced.

Shiny Suit smiled blithely and, through Ion, ventured that the battle should be over in two to three days. It was fortunate for him that Francis only had prop weapons within reach.

In the gypsy camp, one of the charges went off by itself. A pathetic phut sent out a choking cloud of violently green smoke. Trickles of flame ran across fresh-painted flats.

A grip threw a bucket of water, dousing the fire.

Robert Duvall and Martin Sheen, in costume and make-up, stood about uselessly. The entire camera crew, effects gang, support team were gathered, as if waiting for a cancelled train.

There was a long pause. The cavalry did not come riding triumphantly back, ready for the shot.

"Bastards," Francis shouted, angrily waving his staff like a spear.

The next day was no better. News filtered back that Meinster was thrown out of the keep and withdrawing into the forests, but that Ceausescu ordered his retreat be harried. The cavalry were not detailed to return to their film-making duties. Kate wondered how many of them were still alive. The retaking of the keep must have been a bloody, costly battle. A cavalry charge against a fortress position would be almost a suicide mission.

Disconsolately, Francis and Storaro sorted out some pick-up shots that could be managed.

A search was mounted for Shiny Suit, so that a definite time could be established for rescheduling of the attack scene. He had vanished into the mists, presumably to escape the American's wrath.

Kate huddled under a tree and tried to puzzle out a local newspaper. She was brushing up her Romanian, simultaneously coping with the euphemisms and lacunae of a non-free press. According to the paper, Meinster had been crushed weeks ago and was hiding in a ditch somewhere, certain to be beheaded within the hour.

She couldn't help feeling the real story was in the next valley. As a newspaperwoman, she should be there, not waiting around for this stalled juggernaut to get back on track. Meinster's Kids frightened and fascinated her. She should know about them, try to understand. But American Zoetrope had first call on her, and she didn't have the heart to be another defector.

Marty Sheen joined her.

He was mostly recovered and understood what she had done for him, though he was still exploring the implications of their blood link. Just now, he was more anxious about working with Brando — who was due in next week — than his health.

There was still no scripted ending.

The day that the cavalry — well, some of them — came back, faces drawn and downcast, uniforms muddied, eyes haunted, Shiny Suit was discovered with his neck broken, flopped half-in a stream. He must have fallen in the dark, tumbling down the precipitous mountainside.

His face and neck were ripped, torn by the sharp thorns of the mountain bushes. He had bled dry into the water, and his staring face was white.

"It is good that Georghiou is dead," Ion pronounced. "He upset the maestro."

Kate hadn't known the bureaucrat's name.

Francis was frustrated at this fresh delay, but graciously let the corpse be removed and the proper authorities be notified before proceeding with the shoot.

A police inspector was escorted around by Ion, poking at a few broken bushes and examining Georghiou's effects. Ion somehow persuaded the man to conclude the business speedily.

The boy was a miracle, everyone agreed.

"Miss Reed," Ion interrupted. She laid down her newspaper.

Dressed as an American boy, with his hair cut by the make-up department, a light-meter hung around his neck, Ion was unrecognizable as the bedraggled orphan who had come to her hotel room in Bucharest.

Kate laid aside her journal and pen.

"John Popp," Ion pronounced, tapping his chest. His J-sound was perfect. "John Popp, the American."

She thought about it.

Ion — no, John — had sloughed off his nationality and all national characteristics like a snake shedding a skin. New-born as an American, pink-skinned and glowing, he would never be challenged.

"Do you want to go to America?"

"Oh yes, Miss Reed. America is a young country, full of life. Fresh blood. There, one can be anything one chooses. It is the only country for a vampire."

Kate wasn't sure whether to feel sorry for the vampire youth or for the American continent. One of them was sure to be disappointed.

"John Popp," he repeated, pleased.

Was this how Dracula had been when he first thought of moving to Great Britain, then the liveliest country in the world just as America was now? The Count had practised his English pronunciation in conversations with Jonathan, and memorised railway time-tables, relishing the exotic names of St Pancras, King's Cross and Euston. Had he rolled his anglicized name – Count DeVille – around his mouth, pleased with himself?

Of course, Dracula saw himself as a conqueror, the rightful ruler of all lands he rode over. Ion-John was more like the Irish and Italian emigrants who poured through Ellis Island at the beginning of the century, certain America was the land of opportunity and that each potato-picker or barber could become a self-made plutocrat.

Envious of his conviction, affection stabbing her heart, wishing she could protect him always, Kate kissed him. He struggled awkwardly, a child hugged by an embarassingly aged auntie.

Mists pool around Borgo Pass. Black crags project from the white sea.

The coach proceeds slowly. Everyone looks around, wary.

Murray: Remember that last phial of laudanum . . . I just downed it.

Westenra: Good show, man.

Murray: It's like the Crystal Palace.

Harker sits by Swales, looking up at the ancient castle that dominates the view. Broken battlements are jagged against the boiling sky.

Harker's Voice: Castle Dracula. The trail snaked through the forest, leading me directly to him. The Count. The countryside was Dracula. He had become one with the mountains, the trees, the stinking earth.

The coach halts. Murray pokes his head out of the window, and sighs in amazement.

Swales: Borgo Pass, Harker. I'll go no further.

Harker looks at Swales. There is no fear in the coachman's face, but his eyes are slitted.

A sliver of dark bursts like a torpedo from the sea of mist. A

sharpened stake impales Swales, bloody point projecting a foot or more from his chest.

Swales sputters hatred and takes a grip on Harker, trying to hug him, to pull him onto the sharp point sticking out of his sternum.

Harker struggles in silence, setting the heel of his hand against Swales's head. He pushes and the dead man's grip relaxes. Swales tumbles from his seat and rolls off the precipice, falling silently into the mists.

Murray: *Good grief, man. That was extreme.*

Rising over Borgo Pass was Castle Dracula. Half mossy black stone, half fresh orange timber.

Kate was impressed.

Though the permits had still not come through, Francis had ordered the crew to erect and dress the castle set. This was a long way from Bucharest and without Georghiou, the hand of Ceausecu could not fall.

From some angles, the castle was an ancient fastness, a fit lair for the vampire King. But a few steps off the path and it was a shell, propped up by timbers. Painted board mingled with stone.

If Meinster's Kids were in the forests, they could look up at the mountain and take heart. This sham castle might be their rallying-point. She hummed "Paper Moon", imagining vampires summoned back to these mountains to a castle that was not a castle and a king who was just an actor in greasepaint.

A grip, silhouetted in the gateway, used a gun-like device to whisp thick cobweb on the portcullis. Cages of imported vermin were stacked up, ready to be unloosed. Stakes, rigged up with bicycle seats that would support the impaled extras, stood on the mountainside.

It was a magnificent fake.

Francis, leaning on his stake, stood and admired the edifice thrown up on his orders. Ion-John was at his side, a faithful Renfield for once.

"Orson Welles said it was the best train set a boy could have," Francis said. Ion probably didn't know who Welles was. "But it broke him in the end."

In her cardigan pocket, she found the joke shop fangs from the 100th Day of Shooting Party. Soon, there would be a 200th Day Party.

She snapped the teeth together like castanets, feeling almost giddy up here in the mists where the air was thin and the nights cold.

In her pleasant contralto, far more Irish-inflected than her speaking voice, she crooned "it's a Barnum and Bailey world, just as phoney as it can be, but it wouldn't be make-believe if you believed in me."

On foot, Harker arrives at the gates of the castle. Westenra and Murray hang back a little way.

A silent crowd of gypsies parts to let the Englishmen through. Harker notices human and wolf teeth strung in necklaces, red eyes and feral fangs, withered bat-membranes curtaining under arms, furry bare feet hooked into the rock. These are the Szekeley, the children of Dracula.

In the courtyard, an armadillo noses among freshly-severed human heads. Harker is smitten by the stench of decay but tries to hide his distaste. Murray and Westenra groan and complain. They both hold out large crucifixes.

A rat-like figure scuttles out of the crowds.

Renfield: Are you English? I'm an Englishman. R.M. Renfield, at your service.

He shakes Harker's hand, then hugs him. His eyes are jittery, mad.

Renfield: The Master has been waiting for you. I'm a lunatic, you know. Zoophagous. I eat flies. Spiders. Birds, when I can get them. It's the blood. The blood is the life, as the book says. The Master understands. Dracula. He knows you're coming. He knows everything. He's a poet-warrior in the classical sense. He has the vision. You'll see, you'll learn. He's lived through the centuries. His wisdom is beyond ours, beyond anything we can imagine. How can I make you understand? He's promised me lives. Many lives. Some nights, he'll creep up on you, while you're shaving, and break your mirror. A foul bauble of man's vanity. The blood of Attila flows in his veins. He is the Master.

Renfield plucks a crawling insect from Westenra's coat and gobbles it down.

Renfield: I know what bothers you. The heads. The severed heads. It's his way. It's the only language they understand. He doesn't love these things, but he knows he must do them. He knows the truth. Rats! He knows where the rats come from. Sometimes, he'll say "they fought the dogs and killed the cats and bit the babies in the cradles, and ate the cheeses out of the vats and licked the soup from the cooks' own ladles".

Harker ignores the prattle and walks across the courtyard. Scraps of mist waft under his boots.

A huge figure fills a doorway. Moonlight shines on his great,

bald head. Heavy jowls glisten as a humourless smile discloses yellow eye-teeth the size of thumbs.

 Harker halts.

 A bass voice rumbles.

 Dracula: I . . . am . . . Dracula.

Francis had first envisioned Dracula as a stick-insect skeleton, dried up, hollow-eyed, brittle. When Brando arrived on set, weighing in at 250 pounds, he had to rethink the character as a blood-bloated leech, full to bursting with stolen life, overflowing his coffin.

For two days, Francis had been trying to get a usable reading of the line, "I am Dracula." Kate, initially as thrilled as anyone else to see Brando at work, was bored rigid by numberless mumbled retakes.

The line was written in three-foot tall black letters on a large piece of cardboard held up by two grips. The actor experimented with emphases, accents, pronunciations from "Dorragulya" to "Jacoolier". He read the line looking away from the camera and peering straight at the lens. He tried it with false fangs inside his mouth, sticking out of his mouth, shoved up his nostrils or thrown away altogether.

Once he came out with a bat tattooed on his bald head in black lipstick. After considering it for a while, Francis ordered the decal wiped off. You couldn't say that the star wasn't bringing ideas to the production.

For two hours now, Brando had been hanging upside-down in the archway, secured by a team of very tired technicians at the end of two guy-ropes. He thought it might be interesting if the Count were discovered like a sleeping bat.

Literally, he read his line upside-down.

Marty Sheen, over whose shoulder the shot was taken, had fallen asleep.

"I am Dracula. I am Dracula. I am Dracula. I am Dracula. I am Dracula! I am Dracula?

"Dracula am I. Am I Dracula? Dracula I am. I Dracula am. Am Dracula I?

"I'm Dracula.

"The name's Dracula. Count Dracula.

"Hey, I'm Dracula.

"Me . . . Dracula. You . . . liquid lunch."

He read the line as Stanley Kowalski, as Don Corleone, as Charlie Chan, as Jerry Lewis, as Laurence Olivier, as Robert Newton.

Francis patiently shot take after take.

Dennis Hopper hung around, awed, smoking grass. All the actors wanted to watch.

Brando's face went scarlet. Upside-down, he had problems with the teeth. Relieved, the grips eased up on the ropes and the star dropped towards the ground. They slowed before his head cracked like an egg on the ground. Assistants helped him rearrange himself.

Francis thought about the scene.

"Marlon, it seems to me that we could do worse than go back to the book."

"The book?" Brando asked.

"Remember, when we first discussed the role. We talked about how Stoker describes the Count."

"I don't quite . . ."

"You told me you knew the book."

"I never read it."

"You said . . ."

"I lied."

Harker, in chains, is confined in a dungeon. Rats crawl around his feet. Water flows all around.

A shadow passes.

Harker looks up. A gray bat-face hovers above, nostrils elaborately frilled, enormous teeth locked. Dracula seems to fill the room, black cape stretched over his enormous belly and trunk-like limbs.

Dracula drops something into Harker's lap. It is Westenra's head, eyes white.

Harker screams.

Dracula is gone.

An insectile clacking emerged from the Script Crypt, the walled-off space on the set where Francis had hidden himself away with his typewriter.

Millions of dollars poured away daily as the director tried to come up with an ending. In drafts Kate had seen – only a fraction of the attempts Francis had made – Harker killed Dracula, Dracula killed Harker, Dracula and Harker became allies, Dracula and Harker were both killed by Van Helsing (unworkable, because Robert Duvall was making another film on another continent), lightning destroyed the whole castle.

It was generally agreed that Dracula should die.

The Count perished through decapitation, purifying fire, running water, a stake through the heart, a hawthorn bush, a giant crucifix, silver bullets, the hand of God, the claws of the Devil, armed insurrection, suicide, a swarm of infernal bats, bubonic plague, dismemberment by axe, permanent transformation into a dog.

Brando suggested that he play Dracula as a Green Suitcase.

Francis was on medication.

"Reed, what does he mean to you?"

She thought Francis meant Ion-John.

"He's just a kid, but he's getting older fast. There's something . . ."

"Not John. Dracula."

"Oh, him."

"Yes, him. Dracula. Count Dracula. King of the Vampires."

"I never acknowledged that title."

"In the 1880s, you were against him?"

"You could say that."

"But he gave you so much, eternal life?"

"He wasn't my father. Not directly."

"But he brought vampirism out of the darkness."

"He was a monster."

"Just a monster? In the end, just that?"

She thought hard.

"No, there was more. He was more. He was . . . he *is*, you know . . . big. Huge, enormous. Like the elephant described by blind men. He had many aspects. But all were monstrous. He didn't bring us out of the darkness. He was the darkness."

"John says he was a national hero."

"John wasn't born then. Or turned."

"Guide me, Reed."

"I can't write your ending for you."

At the worst possible time, the policeman was back. There were questions about Shiny Suit. Irregularities revealed by the autopsy.

For some reason, Kate was questioned.

Through an interpreter, the policemen kept asking her about the dead official, what had their dealings been, whether Georghiou's prejudice against her kind had affected her.

Then he asked her when she had last fed, and upon whom?

"That's private," she said.

She didn't want to admit that she had been snacking on rats for months. She had had no time to cultivate anyone warm. Her powers of fascination were thinning.

A scrap of cloth was produced and handed to her.

"Do you recognize this?" she was asked.

It was filthy, but she realized that she did.

"Why, it's my scarf. From Biba. I . . ."

It was snatched away from her. The policeman wrote down a note.

She tried to say something about Ion, but thought better of it. The translator told the policeman Kate had almost admitted to something.

She felt distinctly chilled.

She was asked to open her mouth, like a horse up for sale. The policeman peered at her sharp little teeth and tutted.

That was all for now.

"How are monsters made?"

Kate was weary of questions. Francis, Marty, the police. Always questions.

Still, she was on the payroll as an advisor.

"I've known too many monsters, Francis. Some were born, some were made all at once, some were eroded, some shaped themselves, some twisted by history."

"What about Dracula?"

"He was the monster of monsters. All of the above."

Francis laughed.

"You're thinking of Brando."

"After your movie, so will everybody else."

He was pleased by the thought.

"I guess they will."

"You're bringing him back. Is that a good idea?"

"It's a bit late to raise that."

"Seriously, Francis. He'll never be gone, never be forgotten. But your Dracula will be powerful. In the next valley, people are fighting over the tatters of the old, faded Dracula. What will your Technicolor, 70 mm, Dolby stereo Dracula *mean*?"

"Meanings are for the critics."

Two Szekeleys throw Harker into the great hall of the castle. He sprawls on the straw-covered flagstones, emaciated and wild-eyed, close to madness.

Dracula sits on a throne which stretches wooden wings out behind him. Renfield worships at his feet, tongue applied to the Count's black leather boot. Murray, a blissful smile on his face and scabs on his neck, stands to one side, with Dracula's three vampire brides.

Dracula: *I bid you welcome. Come safely, go freely and leave some of the happiness you bring.*

Harker looks up.

Harker: You . . . were a Prince.

Dracula: *I am a Prince still. Of Darkness.*

The brides titter and clap. A look from their Master silences them.

Dracula: *Harker, what do you think we are doing here, at the edge of Christendom? What dark mirror is held up to our unreflecting faces?*

By the throne is an occasional table piled high with books and periodicals. *Bradshaw's Guide to Railway Timetables in England, Scotland and Wales*, George and Weedon Grossmith's *Diary of a Nobody*, Sabine Baring-Gould's *The Book of Were-Wolves*, Oscar Wilde's *Salom*.

Dracula picks up a volume of the poetry of Robert Browning.

Dracula: *"I must not omit to say that in Transylvania there's a tribe of alien people that ascribe the outlandish ways and dress on which their neighbours lay such stress, to their fathers and mothers having risen out of some subterraneous prison into which they were trepanned long time ago in a mighty band out of Hamelin town in Brunswick land, but how or why, they don't understand."*

Renfield claps.

Renfield: *Rats, Master. Rats.*

Dracula reaches down with both hands and turns the madman's head right around. The brides fall upon the madman's twitching body, nipping at him greedily before he dies and the blood spoils.

Harker looks away.

At the airport, she was detained by officials. There was some question about her passport.

Francis was worried about the crates of exposed film. The negative was precious, volatile, irreplacable. He personally, through John, argued with the customs people and handed over disproportionate bribes. He still carried his staff, which he used to point the way and rap punishment. He looked a bit like Friar Tuck.

The film, the raw material of *Dracula*, was to be treated as if it were valuable as gold and dangerous as plutonium. It was stowed on the aeroplane by soldiers.

A blank-faced woman sat across the desk from Kate.

The stirrings of panic ticked inside her. The scheduled time of departure neared.

The rest of the crew were lined up with their luggage, joking despite tiredness. After over a year, they were glad to be gone for good from this backward country. They talked about what they would do when they got home. Marty Sheen was looking healthier, years younger. Francis was bubbling again, excited to be on to the next stage.

Kate looked from the Romanian woman to the portraits of Nicolae and Elena on the wall behind her. All eyes were cold, hateful. The woman wore a discreet crucifix and a Party badge clipped to her uniform lapel.

A rope barrier was removed and the eager crowd of the *Dracula* company stormed towards the aeroplane, mounting the steps, squeezing into the cabin.

The flight was for London, then New York, then Los Angeles. Half a world away.

Kate wanted to stand up, to join the plane, to add her own jokes and fantasies to the rowdy chatter, to fly away from here. Her luggage, she realized, was in the hold.

A man in a black trenchcoat – *Securitate?* – and two uniformed policemen arrived and exchanged terse phrases with the woman.

Kate gathered they were talking about Shiny Suit. And her. They used old, cruel words: leech, *nosferatu*, parasite. The *Securitate* man looked at her passport.

"It is impossible that you be allowed to leave."

Across the tarmac, the last of the crew – Ion-John among them, baseball cap turned backwards, bulky kit-bag on his shoulder – disappeared into the sleek tube of the aeroplane. The door was pulled shut.

She was forgotten, left behind.

How long would it be before anyone noticed? With different sets of people disembarking in three cities, probably forever. It was easy to miss one mousy advisor in the excitement, the anticipation, the triumph of going home with the movie shot. Months of post-production, dialogue looping, editing, rough cutting, previews, publicity and release lay ahead, with box office takings to be crowed over and prizes to be competed for in Cannes and on Oscar night.

Maybe when they came to put her credit on the film, someone would think to ask what had become of the funny little old girl with the thick glasses and the red hair.

"You are a sympathizer with the Transylvania Movement."

"Good God," she blurted, "why would anybody want to live here?"

That did not go down well.

The engines were whining. The plane taxied towards the runway.

"This is an old country, Miss Katharine Reed," the *Securitate* man sneered. "We know the ways of your kind, and we understand how they should be dealt with."

All the eyes were pitiless.

The giant black horse is lead into the courtyard by the gypsies. Swords are drawn in salute to the animal. It whinnies slightly, coat glossy ebony, nostrils scarlet.

Inside the castle, Harker descends a circular stairway carefully, wiping aside cobwebs. He has a wooden stake in his hands.

The gypsies close on the horse.

Harker's Voice: *Even the castle wanted him dead, and that's what he served at the end. The ancient, blood-caked stones of his Transylvanian fastness.*

Harker stands over Dracula's coffin. The Count lies, bloated with blood, face puffy and violet.

Gypsy knives stroke the horse's flanks. Blood erupts from the coat.

Harker raises the stake with both hands over his head.

Dracula's eyes open, red marbles in his fat, flat face. Harker is given pause.

The horse neighs in sudden pain. Axes chop at its neck and legs. The mighty beast is felled.

Harker plunges the stake into the Count's vast chest.

The horse jerks spastically as the gypsies hack at it. Its hooves scrape painfully on the cobbles.

A gout of violently red blood gushes upwards, splashing directly into Harker's face, reddening him from head to waist. The flow continues, exploding everywhere, filling the coffin, the room, driving Harker back.

Dracula's great hands grip the sides of the coffin and he tries to sit. Around him is a cloud of blood droplets, hanging in the air like slo-mo fog.

The horse kicks its last, clearing a circle. The gypsies look with respect at the creature they have slain.

Harker takes a shovel and pounds at the stake, driving it deeper into Dracula's barrel chest, forcing him back into his filthy sarcophagus.

At last, the Count gives up. Whispered words escape from him with his last breath.

Dracula: *The horror . . . the horror . . .*

She supposed there were worse places than a Romanian jail. But not many.

They kept her isolated from the warm prisoners. Rapists and murderers and dissidents were afraid of her. She found herself

penned with uncommunicative Transylvanians, haughty elders
reduced to grime and resentful new-borns.

She had seen a couple of Meinster's Kids, and their calm,
purposeful, blank-eyed viciousness disturbed her. Their definition
of enemy was terrifyingly broad, and they believed in killing. No
negotiation, no surrender, no accommodation. Just death, on an
industrial scale.

The bars were silver. She fed on insects and rats. She was
weak.

Every day, she was interrogated.

They were convinced she had murdered Georghiou. His throat
had been gnawed and he was completely exsanguinated.

Why her? Why not some Transylvanian terrorist?

Because of the bloodied once-yellow scrap in his dead fist. A
length of thin silk, which she had identified as her Biba scarf. The
scarf she had thought of as civilization. The bandage she had used
to bind Ion's wound.

She said nothing about that.

Ion-John was on the other side of the world, making his way. She
was left behind in his stead, an offering to placate those who would
pursue him. She could not pretend even to herself that it was not
deliberate. She understood all too well how he had survived so
many years underground. He had learned the predator's trick: to
be loved, but never to love. For that, she pitied him even as she
could cheerfully have torn his head off.

There were ways out of jails. Even jails with silver bars and garlic
hung from every window. The Romanian jailers prided themselves
on knowing vampires, but they still treated her as if she were
feeble-minded and fragile.

Her strength was sapping, and each night without proper feeding
made her weaker.

Walls could be broken through. And there were passes out of
the country. She would have to fall back on skills she had thought
never to exercise again.

But she was a survivor of the night.

As, quietly, she planned her escape from the prison and from
the country, she tried to imagine where the "Son of Dracula" was,
to conceive of the life he was living in America, to count the used-up
husks left in his wake. Was he still at his maestro's side, making
himself useful? Or had he passed beyond that, found a new patron
or become a maestro himself?

Eventually, he would build his castle in Beverly Hills and enslave
a harem. What might he become: a studio head, a cocaine baron,
a rock promoter, a media mogul, a *star*? Truly, Ion-John was what

Francis had wanted of Brando, Dracula reborn. An old monster, remade for the new world and the next century, meaning all things, tainting everything he touched.

She would leave him be, this new monster of hers, this creature born of Hollywood fantasy and her own thoughtless charity. With Dracula gone or transformed, the world needed a fresh monster. And John Popp would do as well as anyone else. The world had made him and it could cope with him.

Kate extruded a fingernail into a hard, sharp spar, and scraped the wall. The stones were solid, but between them was old mortar, which crumbled easily.

Harker, face still red with Dracula's blood, is back in his room at the inn in Bistritz. He stands in front of the mirror.

Harker's Voice: *They were going to make me a saint for this, and I wasn't even in their fucking church any more.*

Harker looks deep into the mirror.

He has no reflection.

Harker's mouth forms the words, but the voice is Dracula's.

The horror . . . the horror . . .

Hugh B. Cave

The Second Time Around

Hugh Barnett Cave was born in Chester, England, but emigrated to America with his family when he was five. He sold his first story in 1929 and went on to publish an incredible eight hundred stories to such pulp magazines as Weird Tales, Strange Tales, Ghost Stories, Black Book Detective Magazine, Spicy Mystery Stories *and the so-called "shudder pulps",* Horror Stories *and* Terror Tales.

Cave left the field for almost three decades, moving to Haiti and later Jamaica, and he returned to the genre with new stories and a string of modern horror novels: Legion of the Dead, The Nebulon Horror, The Evil, Shades of Evil, Disciples of Dread, The Lower Deep, Lucifer's Eye *and* Forbidden Passage. *His short fiction is collected in the World Fantasy Award-winning* Murgunstrumm and Others, The Corpse Maker, Death Stalks the Night, The Dagger of Tsiang *and* The Door Below. *In 1991 Cave received the Life Achievement Award from The Horror Writers Association.*

In a small New England town, a series of bizarre attacks are being blamed on vampires . . .

9.00 P.M. A lonely road in northern New England, barely two cars wide. Night and road both black as tar except for the area illuminated by the car's headlights.

Suddenly the lightbeams pick out a plodding figure who stops, turns, and lifts a hand in supplication. A stooped old woman, grey haired, the hand wavering before her eyes to shield them from the headlights' glare.

The late-model Buick stops smoothly beside her and its driver leans across the emptiness beside him to open a door for her. He is years younger than she. A college professor from Boston, dark-haired and handsome, Jerome Howell is well dressed in brown slacks, a tan jacket, a white sport shirt. From a thin gold chain around his neck hangs a gold cross.

Professor Howell's hobby – an all-consuming one – is the study of psychic phenomena, and with a whole summer vacation before him and an intriguing mystery to investigate, he is presently in high spirits. Since darkness blacked out the road he has been driving a steady forty miles an hour while thinking of what he will do on reaching his destination.

"Can I give you a lift, ma'am?"

"Thank you! Oh, thank you!" The old woman clambers in and pulls the door shut, then squirms on the seat until she has made herself comfortable. She wears an old-fashioned black dress, a grey sweater, black high-top shoes. "Are you going to Ellenton?"

"Yes, I am."

"Good, good. I was visiting a friend and my husband was supposed to come back for me. I suppose he forgot. We're old and he does that sometimes, poor man." She turns her head to smile at him, but when her gaze touches the gold cross at his throat, she pulls back with a quick little jerk of her shoulders. "I don't seem to remember seeing you before. Do you live around here?"

He shakes his head. Decides to tell her who he is and what he is here for, because she has probably lived in the area long enough to supply some information that will help him in his forthcoming research. But at that moment the lights of a following car flash in his rear-view mirror.

The car has come up behind him at a suspiciously fast speed and is apparently about to go roaring past without even a horn blast to warn him. Always a defensive driver, he jerks his wheel over, causing the Buick to veer to the extreme edge of the road in search of safety.

In the other car, which is an old but souped-up clunker, are two younger men. Monk Morrisey, driving, is eighteen. Dan Clay will be eighteen next month. Both are high school students on summer vacation, jobless by choice but engaged in an ongoing enterprise that earns them more money than classmates who do have summer jobs. Both are of slight build, unshaven, with hair to their shoulders. Both wear boots and dirty jeans and even dirtier khaki shirts.

With its windows rolled up against the evening chill, the clunker reeks of marijuana. Dan has just finished a joint. Monk smokes one as he drives.

They close in on the Buick at sixty-odd miles an hour.

As the other car comes roaring up beside him, Jerome Howell tells himself that no one but a fool or a drunk would be driving that fast on this road in the dark. He swings his Buick even closer to the road's edge to avoid being sideswiped. But despite his defensive manoeuvre, the clunker lurches at the last moment and thuds into the side of his machine, with a sound like that of a sledgehammer striking an empty oil drum.

Oddly, the little old lady seated beside him does not flinch or scream. Apparently unafraid, she only grabs at the dashboard.

The steering wheel spins in Howell's hands as the sandy road-shoulder traps his car's right front tyre. Out of control while he desperately struggles to brake it, the Buick lurches off the blacktop into a shallow, grassy ditch, climbs the far side, and hurtles into a grove of trees.

Howell is a deft enough driver to avoid the first few trees the car seems likely to crash into, but not the next. The Buick strikes that one a glancing blow with its right front fender, rears high on its left wheels, and tips onto its side.

After sideswiping the Buick, the jalopy slowed from sixty-plus so quickly that its tyres squealed on the blacktop and its wheels came close to locking. Bringing it to a halt with its right wheels off the pavement, Monk Morrisey leaned back with a grin.

"Got 'im."

He thrust out his right hand. Dan Clay slapped it with his right, grinned and said, "Them, you mean. There was two of 'em. The driver and a little old lady."

"All the better. Little old ladies wear jewellery sometimes. Let's go."

The two got out of the clunker and loped back along the road to where they could see the other car's headlight-glow among the trees. Scrambling across the ditch, they approached the tipped machine with care.

"They must both be out cold. Or dead, even." Monk's tone said it made no difference to him. "I don't see nothin' movin'."

"Yeah."

Going to the front of the wrecked car, they peered in through the windshield. The driver was bent grotesquely against the door the car was resting on, with one arm limply draped over the steering wheel.

"Where's the old woman?" Dan Clay said. "There was an old woman with him. I seen her." He leaned closer, pressing his forehead against the cracked windshield glass. "She ain't here. Where the hell'd she go to?"

Both backed away from the car and peered into the surrounding darkness for a moment. "Maybe there wasn't no woman," Monk said.

"I seen a little old lady, I tell you! Right there on the front seat, next to this guy!"

"So how'd she get out?"

"How do I know how she got out? She just did, for Chrissake. If she ain't here now, she must've."

"Okay, okay." Monk spread his arms in surrender. "Let's get what we come for."

They peered into the Buick again. There was no way they could crawl under it to open the driver's door. Climbing onto the machine, Dan worked on the high-side door instead. That one was deeply creased from its impact with the tree.

Less experienced predators might not have been able to get even that door open. But after working themselves into a heavy sweat, these two finally succeeded.

Leaning in and reaching down for the unconscious man's right hand, Monk felt for a pulse at the wrist.

"Well?" Clay said.

"I ain't sure. Whaddaya think? Should we –"

"No, no. Leave him be."

"Be better if we –"

"No, damn it. He never seen us. Leave him be but put the mark on him, just in case. Here." Clay took from a hip pocket of his dirty jeans a metal instrument shaped like an extra wide, two-pronged dinner fork with a stubby handle. He and his buddy had designed it themselves and liked to think of it as a miniature devil's pitchfork with the centre prongs missing. He put the instrument in Monk's upthrust hand.

Leaning down into the car again, Monk turned the driver's head to expose his neck and for the first time noticed the gold chain the man was wearing. He broke it off with a quick jerk and thrust it into his pocket. Then with a practised hand he pressed the twin points of the devil's pitchfork into the side of the man's neck until blood oozed out around them.

Withdrawing the instrument, he handed it back up to Dan Clay without comment and went on with his work. This too was routine.

Aided by the light from the dashboard, which like the car's headlamps was still on, Monk squirmed even farther into the wrecked machine and emptied the driver's pockets, pausing only to pass the contents of each up to his companion. Then he emptied the glove compartment. Lots of stupid people kept valuable stuff in glove compartments, he knew from the dozens of cars he and Dan had plundered. Finally he snatched the ignition key, which was one of several on a ring.

"Okay. I got everything."

"You sure?"

"Course I'm sure, for Chrissake. Gimme a hand up."

With Dan's help Monk wriggled back out of the car like a worm from its hole in the ground. Then the two turned to the car's trunk. One of the keys on the ring opened it.

There was a small leather suitcase in the trunk. Dan lifted it out and slammed the trunk lid shut. Both young men then hurried back through the trees and across the ditch to the road. On reaching their clunker, they flung themselves and their loot into it.

Again Monk Morrisey drove. Tonight was his night. While the old car roared down the road, Dan Clay pulled the assorted loot from his pockets and examined it.

"One big, thick billfold." Counting the bills in it, he became so excited he performed a kind of breakdance on the car seat, even with the suitcase across his knees. "Jeez, Monk! More'n five hundred bucks in cash! And a Visa card, two gas company credit cards, a driver's licence, car registration ... The guy's name is Jerome Howell and he's from Boston, Mass." Tossing the billfold onto the back seat, he eagerly turned his attention to the rest of what they had stolen.

That was mostly disappointing. There was a small notebook containing names and notes. The names were unfamiliar and some of the notes were just plain weird, such as "Aleta B, 64, was visited at state inst by Dr. Keller in Aug. Told W she actually saw her brother attacked. Described attacker as tall and handsome, sort of foreign-looking. W says he believes her, but no one fitting that description lives in area." Never much interested in the written word, Dan had no patience for such enigmatic scribblings and tossed the notebook after the billfold.

The rest of the loot from Howell's pockets consisted of cigarettes, some coins, a handkerchief, and a silver lighter that might be worth a few bucks if they could find some dude who wasn't turned off by the initials JDH on it.

The glove-compartment treasures were even more disappointing. This driver, it seemed, kept only road maps and a car-owner's instruction manual there.

As Monk drove on down the road, Dan tackled the suitcase.

It was not locked. He flipped the lid up and took out a book that lay on top of some clothes. A thin book with hard grey covers on which the title was printed in black letters.

"*How to Protect Yourself Against Vampires*," he read aloud. "By Jerome Howell. Hey, that's the name on his driver's licence: Jerome Howell."

Monk stopped scowling at the road long enough to glance at him. "How to protect yourself against vampires?"

"Yeah."

"Jesus. I forgot." Removing his right hand from the wheel, Monk twisted his hips so he could reach into a pants pocket. He pulled out the broken gold chain with the cross on it. "Looka this."

Dan examined it.

"He was wearin' it 'round his neck," Monk said. "I yanked it off to put the mark on him."

"He's that guy those people sent for!" Dan said in a hoarse whisper. "Yeah. He has to be."

"Jeez. Maybe we should go back and finish him off. If he comes to and ain't hurt bad – if he can really do what he come here for – he could put us outa business and ruin our whole summer!"

Monk steered the clunker to the side of the road and they sat for a while to discuss their problem.

They talked about the previous summer. Of how the word "vampire" had become part of the town's vocabulary when the first two townspeople were found with marks on their necks. Of how Dan Clay and Monk Morrisey, even while laughing their heads off at the crazy idea some foreigner named Count Dracula had moved into town, had doped out a way to use the scare as a sure-fire cover for the game they were already playing with out-of-state cars. In the beginning, for God's sake, when the vampire talk started, Monk hadn't even known what a vampire was.

"You must've seen vampire movies on TV," Dan had said in disgust. "Everybody has."

"Maybe, I dunno. If I did, I must've forgot."

"They're dead people who come out at night lookin' for blood. They have to have blood to keep goin'. And when they kill people that way, those people turn into vampires too. Some do, anyway."

Talking about it again now, they looked at and tried to read the book by Jerome Howell, whom certain frightened townspeople had sent for to come and investigate. Many of the words were beyond their understanding, but after flipping through the pages Dan said at last, "The guy is really sold on this junk, y' know. He thinks vampires are for real."

"He's crazy," Monk said.

"Or smart. I bet he gets big money when people hire him."

That settled, Dan tossed the book aside and the two continued their investigation of the suitcase. But there was nothing in it they could sell or use. Disgusted, Dan slammed it shut and threw it on the back seat. "C'mon. Let's go."

"That's it?" Monk groaned as he tooled the clunker down the road again, putting distance between them and the Buick they had wrecked. "Five hundred bucks is all we get tonight?"

"Well, more'n five hundred, like I told you. And the credit cards. Don't forget the credit cards." Dan shrugged. "Hey, it may not be the best night we ever had, but it's okay. We done all right."

"Well, yeah, I guess so."

"And this." Dan held up the cross ripped from Jerome Howell's neck. "Don't forget this."

"He wore that to protect himself, huh?"

"I guess. But it could be worth somethin' for the gold in it. If it's gold."

A little more than an hour after the departure of the two predators, Jerome Howell opened his eyes and asked himself what had happened.

He did not remember.

His head throbbed. He put his left hand to his forehead and discovered there a lump the size of a hen's egg. Just touching it caused a stab of pain as bright as a bolt of lightning. He looked at his fingers. There was no blood on them. He touched his neck, where he felt an odd prickling sensation. His fingertips discovered a pair of punctures in the skin and came away red.

He felt the punctures again, and for some reason the word "vampire" came to mind. Vampire fangs had not actually made the marks, though; he somehow was sure of that without knowing how he could be so positive. Had he been attacked by someone who wanted others to think he was the victim of a night creature?

Why was he here? What car was this, and why was it resting on its side in the dark with its headlights on and dashboard glowing?

The headlight beams revealed a number of pine trees grouped around the machine like giant spiders about to pounce on a crippled insect.

He looked up at the car door above him. Could he boost himself up to it and open it? He must try. Failing in that, he would have to get the window open. Perhaps that would be best anyway. The car had automatic window controls, he noted. He reached for the ignition key.

There was no key in the ignition.

What now?

He was finding it hard to think straight, even to think at all. When he struggled to concentrate, the throbbing in his forehead became all but unendurable. But the struggle finally paid off. Go back to opening the door, his mind instructed. You can pull yourself up to it.

Squirming out from under the wheel, he reached up for the door and found he could not work the release. There was a weakness in his fingers. But with beads of moisture forming on his face and salting his lips, he persisted. The door finally opened an inch.

Now he had to boost or pull himself higher to push it farther open, which meant forcing it up. This took time and increased the pounding in his head, causing him to fight for breath. Then a tree beside the car, apparently the one the machine had sideswiped, was so close that the door would open only part way. He had to stretch his aching body to the limit and crawl out like a damaged caterpillar.

At last, though, he stood outside the machine on ground covered with pine needles and was able to explore his body with his hands.

There seemed to be no major injuries except the lump on his forehead. None that caused any sharp pain when touched, at any rate. Nor could he discover any rips in his clothing. But again, why was he here in this strange place? Whose car was this? Most important, who was he?

He was wearing a tan jacket and had a feeling there should be a billfold in its inside pocket. But the pocket was empty, as were all others in both the jacket and his slacks. Perhaps the plates on the car would tell him something.

He went to look, but learned nothing except that the car was from Massachusetts. Was he in Massachusetts now? Did he live near here, close enough to walk home if he could remember where home was?

The trunk lid was open – perhaps had sprung open when the car hit the tree – but the trunk itself was empty except for a jack and spare tire. Well, maybe something in the glove compartment would help him. Climbing back up on the car with the greatest of care, he leaned in through the partly open door and reached down to the dash.

But, like the trunk, the glove compartment yielded nothing.

Who was he? Where was he? How long would the pounding in his head, apparently caused by the egg-sized bruise on his forehead, keep him from remembering?

Whatever the answers, he had to walk out of here. There was no way he could use the car. So where was the road?

The car ought to tell him that, at least. It must have run off a road into this grove of trees. Assuming it had done so in a reasonably straight line, the road should be over there behind the red glow of its taillights. Not too far away, either. With so many trees around, a machine out of control could not have travelled any great distance.

Had he simply blacked out while driving? Or had some other car forced him off the road and gone on without stopping? And what time was it? He had a feeling there ought to be a watch on his left wrist, but there wasn't. Had he been robbed?

Start walking, he told himself. Just hope to God there's a house not too far away where you can phone for a doctor and a wrecker.

With both arms outthrust like the antennae of a night-prowling insect, he struggled on through the dark and came to a two-lane blacktop road. A pale moon feebly shone through cloud-gaps above it, providing light enough for him to see by. After flipping a mental coin to reach a decision, he turned blindly to his right. Behind him the lights of the car were still visible among the trees.

He must have walked a long two miles before seeing lamplit windows in a house on his left. No car had passed him in either direction. Wherever this road was, it appeared to be little used.

The windows were three in number and well back from the blacktop. One hundred fifty feet, at least. There was an old wooden mailbox on a post at the end of an unpaved drive. He had to lean close to make out the weathered black letters on it.

CARLETON HODE.

He stood there for a moment gratefully resting, because he had not stopped walking since leaving the car. Had he heard the name Carleton Hode before? He didn't think so. But then, he didn't know his own name, did he? Or where he was from. Or whose car he had been driving. He might even *be* Carleton Hode. Or a neighbour. Perhaps on coming face to face with the people who lived here, he would remember.

Straightening from his slouch against the mailbox, he went plodding down the driveway to the house.

One of its lamplit windows looked out on a long veranda, and the pale shaft of yellow light from it showed him the steps. He climbed them. Approaching the door, he wondered whether he should be honest about not knowing who he was. What would *his* reaction be if some hurt stranger appeared out of the dark and said, "Please help me, I've been in an accident, I don't know who I am or where I'm from or where I was going when it happened"? Would he let such a person in or slam and lock the door and phone the police?

I could give myself a name, he thought, but shrugged the thought aside and looked for a bell button. Failing to find one, he knocked. Knocked again. Presently he heard slow footsteps approaching over a bare wooden floor.

How should he respond if the person coming to the door asked, "What do you want?"

The door opened with a slight jerk and he found himself face to face with a small, grey-haired woman in a black dress. She stood there peering up at him, waiting for him to speak. "Good evening," he said. Recalling the name on the mailbox, he added, "Mrs Hode?"

Her expression became a frown. "Who are you?"

Better be honest, he thought. "To be truthful, I don't know who I am at the moment." Feeling weak again, as he had at the mailbox, he put a hand against the doorframe to steady himself. "I've had an accident with my car. Please – may I use your telephone to call for help?"

She leaned forward to peer at him more closely, and he half remembered something. Had he picked up a hitchhiker sometime before his accident? An old, grey-haired woman in a black dress? This very woman, perhaps?

No, no. If anything like that had happened, the person he picked up would never have walked away and left him unconscious, perhaps dying, in a wrecked car. His mind was playing tricks on him.

"Accident?" the woman echoed. "You've had an accident?"

"About two miles down the road. I don't know what happened. When I came to, the car was on its side in a grove of trees and I had this lump on my head."

He pointed to the bruise and she leaned closer to examine it. "M'm. It does look nasty," she said in a thin voice. "Come with me, please."

Closing the door behind him, he trailed her down a lamplit hall to an archway on the right, and through that into a lamplit living room. Or perhaps, in this part of New England in a house as old as this, it was referred to as a parlour. To his surprise, two of its three ancient, overstuffed chairs were occupied by a man and a woman. The man, wearing a dark suit complete with jacket, was tall, swarthy, even handsome in a foreign sort of way. The woman, definitely of old New England stock, was at least as old as his guide and as old-fashioned in her dress. The only other pieces of furniture in the room were two small tables on which stood kerosene lamps with ornate, cut-glass bases and tall glass chimneys.

Mrs Hode – if his guide was Mrs Hode – said to the other two, "This man has been hurt in a car accident and doesn't know who he is."

The pair gazed at him with such intensity that Howell was tempted to turn and run.

"Haven't you a driver's licence?" asked the man, speaking with an accent.

"No, I don't. Or anything else with a name on it. Someone must have emptied my pockets while I was unconscious."

"It would seem you have a problem, then."

"If I might use your phone –"

"To call whom?"

"Nine-one-one, I suppose."

"There is no Nine-one-one here."

"A doctor, then? One who lives within reach?"

"None would be willing to come here at this hour." The swarthy man extended a long, bony finger to point at a brass clock on the wall. "It is past midnight."

Howell was startled. Past midnight? How long had he been unconscious there in the car?

"You had better forget about a doctor tonight." The man's gaze flicked darkly to the woman who had opened the door, then to the other one. "Ladies, I believe what this man needs most is a good night's rest. Don't you agree? I don't know why we can't let him have the spare room for tonight. Then if he is no better in the morning we can call Doctor – ah – Jones." He waited while the two women exchanged questioning looks, then added impatiently, "Well?"

"All right," said the one who had opened the door.

"Yes, I think so," the other echoed.

With bits and pieces of memory struggling to sort themselves out in his mind, Jerome Howell sat silently staring. The two women were sisters, he decided. The man could be the husband of one of them, or just someone living here. Was this the entire household? And were they the Hodes whose name was on the mailbox?

Why did he have such a strong feeling that the Hodes had died long ago, the house had long since been abandoned as old and worthless, and these three had simply moved in recently and taken it over?

The man with the foreign accent was gazing at him. "Well, sir? Do you agree that what you most need is a good night's sleep?"

"With all due respect, sir, I'd prefer to see a doctor," Howell said experimentally. "Is there a cab I could call to take me to one?"

"There are no taxicabs in this small town."

"What town *is* this?"

"Ellenton."

Another jog to his memory. He knew the name Ellenton. But Ellenton what? New Hampshire? He thought so but was afraid to ask. Whoever they were, these people must already suspect him of being unstable. "Well . . . if I can't get to a doctor, perhaps you're right in saying a night's sleep . . ."

"Good." The swarthy man pushed himself out of his chair and took up one of the lamps. He was even taller than he had appeared to be when seated, Howell noted. Even more handsome. Were his clothes a bit newer, less seedy, he might well have attracted attention even in a place like New York City.

"Come with me, please."

Jerome Howell trailed his host up a wide flight of uncarpeted stairs and along a bare upper hall to the rear of the ancient house, where the fellow stopped before the last of several doors and produced a ring of keys. He inserted one into an old-fashioned lock. Strange, Howell thought with a touch of apprehension. How many people kept bedroom doors locked?

Entering the room, the fellow placed the lamp on a bedside table, and by its light Howell saw that the room was a large one. It had four windows. The bed was a massive old four-poster of pine. Completing the furnishings were two ancient chests-of-drawers and a bedroom chair with faded rosebuds on its skirt of chintz.

"The bed is ready," the tall man said in his mellow voice, with just a trace of a smile. "Perhaps you should retire at once, no? You appear to be very tired, sir."

"Are you sure this won't inconvenience you, Mr Hode?"

"I assure you, it is no trouble. Let me get you something to sleep in." Striding to a chest, the man dropped on one knee to open its bottom drawer. "Here now. These will fit you, I believe." He placed a pair of grey flannel pyjamas on the bed and turned to lift a long-fingered hand in farewell. "Goodnight, sir. Rest well."

He went out. Howell heard the key turn in the lock and realized he was a prisoner. A prisoner in a town called Ellenton, in the state of New Hampshire. And suddenly, with the shock of that frightening realization, all the rest of it flooded back into his memory.

He knew his name. He knew he was a vacationing professor of philosophy whose hobby was the investigation of psychic phenomena. He knew he had received a letter from the town of Ellenton, signed by twenty-two of its citizens, imploring him to come to their town and investigate reports of vampirism – especially the rumour that the most renowned vampire of them all, Count Dracula, had chosen to pay the town of Ellenton a visit and was now in residence here.

More and more came back. He remembered he had planned to arrive in Ellenton about three in the afternoon but had been delayed in Portsmouth by car trouble. He recalled that hours later, when it was dark, he had picked up an old woman – one of the two old women now in the almost bare parlour downstairs. Then an old clunker of a car had run him off the road – perhaps deliberately – and when he regained consciousness in his wrecked car, his passenger was no longer there. She could hardly have escaped injury, but still she had vanished.

And now this house. And this tall, thin, handsome man who could easily be the Count Dracula of history, written about so vividly in Bram Stoker's famous novel, and described in the letter the Ellenton group had sent him when soliciting his services. And the locked door. Shaking with fear, he hurried to the door and tried to open it.

It would not budge.

A scratching sound at his back caused him to lurch about in panic and look at the windows. All along, he had been telling himself he did not trust this house or these people, and should not risk going to sleep here. Now he knew he should not have ignored those instincts!

Dark shapes had appeared at all three windows, blocking out the faint wash of moonlight. Were they birds or bats? Bats, of course! Huge ones with monstrous wings and ugly, mouth-agape heads. In each of the three mouths gleamed a pair of dagger-like fangs.

Simultaneously the three hurled themselves at the bubbly old window panes.

Despite his years of research, he half expected an implosion of shattered glass but there was none. The winged things passed through the panes without breaking them. The only sound accompanying their rush was the wet-towel flapping of their wings.

With an ear-splitting cry of terror Howell hurled himself at the locked door. It shuddered under the impact but would not yield. Flung back, he fell to his knees, and as he jerked about to face the intruders, a last lingering memory returned to him.

In wild desperation he clawed at his throat, where a golden cross should have been dangling from a golden chain.

The cross was not there.

But seconds later the fangs were. Three gleaming pairs of them, driving deep into his neck.

When he awoke, he was lying on the bed and the tall, handsome foreigner sat there beside him, smiling down at him. "There are some things you should know before you go on with your life here," the fellow said calmly. "Things about life itself, if I may. Do you recall being run off the road by two young men on your way here?"

"Yes," Howell heard himself saying.

"You were not their first victim, of course. For quite some time now they have been robbing strangers who passed through here – frequently killing them in the process, as they so nearly killed you. And we, my two aged ladies downstairs and I, have been blamed for these atrocities because the two young men make it seem that those attacked are the victims of vampires. You yourself have their false vampire mark on your neck, in case you haven't noticed."

He paused, shrugged, then leaned a bit closer. "Sadly, these two young criminals are not remarkable in this day and age, friend. Just listen to the news any evening on television or read it in the daily papers. A fifteen-year-old youth rapes and kills his grandmother, and who cares? A girl in Texas, only twelve years old, beats to death an infant barely able to walk. Mere children burn down a house because they decide they don't like the man who owns it. All over this sad country, all over the world, insane violence increases while those who should be trying to stop it shrug their shoulders and look the other way."

Howell lay there staring up at him.

"So the two ladies downstairs sent for me, and I came," continued the man with the accent. "Not to stay here long, you understand, but to help if I could. Because someone must step in to put a stop to these horrors. Don't you agree, Mr Howell?"

To Howell's surprise his mind was functioning normally again, but he still needed a moment to absorb and evaluate what he had just heard. He frowned then. "But if you do to these people what you always did – what, apparently, you have just done to me – they will become one of *you*, won't they? One of us? Isn't that how it works? The victim becomes a vampire too?"

The other shook his head. "Only when such is desired. Students of the occult – like you, sir – have been making that mistake for years. We need you; therefore you are now one of us. But if we had not needed you, you and I would not now be having this conversation."

"But what – what do you need me for?" Howell asked.

The other reached out to touch him on the shoulder and said with a smile, "You will soon see, friend. Rest, now, to prepare yourself." And suddenly he was no longer sitting there on the bed. Howell, the new Jerome Howell, was alone.

Seven days have passed since Monk Morrisey and Dan Clay ran Jerome Howell's Buick off the road. The two have spent the money they took from the unconscious Howell and are on the prowl again. Seriously, too, because they are out of pot, out of cocaine, out of everything. They spent their last few dollars half an hour ago on beers at a late-night bar.

Dan Clay is behind the wheel this time. Turning his head, he scowls at his companion. "Damn it, Monk, we shouldn'a done it. I shouldn'a let you talk me into it."

"Done what? Wha' you talkin' 'bout?"

"We shouldn'a stopped for beers. Look." Dan thrusts his right arm out so Monk can see the watch on his wrist – the watch they took from Jerome Howell a week ago. "It's almost midnight, for the luvva god. We ain't gonna find nobody on the road this late."

It is a sparkly bright New England night. No clouds. A round, near-full moon transforms the road into a shining black ribbon. On the left, just ahead, is an old wooden mailbox on a post.

Looking up from the watch in front of his face, Monk Morrisey sees something step into view from the driveway there. It is a man wearing dark trousers and a white, long-sleeved shirt.

One of the white sleeves flaps up as the man steps into the road to beg a lift.

Monk's voice gurgles with glee. "Hey, hey! Looka what we got us, Dan! A volunteer!" He makes fists of his hands and pounds his knees. "Ease up, man! Ease up!"

Dan takes his foot off the gas pedal and the clunker slows to a jerky stop. As the man at the mailbox walks toward them, Monk leans forward to peer at him through the windshield.

"Wait, Dan. Jeez. It's the writer guy."

"Who?"

"The guy with the book. The Buick we ran off the road the last time we were out. Don't you remember?"

Dan Clay remembers. The book about vampires. They had thrown it away. And just tonight, when out of money, they had swapped the man's gold cross for their last two beers in that late-night bar.

"We won't get nothin' outa him," Monk says with a groan.

"We already cleaned him."

The beers have made Dan argumentative. "Who says we won't? He could 've got paid by now for comin' here, couldn' he? He's been here a week."

"But he just walked outa the old Hode place, dummy. Nobody in his right mind would be stayin' in a creepy abandoned house if he had money for a motel room."

"It's a roof, ain't it? And if he believes in vampires, he coulda shacked up there 'cause he likes old houses. He just needs a ride to town 'cause we wrecked his wheels, that's all."

"Well, all right," Monk grudgingly concedes. "If you say so."

They wait then in silence then while the author of *How to Protect Yourself Against Vampires* continues his approach. By the time the man leans against the door on Monk's side, the two in the clunker have even begun to grin a little. But their grins freeze into grotesque expressions of terror when the door is violently jerked open and they see Jerome Howell's face up close . . .

. . . and are trapped in their seats by the hypnotic stare of his sunken, glowing eyes . . .

. . . and see the long, gleaming fangs at the sides of his opening mouth.

Brian Mooney

Endangered Species

Brian Mooney is not a prolific writer, but he has been contributing short stories to magazines and anthologies for more than twenty-five years. His first professional appearance was in The London Mystery Selection *in 1971, since when his fiction has appeared in* The 21st Pan Book of Horror Stories, Final Shadows, Dark Voices 5, The Mammoth Book of Werewolves, The Mammoth Book of Frankenstein, The Anthology of Fantasy & the Supernatural, Shadows Over Innsmouth *and* The Year's Best Fantasy and Horror Eighth Annual Collection.

"During most of the 1980s I was working at a Customs station where, among other things, we used to seize a lot of endangered species parts that people were attempting to import," reveals the author. "One day I had the whimsical idea that vampires might be an endangered species because of modern funeral techniques such as embalming and cremation . . ."

Still searching for companionship, Dracula turns to the personal ads . . .

WELCOME TO MY HOUSE! Enter freely and of your own will!

That is correct, I am your "mysterious" host. And you are Miss Roisin Kennedy. Welcome to my house. Come freely. Go safely;

and leave something of the happiness you bring. But come, for you have had a long journey. The night is chill and you must be in need of food and rest.

Please walk this way. We will go into my library, which is comfortable and where there is warmth and refreshment. This great house is old and much of the rest of it is sadly dilapidated. I was told that it was built by one who made his fortune in the 1849 gold rush and who lived out his whole life here as a stingy hermit, neither improving nor renovating. But it is in keeping with my tastes, for I love houses which are old, which proclaim to you of their history.

See, is that not better? A blazing log fire has so much more to offer than other forms of warmth. Its appearance alone can comfort and cheer the weary traveller. I abhor this modern central heating – it is so clinical, do you not think? In the old country the forests were ancient and thick and provided light and fuel for *boyar* and peasant alike. I hear that under Ceaucescu my land is polluted by the effluvia of industry and coal-fired power stations. Such an abomination!

I digress. Accept the apologies of a garrulous old man who sees so little charming and intelligent company. Be seated, here in this wing chair by the fire where it is most comfortable. In a few moments I will join you and we can converse. But first, allow me to serve you. A little cold chicken and salad? Some wine perhaps?

I am rambling away and forget my manners. You, I know, are Miss Roisin Kennedy of Boston, Massachusetts. I have lived in Boston, a charming city. How wild and remote these forests and hills of Oregon State must seem to you, although they comfort me greatly for they are so reminiscent of my beloved Carpathians. Ah, there I go again . . . In my clumsy way, my dear, I am trying to express regrets for not yet having properly introduced myself to you.

My given name is Vlad. I have been known by other names. Once I was called Tepesch but I may be more familiar to you as Dracula.

No, I beg you, do not look so alarmed. You are not in the presence of a madman. You are in none of the danger so common in the movie entertainments of such as Mr Hitchcock. I am speaking nothing but the simple truth. I am indeed the *Voivode* Vlad Dracula, late of Transylvania, late of London, late of . . . so many places.

I am Dracula the terrible, Dracula the arch-fiend, Dracula "the fearsome lover who died yet lived" as one old movie poster described me, Dracula the . . . much-maligned.

You still seem to be a little agitated, which I can understand. Yet you must have courage for having undertaken your long journey into the unknown. A glass of wine, that will soothe you. Here is some good Tokay, one of the finest years. Is that not excellent? And see, I drink with you.

You laugh. That is good. And I know why you laugh. It is from sheer relief. You think that as I am drinking wine with you I cannot possibly be who I say I am. And yet am I not a nobleman of a lineage centuries-old and proud before Columbus set out on his voyages of discovery? Is not wine a natural drink to one such as I? To tell the truth, I can stomach only a little but if I sip slowly all is well.

There, a little more in your glass. And a toast – to our friendship! You must not believe all that you see and read, particularly if it emanates from such a place as Hollywood. I blame a certain clumsy playwright and that terrible old Mittel-European actor with his oh-so-studied poses. "*I do not trink . . .vine . . .*" Hah! A nonsense! As far as I recall, not even Stoker used that. He simply had me say that I had dined and that I did not sup, which was literally true.

What is that you say? I am "*putting you on*"? Ah, I understand: you believe that I am jesting with you. Dracula was a fictional character, you are sure, based loosely on a real-life fifteenth-century tyrant who died in the year 1476 and who anyway is always destroyed in the book and all the plays and movies. If you bear with me, I will explain all that in due course.

First, I must thank you for answering my advertisement and for having the courage to attend this meeting. So few persons, men or women, would have agreed to an assignation with an unknown person in a place so distant and remote.

So, you were intrigued by my wording. That was my intention. "*Reclusive European nobleman, living far from civilization, promises an inquiring soul unique experience, interesting narrative and rich reward. Intelligent young persons only, of sturdy good health, apply to Box Number V1214.*"

The truth is, my dear, that even one such as I can be lonely and at times must have an outlet for a very human vanity. I purposely placed this advertisement in a great variety of newspapers and journals, rightly guessing that many of the responses would be unworthy of my consideration. As it is, I received few replies and was immediately able to dismiss most of them.

Several were obviously from persons who were little more than panders and I admit to an outdated moral outrage towards such creatures, so much so that I was tempted to meet with and destroy them. This was just a foolish whim which would have achieved nothing and I dismissed it.

Others were from persons who seemed to lack the intelligence that I sought or whose cupidity shone through their every word.

There were those urbanites whose idea of "living far from civilization" is that they need travel no greater distance than the edge of the city.

Your letter, though, was interesting. I have it here. I was impressed at the outset by the fact that you took the trouble to write by hand, and legibly at that. In this age of typewriters and other mechanical devices, you demonstrated a rare – an almost obsolete – courtesy. Then your style of writing, your use of language and choice of words, indicated that you are well-educated and intelligent, that you are worthy of my cultivation.

What follows is what decided me. "*I want no rich reward,*" you wrote, "*I was born to wealth and privilege and the consequential first class education and all my life I have wanted for nothing. Yet I remain dissatisfied for I have never had to struggle to attain anything. Everything in life has been handed to me and I am bored.*

"*If you can indeed offer me a unique experience, 'reclusive European nobleman', then I wish to meet with you.*"

You say that you want no rich reward, and yet your time must be recompensed. As promised when I first wrote to you, I have paid your travelling expenses. Your background is wealthy, you say, but it is my experience that even the wealthy can always use a little more wealth. This leather pouch contains a considerable sum in antique gold coins, crowns, thalers, double-eagles and the like, for which I can provide authentic provenance. Distribute them slowly and carefully among a variety of dealers and you will receive good prices without arousing suspicion.

Now, to convince you that I am who I say I am. The human race, whether or not they believe in such as I, call us Vampire, *Nosferatu* – Undead – Monster. I eschew such pejoratives. Were I to choose a description it would be along the lines of "*Homo superior*". There, I did tell you that I have a very human vanity. However, the accepted human terms are convenient ones and so I will use them.

I will offer strands of evidence which I hope will weave themselves into proof. The light in here is low but I am sure that you can note the pallor of my skin. And no, I am not a recently released felon as I believe you may be thinking. Prison pallor is quite different.

Here is my hand, take it in your own. Ah, you are startled. Is not my flesh abnormally cold? Unlike your own fingers which are silken soft and warm with the vibrancy of the *living blood* flowing in your veins. And witness the palms of my hands, the coarse hairs which grow upon them. No human, however hirsute, would have hair growing there.

Unnecessary to say that I do not keep mirrors about me but I believe that my hair and moustache must at the moment be grey, perhaps even white. You nod. A sign of ageing? Or is it, as in my own circumstances, a sign of long abstemiousness? No, I do not offer the lack of colour in my hair as proof but simply point out that it shields more evidence. See, I move the locks aside and reveal how pointed my ears are.

And if I draw back my lips. Observe my canine teeth which are longer and sharper than those of any normal man. Yes, you are right. They could be false, or I could have had special dental work performed to fuel my fantasy. But it is not so. Here, feel the weight of this huge fire iron. How many men do you know who could bend it in two with such ease – *thus*? Now I will offer you two final pieces of evidence which should fully satisfy you that there is no trickery in what I tell you. Come, stand next to me here at the fireside.

See how your own shadow stretches away towards those shadows beyond the pool of light cast by the flames. Where then is *my* shadow? So, I have your interest. Now, I doubt not that in your handbag – forgive me, your purse – you carry with you a small mirror as do all women. Hold it before me. *Where then is my reflection?*

At last you are convinced as to what I am if not who I am, I can see it in your eyes, I can feel it in your aura. There is realization and there is belief and there is fear. Yet underlying the fear I sense a steely determination to see this adventure through and I salute you for it. I chose wisely.

Resume your seat, Miss Kennedy. I may call you Roisin? Then please, take your seat my dear Roisin. In a short space of time you have had so many surprises. At first you probably thought you were travelling to meet an eccentric dilettante, then you had the brief worry that you were trapped with a maniac, and now you realize that you are the guest of an infamous . . . vampire.

I regret that I must test your strength of purpose just once more. As a sign of good faith, I must ask a small *quid pro quo* for my hospitality. It is long since I have fed and I ask for a little of your blood. Please, hear me out. I intend you no harm and upon this you have the word of a Prince. No more than a sip, and then my story.

The choice is yours. If you do not agree, then I will honour your wishes and you may leave immediately with your gold. Although I must point out that the limousine driver who brought you here was instructed not to return until the morning. There is no telephone in this house nor is this the sort of area where one can find a taxicab, either by day or night. Furthermore, the roads are dark and treacherous and there are wild animals. You could so easily meet with a terrible accident if you were to attempt the many miles to the nearest village.

You are willing? Then I did not misjudge you. You have fire and determination and you are indeed a worthy guest. A sip, no more I guarantee. I promise that you will feel no pain; only perhaps a little lassitude, and possibly a tingle of ecstasy. If you will kindly bare your neck – yes, just there where I can see and scent the rich veins throbbing beneath the fine skin . . .

Thank you my dear. That was not so bad, was it? Here, a little more wine to fortify you. You will forgive me if I do not partake this time. I will not sully the bouquet of the wine that *I* have just enjoyed.

Now that we are both comfortable, I will tell you of Dracula and how he comes to be sitting before you rather than being ancient dust long since dispersed by capricious Carpathian winds.

Ask not how I came to be *Nosferatu* for I do not know. I died and then I awoke as I am now. It may be that somehow my behaviour in life marked me, for I freely admit to being a cruel and unrelenting tyrant. But I lived in a different world to the one that you know and I was probably neither worse nor better than many other fifteenth-century rulers. I justify myself by saying that I was a man of my time.

With the condition of Unlife comes enhancements and limitations. My life is eternal, barring interference by those who have the knowledge and there can be few of them today. How grateful I am for your modern scepticism and cynicism.

I have supernormal strength and yet I can pass – wraith-like – through the merest crack in door or window. I can take the form of animals and mist and moonlight and as such go where I will, once I have been invited. The powers of mesmerism and persuasion are mine and I can hold the most strongly-willed person in thrall when I so wish. I can control animals, bending them to my bidding, although I admit to a distaste for domesticated hounds, cringing, fawning wretches that they are. Within limits I can command the elements, bringing about localized storms and fogs and blizzards at will. I regret, though, that I am unable to retard or to stop time.

Balanced against all these is the fact that certain of my extraordinary powers are limited to the hours of darkness. Outside of these times my strength and swiftness remain constant but my ability to change is impaired. I cannot endure certain things held by men to be holy, but again – who today believes, save for a few scattered peasants in the old countries of Europe? Direct sunlight is anathema to me although I can walk abroad on cool and cloudy days. This is the result only of centuries of Unlife and a young *Nosferatu* exposed during the daylight hours would suffer the most agonising death.

You have read Stoker's novel? Good; I feared briefly that

perhaps your exclusive education might have narrowed your mind against works so lacking in literary merit. Know that the book was literally true.

The general belief is that Stoker was inspired by earlier works, such as those of Le Fanu, and that his research among old books led him to select myself as his central character. Not so. The nature of Stoker's work brought him in touch with many people at all levels of society, among them the person he called Arthur Holmwood, Lord Godalming, although that was not the noble lord's true name.

Like many who have endured traumatic experiences, Lord Godalming needed the catharsis of confiding in another, an outsider. In Stoker he found a sympathetic, if perhaps a doubting, ear.

Through him, Stoker became acquainted with the whole of that group. I am sure he did not believe their tale but he could see its potential as High Gothic romance. After long negotiation, all gave him permission to publish subject to concealment of their true identities. Moving in society, they did not wish to compromise their positions.

They handed to Stoker all of their diaries and papers and with careful editing and some dramatic licence these became the novel *Dracula*. To avoid confusion, I will continue to refer to the persons involved by their fictional names.

I am sure that their underlying purpose in giving permission to Stoker was a foolish optimism that the world would come to believe in and take arms against we superior ones. Despite the depth and breadth of his learning, I believe that Van Helsing was naïve enough to seek such an outcome. Stoker was more worldly-wise. He would have realised that those most *likely* to believe – villagers and peasants and suchlike in the Balkans and surrounding lands – were the most *unlikely* to hear of or read the novel anyway. Stoker, I am sure, sought only fame and riches, and good fortune to him.

I know all these things because I made it my business to find out. Of necessity, *Nosferatu* cultivate useful acquaintances at all levels of society. Following the publication and success of *Dracula*, I had a private enquiry agent look into the matter for me. Stoker had been unable to resist dropping hints of the truth to theatrical friends of his and some of these, plied with strong liquor, were loose-tongued.

You are curious, naturally, as to how I escaped oblivion during that apparently final confrontation. The answer is simple. It was not I in that coffin being borne to my home by the Szgany but a simulacrum which I had created. In more modern parlance, you would probably call it a clone.

You see, I realized very early on during my stay in England that I had made two grievous errors. The first was that in my arrogance I was certain that I would remain undiscovered and unexposed there, for was I not in a land of reason in an age of reason, a land where there was no room in the rational mind for creatures of legend?

I brooked no expectation that that accursed nuisance Jonathan Harker would survive. I had surely believed that when and if I chose to return to my native soil I would find Harker to be such as I, a regent to partner my three consorts.

In time Harker could have become a power to reckon within the world, for he was an intelligent and determined man and from such spring the true Princes amongst us. He could have brought others to the fold and . . . But what use bemoaning now, for it was all so long ago.

And again, how could I have foreseen that a mere lunatic-master such as Seward would know a meddling old woman like Van Helsing? A doctor, Van Helsing called himself. *A doctor*! What right has a physician to know more of ancient lore than of his own profession? Forgive me, dearest Roisin. I came very close to losing my temper then. The thought of those interfering quacks still irks me from time to time. Well indeed that they are long dead and beyond *my* justice.

The second of my great errors was that I came, in my own way, to love. Yes, we *can* love, we denizens of the night. And like humans, when we love we yearn for the constant companionship of the loved one. Both Lucy Westenra and her friend Mina Murray – later Harker – attracted me greatly and I determined that both would be mine for eternity. I set out to convert them to this glorious enhancement of life, knowing full well that in their turn they would recruit their own loved ones to swell my empire.

It was when Lucy was destroyed that I realized someone had knowledge and posed a serious threat to me. As a precaution, I took a little of my blood and mingled it with the sacred soil of my homeland to create my replica. The ability to clone is something which a *Nosferatu* knows by instinct. It seems to be a survival instinct inherent when passing from human to superior life, as instinctive as the struggles of a newly-born antelope on the African plain to gain its feet and run. My survival does, *must always*, take precedence over my loves. For I have a supreme importance in the great scheme of things.

As I said, I created my clone and sent it about my business. I am able to control my clones with my mind and their actions are as my actions would be, but when danger lurks then only the clones are in peril. It was the clone which compelled Mina to drink of its blood, it was the clone which made that mad dash for freedom from the house in Piccadilly.

I have admitted to my errors, but they too – Van Helsing and his crowd of whiter-than-white heroes – made theirs. They assumed that the four houses and the fifty boxes of earth comprised the total of my places of refuge. At different times, both Van Helsing and Harker had commented on my astuteness and ability to plan ahead. And yet in the end they so foolishly disregarded their own insight.

I had dealt with a number of English solicitors and agents and there were many more homes and boxes of Transylvanian earth in and around London for me to take refuge. When those wretches were contaminating my resting places with their holy relics, they were doing little more than exposing to me the limits of their knowledge.

I deliberately had the clone confront them, with the very purpose of making them think that my resources were exhausted but for a few paltry pounds. And the fools swallowed the bait. "His mind is that of a child," bleated Van Helsing and his sheep bleated with him.

It was the clone that fled on the good ship *Czarina Catherine*, the clone that they pursued from London to Galatz, from Galatz to the Borgo Pass, from the Borgo Pass to my castle, the clone that was lying in the coffin when the blades flashed down in that so-called "final" sunset of Dracula, the clone which crumbled to dust when its heart was pierced and its head shorn from its body.

What a strange journey that had been, with our minds – Mina's, the clone's and my own – inextricably linked together. I could experience the darkness of the coffin in the ship's bowels, could feel the sick lurching of the waves. I could sense the cold and snow where Mina and Van Helsing camped, could revel in the temptations from my three consorts that Mina, with the old man's aid, had to resist.

I had hopes, almost, that my clone would triumph, for it was a close run thing that final chase and battle. They all thought that the scar of the Sacred Host passed from Mina's brow because of the "death" of Dracula, but really it passed because I chose to relinquish my hold on her. The importance of my survival, you see.

So there I was, safe in London. I decided that my emotions and activities must be curbed, lest Van Helsing and his cohorts suspect that I yet lived. Such abstinence is not so difficult. While a young *Nosferatu* can be dangerously greedy, one such as I may – like the spider – survive with little or no nourishment for a long time, for very many years if necessary. I could patiently outlive my adversaries, even their descendants, for what are decades to one with eternal life?

I surmised that it would take time for the Van Helsing party to return from Transylvania, for they had to bury Quincy Morris, that courageous and hot-headed American, and to recuperate from their ordeal. They believed me to be dead, they knew with certainty that my three consorts were dead and returned to the eternal dust thanks to that accursed old Dutchman, and they had massacred poor Lucy in her London tomb. They would have been in no hurry, for had not the horror ended?

I decided that it would be in my best interests to move away from London, in fact from England altogether. I would spend a few years lying low, perhaps alternating between Paris and one of the great German cities such as Berlin.

Before taking my leave from the land of my near downfall, I carefully reviewed the events of the recent months. One conclusion I did reach was that my boxes of native earth were the most easily traceable clues for their movement relied upon other parties, agents, carriers and the like. And why had it been so essential for me to transport so many boxes? Instinct, perhaps. Could I do without them?

Over a period of several weeks, I experimented. At the end of that time, I had come to realize that no more than a pinch of my consecrated soil was needed for rest and a filled portmanteau or two should suffice for very many years.

I set sail for France in mid-December when the nights were long and such daylight weather as there was would most likely be overcast and gloomy. Travelling on an evening fast packet from Dover, we arrived in Calais well before the morning. I arranged for my baggage to be sent on to Paris, where I had negotiated to rent an old house in a run-down district, and then set out to find refuge for I was weary.

By now I habitually carried several ounces of Transylvanian soil in a pocket for times of need and in principal I could have rested anywhere. But almost always I have a compulsion to seek somewhere old to make my repose.

Assuming bat form I circled the town until on the outskirts I discovered a small church which bore all the outward signs of dereliction. Surrounding the church was its graveyard and into this I descended, taking on my human shape once more.

A heavy, misty drizzle permeated the air and the whole area lacked adequate street lighting which made the pre-dawn gloom impenetrable and unwelcoming – to a human. For me conditions were perfect, presenting no difficulty as I can see in the dark. The churchyard was neglected and overgrown, the graves no more

than shapeless hummocks thick with weeds and surmounted
by time-weary headstones in varying states of decrepitude and
collapse.

I searched about until eventually I came upon a disused family
vault, its outer walls dripping moisture and stained by moss and
fungus growths. Such a place as was perfect for my needs. The vault
door was loose and hanging ajar and inside were niches containing
rotting coffins together with some half-dozen stone sarcophagi in
the centre of the floor.

I heaved the lid from the largest of these and threw out the
mouldering bones which were all that remained of the occupant.
I could stay here comfortably for a day or two before continuing
my journey to Paris.

As I was scattering the pathetic bones, a man's voice, coarse and
querulous, cried out from the shadows. Although his speech was
thick with regional accent, my French is good and I understood
him easily enough. "What's this?" he called. "Who's intruding in
my hideaway?"

From behind another sarcophagus he staggered into sight, an
unshaven ruffian with dulled eyes and rotten teeth. One filthy,
scarred hand clutched an absinthe bottle to his chest and everything
about him reeked of dipsomaniac. "What d'you want? Bugger off,
this is my place!"

"Take great care," I warned him. "You should beware of how you
address strangers for you do not know what they can be capable of.
I need refuge for a day or two and then I will be gone from here.
Until then, disregard me and I will disregard you."

"Oh, a bloody toff," the man sneered, "I'll wager that you can
spare me a few *sous*. Come on, hand over your money." Gripping
his bottle by the neck, he made a threatening gesture.

All the pent-up fury inside me erupted, a fury which had been
simmering since Van Helsing and his cronies had thwarted my
schemes. Seizing the oaf, I dashed him to the floor and he cried
out in agony as bones shattered. "*Non, m'sieu!*" he screamed out,
"I meant nothing by it. The vault is yours, only let me be!"

Reaching down I pulled him to me like a rough child hugging
a kitten, and giving no thought to soothing mesmerism I plunged
my fangs deep into his jugular. I had determined to abstain from
gluttonous feeding but realized that one good feast would sustain
me for some time to come. I drank deeply until at last the shrieking
animal subsided, near to expiring. His blood was foul, no doubt the
result of many years of imbibing filth, but it would have to do for
the while.

Then I cursed myself for what I had done, not from remorse

– for this is an emotion foreign to me – but for the fact that I had infected a creature not worthy to join the ranks of *Nosferatu*. Casting him down, I tore aside his ragged shirt, ripped open his body and shredded the still living heart with my talons. At last, rage abated, I was calmer. Leaving the carcass where it had fallen, I settled myself into the tomb and rested well.

In Paris I was met and greeted by a neat and prissy little man, Monsieur Jeanmaire, the agent through whom I was to rent my new home. He took me in his carriage and gradually we passed from the fashionable thoroughfares through streets which became meaner and meaner and more crowded, from these into places largely abandoned and housing only vagrants and the very poorest, until at last we reached my proposed new abode.

It was a four-sided house – probably imposing a century or so previously but now heading towards ruin – standing in several acres which were overrun with tall grasses, tangled weeds and ancient trees, dark and gnarled and leafless. The grounds were surrounded by a high brick wall topped with sharp iron spikes which were in surprisingly good condition.

"This appears to be admirable," I told Jeanmaire. "I must explain that I am a scholar and a recluse and I will brook no disturbance. Can you guarantee me the solitude I require in this place?"

"The locals consider it to be a haunted house, *m'sieu*," he replied, pressing a delicate hand to his mouth to suppress a little snigger. "Believe me, none will so much as venture beyond the gateway."

"Let me see inside," I commanded.

The interior, unmodernized and unfurnished, comprised six rooms on each of two floors together with several large basements, dank-smelling and dungeon-like. Thick wooden shutters, through which only the merest glimmer of daylight penetrated, were fastened over the windows, while the dust of years lay thick everywhere, turning opaque the festoons of cobwebs hanging from ceilings and walls. I was exceptionally pleased with the basement which was well below ground level and which I could fortify with ease.

I told Jeanmaire that I would take the property and at the rent asked, offering to pay a substantial sum in advance.

The agent toyed with his silly tooth-brush moustache, a look of doubt on his face. "Herr Szekely —" (for such was the name I had assumed) " —is obviously a man of quality," he said. "Possibly even of the nobility. To offer the Herr such a place, even although it is as stipulated, does not seem right. I can find the Herr somewhere far more suitable at very little more rent."

"The rent is irrelevant," I told him. "The house is what matters."

He continued to look doubtful and started to extol the virtues of other properties on his books, properties situated in places far more appropriate for one such as I. I needed this man's trust, at least for the present, and only a plausible explanation would allay his doubts.

"I am a refugee from my own country," I told him. "There I have offended certain high-ranking individuals who find my philosophy too radical, too threatening to their position, and who would be only too pleased to see an end to me. You will understand, sir, for has not your own lovely country had its own upheavals? I need a place to dwell where their agents would least expect to find me."

He spread his hands in that peculiarly Gallic all-purpose gesture of accord. "*M'sieu, je comprend.* Your position is safe with Jeanmaire et Cie where discretion is a byword."

"One final thing, friend Jeanmaire. Were I occasionally to need a . . . certain companionship, where would I best go to find it?"

Ever since my attack on the vagabond in the Calais tomb, I had given serious thought to my needs. I have mentioned, Roisin, that I can abstain from feeding for very long periods; yet there is always a danger that a combination of long fasting coupled with a sudden rage can make me act carelessly.

I had decided that to lessen the chance of my making indiscriminate attacks on humans, the most sensible solution would be for me to avail myself of the services of a bordello, where from time to time I could take a little discreet nourishment without any lasting effect upon my companion of the evening.

Jeanmaire pursed his lips in a diplomatic smile. "I hear that the most popular establishment with gentlemen of quality is Madame Charmaine's, close by to the Bois de Boulogne," he said. He took a card from his pocket and scribbled an address on the reverse.

And so it was that I came back to settle in Europe for a number of years. Once established in Paris, I journeyed to Berlin where, in the alias of Le Comte de Ville, I rented a similar property and alternated my time between the two cities. Unlike a human, I need little in the way of material comfort and furnishings in my homes were kept to an essential minimum: a chair or two, table or desk, some bookcases.

I acquired books, subscribed to various popular journals and through various means I was able to smuggle much of my wealth and chattels from Transylvania. (I was pleasantly surprised that these were intact, for had I been in the shoes of Van Helsing and others I would have had little compunction in looting the castle. English gentlemen such as Godalming and Harker are strange: they will happily loot whole nations and yet leave the private property of a defeated enemy intact.)

To have once again a substantial library pleased me greatly and I resumed my studies: languages, history, politics, the arts and the sciences, I absorbed all with equal facility.

Within several weeks of taking residence in Paris I asked for an appointment to meet Madame Charmaine, the brothel keeper. Reaction at first was cool, the procurer – obviously with ideas far above her station – accepting visitors only on the basis of personal recommendation. By return I sent a sealed packet containing an appetite-whetting sum in *louis d'or*, which must have been sufficiently personal for the woman for she consented to meet with me almost immediately.

The establishment was in a large mansion house, florid and gaudy with many formally attired servants and a resident orchestra. Décor in the public areas was crimson and gilt rococo and the furnishings plush, the whole well lit by magnificent Italianate chandeliers. A pompous butler with a sergeant-major's moustache and side whiskers led me to the proprietor's sitting-room, which was in very much better taste.

Madame Charmaine herself was a handsome fleshy woman who would probably have made good feeding if that had been my agenda for her. But as with Jeanmaire, I needed her as a friend for now. She offered me an elegant hand which I took, fleetingly touching my lips to it. I saw that my letter with the small heap of gold coins lay on a fine Louis Quatorze desk at one side of the room.

"Please be seated, sir," she invited and when I had taken a chair continued, "And how can I serve you, Herr . . . Szekely?"

"I wish to purchase occasional services in your house," I told her. "My needs and tastes are unusual and while not prepared to discuss them, I will pay handsomely. Before I proceed, are you prepared to accept me as a client?"

"*M'sieu*, very many of my clients pay handsomely to satisfy bizarre needs and tastes," the woman said. "My only conditions are that I am satisfied of your ability to pay and that none of my little ones suffer permanent damage."

I placed a bag containing more gold in her lap and she blinked rapidly when she had loosened the draw-string and examined the contents. "As to the other condition," I said. "You must accept the word of a . . . gentleman. You will find that your employees may need to rest for several days after a visit from me, but my fees will compensate for their lost time.

"And now I must set certain conditions of my own." She nodded acquiescence and I continued: "I will come here infrequently, perhaps three or four times a year and then only with ample notice. The sex of whichever employee you choose is immaterial but they must be young, strong and in perfect health. Do not deceive me on this point.

"Under no circumstances will I use the same employee twice. Whomsoever I patronize is to wear neither jewellery nor ornament of any kind, neither is the allocated chamber to have any kind of mirror, ornament or picture. For what I will pay you, I consider these conditions reasonable. I hold you personally responsible for checking them when I am to visit. Do not be tempted to act contrary to my instructions, for then you will incur my displeasure and I assure you, Madame, you would not enjoy that. I will contact you in the very near future; until then, I bid you goodnight."

In time I made similar arrangements with a superior house in Berlin and so I lived for more than ten years, contented with my books and my studies and my occasional light feedings.

In my feedings I took every precaution to ensure that there would be no future embarrassments. I would place my companion in a deep trance and take little more than half-a-litre or so of blood. Then – satisfied if not sated – while my companion still slept I treated the wounds with holy water which I had bribed a mendicant to obtain for me. The water I kept in a gold flask and was very careful that it did not spill upon my own flesh.

It was in 1911 that the first sign of a long-term purpose altered my apparent course in life. I had paid one of my visits to the brothel and was about to leave when the butler approached. Bowing low, he told me that Madame wished to confer with me in private. This was a singular event. In the time that I had been visiting her house, we had made little contact which is how I had wanted it. We both adhered to our pact and the stated conditions and there was no reason for us to meet. At most we exchanged reserved greetings if we happened to pass each other on the stairway or in the salon.

With some asperity I agreed, and the servant led me to Madame's sitting-room. When he had gone and the door was firmly closed, Madame Charmaine politely offered me a glass of wine. With equal courtesy I declined.

"Forgive me," she said with a coquettish laugh. "But of course you do not wish for wine. After all, you have just feasted on blood, have you not?"

A surge of rage sprang into my breast, a feeling that I had not experienced for many years. In the old days, that emotion was the precursor to a frenzied killing. Controlling an impulse to rend and tear the impudent creature, I asked: "What do you mean by that?"

There was an audible tremor in her voice. "After all . . . Herr Szekely . . . You are Undead, are you not?"

I have heard that when fury shows in my face it is a frightening sight, demonic in its intensity. So must it be, for the woman flinched back from me, her face turning white beneath her mask of rouge. She edged her way to the desk and pulled an accursed cross from the drawer. With an effort I held back from her.

"What is this to be?" I snarled. "Extortion?"

"Not at all, *m'sieu.*" Her voice was terrified but she stood her ground, certain of the power of the object in her hand.

"Then what? And how did you know? I have conditioned your employees to remember nothing."

"How did I know, *m'sieu?* After all these years? There were so many signs, and I am not ignorant of those.

"The pallor of your flesh and its dreadful chill that one time you kissed my hand. Never the same whore twice. Your insistence on the lack of personal and room decoration – terrified, I suppose, that you would be faced with a crucifix or a religious painting. Always the tiny scars on neck or breast or wrist, as if cauterisation had taken place. It adds up. And besides, did you believe that you are the only one?"

"What do you mean?" I stepped forward, prepared almost to risk the white-hot touch of her cross.

"One other of my regular clients is an Undead, *m'sieu.* And he has once or twice brought a guest. He wishes to speak with you. He is here, in my boudoir. I will leave you together and you can rely on my total discretion. The other pays me well, has done so for more years than I have known you. I keep the cross only to ensure that he does not forget himself."

In bygone days I had heard of other *Nosferatu* using human servitors, holding them in thrall with the promise of immortality to come. I have never done such a thing for I would not trust a human to that extent. The madman Renfield was an exception to my rule and then only as a means to an end, a dupe rather than a servant.

I stared intently at the woman until she nigh swooned with terror, then I nodded abruptly. She turned and tapped on the boudoir door before leaving the room, making sure to give me a very wide berth as she exited.

The inner door opened and a figure emerged. I can only imagine that what I saw was like gazing into a mirror. The man was tall and thin, with an aquiline nose, piercing eyes and full ruddy lips which showed a slight protrusion of sharply-pointed teeth. His shoulder-length hair, his small moustache and the neat Van

Dyke beard were all iron-grey in colour. But whereas I favour all
black raiment, the other was clad in a white ruffled evening shirt
with scarlet trousers and smoking jacket. There could be no doubt,
though; this man was *Nosferatu.*

"Good evening." He bowed his head slightly, one equal to
another. "I take it that you have been using an alias here. Whom
do I have the honour of addressing?"

I inclined my head in return. "I am Vlad Dracula, Prince of
Wallachia."

"Ah, I know of you. This is an honour for me, my lord Dracula.
I had heard that you were destroyed but I take it that human
cunning was no match for your own." He smiled. "I am . . . I was
in life Armand Jean du Plessis, Cardinal Richelieu."

"Vanity, vanity," I muttered. "I have always supposed myself to
be alone, save for my offspring and they are now destroyed."

Richelieu gestured me to a chair, waiting with respect until I was
seated before sitting down himself. "No, not alone, although there
are but few of us," he said. "I am in regular correspondence with the
others, all men of power in their lifetimes. In your Transylvanian
mountain fastness you were isolated – the others of us were rather
more at the centre of things, being in European countries of
international importance. We have been aware of your movements
for several years now and your discretion has been exemplary."

"And who else is there?" I asked.

"Perhaps six or seven, though we constantly watch out for others.
But their quality and lineage must be perfect. Although unaware of
your true name, your conduct indicated to us that your antecedents
were almost certainly noble. Undead of lesser status we destroy as
unworthy, although they are few now. And who have we among us?
Well, in Italy there are the Borgias, Rodrigo and Cesare. In Germany
my contemporary Wallenstein of Bohemia, in Russia Gudonov, the
Spaniard Torquemada, a couple of others." His smile was grim. "All
of us combinations of princes, statesmen, warriors and religious
leaders. How came we, I wonder, to be gifted with Unlife?

"Still, let us not concern ourselves with that for now – let us be
thankful for what is." His manner became business-like. "I wished to
meet with you, my lord Dracula, for two reasons. The first obviously
being to ascertain your identity, to determine whether you should
live or die." Again, the grim little smile. "I am thankful that we did
not have to pit ourselves against you, for I can only believe that
you might well have prevailed.

"The second reason was to ask of you a special favour. It is that
you leave France, for a very long time, if not necessarily forever. And
to leave also any other place you may visit regularly in Europe."

"Why should I?" I sneered. "Do you consider these lands to be exclusively your demesne?"

"Not at all, you misunderstand me," Richelieu said, "Such is my respect for you that I would not have the temerity to stand against you. I ask you this for the common good. Please bear with me, lord Dracula, for what I have to say is of paramount importance.

"As I have said, we are few. And we are all old Undead, discreet in our predations and careful to ensure, at this time, that we do not create any new Undead. In France and Germany at least, you have been acting in a similar way. For now, I believe it to be essential that we continue in this manner for the world is changing and rapidly.

"Soon, it will be different from anything we have known previously. I truly believe that before long, there will be a great war in Europe – and perhaps more than one – which will have worldwide implications. Kaiser Wilhelm of Germany is ambitious and acquisitive and Austria – Hungary will dance to any tune that he plays. I can see a threat of we Undead becoming extinct, even if only by accident, in such a war, and it is better that we are isolated from each other so that one at least has a chance of survival."

"There is probably much in what you say," I agreed. "Thinking myself to be alone I have worried little about the possible effects of human folly. As long as they remained unaware of me, I was happy to let them do what they would to each other. You are forcing me to reconsider, Richelieu. What would you have of me?"

"Thank you, my lord Dracula." Richelieu bowed. "We would ask you to go to America. The tentacles of a European war are unlikely to reach there and we could thus ensure that one of us – the greatest of us – remains safe. Those of us remaining here will take all possible steps to ensure our safety and I will certainly remain in correspondence with you. One day, and that day may be in the very distant future, our time will come. What do you say?"

I mused upon what Richelieu had said for some time, weighing the options, and eventually decided that he was right on all points. And America was a burgeoning land, probably destined to become a power like any unknown before. Furthermore, were I to make my home in America the chances lessened considerably of Van Helsing and the others discovering that I lived. Finally, America was a young country with a mass immigration policy and the temptation of all those teeming souls was hard to resist for *Nosferatu*, even for one determined to tread with care.

I reached across to clasp Richelieu's hand in agreement.

As it happened, almost another two years elapsed before I set foot in the United States. Careful planning was required and Richelieu – who had established an enviable network of corrupt human officials, a skill honed during his life as Louis XIII's Prime Minister – and I worked closely together. We arranged a network of Swiss bank accounts for me, transferring some of my fortune into these. Agents smuggled the rest of my gold into America, secreting it in a number of caches known only to themselves and me. Needless to say, it was necessary for all of these agents to suffer fatal accidents.

And finally we disposed of my French and German real estate. But that was near to the end of my days in Europe. I regret that Monsieur Jeanmaire and his German counterpart also died mysteriously, as did the brothel master in Berlin. Madame Charmaine was sufficiently in Richelieu's power to be permitted to live, for the time being.

During my remaining time in Europe I met with some other *Nosferatu* of Richelieu's band and we formed . . . well, we *Nosferatu* do not have friendships as such, but we formed powerful bonds and alliances. I was particularly taken with the Borgias, for their iron control of Italy had not been unlike mine own in my lands. Rodrigo, who in the latter days of his human life had been Pope, was breath-taking in guile and hypocrisy.

I told this powerful group about my sally into England and of the troubles which had beset me there, warning them to be wary in all ventures lest Van Helsing and his band of compatriots were again aroused by the passion of the hunt.

Although I would be entering America in non-human form, I was provided with skilfully forged papers showing that I had been granted status as an American citizen in 1895. And so it was that towards the end of my fifth century in this world, and like other emigrants before me, I departed my native continent to begin a new life.

I travelled packet rather than passenger, on a boat called *The Maine King*, its crew comprising hard-headed Yankees rather than superstition-ridden fools such as had manned the *Demeter* when I took passage to England. The captain had been instructed that I was an elderly and eccentric invalid who would spend the whole of the voyage in the seclusion of his cabin. Meals were to be left outside my cabin by the steward; these were sent through the porthole to the fishes during the hours of night.

The journey was uneventful but not too irksome, for with the passing of centuries one learns a certain patience. I whiled away the long hours of day and night, the long, long sea-miles, studying literature and maps of my new homeland, so that by the time we made landfall I probably knew as much about the continent and her great cities as did most of her native sons.

The first port of call in the United States was the city of New Orleans where one of my many caches of gold was stored. I slipped ashore at night – the tide being on the turn – in the form of a great wolf, easily evading the officials and labourers who, with startled cries, tried to corner me. Some shots were fired but the only bullet which struck passed through my body as if through a shadow.

I needed sustenance, for I had fasted very many months prior to embarking on *The Maine King*, and this was provided fortuitously by a huge dog which attacked me as I loped through mean and noisome dockside streets and alleys. The blood of animals is not so richly satisfying as that of humans – rather like, say, cornmush when one is accustomed only to the finest viands – but it fills the belly and has the added advantage that animals, being soulless, do not in their turn become as we *Nosferatu*.

I will not weary you with details of how I found a home. Suffice to say that I discovered an old and derelict property a little way out of the city and purchased it. Although they are nothing like Europe, I did enjoy the Louisiana wilds with their strange mists and bustling animal life and the swathes of Spanish moss draped from the trees like huge spider webs.

Again, I made arrangements at a brothel to satisfy my need for food. This time the whoremonger was a native-born American of Sicilian descent, a member of the Black Hand. Unlike his European counterparts he cared nothing for his employees, regarding them as no more than money machines. I would be safe from unwanted inquiry.

A few more years passed uneventfully The Great War raged in Europe but my fellow *Nosferatu* survived and Richelieu corresponded regularly, addressing his letters to Mr Newman, Poste Restante, New Orleans. Two pieces of news gave cause for elation. One was that Van Helsing had died in old age, choking on a fish-bone, very soon after I had left France. The other was that both Lord Godalming and Dr Seward had perished in the war: one at Ypres; the other at The Somme. The war passed in time and the world again lapsed into peace, although Richelieu said that all European countries were less happy places now.

It was in 1922 that I once again became obsessed with a woman, overwhelmed by that occasional mad lust to conquer, to engulf, to become as one for an eternity. Not since Lucy and Mina had I so desperately wanted a woman to become my blood consort.

I often stalked the night – using my power to distract attention from where I was – observing the world about me. I would visit taverns and vaudevilles, concerts and plays, even the movies; I would eavesdrop, identifying those who held positions of power and riches; I would ascertain their dwelling places and their friends and servants; I would make sure of all of those snippets of information which might at some time prove advantageous to me.

Thus it was that on a certain night I was attending a society ball at one of the great ante-bellum houses outside of the city. Or perhaps attending is not quite the right expression, for I was outside of the building looking in on them, a predatory cat gazing into the window of a butcher's shop. By and large, the guests seemed to be a tedious crowd, concerned largely with their places in the pecking order, grovelling or condescending depending on whether or not they were addressing their so-called superiors or inferiors.

An orchestra somewhere in a background salon played Strauss and Lehar and other waltz music for men in white ties and tails and women in ball gowns to dance to. My attention was caught by a burst of merry laughter from a group of younger women who were watching a similar group of young men preening and displaying in an elaborate social courtship ritual. Who says that we are so different from the animals?

The young women, richly varied in size and colouring, were all beautiful in their own ways, all of them flushed with the rich blood of life. I could almost hear the blood pumping endlessly around those lovely nubile bodies, almost inhale its warm rich coppery aroma, almost taste the thick succulence upon my palate. I turned away lest greed overcome me.

The night was fine and clear, the sky an ebony jeweller's cloth displaying a richness of diamond stars. Except for where light spilled from the house, the vast garden was a patchwork of shadows cast by great clumps of trees and shrubbery. I sat upon a stone bench, listening to the darkness, its multitude of sounds – muted, nigh non-existent, to humankind – a concerto to my ears.

Suddenly voices were raised in argument. From beneath a nearby group of magnolias I caught the whiff of a woman's scent and the stronger odour of a young male in passion, and my night-keen eyesight picked out a couple struggling a little in the shadows. Her voice was filled with indignation, his with a drunken desire.

"Haydon Lascalles! You just keep your hands to yourself and leave me be! I'm just not interested in you that way!"

"C'mon, honey, you know you want it really," was the slurred reply. "Stop making such a damned fuss and give me a kiss."

The woman was now fighting harder against the beefy and immature oaf who was attempting to embrace her, his clumsy strength slowly prevailing. As I stood, preparing to intervene, the woman raised her hand and slapped his face hard, at the same time screaming aloud.

"You goddamned bitch!" he bellowed. He pulled her towards him with his left hand, in the same instant raising a massive right fist.

As I rushed towards them, I became aware of others pouring out of the house behind me and instantly quelled my intention to kill the importunate fool. Instead I seized his collar and threw him to one side. To one of my supernormal strength his bulk was nothing and he flew from me as if he were a child, landing heavily on his back.

He glared up at me and without moving from the ground blustered: "Fifty years ago I'd have duelled with you for that, old man!"

"And fifty years ago, I would have killed you," I told him coldly. My face must have contorted into a dreadful mask for the pathetic wretch caught his breath in sudden fright and I could sense the blood draining from his fat face.

I turned to the woman and – were I human, you might have said that I had fallen in love at first sight. Latin races call it the thunderbolt. She had heavy dark hair falling about high cheekbones and slightly oval eyes which reminded me of the Slavic women of my native land. Cheeks were flushed with blood, full scarlet lips were parted slightly and her body radiated wrathful heat. But it was not just the outer beauty which called to me, for that never was an imperative consideration when choosing a mate. It was an inner and indescribable thing, something which always makes me certain that someone – man or woman – is a fit consort for *Nosferatu*. My hunger *screamed*.

"What's going on here?" The speaker was almost a caricature, the archetypal Southern colonel, tall, skinny and sun-withered, hair white and goatee beard long and wispy. His posture cried out suppressed rage as he glared from the sprawling youth to me. Another man, a similar type but shorter and somewhat stout, pushed his way through the small crowd to pull the young man to his feet.

The woman clutched at the Southern colonel's arm. "Daddy, Haydon was molesting me and this fine gentleman very bravely came to my rescue."

The Colonel's face purpled and he stepped threateningly towards the miscreant. The second man stopped him. "I'll deal with this, Deschamps. He's my son. My sincerest regrets, Miss Josephine. When Haydon sobers up, I'm sure that he will be pleased to make a public apology."

He slapped his son hard on the cheek. "Get home, you're drunk and a disgrace!"

Haydon Lascalles retreated several yards then turned to point a shaking finger at me. "I'll see you again some day. Then we'll find out how tough you really are."

"Excuse him, sir, he's young and foolish," said Lascalles senior. He pushed his son away, telling him once more to get on home.

I bowed slightly. "Does the tiger find it necessary to pardon the yapping of the jackal? It is forgotten, sir."

The man called Deschamps grasped my hand and released it almost immediately, as if startled by its chilled strength. "My gratitude, sir. I am Georges Deschamps and this is my daughter Josephine."

"Szekely. Count Szekely. A very recent resident of your beautiful and great land." I bowed to Josephine Deschamps and took her hand to kiss the fingers lightly. It was as well that the still curious crowd had not dispersed, for I yearned to lap avidly at her blood.

"Again, my thanks, Count," said Deschamps. "Haydon Lascalles is a boorish wastrel who merits a sound thrashing."

"In my day I would have—" I stopped myself in time. I had been about to say that in my day I would have had him impaled and that had he taken less than two days to die, the executioner would have joined him on the stake. I smiled a little in the dark, relishing memories of those lost, cruel times. "In my day I would have been honoured to thrash him," I concluded.

Deschamps pressed something into my hand. "My card, sir," he said. "You will be a welcome guest in my home. Perhaps, Count, you will honour us with a visit very soon." *An invitation—my sanction*!

"Alas, sir, business is to take me away for some weeks," I lied. "But when I return . . . well, now that you have so kindly invited me, I doubt you will be able to keep me away."

We all laughed at this supposed pleasantry as I made my farewells. The pathetic foolishness of humans. How easy they can make it for we *Nosferatu*. Now that I had received Deschamps' gratitude-impelled invitation, nothing could gainsay me entrance to their dwelling place. And I would act upon that invitation, sooner than they could know, to dine with a member of their family. As I walked away from them my tongue lapped at lips and fangs as if I were a beast of the forest confronting a helpless fawn.

Despite the passions tearing at me, I did not plunge in rashly as would have done a young *Nosferatu*. No, instead I spent several evenings and nights reconnoitring the Deschamps home, merging in with the light ground mists which crept lazily through their property, exploring the layout of house and gardens, casting forth my mind to identify and know family members and servants and their locations during those crucial nocturnal hours. Containing my patience was a burden, for I was torn by the almost irresistible cravings which torment my kind in these circumstances.

At length I chose my night. Generally the household retired at about midnight but I stayed my hand with difficulty for another hour or so beyond the time when I sensed that the last occupant had fallen asleep. At the end of this lull I made my way to that part of the house below Josephine's own balcony and bedroom window.

I scaled the outer wall with ease, instinctively finding finger and toe holds imperceptible to humans, gaining the balcony within brief moments. Despite the night's humidity windows and screens were firmly closed, doubtless to prevent access of pestilence-ridden night-flying insects. The family were patently unaware of other, more potent, dangers of the night. The windows were neither let nor hindrance to me and I slid with ease through the tiny gaps available.

The moon was full that night and shed its golden light into Josephine's chamber, casting chequered shadowy patterns on floor and walls almost to ceiling height. The apartment was huge—as becomes that in the home of a wealthy family—and was well appointed with fine antique furnishings, the centrepiece being a fine leather-topped escritoire with chair upon which a silken gown had been carelessly tossed. Against the wall opposite the windows was a vast and solid four-poster bed with heavy drapes held back by loops of silken cord.

There, in charming disarray, lay my sleeping Josephine, mane of hair spread across fine lawn pillows like dark weed in a milky sea, a single sheet pushed back to well below her waist. Her soft lips were parted and with each gentle breath she took I could hear the Lorelei song of virgin blood.

With my mind I summoned her to wakefulness and slowly she roused, stretching lazily and gazing around the room until she spied me there at the window. With a gasp she sat up, as if about to scream for help. I placed a finger against my lips, imposing silence upon my victim, my love.

For seconds only she resisted and then yielded, mentally and physically, relaxing back against the pillows, eyes shining in terrified fascination. She made but one more sound. "You!" she gasped.

For long minutes I did no more than stand and watch, partly to appreciate her beauty and partly to whet my appetite to the full with anticipation. Then in response to an imperious gesture of my hand, Josephine slowly loosened the top of her night-gown, drawing it aside to reveal one perfect breast, the dark nipple stark against the white flesh. I could see the gentle throbbing of a vein in her neck. I settled by her side, taking one hand in mine to kiss it gently.

"This is a dream," she whispered.

"It will be but as a dream," I told her. "A recurring dream of which you will have no memory. And from the dream you will slip into the longest sleep of all, a sleep from which you will awake immortal to take your proper place at my side."

I lowered my head and drank deeply, more deeply than I had intended that first night but love knows few restraints. I drank my full and more from the fountain of that wine which gives life to us all whether *Nosferatu*, human or animal. During the day that followed and the days following that, I rested more completely than I had rested for many long years.

It took Josephine Deschamps one week to die. The family physician and the specialist he consulted were no Van Helsings. They puzzled over their patient at the beginning and they puzzled until the very end. They assigned nurses to her day and night but they were no obstacle for I needed to do nothing more than entrance them deeply before coming to Josephine.

On that final night I was at the bedside studying my soon-to-be consort. Her flesh was pallid and drawn, the sole colour being two bright spots of fever on the now skeletal cheekbones. The eyes which looked back at me glittered madly, while pale lips pulled back from hueless gums and white teeth which were taking on the sharper aspects of *Nosferatu*.

"Soon, my love," I reassured her.

"Soon, my master," she replied, voice weak and resigned.

I took nourishment from Josephine for the final time then opened a vein in my wrist, holding it to her mouth so that in turn she could drink. She clutched fiercely at my hand, like a feeding baby clutching at the mother's breast. Then she collapsed back. She would be dead by dawn, I knew. Then it would be but a short wait until the rebirth.

I knew that funerals tend to be held swiftly in the Southern States, such is the corruptive quality of the climate. I also knew that because of flood risk in the local environs, interments were frequently above ground in stone niches. I guessed that a family of status such as Josephine's would have its own crypt somewhere in or near the city and I had spent a little time searching for this. When I did find it, I was pleased with it, for it was a large, plain edifice, unadorned save for double bronze doors and a simple plaque inscribed: DESCHAMPS.

Josephine's mortal remains were taken to a funeral parlour

popular with the wealthy. Late at night, after the last mourners had gone, I slipped in to view the body. I told the attendant mortician that I was a family friend just returned from Europe and that having heard the sad news I was constrained to pay respects. He led me to a tiny chapel where the open casket rested on a bier beneath a wall-mounted cross. I dared not approach too closely; to allay suspicion I mendaciously explained to the attendant that I was a Mussulman.

Nonetheless, I could see Josephine clearly enough from where I stood and noted that cheeks and lips were full and red with apparent good health, that a little smile seemed to touch the wonderful mouth. I was pleased with this, for the signs were now there that she was *Nosferatu*. Resurrection varied in my experience but it was unlikely to be more than three or four days before she emerged from the tomb, ravenous and ready to be tamed and tutored.

The day of the funeral was dull and heavily overcast and I watched the actual interment from beneath the shade of a grove of trees beyond the graveyard. I began my vigil that night and for several nights thereafter, shielded by localized fog which I had summoned to the area. There was no sign of Josephine emerging but I remained calm for I know how very much the return can vary from person to person.

You may wonder at my apparent unconcern, but the truth of the matter is that it is a far better thing for new *Nosferatu* who have been entombed to make their own way to freedom. It is an essential part of the process of discovery.

After the fourth night I began to feel alarm and by the sixth night I could only conclude that something was seriously amiss. Perhaps some bumbling primitive had sealed Josephine's coffin with a cross, inadvertently denying her release. I had to discover the truth for myself and find some way to release Josephine from her prison.

I passed through the knife-edged gap in the bronze doors and entered the resting place of several generations of Deschamps where each coffin was sealed into the vault wall by a stone slab. Each of these was adorned solely with the name of the occupant, as a quick search revealed with the newest, deepest incision: JOSEPHINE DESCHAMPS 1901–1922.

I ripped the slab from its place and revealed the casket which I lifted down carefully. I scrutinized the external dimensions but could see nothing like cross or religious icon which might have held Josephine helpless and immobile. I tore away the lid, the deeply sunken screws screaming in protest as I did so.

Josephine lay there peacefully, still with the healthy look that I had observed in the funeral parlour. It was now well into the night and she should have been responding to the initial cravings for human blood. I examined her carefully but could see no visible signs of Unlife. Baring my chest, I incised a vein and blood spurted freely. Lifting Josephine to me, I pressed her mouth firmly to the wound.

She did not respond, hanging limp in my arms with blood trickling down unmoving lips to stain the front of her burial gown. I touched her cheek in wonderment and noticed a greasy feel beneath my fingers. Swiftly I rubbed and her face became a mask, smeared as if by the bloody tears of a clown. *She was masked by rouge and paint!*

I laid my mouth to her neck but barely had my fangs penetrated the cold flesh than I was assailed by a foul chemical stench. I tore the gown from the young body. Her torso, from shoulders to pubis, was marred by a hideous Y-shaped cut, crudely stitched. There was no blood inside my darling, only a noxious preservative.

Embalmed! She had been embalmed! Her heart and entrails had been ripped out and she had been filled with some disgusting laboratory concoction. Josephine was nothing now, nothing more than a ruined husk. Emitting a bestial howl of frustration and rage, I ripped the corpse limb from limb, strewing its parts about that dreadful chamber of the dead. Grief unassuaged, I tore the Deschamps vault apart, destroying coffins and scattering bones and cadavers until there was nothing left for me to ravage.

Had the perpetrators of this vile outrage been cast before me at that moment, I would have made them suffer until they were crying for the ecstasy of death! I thought of the time when as a human ruler I had dined amidst the twenty thousand I had caused to be impaled after a memorable battle. Their anguish would have been as nothing to what I could have inflicted on that night in the Deschamps vault.

Sitting among the carnage I had wrought, I gradually regained some composure. The outrage had been committed and there was nothing now I could do about it. Night was drawing on and although an hour or more to dawn, I should leave before sunrise when my powers would wane.

I stepped forth from the ruin of that shattered sepulchre into slender veils of mist which still blanketed the place. I did not immediately metamorphose into bat or wolf but made my way instead towards the high gates of the cemetery entrance where at last I emerged into clear air. Without warning a beam of light shone suddenly into my face and eyes, momentarily dazzling me although I was able to make out a trio of shapes beyond the glare.

For an instant I thought that I had encountered a police patrol until I heard a familiar voice, triumphant with tipsy and malicious glee.

"Well, look what we got here boys. It's the old feller who interfered between me and my girl. I told you I thought I'd seen him hanging around here." My eyes had adjusted quickly and I could now see beyond the flashlight's brightness. Haydon Lascalles had two friends with him, as big and burly as himself, and his courage was proportionately greater.

"Now my Josephine's gone," he was saying. "And gone without even knowing what a good man I'd have been to her. And it's all this bastard's fault. Reckon he's a damned pervert too, always hanging around cemeteries. What we gonna do about him?"

"You sure this is him, Hay?" said one of the others. "He don't look so old to me."

"It's him right enough, Brad. Must have been using hair colouring." Lascalles sneered at me. "You think that hair dye would get you a nice piece of young ass, Granddad?"

I stared hard at the trio, barely controlling my ferocity. "Do not arouse me," I hissed at them. "Walk away now and you may all live to see another sun rise."

My tone had an effect on the third youth, the one holding the flashlight, for he sidled a step or two back. "Let's leave this, we can tell the cops about this guy creeping round the graveyard at nights."

"Hell, no!" Haydon Lascalles leapt at me, swinging a huge hunting knife he had snatched from beneath his coat. The weapon passed through me harmlessly and I gave a harsh laugh. Disarming my impassioned assailant, I retained an easy hold on him while disembowelling the one called Brad with an upward sweep of the keen-edged blade. Dashing Brad's corpse aside, I seized the third man—who was striking at me with the flashlight—and snapped his spine. He fell to the ground, writhing and emitting pathetic mewling noises.

The reek of fresh gore from the gutted carcass that had been companion Brad was too overpowering for me to ignore. Pulling Haydon Lascalles close, I laughed into his face before striking at his throat. He barely had time to glimpse my fully exposed fangs, barely had time enough to recognize his fate and die wailing for mercy; but time enough he had to be plunged into a mental maelstrom of Hell.

Cowardly bully and wastrel Haydon Lascalles may have been, but his blood was thick and strong as it gushed. Young blood, invigorating blood, blood filled with vitality, *blood*—the well of all power. I drank until bloated, until I could feel hot streams overflowing teeth and lips to pour in rivulets down my chin. Then I twisted his gaping head from his shoulders, tossing it contemptuously to one side.

The one with the broken back had remained conscious throughout his friend's death and his horrified eyes, from which bitter tears streamed, bulged at me. I stirred him with my foot as I glanced at the sky. There was time a-plenty and I was strong from my repast.

Wordlessly I began to call upon certain little friends and allies in their subterranean haunts and could hear their answering cries, as yet too highly pitched for the cur cowering before me. But soon he would hear, oh yes, soon . . .

They came pouring from the gutters and the sewers and from the very tombs themselves, pouring in their hundreds and thousands, squirming, furry little bodies jostling and struggling and fighting for position.

And as I directed my little friends, the rats, the crippled man heard and understood and began to scream. He was still screaming when the tumbling ravenous masses swarmed over the three bodies and sharp little teeth began to rend and tear at their master's gift, at the bountiful and unexpected feast . . .

I rested for some weeks thereafter, replete and rejuvenated, but still rankling at the loss of a worthy mate. I needed to know more about how Josephine had been stolen from me and finally visited the funeral parlour from which my love had taken her final journey.

I sought out the mortician who owned the company and interviewed him in his sumptuous office to the rear of the premises. Here, where no doubt he received all of the grieving loved ones, the air was scented as of flowers, but with my finer senses I could detect the malodorous fetor of the preparations he had used to destroy my Josephine.

"I have come here from Europe with my family," I told him. "And now it seems that soon my father will die. I wish to ensure the finest funeral for him and I was recommended to you by Mr George Deschamps. I have been advised that in your mighty and progressive land, it is the done thing to embalm the deceased. In the old country, you understand, we lack such sophistication."

"Indeed, sir," said the mortician, an ingratiating smile upon his thin lips, thinking I suppose of the gold he could extort from me when he entombed my non-existent father. "Anybody who is anybody now insists upon embalming for their dear departed ones. It is not a cheap process but we guarantee full satisfaction. As you were recommended by Mr Deschamps you are aware of his own recent bereavement. Sir, his poor daughter was a triumph of my art. By the time that I had finished my task, she was as if she slept. I take great pride in my skills and my work, sir."

I could not hate this man, for he was nothing other than a hired lackey. I did kill him, of course, but quickly and mercifully.

I moved away from New Orleans after that. I moved a great deal, in fact, never staying for more than three or four years in one place. I fasted a great deal, only feeding when absolutely necessary. I preyed upon animals or society's outcasts, always destroying the latter when they were no longer of use to me. I stayed away from small towns where people tended to know each other well. Large cities or remote wild places, where both predator and prey could remain well hidden, were the most suitable places for me.

I continued to take a great interest in world events and politics and kept up my correspondence with Richelieu and the others. We discussed the likelihood of war breaking out afresh in Europe, agreeing that the rise of National Socialism made this inevitable. Throughout the thirties they made certain arrangements and by the time that Hitler invaded Poland all were safely hidden in those lands most likely to remain neutral. Like myself they continued to live with discretion.

The Nazi hordes swept across Europe, wreaking death and destruction on a scale unthinkable to those of us who were ancient warriors. At my most tyrannical, I could not have matched them.

Jonathan and Mina Harker both died in their seventies, not of natural causes but in a bombing raid on the City of Plymouth. Their son Quincy was apparently most valorous at the Normandy landings and was awarded the Victoria Cross, posthumously. I salute his memory.

I found my next Josephine–or, I should say, Josephines, for they were twins, brother and sister–in the early nineteen-fifties in Madison, Wisconsin. Both unmarried, both Doctors of Philosophy at the University, they were scions of an old and wealthy family. This time it was not a matter of the Thunderbolt but a cold recognition that these two, with proper control and guidance, had the potential to become great *Nosferatu*. They cared for little save their work and each other and treated all about them with a cold aristocratic hauteur which amused me greatly.

I took my time with these two. Many months passed before they died and by the time they did so, both their physician and their family's mortician were fully under my control. The physician stipulated that an autopsy was unnecessary, he having been treating both for pernicious leukaemia. The mortician was fully persuaded that he had completed embalming the two, whereas he had done no more than apply paint and powder to the bodies. They were mine!

Their funeral took place upon a bright spring day, and that evening I went to the church where the service had taken place. I began to search the adjoining cemetery for the freshly dug graves and while I was doing so a custodian approached and asked if he could help me.

"There was a brother and sister buried here today," I said. "From the University. I wish to pay my respects at their gravesides."

"Their graves, sir?" The custodian looked puzzled. "Didn't you know that they were cremated? So many families prefer that now . . ."

It may have been an expression of incandescent rage upon my face or it may have been the hideous grinding of my teeth which frightened the man, for he scuttled away from me, glancing back once in terror.

Once more my schemes were frustrated! What was it about these humans? So pitifully weak compared with such as I and yet somehow they consistently managed to impede my way. Embalming and now cremation. Such irony.

Had Richelieu been correct all those years ago? Were we *Nosferatu* doomed to extinction, were we to become an endangered species partly because of our insistence on quality for our offspring, partly because of the changing ways in which humans disposed of their dead? Our very nature demanded that we should be a dominant species and yet here we found ourselves in a parlous position akin to the tiger and the whale.

I moved from place to place in America, engaging upon a great study of their funeral rites. I frequented morticians' premises and mortuaries and graveyards. I attended the funerals of acquaintances and strangers and visited morticians' colleges listening to lectures and observing training. I immersed myself in the human rites of death.

And everywhere it was the same. Those worthy of becoming *Nosferatu* were invariably embalmed or cremated, or even both. Only the poorer people, those unworthy of my attention other than as cattle, continued to be buried in a natural state.

You may wonder why I did not simply use such creatures and then move on, leaving them to their own devices. I have mentioned that a young *Nosferatu* is driven by insatiable appetite. Consider the old conundrum of shoeing a horse: it needs four shoes, each with eight nails and you charge a penny for the first nail, two pennies for the second, four pennies for the third and so on. Calculate and you quickly realize that the cost is prohibitive. And so it would be with new and uncontrolled *Nosferatu*. Soon there would be a world empty of all but *Nosferatu*, which is unthinkable.

In Europe, even, according to my allies, embalming and cremation have become the accepted way, and they too have undergone the loss of potentially excellent consorts.

Another irony is that the human race–those, that is, who believe in or believed in us–hold us to be monsters. And yet, Roisin Kennedy, consider the twentieth century and then ask yourself just how monstrous we really are. Look upon what the century has given you: Hitler, Stalin, Mao-Tse Tung, major monsters all, wreaking so much more havoc than would any intelligent *Nosferatu*.

And your minor monsters. Amin in Africa, Pol Pot in Asia, even in my own land the dreadful Nicolai Ceaucescu. And the almost invisible monsters: the scientists who develop more and more terrible weapons, the men who sell such weapons, the so-called "good" politicians who are prepared to advocate the use of such weapons. Tell me, how is it that such men can be considered more human than one such as I? *How?*

I wandered from place to place, here and there renting tumbledown properties unwanted by others, often spending long periods in a state not unlike hibernation, emerging to find myself ever more disgusted with humanity and what they were becoming.

At last I discovered this State of Oregon, and this house which called to me; it is one of those rare dwelling places which seems to be a part of the land on which it stands, seems to spring from the soil. So it was with my fortress in Transylvania which felt as if it grew from the very rock upon which it stood. And so it is with this house; although not old in the sense of which I am old, it is old within this land of America and it grows from the fertile ground like the forest around it.

For many years now, we superior *Nosferatu* have remained inactive. We have observed the world and what is happening to it and we can no longer condone it. We have debated carefully among ourselves and we have reached an important conclusion. There has been too much of the human monster.

The time has come for us to re-establish our rightful place. It will not happen immediately, for we move with stealth. However, we have set in hand a series of stratagems whereby we *Nosferatu* will move surely and inexorably, taking ourselves away from the path of the endangered species to the high road of a dominant one.

When our current plans reach fruition, perhaps by the end of this century, almost certainly no later than the second decade of the next, the world will be a place of enduring peace, controlled by *Nosferatu*. The human race will remain unaware of us, yet they will be our slaves and our livestock. *Homo superior* is about to come into his own: *requiescat in pace, Homo sapiens*!

And that, dearest Roisin Kennedy, is my narrative. As yet you can have little inkling of how good it has been for me to talk with you. Human or *Nosferatu*, the need to share one's dreams and ambitions with another becomes sometimes pressing. You wonder about the unique experience I promised you. As for that, you have already experienced it. But have patience and I will explain in a moment.

Do you not notice something different about me? Ah, exactly. I look much younger, I am less thin and my hair and whiskers are darker.

When describing to you my *Nosferatu* powers, I mentioned my regret that I am unable to halt time in its relentless progress. I do have the ability, though, to give the illusion that I have stopped time. Tell me, Roisin Kennedy, how long have you been here? I see, one night.

Will it astonish you, lovely Roisin, when I tell you that you have been here for considerably more than a week? It is with the power of the will, the strength of the mind, that I create my illusions, that I make you believe little more than a few hours have passed. As for your unique experience—*why, you yourself are now Nosferatu.*

You have awakened from death to a superior state of life. Soon you will thirst and I will control the appeasement of that thirst. Carefully at the outset, until like a new child you come to learn and practise self-control.

Understandably you are unsure whether or not to believe me. Why not take that delicate little mirror from your purse once more and confront your image. There—*see*! Why, you have shattered it into pieces with the force of your throw. Faugh! do not concern yourself with that. It was but a human bauble for which you no longer have any use.

I gave my word of honour that I intended you no harm? Well, I do not consider that I have done you harm. I have released you to a higher plane of life, and what is the harm in that? Seduction is preferable to force as you will discover.

Now listen closely to me. The dawn of a new world order approaches and you can be—are intended to be—a part of it. Among others around the world, you were *chosen*.

Do you recall how it was that you first saw my newspaper advertisement? Precisely, it was shown to you by a friend who knew how your vitality was ground down by ennui. In effect, an agent of mine prepared to sell her friend for . . . well, shall we say thirty pieces of silver?

There are others. Throughout this immense land of yours, others—more than at first I allowed you to believe—have answered my call and are awaiting the invitation to visit with me. All of you were selected with care, in the way that a breeder would select the finest stock: for intelligence, for positions in life, for family power and for influence.

Your own family, Roisin, has wealth and power and influence in abundance. In the past, some have aspired to the most exalted positions of status in the land, some have achieved them. They can continue to do so. Those who have no direct power are frequently power brokers. With you as my consort I can infiltrate that family and use them, just as together *we* will infiltrate and use the families of the others who will come at my summons. With you as helpmeet, those who wait so eagerly to meet their "reclusive European nobleman" can be altered so much more quickly. Our offspring, Roisin, will be awesome, mighty. Soon we will have puppets in the most influential positions in government and finance and society. And through them we will rule.

The web of the *Nosferatu* is spreading, its strands adhering and corrupting wheresoever we require them to. Throughout Europe Richelieu, the Borgias, the others, have all ensnared new subjects from the highest echelons. There may be in existence other worthy *Nosferatu,* perhaps to the east, and we seek to ferret them out and bring them into our alliance. We cannot be stopped, we *will not* be stopped. And none will be aware of this silent acquisition. Who was it who said that Satan's greatest trick was to make mankind not believe in him?

You appear to be horrified. So are we all when first we awaken to this enhanced existence. But then comes the hunger and the awareness, and the horror soon passes. Your initial reluctance is understandable, though, and I will not compel you into my Empire. I will be American, democratic; I will offer you free choice.

It is dawn now, and having feasted well I go to rest. You died and were reborn within this room and it must be your temporary abode. In time, and if your decision is to become one with me, to become Dracula's first consort both in his New World dominions and in the Greater World, then I will arrange a more fitting place for you to rest.

If you do not wish to join with me, then so be it: there is a way for you to end it. You will see that the windows are well covered with heavy velvet drapes. Outside the sun is rising and it promises to be a fine, bright day. When I have retired, you may–if you wish–draw aside those drapes to enjoy that brilliant sunshine.

   I do hope that you will not choose such a course, dearest Roisin, *for we are the future.*

Roberta Lannes

Melancholia

Roberta Lannes is a native Southern Californian. Since 1971 she has been teaching English, fine art, graphics, journalism and various literature courses in junior and senior high school.

Her first horror story was published in Dennis Etchison's anthology Cutting Edge, *since when her short stories have appeared in such magazines and anthologies as* Fantasy Tales, Iniquities, Pulphouse, Lord John Ten, Alien Sex, Splatterpunks I and II, The Bradbury Chronicles, Still Dead: Book of the Dead 2, Deathport, Dark Voices 5, Best New Horror 4, The Year's Best Fantasy and Horror Seventh Annual Collection, Dark Terrors, Off Limits: Tales of Alien Sex, Golden Tears Ruby Slippers, Darkside: Horror for the Next Millennium, Love in Vein II, Lethal Kisses, The Mammoth Book of Frankenstein *and* The Mammoth Book of Werewolves. *A short story collection,* The Mirror of Night, *was recently published by Silver Salamander Press.*

Like nearly everyone else in Los Angeles, Dracula is in therapy . . .

THAT I AM bereft, perhaps insane with grief and melancholia, is beyond dispute. That I seek to take my own life as a result, may be up for contention, but it is my choice. What I leave behind, here, is a sort of last will and testament. More testament than will, since all that I leave is the myth, and mystery.

I, Dracula, Prince of Darkness, have lived too long a life, full of depravity on a par with no other, compulsions beyond what the great artists of pain might imagine, and a loneliness that, until recently, lies deep within me, unexamined. I have hurt many, killed some, and left others with the same affliction from which I suffer. In all my memory, I've brought true joy to only one. And that one is gone. I have no more reason to go on.

Ironically, it was to love that would become my ruin. To love, and to enter analysis.

Most know my history, or a version of it, but no one knows of the last thirteen years. No one but myself, Ashley Lark Hibbert, and Dr Alex Bloward PhD, psychologist. I am telling it here so my death might be understood, and in that, so my life.

I have worked nearly my entire existence, which will destroy the myth of my endless independent wealth, but perhaps will show all that this Dracula was far more worldly, resourceful and diverse than imagined. When I came to the City of the Angels, I found my calling working the graveyard shift at a shelter for homeless and runaway children in Hollywood.

I have never been fond of children, but I found the bedevilled souls who ended up in the haven on Las Palmas to be clever, wicked and defiled, and therefore fascinating. That they were also wounded from this experience on the streets, and abusive homes, was of no interest to me. I wasn't called to heal the poor bastards, just watch them sleep and keep others from wandering in to sell drugs or seduce a sorry body.

There, I met Ashley. She came in writhing and hollering in the hands of two Christian Soldiers, a group of evangelical teenage pus-faced fanatics who "cleanse the streets of Sodom" as part of a volunteer army "sent from God". She was tall, blonde, skinny, and no different from most of the kids brought in by the Christian Soldiers, a prostitute.

Sitting in my office, which amounted to nothing more than a corner of a room strewn with tatami mats and sleeping bags inhabited by teenagers, I watched as they threw her into the intake seat across from me. Some of the sleeping lot woke and complained, but most snored on. They held her as I retrieved the proper forms from my desk and wearily began the futile process of writing down a string of false information, all of which would later be nothing less than confusing if used in the actual attempt of locating the girl.

"Name?"

"Princess Daisy." She snarled at me.

I wrote it down. "Age?"

She stared at my writing. "Fifty."

I wrote that as well. "Address, if any?"

"Address . . . you've got to be kidding. Hell, the corner of Hollywood and Vine. That's as good as any. The motel around the corner. What difference does it make? I'll be back on the street in an hour . . ." She rolled her eyes.

"We're not the police, Miss Daisy. We don't release you. We don't hold you, either." I frowned at the burly idiots holding her. They loosened their grip on her and she rubbed her arms.

"You two can go. I'll handle the princess here." I smiled as vacantly as I could manage.

When they were gone, Ashley, then the princess, looked around at the sleeping forms and took me in more carefully.

"What is this place, a hostel?"

"It's a shelter. A place for runaways to crash so they don't have to sell themselves. The bullies for Jesus seem to think it's easier to dump the lowlife here than take them into the church. I'd have thought they wanted to save them. Isn't that what their sort do?"

She was squinting at me in the dim light. "Wow, a deep thinker. Great. So I can go?"

"You can go. You can also come back anytime you want to. It's relatively clean, dry, and sometimes there's even food and clean clothes donated by some Samaritan. Nothing worthy of a fashion statement, but it beats shoes with holes in them. And then there's my scintillating company. As you can see, I don't have anyone to converse with at these hours."

"Yeah, well, then, bye." She stood, turned to go, then looked back to me. "By the way, my real name is Ashley."

"Nice name. Mine's . . . Vlad." Sometimes I use that name, though we were never the same person. One of many of my myths I resent.

"Vlad? Russian, right?"

"Romanian. But I've been in this country a long time."

"Sure, I'll come visit sometimes. When it gets slow . . . you know, out there." She pointed girlishly to the streets.

"Whenever." I was clearly disinterested, which somehow intrigued her.

She sauntered out into the fall night, and I wasn't to see her for a ridiculously long three hours. When she returned, she was bruised on her forehead, cheekbone, and had a nasty welt on her neck. I enquired if she wanted medical attention, but she asked only that I sit beside her while she slept on the only mat left available. I said I'd watch her, but that I needed to be at the desk for the phone, and such. She shrugged, but I could see she was hurt.

I left at six and she was snoring as loudly as the next guy.

Ashley began haunting the shelter, but only after she'd earned out the night. Sometimes she'd try to engage me in conversation, but mostly I sat listening to her tales of torrid and tragic family dysfunction. She was fifteen, and already had seven years of therapy behind her.

At first, she interested me no more than any other bastard who fell into the shelter. I was simply doing my job, earning enough to keep a dark room for the daylight hours. I had my free time to ferret out a good vein before I went to work. Perhaps that was why, in part, I was often lethargic and uncaring with the kids. That and I simply have never spent enough time with anyone to develop an attachment or emotional bond.

Then, Ashley got pregnant. I hadn't seen her for nearly four months. She was different. Bulging a bit at the belly. And she glowed. Had put on weight.

A Madonna. That's what she was.

Ashley sat down, put a stuffed make-up bag on the desk and sighed. "Vlad, you're my only friend. I need a place to live until my baby's born, and then I'll split. I have enough money to pay part of the rent. I don't do drugs, but your sort never believe that anyway. Would you take me in?"

Maybe it was the way she looked. That I hadn't had a meal in twenty-four hours. Or gradually, I'd come to miss her and felt some kind of connection to her after all this time. Regardless of why, I said I would.

It didn't dawn on me until I left for home at six that I would have to tell her who I really was, and assure her silence before she could stay a night. Or day. Seemed we both worked at night and might sleep all day. An auspicious sign.

I sat her down in the dinette and paced as I explained.

"Okay, here's the story. Don't interrupt me. My name is Dracul, I am a count from Transylvannia. I am commonly known as Count Dracula, and I'm far older than I can remember. I am a vampire, I survive because I live on human blood, and I can't have you living here with me unless you understand that if you tell anyone this truth, you endanger my very existence. And ruin your chances for having a place to stay, since I'd have to leave, and you'd be summarily put back on the street."

She grinned. "Helloooo, Halloween was in October. This is March?"

I froze. "You don't believe me?"

"Besides the fact that you have very long, ink-black hair you keep tied up in a band, have skin that's clearly never seen the sun, and eyes the colour of kiwi, I'd just say you're a very weird guy who needs to believe he's a guy who turns into a bat. Fine, just don't be drinking my blood, okay? I need to keep some to feed junior, here." She nodded down to her belly.

"You don't believe me." So few had known the truth in the past, and all were in awe when they learned it. I didn't know how to approach her incredulity.

"Does it matter? I need you. You could be Napoleon for all I care."

She was right. It didn't matter. I listed my rules for living with me, and she shrugged at all of them.

"Anything's better than living with my family. I sleep all day, too. But I'll be eating a lot. I can't seem to help that. But I won't bug you. Promise. I'm actually grateful."

She looked at me then with something I came to learn later was love. Gratitude isn't love, though that was there as well. Dr Bloward taught me that.

For three months we lived together. I grew more and more fond of her, to the point of distraction. I found it difficult to concentrate on my seductions in order to feed. I got sloppy, and I admit, a bit too preoccupied and aggressive. I nearly killed a woman in Los Feliz. When Ashley had the baby and gave it away, her sadness and guilt became mine. We were becoming something of a family, albeit an odd one.

It became obvious after a few weeks that it was time for her to leave, as she'd agreed. To go back to the streets, selling herself, I imagined. Yet neither of us said anything, me because I'd come to care about her as much as I could anything, and she, I learned later, was thoroughly and blissfully in love. So she just stayed.

One early evening, when I was about to go out to find my sustenance, she sat down on the bed as I dressed.

"You think of me as a sister, don't you." It was a statement.

"I don't know . . . I've never had a sister. Do you? Think of me as a brother?"

She chuckled. "I think knowing you're hundreds of years old sort of kills that notion, even if you look like a man in his late twenties."

"Oh, so now you believe me . . . Well, does this notion include not thinking of me as a potential lover?" My preternaturally still heart fluttered.

She squinted at me just then. "I'm . . . afraid to think of you that way. I don't know why."

"As am I afraid to think of you that way."

She brightened a bit. "You've actually considered it?"

My turn to brighten. "Well, yes, of course. You haven't then?"

"Oh, hell, yes, I have. I'm just afraid to . . . you know, do anything about it."

"We are good together, aren't we." It wasn't a question, either.

She nodded vigorously. "Yeah, really good. But can we . . . you know . . . *be* together? A vampire and a regular girl?"

I was suddenly young, recalling my youth with a longing I'd never known. Had I felt this way once?

"I don't know, Ashley. Do you want to find out?" Please, I thought, please.

"Could we? Vlad . . . I don't want to go back out there. I want to stay with you."

"Ashley . . ." I opened my arms and she leaned warmly into me.

The concussion of two conflicting feelings overwhelming me was almost unbearable. Somehow, in the months we'd lived together, we'd stayed sufficiently apart to keep my blood hunger at bay. My lechery had not so easily been contained. Suddenly, now, my appetite and my profound lust battled for preeminence. Under my nose, her jugular pulsed, and her pink and luscious girl-skin gleamed radiantly, voluptuously. The scent of her made me swoon. I thought, for so long, I couldn't feel anything. Now I'd been tossed into a whirlpool of emotions.

"Kiss me." She turned her face up to mine.

My feeding incisors began extending, and I salivated, ready for blood. I could feel my eyes burrowing into hers, turning her into a helpless victim, not a willing partner. Could I ever simply make a woman my lover?

My Ashley froze, put her hands on my shoulders and pushed me to arm's length. "You asshole, I'm not going to let you turn me into a snack. I want to be your lover."

Oh, the spirit of the her! I still reel at her memory. The Prince of Darkness's wiles weren't going to work on such as this worldly girl.

"I know, Ashley. My body's taking over. I have no idea what to do."

She grinned. "I love it when you get all little-boy lost, and stop being that big old stuffy Dracula."

"All well and good, you're happy, now. Have you any suggestions for how we can get around this . . . hunger?"

She cocked her beautiful head and thought. Clever girl. "Well, after you eat, you don't want to eat again for nearly two days. Why don't you go feed yourself and then . . . we'll see."

"Brilliant. I'm on my way." And so I left Ashley sitting on my bed, waiting for her loverboy to return.

If only I knew then what I know now.

We walked into Dr Bloward's office two months later, both of us miserable and wanting to make our union work. Ashley did the talking that first session, since she was the one with years of experience at the hands of a shrink.

As I sat back, eyeing the man who carried his balding, portly, self with the wariness of prey, Ashley explained our plight.

"Well, we've been together for about two months. At first it was great. The sex was unreal, the passion glorious, and the love was . . . like nothing I'd ever known. You should know right up front, I'm not yet eighteen, but I've been on my own and a prostitute for three years, so I am totally cognizant of my choice in being with Vlad. We have both had to overcome previous baggage to be together, but some of it just feels like we're stuck in cement."

Alex, as he asked us to call him, turned his beady eyes on me, and asked me if Ashley had given a reasonable assessment so far. I nodded.

"Are you ill, Vlad?"

Ashley piped in. "Oh, yeah, I guess we have to get that out in the open, too."

"HIV?" Alex frowned a bit.

"No, he's a vampire." She saw the incredulity in his eyes. I saw the fear.

He chose to respond clinically. "And how long have you believed yourself to be a vampire, Vlad?"

"I have *been* a vampire for over three hundred years. I've forgotten my childhood, much of the past. I know this is stretching credulity for you, especially since your profession is trained to vet out the psychotic or schizophrenic who believes he's something or someone else other than he is. I can only assure you I am, unhappily now, a true vampire." I looked away. Not ashamed, but unwilling to see the look of derision on his face.

"You've forgotten your childhood?" I turned to him. His fingers were stroking his chin, considering. "What do you know of your parents?" Like ditch-diggers shrinks are, plumbing the bowels of one's psyche for pay dirt.

And so our first few sessions went. Ashley or I talking about what we could recall of our childhoods, chronicling our declines. I grew comfortable with him quickly, which Ashley said was a mark in his favour, since her experience of therapists was that when she felt weird with one, she knew he or she was no good. I trusted her experience implicitly.

It was during our tenth meeting we finally told him our difficulties. I was eager to be the one to spill it. Quite unlike me, but I was changing even then.

"It has to do with jealousy, mostly. You see, I am out from dark until ten or eleven at night feeding. I don't kill my donors, haven't for centuries, but I must seduce them close enough to make a meal from their jugular, or another prominent vein or artery. Ashley resents this, which I completely understand, but I cannot live any differently. If I don't acquire a donor, I won't feed. If I don't eat, I can't live.

"As for me, Ashley has taken to using the hours before we are together in the evening for supplementing our income with hooking. While I am aware her having sex with another man is a performance of sorts, as are my own seductions, I feel she should find other work and keep herself for me. I do not, I will point out, do anything more than kiss a woman, and only if she appears to expect it."

"How do you see what Vlad is telling me, Ashley?"

Her arms were crossed on her stomach and her foot was pumping. "Well, he certainly is articulate, isn't he? And to think English isn't his first language . . ." She glared at me a moment. "Yeah, he's right. I'm jealous and he's jealous. We're both so fucking insecure, we can't love each other right." She began to cry. "Help us, Alex. I love him."

I reached for her hand and she took it, her face going into my chest. She sobbed for a few minutes while I stroked her head.

"I can see you love and care for each other. We need to separate the issues between you into Vlad's and Ashley's, not the unit of the *us.*" He proceeded to show us how our old "tapes" of conditioned response and reaction reflexes were controlling us, and how we might get free of them.

It took Ashley four years to learn that she was terrified of losing me, needed to control me, had to learn to accept that my seductions were nothing more than calling a cow in for the slaughter, and that her anger was behind her prostituting herself. Not some imagined need for financial security. When she got it, she got it. She turned to acting lessons at a local theatre while I was out feeding, and began to get parts in equity plays.

For me, it took six years to learn that I was living in denial of

MELANCHOLIA 215

my emotions for so long I had no self, no ego, and therefore no one to respect in myself. I also intellectualized Ashley's jealousy as insignificant. I also tended towards an antisocial personality, and needed to acquire a sense of purpose in my life beyond food, sex, and the love of a beautiful woman. He also suggested I find another manner of acquiring blood that would put my relationship first, and not allow my sustenance to be lessened.

It seemed that after seven years together, I, the Prince of Darkness, and Ashley Hibbert, were making a go of a real relationship. Everything was wonderful. Ashley was about to star in a television series, and I had become a reader for the Braille Institute. I was feeling fulfilled, as was she, and our love life was renewed with passion and devotion.

Alex told us we didn't need him anymore, and off we hurried into a new wall. Too embarrassed to return to face him, I kept my new discomfort to myself.

Ashley was an instant little star. Because we agreed she wouldn't allow anyone access to me or to know about me, she fell prey to every hip single guy or unscrupulous married man in town. She resisted them all, but their curiosity had to create some answer for her rejections or their egos couldn't take it. The tabloids had fun with speculating on her gender preferences, and she soon had to devise dozens of circuitous ways to get home to me. All of this exhausted her, but she remained devoted.

Somehow, this annoyed and finally angered me. Her complaints she was too tired to make love grew in number, and the time apart due to her change in sleep cycle from mine multiplied as well. I suffered this in silence. After all, she loved me. I was nothing anymore without her.

She sensed my troubled heart and soul and begged me to go back to Alex. Ashamed, but determined not to lose my Ashley, I humbled myself back into my nine o'clock appointment.

Alex listened, more fascinated now than ever. Ashley said she'd go with me, but she was always too tired. Alex said I should work on myself, and during hiatus, she'd come in. He trusted her sincerity in wanting to save our relationship. So, I went alone.

What a mistake. I delved into the psyche of the most perverted compulsive the world's ever known. Alex was elated in this process, while I only grew more and more depressed.

"When will this melancholy leave me, Alex? I am no good to Ashley when all I want to do is mope around the house when I am awake, and sleep too many hours in the day."

"Vladdie, depression is the valley in the walk of life. You and Ashley hiked up a steep mountain together and while her road is still in ascension, she will grow depressed as part of her walk. You, my friend, are in the period of time when all you've learned has pitched you into a world where things are no longer familiar. You don't know yet where you're going, but the past is behind you. Trust that in time, you will be moving up the side of another mountain. This time to greater heights."

"And how long should I give this *valley*?"

He chuckled warmly, always assuming I was kidding around when I used his words in the mocking manner I had.

"If you're still feeling blue in a year, I'd say we should try tricyclics on you. There are antidepressants around that could wipe this dysphoria right out."

"Pardon my naiveté, but wouldn't it be a helpful thing for me to take an antidepressant now, while I'm newly depressed?"

Again he chuckled. "Dear Vlad, you don't want to run from these negative feelings. They're just as valuable as your positive feelings. You grow from fully experiencing both of them. All of them. Don't you enjoy your emotions now that you have them?"

I found myself studying his neck, seeking a pulse under his thick skin.

"Well, frankly, no, I don't. And I'm afraid Ashley will leave me if I continue to be a sucking vortex of negativity, as she calls it."

Alex mused over this. He had the habit of appearing to stare at me blankly, but that analytical mind was always working. Working. "Isn't that telling . . . a sucking vortex. She's admitting to her co-dependence in this depression of yours. Tell her I want her here next session, even if she has to drink a gallon of coffee."

Ashley was reluctant, only because, she said, she didn't want to confuse her television personae with her evolving self. But she went. We were back to our weekly sessions, endless and intense discussions at home, our language peppered with psycho-babble.

The years in love and therapy continued. Ashley's show was cancelled, and she developed anorexia. My depression was unaffected by medication, and Alex got fatter, older, and richer on us. He even put Ashley into a thirty-day residential program for eating disorders, while I began combing the city in bloodlust, growing sloppier by the night.

My evolution was becoming my undoing. I was decompensating. Dracula was not meant to be self-aware. Guilt and remorse lived in me like parasites, sapping my motivation for living. I could barely recall what it felt like to know a positive emotion. My anger at my ignorance in this ate at me as well.

On Ashley's twenty-eighth birthday, she insisted she never looked better, and would I please marry her. I blinked at her. She knew

I couldn't marry. Wouldn't marry. I was working on that part of commitment phobia as her birthday neared.

"No, no, Vlad, you don't understand. I want you to drink my blood and let me drink yours. I want to remain this way for eternity with you." She took my chin in her hand and batted her lashes at me. "It may take that long for us to resolve all our issues in therapy, yes?"

I spun away. "God, Ashley, how can you think of spending eternity with a depressed partner? It is a comfort to me to think one day you will be free of this burden in your death, if you don't choose to leave me first."

"Turn around you ancient bag of psychological torments, and look at me." I did. "I love you. I've not stopped loving you. You will not be depressed forever. Alex said so."

I hated to correct her. "He said that it is not uncommon for someone to be depressed a month for every year they were abused or tortured or whatever their trauma. Darling, I've lived far longer than most psychology texts have been around, and that means I could be depressed for decades."

"And what if I choose to work with you in this?"

I was suddenly tired, weary of working on myself. Exhausted at searching for myself. I hadn't yet found anyone within me worth being glad about. Her enthusiasm was born of her mortality and dogged faith in our love. My affection for her couldn't have been more at that moment.

"I love you, Ashley, but I'm afraid I love you too much to allow you to attach yourself to an emotional cavern of gloom for eternity. I'd rather let you go, than do that to you." I regretted saying that as soon as it left my lips. How could I not see then the manipulation? It was shouting in my face!

"Oh, Vlad, you're so noble. But I want to be immortal. Please. I mean what I said. I'm not bullshitting you." She set her manicured fingers on her perfect hips.

Three sessions later, I'd been convinced, even though I couldn't summon the ecstasy I knew I should be feeling at the prospect of eternity with her. With that we went home to Ashley's grandly theatrical production of the Big Seduction. She wanted to be reborn in splendour.

A thousand candles, twenty pots of smouldering incense, silk sheets, sultry music, and a table of delicate sweets awaited us. I knew as I went through the motions, that it was wrong, that my dammed emotions weren't going to spring a leak in time to make this glorious for me as well. Ashley, contrary to my experience, was ardently amorous.

When it was over, I found myself wishing to stand in the face of the sun at dawn. Ashley was sick as hell for awhile, but rebounded as I knew she would. I also knew how being immortal would come to change her. I simply hadn't imagined the speed at which that metamorphosis would occur.

It was less than a week later when she called me into the bedroom where she reclined in all her bored immortal beauty. "I don't like you anymore, Vlad. Whining, moaning, telling me all the time how you miss your old self. Well, I miss him, too. I'm leaving. I want to find someone who can keep up with me, who can feel joy and smile. It's been years since I heard you laugh."

I couldn't say I was stunned. I suspected this was coming. I tried a hollow chuckle. It failed as miserably as our union.

What I hadn't expected was how her leaving would be as a stake to my heart.

Alex continued to treat my ennui, and I continued to lose what desire I had left to go on. He tried to put me in a psychiatric hospital, but I had to remind him I would be a danger to the patients, and it would jeopardize my anonymity. He relented.

So you can see, can't you? Once the most feared and most fascinating of monsters in the known world, I've become a pathetic mass of neuroses, pathologies, with an apparently endless road ahead of me towards an iota of peace and a cohesive self. I've even lost interest in eating. What is the point? I can't even live up to my myth anymore.

When I'm gone, I ask only that you not tell the truth of my downfall, the demise of the Dracula the world still clings to with trepidation. Allow my legacy to live on.

I leave this world without regrets, and I have found some measure of peace. I made my last appointment with Dr Alex Bloward, and told him of my plans. He did his duty as a psychologist and insisted on committing me for my own protection. It was while he was on the telephone ordering the ambulance, I ripped out his throat and eviscerated him.

The condemned are always given whatever they ask for their last meal, and I couldn't have asked for better.

Lisa Morton

Children of the Long Night

Lisa Morton's screenwriting work includes Meet the Hollowheads *(aka* Life on the Edge) *and* Adventures in Dinosaur City *(aka* Dinosaurs)*. More recently, she has scripted various episodes of such animation shows as Disney's* Toontown Kids, Sky Dancers *and* Dragon Flyz, *and she is currently working on a series about vampiric cars that suck fuel! For the stage she has adapted and directed Philip K. Dick's* Radio Free Albemuth *and Theodore Sturgeon's* The Graveyard Reader, *and she has also written and directed her own one-act plays.*

Her short stories have appeared in Dark Voices 6, The Mammoth Book of Frankenstein, Dark Terrors, 365 Scary Stories, *and an illustrated chapbook entitled* The Free Way.

Dracula finds himself ever more disgusted with humanity and what it is becoming . . .

"C'MON, TET, YOU know you can't spend the night here."

The ragged man in filthy combat fatigues looked up from under his thin stringy hair. His real name was John Douglas Black, but he'd earned his street name by begging passersby to "spare some change for a vet, man, I was in the Tet Offensive, had the skin on my back torched by napalm." Tet didn't appear to have any war injuries, but, on the other hand, no one had ever seen his back, either.

Tet staggered to his feet, half-leaning against the wall beside him for support. The two beat cops eyed him with a mix of disgust and pity, then the female one leapt forward to steady him when he almost fell.

"You alright, Tet? We can take you to a clinic, get you some help . . ."

Tet flinched away from her hand. "Already been. They couldn't do shit for me."

The cop reluctantly let her partner lead her back to their car, the game finished for tonight. It was always the same – they knew Tet was one of the harmless ones, didn't really want to roust him, but if they didn't some Yuppie on his busy way back from the video store would complain, then they'd have to arrest Tet. It was easier this way for everyone.

Except Tet really *did* need help. Something was wrong with him. Every morning he awoke feeling weaker, more feverish. He wondered if he'd caught some disease from a rat – there were bite marks on his wrists, small gaping pink spots standing out from the grime.

Tet reached the side street and turned the corner. There was an alley down here that was little more than a walkway and trash storage between buildings. Tet could store himself there with all the rest of the garbage and no one cared.

He stumbled past the first two dumpsters, then let himself collapse. He was almost asleep when he realized he wasn't alone. He looked up blearily and made out a figure standing over him, a silhouette. Then the blackness was dropping beside Tet, and he heard a noise, a hideous noise like a cross between a guttural laugh and an animal snarl.

He realized he'd been hearing that sound every night for nearly a week.

"Hey man, leave me alone, I got nothin' –"

They were the last words Tet said before his throat was torn out.

It was an evening in early November 1917 as he strode across the French plain. When the war had finally washed up against his Carpathian hillsides a year earlier, the smell of blood had begun to work on him, drawing him down from his aerie. He had returned to his homeland ten years earlier, disenchanted and dismayed by London society, and had lived in solitude for a decade, content to feed only on the occasional gypsy or stray traveller.

But then, as the war spread and his native soil was seared and smeared with gore, he became aware of his own hungers. And so he finally followed them until they led him here, to the battlefield of Ypres, on this fall night.

He had spent last night and today in an inn a hundred miles away, and had flown here after sunset. He touched down on a small hill on the edge of the conflagration, and was mildly surprised to find himself shocked by the carnage. In his own battles he had seen wholesale slaughter, but never this devastation of the land. He remembered this area from fifty years earlier; it had been thick with vegetation, a dark green that rustled with life in the night breeze. Now he saw only brown mud, broken metal and broken men.

He descended into the foggy yellow hell of mustard gas, unaffected but not unrepulsed. Even so, he was drunk on wafting copper scent and the moans of the dying. He bypassed mounds of corpses until he came to a man still alive, missing a leg, dragging himself through the clutching filth, gas mask making him look like an insect, a carrion fly.

The Transylvanian fell on the man, tearing the gas mask loose to fix on his throat. The soldier clawed feebly as needlepointed teeth slid into his skin, and then he gave in gratefully as death finally overtook him.

And when the Transylvanian had drained the man, he swam to his feet, head reeling, and let his predator's instincts bring him to the next one . . . and the next . . . and the next, ten years of starvation erased in one night . . .

Until, in his ecstasy, he did not realize that he had fastened upon a man dying of gas poisoning. And suddenly he was on his knees, vomiting up tainted blood with good, helpless as wave after wave of spasm forced the precious fluid from him, until he lay as weak as one of his victims, as barren as the land. Sunrise found him rolling into a trench and covering himself with corpses to escape the light. And although he survived, undiscovered, to rise again at dusk and flee back to his comfortable coffin . . .

. . . Something else in him had begun to die.

Jackson didn't want the job. A bum who'd had his throat ripped out, probably by some other bum's rabid dog. It could've been easily written off, except that the coroner had found the body almost completely drained of blood and ruled it a homicide.

They'd had other cases of homeless death in the last year, and a higher-than-normal percentage had died of blood loss. Some had been found with small animal bites on the throat or wrists, but the M.E. suggested they'd been dying in the alleys for some time, and rats had hastened the process along.

But clearly no mere rat had torn out John Black's throat, and so now they finally had to accept the possibility of a serial killer. Some nut stealing blood to sell, or experiment with, probably. Jackson didn't really care – he had more important cases to deal with. A double homicide of a wealthy couple in Hancock Park. A drive-by in Hollywood. A rape-mutilation-murder in Silverlake, a victim who had left behind three young children. Who gave a shit about a fucked-up friendless ex-vet on the streets? He intended to file it in the back of the unsolved cases as quickly as possible.

That is, until *she* walked in.

It was after eight-thirty on a Tuesday night. She appeared unannounced, asking if he was the one in charge of the John Black case.

He didn't even think to ask how she'd gotten past the main desk and all the barriers from there to here without anyone notifying him, he was so stunned by her.

She was the most beautiful woman he'd ever seen.

Flawless, gleaming pale skin, a perfectly-sculpted face framed by undulations of auburn hair, a lovely shape draped in leather and jewels.

"Excuse me – are you the one in charge of the John Black case?" she asked again, and he realized she had a British accent, very uppercrust and old-sounding.

"Yes, sorry. Cal Jackson." He paused, surprised to realize he was nearly speechless in this woman's presence. "And you are . . . ?"

She entered his office, closed the door behind her and seated herself in a guest chair. "You look awfully young to be a homicide detective."

Jackson blinked, then took his chair. "I'm older than I look."

For some reason she laughed.

He went on, "I was one of the youngest officers ever promoted. That was four years ago."

"So you're good at what you do?"

"Yes," he answered.

She nodded, considering. Now that the initial shock of her was wearing off, Jackson was becoming impatient. "Do you have some information on the case? I'm frankly surprised anyone even knows about it."

"Yes," she smiled slightly, "it was buried in the paper, wasn't it? Apparently poor Mr Black didn't rate better. Even though he was drained of blood."

Now Jackson leaned back, interested. The blood draining wasn't public knowledge. He picked up a pencil. "Just what do you know about Mr Black?"

She rose to go. "I'll be back."

Jackson lurched from his own chair, seeing more than an answer to a case walking from his office. "Wait, I didn't even get your name!"

"I won't tell you my married name, Detective Jackson, but you can call me –"

". . . Lucy."

Sometimes the name pushed its way out, torn from somewhere deep inside him even though it meant nothing now. Everything was nothing now. He existed, undead, not living at all; he went on only for the taste of the blood, the rich metallic tang of it, the sweet numbing as it filled him. He did not even bother to disguise his kills any more, as he once had. He had been clever, so clever, at erasing his marks, disposing of bodies, stealing the blood so slowly that doctors called it disease rather than murder.

And he had excelled at murder. As a living prince, he had been a warrior, a great defender of his country and a dispenser of terrible justice. The ground around his castle had run red with the life of his enemies, and his people had named him *Dracula* – Son of the Dragon. His cruelty – impalings, disembowellings, slow tortures – had become legend.

And yet the pain had been inflicted only on enemies, always in the name of preserving his land.

Wallachia . . . another name that sprang unbidden to his lips sometimes. Another name, like Lucy or Mina, that brought him comfort, a minor peace. Sometimes when he woke at sunset, the names were there and for a second he remembered what they were and had meant to him. Then time intruded again, and they were all gone, and only he was left, alone in an era when his name was a Gothic romance and his evil small.

So it was every dusk that his madness returned.

He no longer slept encrypted in a glamorously-ruined abbey or castle. Now his daytimes were spent in the roach-infested attic of an abandoned theatre in a Western city of the New World. Once he had admired the theatre's crumbling art deco facade, but that had been when he still had enough mind left to admire things. Now he just knew it as the place he returned to each morning, and left each night.

This evening he drifted away from his lair, his form an insubstantial mist carried by a hot Santa Ana wind.

He did not have to search far. A freeway underpass. Three underage addicts handling hypodermic needles with trembling fingers. He waited until they fell back in heavy joy, then took his form. One of the trio saw something, a smoke that became a man, a man dressed in tattered, heavily-stained clothes, with burning eyes and sunken features. He took the first two, then turned to the third, who was so far gone he had not even noticed the deaths of his companions.

The boy wore a Star of David about his neck.

It was gaudy, heavy cheap metal on a thick chain, probably purchased as costume jewellery, but the power of the symbol held nonetheless. Although it was not the symbol of good from the Prince's mortal religion, and thus held no fear for him, something about it stopped him from attacking the boy. He left him there and floated away, vaguely troubled somewhere in the back of his mind, old memories stirred up that disturbed his dreams all the next day . . .

Lucy did come back the following night.

Jackson had spent a sleepless day thinking about her. Trying to sleep, but impossible with her image burned into his mind's eye. He gave into fantasies, speculations – *she murdered her husband she wants a new lover she will seduce me I'll let her yes.*

It was just after ten p.m. when she arrived, as maddeningly-beautiful as she'd been the night before. Once again she glided into his office, apparently having been invisible to the desk sergeant and the other homicide detectives.

"Good evening, Detective Jackson."

"Hello, uh –"

She sighed. "My name is really Lucy MacArthur – Mrs David MacArthur, if you must know."

Jackson knew the name. "David MacArthur . . . some big film guy, right?"

"Music. He runs CM Records."

Jackson nodded, feeling somehow rejected. *Christ, that explains the money,* he thought.

"But I'd really like it if you'd call me Lucy. Please."

He couldn't help but return her smile. "Okay, Lucy. Now let's talk about Mr Black."

"Fine. Surely the word *vampire* has been suggested in connection with this case."

"Surely," Jackson responded. "I've heard my share of Count Dracula jokes in the last few days."

"Well, let me assure you, Detective, that you won't hear any from me."

She considered, then rose and turned the blinds down on the glass around his office so it was hidden from view of the rest of the station. He started to rise in protest. "I don't know what you think –"

He was halfway out of the chair when she looked at him and said, calm yet rockhard resolute, "Sit down."

Jackson was shocked to discover he *was* sitting, without remembering moving his legs. She was across the desk from him, watching.

"I'm sorry, but if I try to tell you who you're seeking – if I try to tell you who *I* am – you won't believe me. I must show you."

"Show me . . . ?"

Then she moved so fast he didn't see. He only knew that suddenly she was standing over him, her hands on his shoulders, her exquisite face near his –

– and she was baring a mouthful of fangs at him.

The rational part of Jackson knew he should doubt – *plastic fangs, movie props, big deal, he'd seen better in Christopher Lee movies* – but somehow he didn't doubt. He knew they were real. But what that made *her* –

She closed her mouth and stepped back from him.

"You're . . . why are you showing me this?," Jackson gasped.

She reseated herself, as if nothing had happened, as if she hadn't just shattered Jackson's well-ordered, rational world. "So you'll believe me. I need you to believe me, because what I intend to do, I can't do alone."

"You're a vampire," he stated.

"Yes. I'm glad you're taking it so well."

Jackson saw his holstered pistol hanging nearby, but knew he could never beat her to it. "That was you who made me sit, wasn't it?"

"Yes, but please understand – I'm not here to hurt you or control you. I'm here to help."

"Are you dead?," he asked, trying to sound reasonable.

"Yes. I died in 1893."

"And you've survived all this time by . . ." He couldn't say it, looking at her, seeing her beauty.

"Drinking blood."

"I thought you said you were married, to –"

"David. I am. He . . . accepts my condition. He provides me with servants, associates, groupies . . . I don't kill, though. They all just think it's some sort of . . . decadent game. Something the rich indulge in."

"You've never killed?," he asked.

"Not since I left England. That was when I realized it wasn't necessary."

"But the man we're after . . ."

She looked away, her gaze clouded. "Kills very matter-of-factly

– or he did, once. He killed *me*, in fact, but now . . . he doesn't even know any more. He's gone quite mad, I think."

"And he is . . . ?"

She took a deep breath, then exhaled it:

"Dracula."

It was 1943, and the world was at war again.

After the last conflict, he had fled back to the Carpathians, but then had been lured down again by the end of the hostilities and the beginning of a new, more elegant era. It was a time of youthful jazz, new tolerances and free design. He stayed, even after the stock market crash, which he neither understood nor was affected by. He travelled the great European cities, in the company of other royalty, like himself. He watched in mild amusement as a ridiculous little man named Hitler rose to power in Germany; his warrior's soul admired the new German spirit of patriotic pride and discipline . . . but when the German forces began to overrun the land, he felt something curdle within him, a thick gathering of apprehension at the useless losses to come.

For a while he went back to London, but when the bombings began he left; immortal under most circumstances, even he feared the power unleashed by the German planes.

He was heading home, surrounded by a caravan of hired mercenaries, when he was distracted one December night in 1943. The source of the distraction was a noise, coming from the east, a sound vaguely like only one other he had heard centuries ago, when still a mortal prince. It was, in fact, a sound he had inspired then.

It was the sound of many voices wailing in agony.

Intrigued, he became airborne and followed the noise. As he neared it, the air around him changed, thickened until it became almost gritty; it stank, filling him with a sickly sweet disgust. He knew that stench. And when he saw the tall chimney stacks belching fire and ashes into the night sky, he knew the source.

He flew closer, circling unseen over a Hell he soon realized was far beyond any he had ever created.

Trucks were pulling into a courtyard not far from the buildings – the crematoria, he knew them to be – with the flaming chimneys. The trucks were full of women. Even though it was below freezing, the women were naked. They were badly emaciated, some with open sores and wounds, others bearing bruises that attested to beatings. A few had died already.

As the trucks stopped, the women – there must have been seventy-five or eighty crammed into each bed – were herded toward openings to walkways that led below ground level.

The women were wailing.

He watched as the trucks finished unloading, the entrances were sealed, and toxic crystals dropped down through pipes into the ground. He heard the cries of the Damned escalate, then finally fade out and cease altogether. In a few moments, the doors were opened and men in gas masks began carrying bodies out, stacking them for the short trip to the crematorium.

He knew, of course, of the German Konzentrationslager, the 'KZ' – everyone in his circles did. But they had been told these were labour camps, to detain the Jews and other "racially-inferior" peoples until they could be relocated. Now, as the truth impacted fully on him, he felt a great rage. He was furious at this squandering of a most delicate resource, the useless waste of blood. He would stop this, make them feel the wrath of a true prince . . .

He set foot on the frozen soil and approached the first uniformed man he saw.

"Who is your leader here?," he asked in thickly-accented German.

The man drew his pistol before he fell under the power of the vampire's hypnotic gaze. Then he just used the pistol to point.

"The Hauptsturmfuhrer,*" he mumbled.*

The Prince turned to look, and made out buildings, newly added to one of the vast crematoria. Lights flickered within, silhouettes moving in front of them.

He became mist and drifted to the nearest door, moving unheeded past several soldiers. Down a hallway, drawn by voices to a doorway. Inside, the smell was of cleaning fluid and formaldehyde.

Four men were there. The room was a laboratory of some sort, equipped with sinks and cabinets, stainless steel instruments and gleaming chrome tables. Of the four men, three were in white lab coats; the fourth wore a full-length black leather overcoat, a skullshead-SS cap, and was smoking, listening as one of the other men spoke.

". . . extensive ulceration of the small intestine, such as is typical in the third week of typhoid fever. You will also note the swelling of the spleen –"

There were, altogether, ten wheeled tables in the room. All held corpses.

Five pairs of twins.

All children, none older than eight.

All carefully dissected. All had had their eyes removed. One wall held a board to which pairs of human eyes had been pinned, like butterflies, carefully sorted by colour.

The smoking man finished glancing over the report he held in his other hand and looked up, nodding in approval.

"Is the report satisfactory, Hauptsturmfuhrer?"

"Most satisfactory. Invaluble, in fact. I want these –" he gestured at the twins on the nearest table, "– packed carefully and shipped to the Kaiser Wilhelm Institute in Berlin. Mark the shipping crates 'War Materials - Urgent'. Do you understand?"

The men in white coats glanced at each other, then the one in charge answered, "Yes. And the rest?"

The man in leather murmured off-handedly, "Dispose of them." He was gazing down at the twins, bobbing on his feet excitedly.

The men in the stained lab coats waited nervously.

The mist in the corner was consumed.

Madness.

This place was madness, impure and unsimple, and he gave himself over to it. He congealed in an eyeblink and exploded through the men, hurling them aside easily. The one in leather pulled a gun and fired at him, clumsily killing one of the doctors instead. The Prince barely noticed, so intent was he on the one he held before him, the one who had relayed the 'report'.

"Why have you done this?," he snarled.

The man shook violently, barely gasped out, "Please, we had no choice, they would kill us like our brothers if we didn't –"

"Your brothers?" He nodded at the dissected corpses, "These are your own people?"

The man did not reply. The look in his eyes was his answer.

In two seconds his headless body was flung aside, the Prince holding the head aloft, blood streaming down his chin.

In five seconds the last of the white-coated doctors was dead, his throat gone.

He rounded on the man in leather, who fired his pistol until the hammer clicked on empty chambers. There were shouts and running feet in the hallway outside, but the Prince gestured and the door slammed shut. Then he began to move towards his final victim, savouring the exquisite terror.

"Before I kill you, slowly and painfully, I ask of you one question: Why do you deserve to call yourself human?"

The man reached behind him, seeking a weapon, and the leather coat was tugged open.

There was a cross on his chest.

Even though it was not a true crucifix, the Iron Cross medal held enough of the symbol's power to repel the vampire. He fell back, averting his gaze, his eyes stinging.

The potential victim hesitated, then laughed as he sensed he was out of danger. "You – you recognized me! You saw my medals and suddenly knew who I was. Now you cower from me, like the rest of your inferior kind!"

The Prince couldn't face his accuser directly, but he could spit out, "How dare you –"

"I dare," responded the German, "because your accent marks you as a Slav, and as such second only to the Jews as a degenerate race, although I admit that you have some personal power. You will make a most interesting display for the Institute."

Outside, a shot sounded. The lock exploded and the door burst inwards. The Prince took the first guard through and tore his throat out.

The Nazi watched in horrified fascination. "What are you?"

The Prince threw the soldier's drained body aside and stood in the doorway. "I am," he answered, "by comparison, a very small nightmare."

With that his form altered, becoming a winged creature of the night, and he left the accursed place.

Three years after the war had ended and the German horrors had been disclosed, he saw a picture in a newspaper of an escaped war criminal. He recognized him from that night, the blandly handsome features, the gap in the front teeth, the Cross pinned to the chest (the most ironic and perverted use of that symbol imaginable). Now the monster had a name:

Dr Josef Mengele.

Mengele escaped, but the Prince, ageless and deathless, was not so fortunate. He was captured and cruelly taunted by what Mengele had unleashed at the place known as Auschwitz.

She'd left last night, after revealing the name to him. Now she was back, and Jackson looked up without surprise from the cheap paperback novel he was reading.

She saw the cover and smiled wryly. "Obviously you believed me."

He closed the book and gestured with it. "You know, Lucy dies in this."

She smiled again and sat, not in the chair but on a corner of Jackson's desk near him, her crossed legs brushing his. "Staked through the heart. Ouch."

"Then you aren't this Lucy."

"Oh, yes I am," she began, "but that book . . . a ridiculous collection of half-truths, a Victorian fiction at best."

He waited, and after a moment she went on. "In the book I have three suitors. Very flattering, but not very true. There was only one. His name was Bram Stoker."

Jackson blinked in surprise. "Stoker?"

"Yes. That night, in the crypt with that terrible old man, Van Helsing . . . Bram sent the professor outside, claiming he wanted to be alone. The professor left, Bram raised the stake – and then couldn't do it. He was a coward, my dear Bram was. I heard him, as I lay helpless in the coffin, tell the old man that the deed was done."

"And Van Helsing believed him?"

"No. I'm sure he intended to come back and finish me alone after they were done with the Count, but the Professor did not survive the encounter."

"Dracula killed him?"

"He didn't get the chance – heart attack."

Jackson considered, then asked, "So why did Stoker rewrite the truth so heavily?"

"Isn't it obvious? Bram's entire reason for writing his quaint book was to expunge his guilt."

"So Dracula drank your blood and you became like him."

"It isn't that easy, Detective, I assure you. He drained me to the point of death, then made me drink of his blood. You needn't worry about his victims – they won't be coming back unless he transformed them, and frankly vampires don't like the competition."

"But he turned you."

"Yes," she said, and for the first time Jackson saw her jaded irony fail, "I suppose he loved me."

Jackson looked closely at her, her legs sliding from under the folds of the silk skirt, then forced his gaze up to meet hers. "In the book you were feeding on children."

She did look away, with a shame that actually surprised him. "I was . . . you have to understand that I was like a newborn myself, cast into a strange new life without guidance. Dracula was being pursued then and couldn't help me. After, though, he did come back. He gave up on Mina and came back to me. He taught me how to use my new gifts, and made me remember who I'd been. He took me to London. We even become part of society . . . but then he left. He grew tired of the people, the cities. He was homesick. So he left and I stayed. We haven't been together since."

"Why do you think this," Jackson gestured at the files on the desk, "is him?"

"I did see him two months ago," she began, her voice barely above a whisper. "He must have found out I was married to David, a mention in a magazine perhaps. One night he appeared outside my bedroom window. He was half-formed, hovering, just . . . watching. He didn't come in, or speak. After a while he just . . . drifted away. He was very lost."

Jackson waited until she could look at him again before saying, "Even if it is him . . . what do you want? Do you think you can save him?"

"Oh no, Detective. I want you to help me kill him."

Before Jackson could react, she was bending over him, one hand gliding down his shoulder. "Why aren't you married, Detective Jackson?"

His shoulder jerked away from her touch. "Who said I'm not?"

She picked up his left hand, held it up between them. "No ring."

He had to admit, "Okay, I'm not. But you are."

She was pulling him out of the chair now, to his feet, her arms going around his waist. "I've been married eight times this century. It's a convenient cover for the way I have to live, and provides me with income."

"And that's all?," he asked, as her hands moved up his back.

"Let's just say I . . . do seek my pleasures elsewhere."

A few seconds later, when her teeth slid easily into his throbbing neck, it was the greatest moment of Jackson's life.

Another sunup . . . another sundown . . .

Even though he had fed the night before – completely drained two of them – he hungered again. Maybe it was the drugs he had ingested with last night's blood, or, more likely, the blood itself was the drug. Only when he was taking in the sweet, rich essence did the pictures in his mind fade. Only then could he rest in peace.

He left his sanctuary and let the night wind take him.

A third floor window in a downtown hotel. One of those to which the government housing programme paid $400 a night to shelter its indigent.

He entered. Two men were passed out drunk on cots in the first room. He took them both without a sound and moved on. In the next room a woman saw him and started to scream – until he ripped her throat out. A third man there. On to the next room . . . and the next . . .

He came to a family, parents and three young children, all sleeping in two beds, only a curtain separating them. He took the parents silently, then tore the curtain aside and faced the children.

The children . . .

The world in 1969 had belonged to the children.

Dracula had finally forsaken his dreary, war-torn homeland for the New World. That had been in the fifties, a time he had found depressingly dull and spiritless. But his financial fortunes had multiplied enough to keep him there.

And then times had changed again, as they always did, and he felt reborn. It was summer 1969, the City of Angels. He was now fabulously rich, constantly surrounded by gorgeous young people dressed in flamboyant clothing. It amused him that their colours were DayGlo. He loved the lively music, the open sexuality, the intense communal gathering that took place on the Sunset Strip every Saturday night. He owned movie studios, record companies, apartment buildings and one old art deco theatre, which he planned to renovate soon. He dressed in velvets and silk brocades, frequented the Whisky and the Velvet Turtle, and his head reeled with LSD-laced blood. He became a figure of mystery and intense speculation among the Strip's habitues, and so was very popular.

All in all, it was a great time to be undead.

It was late on one of those same Saturday nights when he smelled something wafting down from the hills above and to the west. It was something that cut through the haze of marijuana smoke, something he had not smelled since the last war: Blood, newly spilled, a great quantity. It was nearly four in the morning. He was just leaving his last club of the night, accompanied by two staggering youthful companions. He planned to invite them to his limo, ply them with hashish, then taste them both, taking only a little, leaving them to spend the rest of the evening passed out in the rear seat while he flew home just before sunrise. His chauffeur, whom he liked to call "Renfield", was exceedingly discreet.

But the scent, impossible for mortal senses to define, tugged at him, a pull as old and natural as the killer instinct. He halfheartedly excused himself from his prey, moved like a sleepwalker to a dark corner, and there transformed.

On batwings he followed the aroma north, past the Strip, into the hills. Over the sprawling mansions of Beverly Hills, past the winding Coldwater Canyon, up to a place where Christmas tree lights twinkled incongruously in the warm night. He sat down nearby, on an expanse of lawn, nearly swooning from the proximity of the scent.

It did not take him long to find the source. There were two bodies on the front lawn, one man and one woman. They had been stabbed, butchered. In a car in the driveway, a third corpse reposed over the steering wheel, bullet holes a testament to his life's end.

But the inside of the house was where the strongest smells were emanating from, and, in a daze of lust and repulsion, Dracula followed the bloodscent.

There was gore everywhere, on walls, on floors, on furnishings. He turned off a short entryway into a living room, and saw another man and woman. They, like the two outside on the grass, had been savaged, mindlessly stabbed over and over, obviously within the last hour or two. The length of rope connecting them, each end knotted around their necks, showed they had also been hanged. An American flag was draped over the back of the couch.

Dracula ignored the masked body of the man and moved to kneel by the woman. He looked at her face, heartrendingly beautiful even in death, and thought: I know her.

It took a moment for his mind – a mind filled with thousands of faces, collected over centuries – to process her image. Then it came to him.

Of course. He had seen her two years earlier, in a film. A vampire film.

An absurd film, but well-crafted and not without its merits. He had thought her beautiful even then.

Now she lay at his feet, victim of a slaughter so terrible it left even him, history's great parasite, sickened.

As he looked down, he realized something else: She had been pregnant, quite far along. And the child within her . . .

No!

It had been, astonishingly, untouched by the attack, and was moving feebly. He let his fingers rest on her swollen, scarlet side, while emotions he had not felt in over twenty-five years flooded to the surface: Hatred, compassion, disgust, but mostly rage. Rage. Rage.

The child stopped moving.

The first light of false dawn was glowing in the sky outside as he staggered up, the night over. He left the house the way he had come, out the front door. It was only then that he saw the message scrawled there, scrawled in blood which his senses told him belonged to the exquisite corpse within:

PIG

It rang in his head as he found his way home.

PIG

All that warm, rich life reduced to a word, a word describing a filthy farm animal.

PIG

When he took to his coffin, it was still there. And during the day that followed,

PIG

It became the axe that found the cracks already widened in his carefully-kept sanity, and five centuries were shattered with the final stroke.

"You're sure this is it?"

Jackson shone his flashlight around the interior of the deserted theatre, seeing only splintering wood and peeling plaster.

Lucy came up behind, entwining herself around him. "Yes, but don't worry - he's not here right now."

Jackson had spent the rest of last night and today in a drained, rapturous haze. He kept recalling the rush that had filled him as she'd taken him, like an orgasm igniting every cell of his body. She hadn't taken that much, not even enough to cause him to lose consciousness.

What he'd lost was his soul.

He could think of nothing but her. And a part of him hated her for that.

He'd received the call about the massacre at the shelter early, not long after he'd arrived home. It looked like the skid row killer – Dracula, he forced himself to think the name – had gone mad, killing

ten adults and one toddler, and injuring two children. Jackson had
gone to the hospital to question the tiny victims, but they were in
critical condition, comatose, probably dying.

And all he'd thought about was her.

She'd come to him as usual, except this time there were no
words. An embrace, a long kiss, the slick warmth of her tongue
on his, her teeth at his neck, then in . . .

Later, she told him they would kill Dracula tonight.

He drove her unquestioningly to the theatre. He didn't even
feel astonishment when she lifted him in her arms so they could
enter over the ten-foot boards blocking the entrance.

Her plan was to locate Dracula's coffin, hide until he had returned
and dawn was at hand, then open the shopping bag she had brought
along, remove from it a wooden stake, and drive it through Dracula's
heart. Then, to be sure, they would drag his body into morning
sunlight, and Jackson would hold it there until the remains were
completely obliterated.

When Jackson objected – "But the sun" – Lucy had assured him
that she had no intention of sacrificing herself. She would occupy
Dracula's coffin, safe from the light, watched over by Jackson, until
the next dusk.

Now they stood in the vast, echoing space that was the old theatre,
Jackson's senses afire where she touched him, desolate when she
removed herself.

"The coffin is somewhere above us. I can smell it."

The scent led them back into the lobby, through a door on
which fading letters read PRIVATE, and up stairs to a long corridor.
Offices, rehearsal rooms and tech booths lined the hall; a door at
the end opened onto a large storage space for set pieces, flats and
props. Jackson saw a black square overhead, and nodded at it.

"A painted-over skylight. That's good for us."

Lucy barely acknowledged him, then fixed her attention on
something else.

"There it is."

She pushed past cobwebbed couches and coatracks, rusted lamps
and shattered mirrors, to where a coffin rested in a far corner.

It was hardly what Jackson had expected. An ebony box that
had once been highly-polished, but was now as tarnished as the
dilapidated pieces around it. No family crest or crouched gargoyle
marked it. It looked as if it belonged here, a simple prop that
could have graced any number of plays, but now lay dusty and
forgotten.

Lucy opened it and turned away, flinching. Even Jackson gagged
at the stench.

The inside of the coffin was painted brown with layers of dried blood.

"God," Lucy muttered, stepping back, "he has become a monster."

She sagged into a chair that barely supported her weight. She covered her face with one hand and looked away from him.

Jackson realized she was sobbing.

"Lucy . . . what . . ."

He knelt by her, caressing a leg.

"Seeing him this way, what's become of him . . . I knew it would be bad, but this . . ."

"Then we're doing the right thing."

Lucy tried to look up, nodding. "We are, but . . . it's still hard for me. I loved him so."

Jackson pulled back from her as if she had struck him. "You . . . *loved* him? But he –"

She cut him off, almost irritated. "Yes, I loved him. He's the only one I've ever really loved. He gave me my life, how could I not love him? No one could ever mean to me what he does. All the rest, they're just . . . ghosts."

"Including me?"

Lucy stood, realizing her mistake, turning to him with a poor attempt at a smile. She put her arms around him, but he was stiff. "It'll be different when I'm free of him . . . and you'll be the one who's there when that happens."

Jackson let himself be drawn into her embrace, gave his senses over to her . . . but his mind was replaying what she'd said, and weighing chances.

For the first time since his resurrection, he had no desire to feed.

He floated, insubstantial, over the city, dimly aware that he was searching for something. Whatever it was – romance, reason, adventure, simplicity – it was not to be found, not in this place or time. His ways were completely dead, and not even blood would comfort him now.

When the horizon began to pale, he saw the colours there preceding the coming of the sun, and made his first truly conscious decision in days, maybe years:

I will greet the light this morning.

But, as the sky turned pink and gold around him, it was his unconscious instincts that took over, the primordial will to survive that told humans to breathe and his kind to flee the day. And so it was, with an inward scream of disappointment, that he realized he was once again in his coffin prison, the lid closing over him, sealing him away from the release promised by the light.

They had watched silently as Dracula had entered the room, mist seeping through a ceiling vent into the coffin, then coalescing into a gaunt figure who reached a hand up to pull the lid shut.

Now Lucy handed a stake and mallet to Jackson; he took them, half-numb with the sudden realization that she had always meant for *him* to do this. She crept up to the coffin now and paused there, her face unreadable. Then, finally, she laid her fingers on the lid, looked to Jackson and mouthed two words:

The heart.

Jackson nodded, then tightened his grip on the arcane tools and waited.

She flung the lid back.

Jackson looked down and froze.

The thing in the coffin was neither the handsome vampire prince of cinema nor the rat-faced historical Vlad. No, what Jackson saw was a hollow-eyed and stained spectre, past all delusions of vanity or care, clad in clothing so old and stained it was impossible to identify either colour or style. Dracula exuded neither menace nor allure, just great age and sad, apathetic madness.

A cry of dismay escaped Lucy.

Dracula's eyes opened. They fixed on Lucy's.

"My Prince . . . ," she breathed.

There was no response. Without breaking her gaze, Lucy ordered Jackson: "Do it."

Jackson moved the tip of the stake over Dracula's chest, guessing where the heart would be. He settled the point and raised the mallet, gathering force for the blow.

Dracula's features clouded over, and he spoke one word.

"Lucy."

Lucy cried out again, and saw Jackson swinging the mallet. "Wait –!"

She was too late. The mallet struck the wooden stake with enough force to drive it all the way through Dracula's body. Cold blood splattered Jackson's hands and arms, but he pounded the stake a second time, to be sure.

A long hiss was the only sound. Then even that was gone.

Lucy stared, aghast. Jackson dropped the mallet and started to reach for her, but pulled back, seeing his gore-covered fingers. Instead he moved up to her, so close he could feel her trembling.

"Lucy," he said softly, "you know it had to be done."

She wouldn't look at him.

He bent to pull the body from the coffin, to let the sun send it to its final rest, but Lucy suddenly turned on him, pushing him away so roughly he staggered. "No! I won't let you touch him!"

She closed the lid gently.

"What about you? The coffin . . ."

"I don't need it," she answered in a voice as cold as his blood had been. "There's an old trunk in the corner. I'll use that."

She kissed the ebony surface gently, let her fingers rest there for a moment, then crossed to the trunk.

"You won't touch him," was all she said.

Jackson nodded, and she lowered herself in, closing the darkness around her. He waited a few moments, to be sure day had painted the world outside, then he hefted the coatrack up. A few thrusts shattered the black-coated glass overhead, and rich morning sunlight streamed into the room.

He walked back to the trunk and positioned himself at the far end. He pushed until it lay full under the sun, and then he opened it.

Lucy barely had time to scream before the burning began.

When she sprang halfway up, he pushed her back down and held her there while she writhed beneath him. When her struggles began to weaken, she looked up at him, her skin black and blistering, and asked why.

A thousand reasons flooded Jackson's mind:

Because you'd have come to hate me for what I did today

Because I'm just a ghost

Because you used me

Because you didn't love me

Because you're a monster, just like he was

Because you don't belong here

But he said nothing.

When it was over, he turned to the coffin and scraped it across the floorboards a few feet at a time, his muscles straining. Once gold pooled over it, he flung the lid open, ready for anything, except what he saw:

The coffin was empty, nothing left of the vampire prince but the dried blood and the stake.

Jackson stared for a long time. *He disintegrated from the staking.* It had to be true. *He was so old there was nothing remaining, not even ash.*

After a time, Jackson convinced himself. His mind moved onto other matters and he left. There was, after all, still something to be done.

He spent the next day checking on all of Dracula's known victims over the last two years. All from Tet back had been cremated. One of the young junkies had been given over to his parents for burial, but that had been after three days spent in the county morgue. The victims from the shelter massacre had likewise been cremated by the county. He crossed them all off.

Next he drove to a costume shop, purchased a wig, moustache, and dark glasses. A thrift store provided a long coat. He managed to check out a car being held in connection with an armed robbery.

Then he drove to the hospital.

The two young survivors of the shelter massacre were still unconscious, in critical condition. In his disguise, Jackson slipped easily into their room, unseen.

He had already examined them, noted how they had been left strangely untouched, compared to their elders. Even the child who had died had not been torn apart, but had succumbed to shock. The only mark these two bore were tiny pinpricks on their necks.

It was possible that even Dracula had been incapable of mutilating a child . . . or perhaps he had appropriately applied the ancient urge to procreate to children.

Jackson wasn't taking any chances. He could not suffer a possible monster to live . . . and so he removed the two stakes from beneath the long coat.

It was done quickly and quietly, then he was gone before anyone knew. He realized he hadn't needed the borrowed car after all, but then again, if nothing else, Lucy had taught him not to risk unnecessary self-sacrifice.

He thought it was done now. He didn't even mind that no one else would ever know what a hero he'd been, how he'd driven the shadows out. Even if the children had been untainted, Jackson could rationalize that survival would only have meant lives of poverty and misery, ever-increasing violence and tragedy. And if Dracula had escaped (*it isn't possible*), he was hopelessly mad, in a world of madness.

Jackson, on the other hand, would face that world and, if he had to, meet it every step of the way.

Nicholas Royle

Mbo

Nicholas Royle is the author of more than seventy horror tales, several of which have been regularly selected for the anthologies The Best New Horror, The Year's Best Fantasy and Horror *and* The Year's Best Horror Stories.

Other recent appearances have included Dark Terrors *and* Dark Terrors 2, Twist in the Tail: Cat Horror Stories, Love in Vein II, The Mammoth Book of Zombies *and* The Mammoth Book of Werewolves. *He is the award-winning editor of such anthologies as* Darklands *and* Darklands 2, A Book of Two Halves *and* The Tiger Garden: A Book of Writers' Dreams, *and is also the author of three novels,* Counterparts, Saxophone Dreams *and* The Matter of the Heart.

As the cracks widen in Dracula's carefully-kept sanity, he escapes to the African continent . . .

IT WAS A question of arriving at the right time. You didn't necessarily, for example, turn up at the same time each evening, but juggled various considerations, such as the heat, the number of clouds in the sky, even what type they were, whether they were cumulus or stratus or cirro-stratus – stuff like that. You wanted to turn up just at the right moment, just in time to get a seat and a good view and not a moment too soon. After all, the terrace of the Africa House Hotel was not a place you wanted to spend any more time than you absolutely had to. It simply wasn't that nice.

It wasn't nice partly because you were surrounded by all those people you had gone to Zanzibar to get away from – white people, Europeans, tourists; *mzungu*, the locals called them, red bananas. White inside but red on the outside, as soon as they'd been in the sun for a couple of hours. Apparently there was a strain of red-skinned banana that grew on the island.

And partly because the place itself was grotsville. In colonial days, the Africa House Hotel was the English Club, but since the departure of the British in 1963, it had been pretty much allowed to go to seed.

But you didn't go there for the moth-eaten hunting trophies on the walls, or the charmless service at the counter, but to sit as close to the front of the terrace as you could, order a beer and have it brought to you, and watch the sun sink into the Indian Ocean. Over there, just below the horizon – the continental land mass of Africa. Amazing really that you couldn't see it, thought Craig. It didn't really matter how far away it was – twenty miles, thirty – looking at it on the map, Zanzibar Island was no more than a tick clinging to the giant African elephant.

Craig ordered a Castle lager from the waiter who slunk oilily around the tables and their scattered chairs. He was a strange, tired-looking North African with one of those elastic snake-buckle belts doing the job of keeping his brown trousers up. Similar to the one Craig had worn at school – 8,000 miles away in east London.

He didn't like ordering a Castle, or being seen with one (they didn't give you a glass at the Africa House Hotel). It was South African and everyone knew it was South African. He supposed it was all right now, but still, if people saw you drinking South African beer they'd assume you were drinking it because that's what you drank back home. In South Africa. And whereas it was all right to buy South African goods, it still wasn't all right to be South African.

And Craig wasn't, and he didn't want anyone to think he was, but not so badly that he'd drink any more of the Tanzanian Safari, or the Kenyan Tusker. One was too yeasty, the other so weak it was like drinking bat's piss.

This was his third consecutive evening at the Africa House Hotel and he was by now prepared to let people think he was – or might be – South African. He wasn't staying there, no way, uh-uh – he was staying at Mazson's, a few minutes' walk away. Air-con, satellite TV, a bath as well as a shower – and a business centre. The business centre was what had clinched it. Plus the fact the paper was paying.

Craig slipped the elastic band off his ponytail and shook out his fair hair, brushed it back to round up any strays, and reapplied the elastic. He took off his Oakley wraparound shades and pinched the bridge of his nose between thumb and forefinger. Stuck them back on. Squinted at the sun, still a few degrees above the bank of stratus clouds which would prevent the Africa House Hotel crowd from enjoying a proper sunset for the third evening in a row.

From behind his Oakleys, Craig checked out the terrace: people-watching, with a purpose for once. News of the disappearances clearly wasn't putting these tourists off coming to Zanzibar. Mainly because there wasn't any news. Not enough of a problem in any one country to create a crisis. One weeping family from Sutton Coldfield – "Sarah just wouldn't go off with anyone, she's not that kind of girl"; a red-eyed single mother from Strathclyde – "There's been no word from Louise for three weeks now". It wasn't enough to get the tabloids interested and the broadsheets wouldn't pick up on it until they were sure there was a real story. A big story. No news was no news and, by and large, didn't make the news.

Craig had latched on to Sarah's story following an impassioned letter to the editor of his paper from the missing girl's mother. He was a soft touch, he told his commissioning editor: couldn't bear to think of those good people sitting on the edge their floral-pattern IKEA sofa, waiting for the phone to ring, weeping – especially not in Sutton Coldfield. But MacNeill, who'd been commissioning pieces from Craig for three years, knew the young man only attached himself to a story if there was a story there. And since he was between desk assignments anyway, MacNeill let him go. On the quiet, like. Neither the Tanzanian government nor the Zanzibari police would acknowledge the problem – too damaging to the developing tourism industry, ironically – so Craig needed a cover, which Craig's sister, the wildlife photographer, came up with.

The Zanzibar leopard, smaller than the mainland species, was rumoured by some to be extinct and by others to be around still, though in very small numbers. One of the guide books reckoned if there were any on the islands, they had been domesticated by practitioners of herbal medicine – witch doctors to you and me. The Zanzibari driver who collected Craig from the airport laughed indulgently at the idea. And Craig read later in another guide book that witchcraft was believed to be widely practised on Pemba Island, 85 kilometres to the north of Zanzibar though part of the same territory. Though if you tried to speak to the locals about it, they became embarrassed or politely changed the subject. But that was Pemba, and the disappearances – thirty-seven to date, according to Craig's researches – were quite specifically from Zanzibar Island.

Thirty-seven. Twenty-three women between seventeen and thirty, and fourteen men, some of them older, mid-forties. From Denmark, Germany, Austria, Britain, France, Italy, Australia and the US. Enough of a problem as far as Craig was concerned. He was torn now, he was ashamed to admit, between wanting the world to wake up and make a concerted effort (thereby, hopefully, securing the earlier recovery of Sarah, or Sarah's body, and thirty-six others) and hoping he would be the first to break the story.

The cover. A naturalist based at the University of Sussex, Craig's brief was to confirm whether or not leopards still lived wild on the island. They'd even put Sussex's professor of zoology in the picture, for a consideration of course which they called a consultancy fee, so that if anyone called from Zanzibar to check up on Craig, they'd find him to be bona fide.

That afternoon, Craig had visited the Natural History Museum, quite the bizarrest of its type in his experience. Glass cases full of birds, presumably stuffed birds, but not mounted – lying down, recently-dead looking, their little feet tied together with string. Tags to identify them. Their eyes dabs of chalk. In a grimy case all on its own, the bones of a dodo wired up into a standing position. A couple of stuffed bats – the American Fruit Bat and the Pemba Fruit Bat – ten times the size of the swallow-like creatures that had flitted about his head as he'd walked off his dinner the evening before. A crate with its lid ajar: when he opened it, a flurry of flies, one he couldn't prevent going up his nose. Inside, a board with three rats fixed to it – dead again, stuffed presumably, but with legs trussed at tiny rodent ankles. No effort made to have them assume lifelike poses. No bits of twig and leaf. No glass eyes. No glass case. He dropped the crate lid.

Oddest of all: row upon row of glass jars containing dead sea creatures and deformed animal foetuses, the glass furred up with dust and calcified deposits, so you had to bend down and squint to make out the bloodless remains of a stonefish, the huge crab with the image on its shell of two camels with their masters. The conjoined duiker antelopes.

And the stuffed leopard. They hadn't done a great job on it. The taxidermist's task being to stage a magic show for eternity: the illusion of life in the cock of the head, the setting of a glassy twinkle. The Natural History Museum of Zanzibar should have been asking for their money back on this one. You could still see it was a leopard though. If you didn't know, you'd look at it and you'd say leopard.

Craig examined it from every angle. This was what he was here to find. Ostensibly. It couldn't do any harm to have a good idea what one looked like.

Up on the terrace, the touts were working the crowd – slowly, carefully, with a lower-key approach than they tended to use down in Stone Town. In Stone Town the same guys would shadow you on the same streets day after day.

"Jambo," they'd say.

"Jambo," you'd reply, because it would be rude not to.

"You want to go to Prison Island? You want to go to the East Coast today? Maybe you want go to Nungwi? You want taxi?"

You ran the gauntlet going up Kenyatta Street and never had a moment's peace when you were around Jamyatti Gardens, from where the boats left for Prison Island, its coral reefs and giant tortoises. He'd read the books all right.

"Jambo." The voice was close to him. Craig sneaked a look around as he necked his beer. A young Zanzibari had moved in on a blonde English girl who had been sitting alone. The girl smiled a little shyly and the youth sat down next to her. "The sun is setting," he said and the girl looked out over the ocean. The sun had started to dip behind the bank of cloud. "You want to go to Prison Island tomorrow?" he asked, pulling a pack of cigarettes from his pocket.

The girl shook her head. "No. Thanks." She was still smiling but Craig could see she was a little nervous. Doing battle with her shyness was the adventurous spirit that had brought her this far from whichever northern market town she'd left behind. She was flattered by the youth's attentions but could never quite forget the many warnings her worried parents would have given her in the weeks before she left.

The tout went through the list and still she politely declined. In the end he changed tack and offered to buy her a drink. Craig heard her say she'd have a beer. The youth caught the waiter's eye and spoke to him fast in Swahili. Next time the waiter came by he had a can of Stella for the girl and a Coke for the tout. Craig watched as the girl popped open the Stella and almost imperceptibly shifted on her seat so that her upper body was angled slightly further away from the boy in favour of the ocean. Maybe she shouldn't have accepted the beer, thought Craig. Or maybe it was old-fashioned to think like that. Perhaps these days girls had the right to accept the beer and turn the other way. He just wasn't sure the African youth would see it like that. Whether he was a practising Muslim – the abnegation of alcohol told him that – or not.

A high-pitched whine in Craig's ear. A pin-prick in the forearm. He smacked his hand down hard, lifted it slowly to peer underneath.

Craig started, then shuddered; never able to stand the sight of blood, whether his own or anybody else's, he had once run out of the cinema during an afternoon screening of *The Shining*. He had fainted at the scene of a road accident, having caught sight of a pedestrian victim's leg, her stocking sodden with her own blood. She survived unscathed; Craig's temple bore a scar to this day where he had hit his head on the pavement.

The mosquito had drunk well, and not just of Craig either. His stomach turning over, he quickly inspected the creature's dinner which was smeared across his arm, a red blotch in the shape of Madagascar, almost an inch long. Craig wondered whose blood it was, given that the mozzie had barely had enough time to sink its needle beneath his skin. Some other drinker's? Craig looked about. Not that of the Italian in the tight briefs, he hoped. Nor ideally had it come from either of the two South African rugby players sitting splayed-legged at the front by the railing.

He spat on to a paper tissue and wiped his arm vigorously without giving it another look until he was sure it had to be clear. The energy from the slap had been used up bursting the balloon of blood; the mosquito's empty body, split but relatively intact, was stuck to Craig's arm like an empty popsicle wrapper.

This bothered him less than the minutest trace of blood still inside the dead insect's glassy skin.

When he looked up, the blonde girl had joined a group of Europeans – Scandinavians or Germans by the look of them – and was eagerly working her way into their telling of travellers' tales, while the young tout glared angrily at the bank of clouds obscuring the sun, his left leg vibrating like a wire. Craig hoped he wasn't angry enough to get nasty. Doubted it – after all, chances were this sort of thing happened a lot up here. The kid couldn't expect a hundred per cent strike rate.

Craig gave it five minutes, then went over and sat next to the kid. Kid turned around and Craig started talking.

Ten minutes later, Craig and the kid both left, though not together. Craig was heading for Mazson's Hotel and bed; the kid, his timetable for the following day sorted, having spoken to Craig, was heading home as well – home for him being his family's crumbling apartment in the heart of the Stone Town, among the rats and the rubbish and the running sewage. To be fair, the authorities were tackling the sewage, but they hadn't yet got as far as the kid's block.

The group that Alison, the blonde girl, had joined was approached by another tout, an older, taller fellow. More confident than the kid, not so much driven by other motivations, less distracted – he had a job to do. With her new companions, Alison was not so nervous about getting into the trips business. She wanted to go to Prison Island, they all did; they looked around to include her as the tout waited for an answer, and she nodded, smiling with relief. Turned out they were German, two of them, the two girls, but naturally they spoke perfect English; the third girl and the boy, who appeared to be an item, were Danish, but you wouldn't know it – their English, spoken with American accents, was pretty good too.

"We were just in Goa," said Kristin, one of the German girls. "It is so good. Have you been?"

"No," Alison shook her head. "But I'd like to go. I've heard about it." She'd heard about it all right. About the raves and the beach parties, the drugs and the boys – Australians, Americans, Europeans. It had been hard enough to get permission to come to Zanzibar, especially alone, but her parents had accepted her right to make a bid for independence.

"Ach!" shouted Anna, the second German girl, flailing her bare arms as she failed to make contact with a mozzie. "Scheisse!"

"Where are you staying, Alison?" asked the Danish boy, Lief, his arm around his girlfriend's shoulder.

Alison named a cheap hotel on the edge of Stone Town.

"You should move into Emerson's House," Lief's girlfriend, Karin, advised. "That's where we're all staying. It's really cool. Great chocolate cake . . ." She looked at Lief and for some reason they sniggered. Kristin and Anna joined in and soon they were all laughing, Alison included. Their combined laughter was so loud they couldn't hear anything else.

People started to look, but, leaning in towards each other, they could only hear their own laughter.

Popo – the kid – picked up Craig outside Mazson's at nine the next morning in a battered but just about roadworthy Suzuki Jeep.

"Jambo," he said as Craig climbed in beside him. "Jozani Forest."

"Jambo. Jozani Forest," Craig confirmed their destination.

They rumbled out of town, which became gradually more ramshackle as they approached the outskirts. Popo used the horn every few seconds to clear the road of cyclists, who were out in their hundreds. No one resented being ordered to make way, Craig noticed, as they would back home. Popo's deft handling took the Jeep around potholes and, where they were too big to be avoided, slowly through them. Most of the men in the streets wore long flowing white garments and skull caps; as they got further out of town, the Arabic influence became less pronounced. The women here wore brightly coloured kikois and carried unfeasibly large bags and packages on their heads. Orderly crowds of schoolgirls in white headgear and navy tunics streamed into schools that appeared to be no more than collections of outbuildings.

Between the villages, banana plantations ran right up to the edge of the road. Huge bunches of green fruit pointed up to the sky, brown raffia-like leaves crackled in the Jeep's draught.

"You look for Red Colobus monkey?" Popo asked without taking his eye off the road.

"I told you last night," Craig reminded him. "Zanzibar leopard. I'm looking for the leopard."

"No leopard here," Popo shook his head.

"I heard the witch doctors keep them."

"No leopard."

"There are witch doctors, then?"

Popo didn't say anything as they passed through another tiny village, crowds of little children too small to be in school running up to the Jeep and waving at Craig, old men sat under a shelter made out of dried palm leaves. The children shouted after them: "Jambo, jambo!" Craig waved back.

"In Jozani Forest . . ." Popo said slowly, "Red Colobus monkey. Only here on Zanzibar."

"I know," said Craig, wiping his forearm across his slippery brow. "And the leopards? The witch doctors? I have to find them."

"No leopard here."

He wasn't going to get much more out of Popo, that was clear. When the kid swung the Jeep off the road, he reacted swiftly by grabbing his arm, but they had only pulled into the carpark for the forest. He let go of the kid's arm.

"Sorry. Took me by surprise."

Popo blinked slowly.

"No leopard here," he repeated.

The noise of the boat's engine, a constant ragged chugging, made conversation impossible. There was no point trying to make yourself heard, but that didn't stop Lief from occasionally mouthing easily understood remarks about the choppiness of the water, the heat of the sun.

The others – Karin, Anna, Kristin and Alison – grinned and nodded, although Alison's grin was a little forced. Her trip to Prison Island was always going to exact a price, even though it was only supposed to be a half-hour hop: Alison could barely walk through a puddle without getting seasick. As the 25-foot wooden craft took another dive off the top of the next crest, she lurched forward and felt her stomach do the same, only, it seemed, without stopping. She retched, assumed the crash position, fully expecting to be ditched in the drink. It didn't happen. The boat lumbered up the next heavy swell, perched an instant at its arête, and plummeted into the trough. Alison groaned.

The two Danes were chattering excitedly in their own tongue, clearly having a ball. When she looked up, Alison saw Anna and Kristin smiling down at her. "Are you okay?" one of them asked and Alison just managed to shake her head. "It's not far to the island," Anna said, looking forward, but the boat pitched to port, throwing her off her feet. She tumbled into Alison's lap, Alison dry-retching once again.

"Oh God," she moaned. "I can't stand it."

"It's not far now," Lief tried to reassure her, although he was puzzled as to why they had shifted around so much that the bow was now pointing out to sea.

"Where are we going?" Anna asked, of no one in particular, once she had picked herself up off the duckboards.

Now Kristin demanded "What's going on?" as the bow swung around several degrees further to port. Their course could no longer be even loosely interpreted as being bound for Prison Island. "Where are you taking us?" she shouted at the boat's skipper, a lad no more than eighteen sat in the stern, his hand on the outboard throttle.

They were now heading into the wind, and spray broke over the bow every seventh or eighth wave. Alison had started to cry, tears slipping noiselessly over green cheeks. Her mouth was set in a firm, down-curved bow, her brow creased in determined abstraction.

Lief rose to his feet unsteadily and asked the skipper "What's going on?" The 18-year-old just stared at the horizon. "We want to go to Prison Island. We paid you the money. Where are you taking us?" Still the guy wouldn't look at him. Lief leaned forward to grab his arm but found himself jerked back from behind. The other African, who had been squatting in the bow, motioned to Lief that he should sit down. The fingers of his left hand were wrapped around the stubby handle of a fisherman's knife.

"Sit," he ordered. "Sit." He looked at the girls. "Sit." He pointed at the wooden bench seats and everyone complied. Now Anna had started to weep as well and was not so quiet about it as Alison.

"Hands," the boy barked, his jaws snapping around the rusty gutting blade and grabbing at Lief's wrists. With a length of twine he quickly tied Lief's hands behind his back before any of the girls had the presence of mind to knock him off his feet while he had his hands occupied and was temporarily unarmed. They would live to regret this missed opportunity.

Anna and Kristin were almost paralysed with fear. Alison was within an ace of throwing herself overboard, believing that to be actually in the water could not be worse than being in a boat on it. Still the boat struck out against the direction of the incoming waves and soon they were all soaked from the spray over the bow. The boat climbed and plunged, climbed and plunged. Alison leant over the side and was quietly sick; she hoped it would make her feel better. It was funny how not even mortal fear could distract her from her seasickness.

Neither, it transpired, could the act of vomiting. If anything, she felt worse, and when the boat slipped around several degrees to port and took the waves side-on, she liked it even less. Each time the narrow craft leaned to either side she thought she was going in – again she considered doing it deliberately. Anna and Kristin were both crying, staring alternately at each other and at Lief, who was ashen-faced. Alison justified her intention to jump ship by interpreting the others' introvertedness as being an atavistic retreat into their original social groupings in the face of extreme fear. They would no more try to save her life than they would that of one of the two kidnappers, she reasoned. How long had they known her? Twelve hours. What kind of bond grew in such a short time? Not a lasting one.

She remembered what her mother had once told her, when they'd taken the ferry to Calais. "Look at the horizon," she'd said. "Watch the land. Don't look at the water." Thinking of her mother only brought fresh tears and looking left at the palm-fringed shoreline of the island some half a mile away made her feel no better. There was no way she would ever be able to swim such a distance, not even if her life depended on it. And seasickness had to be better than either drowning or being eaten by hammerhead sharks – she'd done her homework and mother nature's bizarrest-looking fish was known to nest in several of the bays around Zanzibar.

She leaned forward again in order to sneak a look at the African boy who had gone back to the bow now that Lief was tied up and neither she nor any of the three other girls appeared to be capable of making a move against him and his mate. He appeared to be searching for something on land at the same time as casting quick little glances back at his captives. If she wasn't mistaken, Alison thought he was nervous. She wondered if they could turn that to their advantage. Maybe he was new to this game, whatever it entailed.

"Listen," she addressed the others, "we've got to do something."

The three girls looked up, whereas Lief retreated further inside himself. He looked as if they might have lost him. Were it not for him, they could have all jumped overboard on a given signal and helped each other to shore. But with his hands tied behind his back, Lief would be unable to swim and the logistics of trying to drag him, lifesaving-style, over half a mile even between them seemed insurmountable.

Karin and Anna were still crying; Kristin had stopped and was calmer. "What can we do?" she wondered.

"Hey!" the boy in the bow shouted at them, brandishing his knife.

"We could all go overboard and take Lief with us," Alison whispered. "See if we can make it to the shore. Or we rush one of them, try and overpower him, knock him in, whatever. We've got to do something."

"Even if we jump in, they've got the boat, they would easily catch up with us."

The boat tipped suddenly as the boy from the bow skipped over the wooden cross-seats towards them and, sweeping his right arm in a wide arc, connected with Kristin under her jaw, knocking her completely off balance. Alison watched in horror as Kristin teetered for a second close to the gunwhale, unaware of the seventh wave about to hit the boat on the starboard side. A scarlet stripe had been drawn on her cheek by the boy's knife which had been in his hand when he hit her.

The wave smacked into the side of the boat and she was gone in a flash, vanished.

"No!" Alison screamed, clambering over to that side of the boat and leaning over. Kristin had been swallowed by the waves. Shock, presumably, having rendered her incapable of reaction. She must have taken her first breath only after hitting the water.

"You murdering bastard! You fucking . . ."

Alison leapt at the youth in her fury, but he grabbed her slender wrists and held her at bay, grinning while she struggled. She tried to kick him but he threw her down on to the bottom of the boat where she scrambled for safety as he leaned down over her threatening with the knife.

"No more," he said.

Kristin's friend Anna had clasped her arms around her knees and was rocking to and fro on her seat, moaning softly. Karin was sobbing, caught between trying to protect Alison and looking after her distracted boyfriend.

When he was satisfied the threat to his and his partner's authority had diminished, the youth returned to his post in the bows, occasionally shouting remarks back to the stern in Swahili.

Alison climbed back on to a seat, unable to control a violent trembling which had seized her limbs. She kept visualizing Kristin washed up on the beach: she would appear not to be moving, then would cough up a lungful of sea water and splutter as she fought to regain control of her breathing. When the images were blacked out by another sickening swoop down the windward side of a wave, she knew that Kristin was dead. She might eventually get washed up among the mangrove swamps of south-western Zanzibar, but her bones would have been picked clean by the hammerheads.

The boat shifted around dramatically on a shout from the look-out boy. They were heading into shore. Alison doubted whether Lief would even be able to walk.

Jozani is the last vestige of the tropical forest that had at one time covered most of the island. The Red Colobus monkeys make it a tourist attraction, but the monkeys conveniently inhabit a small corner of the forest near the road, not far from one of the spice plantations. Visitors are taken out of the car park, back across the road and down a track to where the monkeys hang out.

The first monkey Craig saw was not remotely red.

"Blue monkey," the guide said. "Over there," he pointed through the trees, "is Red Colobus."

Craig saw a number of reddish-brown monkeys of various sizes playing around in the trees; leaping from one to another, they made quite a racket when they landed among the dry, leathery leaves.

"Great," Craig said. "What about the leopards?"

The guide gave him a blank look.

"You want see main forest?"

"Yes, I want see main forest." He followed the guide back to the road and into the car park. The tour around the main forest, Craig knew, would only scratch the surface of Jozani.

"My driver can guide me," Craig said, slipping a five dollar bill into the guide's palm. "You stay here. Relax. Put your feet up. Get a beer or something."

The guide looked doubtful, but Craig beckoned Popo across. He walked slowly, with a loose stride, long baggy cotton trousers and some kind of sandals. "Tell him it's okay," Craig said to Popo. "You can take me in."

After a moment's hesitation, Popo talked rapidly to the guide, who shrugged and walked back to the reception area defined by a bunch of easy chairs and some printed information and photographs pinned up on boards.

"Let's go, Popo."

Popo headed into the forest.

They followed the path until Craig sensed they were starting to double-back on themselves. He stopped, pushed his sunglasses up over his forehead and lit a cigarette.

"I think I want to head off the path a little," he said as he offered a cigarette to Popo.

The African took a cigarette, and lit it, the $100 bill folded around the pack not lost on him.

"Do you want to take the whole pack?" Craig asked. "I have to head off the path a little way. Leopards, you know?"

"No leopard here." Popo's hand hovered in mid-air.

"Witch doctors then. You interested or not?" Craig offered him the bribe again and nodded in the direction he wanted to go. Popo took the pack of Marlboro, slipping the cash out from underneath the cellophane wrapper and folding it into his back pocket. Then he led the way into the forest proper. After a few yards he knelt down at the base of a tree. Craig knelt down beside him and looked where the kid was pointing. There were dozens of tiny black frogs, each no bigger than a finger tip, congregating on some of the broader fallen leaves.

"Here water come," said Popo. "From sea."

"Floodwater?"

"Yes. No one come here. Dangerous."

"Good. Let's go on, in that case."

As soon as they hit the sandy bottom, the youth in the bow jumped out and tugged the boat up on to the beach. The kid in the stern pulled up the outboard. Three gangly, raggedy youths walked across the beach to meet them. Alison, Karin, Lief and Anna were forced out of the boat at knifepoint and the two youths exchanged a few words with the newcomers before turning their boat around and pushing off from the shore.

Alison, Karin and Anna had to walk with their hands on their heads to the treeline; Lief's hands were still tied behind his back. His face betrayed no emotion. Alison was amazed he'd been able to get up and walk. As for Alison, her legs had turned to rubber, despite her small relief at being on dry land. Their new captors were also armed and ruthless-looking.

The wind blew through the tops of the palm trees, an endless sinister rustling. But as they trooped into the forest, the palms thinned out, their place taken by sturdier vegetation. The canopy was so high it created an almost cathedral stillness. All Alison could hear now, apart from their shuffling progress through the trammelled undergrowth, were the occasional hammerings of woodpeckers and the screams of other, unknown birds. From time to time, on the forest floor she would spot sea shells glimmering through the mulch. She jumped when she almost walked into a bat, only to discover it was a broad, brown leaf waiting to drop from its tapering branch. She swiped at it and when it didn't instantly fall she went ballistic, swinging her arms at it as if it were a punchball. The party halted and two of the African youths came towards her, their knives at the ready. She peered over the edge of sanity at the possibility of panic, stood finely balanced debating her options, caught between self-preservation and loyalty to the group.

Before she knew what she was doing she had taken flight. One of the youths might have taken a swing at her, the point of his knife flashing just beneath her nose. She couldn't be sure. Something had happened to spur her into action. Action which she instantly regretted, mainly because it was irrevocable and she knew she would never outrun the local boys; also because she had deserted her companions, which according to her own code of honour was unforgivable. Yet she couldn't be sure they wouldn't have taken the same chance. Indeed, by running, she had created a diversion which, if they had any sense, they would exploit.

These thoughts flashed through her mind as she crashed through the forest, her flesh catching on twigs and bark and huge serrated leaves yet she felt no pain. Adrenaline surged through her system. She couldn't hear her pursuers but she knew that meant nothing. These boys would be able to fly. Whatever it took, to render her bid for freedom utterly futile.

As soon as they heard the drumming, Popo became jittery. Craig didn't give him more than five minutes.

"What is it, Popo?" he asked him. "What's going on?"

"Mbo," was all he would say, his eyes darting to and fro. "Mbo."

It was faint, still obviously some way off, but unmistakably the sound of someone drumming. It wasn't the surf and it wasn't coconuts dropping from the palm trees, it was someone's hand beating out a rhythm on a set of skins. A couple of tom-toms, maybe more, the kind of thing you played with your hand, sat cross-legged – whatever they were called. Craig hadn't a fucking clue. As for Popo, he was out of there. Craig didn't even watch him go, back the way they'd come. His hundred bucks had brought him this far, which was all he'd wanted the kid to do.

A mosquito whined by his ear. He brushed it away and walked on, moving slowly but carefully in the direction of the drumming.

He stopped when he heard another sound, coming from over to his right. Another, similar sound, but more ragged, less musical. The sound that would be made, he realised, by someone running.

Craig's mind raced, imagining somone running into danger, and he was about to spring forward to intercept the runner, whom he still couldn't see, when he saw hovering in the space in front of him a whole cloud of mosquitoes.

They shifted about minutely, relative to each other, like vibrating molecules, seeming at one moment to dart towards him, only to feel a restraining influence and hang back. Because of the noise of the fast approaching runner he couldn't hear their dreadful whine, but he imagined it.

And the runner appeared, crashing her way through the trees, arms and legs flying – a young girl, the young girl from the Africa House terrace, Craig realised – heading straight for the source of the drumming.

"Hey! Stop!" Craig shouted as the swarm of mosquitoes swung its thousand-eyed head to follow the girl's progress. The whole cloud tilted and curved after the girl. She screamed as they crowded around her head: hardly could she have announced her arrival any more extravagantly. Not that Craig had any idea who or what was responsible for the drumming, nor whether they represented a threat. He just had his instincts.

The girl had a head start on him. He ran as fast as he could but couldn't close on her. Too many long lunches in The Eagle. Too many fast food containers in the bin under his desk. His heart beat a tattoo against his chest. He thrust his arms out in front of him to catch a tree trunk and so managed to stop short as the girl burst through into a wide clearing, the mozzies still shadowing her.

His hand-drums lying scattered at his feet, the drummer rose to his full height – six foot something of skin and bone, unfolding like some med student's life-size prop. He was a white man, although it was impossible to judge his age. His feet and lower legs were bare, but the rest of him was clothed. Craig rubbed his eyes, which had started to go funny. Perhaps the heat and the exertion. The fear, maybe, which he acknowledged for the first time, his pulse scampering. The man's coat constantly shifted in and out of focus, like an image perceived through a stereogram. Either there was something in Craig's eyes obscuring his vision, or some filmy substance, spider's web or other insectile secretion, draped across the undergrowth between him and the clearing. The tall man moved closer to Alison, who shrank away from him. He peered at her with bulging eyes that indicated thyroid disorder. His coat settled organically around his coat-hanger shoulders. Alison screamed and the coat shimmered. She lashed out with her right hand, drew a swathe through the living, clinging coat of mosquitoes. They swarmed about her head for a moment, mingling with the swarm that had aggravated her, before gravitating back to their host.

The man's movements were slow. He seemed to make them reluctantly, as if he had no choice. His face was too sunken in the cheeks and uniformly white to betray any emotion. Stepping back from the girl, he picked up a long bone-white blood-stained instrument from the floor by his drums and strapped it over his skull. The false snout, a foot long by the look of it, wobbled hideously as he approached the girl again. The base of it – the knuckle joint, let's face it, the thing had been fashioned from a human femur – rested against his mouth. He blew through it, a low burbling whistle, at which the mosquitoes became markedly less agitated and settled around him; Alison sank to her knees in a dead faint and he snuffled about her prone body.

Craig was furiously considering what action he could take when a further crashing through the undergrowth announced the arrival of Alison's friends from the Africa House, bound and led by three tough-looking African youths who each mumbled what appeared to be a respectful greeting to the tall man – "Mbo," they each seemed to be saying.

Lief, the Danish boy, had remained unresponsive throughout the trek from the beach. His girlfriend, Karin, was trembling with fear and continuous shock; Anna simply screamed whenever anyone came near her. Two of the youths took hold of Karin and Anna and laid them out flat on the ground. Grabbing lengths of dried palm leaves, they wound them around the girls' ankles, going around and around several times, then over the loop in the other direction between the legs until they were secure. They left the arms. The third African youth swiftly bound Lief's ankles in the same manner. Craig had to strain to see where the three were taken: beyond the lean-to on the far side of the clearing. But what lay hidden there, Craig could not see.

The tall white-skinned man was still inspecting Alison when one of the youths returned and started to bind her around the ankles as well. The man sat down once more upon the ground, his legs becoming dismantled beneath his hazy coat like a pair of fishing rods being taken apart. He picked up his hand-drums and began to play.

Craig took advantage of the noise to retreat a few yards from the edge of the clearing back into the forest. Twenty yards back, he crept around towards the back of the camp. It took him a while, because he had to move slowly to avoid alerting anyone to his presence, but he got there. Then it took him a moment before he recognised what he was seeing, even though this was what he'd been looking for. What he'd come to Africa for.

They hung from the branches of a single tree. Like bats.

Like bats, they hung upside down.

Like bats, or like the poor creatures Craig had seen in the museum in the town – bound, each one of them, at the ankles. Three dozen at least.

Most of them were completely drained of blood, desiccated, like the Bombay duck Craig would always order with his curry just to raise a laugh. Husks swinging in the breeze. Wind-dried Bombay duck. Long hair suggested which victims were female, while bigger skeletons hinted at male – but there was no way of telling with most of the poor wretches.

Nearest the ground hung the recent additions – Karin, Anna, Lief. Craig heard the tall man coming around the side of the hut, before he saw him. The wind was not strong enough to drown out the whining concert of the mosquitoes the tall man wore around himself like so many familiars. His own insectile eyes protruded as he looked at his new arrivals, all strung up and ready for him.

Behind him came two of the youths carrying Alison.

The tall man, wearing his bone nose-flute, took a tiny step towards Anna, whose screams were torn out of her throat at his approach.

I could already smell the coppery tang of blood even before the ancient ectomorph in the coat of mosquitoes prodded the young girl's throat with the sharpened femur he wore strapped to his head.

Craig was ashamed at himself, but couldn't stop the opening sentences of his eye-witness account forming in his mind.

I was smelling the blood he had already spilt. I must have smelled it on him or in the air, because the ground beneath my feet nourished no more exotic blooms than the surrounding forest, for he spilled no blood. This exiled European, this tall, spindly shadow of a man – scarcely a man at all – drank the blood, every last drop. It was what kept him alive. I sensed this as much as deduced it as my eye ranged across the bat-like corpses suspended from his tamarind tree. At the same time I felt a shadow fall across my heart, from which I knew I should never be free, even if I were somehow to effect an escape for myself and the youngsters who had joined the monster's collection.

This was Craig's problem now. The purple prose would die a death at the hands of the paper's subs – but thinking of it in terms of the news story he had come out here to investigate helped him distance himself sufficiently to keep his mind intact, to remain alert. Whatever the odds stacked against him, he still possessed the element of surprise.

While he was still thinking, racking his brains for an escape route, the tall man's head jerked forwards, driving the tip of his bone-flute into the hollow depression of Anna's throat. Blood bubbled instantly around the puncture then disappeared as it was sucked down the bone. Craig forced his eyes shut, fighting his own terror of spilt blood. But he had heard the man's first swallow, his greedy gargle as he tried to accommodate too much at once. Craig had always believed himself the hard man of investigative journalism, hard to reach emotionally – his bed back home never slept two for more than one night at a time – and impossible to shock. His fear of the sight of blood had never been a problem before; he avoided stories which trailed bloody skirts – car wrecks and shoot-outs – not his style.

As he retched and tumbled forwards out of the concealing forest, he knew this was a story to which he would never append his byline: firstly, because he wasn't going to get out alive, and secondly, even if he did, the trauma would never allow him to relive these moments.

Two youths pounced on him, jabbering excitedly in Swahili. A third youth darted into the forest in search of any accomplices.

As the youths bound his ankles, Craig watched the tall man gulp down the German girl's blood. He drank so eagerly and with such vigorous relish, it was possible to believe he completely voided her body of all nine pints. His cheeks had coloured up and Craig thought he could see a change in the man's body. It had filled out, the mosquitoes that clung to him no longer covered quite so much of his grey-white nakedness.

He wondered when his own turn would come. Would the tall man save up his victims, drink them dry one a day, or would he binge? Already, he had turned to Alison, swinging from her bonds as she tried desperately to free herself. She was a fighter. Karin sobbed uncontrollably alongside, and Lief was wherever he had gone to while they were all still on the boat. As Craig was hoisted upside down and secured by one of the youths, he thought to himself it would be preferable to go first. As if sensing his silent plea, the tall man twisted around to consider the attractions of his body over the girl's.

Popo's approach was swift and silent. The first any of those present knew of it was an abrupt cacophony: the crashing of bodies through dry vegetation, the deep-throated growling of hungry beasts, the concerted yells and screeches of our rescuers. Visually I was aware of a black and gold blur, flashing ivory teeth and ropes of saliva swinging from heavy jaws as the leopards leapt.

Popo saved my life at that point – the exact moment at which the old Craig died. It was necessary, if I were to survive. The hard-nosed journalist was as dead as the corpses swinging in the breeze higher up in the tree. He would not write up this story, I would – but not for a long time, and not for the newspapers. It's history now, become legend, myth – just as it had always been to Popo and the men of Jozani.

Those who survived it – and they are few – speak of it rarely. Lief lives quietly, on his own, in a house by the sea in his native Denmark. Karin, his former girlfriend, has returned to Africa as an aid worker. Most recently she has been in eastern Zaire: I saw her interviewed on the TV news during the refugee crisis. I have no contact with either of them. Alison and I tried to remain in touch – a couple of letters exchanged and we met once, in a bar in the West End, but the lights and the noise upset us both and we soon parted. I have no idea where she is now or what she is doing.

I left my reporter's job on medical advice and spent some time fell-walking in South Wales until I felt well enough to return to work, but on the production side this time. I never have to read the copy or look at the pictures – just make sure the words are on the page and the colours are right.

I go to Regent's Park Zoo every so often to look at the leopards. Watching them prowl around their cages reminds me of the moment in my life when I was most alive – when I saw, with an almost photographic clarity, one of Popo's leopards take a swipe with its heavy paw at the bloodsucking creature's midriff. There was an explosion, a shower of blood, Anna's blood. His skin flapped uselessly, transparently, like that of the mosquito I had swatted against my arm on the terrace of the Africa House Hotel.

Popo and his men – witch doctors or Jozani Forest guides, I never found out – untied us and lowered us safely to the ground. Later that evening, after the police had been and started the clear-up operation, Popo himself took me back to Zanzibar Town in his Suzuki. On the outskirts of town he brought the vehicle to a sudden halt, flapping his hand about his head as if trying to beat off an invisible foe.

"What's up?" I asked, leaning towards him.

"Mbo," he muttered.

I heard a high-pitched whine as it passed by my ear. I too lashed out angrily.

"Mosquito?" I asked.

"Mbo," he nodded.

It turned out I had got the little sod, despite my flailing attack. Maybe it was just stunned, but it lay in the palm of my hand. I was relieved to see that its body was empty of blood.

"We call it mosquito," I said and I shivered as I wondered if we had brought it from the forest on our clothes.

For months later, I would discover mosquitoes, no more than half a dozen or so, among the clothes I had brought back from Zanzibar. So far, they have all been dead ones.

Paul J. McAuley

The Worst Place in the World

Paul J. McAuley's first major success as a writer was in 1988, when he won the Philip K. Dick Award for his début novel, Four Hundred Billion Stars. *Subsequent books include* Secret Harmonies, Eternal Light *(shortlisted for the Arthur C. Clarke Award),* Red Dust *and* Pasquale's Angel *(winner of the Sidewise Award for best long form alternate history), the short story collections* The King of the Hill *and* The Invisible Country, *and the anthology* In Dreams *(co-edited with Kim Newman).*

He won the 1995 British Fantasy Award for his short story "The Temptation of Dr. Stein" (from The Mammoth Book of Frankenstein*), and also the 1996 Arthur C. Clarke Award for his novel* Fairyland.

Shocked back to sanity, but with his blood now contaminated, Dracula begins to rebuild his power-base from Africa . . .

IT IS A square room twenty feet on each side, with a small, high window blocked by bars and wire mesh. A broken-down cinema projector squats in the middle of the room, its electrical guts ripped out, its lens missing. The concrete floor is filthy, and awash with sewer water in one corner; the unpainted breeze block walls are streaked green and black with algae and mould. Old blood scabs a patch of the floor; Harry Merrick can smell it, strong as spoiled meat, above the fresh blood which spatters his clothes. It is a terrible place, but after the hot, black horror of Block A it seems like the bridal suite of the Hilton International.

"You a political now," one of his guards says. Her shiny black skin is puffed and loose, like that of a three-day-old corpse. Bristles sprout in tufts from her chin and neck; yellow tusks pierce her upper lip. She wears camouflage fatigues and mirrored sunglasses, and aims her M16 with awkward, clawed hands while a shivering medical orderly, stinking of fear, takes a sample of Harry's blood. The man gets the vein on the third attempt, leaving a bad haematoma in the pit of Harry's elbow that begins to disperse even as the barrel of the big syringe fills with dark blood. The orderly plunges the syringe into an ice bucket and scurries away, mocked by the guards.

"That won't do you any good," Harry says. "Loses its goodness as soon as it leaves my body, turns to black powder in a few minutes. Tricky stuff, blood."

"We do magic with it," the woman guard says. "Bad magic. *Black* magic."

Another woman, as monstrous as the first, unlocks manacles Harry could have parted with a twist of his wrists. But there are too many guards and dogs between here and freedom, and some of the guards are as strong as he is.

The guard licks at the weeping sores around the bases of her tusks. Her tongue is bright red, and forked at the tip. She says, "The Count comes for you soon. Then maybe we stake you and cut off your head."

"I look forward to it," Harry says and straightens up. A mistake. The guard reverses her rifle and thumps Harry in the kidneys and then, when he doubles over obediently, in the back of his head.

"Animal," the guard says. "Killer. *Leech.*"

A human guard fixes a crucifix to the wall and then the door is slammed and double-locked, and Harry is left alone with his shame.

Harry first heard of the Count a month before he was arrested. He had gone to the almost empty market to try and buy fresh fish and vegetables for the bar's kitchens. The war, so long a rumour far away in the south, had finally reached the capital, following on the heels of the swarms of refugees.

The rebels had crossed the border two months ago, had quickly taken the iron mines and begun a slow push towards Lake Albert and the capital. At first the rebels' advance had followed a strict tempo. They would take a town and pause, regrouping and strengthening their position, then move on again. But recently the rebels had split into two unequal groups, the smaller more disciplined and more efficient (their leader, Prince Marshall, who had taken to telephoning the BBC World Service with boastful accounts of skirmishes inflated to battles, drove about the front in a jeep, shooting any of his troops who paused to indulge in looting), and the pace of the advance had quickened. Before the split in the rebel ranks there had always been food available in the capital if you could pay the price, preferably in US dollars, but now even the staples of rice and manioc were running low.

Harry Merrick had done his best to keep his bar operating normally, even if it meant dipping into his reserves to match inflated war prices. It was a matter of keeping up appearances. The bar was Harry's refuge – had been for thirty years. It was popular with expatriots and the corrupt businessmen, government officials and army officers who had flourished under President Weah. The whores were clean and young; the booze was unadulterated; the food was good, thanks to Francis, the Fela cook. But the army, since the *coup* principally of the President's tribe, had started to round up Fela men, because both Prince Marshall and Leviticus Smith, the leader of the main group of rebels, were Fela. Harry's cook refused to go out after two of his uncles were arrested and shot, and so Harry had taken over the buying duties.

The capital's food market was a maze of tin-roofed stalls beside the ferry terminal, with the eight storey National Bank, the tallest building in the country, on the other side of the wide lakeside avenue. Normally, the market was bustling from dawn until dusk, but lately less than half the stalls were open, and those half-empty. Harry, in sunglasses and wide-brimmed bush hat to protect him from the early morning light, was haggling over a cage of scrawny chickens when the army truck drove up.

The Bureau of State Research had maintained a low but constant state of terror in the capital since the *coup d'etat* five years ago. President Daniel Weah was a vain, badly educated man with an inferiority complex matched only by his greed and ruthless cunning. He had killed all his fellow plotters in the confusion after the *coup* and assumed total power as President-For-Life, although he still held his former army rank of sergeant. One by one, he had removed the government officials and ministers of the old regime and replaced them with badly educated men from his village. The Chief Justice had been shot in court; the Minister for Defence and two senior army generals had died when their helicopter had been brought down by a heat-seeking missile near the border; the head of the TV station had been blown up by a car bomb that killed sixteen passersby and wounded more than fifty others. Prominent business men had been assassinated, too, and the state had appropriated their assets; like many other small businesses, Harry paid his taxes directly to a bagman who came around every week and who had an uncanny knowledge of the turnover of the bar.

None of this was particularly exceptional for a post-revolution African country in the early 1980s, but after the rebels took the south, the army began its own terror campaign. Soldiers of the two tribes which had previously held power in the country were disarmed and herded into camps; more than a hundred were killed when they had tried to break out of their barracks. Bodies appeared at intersections with their severed heads in their laps, seeming to watch the thin traffic go past. No one dared remove them. A missionary was shot in his church because he had given shelter to the families of two disappeared army officers. Checkpoints were set up at every road out of the city and if someone was detained they were never seen alive again.

Despite the terror and the pincer-like advances of the two groups of rebels, most of Harry's acquaintances in the golf club, the focal point of the expatriate community, were of the opinion that the President would survive. These were men who had lost almost everything as the economy dwindled away into the pockets of a very few, but like a gambler who stakes everything on a final throw, they refused to believe that they were out of the game. Harry himself thought that the President was smarter than he looked. Daniel Weah might be a swaggering bully who behaved like a cattle herder who had just come to the big city, but that was an act. He played dumb, but was shrewd and well-advised, and always pretended to listen to the elders of his own tribe. Now, though, it seemed that he was losing his grip; a few nights ago he had had to appear on TV and explain that the massacre at the barracks had been due to rebel infiltrators, which no one believed at all.

When the army truck pulled up by the side of the road, the crowd parted for it with alacrity. It was a Bedford ten tonner with a heavy grill over its radiator, its cab and the canvas cover over its loadbed splotched brown and green. Soldiers jumped down, lifted a man's corpse out by its arms and legs, and dropped it onto the tin counter of an empty butcher's stall. Then the truck pulled away, soldiers clinging to its sides and whooping with laughter at their joke and firing their M16s into the air even though so-called happy shooting had been banned to save ammunition.

The corpse wore only ragged trousers. It had been severely beaten, and shot in the back of the head. An iron rod had been pounded into its chest, and its hands and feet had been cut off. Something horrible had happened to its mouth; it looked like someone had broken the jaw and stretched it, then hammered crooked ivory nails into the gums and through the cheeks. The crowd looked at the mutilated corpse, murmuring to each other. Harry, shocked, pushed his way out of the circle, and was hailed by the French journalist, Rene Sante.

As usual, Sante was brimming over with gossip and rumours. He was indefatigable, a stringer for half a dozen newspapers and one of the major American TV networks. He had been at a dinner for the remaining ambassadors last night, he said. The President had worn his sergeant's uniform, his blouson heavy with ranks of medals he had awarded himself. Before the dessert course he had made a speech.

"He said he would deal the rebels a blow from which they could not recover," Sante told Harry. "There's talk he plans to napalm the front line villages. He also said that there were no shortages, that thieves had stolen the riches of the country and he would soon arrest them all, and all would be well. Then he took a spoonful of his dessert and got up and left. He gets bored at those things, my friend. I've been to about twenty, and I've never once had dessert. It was ice cream, too – I haven't had ice cream for a month. I think," Sante said, lowering his voice, "that there is not long left. They say he has brought mercenaries in, and that's always a desperate move. The population never likes it because it reminds them of the worst excesses of colonialism, and there's always the risk that they'll go out of control."

Harry and Rene Sante were sitting at a cafe table on the other side of the market. The journalist was sipping from a beer; as usual, Harry had bought iced tea which he didn't touch, except occasionally to hold to his forehead. He was grateful for Sante's chatter because it helped him not to think about the corpse and what it might mean. The day was brightening, and splinters of light penetrated the lenses of his dark glasses like slivers of hot silver; he could feel his exposed skin begin to tighten. He told Sante that last night a TV journalist from CBS had been drinking at the bar.

Sante nodded vigorously. He was a small wiry man, full of energy. He wore a travel-stained safari jacket, its pockets bulging with canisters of film, cassette tapes, spare batteries. He had set his three cameras on the rickety tin table. He was pleased to have caught the dumping of the body; he thought he could sell it to *Paris Match*. It was a parable of the African situation, Harry thought.

The army and the journalists fed on horror, and the ordinary people went hungry.

Sante said, "I know the guy from CBS. He's just been with Leviticus Smith. Smith is boasting that the war will be over in six months. He says he will be President for two years, and then he will think about elections. You should consider of getting out, my friend."

"I'm comfortable here."

After the *coup*, Harry had been tempted to give up the bar and start over somewhere else, but things had quickly settled down. Humans were creatures of habit, and old habits and customs persisted despite the bursts of energy which suddenly and unpredictably overwhelmed their precarious social structures. They had no patience; they didn't have the long view. They saw only what was before their noses, and lived for the day. Harry was able to live amongst them so easily because they twisted facts in their own minds to fit their preconceptions.

Even Rene Sante, who lived off his wits, was easy to fool. He saw Harry as a kind of fellow traveller, not exactly an ally, nor even a friend, but someone who had a common interest in the mixed currency of gossip and rumour and fact by which stringers survived. To Harry, the journalist was neither prey nor a threat. Harry would never drink from him, but Rene yielded to Harry all the same, too ready to spill what he knew.

"There's a new thing I saw," Sante said, drawing his chair closer to Harry. "It was in front of the army barracks. Four men, on stakes."

At first, Harry thought Sante meant that the men had been tied to posts and shot and left as a warning; a few days ago a dozen men had been hanged from lampposts along the main commercial street, with placards tied to their chests proclaiming them to be saboteurs. But Sante said no, this was different.

"These are stakes about eight feet long, sharpened at one end. The men have been lifted onto them and dropped so the stake pierced the – how do you call it? – the asshole. It went all the way through one, came out of his chest. All three were officers. One was a major I knew vaguely. They say it's the President's new advisor, the mercenary they call the Count."

Harry is left alone in the small square room for ten days.

The bars at the window are coated with silver. He burns his left hand badly; the old wound in his side, between the fourth and fifth ribs, aches in sympathy.

At intervals guards bring in vegetable slop heavily flavoured with garlic. Another pointless insult, like the crucifix. Harry has not needed to eat for forty years.

He managed to drink a little from one of the dying men in the cell in Block A before the guards pulled him out, but in a few days his thirst begins to return. He catches a rat on the first night, but after that the rats keep away, although they had the run of the cells in Block A. He keeps the worst of the thirst at bay by eating the cockroaches and centipedes which infest the room, crunching down a dozen at a time, savouring the small bitter sparks of life and spitting out pulped chitin, but the thirst persists, a low level ache, a hollow in his belly. His bones feel brittle, their cores hollow. He tries to exercise. His muscles clench weakly, like tattered grave shrouds on his dead bones, but he knows he has to keep up his strength. Someone has been turning humans, making an undead elite within the army. The Count, the President's advisor. Harry has a black dread that he knows who the Count is, but he tries not to dwell on it. He'll find out soon enough.

He spends most of the time in deep black dreamless sleep, curled up tightly in the corner beneath the oblong slot of the barred window, where the hot, heavy African sunlight cannot find him. Where he is safe from the memories of what he did to the twenty men in the cell in Block A. Where he is safe from his past. Still he weakens, hour upon hour. He needs the life in hot sweet salty human blood. Even in his sleep he can feel the tides of blood moving through the bodies of the guards and the prisoners in this terrible place, each a secret sundered sea. The thirstier he grows the more sensitive he becomes. He can hear the wary rustle of the rats in the spaces behind the walls, the conversations and laughter of the guards, the sighs and moans and rattling breathes of the prisoners in the cells in Block A, the music played by a radio in the old gymnasium on the other side of the compound where the officers lounge, drinking beer and whisky, and the rattle of the vultures on the tin roof. Every night two or three prisoners are tortured until they confess to the truth of the accusations made against them by the security force (and everyone screams, and pleads and finally confesses to stop the torture; Harry can hear every word) and then are led out – either to the cinder track behind the prison block where they are made to kneel in front of the wire fence in the harsh glare of the lights on the tower and are shot in the back of the head by an officer, or to a waiting truck which drives them off to some public place where they are impaled as a lesson to the populace. Harry hears it all, and wider, further, the agitated stir of the city, and the rattle of small arms fire and crump of mortar rounds in the suburbs as the two groups of rebel forces engage with the army to the east and west.

And on the tenth night, precisely at midnight, he hears the limousine sweep into the compound and the panicky flurry of the guards as they spring to attention, the steady tread across cinders, down the stairs, along the corridor, the heavy presence growing nearer and nearer, like a thunderstorm racing across the plains. Harry feels a fluttering panic, an echo of the horror the rats feel about the monster in the cell in Block B, who is his own self. The steady tread fills his head, and then the door slams open like all the graves of the world opening at the Last Trump and the Count is in the cell, a tall dark upright figure filling the little room with his presence, with only the broken projector between him and Harry.

"Fe-fi-fo-fum," the figure says. The voice is deep and resonant. It fills the cell; it resonates in Harry's hollow bones. "I smell the blood of an Englishman."

Impalation became the chosen form of public execution. In front of the post office; along the square between the Presidential Palace and the edge of the Park of the People's Liberation; by the entrance to the ferry terminal. Stakes with rounded points were used in the last place, and when Harry went past one evening two of the men were still alive, screaming to be killed. None of those watching dared go near because of the soldiers who sat around the bases of the stakes, smoking and drinking beer and gambling.

Harry had seen this before, soon after he had been turned. The resistance band of Szekeley gypsies had impaled every German, dead or alive, they took in ambushes.

By now, it was common knowledge that the President had abandoned the advice of his tribal elders for that of the mysterious Count, who was rumoured to be Polish or East German. The Count was going to bring in communist troops to clean out the rebels in the south, it was said; the President was opening his Swiss coffers to pay for helicopter gunships, T45 tanks and SAM launchers. Harry's cronies at the golf club began to revise their opinions. They didn't want the President to win the civil war if it meant that the communists came in, but it didn't seem possible that he could win without outside help while his army tore itself apart along tribal divisions.

The evening after Harry saw the men writhing on blunted stakes, Rene Sante confided the latest scandal with glee. The President's wife had fled to England with her entourage, and when her bags had passed through the X-ray machines at the terminal they had been found to be stuffed with money and jewels. The Canadian aircrew had refused to fly the jet back because they had not been paid.

"Otherwise the President would be gone on the next flight," Sante said.

Harry, who had been listening distractedly, wasn't so sure. He wasn't surprised that the President's wife had fled while she could.

She was a silly vain creature who had never been comfortable with the role of consort of the head of state. On one famous occasion she had invited the wives of the ambassadors to lunch. There had been no food, only gin and whisky, which the President's wife and her lady friends had drunk neat. There had been a six piece band of soldiers who, dressed in camouflage fatigues, played reggae at ear-splitting volume. After showing off the state rooms and the view of the gardens from the balcony of her bedroom, the President's wife had announced to her guests, "Now, girls, we're gonna shake our booties." The ambassadors' wives had gamely tried to match the wild gyrations of the President's wife and her entourage, but after two numbers they had been dismissed, and they had never been invited again.

Harry thought that the President loved power too much to run. It wasn't a communist takeover or even a rebel victory that he was worried about, but the nature of the mysterious Count.

His worst suspicions were confirmed a few nights later, when an officer of the Bureau of State Research came into the bar. Harry was sitting in his usual place at the far end of the bar, a slight, pale, silver-haired figure in a white linen suit and a black silk shirt, a gin and tonic going flat by his elbow. The packed crowd of business men, hustlers and whores parted as the officer, ugly and bull-shouldered, his shaven head gleaming in the purple fluorescents, made his way towards Harry. He wore crisp fatigues and mirror sunglasses and carried an Uzi slung over one shoulder. The Senegalese house band faltered for a moment, then picked up the beat, watching the officer warily; the go-go dancer in the gilt cage above the band was watching too.

Harry called for a drink to be sent over, double Johnny Walker on ice. He expected nothing more than a crude attempt to sell him confiscated ghat or cocaine at an inflated price, or a shakedown he could defuse by paying a dash now and complaining to the chief of police tomorrow.

But the officer ignored the drink. He leaned close to Harry and showed his needle-sharp teeth. The eyeteeth were hooked like a cobra's. It was then that Harry realised the man was not breathing.

"The Count is interested in you, Mr Merrick," the officer said. "He believes you and he might be related." Then he spat into the whisky and turned and walked through the crowd and out of the door.

Harry closed the bar early, packed a bag and had one of his boys drive him to the airport. An Air Guinea 747 was leaving in the morning, and he had bribed the booking office to get a seat.

He got as far as the second checkpoint. Out on the airport road, at midnight, figures materialised from the darkness beyond the guttering flares and the drum of burning oil-soaked rags which lit an armoured personnel carrier parked across the two-lane highway. They seemed to flit down from the palms which lined the road. Six women in loose-fitting fatigues, armed with machetes and M16s. At first Harry thought they were wearing masks, with glaring red eyes and long crooked teeth set in jaws far too wide to be human. Then his driver screamed.

They took the boy there and then, three of them feeding on his living body like turkey vultures, ripping and lapping. Harry tried to run, but the women were stronger and faster than mere humans. They bound his arms with cable and took him to the security compound at the far end of the Park of the People's Liberation, where in colonial days the daughters of civil servants had played tennis. Harry was thrown into a room crammed with prisoners.

And then the terrible thing happened.

The Count sweeps aside the projector as if it is a *papier-mâché* toy; it smashes to flinders against the wall. Harry is pressed right up against the filthy breeze blocks under the window. Moonlight falls over his shoulder and shines on the Count's knife-thin bone-white face. The nostrils of the Count's long, aristocratic nose flare, and he says, "An Englishman, but with gypsy blood in him."

Someone else has followed the Count into the room, but Harry does not see him until he speaks. It is as if he has materialised out of the Count's vast shadow.

"It's as I said, master. The Szekeley lineage, a direct descendent."

A small man, pale, hairless, hunched in a green surgeon's gown. His eyes gleam red and wet behind slab spectacles.

"I thought them all dead," the Count purrs. He makes a single step, and Harry is lifted into the air. He can feel the silver-coated bars burning the air a bare inch from the back of his skull. The Count's bone-white face fills his vision.

"Tell me, little one," the Count says. "Tell me how someone as pathetic as you became one of my children."

Harry made all kinds of resolutions and promises to himself in the first days after he was taken prisoner. He made them all over again after the terrible thing in the cell in Block A. They melt like ice in sunlight before the actuality of the Count. The story tumbles out of him, drawn by the Count's red gaze. He tells the Count how he fell through the black air over Yugoslavia. He tells him how he nearly died, and how he was saved.

1943. Harry Merrick was twenty-three. A lieutenant in the Special
Air Services, an explosives expert. He was being flown towards a
drop behind enemy lines when a stray unit spotted the little plane
and strafed it with machine-gun and rifle fire. A lucky shot hit a fuel
line. The pilot was killed. Harry was hit. He jumped, and found the
bullet which had shattered his left kneecap had also passed through
his parachute. It tore apart when it opened. Harry plunged through
freezing black air and crashed through fir trees and landed in a bank
of snow, lacerated, bleeding heavily, dying.

And they came. The strong, beautiful people, swift and fierce as
wolves. They killed the Serbian patrol which had been slogging
up the mountain side towards Harry. They found him and took
him back to their cave. A girl slit her wrist and he fed from her,
hardly knowing what he was doing. He thought she was his fiancée,
Catharine. He died, and he was reborn.

"The Children of the Night," the twisted little man in the green
coat says. "You see, master? You see?"

"Let him tell his story, fool. Tell me, little one. What happened
to them?"

They called themselves the Children of the Night. They were from
Romania, they said, a place called the Borgo Pass. They had fled
from persecution sixty years ago, and now they were fighting the
Fascists because thousands of their human brothers and sisters had
been killed in the death camps. They were undead, but they were
also gypsies; the girl who had saved Harry, Eva, said that the two
types of blood, gypsy and that of their father in darkness, mingled
in them and gave them a hybrid strength. She was more than a
hundred years old but looked like a girl of eighteen, with an elfin
face and a fall of black hair. She ran like the wind, calling the
wolves of the mountains around her. The metal frame stock of
her Sturmgewehr 44 assault rifle was notched with more than three
dozen kills.

Reborn, Harry fought alongside Eva and her compatriots. The
gypsies specialized in hit-and-run raids and ambushes. Harry devised
ways of blocking roads with the minimum of explosive. They killed
without mercy for they would not drink the blood of their enemies,
impaled the corpses and the wounded on stakes as a sign of their
vengeance. To feed, they ran with the wolves, bringing down deer
and wild boar with teeth and nails, drinking the hot blood of their
prey but never killing. It was a pure, clean way of life. There were
eight of them. Eva and Maria and Illeana. Ion and Little Ion, who
was also called Savu. Mircea and Viorel and the oldest (although he

looked no older than Eva), calm grey-eyed Petru, who could turn himself into a wolf. They were all killed. Only Harry survived.

It happened in the last days of the war. It was very hot, and the short summer nights restricted their activities. There was a great deal of traffic on the roads heading north. Victory was in the air – to the south, each night, there were rumbles and flashes as allied bombers dropped their sticks of high explosive on the retreating Fascists.

A raiding party came in the day, when the Children of the Night were asleep. Twenty, thirty of them, Croatian peasants who were once their allies. Desperate dirty scared men in a medley of torn uniforms, some armed with no more than scythes or pitchforks, one carrying an ancient blunderbuss. But most had rifles, and silver bullets. They knew what they were dealing with. Harry slept at the back of the cave; as a newborn he could least stand the daylight. When the humans poured in, shooting wildly, he took a stray round that passed clean through his side. Maddened by the violent pain of the silver-tainted wound, Harry ran right through the attackers, ran through burning sunlit air and plunged down the steep side of a ravine, coming to rest in a deep bank of ferns in the shade of pines that clutched at rock with twisted roots.

It took three days for Harry's bones to knit (the wound in his side would not heal, and bled a thin black gruel). He climbed the steep cliff, found the shrivelled blackened bodies set upright on stakes. The heads had been taken. The bodies looked as if they had been rescued from a furnace; sunlight had burnt them to bone. Eva and Maria and Illeana. Ion and Little Ion, who was also called Savu. Mircea and Viorel and calm grey-eyed Petru. Harry couldn't recognise any of them.

"They were strong," the Count says. "They were my children. What music they made, in the mountains!"

"Listen to my master," the crooked little man tells Harry. His tongue is black, and too long. His left arm is withered, the hand swollen and fused into something like a lobster's claw. He scuttles up the wall to avoid a blow from the Count. He says, peering down from the corner between wall and ceiling, like a gecko, "He is a great man and I will make him greater."

"My children were beautiful," the Count says. "My brides were lamia who could turn the heart of the staunchest Christian; my Children of the Night were splendid, swift and strong. Even the cold English rose I claimed as my own was magnificent. Now my blood makes only sterile monsters, but soon it will be as it was."

"It will be as it was," the little man says, scampering along the ceiling until he is above his master's cold white face. He has extruded talons narrow and sharp as knife blades from fingers and toes. "My master's blood is tainted, but I will wash it clean."

The Count casually swats him away, and he crashes through the doorway into the guards. The Count turns his red gaze upon Harry, who tries and fails to meet it.

The Count's voice lowers to a silky rumble. "And you, little creature. To find you here, wasting your inheritance. Why do you want to be what you once were? You should rise above it, splendid and terrible! Are you a coward?"

"I'm simply trying to make a living, like the next man," Harry says.

The Count laughs. "You waste yourself in a silly little pretence. Accumulating gold, sipping the blood of whores. Who have you turned? Where are your get? Are you afraid you cannot control them? I will teach you!"

Harry shakes his head. He tried to turn someone once. It went horribly wrong.

"You English have no heart. No passion. You will learn. You will learn from me. When I was alive I commanded thousands. I swept the Turks from the battlefields. I was so powerful that death could not claim me. I refused it. And in my undeath I grew greater still, with thousands of loyal children."

The Count falls silent. He is possessed by his past.

"You will be great again," the crooked little man says. He has crept back into the room, as a loyal dog creeps back to its master after a whipping. "I promise it."

"He tampers with our blood with his genetic science," the Count says. "He says he can cure me. He needs only much gold, and a little time."

"Science is expensive," the crooked little man says, "but it is very powerful, master. Once I properly understand how the blood of posthumous animates transforms the DNA of the living, then I will understand what has gone wrong. I can fix it."

"Silver," the Count says. "They poisoned me with a silver stake, but ran away before they finished me. Cowards! But I recovered. It took decades, but I regained myself. So I won after all, but their pollution lingers still in my blood."

Harry understands. After the Children of the Night were killed, he lay in a torpor for three years, reviving to feed once a month or so, until he recovered from the glancing wound caused by the silver bullet. If it had lodged in his body it would have killed him. He cannot imagine the strength of will the Count must have applied to regenerate with a silver stake piercing his body. Harry learned a lot about the Count from the gypsies, and later he read the standard text. The Count is a monster in every way, father of lies. He was a monster when human, so afraid of the true death that he would do anything to cheat it. Far from sweeping Turks from the battlefield, he had always run away at the first hint of defeat. And he has run from death, clinging to life with every ounce of will.

Harry shares that lust for life. It possesses him. Undead, he cannot imagine an ending to his appetite. He will do anything to survive. He has always known that, although the terrible thing which happened in the cell in Block A still shocks him.

All the time he has pretended to be human, almost forty years, the beast has lain just beneath his skin. He has been like a patient with a disease in remission. It has inhabited him quietly, and he has accommodated to its symptoms, but suddenly it has broken out again.

The Count's gaze pierces Harry through and through.

"You thought you could pretend to be human," the Count says, "but you know now what you are. I put you in the cell in Block A to teach you that."

"They would have killed me," Harry says. "I did it to save my life. Any man would have done the same, if placed in danger."

"Yes, but the life to live is unbreakably strong in you. You will serve me, Harry Merrick, because the will to live is so strong."

"I would rather die than serve you."

"You sought refuge amongst humans as humans seek consolation from religion."

The Count's arm shoots out across the room, longer than any human arm should be. He wrenches the crucifix from the wall, plucks the pale figure from it and thrusts it into Harry's face; it bursts in the Count's fingers, and ivory dust stings Harry's skin and eyes.

"So much for religion," the Count purrs. "I could skewer your heart with this cross, but I am merciful."

"I rather think you've aligned yourself with the wrong side," Harry says. "The rebels will find you."

"Not at all. We have captured one of their leaders and many of his men, and we will make them our brothers with your blood. We will destroy the other rebels, or welcome them into our family. There are no trivial divisions amongst us. You must know that. We are all blood brothers." The Count turns away from Harry. "Bleed him now and let him grow thirsty. Then he will learn what he is!"

The crooked little man taps a vein of Harry's right arm, filling a litre bottle with dark blood while two undead women hold Harry down, stroking his body and kissing and nipping him in a parody of lust. They leave him dazed and weak. He finds enough strength to crawl away from the patch of sunlight that falls through the silver bars.

After he was captured on the airport road, Harry was put in a cell with twenty human prisoners. He was the only white man there. He lasted eight days before the terrible thing happened, almost as bad as what he had done to Catherine forty years ago.

Each night two or three prisoners were tortured until they confessed and then taken out to be executed. Each day two or three new prisoners, dazed and bleeding from beatings, were thrown into the cell to replace those executed the night before. A few were there on criminal charges, but most had been arrested because they were of the wrong tribe, or because they owned something an army officer had taken a fancy to, or because they were relatives of someone who had already been arrested. A few shouted at the guards, trying to reason with them or bribe them with promises, and one or two prayed wildly, calling on God and all his saints to save them from injustice, but most slumped with a sullen air of acceptance of their fate.

Harry was surrounded by the heat and strong beating hearts of human beings, and his thirst grew unbearable. At the end of the eighth day he could bear it no longer. He had enough sense to wait until the hour before dawn, when the prison block was as quiet as it got. He slid over to an old man who had been thrown in the cell that evening, stupefied by a savage beating. He calmed the man and slit a vein in his wrist with his eye teeth, but he had barely begun to lap the blood, thin stuff soured by spent adrenalin, like wine on the turn, when another prisoner saw what he was doing.

The man was a long distance truck driver, strong and alert despite the month he'd spent in the cell after his truck and its cargo of cigarettes had been liberated. He grabbed Harry from behind and slid a shiv made from a bit of sharpened wire through his ribs into his heart. Harry tore out the shiv and killed the man with an SAS trick, thrusting two fingers up his nostrils, driving broken bone into his forebrain. The quick struggle woke the other prisoners and he killed them all too, in a black/red confusion of screams and shouts and blows.

Then the guards came. He was taken across the compound to Block B, bled, and left alone until the Count came for him.

Weakened by loss of blood and his mounting thirst, Harry is anchored to the present only by the alternation of light and darkness. Each day, he sinks into the oblivion that is deeper than sleep; each night, he is visited by the twisted little undead in the surgeon's gown, the Count's assistant.

His name is Lomax. He is an American biochemist who tracked the Count down and offered his services. Amazingly, the Count did not kill him; perhaps Lomax's willing subservience reminded the Count of the human agent of his British adventure. Lomax was not transformed by the Count, or by his women, but by what he calls a recent laboratory accident. He has been experimenting on the blood of what he calls postanimates, has discovered how to keep it alive and whole by mixing it with a soup of haemoglobin and plasma enriched with glucose and potassium chloride. Each night, he takes a little more of Harry's blood, despite Harry's protests that it will kill him.

Lomax is garrulous. He wants to share his secrets. Each night Harry listens, barely understanding, to his theories.

"We will feed you soon, Mr Merrick," Lomax says. "We need you. You are of the same blood as my master. It runs pure in you, direct from his younger self through the gypsies to you. It has not been contaminated by silver. You must cooperate, Mr Merrick. It will be easier for you."

"Humans say we are cruel, but it seems to me that science is crueller."

Lomax ignores this sally. "You have seen my master's get. You see what his women are like. Warped is a kind word. Although he transformed them by the old way, they do not have the capacity to make get of their own. The women are feral creatures and useful, but they are limited. I have experimented with direct injection of my master's blood and that of his get into subjects, but the transformations were too violent and created only monsters, thing turned inside out yet still living, and worse. Injection of your blood gives better results, but they are still . . . disappointing."

"It should be done with tenderness and desire," Harry says. He is disgusted by Lomax's enthusiasm.

The crooked little man giggles. "True, true! There is a change in the blood of the donor that is necessary to initiate a successful transformation of the recipient. Something hormonal, perhaps. If I locate it perhaps I could define what love is."

"I rather think that you confuse desire and love, Dr Lomax. Our desire is closer to hunger than to love. After we sate our desire we want our victims to love us, but we do not love them."

After Catherine, Harry has never been tempted to turn anyone else, but he knows that the Count would change the whole world if he could. He is a monster of ego. He believes he can make anyone love him. He wants Harry to love him.

Harry believes that the Count visited him earlier that night, the third since he was transferred from Block A. At least, Harry seemed to wake, seemed to see a dark figure standing in the open doorway, staring down at him. How long had the Count been watching? Harry tried to frame a question, his dry lips splitting in a dozen places, but the figure was gone. A few moments later something darkened the moonlight that fell through the barred window.

Harry waited for the Count to return, listening to distant gunfire and wondering if the rebels might soon capture the security compound and free or kill him. But the Count did not come back. When at last the cell door was unlocked, it was to allow in Lomax.

"At first I thought it was an infective agent," Lomax says now. "A DNA virus which added genes to human cells at the point of death. Now I am inclined to believe it is something which switches on existing genes. There are things called homeoboxes in our chromosomes, stretches of DNA which code for related proteins which link together to carry out a particular task. Expression of a homeobox is induced by an activator, a substance which causes the control gene to make a protein which switches on the other genes. I think that the blood of the postanimate contains such an activating substance. A flavonoid, perhaps. Whatever it is, it is highly sensitive to silver."

"You are dying, doctor. I can smell it."

Lomax lifts the club of his arm. The skin has transmuted to a hard semi-transparent substance something like horn. "In my case, the sequence may not have been fully activated. Perhaps there is more than one homeobox involved. There are many sequences in the human genome which appear to code for nothing at all. Junk DNA, it's called. But perhaps it isn't junk. Instead, it may be a relic of our evolution. Perhaps our ancestors were all like my master, a race which lost its nobility by a genetic accident."

Lomax's eyes gleam red and wet behind his slab glasses. He says, "Humans pretend to be rational but they are tormented by their animal selves. They are badly knit together, torn apart by a thousand different impulses. But we know our nature completely. It is simple and pure. Hunger, hunger for life. That is all we must satisfy. It frees us from the mess of sex and tribal hatred. All of our kind are one, even the least. Even me."

"Kill me," Harry says. "Do it cleanly. Not like this."

"Oh no, you are necessary. There have been . . . problems with our recent converts. One or two have escaped tonight. But I can overcome problems. It's just a matter of time. You will feed tonight, and I will come again tomorrow."

Lomax signals to the guards, and takes out the hypodermic.

After Lomax has packed the blood-filled hypodermic in ice and left, the guards push a man into the room. They screech with glee and lock the door.

The man is tall and muscular, dressed in a ripped tunic with colonel's bars on the shoulders, and torn fatigue trousers. His face is swelling with bruises and he is bleeding from a bad cut over his right eyebrow, and the smell of his sweet blood fills the little room. He moves quickly, ripping a spar from the ruins of the projector and holding it in front of him like a javelin.

"Wait," Harry says. He climbs to his feet. His eyeteeth prick through his gums, and his jaw aches with the effort of keeping it from unhinging. His fingernails have lengthened into curved talons and he jams them into his palms; the pain makes him cry out, but helps keep the red mist of his mounting thirst at bay.

"I know you," the Colonel says. Despite his bruises and torn clothing he has a commanding dignity. His gaze is steady, and he firms his grip on the spar. "You own the bar on Freedom Avenue. The guards said that you are a monster."

"I would agree with them."

"The guards said that you will tear out my throat and drain the blood from my body."

"I need to feed, but I do not have to kill you to do it."

"They said you killed twenty men with your bare hands."

"Yes, I did. I am not proud of it, Colonel. That's why I'm trying not to kill you."

"Then keep trying, Mr Merrick."

"I believe we can help each other," Harry says, and explains about the silver bars at the window.

They work through the night. Harry extrudes razor-sharp talons to excavate the mortar around the window; the colonel, Milton Tombe, uses the spar to lever at the bars, rocking each one back and forth until they are loosened so that he can pry them out with his bare hands. The bars are deeply embedded and it takes a long time to remove each one. While they work, Colonel Tombe tells Harry that he was part of a group of army officers who wanted to kill the President and sue for peace with the rebels.

"There was an order two days ago that we should return to our barracks for special medical treatment. We were told it would make us invulnerable to bullets. Well, I was educated at Sandhurst, and I have a degree in chemistry from our own university, Mr Merrick, and I do not hold with superstitions. I held my position, and yesterday a friend of mine came roaring up in a jeep. He was almost hysterical. It seems that the fourth brigade had been injected with something that turned them into monsters. Most had died, he said; the rest went mad, rampaging through the streets. In the confusion, some captured rebels escaped, and were fighting with the President's guard. I knew about the monstrous women the President has surrounded himself with. I thought they were the products of steroids, or some other muscle-building treatment. Until now, I did not believe that they drank blood. One hears these things about other troops. They make empty boasts to try and unnerve their enemies. It seems that I am wrong."

"They took my blood," Harry says. He is sitting in a corner while Colonel Tombe, stripped to the waist and shining with sweat, levers at a bar. It is near dawn, and they have removed only three of the dozen bars. "That's what the soldiers were injected with. And the rebel prisoners, too."

"Then it's true your kind make more, by biting men?"

"You would have to drink a little of my blood, and I would want to turn you. I've never wanted to do that to anyone. At least, not for forty years."

It has to come out of desire, he thinks. The Count has desire enough to fill the world, even if it was only to create so many mirror-images in which he can admire the warped reflection of his own self. But Harry has no desire left; after the disastrous tryst with Catherine, he lost everything but his thirst.

"The President wants to turn all the army into monsters. The army is fighting against itself," Colonel Tombe says. "And in the middle of the confusion the rebel leader, Prince Marshall, has escaped. My brother officers and I went to plead with the President to stop this madness, and we had determined to kill him if he refused. But when we got to the palace grounds a white man swept down upon us, and killed everyone but me. It was the President's advisor, and I think he has killed the President, too. Meanwhile, the rebels led by Leviticus Smith advance apace. They took the power station and the oil depots three days ago. There!"

The bar has come loose. Colonel Tombe weighs it in his hand. "I could kill you with this, you say?"

"If you tried, I would probably kill you first." Harry gets up and starts to score the mortar around the next bar, working carefully but quickly. After a while, he says, "I think the President is still alive. The Count will need a human figurehead to deal with the outside world."

"The UN was sent away." Colonel Tombe starts to lever again. This time the bar comes away almost at once. "We will have to ask them back, to mediate. Are you all right, Mr Merrick?"

"I am trying hard not to think about how thirsty I am."

"They took blood from you." Colonel Tombe looks shrewdly at

Harry. "You would not turn me into one of your kind if you fed from me?"

"Believe me, it's the last thing I want to do."

Colonel Tombe loosens the collar of his tunic, baring his muscular neck. "Then I will think of it as a blood transfusion."

After Harry awakened in the cave in the mountains, cured of the worst of his wound, he made his way to England and the dim memory of his fiancée. It was 1948, the coldest winter in memory. He found that Catherine had married, supposing him dead, and he killed her husband and took her, tried to make her over. But he did it not from love, but from a desire for revenge: for her infidelity; for the loss of what he had once been. She became a monster, and he killed her, bursting her head between his hands. On the run, he spent an evening in a cinema, and the first film of the double bill, *The Vampire's Ghost*, a poor melodramatic thing, gave him the idea of finding a new life in Africa.

He has been hiding from what he has become ever since.

Harry slits a vein in the Colonel's forearm and drinks deeply. He could drink forever, but he pulls himself away after only a few minutes, licking the film of blood from his sharp eyeteeth with his roughened tongue.

The two men stand face to face in the growing light of dawn. The Colonel wraps his fingers around the slit in his forearm. At last he says, "It won't stop bleeding."

Harry explains about the anticoagulants in his saliva, and rips a strip from his shirt and binds the wound. The smell of blood on the Colonel's fingers is heady, but he resists the temptation to blot it up with his tongue. It would not be seemly.

He says, "We should rest. I can't work in the daylight. It burns as badly as silver, and the human guards will come, I'm sure, to see if you are dead."

But the guards do not come. Harry and Colonel Tombe sit at opposite sides of the little room, Harry under the window, Colonel Tombe by the door. Harry falls into a stupor, and wakes in darkness to find the Colonel working at the bars again.

The Colonel hears him stand, and turns quickly. Harry laughs, and says, "You could have killed me while I slept."

"We need each other, Mr Merrick."

"Yes. Yes, I suppose that we do."

They renew their joint attack on the barred window. The last bar comes away after midnight. Harry reaches through and crumples the wire mesh and climbs through into the warm night, then helps

Colonel Tombe scramble out. The compound is lit only by moonlight. Dogs are barking nearby, and further off there is the crackle of small arms fire. To the west, a sullen red glow stands behind the roofs of the dark city.

It is the oil depot, Colonel Tombe says, and adds, "Perhaps the rebels are close at hand. It would explain why the guards have run away."

"We should wait for the rebels, perhaps."

"I would not make myself a prisoner. Besides, I think they would kill me. Come with me or stay."

"Lomax didn't come tonight. I wonder why?"

Harry and Colonel Tombe run across the wide cinder yard to the tall wire fence without raising any challenge. Colonel Tombe pauses and says that the fence is electrified; Harry laughs and grabs it with both hands and tears it apart. Like the city, the prison compound is without electricity.

The compound is on the far side of the park which was made from the grounds of what was once the Governor's Mansion. They run a long way down the road through the park until the Colonel must stop, breathless. With fresh blood in his veins, Harry thinks that he can run forever.

"We'll find my men," the Colonel says, when he has his breath back. Moonlight slides like oil over his black face. He is smiling. "By God, I will deal them a blow they won't forget."

Harry does not have to ask if he is talking about the rebels or the President's – the Count's – undead army. He says, "Use silver bullets. Even if they look completely dead, cut off the heads, or they'll heal. Find out where they hide in the day. Newborns can't stand daylight."

"We'll work together against this. I could arrest you, but I hope that you will volunteer."

Colonel Tombe still carries the metal spar. Harry snatches it up, bends it in two and tosses it into the darkness. He shows his teeth, and the big soldier takes a step backwards. Harry says, "Don't follow me, Colonel. I have business of my own. Family business."

Then he turns and runs, so fast he might be flying through the night. He hears the Colonel shouting after him, but he runs on, faster and faster, towards the Presidential Palace.

There is a line of tall, graceful royal palms at the edge of the park. The road is littered with fronds chopped down by small arms fire. Spent cartridges and scraps of metal and bits of broken glass lie everywhere. The bodies of a dozen soldiers lie in an untidy heap beside a checkpoint of concrete-filled oil drums and razor wire.

Harry moves forward cautiously. Seven bodies are impaled on stakes between the scaly trunks of the palms: the Count's women, and the Count's assistant, Lomax. One of the women is still alive. She writhes slowly, hissing and arching her back, trying to lift herself off the wooden post which has pierced her vitals.

Harry asks her what happened, but she only spits blood in his face. Beside her, Lomax stirs and groans on his stake. He has lost his slab glasses; his surgeon's gown is stiff with his own blood. "Kill me," he says. "Oh Christ please kill me."

"Tell me about Prince Marshall."

"You are my father," Lomax gasps. Black blood dribbles from his mouth. His feet kick at the stake. His hands are bound behind his back. "Have mercy."

"How many did you change? How many escaped?"

"Yesterday. We fought them through the palace. Please." He rocks a little on the stake and screams. "Please. I can't get free."

"You've probably healed around it. Where is the Count?"

"Hiding from your children. High above." Lomax's red eyes are staring up at the Gothic wedding cake of the Presidential Palace.

"You told me that humans are less than us because we are perfect expressions of our genetic inheritance. I think you are wrong, Lomax, and your master is wrong, too. At some point in the past humanity overcame beastliness, but in us it has burst out and erased everything that made us human. We are not stronger because of our thirst, but weaker. A good man has just shown me that."

But in his torment Lomax hasn't heard Harry's speech. "Please," he whispers. "Please. Father, forgive me . . ."

Harry relents. He hauls on Lomax's feet with all his strength until the point of the stake bursts the crooked little undead's heart. Lomax gargles a fountain of blood that boils away to black dust even as it spatters the ground.

The square beyond the park is eerily quiet, but Harry knows he is being watched. He makes the best of it, straightening his shoulders and whistling "Lily Marlene" as he marches around the empty plinth in the centre of the square, the hub of the traffic circle where, until the country gained its independence fifteen years ago, a statue of Queen Victoria stood.

Man-sized creatures hang in the branches of the huge coral trees on either side of the gate in the iron railings around the palace; they drop to the ground as Harry goes past. He hears the distinctive sound of a machine gun being locked and loaded, but walks on across the gravel of the courtyard. The President's black armoured Mercedes sits on burst tyres before the steps of the palace, its doors flung wide, paint knocked from craters in its armoured bodywork, its bullet-proof windscreen starred. Harry starts up the steps, and then the watchers rush him, and carry him forward.

Harry doesn't resist as he is bundled through state rooms to the President's office. The palace is as dark as the rest of the city, but Harry can clearly see the many bodies lying in the shadows. Most are human, mutilated around the throat or decapitated.

The President's office, familiar from many TV broadcasts, is hot and stinking, and crowded with the undead. Candles burn everywhere, clustered in elaborate gold or iron candelabra or stuck with their own wax to the polished walnut grain of the expensive ormolu bureaux. Faces like half-melted animal masks turn to stare at Harry as he is hauled through the tall double doors. He realizes with a mingled thrill of horror and excitement that these are the fruits of Lomax's experiments with his stolen blood. Most are blotched unevenly with patches of dead white pigmentation. One sprouts a tangle of teeth in a mouth that gapes so wide the heavy jaw rests on its chest; another, in a soiled bridal gown, has a face ridged with cartilage, ears grown into ragged leather flaps that fall over its shoulders and trail on the ground; yet another has a head that has shrunken to little more than a long pangolin's snout set with crooked rows of ivory needles from which a green slaver constantly drips. Even though they can only be a few days past transformation, all, even the most human, are in advanced stages of decay, with weeping sores and ripe bruises and softening skin like over-ripe mangoes. The air is heavy with the smell of gangrene; the deep-pile carpets are sticky with blood.

The undead are all staring at Harry, but he stares at the two figures separated by the polished mahogany plane of the big desk at the far end of the room.

A man wearing only tracksuit trousers is handcuffed to a chair in front of the desk. His black skin shines with sweat; his chest and back are covered with welts and bruises, and his head hangs down. He is breathing heavily.

Behind the desk, the leader of the undead lounges in a pneumatic black leather chair. His face has grown a wolfish snout, but Harry still recognizes him from the tribal scarification which decorates his distorted cheeks, and the trademark red beret.

Prince Marshall, leader of the breakaway rebel faction. He wears a necklace of hand grenades. He grins, red tongue lolling in elongated jaws, and beckons Harry forward with a lazy gesture. An undead woman in fatigue trousers, a bristling pelt growing thickly over her bare breasts, mops at his forehead with a handkerchief.

The undead murmur amongst themselves and make way as Harry crosses the room. One, its arms and legs fused into fleshy flippers, scampers towards him and flops down in a parody of obeisance. There is a human amongst them, in a safari jacket with bulging pockets. It is the French journalist, Rene Sante. His sallow face is strained and pale. He is carrying a video camera the size of a small suitcase on his shoulder, and squints around at it at Harry.

"My god, Harry," he says, "what are you doing here!"

"I see you are working," Harry says. "How much will you make from this, I wonder?"

"They killed the CBS crew, Harry!" Sante is crying. "They only let me live because they want a record of this."

"For history," the undead rebel leader behind the desk says. His voice is rich and deep, and carries through the cackles and mutters of his undead followers. "We show the world what this traitor has done to his country. Keep filming, little Frenchman. I will let you go, I promise, but only if I like your work."

One of the undead, quills of bloody bone hanging around his face, lifts up the head of the man in the chair. It is President Daniel Weah.

"He tried to make us his zombies," Prince Marshall says, "but he only made us strong. We acknowledge the strength in your blood, Mr Merrick. You are a great magician, even if you are a white man."

"It will destroy you," Harry says.

Prince Marshall smiles wolfishly. "Oh, I don't think so."

Daniel Weah licks his lips and looks around, blinking in the glare of Sante's video camera. "Undo the handcuffs," he complains. "They give me a lot of pain. I can't think with them on."

The rebel with the ruff of bone quills smacks Weah around the head, and the other undead crowd forward, chittering amongst themselves.

"He tried to run away," Prince Marshall explains. There is an uncapped bottle of whisky on the desk and he swigs from it and spits it in a fine spray across the desk into Daniel Weah's face. "This stuff tastes of piss and petrol," he says, to no one in particular.

Harry says, "I can explain what has happened to you, but you must let the humans go. This isn't between them and us. You must understand that they are not our enemies. It is the Count we must fight."

"We will catch him," Prince Marshall says. "We will catch him and put him on the stake next to his creature. Then we will drink your blood again, and grow even stronger."

They do not know what they are, Harry realizes in horror. They were changed too quickly, while they were still vigorous. Usually the change is effected only at the point of death of the victim, after a long dance of seduction, after many little feedings, and with blood fed directly from a vein of the seducer. These creatures were changed by injections of his stolen blood; no wonder they are rotting where they stand.

"Don't argue with them, Harry," Sante pleads.

Harry turns on the reporter. "You're as bad as them, feeding on horror. Put down the camera. Walk away."

"They'll kill me!"

The undead laugh and cheer, and Prince Marshall takes out a blue steel automatic and fires it into the ceiling and leans through the cloud of gunsmoke and yells, "I want information! I want to know the truth! You will film the truth for history, Frenchman, then you will go!"

The half-naked woman wipes Prince Marshall's forehead with her cloth. He is sweating blood.

Daniel Weah's head has slumped down again. Now he raises it and looks around and says, "I'll tell you the truth, but you must loosen my arms. They pain me. Prince, Prince, just listen to me. I'll tell you, but loosen my arms."

Two undead hoist the President upright in the chair; others crowd around. One, wearing a black cocktail dress ripped at the shoulders and a Hermes scarf in his hair, shows a mouthful of fangs at the camera. They are growing thirsty, Harry realizes, but they don't know it. The room seems hotter, smaller, full of lurching shadows.

A kind of interrogation gets under way. Sante tries to hold the video steady, although his hands are shaking. At some point he has pissed in his pants; Harry can smell it. He flinches when Harry puts a hand on his shoulder, then whispers from the side of his mouth, "This is the worst place in the world, Harry. We're both going to die."

Harry remembers what Lomax told him, and can't help laughing. "The worst place in the world, my friend? It lives inside us all, human and undead."

Prince Marshall has become distracted by an argument with one of the undead. He shouts, but Harry can't hear what he is shouting because the rest of the undead are shouting, too. Suddenly the rebel leader shoots the nearest; the man is knocked back by the impact of the bullet, but he remains standing and begins to laugh wildly, tearing open his khaki blouse to show off his wound.

"You see!" Prince Marshall yells, leaning over the desk and brandishing the pistol in Weah's face. "We are unkillable!"

One of the undead rips a string of juju fetishes from around Weah's waist and crunches the knots of feathers and small bones between sharp teeth.

Weah begins to plead. "Gentlemen, gentlemen. Please listen to me. We are all one. We are all brothers."

"That man won't talk," Prince Marshall yells. "Bring me his ear."

One of the undead slices at Weah's left ear. Weah howls and tries to get loose, but he is held fast. The undead soldier tosses the scrap of gristle to Prince Marshall, who chews it with gusto.

Daniel Weah groans. Blood runs from his mutilated ear, mixing with the sweat on his chest. Harry can smell it, and his eyeteeth prick his gums.

"I'll ask again," Prince Marshall says. "What did you do with all the money? What did you do with the economy of our beautiful country?"

Weah says, "You know, gentlemen, if I told you, you wouldn't believe it."

"Confess to the people," Prince Marshall says. "Tell them where you keep their money."

"I was always working in the interest of the people. I keep only one account."

"The number. What is the number?"

Harry realizes that Prince Marshall wants the access code of Daniel Weah's Swiss bank account.

"I don't know." Daniel Weah lifts his head, squinting in the harsh light of the video camera. "Loosen my arms, please. I can't tell you while my arms are tied. Please, my ear is cut and my arms pain me."

This throws the undead, and they begin to argue amongst themselves. Prince Marshall watches, sunk in the black leather chair, sweat and blood mopped from his brow by the woman.

"The Count," Harry says. "The Count will drain the account if you don't stop him." He steps in front of Weah and addresses the throng of undead. "You are all my children. You are all changed by my blood. What you once were is irrelevant. What you wanted when you were human and alive is irrelevant. Listen to me. It's more important to stop the Count than pursue your revenge."

Prince Marshall yawns, showing the stout yellow teeth that crowd his elongated jaw, and idly waves his big automatic. "I don't care about this Count. His creature changed us, but we were stronger than his European science. We escaped, and we are the strongest army in this country." His followers howl at this. Prince Marshall shouts over their noise, "This man claims he is our father. Let him show it. He'll change this so-called President, and then maybe we'll believe him!"

Harry is seized and whirled around. He struggles, but two of the undead hold his arms and another has wrapped an arm around his neck so that he cannot breathe. But breathing is only a habit; Harry doesn't need it.

His head is forced down, an inch away from Daniel Weah's neck. The smell and heat of the man's blood is dizzying. Harry sees only red, with the light of the video camera blazing behind it. His teeth cut his lips.

Prince Marshall comes around the desk and shouts into Weah's mutilated ear. "The number! Tell me the number or he bites you and makes you one of us!"

"I don't know it!"

"It doesn't work like that!"

"Do it!" Prince Marshall screams. "Do it!"

Harry does it. He tears out Daniel Weah's throat, spits the lump of flesh into Prince Marshall's face, and opens his mouth to the rich gush of blood. It runs like electricity through his body. He can feel every cell opening to it. Then he's thrown aside. Maddened by the smell of blood, most of the undead are trying to get to Weah's body. Prince Marshall knocks two aside, shoots a third in the head.

The light of the video camera waves across the ceiling; the undead rebel in the wedding dress is attacking Sante. Harry plucks off the rebel, breaks his back, throws him into two more. Someone hacks at Harry's leg with a machete; he rips it from the rebel's hands and whirls and takes off Prince Marshall's head in a clean sweep.

The undead howl. Harry picks up Sante by the collar of his safari jacket with one hand, grabs a discarded AK-47 with another and fires it point blank into the floor-to-ceiling drapes behind the desk. The muzzle-flash sets the heavy material on fire; Harry dashes whisky over the flames and they roar up to the ceiling.

When he turns, the crowd of undead kneels in a ripple of movement that spreads from front to back. Firelight reddens their twisted faces as they stare up at him. Harry plucks the camera from Sante, smashes it, rips out the tape cassette and tosses it into the fire behind him. He walks Sante through the adoring rebels, the wound in his leg ripping wide with each step, and slams and locks the tall doors shut behind him.

Sante is crying. As they pass through the dark staterooms he says in French, "What are you? What are you?"

"I used to think I was a monster," Harry says. "Now I'm not so sure. What I've become sleeps inside you, waiting only for blood to waken it. I'm as human as you, Sante. My thirst made me forget that."

At the stairs, he pushes Sante forward so that the journalist stumbles down the first few steps. Invigorated by the President's blood, Harry feels stronger than he ever has. Already the wound in his leg is knitting over; he can feel the muscle fibres swarming together. He tells Sante, "I'd like to say that this could be the beginning of a beautiful friendship, but I have unfinished business. There's a Colonel. Milton Tombe. Find him and tell him to look for the Count. These things won't live long, but if the Count escapes he will start this again. Run, you fool. Run!"

Sante looks at Harry. He seems to want to say something, but then he thinks better of it and scampers away down the stairs. Harry can hear the undead banging at the locked doors. They'll break through soon enough, but it doesn't matter. Without a leader they'll be easy prey for the army.

Lomax claimed to know where the Count is hiding, and Harry, remembering calm grey-eyed Petru, who could turn himself into a wolf, remembering the claims of the standard text, thinks that the crooked little undead was telling the truth.

Harry runs up the stairs, with smoke from the burning rooms thickening around him. Beyond a plywood door, a service stair leads up to the roof. On one side, the glow of the fire illuminates clustered pinnacles and turrets; at the far edge of the other side a dark shape rises up against the thin grey dawn light. Harry raises the AK-47 and begins to fire as he runs forward, sweeping the muzzle of the weapon back and forth until it jams.

The figure is gone. Harry leans over the parapet but the courtyard below is empty except for the shot-up Mercedes. Perhaps it was never there, he thinks, but a moment later, a dark shape flits across the blood-red disc of the setting moon, heading westward, chasing the night.

Harry turns back to face the east, to wait for the cleansing light of the rising sun.

Guy N. Smith

Larry's Guest

Guy N. Smith was first published at the age of twelve in a local newspaper. Following a career in banking, his first novel, Werewolf By Moonlight, *appeared in 1974.*

Since then he has published nearly ninety books in all genres, although he is still best known for such horror novels as the bestselling Night of the Crabs *(and its five sequels), plus* The Sucking Pit, The Slime Beast, Bats Out of Hell, Satan's Snowdrop, Abomination, The Festering, Carnivore, Witch Spell, The Knighton Vampires, The Dark One *and* Dead End. *He has also written a number of non-fiction books on countryside matters, westerns, crime and mystery thrillers, and a series of children's animal novels under the pseudonym of "Jonathan Guy". His* Writing Horror Fiction *is a recent manual for aspiring authors.*

Returning to England, the Count discovers that things have changed during his absence . . .

LARRY STUMBLED panic-stricken out of the old underground air-raid shelter at the bottom of the garden, almost screaming his terror aloud. Overhanging laurel branches reached out like cold wet hands to stroke him; he hit back at them. His breath came in short gasps, his heart was beating faster and faster.

Then, to his sheer relief, the house loomed up ahead of him and he staggered in through the open back door, every ounce of his sixteen-stone frame trembling, his heavy-jowled unshaven features ashen. The wicker chair in the corner of the cluttered kitchen creaked alarmingly beneath him as he fell into it.

Oh, please God, it was all in his imagination!

Then he heard the kitchen door creaking slowly open, peered through the gloom and cringed from the stooped silhouette that was framed against the wan light from the hall.

No, please!

"Larry, are you all right? You were very out of breath when you came in. You haven't been . . ."

"I'm okay!" The hoarse whisper came from his quivering lips. He had only to move a yard and his mother was asking him if he was all right, shuffling to check on him like some grotesque ghoul. She was beginning to go senile, but that wasn't surprising at eighty-six. He had wasted the best part of his life staying at home to look after her, all for a miserable inheritance that he might not even get if she out-lived him.

"Go back into the lounge, Mother, it's nearly time for your television programme. I'll bring your tea shortly." *And just leave me alone,* he added silently to himself.

He heard her going back through the hall. Jesus, he didn't get a minute's peace these days. She still thought he was twelve instead of fifty-two. Right now, though, he had more important things to think about.

Like that coffin out there in the disused wartime shelter which he used as a darkroom for his amateur photography. Jim had dumped it there, of course. Who else? It *had* to be him. For some months now Larry had allowed Jim to store crates and boxes in there. Temporarily, of course – booze and cigarettes brought back from transcontinental haulage trips. It had seemed a fair arrangement; one day the shelter would be full, the next it was empty. Jim had regular customers for his contraband – pubs and off-licences presumably. Naturally, Larry's mother didn't know what was going on and she wasn't likely to find out. She couldn't even walk as far as the shelter with her arthritis and osteoporosis and, even if she somehow managed to, she was almost blind with cataracts. There was no fear of her finding out.

There was always an envelope left for Larry on the shelf inside the entrance after Jim had been to collect his latest cache. Twenty

or thirty pounds, sometimes forty. It was money for old rope.
Until now.

But what was a bloody coffin doing in there? Finding that hadn't
done Larry's blood pressure a whole lot of good. He had just had
one glimpse of it when he flicked the light on, then he had fled.
It wasn't a new coffin, in fact it looked quite old – like it had been
lying around for some time. Larry almost thought that it might have
been dug up from some graveyard. An exhumation. No, surely not.
There wouldn't be a corpse in it. Would there? No, of course not,
Jim wouldn't be into selling dead bodies, would he? Larry blanched
at the thought, remembering that movie about Burke and Hare. He
shuddered.

Then he guessed what it was all about, and realization brought
with it a flood of relief. Jim had used the coffin to smuggle cigarettes
and that thought made Larry feel a whole lot easier. It was ideal for
the purpose. Maybe the customs were having a purge on small-time
smugglers and what better than a coffin to allay suspicion? They
weren't likely to open *that* up! Larry almost laughed aloud at the
thought.

All the same, Jim might have told him, it could have given Larry
a bloody heart attack! Maybe he would give Jim a call just to put his
mind at rest, check that there was nothing sinister about the coffin.
No, Mother would overhear. Her limbs and her eyesight were in a
bad way, but there was nothing wrong with her hearing. Doubtless
Jim would take the coffin away tomorrow and there ought to be
an extra tenner in the envelope for something like *that.*

Larry glanced around in the failing light. He had gone out to
the shelter to fetch a film which he had developed earlier in the
day, but in his sudden fright he had left it behind. He needed
that film, he wanted to check the negatives. There were a couple
of autumnal landscape shots which he might be able to sell to a
magazine. His mother always kept him short of money. That was
her hold over him. You'll get it all one day, Larry, so just you look
after me in the meantime.

He would have to go and get it, then.

He glanced out of the window into the wilderness of the garden
and saw that it was not quite dark yet. Once night had fallen there
was no way he would ever go out there. It wouldn't take a minute,
the strip of developed film was suspended from a clothes peg just
inside the doorway. His heart started to speed up again.

Go on, it's now or never. There's nothing to be afraid of. Really,
there isn't.

"Are you sure you're all right, Larry?" His mother's concerned
voice came from the lounge.

"I'm fine."

"Where are you off to now?"

"Just fetching some film from the shelter."

Her hearing certainly made up for all her other shortcomings.

"Can't it wait till morning?"

"No, I need it." He slammed the back door after him.

It was deep dusk and it would be fully dark in ten or fifteen minutes. The laurel branches reached out for him again as if they wanted to drag him into the shelter. He shivered, slapped back at them, stumbled on the uneven ground and almost lost his footing.

"Damn!" He yelled his fear and frustration out loud as he just managed to regain his balance. "And damn Jim, too, for bringing that bloody coffin here. He might've asked first, it's only good manners. Give him an inch and he takes a bleedin' mile."

He thought he had left the shelter door open in his flight, but it was firmly closed now. The latch was stiff; he had to force it, and it clanged as it came free. The door creaked open. It was pitch dark inside, but he could not remember having switched the light off. Obviously, he must have done so. He hesitated, almost changed his mind – he didn't really need that film tonight, tomorrow would be soon enough. Still, having come this far . . .

A faint noise had him stiffening, as is somebody had moved in the bowels of this World War II edifice. Larry's mouth went dry, his pulse raced and his temples throbbed. It stank inside here, stale and musty and . . . something else which he could not quite place, an odour that was like damp earth. Well, this shelter was underground so it was no wonder that it smelled earthy.

Definitely, something moved. Rats, probably. His flesh crawled, he hated rats. He had seen one in here once before. No, it wasn't rats, it was too big and heavy. Jim, in all probability, come to collect his illicit cargo. At least he would get rid of it tonight. It must be Jim.

"Jim?" Larry scarcely recognized his own voice. The name echoed in the confined space, came back at him.

There was no answer. Just a soft footfall. Larry tried to peer inside the shelter but it was too dark to see. Then he had a sudden thought which, in its own way, was a relief. Maybe Jim had something *really* illegal in that box – like drugs – and he was hoping that Larry hadn't found it. Just an overnight storage, and he might even try to dodge paying, too.

"That you, Jim?"

Whoever it was breathed deeply, an intake of breath which was released in a low hissing sound. Larry almost fled back to the house.

Once indoors he would lock and bolt the doors, the way he always did at dusk.

But he stayed. Maybe it was the thought of the money – which Jim might not leave if he thought his visit had gone undetected – that held Larry there. Or perhaps he was too shaken to flee. Whatever the reason, Larry stretched out a trembling hand, located the rusted, cobweb festooned, power point and flicked on the light switch.

Larry was momentarily dazzled by the unshaded bulb, and he averted his head while his eyesight adjusted to the brightness. Then an inarticulate cry came from his lips as he stared in disbelief.

A man stood in the centre of the small brick-built underground chamber, his dark clothing starkly outlined against the dirty whitewashed walls. It certainly was not Jim! The stranger was much taller than Larry's acquaintance – he must have been well over six feet. A garment was draped around his shoulders. It might have been a loosely worn topcoat or an old-fashioned cloak.

His hair was brushed straight back, flecked with grey, but it was the expression on his features which filled Larry with a new dread. The cheeks were hollowed and the mouth was so red that it might have been smeared with lipstick. Strong white teeth were bared in either a smile or a snarl, Larry could not be sure which.

Yet it was the eyes which terrified him most – twin orbs that glowed redly, that seemed to bore into him and read his innermost thoughts. Larry swallowed. This time he would most certainly have fled but for the fact that his legs had suddenly gone so weak that he doubted whether they would be able to bear his weight much longer. He gripped the shelf, held on to it for support. Oh, what a fool he was to have returned to the shelter!

"Good evening," the mysterious stranger flicked at particles of dusk which adhered to his long cloak. His lips were stretched stll further, revealing twin canine teeth that glinted in the stark light. "I trust you will forgive this intrusion. It is not by choice, I assure you."

"That's . . . that's all right", Larry stammered. It wasn't, but he was, not going to argue with this guy. The other had a hint of a foreign accent; doubtless, Jim was involved in this. Perhaps he had taken to smuggling illegal immigrants.

"What country is this?" Those eyes fixed Larry with an unwavering stare. He did not want to look into them but he found himself compelled to meet the other's gaze.

"England," Larry gulped. So the guy was foreign and doubtless he had travelled here inside that . . . Larry forced his eyes away, stole a glance at the coffin. The lid was propped open and he saw that the interior was lined with red velvet and silk. A nauseating stench wafted from it, like a rotting corpse had lain within. It probably had. Jim had dug the coffin up, dumped the contents and used it to transport this weirdo here.

"England . . ." The other's eyes appeared to glaze over. "I knew that country . . . a long time ago."

He's cooked, Larry thought, crazy as a coot. Maybe it's some kind of game to scare the shit out of folks. He started, eyed the stranger again and his guts balled. There *was* a similarity, more the attire and the posture than facially . . . a definite likeness to a character he had seen in a number of late night movies, portrayed by a variety of actors. Well, if this stranger was acting out the part, that was why he looked so much like . . ."

"May I prevail upon your hospitality?" There was a smoothness that blended into presumption, adding to Larry's unease. "I shall need a dwelling place during my stay in England."

"My . . . mother doesn't allow anybody to stay overnight. We don't have a spare bedroom." That was because all the rooms were piled with Larry's junk. He never threw anything away.

"Oh, this place is more than adequate," the man waved a hand. "Everything that I desire. And I will pay you handsomely for your hospitality." His other hand delved into the folds of his clothing and reappeared with a shining coin held between two fingers. "On account, sir, and I will pay you more in due course. Go on, take it."

Larry's outstretched hand shook. The coin was unbearably cold, like buried treasure that had been unearthed. He guessed it was gold, but its markings were unknown to him. Whatever part this guy was enacting, at least his money seemed genuine. Larry felt a shiver running up his spine. He didn't know what the coin was but it was certainly no fake. It cast a sinister reality upon this bizarre encounter.

"All right," Larry's teeth chattered when he spoke. "But only for a short time." If necessary, he would call the police tomorrow.

"Of course." Those huge sharp teeth flashed another smile. "Just until I . . . *acclimatize.* I shall go forth, explore this strange land and ascertain whether or not it is to my liking. If so, then I shall endeavour to find some place to live which is in keeping with the lifestyle to which I am accustomed in my homeland."

Larry nodded. There were questions which he refrained from asking for fear of what the answers might be. This guy could doss down in the shelter overnight. Then tomorrow, in full daylight, he would reassess the situation.

He turned away, stumbled from the shelter, and made his way back indoors. Only then did he remember that he had still not collected his strip of drying negatives. They could go hang, literally. There was no way he was going back in there tonight.

Larry's mother always retired for the night around ten o'clock. She would go upstairs, a step at a time, clutching the bannister all the way, and then spend another hour undressing and doing whatever she did in her own bedroom. Larry rarely went to bed before the early hours – there was little point when there was nothing to get up for the following morning. Usually he watched a late movie or a video. But not tonight.

He had checked and rechecked that all the doors were bolted and locked. He was not in the mood to watch a film, certainly not one of *those*. He sat in the kitchen, glancing uneasily around. It was disconcerting to know that some nutter was camped out in the shelter, but at least the other couldn't get into the house tonight.

Larry studied the coin which the stranger had given him. He was certain it was gold but its origin remained a mystery. It was very old and therefore likely to be very valuable. Even so, it was small compensation for having to tolerate this madness.

He made up his mind that he wasn't going upstairs tonight. Somehow, asleep in bed, one was vulnerable. Far better to doze in the chair.

Larry slept fitfully. In his uneasy dreams he saw looked into those glowing red eyes, heard that awful hiss.

He woke up with a start and smelled his own sweat. He looked around the room but there was nobody there. It was that on-going nightmare that had disturbed him . . .

Somebody was tapping on the outside of the window.

Larry blanched. He thought about going through to the hallway and phoning the police. But it might just be night moths flapping against the window, attracted by the light from within. In which case Larry would look like a bloody idiot when the Bill arrived.

The tapping continued, more insistent now.

Larry knew he would have to take a look, he couldn't stand this all night. His legs were shaky as he heaved himself up out of the chair and crossed the room unsteadily. His trembling fingers rested on the frayed curtain. He didn't want to look, he didn't dare. *Something* made him.

Larry screamed as he stared into the sallow features pressed against the other side of the pane – as he looked into those bloodshot eyes and recoiled from an angry snarl.

He should have let the curtain fall back into place, and either returned to his chair or else gone through and phoned the police. He did neither. Just stared into those hateful, commanding eyes.

"*Let . . . me . . . in.*"

Larry obeyed, and then the tall imposing figure of his unwanted guest was standing over him in the kitchen, breathing foul fumes that made Larry want to retch.

"What *is* this place you call England?" the stranger demanded. He was clearly angry and disturbed.

"What . . . what d'you mean?"

"Where are the horses and carriages? What are those machines that hurtle by at unbelievable speed, apparently without horses to pull them? And larger ones, like monsters on wheels?"

Jesus, he was screwy, this one! "They're cars," Larry explained. "Cars and lorries. Driven by petrol."

"Petrol?"

Christ, just where did you start? Larry didn't know.

"I attempted to discover a town, where I might find what I seek."

"The town's less than two miles from here, straight down the main road, you can't miss it. But everything'll be closed now."

"I need a woman," the tall man was trembling with undisguised lust. "A comely wench. But I cannot, I dare not, enter this place you call a town with its strange bright lighting and carriages that travel without horses. I need your help, and I will gladly reward you." As if by magic another of the strange gold coins appeared and was held up in front of Larry's eyes. "Find me a wench!"

"There's a red light area in town. The prostitutes solicit at all hours of the night." Larry knew that because he had driven around the streets once or twice. He just had not had the courage to stop. "You'd find one easy enough if you . . ."

"Go and bring one back for me!"

Larry felt weak and scared for another reason now. Kerb crawling was a dangerous occupation – there had been a big feature on it in the local newspaper.

"*Go!*"

"Give me half an hour and I'll see what I can do." Larry did not have a choice. His mother should be fast asleep by now. If he rolled the Mini down the drive and didn't start it until he reached the road, he probably wouldn't awaken her. His greatest fear was that a patrolling police car might stop him.

"Bring her to my abode – a whore who will be honoured above all others, for she will have been singled out to become Count Dracula's chosen one."

So this idiot was acting out his Dracula fantasies, just as Larry had thought. He might even have made it as a ham actor in some low budget movie, he was good enough for that. He looked and acted the part even if he was a bit grubby when compared with the professionals. He was scary, too. Which was why Larry was anxious to appease him. There was a tart who worked the lower end of Bingley Street. Only in her teens, but she'd been there on every occasion Larry had made a tour of the red light area. If she happened to be there tonight, then it should be quite easy to pick her up and bring her back here.

It was.

It was only the ten pounds up front that made Larry's task relatively easy. The girl was clearly suspicious. She usually took her clients to a piece of waste ground if they were just after a quickie. A longer session, back at her place, cost more, but she didn't like going off to an unknown destination. However, with the promise of a further payment, she reluctantly agreed. She called herself Sally Ann and had an escalating drug addiction to finance, which she was open about. "What's wrong with the 'ouse?" She glanced behind her at the silhouette of the big house as she clutched Larry's hand. She gave a gasp of fear when a branch of cold wet leaves touched her bare legs.

"I don't like this."

"It's an annexe."

"A what?"

"An outside place where our lodger lives. He's a very wealthy man and I'm sure you'll be well paid."

"Better 'ad be," she shuddered. "This dump fair gives me the creeps."

Sally Ann held back in the entrance to the air-raid shelter, but Larry pushed her forward. She gasped aloud when she saw her client. She might have screamed and tried to make a run for it, but his glowing eyes fastened on her, appeared to hypnotize her. He reached out, grabbed her wrist and dragged her towards him.

As Larry let himself back into the house he heard her muffled screams from below. Calling the police was out of the question now – he had become an accomplice of this strange man whose sexual fantasies led him to play the role of Count Dracula.

That's what they were, Larry decided – sex fantasies, lived out to the extreme. The guy was just a dirty old man. All the same, it was both worrying and frightening.

There was no sign of life from the shelter next morning. Larry watched and waited, oblivious to his mother's witterings.

"Larry, you'd better pop into town. We need some more bread and . . ."

"I'll go tomorrow, Mother, we can manage until then."

"You'd better do some cleaning, this place is starting to get dirty."
It *was* filthy, had been for weeks, but she only noticed it when it became very bad.

"I'll do it later."

He kept watch from the landing window which overlooked the rear garden. The shrubs and trees were so overgrown that the shelter entrance was hidden from view, but he would be able to see anybody leaving in the direction of the house. He just hoped, if that happened, that his mother wouldn't hear them. But there was no sign of anybody, and he certainly was not going out there to look.

The day wore on. The morning drizzle cleared and weak sunshine broke through the cloud formation. And still there was no movement from the shelter.

The afternoon was misty – in all probability a fog would roll in with darkness. Larry became increasingly uneasy. What was going on out there? Had they left via the rear garden, gone through the woods at the back? Had "Dracula" moved on to another abode and taken his comely wench with him – plied her with gold coins for her company and favours. If that was the case, good riddance to both of 'em!

"I'm going up to bed now, dear." Larry's mother leaned in through the kitchen doorway. "Don't you be too late coming up yourself. I didn't hear you come to bed last night and I lay listening for hours."

"Mother, I'm turned fifty . . ." Oh, Christ, what was the point?

Larry decided to spend the night in the kitchen again. He was exhausted and yet sleep eluded him. He was kept awake by the nagging expectancy of another tapping at the window, pulling back the curtain to stare into the awful countenance of . . .

A tapping came on the window, fainter than before, not so insistent. Larry knew that he had to go and look. He steeled himself for the inevitable – those burning eyes and blood-red lips, a faint hissing that clouded the glass. Another demand, another whore.

But it wasn't the strange lodger at the window. Instead, it was the prostitute who called herself Sally Ann, looking radiantly beautiful and smiling at him with full, soft lips.

"Let me in, Larry", she mimed.

On this occasion there was almost an eagerness in his obedience. He put a finger to his lips and just hoped that his mother wasn't awake and listening. At least the girl was alive and unharmed. His own worst deed was that of procuring a prostitute for another person. Mother would never survive the shame, and that might not be a bad idea.

"Where is *he*?" Larry asked as he let her into the house and locked the door behind her.

"Don't you worry about him." She stretched up on the balls of her feet and her soft lips brushed his own. "You'n me've got the whole night ahead of us, Larry."

Larry had never really had a girlfriend before, just the odd one-night stand that had ended up in frustration and disappointment. All his attempts to get what he wanted most in life had been thwarted, either with lame excuses or downright refusals. Until now.

Sally Ann made the running. Her deft fingers removed his soiled clothing and she didn't even appear to notice his unwashed body or his obesity. She flaunted her own nakedness, teased him, then finally came astride him.

Larry groaned his pleasure aloud. She didn't *have* to do this, she wasn't getting paid for it. So she had obviously taken a shine to him. Mother wouldn't approve, but tonight was Larry's night of pleasure and tomorrow could look after itself.

He knew he couldn't hold back any longer and Sally Ann knew it too. Her beauty, her seductive smile, was a blur as he hit his peak. She writhed with him – they were like a duo of experienced ballet dancers who knew each other's every move and went with it. Her lips found his then, slid a soft warm path down to his grimed neck. And bit deep.

It hurt, but he didn't mind. He sensed the sticky warmth of his own blood. A love bite was a mark to be proud of when one had turned fifty.

They embraced again and he felt drowsy.

With the coming of daylight, she returned to her Master in his underground lair and Larry retired to his bedroom. Some time later his mother knocked on the door and enquired if he was all right.

"Just a migraine," he answered sleepily.

"Then you stop in the dark all day", she said. "I can cope."

Truly he must remain in a darkened room throughout the daylight hours – not just today but every day from now on. Larry understood that only too well.

When darkness fell, he and Sally Ann would return to Bingley Street where there was work to be done. Her clients and his whores would swell the ranks of the undead whom the Master could command from his small tomb on English soil. Here the Count would learn to cope with a society that was a far cry from the one he remembered. And that society, too, would change and adapt. It would take time, but nobody would be overlooked.

Perhaps even Larry's mother would be granted eternal life in her twilight years. Larry cringed at the thought, but the decision was not his. He was merely a slave to the Master now.

Jan Edwards

A Taste of Culture

Jan Edwards's reviews are regularly published in Starburst *and* The British
Fantasy Newsletter. *She recently produced and edited the chapbook* Silver
Rhapsody, *commemorating the 25th anniversary of the British Fantasy
Society, and she has short stories forthcoming in* Visionary Tongue *and*
Dark Horizons.

*"I got the idea for this story after going to the fair on Brighton pier with
my autistic daughter," she reveals, "and noted how her eccentricities that
so often attract disparaging looks and comments from strangers, were not
noticed – or perhaps more readily tolerated – in the fairground atmosphere. It
started me thinking that the fair, with its manufactured* bonhomie, *might
be the perfect place for any social outcast to mingle unnoticed. Somewhere
the Count might go for a night off."*

Dracula gradually becomes accustomed to his new surroundings . . .

HE WAS HUNGRY. But the first stand, crudely painted in garish
colours, proclaimed its contents to be "Earth Friendly". He averted
his eyes. This was England. Roasting oxen and warmed bread – that's
how it used be at English country fayres when he had visited them

in years past. Now it was all lentils and tofu and other vegetarian creeds that offended him deeply.

He shrugged lightly and moved around the gathering's perimeter to gauge the extent of delicacies on offer. Darkness had only just fallen and he was in no hurry – happy to feel, if not part of the crowd, then at least in contact with life; not merely humanity, but life itself: and the music that rose all around him, so vibrant, so invasive with its rapid, heartbeat rhythm. It pleased him greatly. These modern sounds were unfamiliar to him, but then every generation renewed the angst of misunderstood youth through its Art. It was part of the mystique of life.

He moved on, admiring the scenes before him. People, and so many of them in such a small place, and so varied. His stomach muttered discontent, reminding him he had to fill the void before he could think of doing anything else. What would a fayre have to offer other than sweetmeats doled out for infants and would-be infants alike?

He could see any number of options. Chinese? No. He had never found them satisfying. Italian? Maybe not – even the smell of garlic gave him indigestion.

A tall black woman brushed passed him, her cinnamon-scent lingering with him as she walked away. He paused, rotating slowly to follow her progress, until she vanished into the crowd. He'd follow if she were alone – the bulky lad trailing behind her could be a stranger; but somehow he doubted it.

The lights on a ride close by him so stung his eyes with their flaring intensity that he had to raise a hand to block the worst of the glare. Maybe he was getting too old for all this frivolity. Perhaps he would skip all this noise and settle for a liquid supper, like in the old days when life was so much simpler. There was an inn on the far side of the green. Quiet in comparison to this mêlée, but suitable. He'd find something there. But a companion? He never drank alone. It was not civilized.

He cast around for an easier option, and almost blundered into a burger-stand. He shuddered at an abomination surpassing tinned spaghetti and, reeling away from the hideous stench, quite literally stumbled into a small, lone figure huddled in the shelter of the vehicle, borrowing warmth from the occupant's vile trade.

Engrossed in the contents of her purse, the young woman was unaware of his presence until she looked up, face flushed under the fairground lights. She was an open invitation. Wide deep green eyes, and soft flawless skin made more tempting with its painted-on beauty. And a neck that arched in slender elegance as she looked up into his own dark eyes.

"Oh! Pardon Monsieur." Her voice was low, but oddly childlike in her surprise at his sudden appearance.

He bowed low, and smiled, anticipating a treat he hadn't thought to find in Britain's rural wilderness. It didn't matter where on this earth he found himself, it would always be hard to beat a good French red.

R. Chetwynd-Hayes

Rudolph

Ronald Chetwynd-Hayes has been called "Britain's Prince of Chill". He is the author of twelve novels, twenty-four collections of stories, and has edited twenty-three anthologies. His books include The Unbidden, The Elemental, The Monster Club, The Partaker, Tales from the Dark Lands, The House of Dracula, Dracula's Children, Tales from the Hidden World, Hell is What You Make It, The Psychic Detective, Shudders and Shivers *and* Something to Suck: The Vampire Stories of R. Chetwynd-Hayes, *as well as twelve volumes of* The Fontana Book of Great Ghost Stories *and six volumes of* The Armada Monster Book *series for children.*

The author of two film novelizations, Dominique *and* The Awakening *(the latter based on Bram Stoker's* The Jewel of the Seven Stars*), his own stories have been adapted for the screen in* From Beyond the Grave *and* The Monster Club *(in which the author was portrayed by actor John Carradine). In 1989 he was presented with Life Achievement Awards by both the Horror Writers Association and the British Fantasy Society.*

Sometimes even a vampire needs someone to look after him . . .

SINCE YOU INSIST on my telling all – as the saying goes – I'll start from the beginning. Yes, I think that's best. Someone should know what's going on, even if I can't believe half of it myself. But I've got to, seeing as how most of what I'm going to tell you happened to me. Me, Laura Benfield, who at thirty-seven years and three months, lived quite comfortably on a small income my mother had left me, together with the house.

Then I did a part time job, nothing strenuous you understand, for I'm not all that strong, just addressing envelopes for a mail order firm three days a week. Then that bastard Michel Adler came into my life and lit a bomb under me.

What? No, I don't mean literally. For God's sake! But it would have been kinder if he had. Handsome bastard he was. Looked like Errol Flynn in *Captain Blood* that I saw on telly twice. And charm! He could bring the birds down from the trees and worms out of the ground and get 'em to play hop-scotch together.

I met him at the Byfleet Social Club when I was sweating on a full house at bingo. I was just one number missing – legs eleven it was, but of course with my luck a cow from Tyburn Avenue got it. Not legs eleven, but five and three, fifty-three, which filled her house for her.

Then I hears this voice, all soft and gentlemanly like, say:

"Damn bad luck, old dear," and turning I sees him for the first time.

You know I went right weak at the knees, there and then, me who normally would never talk to a strange man. He had grey eyes, the sort that sort of twinkle and seem to be full of mischief. Know what I mean?

Well, not to make mincemeat out of a cold sausage, when he suggested we have coffee in the club room, I accepted like a shot and made sure Maud Perkins saw me hanging on to the arm of this sexpot, although when we were seated side by side near a ruddy great mirror that some sadistic bastard had stuck on the wall so that it took in the entire room, I began to ask myself where the catch was.

I mean, every woman there from sixteen to eighty was giving him the what-about-it-sign and I – let's be honest – had nothing bedwise to offer. There again they do say beauty is in the eye of the beholder, so I thought maybe my eye was missing out on some of my beauty. Any road that was the only explanation I could think of, for boy, did he give me the treatment.

After pouring coffee down me, he suggests dinner in some quiet restaurant wouldn't be out of place, he having not eaten since breakfast, due to being run off his feet by business commitments. It seemed that he had popped in the bingo club to unwind, for hearing numbers shouted out over a loud speaker had a relaxing effect on him. He also said it was the play of my features that directed his attention to me, suggesting as they did I had a beautiful soul which was reflected in my eyes.

No one has ever talked to me like that before and although you may think I'm a silly 'apporth to be taken in by stuff like that, just you remember that in every plain, dull woman, there's a beautiful, interesting one trying to get out. And he knew how to order a good dinner and wines with names I couldn't even pronounce, and when he left the waiter two pounds as a tip, I thought he must really be on the top shelf spondulics-wise.

Then he took me home and I felt awful about inviting him in, for the place hasn't seen a decorator's brush since my mum died and truth to tell, I'm no great dab at housework. But he – Michel – only laughed and said the house had character and personally he had no time for your spotless and everything in its place living unit, where it was impossible for anyone to feel comfortable.

Well, I had nothing in the house in the booze line, except for a few bottles of brown ale and I couldn't offer him that after all the wine and liqueurs he'd lashed out for on me. But he said he just as soon have a cup of tea, which he made, after telling me to sit down and put me feet up.

Then we talked. Even now, I have to admit that man had a wonderful brain. He told me all about the stars and how this world is only one among millions of suns and things and there must be billions of civilizations and one day clever, but funny-looking creatures will either visit us or we'll visit them and . . ."

Sorry. I didn't mean to break down like that, but when I think how things could have been if he hadn't turned out to be a crook, me heart's fit to break.

Anyway he came to see me quite often and took me out once or twice a week, always somewhere swanky, but there was one thing I thought was strange. After he'd paid the bill, he entered the amount in a little black book. He said it was so he could claim it back against tax, which didn't sound right, for a friend once told me that you can only get tax rebate for entertaining foreign buyers, but I didn't say anything, just supposed he knew his business best.

Then he got to talking about money, saying that lots of people did not realize they were sitting on thousands, until the matter was brought to their attention.

"Let's take your case, Laura," he said, "that house of yours, you could raise forty thousand quid on it any day. Invested by someone who knows his business, you could double it within six months, pay back the mortgage and use the extra thirty thou for further investments. That kind of thinking has laid the basis of many a fortune. I know – that's the way I started out."

Honestly it sounded right, particularly the way he put it, and when I said I wouldn't like to mortgage my mum's house, he said fair enough, he was only talking about what could be done, but God forbid he should influence me in any way. But if I should ever consider the idea, he'd be pleased to help me.

The seed had fallen on fertile ground, if you get my meaning. All of us could do with some more money, and the very thought of having thirty thousand nicely invested made me feel good. So one day I said I'd like to investigate the possibilities a little further – and that was it.

He cleaned me out in three weeks. He did all the paperwork – all I had to do was sign, the milkman witnessing my signature. First the mortgage on the house, then liquidating my little investments, for Michel said they were only chicken feed and he'd do much better for me. He explained for tax reasons all the money would be paid into a bank account under his name . . .

Thank you for the handkerchief, sir, these little lace things he brought me are no good when you shed buckets as I've been doing over the past few months.

What? Of course . . . well I had to get myself a proper job, didn't I? I mean I was down on my uppers. The house gone, me in a shabby bed-sit and not a penny coming in. I got taken on by a local store, but I wasn't really fitted for it. Me ankles swelled up with all that standing and when the customers got nasty, I answered back, which didn't please their mightinesses on the sixth floor, so I was soon out on my ear.

Then I read this advertisement. See? I've got the newspaper cutting here:

COOK HOUSEKEEPER required by single gentleman. Live-in all found. Salary by negotiation. Ring Mr Rudolph Acrudal 753. 9076.

As I've said I'm not all that good at housekeeping, but I'm not all that bad at cooking, so long as no one expects anything fancy. And with a single gentleman there's no woman to find fault – so why not?

The voice that answered the phone sounded genteel, which reassured me, for I find educated gentry are more easily pleased than your jumped-up-come-by-nights, and it was agreed I should come round right away, so I gave Mr Acrudal (pronounced Ac-ru-dal. I must say it took a bit of getting used to) my name and hired a taxi, for it's just as well to give the impression that you're not hard-up when applying for a job, and got myself driven to the address the gentleman had given me over the phone.

An old Victorian terrace house it was, four storeys high including the basement, with a flight of cracked grey steps leading up to the front door. The place didn't look so much run down as neglected, and I could imagine an old bachelor who just couldn't be bothered to have it done up.

He answered the door – Mr Rudolph Acrudal – a tall lean man who could have been any age. Honestly, I couldn't make up my mind if he was a worn-out thirty, or a young seventy. He had a mass of black hair sort of sprinkled with white, as though he had been painting the ceiling and splashed white paint over his hair.

High cheekbones and a hooked nose and two long eye-teeth that dimpled his lower lip, which I might as well say were black. The lips I mean. His ears tapered to a sharp point at the top, making him – what with sunken black eyes – look like those old prints of the devil. He wore a tight-fitting black suit that included stove-pipe trousers. True. I swear on oath. He jerked his head back and forth several times and then said in a rusty kind of voice:

"Miss Benfield – yes? Good. Come in – don't just stand there. The sun may come out at anytime and that won't be good for my health." And he all but pulled me into a hall that stunk of damp and what could have been burnt fat, and where every floorboard creaked when you took a step forward, to say nothing of the odd flake of plaster that floated down from the ceiling, particularly when Mr Acrudal slammed the front door.

He led the way into a front room that looked even worse than the hall, being mostly dominated by a giant old desk and a mixture of books and papers that lay everywhere? Honestly I thought for a moment it was the dumping area for Let's-have-all-your-old-books-and-newspapers-week. But he upended one wooden armchair, so that everything on it – including a huge tom cat – slid on to the floor. He half sat on the desk and gave me the doings.

"My wants are simple. Breakfast – black pudding on toast. Lunch – pig's blood mixed with lightly done mince. Dinner – the same. Nightcap – a glass of pig's blood." He looked at me intently. "How does that strike you?"

I spoke boldly – it always pays in the long run: "Well, sir, it wouldn't suit me, but if that's what you want – I'll try to make it as tasty as possible."

He jerked his head up and down and I could swear he was dribbling as though the very thought of his favourite diet had started his mouth watering. "Good. The last housekeeper I had, heaved up when she saw me shovelling in the mince and blood. That's settled then. You have a free hand. Make sure I'm fed and moistened three to four times a day and you can do what you like."

I said, "Thank you, sir. I can see there's plenty to do. And where will my quarters be?"

"Wherever you care to make them. Plenty of empty rooms on all floors. I use this one and the one next door. No need for you to go in there. As for money . . ."

"I was about to mention that, sir."

He bent down and brought forth a large old carpet-bag from beside the desk, which he dropped in my lap. When I opened it I found wads of bank notes – fifty pounds, tens and fivers. Mr Acrudal waved a dirt-grimed hand.

"Pay yourself a hundred a week, then take whatever is needed for housekeeping."

I shook my head firmly. "That won't do at all, sir. We won't know where we are. I'd like you to keep this bag somewhere safe and pay me whatever is required each week."

His face – white as a pig's belly – took on a real bad-tempered expression and I thought to myself: I wouldn't like to cross you, me lord, that I wouldn't. For now, his face from dead white turned to a light grey. Very off-putting it was. Never seen anything like it before. Then he kind of spluttered out words it took me some time to understand.

"Don't . . . ar . . . r . . . g . . . u . . . e with . . . me . . . m . . . m . . . e w . . . o . . . m . . . m . . . a . . . n . . . D . . . o . . . o . . . o . . . a . . . s . . . I . . . say."

He scared the wits out of me and I was about to give him a piece of my mind and then walking out, when I remembered the cold bed-sit and the two quid and small change in my handbag, so I nodded like an idiot and said: "All right, sir . . . calm down. I'll make a note of all the money I take and let you have a statement once a week."

He did calm down, but appeared to be tired out as though the outburst had drained him.

I got out of the room as fast as my legs would take me and after I had cooled down a bit, began to explore the house. The kitchen I found in the basement, if the grease-lined hell-hole could be identified in any way as a place for preparing food. Do you know there was an old rusty iron range that heated an antiquated boiler with a tap on one side. A plain deal table collapsed when I tried to move it. Damp rot had done its worst to the floorboards and I almost broke an ankle when my foot sank into rotting wood. I made up my mind then and there – the kitchen was a write-off.

I chose a room two floors up that commanded a view of the

overgrown back garden and decided to take a thick wad of notes from that bag and buy a portable oil stove and a complete set of saucepans.

But number one question. When did the old devil want feeding next?

I looked at my watch and saw that the time was twelve-fifteen, so it would be reasonable to suppose that lunch – pigs' blood and mince – should be served around one o'clock. Frankly I lacked the courage to ask Mr Acrudal where the nauseating mixture could be found – or obtained, but finally I went down into the hall and found a gold-coloured round tin that contained around three pints of thick blood and a bulging newspaper parcel.

I could sympathize with my predecessor who heaved when she saw her employer tuck into this muck, particularly when my nose told me the mince – and maybe the blood as well – was most definitely off.

I washed an iron saucepan as best I could, bunged the soggy mess into it and actually managed to stew it over an old hurricane lamp I found in one corner of the so called kitchen.

I did my best to flavour this horrible concoction (boiling blood explodes into evil-smelling blisters) with pepper and salt, plus a nutmeg I found the large cat playing with, while pretending fat healthy maggots weren't being done to death down below.

At one o'clock precisely I carried a tin tray on which slid back and forth a deep bowl containing bubbling, flavoured, blood-seeped, spicy mince. I had also succeeded in washing a dessert spoon, and after pushing the door open with my right knee, lurched across the littered floor to where the old-young man sat behind his desk. He really brightened up when he saw me with the tray and when I bunged it down in front of him, he grabbed the spoon and began shovelling the mess in.

It was a dreadful sight and sound. Slop-slub-lip-smacking with what missed the target dribbling down his chin. When the bowl was half empty he paused for breath and expressed sincere appreciation.

"The best blushie I've tasted in years, Miss Benfield. You are talented . . . so talented. Just give me the same for dinner and we'll get along famously. I knew by your smell that we'd haunted the same track."

I said primly, "So pleased to give satisfaction, sir," and backed out of the room. I didn't know what he meant by smell and could only regard the remark as some kind of insult.

Having taken care of my new employer's requirements, I began to sort out my own. I explored the house from attic to basement and confirmed my original opinion that neglect had resulted in devastation, but a few weeks' hard work could make the place at least livable again. But not by me. As money seemed to be no object, I decided to dig well down into that carpet bag and hire a cleaning firm; the kind of organization that takes care of offices and showrooms. In the meanwhile I turned out a small bedroom on the third floor, took over a quilted double divan that must have cost a pretty penny when new, shook the dust out of some red blankets, unwrapped pink sheets and pillow-cases that sometime in the past had been sent to a well known laundry.

I uncovered three bathrooms – literally – and threw their contents out of a landing window and watched them land in an enclosed dank area. Two tubs had to be written off as what appeared to be cinders and wood ash had been thrown into at least six inches of water, resulting in corrosion that in some places had eaten through the metal. But one was still in reasonable condition and I managed to scrape it clean and plug two holes with putty that I found clinging to the banisters. By five o'clock that part of the house that I would be using was at least clear of surface rubbish and filth and I was free to think of my own needs.

I visited Mr Acrudal and to my disgust found he had licked the bowl clean and by his greedy enquiring look clearly thought I had brought a replacement.

I said, "Sir, I will need money, mainly for food for myself and having this house cleaned from top to bottom."

He put his head on to one side and looked not unlike an intelligent dog that it trying to understand what it is being told to do. Then there came from his throat what I can only describe as growled words.

"Cleaned ... from ... top ... to ... bottom?"

"Yes, sir. If you'll forgive me for saying so, the place is a disgrace the way it is. I was thinking of engaging a cleaning company."

"More than two strangers ... strangers ... in ... the ... house?"

"Well, there's no way I can do all the work myself and we can't leave it the way it is."

He reached down and produced that carpet bag again and dumped it on the desk. He fumbled around inside for a few moments and brought out a bundle of fifty pound notes that must have totalled at least seven hundred pounds. Then for the first time so far as I was concerned, he got up and eased his way round the desk, clutching the money in one hand and supporting himself with the other. I think there was something wrong with the left foot – or rather I thought so then. In fact as he drew nearer I couldn't dismiss the thought that he was in some way deformed, terribly deformed, although a slight limp was the only outward sign.

Then he was close up – breathing on me.

I all but choked on the stench of decay that might have seeped through water-logged churchyard loam. I retreated back one step, before his right hand formed a band of steel round my left arm and jerked me forward until our faces were only a few inches apart. Then he smiled, a strangely sweet smile that revealed beautiful white teeth and instantly I forgot his grotesque appearance, the foul breath and the oddness about him; instead I became aware of a rising wave of excitement that later made me distrust my own senses. His voice came quivering from his open mouth as a thrilling whisper.

"Do whatever you wish . . . at all times the house is yours, but never . . . never . . . allow strangers . . . to cross my threshold." His smile became more pronounced and such was my fascination I could even ignore those long eyeteeth. "Please understand that. If work is too much . . . leave it. Confine yourself to preparing the so excellent blushie and I will demand no more."

He released me, thrust the money into my hand, then returned to his chair and became engrossed in reading what looked like an old document.

After a while my limbs became once again capable of movement, so I bolted back into the hall and took refuge in the room I had requisitioned for my own use. The bundle of money still clutched in my left hand forbade all thoughts of decamping and making for the nearest YWCA for even the most incorruptible soul must surrender to greed when loot is constantly thrust into its vicinity.

But there was another reason why I would find it increasingly more difficult to leave this house, no matter how fearsome it might become.

Rudolph Acrudal was without doubt ugly, repulsive and sinister, but I knew now he radiated some kind of charm that sooner or later I would find irresistible.

I got some kind of routine working – and surprised myself.

Mr Acrudal's rations came from the local butcher, who dumped can and parcel on the top step each morning, plus whatever I ordered for myself. I may add my spiced blushie so pleased my employer that he would eat nothing else – not even the black pudding, a fact that aroused the interest of the butcher when I paid him every Friday morning.

Having done things to an elaborate cash register, I was given a printed receipt, before a red face creased into a wide confidential grin.

"Tell us the truth, love. What the 'ell does he do with all this blood and mince? I mean it's not as though it comes from fresh meat. From the beginning I was told it must be high. Straight up. Warm, runny and smelly. And the blood – thickish."

I always started out by giving the same answer: "That's Mr Acrudal's business and mine," but after a while the need to talk to someone who is nice to me, got the better of discretion and I finally admitted I had to cook the horrible mess which Mr Acrudal was so kind as to say he enjoyed. And although Mr Redwing – that was the butcher's name – expressed disbelief, I could see he wanted to believe and pass on what he believed to an enthralled public.

Then while carving me a nice piece of topside: "No one seems to know what he looks like, him never coming out in daylight. Is it true he has 'orns under his hair?"

Of course I could only gasp: "Of course not. It's not as bad as that. Don't be silly."

I think it was about then that I became aware that the house was being watched. Not openly, but sometimes from a parked car, or the shadow cast by an old tree. Dark, squat, round-shouldered men was the only impression I got, never actually seeing them close-up, you understand. I wasn't all that worried, assuming that such was the interest as to what took place in the house, some nosy parker – or parkers – were hoping to catch a glimpse of Mr Acrudal at one of the windows.

I started another kitchen on the first floor, buying one of those elaborate oil stoves complete with oven and grill; and a table high fridge and sink unit. Getting the sink connected up without letting Mr Acrudal know, took a bit of organizing, but I did it by donning a boiler suit and putting in an occasional appearance in the Master's room, complaining how wrong it was for a woman to have to do this kind of work without help.

He never commented, but tried to hide behind a massive tome that looked as if it had been stored in a damp cellar for a few years. In fact all the books in that room gave me that impression. Any road, by the end of the first month I had made myself as comfortable as the surroundings would permit and more or less adapted to what could only be called a bizarre situation. But that failing that my dear mother had so often stressed – had killed the cat – namely curiosity – would not give me any peace.

For example: he had never allowed me to see his bedroom or so much as move a book in that awful room where he spent so much of his time.

So I gave the rest of the house a good going over, and got the impression Mr Acrudal had been there a long time.

I found newspapers going back to 1870, some announcing the abdication of Napoleon III. Cupboards were crammed with them, some seemingly unopened, others with rectangular holes where paragraphs and entire columns had been cut out. I unearthed books bound in plain covers lacking both title and author, the script in some foreign language which I would never understand in a thousand years.

I was about to replace one when I saw a piece of paper sticking out from the middle pages, thrust in hurriedly I would imagine as a book marker, which turned out to be a letter written – thankfully – in English.

I would have you believe me, Sir, that I do not as a rule pry into other people's correspondence; my mother raised me properly but when you're eaten up by curiosity and badly want to know who – what – your employer is, you'd be a saint – which I beg leave to say I'm not – not to read a few lines scrawled on a piece of paper.

I can remember every word.

> *Rudolph, a word of warning: Total abstinence of essential fluid will age a body that should retain youth for night on eternity. Waste not the gift our sire gave you. The blushie diet will only sustain.*
>
> H.

And that was all. I put the paper back in the book, then settled down to have a good think. When I was a kid my dad was always swearing to practise Total Abstinence, which meant not drinking booze in any form whatsoever. His good intentions were usually drowned in about fourteen days.

But I had never heard booze called essential fluid – although my dad might have thought it was – and certainly couldn't entertain the idea *not* drinking the stuff would age the body. Quite the contrary I would have thought.

And my employer's diet was mainly blood and rotten meat. Blushie. To my mind the only nourishing meal he ever ate was his early morning black pudding – or blood sausage as I've heard it called. But now he'd given that up.

Blood!

It would seem that my employer needed blood in some form or another to sustain life, but according to H he wasn't getting it in right quantities – or quality. In other words he wasn't getting the right kind of blood.

Yes, sir, I've seen my ration of horror films and my mind came up with the question: What kind of being needs a diet of blood to exist? – and supplied an instant answer.

A vampire.

And it was no use calling myself a silly twit and repeating "Vampires don't exist" over and over again, for my bloody brain came up with another question: How do you know they don't exist? And I remembered the long eye-teeth and suddenly imagination created a fantasy-picture, complete with sound, touch and colour. I was being held by one large hand while the other tore my dress leaving by throat bare, hot stinking breath on my skin; then came a sharp pain and I became as a virgin on her wedding night, terrified, gasping – and shuddering with ecstasy.

"We were reckoning the other day," Mr Redwing said, adjusting his straw hat to a more becoming angle, "that your boss must have eaten his weight in rotten mince several times over. Doesn't he have any vegetables? Or salad?"

I'm not good at lying so I just shook my head.

"Thought not. My missus says if you just eat meat and nothing else, you're in line for scurvy. Like they did in Nelson's navy. Hope you look after yourself, love."

"I do that. Plenty of salad and fruit. But is that true about scurvy?"

"Sure thing. Ask any doctor. Must have a balanced diet."

After the lapse of three days I had come round to ridiculing the very idea of Mr Acrudal being a vampire. Or at least half convinced myself I was ridiculing the idea, which is almost the same thing. But certain facts could not be erased, particularly my employer's strange diet and the damned letter, which for my peace of mind, I should have never read.

Now Mr Redwing's little snippet of information had set fire to the dry grass of conjecture, highlighting the fantastic more vividly than ever. If a hundred percent protein diet resulted in scurvy, then Mr Acrudal should have been dead long ago. If one thought about his health at all, the only reasonable assessment must be neither good or bad, but Acrudal-normal.

So far as I knew he took no exercise, the only movement being from workroom to bedroom, with periodical visits to the bathroom. Presumably he washed there, but I was willing to swear he never took a bath or shaved. I assumed that his hair must grow, that is to say on his head, but his face remained smooth, which made me wonder if there was any hair on his body at all.

I had been in the house just over three months when Janice turned up.

She let herself in the front door, having it appeared her own key. A pretty, impudent teenager – or so she seemed – dressed in a white jersey with red stripes and a pair of well-washed jeans. Black, wind-blown hair, thick eyebrows and dark sparkling blue eyes. A broad intelligent face that seemed to be always lit by a faintly mocking smile, and really beautiful white skin that positively glowed with obscene good health. I noticed she had large well-shaped hands. When she spoke her voice had a brittle quality, enhanced by a slight foreign accent.

"Hallo, don't tell me you're the new cook and bottle-washer! I'm Janice, sort of niece to old thingy."

I said, "I'm pleased to meet you, miss. I've been Mr Acrudal's house-keeper for three months now. I'll inform your uncle you're here."

She laughed, a lovely soul-warming sound in that dreadful house, and shook her head until the black hair bounced.

"No need. I'll surprise the old sod."

And while I was shaking my head, for I've no time for bad language, to say nothing of disrespect for elders and betters, she pranced along the hall and without so much as a tap on the door, entered her uncle's room.

I heard a roar that had much in common with a lion suddenly spotting an extra and quite unexpected meat ration. When I arrived at the open doorway, I was greeted by a spectacle that both shocked and angered me.

She – Janice – was sitting on his lap and he had pulled the jersey down from her left shoulder and was pressing his lips into the white flesh, and she – brazen hussy – was laughing with head well back and turned towards the door, so that she was looking directly at me. To this day the picture is etched on my memory. The young girl with laughter expressed in every line on her face and Mr Acrudal pressing his lips into her bare shoulder, as though he were preparing to eat her.

And another smell had been added to those which already pervaded the house – the smell of lust. But not the healthy lust that even a left-on-the-shelf type like me can understand, but something alien – foreign I think that means, sir – that made my flesh crawl. But I couldn't move, just stand there watching them; and gradually there came to me another emotion that filled me with self-disgust.

Jealousy.

I wished with revolting envy he was doing it to me.

The spell was broken when that wool jersey ripped exposing most of her back, for then she flowed off his lap, rolled across the floor, then sprang to her feet with one graceful bound that would not have disgraced a sleek, well-conditioned cat. She stood staring down at Mr Acrudal in his chair, her hands raised, the palms facing him.

"Steady on." Her voice held a hint of menace. "I'm one of the family, remember? So far – so good – or bad. And humey eyes are watching and the thing is going green."

And she turned her head and grinned at me in such a fashion my hand itched to decorate her smooth white cheek with my finger-prints. But at least anger had set me free and I was able to run up to the makeshift kitchen and there whisk two eggs with a fork, consoling myself with the thought that if the young bitch wanted lunch, she could get it herself.

She came up some ten minutes later, the jersey pinned together with a safety pin, but still not doing much to cover the left shoulder.

I said, "Yes, miss, anything I can do for you?" in a tone of voice that suggested I'd prefer her room to her company. At least that's what I intended to convey, but it didn't have any effect. She gave me another impudent grin, then sat on the table, swinging one leg.

"Have you got hot pants for the old sod? Don't get aereated, they all do, even if he is off-putting. You'll go crawling back regardless."

"You insolent slut."

She leaned over and actually tickled me under the chin. "Am I? I expect you'd like to belt me, wouldn't you? But don't try it on, I could break your back in three different places before you'd raised a hand." She giggled and put her head on to one side and I couldn't help admitting how pretty she looked. "Funny how you humes pretend horror, but drop your knicks when one of the Count's by-blows breathes on you. It's the smell what does it. Gets the old glands going."

I sat down on a chair and took a shuddering breath and although I knew the veil must be torn from the face of truth, nevertheless curiosity fought a bitter battle with dread. Eventually I asked:

"What's all this in aid of, miss?"

How the little bitch laughed. Came right up close and ran one large beautiful hand down my leg, so that the desire I had kept so well under control, broke free and flooded my loins with liquid fire. And the safety pin must have come unfastened for the torn jersey slipped down from her shoulder and I could see one rounded breast – and oh, my God! I didn't know where I was or what kind of machinery was ticking away in my body, and the house was saturated with evil – well it must have been, only what the hell is evil? – because how else were such thoughts belting around in my brain. Then her low, thrilling voice with its slight accent, spoke again.

"Oh, come off it. Don't tell me you don't know the score. Been in the house for three months or more, looked at him, smelt him, and not known him for a second generation vampire? The count's son? Sooner or later you'll be down under him taking the shagging of a lifetime, so that in around a year you'll drop a little humvam."

I screamed, "No!" and her laughter should have choked her.

"Yes. Yes ... yes ... yes. He likes the over-ripe, retarded type. The spark in the belly waiting to erupt into a mighty flame. After a session with my Lord the Prince Rudolph, my sort of uncle, a stallion won't satisfy you. But," she leaned over and inserted one long finger into the crease between my breasts, "guess what. He, descended from the most ancient line in the world, is ashamed of being what he is. Son of the vampire king. He won't partake from the neck, or even intake vital essence from a bottle. Makes do with pig's blood and rich mince. That's why he looks so weird. And all he's got to do is imbibe once – and, oh boy, you'll see the difference. He almost gives way when I get to work on him, but no way. I don't mind slap bot and fumble, but no give with the vital. Well, it wouldn't be decent."

I took a firm grip of my reeling senses, drove a shaft of iron through my quivering soul and transformed a spoonful of courage into a little spear of anger.

"You're a dirty little trollop, miss. At least that's what my old mum would have called you. You must have a mind like a cesspool, only it's probably so twisted you can't tell the difference between fact and fancy. Me, I'm going to hang on to my sanity and assume that dirty old man is over the edge, or if you prefer, up the pole, then get the hell out of this place."

She patted my cheek and I smacked her hand away. "You can't. No way. You've let him come real close and the smell of him is in your blood. And just supposing you were real strong and managed to get away – the pack would get you. The pack of shadmads. Or maybe as you're someone special – vammads. They've been watching the house since you arrived. Looking after you. Once they get on your track they never let up until you're a flabby bag of nothing in the gutter. No hume ever lives to spill the beans on the family."

I closed my eyes and muttered a kind of prayer.

"Let me disbelieve now and know I am protected by invisible angels and can never be pulled down. Never."

Her giggling flooded my being with cold wavelets and for the first time I knew my soul was confined in a castle that crouched half way up a flame-tipped mountain, where it waited for death to set it free. And in the valley there waited the demons, the unnamed, who feed on immortal essence, and breathe their fire-dreams into our sleeping brains.

Large beautiful hands stroked my naked thighs and I screamed total, absolute surrender.

"Take me to him," I screamed. "Take me to him."

She purred a soft little chuckle.

"That's why I came. Uncle Rudolph must be up and around soon, there's so much for him to do. Help bend time for example. And he must have that what is essential for him to look young again."

She was behind me, her hands on my breasts, guiding me out of the room, down the stairs. Realization of what lay in store made me struggle when we crossed the hall, and the mere sight of him – immortal son of Dracula – seated on the desk, exploded a fear bomb in my stomach and I passed into a fire-streaked darkness where the five senses merged into one, or took on an extra.

Tell me, sir, you might know, is it possible for all of us to have extra senses that sleep within our bodies, but could be awakened if the conditions are right – or wrong?

They – Mr Acrudal and the young bitch – did something to me, for it seemed as if I slid down a tunnel through days, weeks and months, even years, and only allowed me to pop my head up through a ventilation hole, once now and again.

Did they bury me? If not, then how is it I can still remember the cloying dampness pressing on me everywhere; breathing rich soil that gave me a joyous half-sleeping life. Every now and again I became aware of one of their faces gazing down at me, his grown strangely young, glowing with a special kind of beauty that I suddenly realized had always been lurking just beneath the surface.

My blood gave a deeper red to his lips, my vital essence lit candles in his eyes; weakness fought tingling strength in my veins, blood had been replaced by something more interesting. Strangely, I cannot remember during that twilight period being other than happy. Or if not happy, then blissfully content. I became dimly aware that somewhere along the road to eternity I would take a dark turning and never come back, but even that prospect could not mar the safely insulated present.

I came to understand, sir, that fear and even dread can so easily change from black to bright red. Can you understand that?

The birth pangs were muted.

Like having a tooth pulled when the cocaine hasn't quite taken effect. I mentioned that dread had changed from black to bright red, well, during the birth I existed in a red mist. I could see the young bitch (only she wasn't young), moving about, feel her hands on me, forcing my legs apart, but when she and Mr Acrudal spoke, their voices seemed to come from a long way off and I couldn't understand a word they were saying.

The explosion that tore my guts apart rocketed me into full

consciousness for around two minutes and I felt the agony, the pure seething terror and knew . . . knew – knew exactly what I was giving birth to, but then he, Mr Acrudal, Prince Rudolph, filled my brain with wonderful pictures, so that fear, the pain, the knowledge, were banished and I was permitted to sink back into my nice cosy insulated happiness.

I awoke in my own bed.

That which had come from my body was confined to a black wooden cradle and when it raised its head and spat at me, I screamed and strained at the broad straps which only permitted limited movement. Even now, sir, when more immediate horror whimpers just beyond that door, a cold shudder sends limb freezing dread down my body, when I think of that tiny face twisted up into a grimace, hissing like a snake, then spitting . . . No, please don't ask me to describe it. Please don't . . . Thin and white, two jutting teeth, black gleaming eyes . . . yes, like those of a snake. A black mamba . . . Rudolph was very gentle with me – the young bitch had disappeared for time being – and he explained over and over again that *it* would improve beyond recognition in time, become beautiful, as did the entire race down to the fourth generation. The right nourishment took care of that. But . . . but – I will be all right, sir, in just a minute – but I must tell you . . . must . . . he said for the first few weeks I must . . . feed . . . feed it . . . but . . . he explained wonderfully . . . it was not milk it needed . . . so it wouldn't suck . . . but bite . . . chew . . . chew . . . sometimes nibble . . . nibble . . .

After two weeks they took the thing I had bred away from me, which may have saved the remnants of my sanity, for it had begun to develop tiny claws on fingers and feet, although I was assured that they would soon disappear, being in fact the equivalent of milk teeth.

Rudolph – how beautiful he had grown – fed me on stewed mince and maybe because I didn't think about it too much, it tasted quite nice and most certainly did me good. I put on weight and when I was quite strong – and not before, for he really was most considerate – the Prince took my left hand in his and explained all I needed to know.

Actually all he wanted was to live a quiet eternity writing a history of his illustrious family, but it would seem it was his duty once now and again, to father an offspring, which would be a half-breed, but help spread the Dracula blood among the humes. Only a woman who could remain in that dreadful house for not less than three luna months, was suitable for vam breeding.

Rudolph bared his sharp white teeth in an engaging smile that I found to be so irresistible. "You are to be congratulated, my dear. Many were interviewed, few were chosen."

"And what happens to me now?" I asked.

He sighed deeply. "Why did you have to ask that question? Whatever answer I give is certain to hurt. I should put you down, but I lack the necessary ruthlessness. So, I am going to set you free. Whatever happens will not be the result of my action. Take my advice, get well away from the house. Travel by day. The pack are not happy in daylight and whimper most piteously when caught under the naked sun. I cannot give you hope for a long life, for that on reflection will not be desirable, but you may derive some satisfaction in evading the pack for a quite considerable period.

"Tell someone of your experience if you so wish and it eases your mind by doing so. No one will believe, but a version may be passed on and that will give birth – in the fullness of time – to an interesting legend. But of course should someone even half believe and start to investigate – more work for the pack."

The pack.

He always pronounced that word in a peculiar way, as though it were distasteful to him and its implication something no gentleman would ever consider. Oddly enough, I did not even think about it, although at the back of my mind I knew what eventually my fate would be. The young bitch had told me plainly enough.

Instead, I began to wonder who prepared the wonderful meals that were served up on a wooden tray and came to the conclusion it must be Rudolph. A gifted family and, when necessary, domesticated. After all, the original count cooked excellent meals for Jonathan Harker and made his bed into the bargain. Yes, he actually gave me *Dracula* to read.

Then came the morning when he kissed me on the lips and as always my legs turned to jelly and you would never believe how young and beautiful he looked.

My luggage stood in the hall, but I couldn't really believe I'd have a use for it – not now. The young bitch opened the door and I ignored her impudent grin, but I will confess I'd go to my end more happily after an hour alone with her, just supposing she was tied down or something.

"Goodbye," Rudolph whispered. "There's plenty of money in your handbag. More than you'll ever need."

A taxi stood waiting and someone – Rudolph I suppose – carried my luggage out and piled it at my feet. Then I was away and again knew nothing until the cab drew up outside a rather dingy hotel. The driver spoke over one shoulder.

"The Imperial, ma'am. That was were I was told to bring you."

I must have blacked out or maybe time-jumped forward a few hours, for I remember nothing more until finding myself lying on a double bed looking up at a cracked ceiling.

And you want to hear something really weird? I was homesick for that awful old house and Rudolph and the young bitch. I think I must have passed around three days eating and sleeping, and quite possibly have remained in that hotel until my money ran out, if I had not seen them from my window.

It must have been early evening for the street was silver-gold with lamplight and I could easily see the black car standing opposite with three or four figures leaning against it, staring up at my window. Dressed entirely in black, with long dog-like faces; jutting mouths, black lips, flattened noses, tapering ears and gleaming red-tinted eyes. I breathed one word:

"The pack!"

I'd forgotten them.

I sat by the window and watched them all night. So far as I could see not one moved until the first streak of dawn lit the grey roofs. Then they all piled into the car and drove away.

I left the hotel ten minutes later and have been more or less on the move ever since. But the pack have never really been far behind and I've no doubt are somewhere in this vicinity now. I've seen them several times, but they keep their distance, because I suppose I'm not quite ready for the kill yet. When I leave, sir, it might be well if, for your own sake, you waited for a while before leaving. Don't let them think you're at all interested in me. But you may be safe enough, for Rudolph said I could tell my story, but it's best not to take risks.

Well I'll be on my way. Thank you for being such a good listener – and, yes, buying me that drink after that silly fainting spell. They'll be calling time soon, so you can go out with the crowd. Lovely full moon tonight . . . wolf moon I've heard it called. Good luck, sir . . . good luck . . .

Graham Masterton

Roadkill

Graham Masterton was a newspaper reporter and editor of Mayfair *and* Penthouse *before becoming a full-time novelist with his 1976 book* The Manitou *(filmed two years later).*

Since then he has written more than thirty horror novels and dozens of short stories, as well as historical sagas, thrillers and bestselling how-to sex books. In 1989 he edited Scare Care, *an anthology of horror stories to benefit abused and needy children, and recent books include* Burial, The Sleepless, Spirit, Flesh and Blood, The House That Jack Built *and he is currently working on a new series of supernatural novels for young adults,* Rook, *set in a community college in Los Angeles. His short fiction has been collected in* Fortnight of Fear *and* Flights of Fear.

Even a vampire cannot always halt the march of progress . . .

HE SLEPT, and dreamed . . .

He remembered the blood, and the battles. The extraordinary clanking of swords, like cracked church bells, and the low hair-raising moan of men who were fighting to the death. He remembered how sharpened wooden stakes were thrust into the cringing bodies of weeping men, and how they were hoisted aloft, so that the stakes would slowly penetrate them deeper and deeper, and they would scream and thrash and wave their arms in anguish. He remembered how he had looked up at them, looked them in the eye, and smiled at their pain.

He remembered his own death, like the shutting of an owl's eye; and his own resurrection. The strange confusion of what he had become; and what he was. He remembered walking through the forests in torrential rain. He remembered arriving at a village. He remembered the women he had lusted after, and the blood he had tasted, and the wolves howling in the dark Carpathian mountains.

He remembered days and nights, passing as quickly as a flicker-book. Sun and rain and clouds and thunderstorms. He remembered kisses thick with passion. Breasts running with rivulets of blood. He remembered Brighton in the sunshine, and Warsaw in the fog. He remembered heavy, seductive perfumes, and women's thighs. Carriages, cars, railway-trains, aeroplanes. Conversations, arguments. Telegrams. Telephone calls.

It went on for ever, and sometimes he lost track of time. Sometimes he had written letters to some of his closest friends, only to realize halfway through that they must have been dead for two hundred years. He had hunched over his desk, in such a spasm of grief that he could scarcely breathe. He had stopped writing letters – and, even when he received them, which was very rarely, he didn't open them any more.

But every day a new day dawned, and every night the sun went down; and almost every dusk he pushed open the lid of his casket and rose from his bed of friable soil to feed on whoever he could find.

One night, early in October, he opened the cellar trap to find that the hallway was empty. All the furniture had gone. The hallstand with its hat-hooks and mirrors; the Chinese umbrella-stand beside the door. Even the carpets had gone. He stepped out onto the bare boards in his black, highly-polished shoes, turning around and around as he did so. The pictures had gone. The landscapes of Sibiu and the Somesu Mic. Even the painting of Lucy, with her white, white dress and her white, white face.

He walked from room to room in rising disbelief. The entire house had been stripped. The dinining-table and chairs were all gone, the sideboard gone, the velvet curtains taken down. Everything he owned – his chairs, his clocks, his books, his Dresden porcelain, even his clothes – everything was gone.

He couldn't understand it. For the first time in his existence he felt seriously unnerved. For the first time in his life he actually felt *vulnerable.*

It had been so much easier when he had been able to hire servants – people who could handle the daytime running of the house. But in the past twenty years, servants had been increasingly difficult to find and even when he *had* found them, they had turned out to be demanding and unreliable and dishonest. As soon as they realized that he was never around during the day, they had taken time off whenever they felt like it, and they had pilfered some of his finest antique silver.

One night, in a pub, he had met a builder, a mournful Welshman called Parry, and he had managed to organize some repairs to the roof and a new front gate, but it had been years since he had been able to find a gardener, and the house was densely surrounded by thistles and plantains and grass that reached as high as the living-room window. He hated unkempt gardens, just as he hated unkempt graveyards, but as time passed he began to grow to enjoy the seclusion. The weeds not only screened him from the world outside, they deterred unwelcome visitors.

But now his seclusion had been devastatingly invaded, and he had lost everything he possessed. All the same, he gave thanks that the cellar trap had remained undetected. It matched the parquet floor so closely that it was almost impossible to discern. He was in constant fear that somebody would find his sleeping body during the hours of daylight – not a priest or any one of those scientists who had once hunted the Undead. Real death, when it came, would not be unwelcome. No, what he was afraid of was injury or mutilation. This part of the city, once fashionable, was now plagued by gangs of youths whose idea of an evening's entertainment was to throw petrol over sleeping tramps and set them alight; or to break their legs with concrete blocks. Death he could accept – but he couldn't bear the thought of living for ever while he was burned or crippled.

He went upstairs. The bedrooms were empty, too. He touched the shadowy mark on the wall where a portrait of Mina had hung. Then he threw back his head and let out a roar of rage that made the windows shake in their sashes, and started the neighbourhood's dogs barking.

Shortly after eleven o'clock, he found a girl standing in a bus shelter, smoking a cigarette and chewing gum at the same time. She couldn't have been older than sixteen or seventeen, and she still had that post-pubescent plumpness that he particularly relished. She had long blonde hair and she was wearing a black leather jacket and a short red dress.

He crossed the street. It was raining – a fine, prickling rain – and the road-surface reflected the streetlights and the shop-windows like the water in a dark harbour. He approached the girl directly and stood looking at her, his hand drawn up to his overcoat collar.

"You'll remember me the next time you see me, won't you, mate?" she challenged him.

"I'm sorry," he said. "You remind me so much of somebody I used to know."

"Oh, that's original. Next thing you'll be asking me if I come here often."

"I'm – I'm looking for some company, that's all," he told her. Even after all these years, he still found it went against the grain to approach women so bluntly.

"I don't know, mate. I've got to be home by twelve or my mum'll go spare."

"A quick drink, maybe?"

"I don't know. I don't want to miss my bus."

"I have plenty of money. We could have a good time." Inside, his sensibilities winced at what he was having to say.

The girl looked him up and down, still smoking, still chewing. "You look like a big strong bloke," she suggested. "We could always do it here. So long as you've got a johnny."

He looked around. The street was deserted, although an occasional car came past, its tyres sizzling on the wet tarmac. "Well . . ." he said, uncertainly. "I was thinking of somewhere a little less public."

"It's up to you," she said. "My bus'll be here in five minutes."

He was just about to refuse her offer and turn away when she flicked her hair with her hand, revealing the left side of her neck. It was radiantly white, so white that he could see the blueness of her veins. He couldn't take his eyes off it.

"All right," he said, tightly. "We'll do it here."

"Twenty quid," she demanded, holding out her hand.

He opened his thin black wallet and gave her two ten-pound notes. She took a last drag on her cigarette, flicked it into the street, and then she hoisted up her dress to her waist and tugged down her white Marks & Spencer panties. Somewhere in his mind he briefly glimpsed Lucy's voluminous petticoats, the finest white cotton trimmed with Nottingham lace, and the way in which she had so demurely clasped her thighs tightly together.

He kissed the girl on the forehead, breathing in the smell of cigarette-smoke and shampoo. He kissed her eyelids and her cheeks.

Then he tried to kiss her lips but she slapped him away. "What are you trying to do? Pinch my gum? I thought we were supposed to be having it off, not kissing."

He grasped her shoulders and stared directly into her eyes. He could tell by the expression on her face that she had suddenly begun to realize that this wasn't going to be one of her usual encounters, twenty pounds for a quick one. "What?" she asked him. "What is it?"

"One kiss," he said. "Then no more. I promise."

"I don't like kissing. It gives you germs."

"This kiss you will enjoy more than any other kiss you have ever had."

"No, I don't want to." She reached down and tried to tug her panties back up.

"You're going to go back on our bargain?" he asked her.

"I told you. I don't like kissing. Not men like you. I only kiss blokes I'm in love with."

"Yet you don't mind having sex with me, here, in the street, somebody you don't even know?"

"That's different."

He let go of her, and lowered his arms. "Yes," he said, rather ruefully. "That's different. But there was a time when it was the greatest prize that a man could ever win from a woman."

She laughed, a silly little Minnie Mouse laugh. That was when he gripped her hair and hit her head against the back of the bus shelter, as hard as he could. The glass frame holding the timetable smashed, and the timetable itself was splattered in blood.

As she sagged, he held her up to prevent her from dropping to the ground. Then he looked around again to make sure that the street was still empty. He hoisted her up, and carried her around the bus shelter and into the bushes behind it. He found himself half-climbing, half-sliding down a steep slope strewn with discarded newspapers, empty lager cans and plastic milk-crates. The girl lolled in his arms, her head hanging back, her eyes closed, but he could tell by the bubbles of froth that were coming from her mouth that she wasn't dead.

He took her down into a damp, dark gully, smelling of leaf-mould. He laid her down, and with shaking hands he unzipped her jacket and wrestled it off her. Then he tore open her dress, exposing her left breast. He knelt astride her, lowered his head, and with an audible crunch he sank his teeth into her neck, severing her carotid artery.

The first spurt went right over his shoulder, spattering his coat. The second hit his cheek and soaked his collar. But he opened his mouth wide, and he caught the next spurt directly on his tongue, and swallowed, and went on swallowing, with a choking, cackling sound, while the girl's heart obligingly pumped her blood directly down his throat.

Whether he was driven by rage for his lost possessions, or by disgust for the world in which he now found himself, or by sheer greed, he went on an orgy of blood-feeding that night. He slid into a suburban bedroom and drank a young wife dry while her husband slept beside her. He found a young homeless boy under a railway arch and left him white-faced and lifeless in his cardboard bash, staring up at the sodium-tainted sky. He hated the colour of that sky, and he longed for the days when nights had been black instead of orange.

By the end of the night, he had left nine people dead. He was so gorged with blood that his stomach was swollen, and he had to stop in the doorway of Boots the Chemist and vomit some of it up, adding to the splatter of regurgitated curry that was already there.

He returned to his empty house. He would have liked to have stayed up longer, walking around the rooms, but the sun was already edging its way over the garden-fence, and the frost was glittering like caster-sugar. He raised the cellar-trap and disappeared below.

He slept, and he dreamed . . .
He dreamed of battles, and the screaming of mutilated men. He dreamed of mountains, and forests as dark as nightmares. He thought he was back in his castle, but his castle was collapsing all around him. Chunks of stone fell from the battlements. Towers collapsed. Whole curtain-walls came roaring down, like landslides.

The earth shook, but he was so bloated with blood that he barely stirred. He whispered only one word, "*Lucy . . .*"

It took the best part of the day to demolish the house. The wrecking-ball swung and clumped and reduced the walls to rubble and toppled the tall Edwardian chimneys. By four o'clock the demolition crew were working by floodlight. A bulldozer ripped up the overgrown garden and roughly levelled the hardcore, and then a road-roller crushed the site completely flat.

During the next week, trucks trundled over the site, tipping tonnes of sand to form a sub-base, followed by even more tonnes of hydraulic cement concrete. This was followed by a thick layer of bituminous road pavement, and finally a top wearing course of hot asphalt.

Deep beneath the ground, he continued to sleep, unaware of

his entombment. But he had digested most of his feast, and his sleep was twitchier now, and his eyes started to flicker.

The new link road between Leeds and Roundhay was finished in the middle of January, a week ahead of schedule. In the same week, his property was sold at auction in Dewsbury, and fetched well over £780,000. A Victorian portrait of a white-faced woman in a white dress was particularly admired, and later featured on the BBC's *Antiques Road Show*. Among other interesting items was a Chippendale secrétaire. The new owner was an antiques dealer called Abrahams. When he looked through the drawers, he found scores of unopened letters, some from France, many from Romania and Poland, and some local. Some were dated as far back as 1926. Among the more recent correspondence were seven letters from the county council warning the occupier of a compulsory purchase order, so that a new road could be built to ease traffic congestion and eliminate an accident black spot.

He lay in his casket, wide awake now and ragingly hungry – unable to move, unable to rise, unable to die. He had screamed, but there was no point at all in screaming. All he could do was to wait in claustrophobic darkness for the traffic and the weather and the passing centuries to wear the road away.

Terry Lamsley

Volunteers

Terry Lamsley set the stories in his first collection of supernatural tales,
Under the Crust, *in and around Buxton, in the heart of England's Peak
District, where he lives with his family.*

*Although originally intended to appeal to local readers and tourists to
the area,* Under the Crust *reached the hands of the late Karl Edward
Wagner, who was instrumental in the book being nominated for three
World Fantasy Awards in 1994, and ultimately winning the Best Novella
award for the title story of the collection. In 1996, Ash-Tree Press published
Lamsley's second collection of tales,* Conference With the Dead, *and
the same publisher has recently issued a hardcover edition of* Under
the Crust.

*The author's atmospheric ghost stories have also appeared in such
anthologies as* The Best New Horror, The Year's Best Fantasy
and Horror, The Year's Best Horror Stories, Dark Terrors *and*
Lethal Kisses.

*For a vampire, help can sometimes come from the most unexpected
source . . .*

"I THINK, FOR the first visit, you had better take someone with you. He's probably a nice enough old gentleman, but we don't know much about him."

"Is he very old?"

"I believe so."

"That's a posh street, where he lives. The best part of town. We don't often get called out there. The residents are well off enough to buy better help than we provide."

"Anyone can fall on hard times, Sylvia."

"I assume he is housebound?"

The Volunteer Coordinator nodded. "He had an accident some time ago that has stopped him getting about. Broke his hip, I believe. Something like that. A neighbour informed us he was probably in trouble."

"The independent type," Silvia said. "Too proud to ask for the help he needs. Toffs like that aren't used to talking about their private problems with the likes of us."

"They have to get used to it pretty quickly if they want to take advantage of the services we provide, love," the Coordinator reflected. "He could have to wait months or years for medical treatment. Single, elderly men are not high on anybody's list of priorities. Meanwhile, we'll just have to make an assessment of his needs, and do the best we can for him."

"Poor old soul," Sylvia said.

The Coordinator smiled compassionately, as she did dozens of times each working day, to express the depth of her empathy with her staff, their clients, and the world in general.

"Take Mr Strope along, Sylvia. He's getting bored sitting about in the office with nothing much to do."

"Isn't there anyone else? Someone I know?"

"He requested to be put with you. Says he admires you."

Sylvia pulled a sour face. She had frequently noticed the little man watching her recently. She kept bumping into him in shops, on the street, all over the place. It was almost as though he were stalking her. She was afraid he might have learned some of her secrets.

"There's nothing wrong with Mr Strope, is there dear?"

"Well, just the way he looks, I suppose. And the way he looks *at* me."

"What *do* you mean?"

"He's got a hungry look."

"Are you suggesting he might be a pest? He's been checked. The police say he's clean as a whistle."

"Oh, I don't doubt that."

The Coordinator rested her fingertips together under her chin and gave Sylvia a challenging look. "He's new to the job, but he seems to have his head screwed on: he picks things up fast, and he's keen," she said. "But you don't have to take him if you don't want to, pet."

"I've nothing against him, I suppose," Sylvia admitted.

The Coordinator handed her a sheet of paper with an address written on it.

"Off you go then, poppet. He's got an Irish sounding name, the old chap. O'Cooler, Mr Strope said he thought it was. He took the call. Said it could have been *Doctor* O'Cooler, but the line was crackly. Let me know how you both got on as soon as you get back, won't you?"

Sylvia memorized the number of the house and handed the paper back with a dismissive flourish.

"Of *course* I will," she said primly, and left.

"I don't think anyone in there can hear me knocking because the door's so thick. It's like the entrance to a castle."

They had been on the front step for what seemed a long time.

"Try the bell again," Sylvia suggested.

Mr Strope was about to comply when he suddenly froze in an alert, listening posture. He turned to Sylvia with his eyes wide and his mouth open, as though he was going to take a bite out of her.

"Did you hear that? Something's moving in there."

Sylvia shook her head sceptically.

Strope listened again. "Getting closer," he said. He rapped the door hard with the back of his hand.

Unmistakably, a voice sounded distantly inside.

"*Go away. No tradesmen. No religious bigots.*"

Sylvia was used to outright rejection of this kind. She had long ago learned how to chat and charm her way into the most inhospitable, unwelcoming establishments. It was just one of her many skills. Sure enough, after a few well chosen pleas and blandishments, whoever was behind the door grudgingly agreed to let them in.

They waited patiently, watching the door with speculative antici-pation, until an open hand appeared abruptly through the large, flapless letter box. A big, none-too-clean hand with long, strong square-tipped fingers. Palm up, it bore an ancient key.

The message was obvious. Strope accepted the key, the hand withdrew, and they let themselves in.

It was extremely gloomy inside the house. Sylvia, carefully venturing forth, was expecting this, as she had noticed heavy, drawn curtains at every window as she had approached the huge red-brick Victorian building minutes earlier. No lights were on. Darkness hung everywhere like some solid substance.

A person in a wheelchair, backing steadily away from them down the hallway, was receding into invisibility. They had no alternative but to follow. Somewhere near the back of the house the vehicle turned off into a large room partly illuminated by a single flickering oil lamp. There were a few items of heavy furniture parked round the sides of the room, including a broken and unmade bed, an oak table with candelabra, a quartet of throne-like chairs, a long, low blanket-box, lidded, and resting on six elegant claw and ball legs, and what appeared to be some kind of iron stove, from which a thick pipe or chimney curved up through the ceiling. All these articles except the stove were partly concealed by black muslin drapes that drooped from them at various points, looking for all the world like the snares of some alarmingly overgrown arachnids.

The occupant of the mobile chair, similarly wrapped in a cocoon of peculiarly tailored fustian, whose face had so far not been visible, came to a halt alongside the box, and firmly applied the brake. A masculine voice, plangent, but a little unsteady, like a poorly maintained church harmonium, apologized for not answering the door sooner.

"I was resting. It takes me some time to – to come to myself, when my sleep is disturbed."

"Asleep at eleven-thirty in the morning!" Sylvia thought. "How demoralized the poor man must be." She resolved to do something about that.

"It's alright, mate," said Mr Strope. "Don't worry. We're in no hurry. We've got time on our hands just the same as you have."

The man in the chair turned towards him and, in doing so, revealed his features. He had hard, round, owlish eyes, a thin, hooked nose, and an apparently lipless, discontented, drooping mouth, more sharply down turned on the left side than the right. His long silver hair was patchy, as though his scalp was diseased, and his face shone like polished ivory in the lamp light. His manner was poised, his expression detached. He held out his hand again towards Mr Strope. It obviously wasn't there to be shaken. It took Strope a few seconds to understand the significance of the gesture, before he hurried forward and replaced the key.

O'Cooler solemnly asked them to take chairs and be seated.

Once her great bulk was comfortably enthroned, Sylvia explained who they were and why they had come. "We'll have to ask a few questions about your circumstances first. You've no objections?"

O'Cooler shook his head grandly and turned his full attention on his interlocutor. He reached discreetly into one of the pockets of the rather theatrical garments he was wearing. Sylvia thought he was going to light a cigarette but instead he pulled out a length of dark material and held it across the lower portion of his face as though he expected to sneeze. No sneeze came, and the cloth remained in place. *Bad teeth,* Sylvia speculated. *Pyorrhoea?*

"Now," she said: "Name and title? Have I got it right – Mr – *O'Cooler?*" She spelt it out. "Yes?"

The man in the chair appeared to have some brief doubts about the veracity or accuracy of this most basic information about himself for a surprising number of seconds, but at last he dropped his head vigorously in confirmation.

"And it *is* Mr – not Dr?"

Again a pause, during which Sylvia thought the man might be smiling to himself behind his hand, then:

"Correct," he said.

Sylvia rattled off a dozen questions that were all more swiftly answered. She wondered, as he spoke, which part of Ireland the man originated from. He certainly had a slight accent, she decided. Or should that have been brogue? She found herself becoming fascinated by his almost musical voice. He's attractive, in an unusual sort of way, she decided, in spite of his age.

She tried to get through the questionnaire as quickly as she could, but it was a long rigmarole. She felt the gaze of both men fixed upon her. O'Cooler looked her frankly and calmly in the eye from behind his half-masked face, but Strope, she knew, was covertly surveying the curves of her over-ample body. *My very fat body*, she thought, and squirmed slightly in her chair under the intensity of his wanton gaze. As she did so her huge breasts rippled, and Mr Strope's eyes glowed afresh. She thought she saw moisture emerge on his lips. She had long ago learned that a certain type of man was attracted to and easily became obsessive about extremely overweight women. Little Strope, with his wiry but muscular body, thinning hair, sad but cunningly hopeful expression, and restless hands, was a perfect example of the type. Also, under the surface, there was something fierce and primitive about him that alarmed her. She'd known as soon as she'd set eyes on him he could be trouble, and now here she was teamed up with him, perhaps in extended partnership. *No.* Not that! She didn't want to be unkind, but she would have to do something very positive to discourage him.

"And how did your accident happen?" she asked the owner of the house. "Just the details."

O'Cooler, without reflection, said, "I slipped and fell when I was emerging from my . . ." He seemed to cough then, or so it sounded, and faltered in some confusion for a moment:

"From my *bath*," he said at last, pronouncing the final word with particular clarity.

"The most dangerous place in the home for an old person, the bath," Sylvia observed ominously. "Thought of installing a shower?"

"No." His response was startling: almost a yap, as though the idea was somehow repellent and alarming. He wiped his mouth vigorously, returned the cloth to his pocket, then put his hand up guardedly over his lips. "Certainly not," he added more composedly. "Running water doesn't suit me," he explained.

Which confirmed Sylvia's nasal suspicions that it was a considerable time since he had been anywhere near that element with a bar of soap. Since his accident, perhaps? How long ago was that? She asked him.

"Almost seven weeks," O'Cooler admitted, sounding, for the first time, slightly sorry for himself.

"Since when, of course, you have not been able to get about. Do the doctors give you any hope of recovery soon?"

O'Cooler shuddered. "I am reluctant to submit myself to the investigative considerations of the medical profession," he said.

"You've not *seen* a doctor?"

"No." O'Cooler shook his head grandly, with dignity.

"So you've had no help at all. How have you been coping?"

"Poorly, I'm afraid. My –" he searched for a word, " – my *sister*, Carmilla, has been kind enough to drop in with a little food from time to time, whatever she had surplus to her own requirements, but she is ailing herself. The hole in the ozone layer is affecting all our family. We're very sensitive to that sort of thing, I'm afraid. The implications are serious. It's sapping our strength. Our bones are becoming brittle . . ." He seemed in danger of loosing the thread of his thoughts, but recovered his drift quickly. "Also," he continued, "as an alternative source of nourishment, I've got an arrangement with one of the local butchers, who is a very understanding man, with peculiar tastes himself, and who will deliver in emergencies. But it's not the same thing at all. I'm rather fussy about what I take inside me, if the truth be known," he admitted, sounding somewhat insincerely apologetic.

Sylvia caught her breath and interrupted, "Do you, by any chance, have special dietary needs?" she asked, failing to keep an edge of excitement from her voice. "Or an eating disorder, perhaps?"

"You are astute," O'Cooler acknowledged. "I have suffered from something of the kind for a very long time. I have a problem with solid food. I only take – (he pronounced the next word as though it had five syllables) – liquids." His tone as he made this statement somehow made it obvious he was not prepared to go into further detail about the nature of his problem.

Sylvia wondered what on earth O'Cooler got from the butcher, but decided not to ask. *Bet he has just got bad teeth,* she thought, feeling somewhat let-down. *Well, that could soon be fixed by a visit to the dentist. He's not really,* deeply *sick like I am.* For a moment, she had hoped she might have found a fellow sufferer. Her disappointment made her symptoms tingle painfully through every part of her body. She stood up suddenly, clutching the huge canvas shoulder bag she took with her everywhere, and asked the way to the bathroom.

O'Cooler seemed put-out by this question at first, as though he were unsure if he possessed such a facility. Then, with palpable reluctance, he directed her up the stairs, first left, first right, first door on the right, and handed her a torch. "The battery is very low," he warned, " so don't waste it."

Does he think I'm going to go prying about up there? Sylvia wondered, feeling that perhaps her client had something to hide.

As she left the room she heard Mr Strope say, "Big house you've got here mate. You live alone, don't you?"

O'Cooler confirmed this fact.

"Funny," Strope went on, "because I thought I saw someone leave as we turned the corner to get here."

"An estate agent called earlier, to look the place over: I'm thinking of selling up and moving back to the old country."

"He seemed to be in a hell of a hurry to get away. In fact, I thought he'd jumped out of one of the first floor windows. I think he might have cut himself. Could swear I saw blood on his shoulders."

"Ummm," said O'Cooler, apparently unconcerned. "Well, it's possible, I suppose. He was a clumsy fellow."

Sylvia, ascending the steep stairs, heard no more.

She located the bathroom just as the torch flickered out. Inside, she was relieved to find there was a bulb in the ceiling lamp that responded halfheartedly with possibly thirty watts-worth of illumination when she flicked the switch. She sat down on the toilet without lifting the lid, opened her bag, pulled out a number of plastic bags and lunch-boxes, and began to open them at random. They contained a wide selection of cakes, biscuits, pies, chocolate, meat, and – *other* things. All sorts of other things. Any spare money she had (which was little enough, but she spent it wisely) went on food.

A fast eater, Sylvia dug into various containers and stuffed her mouth again and again. She'd been a binge eater for five years, since she was twenty-two. Severe, insoluble problems with men were the cause, she believed. After a number of disastrously painful affairs she had swiftly gone from being a person who ate too much of what she fancied to someone who obsessively consumed unpleasant food she didn't like, to punish herself for her greed. She had expanded accordingly. Later still, she went on to eating other things that were not good for her at all. She had developed most unusual appetites.

Today she was in such a hurry to indulge herself that she did not, at first, realize exactly what sort of place she had walked into. Gradually, as the first overwhelming gratification brought on by her abandoned self-indulgence began to wane, and self-loathing to wax, she started to take in her surroundings.

The bathroom's ornate fittings were huge, ancient, and covered with filth. She could just see into the bath from where she was sitting. Presumably, it was the one O'Cooler claimed to have fallen out of, but she had her doubts about that. It was quarter full of brown sludge from which protruded dozens of small bones; of birds and other animals, by the look of it. There were feathers, and bits of skin too. They'd been there a long time. Parts of the otherwise bare wooden floor were similarly smeared with pools of this muck, that looked like someone's unsuccessful and discarded attempts at making stew. Sylvia got up and began to prowl around. She wanted to wash her food-besmirched hands, but the sink was almost overflowing with something similar to the substance in the bath, but without the bones. Fungus of some kind, green in colour, floated upon its surface in patches. She turned on one of the taps. Nothing emerged until a trickle of black, shiny insects, who must have been nesting there, fell out onto the gunge below and began to struggle and drown.

Sylvia cleaned herself up as best she could with a tissue, grabbed her bag, and got out of there. The torch glimmered briefly to life again just long enough for her to find her way along the forlorn corridors to the top of the stairs. She descended blindly and ultra-cautiously, edging her way down each level, aware that if she lost her footing and fell her own weight would probably kill her.

The door to the room in which she had interviewed the resident of the house was shut. She knew she had left it wide open, otherwise she would not have overheard the fragment of conversation between O'Cooler and Mr. Strope when she had set out for the bathroom. Still in the dark, she thought perhaps she ought to knock, though she was not sure why she had gained that impression. She tapped lightly, paused, tapped loudly, waited again, then grabbed the handle firmly, wrenched it round, and entered.

She felt at once that the atmosphere in the room had changed. O'Cooler was standing some distance away from his wheelchair now, with his back towards her. He was leaning almost casually on a thick brass-topped stick. His tight shut, downcast mouth straightened into what may have been intended as a demonstration of chilly welcome as he slowly turned to acknowledge her re-entry.

He's really is a very striking man, Sylvia realized: fanciable, even. He hadn't made her *feel* welcome, however. Something was up. She detected a new complicity between the two men, from which she felt herself excluded.

Strope's face no longer bore its usual crafty, somewhat craven look: he appeared thoughtful now, and self-satisfied, as though he had recently achieved something very much to his advantage.

"I couldn't help noticing your domestic circumstances leave a lot to be desired, Mr O'Cooler," Sylvia said firmly, attempting to reassert herself. When O'Cooler made no response, she added, "If you don't mind me saying so, your bathroom contains a number of health hazards and possible sources of infection. Animals are getting in somewhere, and dying there. The air throughout the building will be full of invisible pollutants. Any food you bring in will quickly become contaminated. All kinds of morbid conditions will flourish. Also, the whole building is dark and dangerous. The electrical wiring is a fire risk. The plumbing doesn't work . . ."

O'Cooler stabbed the floor in front of him with his cane and abruptly made his way back towards his chair with a peculiar jerking motion. (*Some limited mobility*, Sylvia noted. *He's not completely helpless.*) His stick and stiff lower limbs formed a tripod that swung from side to side ungracefully. He scuttled along like a spider robbed by a cruel child of some of its legs. When he regained his seat he masked his mouth with his hand again and said, "The animals you saw were used by me in a little experiment, when I first came by my injury. Sadly, only partially successful, I'm afraid. The other things you mention are the least of my problems, my dear. None of that troubles me at all. I have long been used to living in a state of advanced dilapidation. I prefer it. It suits me. I have no use for mechanical conveniences and my lifestyle transcends your modern standards of hygiene."

Sylvia was gratified and encouraged. He had called her, "my dear". She said, "I'd like to be able to offer you a home-help: someone to come in to tidy up for a few hours a week, and maybe meals-on-wheels – "

In spite of his previous statements, O'Cooler showed considerable interest in this proposal.

" – but there's a waiting list and, believe it or not, there are a lot of senior citizens even worse off than you. There's just not enough money to go round, you see. Unless – I don't suppose you are able to afford private assistance . . . ?"

"Unfortunately not. I invested unwisely." O'Cooler said something else angrily behind his hand that Sylvia didn't catch. She thought he mentioned Lloyd's.

"Never mind," she said. "I'm sure we'll be able to help in some way: we can do something to assist you."

Strope spoke up then. "Mr O'Cooler and I had a chat while you were away," he said, "and we've come up with a little plan."

"Oh?" How *very* unprofessional! Mr Strope had no right to do anything of the sort. She was the experienced caring person. It was up to her to decide, with the assistance of the Volunteer Coordinator, what could and would be done to alleviate her client's suffering. Strope knew nothing about such things. He was totally inexperienced. It was unfair to the client to make promises that could not be met. She was sorry, but she had been right to assume he was unfit for the task he had set himself. He'd have to be put in his place. She would, as gently as possible, point out the faults in whatever scheme he had cooked up.

"What *plan*?" she said.

Strope, regarding her greedily, with unconcealed voluptuous satisfaction, seemed delighted with her obvious anger. She realized her flesh was quaking with tension. She attempted to control herself, but made things worse. Strope's eyes rolled slightly, and his hands twitched.

"Well, not so much a plan, perhaps, as an understanding," he said.

"A gentleman's agreement," O'Cooler suggested almost jovially, "made to our mutual satisfaction. Simple, but very ingenious. We all have our part to play," he added, as an afterthought.

Strope gave him an uneasy look, as though he had spoken out of turn.

"And it was his idea?" Sylvia asked, nodding towards the little lecher. She was not best pleased to learn that whatever it was they had in mind apparently included her. "I think I ought to warn you he is in no position to make decisions about your future."

O'Cooler turn his owlish black eyes on the other man and made a sound that was the verbal equivalent of a question mark.

For a moment, Strope's confidence visibly wavered, but, after a moment's reflection, he recovered his composure.

"I'm not the fool you take me for, Sylvia, my love." Strope smirked craftily and pointed at O'Cooler. "I know more about him *and* you, and the habits of both of you, than you might care to hear about."

Sylvia's apple-red cheeks blanched.

"You'd better explain," she said, not at all sure she wanted to learn what might come next.

"A pleasure," said Strope. "It just so happens I live across the road from here. In a first floor flat looking out on the street. Being without work, and broke, I have nothing to do, twenty-four hours a day, but stare out. So I see what's going on. Not much, a lot of the time, but, thanks to this chap, enough to keep me entertained. A single gentleman living alone, or so he would have us believe, in this great castle of a place, who sometimes has night guests who go in but never come out, and who has filthy black smoke pouring out of his chimney at three and four o'clock in the morning, and who buries bags of charred bones in his back garden is bound to provide a bit of novelty interest to someone as bored as me."

"You have been trespassing on my property," O'Cooler observed testily.

"In the public interest," Strope agreed. "You should have been more careful. I didn't have to dig deep: there are bones sticking out of the ground all over the place. I tripped over them. You should have made sure your curtains were properly closed too. I saw what you were putting in that stove."

O'Cooler took his hand away from the lower section of his face and gave his neighbour a cold, dangerous look. His lips jerked down in a way that suggested he had muscles around his mouth that others do not have. Sylvia noticed for the first time how very powerful his jaw looked. She caught her breath. What a *noble* head he had. She watched him, spellbound. She didn't understand what Mr Strope was saying – was hardly listening, because it seemed to have nothing to do with her – but she could see he was upsetting their client, who they had come to help. Before they could start to argue, she said, "I think we can bring this interview to a conclusion now. I have enough information. We will contact you again soon, Mr O'Cooler, when we've put together a package of assistance to offer you. Subject to your approval, of course. Now, if you're ready M: Strope? I think it's time we were going."

"I'm staying here, sweetheart. And you're not going anywhere either."

Strope's tone was extremely unpleasant. Sylvia looked to the aristocratic figure in the wheelchair for support. O'Cooler noticed her appeal, and shrugged.

Sylvia's eyes went slightly out of focus as she considered her situation. Was she at the mercy of these two men? To make things worse, Strope started speaking again, about her now.

"I've been angling to get you to myself for a long time, my love" he revealed. "I've been crazy about you since I saw you eating the five course special in the Corner Cafe, weeks ago. My dream woman, that's what you are, Sylvia. Big as they come, and beautiful with it. But I could tell you didn't think much of me. I smiled at you more than once in the Cafe, when you looked my way, but you didn't even see me. You were too busy eating. Fair enough, I told myself. When you left I decided to follow you, and of course, before long, I got to know *all* about you."

"You spied on me," Sylvia said, contemptuously.

"You bet. Every day, from dawn to dusk. Watching your house was much more interesting than watching this one. I'd got Mr. so-called-O'Cooler's number by then anyway. I had no doubts about who and what he was: all I lacked was some way to turn that knowledge to my advantage."

O'Cooler seemed about to speak, but in the end decided to keep his own council. His owlish eyes watched Strope keenly however, as the little man continued his monologue.

"I almost went up and spoke to you a number of times, but you stared through me, or gave me a haughty look, so I didn't dare. I'm a bashful man, by nature. Anyway, when I realized you did unpaid work for the Volunteers, I saw my chance to get close to you, so I offered my services too. They soon had me on trial, answering the phone in their office. That's when I put two and two together and I saw an opportunity to get you where I want you. It was me that brought the plight of the "poor old gentleman" to the attention of the Volunteer Service. I pretended a call came in requesting help just when I knew you were due to take the next case. It was me that hinted to the Coordinator that you ought not go alone. There was nobody else around who could have gone with you, I made sure of that."

"And here we are," Sylvia said. "I see." She looked again to O'Cooler for assistance, but he had still not taken his eyes off the little man. "What's this bargain the two of you struck?" she asked.

Strope gave her a blissful smile. "Simple. As you so rightly guessed, our friend here has "special dietary needs". Requirements that are not being met, because he can't get about to satisfy them. I can and will provide him with what he requires. In return, he allows me the uninterrupted use of part of his premises for my own purposes. I must have somewhere away from my flat, where I can satisfy *my* needs occasionally. Somewhere my activities won't be overheard."

"Where do I fit in to this agreement?" Sylvia asked, glancing desperately back and forth from what she could see of the inexpressive features of the resident of the house to the gloating, triumphant face of the little man. "I don't understand. What am I going to get out of it?"

Strope move closer to her.

"My undivided attention," he said.

Sylvia snatched up her bag and attempted to leave the room. She was slow on her feet, however, and Strope was as agile as a lizard. He slipped out of the door ahead of her and slammed it in her face. She heard the lock turn.

She turned to O'Cooler. "Are you going to let him keep me here?" she demanded.

O'Cooler's eyes were heavy-lidded – almost closed. He looked tired out. Obviously he wasn't used to such excitement. Not during the hours of daylight, anyway.

"That was one of the terms of our pact," he acknowledged wearily.

Sylvia folded her arm across her breasts in an angrily protective gesture, as though she was preparing to repel boarders. "What's he up to now? Where's he gone?"

"Checking the security arrangements, I imagine. He asked about them earlier. I had them installed some years ago, to stop the more predatory local youths getting in, and other, more welcome people getting out, during occasions when I was forced to absent myself for one reason or another. There are steel bars up at all the ground floor windows, which are made of bullet-proof glass. The outer doors are similarly protected. The whole ground floor can be sealed off from the upper regions at the press of a button."

"So I'm trapped. You're going to let him do what he likes with me?"

"He led me to believe you are not the first, and probably won't be the last, of his victims."

"Well, that's a consoling thought, to be sure," Sylvia snapped.

O'Cooler raised one furry eyebrow at her sharp tone and unexpected irony, then fatigue got the better of him. He held back his head, opened his mouth, and yawned widely.

Sylvia noticed the yawn, and the glint of O'Cooler's fangs.

She was a well-meaning, good-hearted person who tried always to see the best in people. She was the sort who made an effort to keep up a cheerful front, and tried not to dwell too much on the dark side of life. She had to, the kind of work she did, to get through her days. True, she was a bit slow on the up-take, but she wasn't stupid. She was a supremely practical girl, who didn't try to ignore the evidence of her own eyes. And she could think fast, when she had to.

"There's something you should know," she said to the increasingly dormant creature in the wheelchair.

"Mmm." He hardly stirred.

"I was voted "Most Valued Volunteer: 1997" by my fellow workers recently. I got a certificate."

O'Cooler twitched slightly, perhaps with impatience. "Oh: good."

"*Most Valued Volunteer*," she repeated. "I'm an important part of the set-up back there. Very experienced. They need my expertise."

O'Cooler stifled another yawn. "How very gratifying for you."

"They'll miss me soon, if I don't get back. They have your address. Strope slipped up there, in his hurry to get his hands on me, and wrote it down on a piece of paper for my Coordinator. They'll certainly come looking for me. Maybe with the police. I should have thought you were the last person in the world to want *them* snooping around, under the circumstances, especially if Strope was right about what you've got buried in your back garden."

Her words aroused the sleepyhead quicker than an alarm clock could have done. "Are you sure about that?" he spluttered.

"Absolutely. I've been gone a long time already. And, let's face it, you're as much a prisoner here as I am – in your condition, in the middle of the day. There's nobody to help you make your escape in that thing." She pointed to the long, lidded wooden case she had earlier mistaken for a blanket-box.

O'Cooler's composure had vanished: he was wide awake. Sylvia could almost hear the alarm bells ringing in his head. "But if I stay here, and let you go . . . ! That man said if I let him have you, he would bring me food regularly, until I recovered."

"If he promised to lure people here for you to feed on, forget it. He couldn't deliver. And he'd dump me and run, when he'd finished doing what he wanted to me. You'd just have another corpse on your hands for the police to find when they get here."

"I had no option but to believe him or starve."

"But I told you I could put an aid-package together for you myself. Individually tailored to your needs, now I understand exactly what those needs are. We'll work something out."

"Can you give me some details?"

"Okay." Sylvia explained that the Health, Social and other Services were being manned more and more by otherwise unemployed and untrained volunteers who, if they were considered at all suitable, were told to put in plenty of time for nothing, if they wanted to continue to receive benefits. Millions of people were desperate to comply with this scheme, as it offered the nearest thing most of them would ever get to security.

"There's a vetting process they all have to go through, and most of them are worse than useless, as you can imagine. Those, we have to reject. It's part of my job to interview these people. I have access to the names and address of thousands of the rejects, who mostly have no income at all. Consequently, they will do anything, *anything at all*, for a little cash."

O'Cooler fiddled thoughtfully with his walking stick. Out of touch with social and economic conditions in the world outside, he hung on to her every word.

"See what I'm getting at?" Sylvia said, as her bleak revelations sunk into the invalid's brain. "I am in a position to hand-pick any number of reliable – let's call them *donors* – of either sex, who will provide you with a discreet personal and anonymous service, brought to you *in your own home*, for a few pounds a week. I know you made some unwise investments, but you can afford that surely?"

She could see O'Cooler (she still preferred to think of him under that name) was tempted by her scheme. "I can even screen them for your favourite blood group, if you have a preference," she added temptingly.

"What guarantee do I have you will do as you say?" O'Cooler said.

Mr Strope could be heard returning, his boots knocking on the uncarpeted parquet floor in the corridor outside.

"You have my word. As 'Most . . .'"

"Yes, I know: 'Most Valued Volunteer'," O'Cooler snapped, but he had made up his mind. He surprised Sylvia by holding out his big long hands and grasping hers. "It sounds like a bloody good bargain, to me," he said, not really swearing, she guessed. "As you see, I put myself in your hands." He raised her hands to his thin, hard lips, and kissed her fingers. "Here's to our future" he said.

She wondered if he was suggesting they could become friends. More than that, perhaps. The idea was not unpleasant. He had something other men she'd met certainly didn't have. She could do worse. After all, in his way, he was very distinguished. A Count, even.

Strope was having trouble with the awkward key.

"What shall we do about *him*?" O'Cooler muttered, a co-conspirator now.

"Is that stick of yours as strong and heavy as it looks?"

O'Cooler nodded. "And weighted with lead at the top." He handed it over. "When you've finished, I'll dispose of him in that." He pointed towards the oven. "I should be able to manage if I take it slowly."

"I'll try not to kill him outright. There's not much to him, but he should provide you with a snack before he goes."

The aristocratic invalid nodded his approval and gratitude. "Very considerate of you."

Beyond the door, Strope dropped the key and cursed.

Sylvia took the opportunity of this delay to lean down close to O'Cooler's ear and quickly explain the nature of her own eating disorder: in particular, about the *other things* she had developed an appetite for recently. It was time, she felt, to exchange confidences: to form a bond.

At first, O'Cooler looked a little taken aback.

"Well," he said at last, "who'd have thought it? But, if that's the way things stand with you, I'll save the heart and lights, and the, er, other bits."

"If it's not too much trouble," Sylvia whispered. "I'll have to get back to report to my Coordinator soon. I'll tell her you don't require our assistance after all, and that Strope has decided he doesn't want to continue with this sort of work, but I'll try and call round for them later, while they're fresh."

The key clicked and turned at last.

Moving surprisingly quietly for someone her size, Sylvia took up position behind the door.

She winked at her new friend, and raised the bronze-tipped stick high above her shoulder.

John Gordon

Black Beads

John Gordon joined the Navy from school and served on minesweepers and destroyers during World War II. After the war he became a journalist and worked on various local weekly and daily newspapers in East Anglia and Plymouth.

His many books for Young Adults include such novels as The Giant Under the Snow, The House on the Brink, The Ghost on the Hill, The Waterfall Box, The Edge of the World, The Quelling Eye, The Grasshopper, Ride the Wind, Secret Corridor, Blood Brothers *and* Gilray's Ghost, *plus the collections* The Spitfire Grave and Other Stories, Catch Your Death and Other Stories *and* The Burning Baby and Other Ghosts. *He has also written his autobiography, entitled* Ordinary Seaman.

The darkness can hide so many secrets . . .

RICHARD APPIAN WAS reclining full length in the swing seat when he raised the question of the break-in. "It's hardly serious," he said. "Just enough risk to be entertaining."

Angela watched him drink. He was really very handsome. Coppery hair cut short, a strong neck and broad shoulders. He was aware of his size and he used it; that was part of his attraction. He faced down anyone he met, his small blue eyes glinting with what at first appeared to be friendliness until suddenly his smile would broaden and his victim would realize, too late, that Richard Appian had marked him down. It thrilled her.

"Ricky," she asked, and her voice was languid, "does the old lady have anything you particularly want?"

"Her place is a treasure house," he said. "Nothing has been touched for fifty years. You'll love it."

And she would. The past was a deep well of mystery to which she was drawn. Even her clothes showed it with a tendency to be slightly out of date. But he liked a woman to look feminine, by which she knew he meant helpless and compliant, and he always maintained that it was the simplicity of her dress, the fitted waist and flared skirt that had at first attracted him. That, and the strange circumstances of their initial meeting.

"Black beads," he said. "She's bound to have ebony beads somewhere."

She chided him at that. "Black beads are Victorian," she said. "Far too old." And yet he had struck a chord; she could see herself with a double string of heavy black beads reaching to her waist. It was a childish thought from far back. "You have read my mind once more," she said.

His smile, which would come and go like a shutter opening and closing, remained open to show the whiteness of his teeth. He was so superbly at ease, stretched out in the shade of the swing's awning, that her heart gave the strange little skip she had recently learned to live with and then ran away in palpitations that left her gasping. Which made her prettily defenceless, he thought.

"But you don't actually *need* anything, Ricky," she murmured, turning her head away to look across the wide lawn where the trees made tents of restful shadow.

"What I *need*," he said, "is what I *want*. And what I want is to have you with me when I go there."

"But why?" They sat in the shade of a cypress behind the house, but even there the glare of the sun had made him put on his dark glasses and she could not see the expression in his eyes. "Why, Ricky?"

"Because it would please me." Beneath his invisible gaze his lips wore a smile. "Because you never let me take you home."

"But I do." Enormous weariness made her close her eyes. She did not wish to make yet more excuses for not allowing him to take her further than the entrance to the apartment building. "It's such a small place," she said, "you wouldn't like it." It was so dark and narrow it had taken her a long time to get accustomed to it. He wanted to know too much, too many of her secrets.

He watched her. She sat upright, except for the gentle curve of her spine, and her hand drooped over the arm of her chair holding her glass by its rim as if it was almost too heavy for her slim fingers. Her pale lethargy emphasized the dark beauty of the eyes which slid away from him to look towards the house. He had never lived anywhere else; there was space for him, and to spare, and it was easier for him to take part in the family's business if he lived at home – in the style which suited him. He sought to impress her even more. "Mrs Grayson's house is much larger even than this," he said, "and we shall have it all to ourselves."

"But it will be dark." She did not look at him. She knew what was in his mind. Taking her to a strange empty house in darkness excited him, but he was reluctant to admit it to her. A faint contempt stirred in her that he should hide his desires by pretending to be a thief.

"All you will have to do is hold the torch," he said.

"But what if we should be surprised?"

"That's impossible. Mrs Grayson is in a nursing home and won't be coming back. Ever."

"I shall be a liability," she protested. "I can't climb, I can't run." By tormenting him she put an edge to his determination, but she herself tingled with pleasure at the danger and it diminished the dragging tiredness that besieged her.

"There is no need to climb through windows. I can get a key at any time I want. We have known her for years, and she'll never know what's missing."

"I'll be useless – I get so breathless." She frowned; it had not always been so.

"You won't even have to climb the stairs." The dark lenses looked on her and she knew the expression concealed there. She had seen it before on another face, in another place. She lowered her eyes and allowed him to betray what was in his mind. "A big house all to ourselves," he said. "I shall carry you up the stairs in the dark." He hesitated. "If you would like that."

When she said nothing he sought to justify himself. "You mustn't forget I have carried you before." He saw her eyelids flicker as if she did not remember. It was a game they played. "My old dog Wolf found you," he said. "In the woods lying among the dead leaves. He thought you were dead, too. We both did."

"I was merely comfortable." She dipped her eyes. "I was asleep."

"How was I to know? I lifted you up, and you were as light as air."

"Not everyone would find me as light as that; you don't know how strong you are." She was never sure she should remind him of his strength; she had seen others afraid of it. "Then you woke me."

"Not by picking you up." She had remained asleep in his arms.

"Perhaps not, but I felt your breath beneath my chin."

"I thought I saw a pulse in your neck."

"I felt your breath, and it was time to wake."

"Strange meeting," he said.

He watched as she, remaining silent, raised her glass to drink. The wine had a deeper red than her lips. He became bolder.

"We shall go to old Mrs Grayson's house. There may be a dress you can wear . . . Mrs Grayson had a daughter."

"Black beads," she said. "Just black beads; nothing else."

His sigh was soundless, and they did not look at each other. He was having his way and she was permitting it.

Somewhere out of sight a car squeezed the pebbles of the drive. "My mother," he said. "There will be trouble."

"Because of me?"

"Indirectly."

Mrs Appian came around the corner of the house and saw them. Peevish lines puckered her mouth.

"I thought you were in the office today, Richard." She did not glance at Angela.

"I phoned them first thing and told them what to do."

"But you know your father likes one of us to be there when he is away. It is the only way to run a business." Mrs Appian, soberly dressed and trim, but with a bright scarf at her throat, looked at the drink in Angela's hand, and then at Angela's clothes. The girl's long dark hair contrasted strongly with her pale skin, and she hardly seemed to have the energy to smile. Why were his girl friends always so docile? Maybe it was just as well, considering his temper. But this one was a worry. "Are you quite well, my dear?" she asked. "There's not a scrap of colour in your cheeks."

Her son got to his feet. "That's why I gave myself a day off, Mother. I'm looking after her." He turned the conversation. "And where have you been today – the hairdresser?"

"I have not." The softly gilded waves of her hair, not as pliant as they appeared, moved in a body with her head. "I have been to see poor Mrs Grayson."

"Strange," he said, "we have just been talking about her. Drink?"

"My usual," said his mother. "And what have you two been saying?"

He looked back over his shoulder as he stepped through the open french windows. "I have been telling Angela that nothing in the world would induce me to go to that gloomy old mansion of hers. I would be far too scared."

Mrs Appian laughed, and thought it necessary to defend her son. "That's nonsense," she said to Angela. "He's as brave as a lion, especially in dark places. He always has been."

"He's far too brave for me." Angela lowered her eyes. "He frightens me." And Mrs Appian saw that this strange girl was, in fact, foolishly afraid of her son.

"Let me tell you what he's really like," she said as she accepted the drink he had brought for her. "And, Richard, don't you dare interrupt." She tugged at his hand as if that would make him obey. "One day when he was still a little boy he went missing and we searched and searched until it got dark and he was nowhere to be found. I was frantic. And then, I don't know why . . ." she looked up at her son ". . . it must have been a mother's intuition, but I was convinced he must have gone round to Mrs Grayson's house, even though she was on holiday. And there we found him, inside, sitting at the foot of the stairs in the great empty hall . . . sitting there in the dark all by himself as though he wanted to spend the night there."

He laughed. "So you see, Angela, I have the soul of a thief – I broke in."

"Nonsense!" His mother slapped at his hand. "I had the key and you had borrowed it."

"Stolen it to break in. That's what I'd done."

"Don't be perverse! You had just heard the dreadful story of Mrs Grayson's daughter and it had affected you and made you sad. But you told me you had only gone there as a dare."

Angela had hardly been listening. The heat and light made her head ache and her limbs were limp and lifeless and she wanted to be elsewhere, but she had to ask a question. "What happened to Mrs Grayson's daughter?" she said.

"Nobody knows," said Mrs Appian. "She disappeared long ago, more than fifty years now, and has never been seen since." Once again she turned her eyes on Richard. "But this young man of mine was convinced as soon as he heard the story that she was dead. What a mournful child! And there he was, all alone in that great gloomy old tomb of a house, as if he was waiting for her!"

"Were you?" The words made Angela's heart rock. They had escaped against her will.

"Maybe." There was a smile on his lips below the blank lenses. "Who can tell?"

"He was so cold and pale," said Mrs Appian, "you can't believe it to look at him now, the great ox."

"I am the pale one." Angela knew that her smile was thin and wan, and Mrs Appian responded.

"You don't look at all well," she said, but her sympathy had an extra purpose. "Why don't you take her home, Richard? The poor girl obviously needs to rest. And then you can call at the office – it would please your father."

He did not attempt to get out of the car when he dropped her at the entrance to the apartment block. There was a sheen of bad temper on his face. "One day you'll invite me up," he said.

It was the one thing she could not do. She had to keep something of herself apart from him; if she surrendered too deeply she would lose him. She smiled, but said nothing and waited until he had driven away before she moved. And then she turned her back on the apartments and walked to where a little church brooded secretively among buildings much taller than itself. A bench in the corner of the graveyard had become a haven for her ever since she had met Richard and the heaviness had overtaken her limbs. She would sit there for hours, neither awake nor asleep, and let her mind drift aimlessly.

But today her hazy wash of thoughts slid and circled but was anchored in one place. She was puzzled by the attraction Richard Appian had for her. A hand went to her throat. Once before she had suffered the formidable anger of a powerful man, and bore the marks, yet she was once more being drawn to someone with the strength to lift her as if she weighed no more than a kitten . . . someone callous enough to rob an old woman. And she had not the will to refuse to help him.

It was dusk when he picked her up outside the apartments. There was a tense excitement in him about what lay ahead, and he only briefly asked her how she felt.

"I spent the afternoon resting," she said. "Sitting among the leaves."

"Like when I first found you." He enclosed her cold fingers in the heat of his hand and she shuddered. "Are you afraid?"

She nodded, but nothing would have made her turn back. It was necessary for her to be with him. "Where is the house?" she asked.

"You must have seen it . . . it's big enough." And when they drove down the broad avenue with the arching trees it seemed familiar to her. "But we can't park here," he said, "we may be recognized."

He drove on and parked in a side street, and as they walked back beneath the shadows of the trees he put his arm around her so that they would be taken as strolling lovers. But he did not kiss her and it was not until they had found the gate into the grounds and were moving through a tunnel of overgrown shrubbery that she made him pause and look down at her. "Leaf mould," she murmured, "can you smell it?"

The scent was in his nostrils. She held her face up to him and their lips met.

"You found me lying in leaf mould," she said, and as their lips lingered she added, "It was like a bed."

He sensed the thrill of fear and longing in her and spoke softly. "There are rooms with beds in the house."

"I shall choose," she murmured.

The moon had dipped near to the horizon, but enough light filtered from the sky to make the grey housefront stand out from the shadows. The windows were deep set in heavy stonework and the door was hidden within a porch. He had a key. "But no one will suspect us," he said, "because I shall smash a window when we leave. It will look like a break-in."

She hardly heard him. Now that there was no turning back she was reckless, and her heart churned. The empty hall opened around them like a dark church, and even though he took care that the heavy door should close softly at their backs the sound was picked up and ran away, echoing across the marble floor.

"It is all ours," he whispered. "You can pick and choose whatever takes your fancy."

"Black beads," she said. "I want black beads." Her heart clamoured in her breast as though she had come to the end of an exhausting journey, and he turned to find her clutching at the wall and barely able to stand.

"There is no need to be afraid," he said with the gentleness he was capable of when his will was being obeyed. "We are alone."

"Take me upstairs." She was aware that her gasping breath told him that she had not the strength to climb.

He picked her up and, cradling her in his arms, carried her across the hall. He trod so softly there was no sound, and as they stirred the quiet air she surrendered. She allowed her head to fall back so that her long, black hair brushed the banisters as he carried her higher. She had dreamt of this as she lay in the woods and the autumn leaves had drifted down. Long ago.

He felt her limbs quiver. "What is it?" he asked.

She did not answer. Long ago she had been in a man's arms, resisting him, thrusting him away but unable to prevent him holding her closer and closer until his lofty forehead and the piercing eyes beneath the heavy eyebrows loomed over her and his mouth had found hers. And then, too weak to struggle, she had gazed up through the dark branches of trees while his lips, softly and moistly, had lain against her neck. A sudden sharp pain had made her cry out, and then the trees had stooped and watched her slide into blackness. It had happened long ago.

"You woke me," she said.

He grunted, not knowing what she meant.

"I was asleep in the wood for a much longer time than you could ever guess." The leaf mould had taken her down into darkness, and she had lain still for year after year as the tree roots explored her and held her fast in the earth. A man had put her there. "And then you came and woke me, Ricky," she whispered.

They came to the landing and a long passage stretched ahead. It was she who, like a child, let her fingers trail along the wall until they found a door.

"Here it is," she said.

The silence of the house was focused on the click as the handle turned and the door swung open. They went through. A sly patch of moonlight stood against the wall at the corner of a dressing table as though it had been waiting for them.

She put her arms around his neck and kissed his ear. "Black beads," she whispered.

She slid out of his arms and went to where the moonlight lay. He heard a drawer open and her little chuckle of surprise. He moved towards her, but she ordered him to wait as she stepped into the shadow of a corner. He heard a soft sigh of garments and then the mirror of the dressing table tilted and the dying moonbeam fell on her where she stood.

She was unclothed, pale and vague, but against her skin two long loops of black beads hung down between her breasts to the shadows of her belly. She allowed him to carry her to the bed.

"The beads," he said, "you knew where they were."

She laughed softly and drew him down. "This is my room," she said. "You have brought me home."

He did not understand, and she did not tell him of the slow revival of memory as he brought her through the hall and up the stairs. His hand touched her cool skin and felt the warmth beneath, and all questions fled from his mind. He was above her and joined to her, and her hands held his head and brought him closer as if to kiss him but, as his head tilted back in a spasm, her lips touched his throat.

The teeth that punctured his neck were part of his pleasure and he, without being aware, allowed her to drink. There was little noise in the room as her lips pressed against him, and as he was drained her heartbeat grew stronger and his grew less and less until it faded and failed.

She left him in the quiet of the night and, with her lips still wet, slipped from her mother's house and returned to where she slept beneath the deep leaf mould.

Joel Lane

Your European Son

Joel Lane is the winner of the 1993 Eric Gregory Award for his poetry. His short stories have appeared in various anthologies and magazines, including The Best New Horror, The Year's Best Horror Stories, Darklands *and* Darklands 2, Little Deaths, Twists of the Tale: Cat Horror Stories, Sugar Sleep, The Science of Sadness, Panurge, The Third Alternative *and* Ambit, *and he was recently the Featured Writer in the seventh issue of* The Urbanite. *A collection,* The Earth Wire and Other Stories, *was published by Egerton Press in 1994 and won the British Fantasy Award.*

" 'Your European Son' was written in six days of continuous work," reveals the author. "I wanted to update the relationship between Dracula and Renfield, who are the two most significant characters in Stoker's novel (who remembers anything about Jonathan Harker?), and also to explore the way in which the Count is both an outsider and a patriarch, rather like a Mafia don. Dracula is also a symbol of central Europe and its combined heritage of culture and violence. He is not 'evil', but he is definitely a criminal."

Dracula's nature demands that vampires should be superior to the human race, and he begins to build his criminal empire . . .

EACH DECADE'S BIG ideas struggle on into the next decade, looking more and more out of place. Then they either die or get revived. Graphic design was one of the big ideas of the eighties: everyone needed it, or thought they did. By the end of the nineties, it had been absorbed into the industries it served, and was no longer any way to make a decent living.

Two years out of college, Richard Wren was a freelance designer living on the breadline. Then a chance conversation in a rough pub near his lodgings in Tyseley got him into a new line of business. The supply side of the black economy. Car parts, office equipment, computer hardware, lifestyle accessories, even medical supplies as well as no end of pharmaceutical drugs ... it all had to come from somewhere. Straight robbery was only a part of it; often the "victim" was involved in the deal, claiming insurance as well as a cut. Or someone was going behind his employer's back. Likewise, getting away with it had as much to do with negotiation as fast cars. It was setting up a job, and clearing up after it, that Wren was useful for. He wasn't a hard man. He was cute, and plausible, and had a certain little-boy-lost quality that wasn't entirely fake. As an added bonus, he knew how to handle computers. A bit of erudition and charm went a long way in the subculture of no-mark petty crime. It helped to smooth the edges and prevent mishaps. Wren's associates weren't into bloodshed: it had no commercial value.

He kept up the day job, such as it was. Appearances counted for everything. Still, the night work enabled him to move to a better flat. He was looking at the posh tower blocks on the edge of the city centre when Matthews, a locksmith with a useful collection of duplicates, told him about the vacant flat in Schreck's house. Wren knew what that meant. All of Schreck's tenants worked for the same firm, and were answerable to him. Not that Schreck was the boss, as such. He was just a good fence. Good fences made good neighbours. Schreck's basement was an almost legendary depot for all things dodgy. Being his tenant meant that you were relied upon. The rent was low, but there were attendant responsibilities. When Wren hesitated, Matthews suggested that it would not be in his financial interests to turn down the offer. Wren signed the verbal contract with only a flicker of unease. He was all for job security. Besides, he was curious.

Schreck had a bizarre reputation. He came from some Central European country no one had heard of, and had been one of Warhol's crowd in late-sixties New York. He'd struggled through the seventies as a rock producer and film technician, before coming to England and getting into business crime (another big idea of the eighties). He'd brought some Warholian theatrical camp with him.

Apparently he was never seen by day, and always wore black fabric: satin, velvet, that sort of thing. His face was dead white, except for the bloodshot eyes and shiny lips. Matthews and the others usually referred to him as the Count – which, after a few drinks, was sometimes slurred to the Cunt. He was as bent as a Shadow Cabinet election, obviously. But it went without saying that he had to be fucking dangerous to get away with all that. Like Ronnie Kray or something.

Wren moved into the house in early summer. It was an old detached house, newly renovated and painted white, with leaded windows that weren't quite transparent. The district was a bright mixture of the fake-suburban and the austerely commercial, both elements having the cold smell of money. But it was only a few miles up the Warwick Road to the flaking white-trash districts of Acocks Green and Tyseley, and more criminal contacts than even Schreck would know what to do with. The landlord was away on business the weekend Wren moved in with his computer, box of CDs and four suitcases full of Top Man shirts and worn-out jeans. But on the Wednesday, just after nightfall, there was a firm knock at the door of Wren's studio flat. "Come in." The door swung open. Schreck was a big man: he had to stoop to get through the doorway, and his handshake wrapped around Wren's knuckles like a boxing glove.

"Nice to meet you," he said. "I hope you'll be comfortable here." He was a well-preserved fiftysomething, with spiky black hair that was going grey above the ears. His eyes were a deep blue, cracked by tiny red veins. The brightness of his lips might have been augmented by lipgloss, or it might have been an anomaly linked to the complete lack of pigmentation in the rest of his face. He was wearing an expensive charcoal-grey silk shirt that, despite himself, Wren felt an impulse to reach out and touch.

They chatted for a few minutes, Schreck taking an intelligent interest in Wren's posters and CDs. He was appreciative of Joy Division, but utterly dismissive of the Cure: "They don't express despair, they fabricate it as a lifestyle option. *Entertainment*." There was a trace of Middle Europe in Schreck's voice: not so much an accent as a weight hanging around the vowels, like a second voice you couldn't quite hear. Behind his deliberate politeness, Wren could sense a rather icy self-possession. The cellar and its rumoured contents weren't mentioned. Rent arrangements were discussed as if this were a purely normal tenancy. Perhaps it would be that easy. But just before leaving, Schreck told him: "Don't go on holiday without letting me know. Even a weekend. It might not be convenient. And trust matters." He let that sink in before wishing Wren goodnight and quietly closing the door.

It was the last and hottest summer of the nineties. Wren had trouble sleeping, and began doing some of his design work at night. His main contract, with a magazine publisher in Birmingham, only required him to be there in the afternoons. He struck up a friendship with one of the sub-editors, a tall blonde girl called Alison; they met for a drink a few times, but she wouldn't get involved with him. Once she phoned another man from the office, and the tone of her voice made Wren realize just how far he was from getting close to her. The heat and lack of sleep helped to turn his disappointment into obsession. The inside of his head was a noticeboard covered with photographs of Alison. If he'd been able to download his compulsive daydreams onto his Apple Mac, he could have designed a whole magazine about her. Whenever he had to go into the office, he felt tense and scared.

The house was a partial escape from the summer. The air seemed thinner somehow, as if the leaded windows did more than just weaken the sunlight. It had once been a Victorian family house, and seemed to recover some of its old character after dark, when the shadows erased the new wood-chip wallpaper from the deep stairwell. Wren's flat, on the second floor, had been a family bedroom once. He tried not to think about that too much. Schreck's late-evening visits became a regular event, with Wren sometimes being invited down to the landlord's ground-floor flat to share a drink and a video. Schreck had a brilliant collection of old films, mostly in black and white: Hitchcock, Polanski; *film noirs* from the forties; Universal horror films with Boris Karloff and Bela Lugosi; German expressionist films like *Nosferatu* and *Pandora's Box*; erotic art-films by Warhol and Fassbinder; trash with a PhD in the architecture of its own back passage. He was particularly enthusiastic about old horror and crime B-movies, and the way they had been used to get subversive and dangerous material past the barriers of a hidebound audience. "True Gothic nightmare camouflaged as *schlock*. Behind the plot clichés and cheap special effects, such a world of ambiguity, guilt, narcotics, lust. Such dark, terrible eyes staring at you." Schreck was inclined to get maudlin when he was drunk. His fridge and drinks cabinet housed a crystal garden of wonders. He and Wren sat for hours in the flickering light of the screen, drinking strong Polish vodka with tomato juice or bittersweet liqueurs that glowed like the moon through clouds.

Wren stored up the cold, stark landscapes of these films to protect him from the burning days. The alcohol helped too, as long as he had an extra hour or so to sleep off the worst of it. Spirits had a power that beer entirely lacked: the effect stayed with you all day, like a rose of ice slowly melting into your gut. A private darkness.

Sometimes he made shallow cuts in his arms with a razor blade and licked the blood, then ran cold water over the skin. It made him feel in control. The occasional robbery helped too, though the firm were keeping a low profile until the nights drew in. Wren enjoyed the strategy aspect of it, the sense of winning a game. His fear of guard dogs, armed security guards, police roadblocks, was sharp but limited. It was easier to live with than the way he felt about Alison. And the sense of discipline reassured him. Whatever they took, including money, came back to the house and was stored in the various parts of the basement for Schreck and his invisible overlords to look after.

One Friday night, after the successful liberation of a few grand's worth of state-of-the-art computer games from an underground depot, Wren and two other thieves celebrated with a night at a private club. They'd invited the security guard whom they'd prevented from raising the alarm to join them, but he'd opted to lay low for a while. The club was dark and echoing, and so humid that it seemed about to rain. It was full of criminals pretending to be businessmen, and businessmen pretending to be criminals. Two young female strippers posed awkwardly on the narrow stage, feigning interest in each other. Around a small table, several middle-aged men were ostentatiously cutting up lines of snow. Wren and the other two sat at the bar, knocking back malt whiskies and Black Russians. A few young women drifted quietly among the tables, waiting. The air was cobwebbed with a predictable desire, like something designed and fabricated on a page of broken light. Wren drank steadily, chewing ice, watching the two mirrorballs pull shreds of colour across the girls' pale faces and arms.

Some time later, he wasn't sure how late, the three of them ended up in a tiny side room with a thin, dark-haired girl wearing a red tunic. There was a black velvet futon in the middle of the floor. Wren felt strangely exposed, aware of the two men watching as the girl undressed him and pushed him down onto the futon beneath her. His hands struggled with her underwear. Then she was kneeling over him, her bony hands holding down his outstretched arms. His companions knelt on either side, watching closely. Wren felt trapped. A mixture of humiliation and joy took him over, reducing him to a living snarl. As he came, he caught her earlobe between his teeth and bit. A metallic smear of blood glued his dry lips to her skin. The girl pulled away, her face tight with rage. Wren licked his lips and watched as the other two pacified the girl with money and apologies. Neither of them touched her.

Occasionally, in the house, he'd see Schreck with visitors or overhear them talking. Mostly, he assumed, it was business. Did Schreck have a boyfriend? There had been a couple of rough-looking teenage lads, but neither had been a regular visitor. Just because people said the Count was queer didn't necessarily make it true. Rumour was a separate kind of reality. Maybe they said Wren was driving his stake into the Count. He did wonder, when he sobered up after one of their late-night drinking sessions, if anything was going on. Drinking buddies were more than friends sometimes, it was a well-known phenomenon. At college, he'd known blokes who were officially straight get ratarsed together and end up cuddling, or even exchanging handjobs. But if Schreck was trying to get him that way, he'd already passed up quite a few opportunities. The thought of Schreck grabbing his balls one of these nights didn't worry him too much. What seemed more likely, and more threatening, was that the old madman was falling for him and might never let him go. There was an edge to their nocturnal films and bottles that Wren didn't understand. It was getting to him. But he didn't know what would happen if he tried to cry off. There was something protective about Schreck, almost motherly. His sharp nails, the mints he chewed to sweeten his breath. Probably a Catholic, or a Jew. How would he treat you if you stopped being one of his family? By late summer, Wren suspected he'd already got into something he couldn't get out of. And then there were the dreams.

It was like an extension of some of Schreck's older films into the monochrome world they evoked: forests, empty streets, crumbling buildings, the moon behind clouds. Tiny figures were scattered across the landscape: either dolls or babies, their faces closed and blank. Tree branches, prams and other debris floated in a disused canal, behind railings almost eaten through with rust. Everything was still, as after some terrible event. Wren (or whoever he had become) was always lost, trying to find someone or escape from someone. The story never revealed itself to him. Somewhere behind a wall, or in the next street, it was still going on. He could just hear the echoes of someone crying, or screaming, or snarling with rage, or groaning in pleasure. But he didn't know where the sounds came from. At some point near the end of each dream, he looked at the moon and saw through a black frame into another world: a darkened room where Schreck's face was watching him. The only colours in the entire dream were the red of Schreck's lips and the deep blue of his eyes, which never met Wren's own.

One night in mid-August, Wren visited a rock nightclub in the city centre. It was billed as a Goth/Alternative/Industrial night. A

damaged mirrorball stood on a concrete pillar at the end of the
street. The club itself resembled a derelict warehouse with speakers
and lights installed at the last moment. The walls were unevenly
coated with posters advertising gigs over the last few years. There
were two similar concourses, each with a long curved bar stretching
from the doorway to the edge of a square dance floor. The music on
the first floor was mostly heavy metal, the music on the second floor
a mixture of goth and industrial. The people dancing on each floor
provided a visual guide to the differences. Wren decided to stick
to the upper venue, for several reasons. After two hours of harsh
music and lukewarm beer served in plastic glasses, his enthusiasm
was waning. Very few of the girls seemed to be unattached; perhaps
they were only here for the music. Feeling lonely and unexpectedly
drunk, he stumbled onto the adhesive dance floor just as a new
track began.

The rapid, scratching guitar caught him by surprise; then he
recognised it. Lou Reed snarling *You killed your European son / You
spit on those under 21*, then a glass breaking, then five minutes of
tense, atonal noise. He'd heard it before, of course; but never
at this volume, or in such an appropriate context. The sound of
a tune broken down painfully into its elements. Wren shut his
eyes and wondered about the future. The clean, computerised life
wasn't going to happen. But what would take its place? Barbarism?
Terror? What instincts had to be accepted before humanity was real
again? The Velvet Underground track was more than thirty years
old, but it was still shocking. Schreck was right about the eighties,
he realized. That era had taken everything that was disturbing
and turned it into a lifestyle option, a product. Now society was
discovering how real it all was. *You better say so long.*

Later, the music became more plaintive and the floor stickier.
Couples folded into the shadows, joined inseparably at the mouth.
There were fewer people dancing. The toilets were a no-man's-land,
splattered with piss and vomit. In a small side room where the bar
only served Budweiser, Wren successfully chatted up a pale young
woman with spiky black hair and a non-human skull tattooed on
her left shoulder. Her name was Lucy. They danced together,
embracing awkwardly, before stumbling around various bits of
human wreckage to the exit. Outside, the night was starry and
relatively cool. They caught the night bus rather than wait for a
taxi. Someone behind them vomited onto the floor. Wren and
Lucy kissed, filling their mouths and nostrils with each other.

They hardly slept that night. Wren was feverish, hungry for
something he couldn't define. Lucy was kind, affectionate, caring.
He wanted none of it. The first time they made love, it took him a

long while to come. The second time, near dawn, he asked her to bite him. She nibbled his tense shoulder. "Harder. *Bite.*" He dug his nails into her spine. Angrily, she bit down hard. When he saw the blood smeared across her mouth, Wren came at once. His entire body ached from the effort. Lucy seemed a bit nauseated. She dabbed at the wounded shoulder with a handkerchief, wincing at her own teethmarks.

In the morning, she left before Wren was properly awake. He washed the bite, put two plasters over it and went back to bed. Having slept through half the day, he felt restless and disorientated in the evening. Towards midnight, he caught a late bus into Tyseley. The inert husks of derailed trains crowded the railway depot, like abandoned chrysalids. Asset-stripping in a crudely literal sense, two years after the selloff. The whitewashed exteriors of old factories and workshops glowed faintly, picked out by the streetlamps. A stray dog foraged patiently in a litter-bin. Here and there, lights behind closed shutters indicated night work – some of it, perhaps, the same kind of night work that Wren and his colleagues were involved in. There were no exposed windows, anywhere. Cars and vans drove along the Warwick Road, none of them ever turning off or stopping.

Wren knew his way around here by night better than in daylight. He walked down a side-street between a Catholic church and a disused canal, the water glinting through battered railings. Where a flattened stone bridge crossed the canal, he could see a patch of wasteground with a boarded-up house and a weeping willow tree. A pigeon groaned from somewhere behind the tree. Wren thought suddenly of the Chinese Willow pattern on bowls he'd eaten from as a child. It was colder than the previous night. He could smell burning wood. Was that a fire in the distance, or just a red security light in a factory yard? He stepped forward until he was under the tree, its long yellowish leaves touching him. Their ends were dry. The sound of machinery, like guitar chords, rose from the bassline of the distant traffic. And then, quite abruptly, the gentle movement of the willow leaves stopped. Wren felt a white breath pass over him, as if he were an image on a screen. There was a faint sound of cracking and tearing; then silence and a cascade of dry filaments, as the tree shed all its leaves at once.

When he told Schreck about his experience with the Velvet Underground song in the nightclub, the landlord smiled gently. "Oh yes. Lou Reed . . . such a gifted boy. In those days. He was so real. David Bowie stole his thunder, of course – but it wasn't the same. Bowie could change his image at the drop of an eyelash, but Reed could change his *soul.* You can hear it in those songs, the danger." Wren didn't tell him about Lucy or the dying tree. In any case, Schreck was away on business a lot of the time now, so Wren saw much less of him. It gave the tenant a chance to sort himself out. The inability to sleep normal hours was messing him up, and the dreams were starting to undermine his waking life. His GP referred him to a counsellor, who kept asking him about his parents. *No*, he thought angrily, *I wasn't abused. I wasn't even scared of them.* But when he thought back to how his parents had seemed – their heavy bodies, their violence towards each other, their nocturnal outcries of love or fury – it was hard not to think of Schreck, because Schreck made him feel like a child. A silent witness.

In October, his contract with the magazine publisher ended. He invited Alison round to his flat for a valedictory meal. Rather to his surprise, she accepted. That weekend turned out to be a slightly inconvenient one for Wren. Schreck and Matthews were both away, sorting out an urgent problem somewhere in North Yorkshire. Wren had been warned to expect a large consignment of hash at some point over the weekend. Schreck had given him the money and the key to the basement. In all probability, the deal had been engineered to test Wren's reliability. It was petty stuff, in all respects: the cash, the weed and the arrangement. Taking the mediocre seriously was what life in the West Midlands was all about. He hoped it wouldn't clash with Alison's visit. Then again, maybe it would give him a chance to impress her – and even an excuse to get her stoned.

Wren spent hours cleaning the flat beforehand. His eyes had become used to a certain level of dirt and rubbish, and the flat seemed unfamiliar without it. He was surprised to discover some rusty stains inside the bathroom door, where the towel normally hung. He must have cut himself one night, probably when drunk, and forgotten about it. Alison turned up punctually at eight, wearing a blue-black coat he'd not seen before. The night behind her was still and clear, stars and streetlamps glowing as if painted in the doorway.

They shared a bottle of white wine and some mushroom pâté, followed by grilled mackerel in garlic sauce. The Velvet Underground's third album, the quiet one, unwound strands of melody from the black speakers at either end of the room. Alison glanced appreciatively round the flat. "This is a really nice place. Bit gloomy though. Like you spend all your time in here with the curtains drawn. All these records, posters, books. Most people, you see their flats and there are no books at all." She smiled, her mouth resting a little tensely on her knuckles. Then her eyes narrowed. "The house is a bit creepy, don't you think? It's so featureless. Like a hostel or something. And there's not enough light."

"The landlord's a vampire," Wren said. "That's why I put garlic in the sauce. To protect you." Alison's eyes widened in an expression of dawning terror. Then she cracked up, giggling hard, and almost choked on a fishbone. Wren jumped to his feet, but she waved him back down and coughed into her hand. "Are you okay?" he asked. She nodded. Her face was flushed; her pale blue eyes glittered with moisture. She ran a hand through her blonde fringe, pulling it back. They stared at each other. Feeling more scared than he could have imagined possible, Wren reached out and touched the back of her hand. She gripped his fingers. Lou Reed sang gently, bitterly, about loss and sin. *Thought of you as everything I've had but couldn't keep.* As Wren stood up and came round the small table towards her, she lifted her face to kiss him.

They progressed from wine to cognac and mint chocolate-chip ice cream. The stereo fell silent. Wren felt somewhat at a loss for words. He'd anticipated making some convoluted verbal pass; but it had happened almost too easily. As if trying to regain control, Alison started to run through her past impressions of him. "At first I thought you were really cute. Kind of naive and impressionable. Then I got a bit scared. You were too intense, and I thought maybe you were a bit strange. The morbid things you used to come out with. Sometimes you'd come in looking really tired, and then be secretive about where you'd been. Like you were in trouble." She laughed gently and kissed him. "But now, I think I've worked you out. This flat . . . it's like a middle-class facsimile of a Gothic artist's garret. You just want people to think you're tortured and strange. It's an image. Really you're cute and naive. You don't know anything about the dark side of life, except what it's meant to look like. Do you?" She drained her brandy glass and gazed at him affectionately.

"You don't know that," Wren said. "You don't know what I feel. You don't always have to experience something to feel it. And maybe I *have* experienced things you don't know about. What I've seen. Been part of. Crimes." *Shut up,* he told himself. Maybe she wouldn't take him literally. But why did women trying to mother him always make him feel violent?

Alison gripped his shoulders and pulled him against her. "I don't believe you've even nicked bubble-gum from a corner shop," she said. "You're just turning ordinary guilt into a fantasy. Confess what you like, I won't believe you." They sat down on the bed together. He slipped a hand under the collar of her shirt. Then the doorbell rang.

A black van was parked outside. A small man in a leather jacket, with the makings of a beard, was reaching up to press the bell a second time as Wren opened the front door. "Mr Robin?" he said. "Wren, that's it. Got some videos for Mr Schreck here. You gonna let me in or what?" Wren stepped back into the hallway. "Never do business in the hall," the visitor said. "You really haven't got a clue, have you?" Blushing, and thinking uneasily of Alison, Wren led the dealer upstairs to his flat. The man's carrier bag contained three video cases. Two of these contained films. The third was packed full of brown fibres that looked like soil. It was labelled AIRPLANE. Brummie humour, you couldn't beat it. Wren took the envelope full of banknotes from his own locked briefcase and handed it to the dealer. Alison looked on impassively from the bed. Wren had to go back down to unlock the front door. "Make sure the bitch keeps her mouth shut," the man said on his way out.

Wren took a deep breath and returned to his flat, where Alison was cautiously examining the video case. "What do you do with this?" she asked, then laughed at the expression on his face. "I don't mean what do you *do* with it, Richard. I mean what are *you* going to do with it, now. I assume you don't own it." They'd underestimated each other. Wren explained about his landlord and the basement. "Come with me," he said. "You might learn something." His need to make an impression was stronger than his instinct for secrecy. It was past midnight; no one would bother them.

The basement was actually a nuclear fallout shelter, adapted by a previous tenant from a more traditional cellar. There was a concealed entrance in Schreck's flat, and another – which Wren had access to – in a shed behind the house. The interior of the shelter was lined with concrete and had about thirty yards of shelving, designed for storage of provisions against Doomsday. There was no food or water there now; but Wren supposed that, if Yeltsin's successor decided to press the button, he and Schreck could spend their last few days smoking wacky baccy, watching porn videos and playing computer games. He led Alison downstairs in the darkness, walking quietly through the hallway to the back door.

Outside, the cold sobered him up rapidly. The shapes of discarded rubbish crowded the garden like a frozen menagerie. There were no herbaceous borders here. The shed was full of old newspapers and bits of damaged pottery. He cleared the tiny entrance to the bunker and keyed in the numbers Schreck had given him on the lock panel. Alison followed him down the steps. He flicked on the dim red light and looked around. Unmarked boxes and packages crowded the narrow shelves. The air was cold and still, more dusty than he remembered. On a low shelf, near the door, there was a row of video boxes. He added the box of cannabis to the end. A small, flattish cardboard box sat alone at the end of the shelf. It was unsealed. He flicked it open, prompted by the same bitter curiosity that had made him search through his parents' bedroom as a child. What he touched, without seeing it, was some kind of mask, like the face of a baby or a cat. It crumbled at once. He shivered violently. "What's up?" Alison said.

"Nothing." He closed the box and turned, putting his arms round her. As they kissed, he saw a tiny red light winking above her shoulder. A hidden camera? Was Schreck recording this? Before he could react, Alison pointed to the far end of the room. "Look. What's there?" A small door in the concrete wall, not quite shut. No handle; not even a keyhole. "Can we get through?" Despite all his recent experience, despite being nine years on from puberty, Wren felt a wheel turning within himself at the thought *It was her idea.* He stepped to the far wall and gripped the edge of the door. It was heavy, but it opened easily. There couldn't be a room beyond it, he realized from the smell of fresh soil.

But there was. It was smaller than the first room, and had no light. In the vague red glow from behind him, Wren could see that all four walls were lined with shelves. On each shelf, there was a coffin. Wren felt Alison step past him. "What the fuck?" The light seemed to pull back, as if it were being repelled or absorbed by the darkness in the room. "Oh, my God. Who are they?" The air was crowded with translucent faces, or many copies of the same face. All mounted like paper masks on impossibly thin bodies. All staring.

It was cold in here, as cold as a deep freeze. Alison turned round. There were dark patches of blood on her cheeks, her neck, her raised hands. "Help me." Something he could hardly see pushed him back into the doorway. "*Please.*" The door closed on him. Wren crouched behind it for a long time, trying to hear. But there was no sound. The door fitted so neatly into its frame that it could almost have been part of the wall. It couldn't be opened from the outside. When he stood up, his eyes were stinging. There was blood in his mouth.

After the bunker, the house seemed like a vast emptiness. Wren climbed the stairs numbly, entered his flat without switching on the light, and stood there for a moment. Then he began to remove his clothes. The cold of underground seemed to have followed him. It was the beginning of winter. He ran a warm bath, took a razor blade from the cabinet and half embedded it in the soap. Then he lay down in the water. The left wrist sliced open as easily as a fish. The right wrist was harder, because he'd cut a tendon or something in his left hand. He made two longitudinal gashes before hitting the vein. Then he rested his head between the taps and watched the blood spreading like two bright flames in the water. Soon he couldn't feel anything but the faint trickle of water from his exposed feet. There was blood in the air now, darkening, clotting above his face. Then two eyes opened in the sky of blood.

Schreck. The landlord gripped Wren's shoulders and pulled him up. The water seemed almost freezing. Gently, he took Wren's left hand and lifted the open wrist to his mouth. Wren felt a tongue probe the edges of the wound. Then Schreck took the other wrist and drank from it. The comfortable haze of blood was receding, and a black emptiness was starting to take its place. Wren felt other wounds open: the old razor-cuts along his inner arms, and the bite-mark on his right shoulder. Schreck leaned over and kissed him firmly on the mouth. He seemed to have more than two lips. There are no revelations, Wren thought. Only more of the same. A monster disguised as itself. He put his arms round Schreck, and felt himself lifted easily from the red water.

Later, he opened his eyes to find himself in bed. Schreck was sitting beside him on the duvet. As Wren looked at him, the landlord picked up a glass and put it in Wren's hand. It was neat vodka, Schreck's own. The best. Wren felt his wounds sting as the alcohol opened up his circulation. Behind the drawn curtain and the leaded glass, it was daylight. Wren tried to smile. "What do you call a cunt with teeth?" he asked, his voice sounding thin and childish.

"I know. Dracula." Schreck glanced at the small table near the bed, the two brandy glasses and crystal dessert bowls. "I'm sorry about her," he said. "My little friends. She's with them now."

"Do you always turn your friends into versions of yourself?"

The landlord shrugged. "Doesn't everyone?" He stroked Wren's hand with a surprising tenderness.

They stared at each other for a while, like a couple making up after a row. Then Schreck asked: "Do you want her back?" Wren nodded. "I'm sorry. You can't be with her. Not that way. You're just not the type . . . But there's a whole world out there for you." Schreck gazed at the curtained window. When he looked back at Wren, there were tears in his eyes. "Richard. I need someone who's not like me. Someone to live for me, love for me . . . and eventually, die for me. To feel the pain I can't feel." He stood up. "I'll leave you now. There's food in your fridge, booze in your cabinet. I've cleaned the bath. All you need to do is rest. If you want me, just knock on my door. I'll wait."

Then he picked something up from the floor and put it on Wren's bedside table, next to the alarm clock. It was the cake of soap with the razor still in it. "Your choice," he said. "There are many ways out. But remember, the real evil is the denial of need. Do what you have to." The door opened and closed softly. Wren blinked at the drying wounds on his wrists. The power to heal. The power to harm. He sat with his arms wrapped across his chest, rocking himself gently. *Father. Mother.* He drank some more vodka and began to cry. He cried until his throat ached and his eyes were burning. When night fell, he was still crying. But he still hadn't picked up the razor blade.

> *The leaves are falling as if from far away,*
> *as if a garden had withered in space;*
> *the way they fall is like saying no.*
> > – Rilke

Brian Stableford

Quality Control

*Brian Stableford lectured in sociology at the University of Reading until
1988, wrote full-time from 1989 to 1995, and is currently employed as a
part-time lecturer at the University of the West of England teaching courses
in 'The Development of Science in a Cultural Context'.*

*He has published more than forty science fiction and fantasy novels,
including* The Empire of Fear, The Werewolves of London, The
Angel of Pain, Young Blood, Serpent's Blood, Salamander's Fire,
Chimera's Cradle, The Hunger and Ecstasy of Vampires *and its
sequel,* The Black Blood of the Dead.

*A prolific writer about the history of imaginative fiction, he was a leading
contributor to the award-winning* The Encyclopedia of Science Fiction
*edited by John Clute and Peter Nicholls, and contributed numerous articles
to Clute and John Grant's* The Encyclopedia of Fantasy. *He has also
published a number of anthologies and volumes of translations relating
to the French and English Decadent Movements of the late nineteenth
century.*

*Having observed the world and what is happening to it, Dracula advances
his plans to re-establish himself and his fellow vampires as the dominant
species . . .*

BREWER HADN'T BEEN in the Goat and Compasses for nearly a year. He didn't need to go into places like that nowadays; he always met his runners on safer ground. His legitimate business was booming and it didn't seem politic to be frequently seen in a pub known to be favoured by dealers, pimps and other assorted riff-raff. There were no big players on view now, though; it was only lunchtime.

He found Simple Simon propping up the bar, looking no fatter and no more prosperous than he ever did, but not looking like a boy on the brink of starvation either. Brewer still thought of Simon as a boy although he must have been well into his twenties by now. Clearly, he was still working – if not for Brewer then for someone else.

"Hello, Simon," Brewer said, taking the youth by the elbow and leading him away from the bar to a booth in the corner. "It's been too long, hasn't it?" While Simon thought about how to answer that he went back to the bar and ordered a couple of pints.

When Brewer carried the tankards over to the booth and set them down Simon had the grace to look slightly guilty, but he didn't look scared. Brewer had never mastered the delicate art of terrifying his pushers, preferring to represent himself as a man who was as gentle and trustworthy as his product. Sometimes, he regretted his laxity. There was always the chance that some under-terrorized imbecile would grass him up if the police put the screws on tight enough.

"It's okay," he said, staying in character. "No threats. I only want an explanation. You owe me that much, at least."

"An explanation of what?" Simon asked, although he knew full well.

"An explanation of why you haven't picked up your supplies lately. I know you too well to believe that you've decided to straighten up, so you've obviously found an alternative supplier. You don't have to tell me who it is, but I need to know what it is you're peddling. I thought I had the kind of product that wouldn't easily be outdone. If my recipe book is out of date I really ought to catch up. It's not the money, of course – it's a matter of professional pride."

"It's not better," the youth muttered. "Not really. It's just different. New."

"You're telling me you're a fashion victim? Some new designer product hits the street and you feel like you have to switch brands in case your mates think your habit's passé?" Brewer tried hard to imply that it was unbelievable, but he knew that it was only too likely.

"It's not like that," Simon said, uncomfortably. "It's just . . . people can be very persuasive."

"You mean they threatened to break your legs if you didn't ditch my stuff and start selling theirs?"

"Not exactly," the boy muttered, unable to muster enough conviction to tell a convenient lie. The trouble with Simon was that he was vulnerable to the mildest forms of persuasion, provided he was approached in the right way.

"It's okay," Brewer lied, hoping that he didn't sound too convincing. "It was bound to happen. It's the hectic pace of technological innovation – not to mention the money that's being poured into neurochemical research. I'm only one man, and I can't be expected to create and supervise the psychotropic revolution by myself. There's room for everyone in a boom market, no need for conflict. This is 1999, after all – we're not Jurassic crack dealers, are we? I just need to know what's going on. Is there any reason why you shouldn't retail my products as well as theirs?"

Simon shrugged awkwardly. Plainly there was.

Brewer wondered whether it might have been optimistic to assume that his new rivals were men like him: civilized people with degrees, well-appointed laboratories and a serious interest in the next phase of human evolution. Maybe the old-time crack dealers were trying to get back into the game. If so, he shuddered to think what their quality control must be like. He stared over Simon's shoulder and let his eyes wander while he wondered how much trouble he might be in.

His wandering gaze was suddenly arrested and held by a trim figure easing its way out of a booth on the far side of the room. His attention would have been caught even if he hadn't recognized the face lurking behind the opaque sunglasses, but the shock of realizing who she was intensified his reaction considerably.

Simon looked around to see what Brewer was staring at, but turned back quickly, as if he were afraid to look upon such a startling profile.

"Does she come in here often?" Brewer asked.

"Sometimes. Still counts a few of the working girls as friends. They say her old man doesn't like it, but he doesn't keep tabs on her during the day."

"Must be the laid-back type." Brewer used the sneer to cover up an unexpected stab of jealousy. For nearly a year Brewer had supplied Jenny with happy pills in exchange for sex, but she had been using too many other things, and she had never quite come off the game. He had dumped her when she had gone far enough downhill not to be special any more. In his experience, nobody ever climbed back up that kind of hill once they'd started to roll, but Jenny now looked *extra* special – far better than she ever had before. That was difficult to believe, given that she must be at least Simon's age, with the sweet succulence of innocence far behind her.

"So laid-back he's creepy," Simon said. "You want to go say hello?"
He didn't really think he was going to be let off that easily, but there
was a distinct note of hope in his voice, doubtless encouraged by
the intensity of Brewer's stare. He wouldn't have got off that easily,
either, if the girl hadn't got up from her seat at that very moment
and started for the door, waving goodbye to her erstwhile friends
– who looked after her with naked envy, but rather less hatred
than might have been expected.

Brewer didn't spare Simon another glance, but he said "I'll be
back" in his best Schwarzenegger drawl. He left the pint he'd hardly
touched on the table.

It wasn't difficult to catch up with Jenny; she wasn't hurrying.

"Can I offer you a lift somewhere," Brewer said, as he drew level
with her.

She seemed genuinely surprised to see him. Perhaps she'd been
too deep in conversation to see him enter the pub and perhaps she
hadn't glanced in his direction while she made for the door. She
stopped and turned to look up into his eyes. Her own eyes were
hidden by the dark glasses but he imagined them blue and clear,
as radiant as her complexion.

"I don't know, Bru," she said, blithely. "Which way are you
going?"

"Any way you like," he said. "It's my afternoon off."

"Nothing cooking back at the lab?" Her voice was gently teasing;
there was no evidence of hard feelings regarding the way their
previous acquaintance had drifted to its end.

"We only do the lawful stuff by day," he told her. "Half the night
too, most days. Difficult to find time for fun and games. The last
civil service lab's due to close next April – not cost effective. Private
contractors like me do all the statutory health and safety work these
days, as well as all the forensic testing. Never been busier."

"Health and safety work? Is that what you call it?"

It was more a veiled insult than a joke. He'd always offered
products that were as safe and as healthy as he could contrive.
He liked *all* his customers to stay fit and well – and happy too.

"Quality control is what I call it," he said. "Making sure that
the goods you buy at the supermarket, or over the pharmacist's
counter, are exactly what they're supposed to be and as pure as
scientific ingenuity can make them. It's vital work in these corrupt
times. There's more money in faking designer drugs than there is
in faking designer jeans or fine wines, and you know how paranoid
people are about their food since last year's pesticide plague. You
look incredibly well, Jenny. I'd never have believed it. You must

have kicked all your old habits." He emphasized the word *all* very slightly.

"Every last one," she said. "Where's your car?"

"In the multi-storey. I *never* park illegally. Where do you want to go? Home?" He started walking again as he said it, pointing the way with a languid finger

"I guess." She must have known that he was burning with curiosity, but she carefully didn't say where home was. "Everything's rosy with you, then?"

"Couldn't be better," he assured her, having no intention of telling her that some rival was taking a big bite out of his synthetics trade. "The revolution is bang on course. The great crusade continues." He always took care to sound as if he wasn't serious when he said things like that, but he was. He didn't see himself as one more drug-peddler in the shark-infested soup; he really did believe that psychotropic chemistry would pave the way for the next step in human evolution. He'd tried to explain that to Jenny a dozen times and more, back in the old days.

"I know," she said, perhaps implying that although she'd kicked the habits which had been destroying her she hadn't given up on everything she bought on the street . . . or perhaps not.

"I hear you're living with a laid-back creep," he said, as they stepped into the lift that would take them up to level nine of the multi-storey. "Only comes out at night – some kind of vampire, maybe?"

She didn't laugh. She didn't even smile. In fact, she turned her head away, as if she didn't want him to be able to read her reaction too accurately. As she moved her head the skin at the side of her neck stretched, and lifted an odd discolouration briefly into view above the collar of her neat black blouse. It looked like a lovebite, but Brewer only caught a momentary glimpse of it before she turned again and it disappeared.

"I'm with someone," she admitted. "I'm not like I used to be, Bru. I learned to apply a little quality control of my own, just in time."

This time the insult wasn't even veiled.

"It's okay," Brewer said, uneasily. "I'm only curious, not jealous. We were never married, were we?"

"No," she said, colourlessly. "We never were."

When she got into the car – without pausing to admire it, although it certainly warranted a certain respect – she had to tell him where home was.

"Docklands?" he echoed, deliberately overdoing the contempt. "I thought even the yuppie dinosaurs had moved out of there. I suppose it's handy for your old stamping grounds, though."

"It's quiet," she said, as if that were explanation enough. Then she looked away, as if she wanted to punish him for wanting to hurt her feelings – but she didn't try to get out of the car again, and she seemed perfectly relaxed as he zigzagged down to the barrier and out into the traffic.

He let the conversation lapse while he threaded his way through the crowded streets, pretending to concentrate hard but continually stealing sidelong glances at her at every junction. She gave him directions in an absurdly overabundant fashion, as if he couldn't be trusted to find his way around the City Security Zone or through the road-works fringing the last of the Jubilee Line extension building-sites.

The place to which Jenny eventually guided him was, indeed quiet – which wasn't surprising, given that it was one of those maximum security buildings with a fiendishly complicated entry system and no ground floor windows.

"Are you going to invite me in for a coffee?" he asked, as she got out. She hesitated, with her hand on the door-handle, as if waiting for some extra inducement. Thinking that he understood, he reached under the seat and released his secret stash. "I can sweeten it for us," he said.

"You're crazy, keeping that stuff in your car," she said. "Especially a thief-magnet like this."

"We scientific geniuses have ways of thief-proofing our homes and vehicles," he said, airily. "We don't need *that* kind of hi-tech fortress." He nodded at the armoured entry-door with all its smart sensors.

She let go of the door-handle without opening the door. "If you're coming up for coffee," she said, "you'd better put the car in the basement. And if you want it sweet, you can have all the sugar you need. Put that stuff back where it came from."

He did as he was told. It would have suited him better if she'd been tempted, but he certainly wasn't going to insist.

It was almost as difficult to get into the subterranean car park as it was to get through the building's main door, and Jenny had to produce two different ID cards to open the doors of the lift which took them up to the apartments – all the way up, as it transpired. Jenny's new man lived in the penthouse.

"The trouble with security," Brewer observed, as they made their ascent, "is that it works both ways. If there were a fire, you'd never get out – and the fire brigade wouldn't be able to get in to help you. Where *I* live it's simple to get in and out, even though it's not easy. *My* security systems are glorious in their subtlety."

"Just like you," she said, with telling sarcasm. Perhaps, he thought, she'd only invited him in to score a few points by showing him everything that she'd accomplished since he dumped her. On the other hand, living in a maximum-security love-nest with a guy that Simple Simon called a creep must have its downside. If she often went back to the Goat and Compasses to pass the time of day with whores whose beat she'd once shared she must be desperate for congenial company.

Brewer wasn't surprised to find that Jenny's boyfriend wasn't home. He was, however, mildly surprised to discover what kind of place his home was. It wasn't particularly plush, considering the rent one had to pay for that kind of situation and that kind of safety, and it was certainly no leftover yuppie's style-trap. All the walls were lined with shelves and all the shelves were fully-laden, ninety per cent with books and ten per cent with CDs: thousands of each. There was an alcove in the living-room fitted out as a workstation with a pair of widescreen PCs whose screen savers swirled different shades of blue and grey around one another in endless mirror-image sequences. Brewer took note of the laser-printer and the idle fax machine, but they weren't interesting enough to warrant close study. The glass in the broad window was heavily smoked; even though the sun was shining the room was distinctly dim.

It would have taken hours to make a detailed study of all the book-titles, but a quick scan told him that they were all non-fiction, with no obvious specialism. The CDs were mostly audio or read-only, but there were at least fifty user-disks. If they weren't just for show, that added up to an awful lot of gigabytes.

"Are you taking an Open University degree or something?" he asked, although he was painfully aware that it left much to be desired as a conversational gambit.

"No," she said, disappearing into the kitchen to put the kettle on. She had finally taken off her sunglasses, but he still hadn't seen her eyes.

"Mind if I use your loo?" he asked, figuring that he would only get eaten away by curiosity if he didn't.

"Into the hallway, second door on the right," she answered, unsuspiciously.

The bathroom was ordinary enough. He turned the taps on while he opened the cabinet and began a scrupulous examination of everything stored there. His trained eye skated over the cosmetics and probed for something that didn't look quite right, something *revealing*. He didn't expect any illegals, or even anything particularly esoteric, but in his experience there were always clues in a bathroom cabinet for an expert eye to decode.

He grinned when he found three pill-bottles without proprietory or prescription labels lurking in a corner behind a flask of skin-conditioner. When he shook the capsules out they didn't have any indicative markings. He picked up three of each kind of capsule, slipped them into the inside pocket of his jacket and turned the taps off.

By the time he came out he'd triggered Jenny's urge to go. When she locked the door behind her he moved swiftly into the kitchen and opened the refrigerator, just on the off chance.

This time the anomaly leapt right out at him. Three non-standard hooks had been installed in the left-hand wall and the grille below them had had two bars removed so that three fluid-filled bags could be hung there. Brewer didn't like to judge by appearances but the straw-coloured fluid that filled the bags looked like blood-plasma – the real thing, not the standard synthetic substitute. He just had time to squeeze a sample into one of the specimen-bottles he always carried with him before moving swiftly back to the living-room and taking up his coffee-cup.

"Well," he said to Jenny, as she came back into the room "you certainly landed on your feet. I'm glad. How did you kick the hard stuff – some kind of substitution programme?" Her eyes were blue and radiant, exactly as he'd expected, and they had a curious *haunted* look that was very attractive – as if they had seen far more than they had ever hoped or expected to.

"Will power," she said, shortly. "You don't seem too have taken too much harm from sampling your own products – but you were always a moderate man. I suppose you've got plenty of girlfriends, just as lovely and every bit as eager as I was?"

"No one special," he said.

"No one is," she retorted. He wondered if it was a philosophical remark or yet another insult, to be understood as including an unspoken *to you*.

"Anyhow," he told her, truthfully, "I don't know anyone as lovely as you. You used to be pretty, all right, but *now* . . . what's your secret, Jenny? I bet those kids you were talking to in the pub would give a hell of a lot to know it." He couldn't help adding: "They must really hate you now."

"It's no secret, Bru," she said. "It was just a matter of getting the shit out of my system. I'm okay now – absolutely clean. Nobody hates me. I don't go back there to rub their noses in it. They know I only want to help."

Saint Jennifer, reformed whore and would-be saviour of fallen women? he was tempted to say. All he actually said was: "Nobody's absolutely clean." He held up the coffee-cup as he said it, to remind her that caffeine was an upper of sorts. The coffee was too strong for his own taste, and he noticed that she was drinking hers black, without sweeteners. She'd always liked it white before, with one or even two.

She didn't dignify his stupid correction with a reply.

"The light in here is distinctly dismal," Brewer observed, feeling that he'd somehow gone five points down in the game and hadn't a clue how to start scoring on his own account. "I don't wonder you feel the need to get out in the sun once in a while, even if you have to go back to your old haunts in search of a bit of company. Don't you have new friends now? Or is your boyfriend the solitary type, outside of bed?"

"You'd probably get on with him well enough," Jenny told him, wryly. "You have lots of interests in common."

Brewer let his eyes travel over the loaded bookshelves. "He probably has interests in common with everyone who has interests," he remarked. "He's obviously a very interested man. Is that why you're at a loose end? Is he out pursuing his interests?"

"He doesn't have a lot of free time at the moment."

"I know the feeling," Brewer said. "Exactly what interests do he and I have in common?"

"Biotech," she said, shortly. After a pause, she added: "Quality control." Now she was being deliberately enigmatic. Her blue eyes were looking up at him from beneath slightly lowered brows. She was fishing for a reaction. Brewer wondered whether she expected him to be flattered by the news that she'd picked out a man like himself once she'd been consumed by conformity and decency – if she *had* been consumed by decency and conformity, and wasn't just a better class of whore than she'd been before.

"Are you happy?" he asked.

"What kind of question is that?"

"Just a question."

"Do you think I was happy before?" she asked, with some slight asperity. "Do you think I was happy when I knew *you*?"

"You were sometimes," he said. "I was the one who gave you the happy pills, remember. I make a good product. You were happy enough when you were under the influence. I just wondered if you were happy now that you don't even take sweeteners in your caffeine-loaded coffee."

"What you're wondering," she said, "is why I invited you up here, and why I agreed to let you drive me home. You're wondering whether you might possibly have got lucky, now that screwing me would count as *getting lucky* instead of trivial commerce."

"I never thought of it like that," Brewer said, as equably as he could.

"No, you didn't. For me, trading sex for the stuff you had to sell was cutting out the middleman, but you really did think that it didn't count as whoring if no actual money changed hands. I never quite understood that."

"I liked you," he said, truthfully. "You were pretty, and sweet. Are you pissed because I never asked you to let me take you away from all the rest of it? I might have, if I'd thought you'd say yes – but you were the one who was just cutting out the middleman."

"I'm a lot prettier now," she said, "but not nearly so sweet. I'm not so sure you'd like me now, once you got to know me." The *haunted* note was sounding in her voice now.

"I'm sure," Brewer told her. He intended it as a compliment, but she didn't seem to take it that way.

"Because nothing else counts except the looks," she countered. "Because getting to know me better couldn't possibly change your mind, which you made up the instant you saw me in the Goat and Compasses. What were you doing there, anyway? I haven't seen you in there before – not for at least a year."

"Looking up an old friend," he told her. "You remember Simon, don't you? Simple Simon."

"Oh, *him*," she said, as if the revelation explained everything.

"He's no worse than the old friends *you* were looking up," Brewer pointed out. "Maybe a cut above, depending how you compare things. Either way, he brought us together again. It really is good to see you, and I really am pleased that you got out of the gutter and started reaching for the stars. Sure you're happy. Who wouldn't be? So why *did* you let me drive you home instead of calling me a shit and kicking me in the balls? If I was just a paying customer before, why give me the time of day now? If you don't want to pick up where we left off –and I assume you don't – you must have some little itch of curiosity needling you. You must at least be interested to know how I am."

"I already asked you how you were," she pointed out.

"So what else do you want to know?"

"How you *really* are. As you say, there's just a slight itch of nostalgic curiosity. Do you know the one thing about you I missed, when you stopped coming round because I was too much of a wreck?"

It wouldn't have been diplomatic to say *the pills* so Brewer said: "My acid wit?"

"Those little rhapsodies about the psychotropic revolution," she said. "*Not* the acidly witty ones, the ones when you forgot yourself just a little, and actually half-meant what you were saying, about a world where biotechnology would save us from ourselves. It was all bullshit, of course, but it was nice that you believed in *something*, even if it wasn't love or honesty or common decency. I was young then, of course. Too young. Do you still believe in it, just a little, or have you become just one more drug-peddler, dedicated to being rich and having a flash car with cunning anti-theft devices?"

"Oh, I still believe in it," Brewer assured her. "I really and sincerely do. I only use the acid wit to cover up that fact. Always speak the truth in a sarcastic tone of voice, and no one will ever find you out."

"No one?"

"Except you, of course. I let my guard down with you. I'm letting my guard down now, or hadn't you noticed? It came crashing down the moment I saw you in the pub. I should be busy breaking Simple Simon's legs, or persuading him that I might if he doesn't shape up, but I never had the heart for that kind of crap, and the moment I saw you . . . well, here we are. This is a *terrible* cup of coffee. How can you drink it black like that?" He put the cup down and moved closer to her, pretending that he was just pointing at her coffee cup.

"Our tastes change as we mature," she told him. She must have known that he wasn't moving closer to point to her coffee cup, but just for a moment she hesitated about backing away. He took that as a green light, but when he reached out for her she froze. He'd gone too fast.

"No, Bru," she said. "It's nothing like that. It really was just curiosity."

He didn't believe her. He took hold of her anyway, hoping that it might be the kind of stall that could still be over-ridden, although he knew that the odds were against him, for the time being. He tried to kiss her, but she wouldn't be kissed. He held her more firmly, but when she stopped struggling it wasn't surrender.

"You'd have to rape me," she said. "I don't think you want to do that, do you?"

He let go of her immediately. It certainly wasn't what he wanted, and it definitely wasn't his style.

"There's nothing I have to offer you any more, I suppose?" he said, not intending it to sound as bitchy as it did. "Nothing you want in return?"

She didn't look angry, but she didn't look apologetic either. "This was a mistake," she said. "It was silly."

"Not that silly," he assured her. "Whatever you were looking for back there, you were more likely to find in me than in those tattered slags you were talking to. You still are. What *were* you looking for? Not just something to relieve the boredom, surely."

"No," she said, positively. "Not just that. And you're right –

maybe I should have come looking for you in the first place. But it's nothing to do with sex, Bru, nor with the stuff you peddle as synthetic happiness. It's something else. You'd better go now."

"Why?" he riposted. "Is it time for your boyfriend to come out of his coffin? Oh, sorry – home from work, I mean. What exactly is it that he does?" He was *almost* tempted to make a crack about the plasma in the fridge, but he knew better. One of his golden rules was never to tell people he knew they had secrets until he'd figured out what the secrets were.

"I wouldn't like to keep you away from your own work for *too* long," she countered. "All those haemorrhoid creams and heartburn tablets have to be kept pure, don't they? And there's always more happiness to cook up while the plant's lying idle. You always were a busy man – that's why your sex life consisted of brief encounters with cheap whores."

The insults were too far out of date to hurt. The new generation of pharmaceuticals was way past the haemorrhoid and heartburn phase.

"I knew the acid wit was what you'd missed most," he came back, as heroically as he could. "You obviously missed it so much you stole the recipe."

He left after that – as politely as he could, given the circumstances.

It wasn't easy to get the car out of the basement, but he managed it eventually. He drove it home, possessed all the while by an icy calm.

He was sure that he'd see her again, even though he'd made such an unholy mess of things. He'd memorized the number inscribed on the phone in her hallway, and he knew she'd probably be on her own during working hours. Next time, he'd have a script ready, and he'd make up all the ground he'd lost.

He had to; it was a matter of pride.

Brewer made no attempt to put the pills or the plasma into analysis while his lab-assistants were still on site. Even Johanna wouldn't have known what he was doing, or why, and she knew better than to ask, but it was his habit to be discreet and he needed the equipment in the main lab to get the job done quickly. Johanna and Leroy weren't in the least surprised that he was still there when they completed the last of their own assignments a mere two hours into time-and-a-half and dropped the results on his desk. They thought of him, half-admiringly and half-pityingly, as a workaholic night-bird.

He bid them both a cheery goodbye, and switched on all

the privacy screens as soon as they were clear of the building.

Once he'd got the first set of analyses started his curiosity faded away into the methodical routines. It wasn't until he was certain that it was a *very* exotic protein that a certain excitement began to force its way through his controlled state of mind. All proteins in the public domain were intrinsically boring; these days, one had to go a long way out of that domain to find anything really weird. This one was from way back in the wilderness.

When the first sample had cleared the initial stage of analysis he set the replicated samples of the second compound going, but he held off on the plasma lest he get into a tangle. The first rule of good lab practice was to take things in order.

As soon as Brewer had an amino-acid map of the first compound, and while he was still waiting for its 3-D configuration, he checked the newest edition of the encyclopedia. He knew that the unknown wouldn't be on file – these days, nobody ever filed anything until they were sure it was worthless, and that usually took a long time – but he expected the book to throw up a few probable template-molecules based on common base-clusters. Practically all novel proteins were designed by computer-programmes which tried to juggle known activity-sites into more interesting or more economical configurations, so it was usually possible to guess what kind of base an innovation had started from and what kind of effect the designer might be trying to enhance.

It didn't take him long to figure out that he wasn't dealing with any of his usual fields. Whatever pill number one was supposed to do it hadn't any obvious potential to mimic or interact with neurotransmitters or amygdalar encephalins. Nor had it any detectable kinship with the currently-favoured avenues of research into cell-repair and tissue-rejuvenation. That probably meant that it had nothing to do with Jenny's new look – but if it had, then it really must be something odd, something unexpected.

It didn't take long to find out that the same was true of type two – by which time Brewer's instincts were beginning to detect a suspiciously *natural* ambience.

Brewer was not at all enthused by the thought that the samples might be nothing more than lumps of raw-material churned out by DNA of unknown function that had been cloned from some obscure plant or bacterium in the faint hope that it might turn out to be interesting. Computerized design hadn't quite driven the old pick-and-mix methods to extinction and there wasn't a nation in the world that didn't have its own mock-patriotic Ark project dedicated to gene-banking as many local species as could be identified, in the faint hope of preserving data that would otherwise be lost to the attrition of routine extinction.

The trouble with *natural* proteins, of course, was that they might be geared to functions which had no relevance at all to human beings, slotted into biochemical systems which had long been discarded by the higher animals – or, indeed, all animals of whatever height. The majority of exotic natural proteins sufficiently stable to be incorporated into pills were structural materials devoid of any real physiological significance. Brewer tried to console himself with the thought that nobody would keep those kinds of samples in his bathroom cabinet, but it wasn't until he had the 3-D configurations, and could trace the pattern of active sites, that he became morally certain that he wasn't dealing with any mere building-blocks for fibres or cell-walls.

Unfortunately, it still wasn't clear exactly what the relevant physiological activity might be. The proteins certainly weren't psychotropics, and if they were cosmetics of some kind they were no common-or-garden patent-avoiders.

When he decided that it was time he put the plasma-like stuff into the system he had been studying his screen intently for at least twenty minutes, virtually oblivious to his surroundings. While he reached out to pick up the specimen-bottle containing the straw-coloured liquid his eyes still lingered on the screen. It wasn't until his groping hand failed to make contact with the bottle that he looked sideways, and then up.

There was no way to tell how long the invader had been standing there, not six feet away, watching him. Brewer had never been so startled in all his life – but he had never before been confronted by anything so nearly impossible. His electronic defences were, as he had assured Jenny, glorious in their subtlety. How glorious, therefore, must be the subtlety of the man who now stood before him, having hacked his way through the undergrowth of passwords and booby-traps?

There was nothing particularly striking about the invader himself, apart from his lustrously pale skin, his remarkably dark eyes and his astonishing aptitude for silence. He didn't seem unusually menacing, although there was a peculiar glint in his near-black eyes which suggested that he might become menacing if crossed.

Brewer desperately wanted to say something that would save a little face, but he just wasn't up to it. All he said, in the end, was: "Who the hell are you?" He was uncomfortably aware of the fact that it was a very tired cliché.

"You've seen me before, Mr Brewer," the unwelcome visitor told him. "Several times, in fact." He had a slight accent of some kind but it wasn't readily identifiable.

Brewer stared hard at the invader's face, certain that he would have remembered those coal-black eyes and that remarkable complexion. He had method enough left in him to realize that if that were so, those were exactly the features he must set aside, in order to concentrate on the rest. When he did that, he got a dim impression of *where* he had seen the man – but, not, alas, the least flicker of a name.

On the other hand, Brewer realized, given what he was doing and the way his uninvited guest had taken the trouble to sit around and wait for him to look up, there couldn't be much doubt about the invader's purpose in coming to call.

"Jenny said we had interests in common," he said, knowing that there was far too much lost ground to catch up but feeling that he had to try. "You see so many people, though – all those seminars, all those cunningly-contrived meetings where clients try to whip up competition in order to drive the tenders down. We were never formally introduced, were we? Funny how we can have so many mutual acquaintances, and not know one another at all."

"I know *you* very well," the stranger said. "I've heard a great deal about you, one way and another." There was suddenly something about his eyes that seemed profoundly unsettling, but there was as much sadness in it as threat.

Brewer, desperate to know exactly how much trouble he was in, tried to fathom the significance of *one way and another*. One way was obviously Jenny – but who was the other? The people Brewer met at conferences and the people he met in the course of his legitimate business had little or nothing to tell. He put two and two together and hoped he wasn't making five.

"You're the guy who's been taking over my runners, aren't you?" Brewer said, "Jenny put you on to them – to Simon and the others. Is that what she was doing in the Goat and Compasses today? Making deliveries?"

The stranger shook his head. "She doesn't make deliveries," he said. "She has nothing to do with that aspect of the business at all – except, of course, that she did give me the information which allowed me to make contact with some of your agents. I only needed a handful of names; the rest I did myself."

"Did she tell you where to find me?" Brewer asked, warily. He wondered whether the accent might be German, or maybe Serbian.

The stranger shook his head. "That was Simon," he said. "You embarrassed him. He told me you were after me – and why you suddenly stopped asking questions. Jenny doesn't know that I know you were at the flat, any more than she knows about the things you took. It was careless of me to leave them lying around, but I simply didn't realize that you might be able to walk through my security systems as easily as I could walk through yours."

That was a scoring point; without Jenny's help, Brewer would never have been able to worm his way into the stranger's flat, and they both knew it.

"Fate seems to have been determined to throw us together," Brewer observed. "Did you pick up my ex-girlfriend solely in order to find out about my distribution system, or did she just happen to give you the idea of making a little extra money that way?"

"What do you make of the proteins?" the other asked, pointedly ignoring the question. "How much have you figured out?"

What Brewer had figured out was that the one advantage left to him might well be that the other man couldn't possibly know how little he knew, so he wasn't about to tell him.

"Jenny's looking very well," Brewer commented, instead. "Rather better than you are, I think – which presumably means that you're testing your freshly-hatched miracles on her before applying them to yourself. Sensible enough, I suppose, but not entirely *sporting*. No wonder Simon thinks you're a creep. You'll want to do a few more runs before you're certain, of course. Better safe than sorry." That was the best he could do without admitting that he hadn't a clue what the proteins were for, or where they might have come from.

"We're not enemies, Mr Brewer," said the man with the disturbing eyes. "We're not even rivals – not really."

Brewer didn't understand that move either. Was the stranger trying to make a deal? If so, he thought, the best thing to do was play along with it. "Sure," he replied. "We're both on the same side: the side of the psychotropic revolution. Marked down by destiny to be the midwives of the *Übermenschen*."

"Jenny told me all about that," the stranger admitted. "She told me that you were sincere but I wasn't convinced."

"Is that why you're here – to be convinced?" Brewer couldn't believe it was as simple as that.

"Not exactly," said the dark-eyed man. "I came out of curiosity. While I'm here, though, I suppose I ought to recover the things you stole, and obliterate all the records of your analyses." He stressed the word *all* very faintly, perhaps to remind Brewer that memories were records too.

"I can understand that," Brewer said. "I'm irredeemably curious myself."

The stranger hesitated, as if he were hovering on the brink of some make-or-break decision. Then, making up his mind, he set the specimen-bottle down on the bench beside him and took something out of his pocket.

Brewer recognised the device immediately. It was a sterile pack containing a disposable drug-delivery device: what the tabloids had taken to calling a "smart syringe" since it had become the darling of all the hardcore mainliners. The instrument wasn't so very smart, but it *was* subtle; its bioconductors could deliver drugs to underlying tissues without ripping up the superficial tissues. Deeper probes did tend to break a few capillaries, but they only left a little round mark like a bruise – or a lovebite.

"Need a fix?" Brewer asked, uneasily.

With a dexterity that might have been admirable in other circumstances the stranger took the cap off the specimen bottle one-handed and carefully transferred the fluid to the barrel of the device.

"Keep your hands on the bench," the stranger instructed him.

Brewer instantly raised his hands from the bench and came to his feet. He wasn't being stubborn or heroic – it was just a reflex, animated by fear. He swung his fist, the way he'd seen a hundred men actors swing theirs in a hundred action-movies.

The dark-eyed man pivoted on his heel, and moved so fast that Brewer couldn't keep track of him. It might have been the blindness of Brewer's panic, but the speed of the man seemed supernatural. Brewer found himself reeling backwards, clutching his stomach. It hurt horribly, but he hadn't yet had the wind knocked out of him and he was able to lunge forward again, as if to tackle the other around the knees.

The second assault was no more effective than the first. The unseen blow to his head hurt even worse than the smack in the belly. It didn't leave Brewer unconscious, but it knocked him down and it knocked him silly. He was on all fours, wondering whether he could get up again, when he felt a foot in the small of his back, forcing him further down. He pressed upwards against the force, but he couldn't resist it. Once he was flat on the ground, with an irresistible weight bearing down on him, he felt the pressure-pad of the smart syringe at his neck.

The contact lasted at least twenty seconds, but there was nothing Brewer could do to break it. It didn't hurt – that, after all, was the whole point of smart syringes.

Brewer was slightly surprised that he was still conscious when the instrument as withdrawn, although there was no earthly reason to suppose that the straw-coloured liquid might have been an anaesthetic. By the time the weight was removed from his back the pain in his head was easily bearable, but he still felt nauseous. He thought it best to stay down until he was sure he could stand up straight. He was dimly conscious of the dark-eyed man moving to the bench where the pills were.

Eventually, he picked himself up, and met the stare of those remarkable eyes. "Thanks," he said, putting on the bravest face he could. "I thought I'd lost my chance to analyse the stuff."

"You've got every chance," the dark-eyed man assured him. "But there really isn't any hurry. Not now. You know where to find me when you're fully prepared for a rational discussion."

Having said that, the stranger simply turned away, walked to the door of the lab, and went out. It shouldn't have been easy to exit the building without the proper codes, but Brewer didn't suppose the unwelcome visitor would get into any difficulties.

A quick check told him that the remaining pills were gone and that the data displayed on his screen had all been dumped. It wasn't a thorough job, though; he probably had enough traces left in the equipment to do another run, and he ought to be able to recover the ghosted data from the hard disk. The dark-eyed man didn't seem to care what Brewer had found out, or what he still might find out. Brewer wondered exactly what the mysterious stranger had meant by "fully prepared". It couldn't be a simple matter of attitude.

Brewer used an ordinary hypodermic to extract some blood from the discoloured patch at the side of his neck, but he didn't start any kind of immediate analysis; he stuck it in the refrigerator and hurried out into the night. He didn't stop until he reached a payphone.

He used a generic phonecard of the kind anyone could buy at the checkout in any supermarket but he was careful to route the call through Talinn; the people whose help he needed preferred to deal with careful customers.

It was so late by the time Brewer got back on the road that Simple Simon was at home, sleeping the sleep of the unintimidated. Unsurprisingly, he was alone. His door had three good locks on it and his window had two, but the glass was so old it hadn't been proofed against solvents, so Brewer was able to get in without disturbing his host and conduct a rapid but thorough search.

He found Simon's supply easily enough, buried beneath the youth's collection of business cards. It was a collection like any other; Simon stripped telephone booths the way younger kids stripped foreign stamps from used envelopes. Brewer pocketed all but a few of the pills. Then he positioned himself by the side of Simon's bed.

He filled a common-or-garden hypodermic syringe that he hadn't bothered to sterilise, and pressed it suggestively to Simon's throat while switching on the bedside lamp. He wished that he'd made more effort to cultivate the expertise of intimidation. No matter how hard one tried to be businesslike, it seemed, there was something about the drug business that resisted rational reform.

"Don't jump, Simon," he advised, as the boy's eyes flew open. "Quite apart from the fact that you'd impale your Adam's apple, you'd get a shot of something very nasty indeed."

Simon spluttered and twitched a bit, but he got the message.

"What is this?" he complained.

"Tell me about Jenny's boyfriend, Simon," Brewer said. "Tell me everything you know, and tell it fast."

"What's in the syringe?" Simon wanted to know.

"Just something to set your nerves jangling. It won't do any permanent damage, but it'll make every kind of sensory experience excruciatingly painful for at least twenty-four hours. If you don't want to live through the most godawful day imaginable, tell me about the guy who's fitting you out with your new supplies. Tell me *everything*, and pray that it might be enough."

Simon had been about to protest that he didn't know anything at all but he changed his mind. "He's a chemist, just like you," he said, as if that might make the news more welcome. "Analyses stuff for the government, or anybody else who pays . . . he says his name's Anthony Marklow, but I don't think he's even English. His stuff's not *better*, just different. I'm not about to stop using yours, believe me. It's just . . ."

"Marklow, Simon. Tell me about *Marklow*. What's Jenny been doing for him? Is she selling stuff to the whores – or giving it away? What is it?"

"I don't know! What's the matter with you? What was all that stuff about not being a gangster, hey? What was all that stuff about *room for everybody in a boom market?*"

"This isn't about economic competition, Simon. It's about something more serious. Marklow's not just hawking happy pills. He's doing something else, and I need to know what it is. *Now*, Simon. What's he doing *as well as* cutting into my trade?"

"How the fuck should I know?" the youth wailed, with patent sincerity. "I just . . . you'll have to ask the girls. Jenny talks to the girls, not to me. If she gives them something, they sure as hell don't tell me."

With the forefinger of his free hand Brewer pulled his collar down and pointed to the side of his neck, where there was a blue mark that would soon turn purple, and then brown.

Simon's frightened eyes followed the gesture with mesmeric concentration.

"Have you seen anyone sporting marks like this?" Brewer asked.

"Sure," Simon told him. "I thought it was funny – the doc doesn't usually shoot stuff into a person's neck, and you wouldn't think the girls would do it to themselves. Why . . . ?" He stopped, evidently wondering how the mark on Brewer's neck had got there but not daring to ask.

"How many?" Brewer wanted to know.

"I've seen three," Simon said, implying that there might be dozens or hundreds more. "Why the neck?"

"Maybe he doesn't have time to get them to roll their sleeves up," Brewer replied, drawing the point of the syringe an inch or two away from Simon's throat. A more likely explanation was that the target was the carotid artery, which would feed the drug straight into the brain – except that his brain still seemed to be working normally. He wasn't high and he wasn't dopey; whatever had been shot into his flesh hadn't been a psychotropic. Maybe the hit had been aimed at one of the brain's associated bodies. If so, the pituitary had to be the favourite with the pineal close behind. The pituitary was the master gland, the dispatcher controlling the hormonal couriers which kept the body in order. The pineal still carried an aura of Cartesian mystery that had intrigued a legion of modern investigators.

Simon freed one of his naked arms from the duvet and reached out to push Brewer's hypodermic even further away. Brewer let him do it; if the boy had known anything more about Marklow he'd have spilled it.

"How long has Jenny looked the way she does now?" Brewer asked.

"Don't know," Simon replied, yet again. "She started coming around three, maybe four months ago. Every three weeks or so. Like I say, she doesn't talk to me. Just to the girls. I didn't know she was with the creepy guy, at first. I saw him pick her up one night. I've seen them together a couple of times since, always after dark. I thought . . ." He trailed off, as if no longer certain of what he had thought.

"Why *creepy*, Simon? What's so creepy about him?" Brewer realized as he posed the question that it might be important. "Creepy" wasn't the kind of word people like Simon usually bandied about; it was a whole generation out of date.

"Short for creepy-crawly," Simon said. "It's those eyes – the way they can make you feel, like spiders running down your spine. He makes out he's being generous – free samples, nice prices – but there's something *behind* it all. Not exactly a threat, not like *you'd better deal or else* . . . more like *I know you better than you know yourself.* What would *you* call him?"

Brewer thought about the impossibly dark, impossibly empty but unsettling eyes. "I don't know," he confessed. He thought about Jenny's miraculously blue eyes and marvellously clear skin, and added: "Whatever he's come up with, it cuts deeper than happy pills or dream machines."

"I could try to get some for you," Simon said. He was obviously anxious to make up for petty treasons past now that he knew what Brewer was capable of, violence-wise.

"You're too late," Brewer told him, grimly. "I already got my free sample." He went to the drawer where Simon kept his collection and grabbed a handful of the advertising cards. He threw them at Simon, then went back for a second handful.

"I want a number, Simon," he said. "I want to meet a girl with a bruise just like mine but older – a *lot* older."

Simon was about to protest that he hadn't any idea which girl went with which card, but he thought better of it. He was a dedicated hobbyist, after all; he had a collector's pride. It took him a couple of minutes, but he found what he was looking for. Brewer took it.

"You'd better get that great gaping hole in your window fixed," Brewer told the boy. "There's a terrible draught in here."

When his staff turned up the following morning Brewer told them to drop everything else and concentrate on a rush job. They didn't ask any questions; they would assume that it was an industrial espionage job beyond the pale of legality but it wasn't the first time they'd done that kind of work and it wouldn't be the last. They went to it with a will; it was a welcome break from the usual routine.

It only took Brewer fifteen minutes to recover the data Jenny's boyfriend had erased. As soon as he had it he passed it on to Johanna. "If you can figure out what they're for," he said. "You win a nice prize. You won't find anything like them in the patent files, but there has to be something, somewhere, which will give us a clue. A protein is a protein is a protein."

"Any clues?" Johanna asked.

"They might be something to do with tissue rejuvenation, but not in any of the conventional approaches."

She raised her eyebrows at that and glanced at the little bladder-packs on his desk, which were full of rich red blood. He nodded. "Same sort of thing," he said. "Field tests are already under way. That's why we have a lot of catching up to do. The compounds you're looking at are probably supportive; I'm going after the chap they support."

That was another clue and she acknowledged it with a nod. She knew that a "chap", in this context, was probably a virus vector – something that had to be kept in a suspension containing living tissue.

If Johanna saw the mark on Brewer's neck she didn't give it a second glance; she probably thought he'd spent the night with a girl. He *had*, of course, spent the last few hours of darkness with a sleepy whore, but she hadn't been in the least amorous. She'd been very expensive, but not by virtue of her business acumen; her reluctance to talk had been perfectly genuine – but she was, after all, a whore. It had only been a matter of fixing the right price.

The whore hadn't known Marklow's name. She'd only seen him three times. He'd been very polite, she said, but there was something about those eyes – as if they could look right *into* you and see the blood coursing through your veins. Jenny had persuaded her to take part in the "secret experiment", using her own improved appearance as a lure. The drug had been pitched to her as a cosmetic treatment, not as any kind of elixir of life: plastic surgery without the knife.

"A couple of days after the first shot I got itchy," the whore had told him. "Jenny told me to expect that, and not to scratch, but I couldn't help scratching a bit. It keeps coming back, especially on sunny days, and I have to wear sunglasses all day except when it's cloudy, but I've got more used to it and the pills help. I feel a bit nauseous too, mostly in the mornings – like I was pregnant. Lost weight nice and steady, but that's partly the high-protein diet. I don't mind the itching, really – it's like I can feel it working. It *is* working."

"Nothing else?" Brewer had asked, insistently.

"Only the dreams," she told him. "Jenny warned me about those, too, but I like them. They're fun."

"What kind of dreams?"

"Vampire dreams. Nightmares, some might say, but they don't scare *me*."

"Vampire dreams? What's that supposed to mean?" Somehow, he'd wished he could be more surprised by the introduction of *that* word.

"Sometimes, I dream I'm a bat – well, not a bat, exactly, but something *like* a bat. Flying by night, seeing but not seeing. Other times, I'm more like a wolf. You should see the moon! Huge and red as blood. It's great. The hunt, the kill, lapping up the blood. If that's how animals feel, I want to come back as a lion. Jenny says it's just the diet, but I reckon it's memories of other lives coming to the surface. Why else would we all have the *same* dreams? These shrinks who take you back to Roman times and ancient Egypt are full of crap. We were animals for billions of years, you know, before we ever became human. Race memory, isn't that what they call it?"

Brewer hadn't bothered to inform her that neither bats nor wolves were numbered among the human race's remoter ancestors. He had agreed with her that shrinks practising past-life regression were full of crap, but hadn't added that in his opinion her own theory was by no means empty of it. He'd been too busy thinking about the dreams. They were the oddest thing of all – and thus, perhaps, the most significant. He remembered the haunted look in Jenny's blue eyes. One reason why she'd taken him home was to make him see how well she'd done since he dumped her, but there had been another. Whatever had been done to her had made her anxious, and a little bit lonely.

Was that, he wondered, the effect of her vampire dreams?

Brewer hadn't felt any itching yet, but he wasn't in any hurry and he didn't intend to go out in daylight until he had the problem cracked, at least insofar as it *could* be cracked by the equipment in the lab. Nor was he intending to sleep, let alone to dream. He was a chemist, after all; he had ways of avoiding the need for sleep at least for a couple of days.

He knew that he couldn't go back to Andrew Marklow without a deal to make, and he wasn't sure yet what kind of deal there was to be made. A promise of silence wasn't enough, for him or for Marklow. Marklow wasn't afraid that he'd go to the authorities – and not just because he figured Brewer couldn't do that without imperilling his own illicit operation. Marklow wasn't afraid, period. Brewer admired that, but it also made him anxious. Despite his chemical expertise, he'd never come close to mastering the art of not being afraid.

As things turned out, it didn't take a genius to locate the stranger in the blood-samples. The "chap" wasn't a virus at all; he was something much bigger. If he'd had a cell-wall he'd have qualified as a bog-standard bacterium but he didn't. The only label Brewer knew that might apply to him was *rickettsia.*

The only rickettsia Brewer knew, even by repute, was the one which caused Rocky Mountain spotted fever, but when he went to the on-line encyclopedia he found that there were a hundred more on record – none of which bore any very intimate resemblance to the one that had now taken up residence somewhere in the vicinity of his brain, and was presumably reproducing like crazy as well as retuning his endocrinal orchestra.

There were, Brewer noted, two significant properties that rickettsias had. Having no cell-walls, they were immune to antibiotics. By the same token, however, they were very difficult to transfer from host to host. That was why Rocky Mountain spotted fever, although incurable, hadn't ever managed to cause an epidemic. People who caught it had it for life – which hadn't been very long in the days before doctors developed palliatives for the nastier symptoms – but they didn't usually pass it on to others. Even their spouses weren't significantly endangered; it wasn't an STD. Theory said you could only get infected through a open cut – or, of course, a hypodermic syringe, dumb or smart.

Brewer hesitated for a few minutes before giving the information he had gleaned to Johanna and Leroy, but he figured that the time for keeping things strictly to himself was past. Until he had been infected himself there'd been no urgency at all. Now that he had found out that what he had was exactly the same as what the whore had – and presumably, therefore, exactly what Jenny had – the urgency was somewhat less than it might have been, but time was still pressing. He needed all the reliable help he could get.

"If you want a DNA-profile of something *that* big," Johanna pointed out, "It'll take us weeks. Maybe months. Even if it's a variant of one of the recorded species we'd have to start from scratch. Nobody's ever sequenced a rickettsia – or if they have, they haven't published. Do you think the pill-proteins are products of the rickettsial genes?"

"No," said Brewer. "I suspect that the pill-proteins are meant to alleviate some of the symptoms of the rickettsial infection." If that was true, it wasn't good news. It meant that he needed the pills himself if he were to enjoy the benign effects of his minuscule passengers without suffering the downside of their presence in his system.

"Infection?" Johanna echoed, anxiously. It was one of the words that always sounded alarm bells in a lab like this, even when nothing was coking but everyday commercial products sent for routine checking.

"It's okay," he assured her. "You can only catch it through an open cut, and it's difficult even then. This one's *supposed* to be benign, but there has to be a catch."

"There's a catch all right," she said – but she was only talking about the '98 protocols regarding the legality of engineering human-infective agents. Nobody expected them to hold, even in the medium term. Everybody in the business knew someone, somewhere, who was working in the confident expectation that the new millennium would bring in a whole new set of rules and regulations, elastic enough to license *anything* provided only that it were done discreetly. Andrew Marklow might be ahead of his time, but not that far ahead of it.

The only problem, Brewer thought, was that breaking into other people's labs and shooting human-infective agents into their carotid arteries couldn't meet anyone's definition of "discretion".

"I don't need a gene map," he told Johanna. "I just need everything we can get before nightfall."

"What happens at nightfall?" she asked.

"I have to see a man about a disease," he replied, as the phone at his elbow began to ring. He picked it up immediately, but it was only a message telling him where to go to collect a message from Talinn.

It was Jenny who answered when Brewer presented himself at the door of Marklow's building, and Jenny who came to the apartment door when he'd negotiated his way through the various layers of security. The first thing she said to him was: "You're a thief."

"And you're a whore," he said, "but we've both been taken for a ride. Your boyfriend always knew I'd come looking for him. He didn't move in on my operation to make a little extra money; he did it to attract my attention."

"Don't flatter yourself, Bru," she replied – but he wasn't flattering himself. He knew that he'd already been pencilled in for recruitment when Jenny's urge to show off and rub his nose in what he'd lost had kicked things off prematurely. Sooner or later, he'd have been invited up here, and presented with a offer he couldn't refuse.

The man who called himself Anthony Marklow was standing by the window looking out over the river. He didn't offer to shake hands and he didn't offer Brewer a drink. Nor did Jenny; she just went to the sofa and threw herself down in an exaggeratedly careless manner she'd probably borrowed from some American super-soap. Brewer remained standing, so that he could meet Count Dracula face to face.

Brewer was reasonably certain by now that Marklow *was* Count Dracula – maybe not literally, but as near as made no difference. His friendly neighbourhood hackers hadn't managed to prove the case – in fact, they'd been so embarrassed about their failure to come up with anything concrete regarding Marklow's true identity that they'd forsaken half their fee, which had only left them enough stuff to stay high till 2020 – but the void of information they'd exposed was far too deep to be any mere accident. The fact that computers had only been around for a couple of generations meant that, in theory, the early history of anyone over fifty could be utterly untraceable, but the absence of anyone behind the Marklow mask was far more pronounced than that.

"You said that you weren't convinced when Jenny told you I was serious about the genetic revolution," Brewer said, when the other transfixed him with those dark persuasive eyes, "but you *did* want to be convinced, didn't you?"

"I was interested," Marklow admitted. "It's time for me to move my personal project on to a bigger stage, and it would be very convenient to have some expert help."

"You took a big risk," Brewer said. "Suppose I were to start looking for a cure? I could find one, you know, given time. Just because ricksettsia are immune to conventional antibiotics doesn't mean that they can't be stopped. Big bugs have little bugs upon their backs to bite 'em . . ."

"And little bugs have littler bugs, and so *ad infinitum*," Marklow finished for him. "It *is* a problem. You're just a small-time hack with delusion of grandeur but there are plenty of researchers out there with the equipment and the knowledge necessary to tailor a virus to attack the agent. I've been safe from harassment for a long time, but the race will soon be on again."

"Again?" Brewer queried. He was pretty sure that he knew what Marklow meant, but he wanted confirmation.

What the vampire meant was there had been a time when he had been utterly ignorant of the nature of his own condition, quite incapable of controlling it. In those days, he must have been very vulnerable, even though the legions of would-be Van Helsings who'd have staked him, beheaded him or burned him undead had even less understanding than he had. Brewer still wanted to hear him confirm all that, and he also wanted to know what sort of timescale they were talking about. He wanted to know how long Count Dracula, *alias* Andrew Marklow, had been undead, because he wanted to know what kind of life-expectancy he and Jenny might now have – or might yet obtain, as the prototype was refined and perfected.

For the time being, though, Marklow had no intention of giving too much away. Fist, he wanted to hear what Brewer had to say – and if the expression in his eyes was anything to go by, what Brewer said was going to have to be good. The age of Jurassic crack-dealers might be long gone, but there were still plenty of individuals in the world who could and would kill without compunction, and without the least fear of reprisal.

"I took a little nap before I came out," Brewer said, hoping that he sounded sufficiently relaxed. "I wanted to see what the dreams were like. I wasn't convinced that anything could actually do that:

play dreams inside a man's head like tapes playing on a VCR. But that's what animal dreams are like, isn't it? In animals the arena of dreams is straightforwardly functional; it's for practising instinctive behaviours and connecting up the appropriate neurochemical payoffs. It's for putting the pleasure into the necessities of life. For a few minutes I even wondered whether the whore might be right and it might actually be an ancestral memory of some kind, secreted into a vector by accident . . . but that still didn't make sense. Bats and wolves aren't related that way."

Marklow nodded, but there was no sign of approval in his brooding stare.

"After that," Brewer said, "I wondered about the possibility of an extraterrestrial origin – alien DNA strayed from a meteorite or a crashed UFO – but that was only because I'd watched too much television. The real answer was much simpler. I only had to remember the *other* disease which operates the same way – and works the trick even though it's a mere virus, fifty genes short of a chromosome."

He paused for dramatic effect. It was Jenny who obligingly said: "What *other* disease?"

"Rabies," Brewer told her. "You see, the rabies virus isn't very infectious. Even if it's dumped straight into an open wound with a supportive supply of saliva it frequently fails to take, and in order to achieve *that* it has to bring about some pretty extreme behaviour modifications in its victims. Hydrophobia, reckless aggression . . . a whole new set of meta-instincts. That's the price of its survival. It's a hell of a clumsy way to get by. Who'd have thought that a mechanism like that could have evolved *twice*? Perhaps it didn't. Perhaps the virus is just a spin-off from the rickettsia. Perhaps what you and I have is the Daddy rabies, and the one the mad dogs have is just the prodigal son."

"I don't have any kind of rabies," she told him, frostily. She wasn't nearly as outraged as Brewer had hoped she'd be.

"No," Brewer said, "you don't – not as long as you keep taking the palliatives. Even then . . . this is a carefully-engineered strain, selected to keep the good effects while losing the bad ones. But Mr Marklow has a kind of rabies – don't you, Mr Marklow? You have the original – the kind of rabies that our ancestors called vampirism."

"I *had* the disease which *your* ancestors called vampirism," Marklow riposted. "Now, I only have a modified form of it which is much more like the strain with which the subjects of my field-trial have been infected. You might say that I'd been cured, provided that you weren't too fussy about the definition of the word *cure.* I've traded an awkward but valuable infection for its civilized cousin, which is equally valuable but far less awkward."

"How much less awkward?" Brewer wanted to know.

"Did you bring the results of your analyses?" the ex-vampire countered.

Brewer pulled a sheaf of papers out of the inside pocket of his jacket. It was only a dozen sheets of A4 but there was a lot of data packed into the dozen sheets and he'd summarized his conclusions very tersely.

While Marklow looked at the data Brewer studied Jenny, searching for the slightest indication of an unfortunate side-effect. The mark on her neck told him that she still needed booster shots – that even if it were shot right into the carotid artery the rickettsia still had difficulty taking up permanent residence in the brain and its associated structures – but that wasn't bad news. If he were to carry forward Marklow's grand scheme for the remaking of human nature he could certainly maintain his supplies of the rickettsia, given that he had a readily available culture-medium.

"That's good," Marklow said, when he'd scanned the familiar information and read the judgmental comments. "Your staff evidently make up an effective team, and you obviously trust them. How much of the whole picture have you let them see?"

"They know that there's a whole new approach to rejuvenative technology and life-extension – and they have enough of a basis to start their own research along the same lines, individually or in alliance. They don't know that the new approach is really an old approach. They know I got the data from somewhere else but they think it was one more commission. They don't know that it was a gift from Count Dracula. They don't know that one of the blood-bags was mine, so they don't know I'm a carrier. *How much less awkward?*"

Marklow smiled. It wasn't a particularly predatory smile. "I no longer have any real compulsion to bite or stab my fellow creatures and apply my slavering lips to the wounds," he said. "The dreams still frighten me a little – I don't suppose I'll ever be able to take the innocent pleasure in them that my new generation of converts can – but they're no longer a curse that I have to fight with every last vestige of my strength."

He paused briefly. The expression in his eyes was unfathomable but his voice was gentle and regretful. "I did have to fight it, you know," he said, sounding as if he genuinely wanted to be believed. "It was the price of survival in the modern world. I had to remain hidden, unknown . . . I had to become a figure of legend, a mere superstition. I saw what happened to others of my kind who couldn't master their appetites. There are a thousand ways to die, you see, even for . . . someone like me. We did our best to spread rumours to the contrary, but our rumours always had to compete with *theirs*. The confusion worked to our benefit, in some ways, but not in others . . .

"I've been alone for a long time, but I knew that science would save me. I knew that there would be a revolution some day that would allow me to transcend my monstrousness and become a true immortal. I knew that when that happened, I could rejoin the human race and become its benefactor, changing evil into good. I knew that there would come a time when I could look for company again – for *congenial* company."

Brewer wasn't sure whether the adjective referred to Jenny, or to him, or to both of them, but he couldn't resist the temptation to feign misunderstanding. "I guess a cohort of whores is about as congenial as you can get," he said, "if you're that way inclined."

He cast a calculatedly negligent glance in Jenny's direction, and saw that he had wounded her, but Marklow remained unmoved. If the ex-vampire was as old as Brewer suspected, he was probably unmovable. He'd probably been undead for a very long time – but at least he'd had nightmares all the while. There had been a taint of Hell in his unholy existence, and might be still, even in a world which was on the verge of conquering all the Hells of old: disease, death, pain and misery.

"Where should I have looked for volunteers?" Marklow asked, in all apparent earnest. "Prisons? Cardboard City?"

"Old people's homes?" Brewer countered, not at all earnestly. "Not sufficiently unobtrusive, I suppose. You do plan to remain unobtrusive, I suppose, even when you start serious marketing. The rich will want to keep it to themselves, of course. They appreciate confidentiality. Vampires, the lot of them – they think of mere human beings as cattle. That's why you thought of me when you wondered how best to expand your operation, I suppose. You think I'm a kind of vampire too, because I sell illegal happy pills to pimps and whores, kids and hackers."

"You're not any *real* kind of vampire yet," Marklow responded, mildly. "You'll have to work at it. It sometimes takes half a dozen shots before the rickettsias are permanently established. But once they're set, they're set for life – and that could be a *long* time."

"How long?" Brewer wanted to know.

"We'll just have to wait and see," Count Dracula told him. "We're dealing with a new strain, after all."

"How good was the old strain?" Brewer persisted.

"I don't know," Marklow replied. "the oldest men I ever knew had forgotten long ago how old they were. Arithmetic hadn't been invented when they were young. Nor had writing – but fire had. Fire and wooden spears. By the time writing was invented the war was almost lost. The rickettsia almost went the way of the mammoth and the sabre-toothed tiger, and the thousand other species neolithic man hounded to extinction. Mercifully, it survived. Mercifully, I survived with it. Now, the new era is dawning. Soon, I won't have to hide any more. Together, you and I and all of Jenny's friends . . . we shall be the midwives of the *Übermenschen*, as you so tactfully put it."

Brewer could see that Jenny felt uncomfortable. She knew that an important boundary had been crossed when Marklow first allowed the word "vampire" to cross his lips. He was exposed now, and so was she. She was afraid – but Marklow wasn't. He had grown out of fear long ago. He still retained the ability to terrify, but he couldn't identify with those he terrified. He gave the impression of knowing more about his victims than they knew themselves, but he didn't. He thought that he was still, essentially, a man – but he didn't know *human* beings at all. Perhaps it had been a mistake for him to try so hard to become harmless, to become a saint instead of a devil.

"Togetherness," Brewer told him, sardonically, "is a wonderful thing."

Bang on cue, the doorbell rang. Not the bell that rang when someone was downstairs, outside the reinforced doors of the building but the discreet chime which signalled that someone was at the door of the apartment.

Marklow knew as well as Brewer did that anyone with the skill to get that far without being detected didn't need to sound the chime – that the gesture was a kind of mockery.

"Don't get up," Brewer said to Jenny. "I think that's for me."

Brewer had instructed the man with the rifle not to take any chances; he had seen how quickly Marklow could move and how powerfully he could hit out. The marksman fired as soon as he was sure of his shot, and Marklow slumped to the floor.

It was the shock of the impact that had felled him but the ex-vampire's attempt to rise to his feet was all in vain. The tranquillizer-dart would have sent a horse to sleep, or even a tiger.

"Look after him," Brewer said, as the collection squad went to pick up the body. "He's an endangered species. Make sure you put him in a nice strong cage – and be careful when he wakes up. I dare say he can still bite, when the mood takes him."

Jenny had got up from the settee. She still looked like a minor character in some Hollywood super-soap, but now she seemed to think that her face was in close-up and that her features had better start running the gamut of the emotions, at least from Alarm to Anxiety.

Brewer held the door open for the man from the ministry. "Jenny, this is Mr Smith," he said, over his shoulder. "He wants to you to give him a complete list of all the friends you introduced to Mr Marklow. It probably won't matter much if it isn't *quite* complete, but you'd gain a good deal of moral credit if it were – and from here on in it would be a good idea not to be overdrawn at the moral credit bank. I told your boyfriend the truth when I said that I could design a cure for what you have, given time and a big enough budget. If you want to hang on to your indigenous rickettsias you'll have to make yourself useful."

Mr Smith didn't smile. Brewer hadn't expected him to. Men from the ministry – *any* ministry – lost their smiling reflexes once they'd been in the job for a while.

"You *bastard*," Jenny said. "You sold us out!"

Brewer put on a show of being deeply wounded. "*I* sold *you* out! You were the one who told your new boyfriend all about my covert operations. You sold him my . . . business associates. You even sold him your old friends, as bankrupt stock at a knockdown price. Then he wanders into my top-security lab, calm as you please, beats me up and shoots me full of bugs – bugs whose not-so-remote ancestors have had him chewing bloody holes in anything and everything warm-blooded for hundreds, if not thousands, of years. Did he really think that was the right way to win me over – or was it your idea? You never did understand human nature, and he must have forgotten everything he learned when he was human himself. Not entirely surprising, I suppose, given that his disease made him closer kin to mad dogs and vampire bats. The only element of social intercourse he mastered was the art of staying hidden, masked by a legend that had become a joke . . . and in the end he even forgot *that*."

Jenny looked back at him with eyes that were almost as piercing, almost as threatening, as Anthony Marklow's – but they were still baby blue in colour, and she hadn't quite enough presence to carry off the act. She wasn't a *real* vampire, after all. She only had bad dreams.

"I thought you meant it," she said, feebly. "I really thought you meant all that stuff about being at the cutting edge of the next revolution – about the quest for immortality, the transcendence of all inherited limitations."

"I did mean it," he told her. "I still do. What do you think I'm doing here? It's a question of quality control. Did you think I could entrust this kind of work, and the rewards that are likely to flow from it, to someone like *him*? He's a fucking *vampire*, for God's sake!"

Jenny's burning gaze flickered from Brewer to the unsmiling Mr Smith and back again, as if to say: *What's he? What kind of quality control does he represent?*

What she actually said was: "Anthony would have cut you in. He'd have made you an equal partner. The establishment won't even cut you in. As soon as I tell this creep what he wants to know, you and I will be surplus to requirements. *They*'ll have it all."

"You watch too much television," Brewer told her. "The government isn't a conspiracy set up to control us. I *voted* for the government. I sure as hell never voted for Count Dracula. And your slang's out of date. Nobody except Simple Simon calls people *creeps* any more – and Simon's so sad he gets off on collecting the business cards from public phone booths."

"You couldn't stand it, could you?" she retorted. "You just couldn't stand seeing me like this. People you throw away are supposed to stay thrown away, aren't they, Bru? They aren't supposed to find someone better, to get their lives back on track. You did this because you're jealous – bitter and twisted and *jealous.*"

Brewer had to check Mr Smith's face to make sure that he hadn't cracked a smirk. Mr Smith was being very patient, even by the standards customarily observed by the establishment's bureaucrats.

"We have to leave, Jenny," Brewer said, quietly. "There are people waiting outside. The have to search the place, collect all *this.*" He waved a negligent hand at the books and CDs.

"They have no right," she whispered – but she didn't press the point. How could she? She knew as well as Brewer did that Anthony Marklow was guilty of any number of crimes, recent as well as ancient. She wasn't innocent herself – not according to the '98 protocols. In fact, she was a dangerous felon, not to mention a willing carrier of an illegally-engineered organism.

Brewer waited for her to fall into step with the man from the ministry and then he followed them, at a respectful distance.

He was confident that Jenny was wrong about him being a fool to trust the legitimate authorities. After all, he really had voted for them – and he'd taken care to post twenty copies of his twelve A-4 sheets to secret repositories all over the world, routed via Talinn and Tokyo, Ratzeburg and Palermo. Given that the net was still in its frontier phase, the chances of his new colleagues being able to locate and destroy them all were pretty slim.

He wished that he'd made more progress in the art of being intimidating, but he knew that even if he'd been a *real* gangster he couldn't possibly have come to a different decision. Even gangsters couldn't be entirely immune to the duties of citizenship; they were as dependent as anyone else on the solidarity and stability of the social order. The way he'd chosen would lead to wealth, and hence to power, as surely as any other – and by way of a bonus he'd have a special kind of fame thrown in.

From now until the end of time he'd be known as the man who'd finally put an end to the evil career of Count Dracula: the man who'd exposed the last undead vampire in the West for what he truly was.

A reputation like that would surely be enough to make eternal life worth living.

Michael Marshall Smith

Dear Alison

Michael Marshall Smith won the British Fantasy Award for Best Newcomer in 1991, his short stories "The Man Who Drew Cats" and "The Dark Land" won two consecutive British Fantasy Awards in 1991 and 1992, and he received another in 1996 for "More Tomorrow" (which was also nominated for a World Fantasy Award).

His début novel, Only Forward, *received excellent reviews and won The British Fantasy Society's August Derleth Award in 1995. He followed it with* Spares *(which was optioned for filming by Steven Spielberg's DreamWorks SKG) and* One of Us.

Smith's short fiction has appeared in The Best New Horror *and* The Year's Best Fantasy and Horror *series,* Dark Terrors *and* Dark Terrors 2, Dark Voices 2, 4, 5 *and* 6, Darklands *and* Darklands 2, Touch Wood: Narrow Houses Volume Two, The Mammoth Book of Zombies, The Mammoth Book of Werewolves, The Mammoth Book of Frankenstein, Lethal Kisses, A Book of Two Halves, Twists of the Tale: Cat Horror Stories, The Anthology of Fantasy & the Supernatural, Shadows Over Innsmouth, Omni, Chills, Peeping Tom *and* Interzone.

As the darkness spreads, it touches many innocent lives . . .

It is Friday the 25th of October, and beginning to turn cold. In the street outside my study window an eddy of leaves turns hectically, flecks of green and brown lively against the tarmac. Earlier this afternoon the sky was clear and blue, bright white clouds periodically changing the light which fell into the room; but now that light is fading, painting everything with a layer of grey dust. Smaller, browner leaves are falling on the other side of the street, collecting in a drift around the metal fence in front of the house opposite. I'll remember this. I remember most things. Everything goes in, and stays there, not tarnishing but bright like freshly-cut glass. A warehouse of experience which will never fade away, but stays there to remind me what it is I've lost.

I'm leaving in about half an hour. I'll post the keys back through the door, so you'll know there is no need to look for me. And a spare set's always useful. I've been building up to it all day, telling myself that I'd leave any minute now and spend the day waiting in the airport. But I always knew that I'd wait until this time, until the light was going. London is at its best in the autumn, and four o'clock is the autumn time. I'll put the heating on before I go.

I'm not sure what I'm going to do with this letter. I could print it out and put it somewhere, or take it with me and post it later. Or perhaps I should just leave it on the computer, hidden deep in a sub-folder, leaving it to chance whether it will ever be discovered. But if I do that then one of the children will find it first, and it's you I should be explaining this to, not Richard or Maddy; you to whom the primary apology is due.

I can't explain in person, because there wouldn't be any point. Either you wouldn't believe me, or you would: neither would change the facts or make them any better. In your heart of hearts, buried too firmly to ever reach conscious thought, you may already have begun to suspect. You've given no sign, but we've stopped communicating on those subtler levels and I can't really tell what you think any more. Telling you what you in some sense already know would just make you reject it, and me. And where would we go from there?

My desk is tidy. All of my outstanding work has been completed. All the bills are paid.

I'm going to walk. Not all the way – just our part. Down to Oxford Street. I'll cross the road in front of the house, then turn down that alley you've always been scared of. (I can never remember what it's called; but I do remember an evening when you forgot your fear long enough for it to be rather interesting). Then off down Kentish Town Road, past the Woolworth's and the Vulture's Perch pub, the mediocre sandwich bars and that shop the size of a football pitch which is filled only with spectacles. I remember ranting against the waste of space when you and I first met, and you finding it funny. I suppose the joke's grown old.

It's not an especially lovely area, and Falkland Road is hardly Bel Air. But we've lived here fifteen years, and we've always liked it, haven't we? At least until the last couple of years, when it started to curdle, when our love slowly froze; when I realized what was going to happen. Before that Kentish Town suited us well enough. We liked Cafe Renoir, where you could get a reasonable breakfast when the staff weren't feeling too cool to serve it to you. The Assembly House, wall-to-wall Victorian mirrors and a comprehensive selection of Irish folk on the jukebox. The corner store, where they always know what we want before we ask for it. All of that.

It was our place.

I couldn't talk to you about it when it started, because of how it happened. Even if it had come about some other way, I would probably have kept silent: by the time I realized what it meant there wasn't much I could do. I hope I'm right in thinking it's only the last two years which have been strained, that you were happy until then. I've covered my tracks as well as I could, kept it hidden. So many little lies, all of them unsaid.

It was actually ten years ago, when we had only been in this house a few years and the children were still young and ours. I'm sure you remember John and Suzy's party – the one just after they'd moved into the new house? Or maybe not: it was just one of many, after all, and perhaps it is only my mind in which it retains a peculiar luminosity. You'd just started working at Elders & Peterson, and weren't very keen on going out. You wanted a weekend with a clear head, to tidy up the house, do some shopping, to hang out without a hangover. But we decided we ought to go, and I promised I wouldn't get too drunk, and you gave me that sweet, affectionate smile which said you believed I'd try but that you'd still move the aspirin to beside the bed. We engaged our dippy babysitter, spruced ourselves up and went out hand in hand, feeling for once as if we were in our twenties again. I think we even splashed out on a cab.

Nice house, in its way, though we both thought it was rather big for just the two of them. John was just getting successful around then, and the size of the property looked like a bit of a statement. We arrived early, having agreed we wouldn't stay too late, and stood talking in the kitchen with Suzy as she chopped vegetables for the dips. She was wearing the Whistles dress which you both owned, and you and I winked secretly to each other: after much deliberation you were wearing something different. The brown Jigsaw suit, with earrings from Monsoon that looked like little leaves. I remember them clearly, as I remember everything now. Do you still have those earrings somewhere? I suppose you must, though I haven't seen you wearing them in a while. I looked for them this morning, thinking that you wouldn't miss them and I might take them with me. But they're buried somewhere, and I couldn't find them.

By ten the house was full and I was pretty drunk, talking hard and loud with John and Howard in the living room. I glanced around to check you were having a good enough time, and saw you leaning back against a table, a plastic cup of red wine hovering around your lips. You were listening to Jan bang on about something – her rubbish ex-boyfriend, probably. With your other hand you were fumbling in your bag for your cigarettes, wanting one pretty soon but trying not to let Jan see you weren't giving her familiar tale of woe your full attention. You were wonderful like that. Always doing the right thing, and in the right way. Always eager to be good, and not just so that people would admire you.

You finally found your packet, and offered it to Jan, and she took a cigarette and lit it without even pausing for breath, a particular skill of hers. As you raised your zippo to light your own you caught me looking at you. You gave a tiny wink, to let me know you'd seen me, and an infinitesimal roll of the eyes – but not enough to derail Jan. Your hand crept up to tuck your hair behind your ear – you'd just had it cut, and only I knew you weren't sure about the shorter style. In that moment I loved you so much, felt both lucky and charmed.

And then, just behind you, she walked into the room, and everything went wrong.

Remember Auntie's Kitchen, that West Indian cafe between Kentish Town and Camden? Whenever we passed it we'd peer inside at the cheerful checked table cloths and say to each other that we must try it some day. We never did. We were always on the way somewhere else, usually to Camden market to munch on noodles and browse at furniture we couldn't afford, and it never made sense to stop. I don't even know if it's still there any more. After we started going everywhere by car we stopped noticing things like that. I'll check tonight, on the way down into town, but either way it's too late. We should have done everything, while we had the chance. You never know how much things may change.

Then, over the crossroads and down past the site where the big Sainsburys used to be. I remember the first time we shopped there together – Christ, must be twenty-five years ago – both of us discovering what the other liked to eat, giggling over the frozen goods, and getting home to discover that despite spending forty pounds we hadn't really bought a single proper meal. It's become a nest of bijou little shops now, of course, but we never really took to them: we'd liked the way things were when we started seeing each other, and there's a limit to how many little ceramic pots anyone can buy.

By coincidence I ate my first new meal just round the back of Sainsbury's, a week after the party. It was after midnight, and I knew you'd be wondering where I was, but I was desperate. Eight days of the chills, of half-delirious hungers. Of feeling nauseous every time I looked at food, yet knowing I needed something. A young girl in her early twenties, staggering slightly, having reeled out of the Electric Ballroom still rushing on e. I knew because I could taste it. She noticed me in the empty street, and giggled, and I suddenly knew what I needed. She didn't run away as I walked towards her.

I only took a little.

You and I went to Kentish Town library one morning, quite soon after we'd got the first flat together. You were interested in finding out a little more about the area, and found a couple of books by the Camden Historical Society. We discovered that no-one was very interested in Kentish Town, despite the fact it's actually older than Camden, and were grumpy about that, because we liked where we lived. But we found out some interesting snippets – like the fact that the area in front of Camden Town tube station, the bit which juts out into the crossroads, had once housed a tiny jail and a stocks. Today the derelicts and drunks still collect there, as if there is something in that patch of ground which draws society's misfits and miscreants to it even now. I'll cross that area on my way down, avoiding one of those tramps – who I think recognizes something in me – and head off down Camden Road towards Mornington Crescent.

I don't understand why it happened. You and I loved each other, we had the kids, and had just finished redecorating. We were happy. There was no reason for what I did. No sense to it. No excuse, unless there was something about her which simply drew me. But why me, and not somebody else?

She was very tall, and extremely slim. She had short blonde hair and nothing in her head except cheekbones. She came into the room alone, and John immediately signalled to her. Drunkenly he introduced her to Howard and I, telling us her name was Vanessa, and that she worked in publishing. I caught you glancing over, and then looking away again, unconcerned. John burbled on at us for a while about some project or other he was working on, and then set off for more drinks, pulling Howard in his wake.

By then I was pretty drunk, but still able to function on a "What do you do, blah, this is what I do, blah," kind of level. I talked with Vanessa for a while. She had very blue eyes, a little curl of hair in front of each ear, and the way her neck met her shoulders was pleasing. That was all I noticed. She wasn't really my type.

After ten minutes she darted to one side to greet someone else, a noisy drama of squeals and cheek-kisses. No great loss: I've never found publishing interesting. I revolved slowly about the vertical plane until I saw someone I knew, and then went and talked to them.

This person was an old friend I hadn't seen in some time – Roger, the one who got divorced last year – and the conversation took a while and involved several drinks. As I was returning from fetching one of these I noticed the Vanessa woman standing in the corner, holding a bottle of wine by the neck and listening patiently to someone complaining about babysitters. I suffered a brief moment of disquiet about ours – we suspected her of knowing where our dope stash was – and then made myself forget about it. When you're thirty all your friends can talk about are houses and marriage; by a few years later babies and their sitters become the talk of the town. It's as if everyone collectively forgets that there's a real world out there with interesting things in it, and becomes progressively more obsessed with what happens behind their own front doors.

I muttered something to this effect to Roger, glancing back across at the corner as I did so. The woman was swigging wine straight from the bottle, her body curved into a swan's neck of relaxed poise. I couldn't help wondering why she was here alone. Someone like that had to have a boyfriend.

Then I noticed that she was looking at me, the mouth of the bottle an inch from her wet lips. I smiled, uncertainly.

We never really spent much time in Mornington Crescent. Nothing to take us there, I suppose, especially after the tube station shut down. Not even really a proper district as such, more an blur between Camden and the top of Tottenham Court Road. I remember once, when Maddy was small, telling her that the red two-storey building we were passing in the car had once been a station like Kentish Town's, and that in fact there were many other disused stations, dotted over London. She didn't believe me at first, but I showed her an old map, and after that was always fascinated by them. York Road, South Kentish Town, Down Street. Places which had once meant something to the people who lived there, and which were now nothing but scar tissue in a city which had moved forward in time.

Then down towards the Euston Road, the part of the walk you never liked. Fair enough, I suppose. It's a bit boring. Nothing but towering council blocks and busy roads, and by then you'd be complaining about your feet. But I'll walk it anyway. It's part of the trip, and by the time I come back it will all have changed. Maybe it'll be less boring. But it won't be the same.

One in the morning. The party was going strong – had, if anything, surged up to a new level. I saw that you were still okay, sitting cross-legged on the floor in the living room and happily arguing with Suzy about something.

By then I was very drunk, and on something like my seven billionth trip to the toilet. I passed you as I left the room, letting my hand fall, and you reached up and grabbed it for a moment before letting me pass. Then I flailed up two flights to the nearest unoccupied bathroom, cursing John for having so many stairs. The top floor of the house was darker than the rest, but I'd worn a channel in the new carpet by then and found my way easily enough.

Afterwards I washed my hands for a while with expensive soap, standing weaving in front of the mirror, giggling at my reflection and chuntering cheerfully at myself.

Back outside again and I seemed to have got drunker. I tripped down the small flight of steps which led to the landing, and reached out to steady myself. Suddenly my mouth was filled with saliva and I had a horrible suspicion I was about to christen the house, but a minute of deep breathing and compulsive swallowing convinced me I'd survive to drink another drink.

I heard a rustling sound, and turned to peer through a nearby doorway. I recognized the room – it was one John had shown us earlier, destined to become his study. "Where you'll sit becoming more and more successful," I'd thought churlishly to myself. At that stage it didn't seem very likely he would commit suicide six years later.

"Hello," she said.

Vanessa was standing in the empty room, over by the window. Cold moonlight made her features look as if they'd been moulded in glass, but whoever'd done it must have been pretty good. Without really knowing why, I stumbled into the room, pulling the door shut behind me. As she walked towards me her dress rustled again, like the shiver of leaves outside my window.

We met in the middle. I don't remember her pulling her dress up, just the long white stretch of her thighs. I don't remember undoing my trousers, but someone must have done. All I remember is saying, "But you must have a boyfriend," and her just smiling at me.

It was insane. Someone could have come in at any moment.
But it happened.

Tottenham Court Road. Home of cut-price technology, and recipient of many an impulse buy on my part. When we walked down it
towards Oxford Street you used to grab my arm and try to pull me
past the stores, or throw yourself in front of the window displays to
hide them from me. Then later I'd end up standing in Marks and
Spencers for hours, while you dithered over underwear. I moaned,
and said it was unfair, but I didn't really mind.

Past the Time Out building, where Howard used to work, and
then the walk will be over. At the junction of Oxford Street and
Tottenham Court Road I'll turn round and look back the way I've
come, and say goodbye to it all. Sentimental, perhaps: but that walk
means a lot to me.

Then I'll go walk down the Leicester Square tube and sit on the
Piccadilly Line to Heathrow.

I have a ticket, my passport and some dollars, but not very many.
I'm going to have to find a way of earning more sooner or later, so
it may as well be sooner. I've left the rest of our money for you. If
you're stuck for a present for Maddy's birthday, incidentally, I've
heard her mention the new Asylum Fields album a couple of times.
Though probably she'll have bought it herself, I suppose. I keep
forgetting how old they've got.

After those ten minutes in John's study I came downstairs again,
suddenly shocked into sobriety. You were still sitting where I had
left you, but it felt like everything else in the world had changed. I
was terrified that you'd read something from my face, realize what
I had done, but you just reached up and yanked me down to sit next
to you. Everybody smiled, apparently glad to see me. Howard passed
a joint. My friends, and I felt like I didn't deserve them. Or you.

Especially not you.

We left an hour later. I sat a little apart from you in the cab,
convinced you'd smell Vanessa on me, but I clutched your hand
and you seemed happy enough. We got home, and I had a shower
while you clanked around in the kitchen making tea. Then we went
to bed, and I held you tightly until you drifted off. I stared at the
ceiling for an hour, chilled with self-loathing, and then surprised
myself by falling asleep.

Within a few days I was calmer. A drunken mistake: these things
happen. I elected not to tell you about it – partly through self-serving
cowardice, but more out of a genuine knowledge of how little it
meant, and how much it would hurt you to know. The ratio between
the two was too steep for me to say anything. After a fortnight it

had sunk to the level of vague memory, the only lasting effect an increased realization of how much I wanted to be with you. That was the only time, in all our years together, that anything like that happened. I promise you.

It should all have been okay, a cautionary lesson learned, but then the first hunger pangs came and everything changed for me. If anything, I feel lucky that we've had ten years, that I was able to hide it for that long. I developed the habit of occasional solitary walks in the evening, a cover that no one seemed to question. I started going to the gym and eating healthily, and maybe that also helped to hide what was happening. At first you didn't notice, and then I think you were even a little proud that your husband was staying in such good shape.

But a couple of years ago that pride faded, around about the time the kids started looking at me curiously. Not very often, and maybe not even consciously, but just as you started making unflattering remarks about how your body was lasting compared to mine, I think at some level the children noticed something too. Maddy had always been daddy's girl. You said so yourself. She isn't any more, and I don't think that's just because she's growing up and going out with that dickhead from her college. She's uncomfortable with me. Richard's overly polite too, these days, and so are you. It's like I've done something which none of us can remember, something small which nonetheless set me apart from you. As if we're all tip-toeing carefully around something we don't understand.

You'll work out some consensus between you. An affair. Depression. Something. I know you all care for me, and that it won't be easy, but it has to be this way. I'm not telling you where I'm going. It won't be one of the places we've been on holiday together, that's for sure. The memories would hurt too much.

After a while, a new identity. And then a new life, for what it's worth. New places, new things, new people: and none of them will be you.

I've never seen Vanessa since that night, incidentally. If anything, what I feel for her is hate. Not even for what she did to me, for that little bite disguised as passion. More just because, on that night ten years ago, I did something small and normal and stupid which would have hurt you had you known. The kind of mistake anyone can make, not just people like me.

I regret that more than anything: the last human mistake I made, on the last night I was still your husband and nothing else. That I was unfaithful to the only woman I've ever really loved, and with someone who didn't matter to me, and who only did it because she had to.

I knew she must have had a boyfriend – I just didn't realize what kind of man he would be.

I can't send this letter, can I? Not now, and probably not even later. Perhaps it's been nothing more than an attempt to make myself feel better; a selfish confession for my own peace of mind. But I've been thinking of you while I've been writing it, so in that sense at least it is written to you. Maybe I'll find some way of keeping track of your lives, and send this when you're near the end. When it won't matter so much, and you may be asking yourself what exactly it was that happened.

But probably that's not fair either, and by then you won't want to know. Perhaps if I'd told you earlier, when things were still good between us, we could have worked out a way of dealing with it. It's too late now.

It's time to go.

I'll come back some day, when it's safe, when no one who could recognize me is still alive. It will be a long wait, but I will come. That day's already planned.

I'll start walking at Oxford Street, and walk all the way back up, seeing what remains and what has changed. The distance at least will stay the same, and maybe I'll be able to pretend you're walking it with me, taking me home again. I could point out the differences, and we'd remember the way it was: and maybe, if I can recall it clearly enough, it will be like I never went away.

But I'll reach Falkland Road eventually, and stand outside looking up at this window; not knowing who lives here now, only that it isn't us. Perhaps if I shut my eyes I'll be able to hear your voice, imagine you sitting inside, conjure up the life that could have been. I hope so.

And I will always love you.

Conrad Williams

Bloodlines

Conrad Williams is the winner of the 1993 Littlewood Arc Prize and the British Fantasy Award for Best Newcomer, and was a finalist for the London Writers Award.

His short stories have appeared in many small press and professional magazines and anthologies, including The Year's Best Horror Stories XXII, Dark Terrors 2, Darklands 2, A Book of Two Halves, Sugar Sleep, The Science of Sadness, Northern Stories 4, Blue Motel: Narrow Houses Volume Three, Cold Cuts II, Last Rites & Resurrections *and* The Third Alternative, *among others.*

" 'Bloodlines' was conceived in an afternoon while my girlfriend, Keri, was at the dentist," explains the author. "I've since discovered that, as a child, her eye-teeth were unusually long and used to rest on her bottom lip when her mouth was closed. This story is for her. I'd also like to thank Kim Newman for going to the trouble of providing me with information about the Count's various pseudonyms."

The new millennium approaches, and Dracula is incarcerated in a maximum-security prison . . .

NAIM PARKED HER Mini as the shadow of an armed guard swept over her. She was twenty minutes early and would have arrived even sooner if she had not stopped off in the park to calm herself down. This was the first interview Salavaria had agreed to since his incarceration. The authorities had green-lighted her application for a meeting first time round and she had been too busy getting her questions right, placating her editor and tying up the loose strings of other stories to fully appreciate the enormity of this liaison.

It was a stifling day. Naim rubbed her forearms gently through her jumper as she crossed the gravel forecourt to the gate. There were two more guards with Armalite rifles slung loosely across their shoulders; one of them was stroking the barrel as he watched her progress. The car that had shadowed her through the Bedfordshire countryside since she slipped off the M1 at Aspley Guise had parked a little distance back from her: a pair of blank faces tracked her from the front seats. Nobody was taking any chances with this gig.

She tried to re-focus her mind: she needed to be as unruffled as possible if she were to come away from the interview with a good story. Her mind flitted over the bloody half-decade of Salavaria's reign of terror prior to his capture at an abandoned railway station in North Yorkshire last winter.

Salavaria, she thought. She had seen the pathologist's photographs. They had followed him through the deep snow, the tracker dogs and the police, to a crumbling stone platform where they found him trying to swallow the heart of ten-year-old Melanie Cartledge, whose body lay in the snow nearby, ringed with an ugly spattered circle of blood and faeces. He had attempted to set fire to her corpse but her clothes were too damp. Her singed hair sent an unbroken line of thin smoke into the sky.

"Shoot me," he had begged them.

A constable from the Yorkshire police had been suspended for six months for trying to brain him with his truncheon.

"Good morning Ms Foxley." A voice touched by synthetic crispness darted at her from the steel doors. There were no windows here.

"Morning," she returned. "I'm here to see – "

"Gyorsy Salavaria. Yes, yes, we know all about that. Could we take you through GeneSync security please?"

She pressed the back of her hand against a matte plate on the door. The plate hummed lightly against her flesh as an IntraScan assessed her DNA. Before it had stopped humming, refreshed its lenses with a self-cleaning spray and disappeared into its housing, the door was opening, sliding down into a socket underground. Three armed guards surged towards her from the inner gloom, and motioned for her to climb on to their Magnabike. After stop/start passage through a series of inner gates, they glided in silence past featureless black walls that seemed to boast a join neither with floor nor ceiling. Large red numbers were stencilled at intervals, interstitial globes breathed pale light against the dull sheen of metal. It was cold in here. She thought she heard a moan.

"Are these the cells?" she asked.

One of the guards regarded her through his black plastic face mask: she saw her own features, tiny and distorted, in its sheen. He nodded and faced front. She followed suit, noting the driver – fused with the cockpit as though he was of its design rather than merely its pilot – bathed in thin green light from the controls. By the time they drifted to a stop, she was thinking of insects.

She stepped on to a bay floored with a perspex-covered grille. It was underlit by brilliant white light. Once her eyes had readjusted to the glare, she could see that the space below the grille fell away hundreds of feet. There were passageways down there; guards walking them like ants in a catacomb.

"This way," motioned a guard.

She was led into a seam in the blackness which opened out into a walkway punctuated by pools of water and potted plants. A man in a red robe waved at her from the walkway's end. His glasses flashed intermittently as though he were trying to signal her a covert message.

"Miss Foxley," he called. "Quite a ride, isn't it? I reckon we should open to the public."

"Professor Neumann?" she extended her hand.

"'Fraid so," he smiled and took her arm. "This way."

His office was accessed via a short elevator ride – the only way in or out of the room, apparently. He seated himself at an expansive desk that supported nothing greater than a chewed pencil, a mug bearing the legend: I'VE GOT PMT and an ornate block of slate with *Professor K Neumann* engraved upon it.

"Can I get you anything? Coffee, tea . . . I've got some Exta-C Lite?" He fingered the ornate whiskers that bracketed his face.

"Nothing thanks." Maybe it was the imminent introduction to Salavaria or the office's spartan appearance that was getting to her, but she couldn't stop shaking.

"Camera six!" called Neumann, stroking his pony tail. A screen, the size of the far wall, fluttered into life.

"I'll be watching the interview, of course," he said. "You'll be perfectly safe. If Gyorsy tries to rise from his chair the seat will inject him with a small dose of fentanyl."

She could hardly hear him. Her eyes were fixed on Salavaria.

He was no longer the strutting, plump monster that had glared from every front page the morning after he was arrested; here was a meagre scrap of flesh, his clothes hanging from him like giant folds of loose skin. His hair had either fallen out or been shorn close to his scalp: the planes and angles of his head stood out in painful detail.

What happened to him?" Naim asked, approaching the screen.

"Guilt, I would imagine, although your guess is as good as any other – and will probably be worth much more in an hour or so. None of us have been able to get a word out of him."

"What? Nothing?"

Neumann shook his head. "Although, he does talk in his sleep. We've got a VA mic in his cell. There are tapes if you'd like to listen."

"Not just now. I'd like to be free of anything that might influence any conversation." She thought of the forensic pictures of Lisa Chettle, his first victim, her remains flapping in the branches of a tree like strips of cloth. "Well, as free as I can make it."

"I understand. I'll give you a copy of the tape to take away. But you'll have to sign a legal waiver agreeing not to reproduce the material in anything you write."

He joined her in front of the screen. He was wearing a sweet, expensive aftershave; it had brought his skin out in reddish bumps. When he spoke again, it was in a conspiratorial murmur as though this room, as opposed to Salavaria's cell, was being bugged. Perhaps it was.

"Before you leave, I could show you my quarters. It might be amusing."

Naim looked up at his florid face and felt a wave of nausea wash through her. She guessed it would be anything but amusing.

He became more animated when she entered, but not much more.

"Gyorsy? Hello. My name's Naim Foxley. Uh, can I call you Gyorsy? You agreed to speak to me?"

"Don't talk to me as if I were an idiot. I know who you are. My brain works okay. Sit."

"Thank you. I – look, I can't pretend ... I'm a little nervous. I'm a lot nervous. I've never ..."

"Never what? Passed the time of day with a serial killer before? Is that what you were going to say? Or something more emotive. A pervert, yes? Or better: a psycho. A ding-dong fucking psycho."

"*Prisoner 2433249. Code breach. Any more of that, Sally, and you'll be on bread and water for a week.*"

He looked up, then closed his eyes and smiled. "Apologies Professor. I was not thinking." His gaze levelled with hers once more. It was not, she noted with some discomfort, unpleasant. "And apologies to you too, Ms Foxley . . . Bread and water, though, that's for your benefit. Prison brutality is not dead, you know. I'll be scarred before the day is out. Batons are still the favoured weapon, even as we reach the end of the century. You'd think they'd come up with something a little more modern. A little more *Star Wars*."

He shrugged her towards the chair opposite. "I'd offer to make you some tea, but I'm not allowed near the kettle," he said. His voice carried some of the authority she'd missed in his physique.

"I'm not thirsty," she said, through a mouth that had become powder dry.

They sat silently, his eyes sad, absent of any mocking of her as she fumbled her interview materials on to the table.

"Where do you come from?"

"Cusmir, in the south of Mehedinti. Romania. Although I lived a great part of my life in Hungary before moving here. In a village, Bitcse, with my grandparents."

She had a bunch of questions ready to recite, designed to bring him out of his shell. What shell? He knew why she was here, his glittering eyes said so. The questions were there for her. They were a runway for her to gather pace before she launched herself at the big one. Now she saw she didn't need it. "Why?" she mouthed, unable to summon a squeak of sound.

"Do you know what it is like to float in a bath of blood?" he whispered. "To sleep in a bed with corpses that cannot close their eyes? Do you know the feeling, when you take something incontrovertibly positive as a life and turn it, with your own hands, against everything that is outlined in its code, to oppose what nature intended?"

There was no gloating in his revelations, no theatre. His voice became drawn and robotic, reciting the delusions of his psychosis as though they'd been scripted for him. She was grateful she didn't have to ask any more questions; he guided her through the misery without prompt. He began to quietly cry through his words, a wetting of the bluish skin beneath his eyes. He looked pathetic, not the man who had torn an unborn child from the womb of Emily Tasker and partially devoured its face while the mother bucked in the throes of haemorrhage.

"I didn't do it for me. I didn't do any of it for me," he said. "I was trying to atone for the actions of my forebears and trying to lay a safe passage for the family I once thought I might have. Imagine," he snorted, twisting his face, "me, The Leech, fathering children. The press would think the pram I sat them in a snack bucket."

She recoiled from the image before it had a chance to solidify. She noticed she had neglected to switch on her Dictaphone; her notebook was bare, the point of her pencil lead sharp. It did not matter – his words were scarring her. She would not forget.

The interview swayed between them, like the pendulum of a clock. Time seemed to condense, become syrupy, as he wove his bland, bitter narrative. At times, he swung in so close she feared she would smell the mealy stench of raw corpse on his breath: she almost cried with relief that he smelled of Potter's throat pastilles. Only when the guards moved in with their weapons cocked did she realize that Salavaria was touching her; she did not have the strength to pull away. When she did, she was aware of a tablet of paper tucked between her fingers.

"I hope I've done enough," he said. "God knows I'm not safe here if I haven't."

"What do you fear?"

"You'll discover that soon," he said, and nodded. "The bureau."

She clenched her hand.

In the relative sanctity of her car, Naim allowed herself a long, whooping exhalation. She had to try three times to fit the ignition key into the fascia but her hands were still shaking. She had forgotten about the piece of paper but now she unfolded it. How had Salavaria been allowed pens, even paper? She had reported on suicides achieved with both. But then she saw that the paper was an ancient bus ticket, small enough for him to have lodged it beneath a fingernail. The message, such as it was, had been written in blood, a spidery trail guided, it seemed, by a nib no broader than the end of a hair. Before she had even recognized the words as a London address, she found herself wondering who had spilled the ink that formed them.

Naim disembarked at Euston and took the Tube to Holloway. There, she crossed the street and walked down Hornsey Road to a mini-roundabout. Gripped by an unease which had come on with the speed of her arrival – she could be gazing upon Salavaria's secret London garret within five minutes – she stopped at a corner cafe for a cup of tea. The address burned against her thigh. She watched as a fat, slow fly landed on a cake by the counter.

While the tea was doing its job, she slipped the tape into her Walkman and pressed the play button. A male voice Neumann's cut in with its cool, precise tones. "Night one. Recording starts 03:45a.m. Second of December 1999."

There was a thick, ruffling noise possibly Salavaria moving around beneath his blanket and then a short span of silence broken by his moans.

"Jesus, no," he whispered. "Lord of Darkness, I beg you, spare me. Spare me. All I did was as an offering for you. It was all in the way of atonement. Leave me in peace ..."

A break in the tape, then Neumann was back: "Night two. Uh, recording starts 01:09 a.m. Sixth of December 1999."

This time the thrashing was more pronounced, accompanied by a tapping sound, a scratching, as of a fingernail on glass. "Go away," hissed Salavaria. "Leave me be. I have atoned."

The scratching increased until Salavaria screamed. It did not sound like the scream of the person she had met a day previously. This was bloody and desperate, the scream of a man who was allowing the fear for his own life out of his body. There was a word too, that he gasped repeatedly, once all the fight had left him.

Oupiere.

There were more recordings in a similar vein, and she noticed they grew more frequent until he was having these "attacks" four or five times every night. On each occasion, he used that strange, almost beautiful word.

Oupiere.

She paid for her tea and stepped into the street. The light was on the wane and a bitter wind was flooding the lanes. She pulled her coat tight around her and walked towards Salavaria's flat. Hornsey Road stretched away from her – a hemisphere of cold light and traffic. Her footsteps thickened around her as she entered the tunnel of the railway bridge. Before she'd passed through it, a second pair of footsteps were marking time with her own.

Naim looked back and saw, about thirty feet away, a tall man in a black polo neck sweater. He was wearing sunglasses with tiny round lenses. Was Neumann having her followed?

In his hand he was carrying a bundle of papers. A black stain soiled the bottom of the package, where he was holding it. He seemed to draw the dark around him, as if he were a magnet for its shade. A thin cloud fussed about his head. It took her a moment to realize that they were flies. She picked up her pace, startled by the panic that had burst in her gut. She fished the keys from her pocket and crossed the road, looking back again when she had reached the opposite kerb. He had not emerged. She ran.

At the communal door, she pressed all the entry buttons until someone buzzed her in. She slammed it behind her before she had a chance to worry about disturbing the other occupants. She had intended to be a little more cloak and dagger. Flicking on the timer light, she took the stairs two at a time, trying to force her breathing to regulate itself. The light died. Cursing, she edged along the worn carpet until she found another switch. How would she get in? Surely he would not leave a key under the rug for her. She had checked before the nonsense of the idea could take hold. But above the architrave she found what she was looking for. When the light had died a second time, she blindly made her way into Salavaria's flat. She stumbled to the window and looked down into the street. The man was there – it was difficult to make him out in the darkness. His face seemed smudged, a thoughtless thumb on a charcoal sketch. She watched as his fingers dipped into his package and pulled something black and wet from it. She saw him duck to catch the morsel between his lips. When he went for a second mouthful, he paused and looked up at the window. A chunk of his supper slipped between his fingers and spattered the pavement by his feet.

"Christ," she said, and moved away.

She felt for a lamp, brushed a hand against its shade, and turned it on. Salavaria's flat leapt back from her. The living room was tidy, if a little dust-coated. She wondered if she should find a telephone and call the police but reasoned that she was being paranoid and that explaining her presence in a flat that was not hers seemed just too much like hard work at the moment.

There were bookshelves containing a selection of modern novels and nineteenth-century classics. There were vases containing powdery flowers. A coffee table was scattered with magazines a year old. Naim could not ignore the smell. It was not unpleasant, and if she had not known of Salavaria's habits, she might not have immediately guessed its origin. She followed the slightly stale, slightly acrid odour to the bathroom where she found a sheaf of human skins laid out in the tub. They were yellowish and brittle, like unscrolled papyrus. In fact, on closer inspection, the simile bore additional fruit: brown ink travelled the grain of the skin, skirting a mole here, a scar there, a tattoo. Naim found it hard to work out what the words said. Not only were they in a foreign language, but the ink had dried and leeched into the skin, spoiling its sense. At intervals, however, she recognised a pattern. Or rather, a letter, a capital dotted around the text with curious frequency.

D.

Behind her, in the corner, shin bones were stacked like so much firewood. There was a human head on top of the fridge, a note to buy more matches pinned to its desiccated cheek. She moved slowly, through the dead centre of the room, anxious not to touch anything. Her breath felt extremely cold in her lungs. She saw a painting of a marigold on the wall, a photograph of Salavaria in the driving seat of a sports car.

There was a small ante-room just off the corridor that adjoined the kitchen to the bathroom. Naim pushed the door back and saw the bureau Salavaria had referred to. It was empty apart from a journal, wrapped in its blue leather binding. To her left, a stack of papers real ones were weighted down by a lump of something she was not too keen to study. She elbowed it out of the way and sat on the high-backed wooden chair which was a little too tall for the desk. It creaked massively. She pushed her focus into the densely knitted text, hoping to forget the cloying horrors around her for the revelations she needed so that she could leave. She had had a bellyful of Salavaria's insanity.

It was hard to read, but the first entry appeared to be dated some time in the last century, 18 – what? Ninety-seven was it? She squinted at the text, running her finger under the elaborately scrawled words. Here and there, passages stood out, not least because somebody – presumably Salavaria – had underlined them.

13th November, 18—

We have been on the road for some ten or eleven days now. This winter wind bites at us with a passion, constantly reminding us of the dead, cold thing we are fleeing. At nights we huddle together, reassuring each other that he is gone for ever, but we never can quite believe it. Pyotr keeps watch while I feed Alexander and help him to sleep. This evening, he asked me why Ubek was not with us. I have dreaded such a moment. For a while I could not answer. I told him, eventually, that she had gone to a better place and had died to save us. The image of her snapped apart in Draoul's hands like so much kindling will stay with me till judgement day. That we had a part in his banishment from this world is a blessing, yet no amount of pain could be too great for that leech, that evil beast. Dear Ubek.

17th (?) November, 18—

A bitter night in the Carpathian mountains. Pyotr has terrible frostbite and raves in his sleep about the night's face. How it folds around him and tries to suck the very life from his lungs. We are having trouble with wolves. They are growing bolder, despite the fires we burn each dusk. Horrible animals, they come up to the very edge of the firelight and growl at us. Their eyes seem almost human. Sometimes they foam at the jaws, this light turning their spittle almost red. Alexander has gone down with a fever. He says he can sometimes see Ubek in the trees, smiling at him and asking him to come and play with her. The sooner we are away from these ill-charmed heights, the better. I long for our home, where we could sit and look across

*at the forests at night, at the lanterns that shone in the fields. So much
ash, now. All ash.*

21st November, 18—
*Pyotr has rallied. The weather has eased off as we come out of the foothills
and approach Sibiu. It seems, watching the sunrise, as if the worst is behind
us. I can almost believe that tomorrow, as Pyotr promises, we will be with his
uncle and safe from the nightmare of this past six months. We pray that
Professor Van Helsing is similarly protected. And yet . . . Draoul seems
as close as the sudden touch in the night from the dead winds blowing
down from the north. I pray for us. I pray for our future families. God
save us all.*

Naim blinked and sat up. The bones in her back crackled with
effort. A light headache had nestled behind her eyes. *Draoul,* she
thought. *Who the fuck is Draoul?* The chill of Salavaria's room settled
into her. She pulled her cardigan more closely around her shoulders
and pushed away from the desk. At the window, she pulled the blinds
apart minutely but the stranger was nowhere to be seen. Her eyes
were playing tricks; a smear of darkness shimmered where he had
stood. Playing safe, she rang for a cab, then tidied up Salavaria's
effects, carefully wiping away her presence with a balled-up tissue.
She did not want to explain her visit to the police when they
eventually grew wise to this place.

A minute waiting was a minute too long for her. She grabbed her
bag and strode to the door. She would hang around in the corridor
downstairs. The smell of corpses was a bitter flood in her nostrils.
Naim opened the door as he was unhinging his immense mouth:
packed with teeth, drifting into the dark of his gullet like those of
a shark. She gasped, stepped backwards. Blinked. He was gone.

She ran across the road, barely checking to see that she had shut the
door behind her. A light rain had begun. It worried her cheek like
the fingers of a playful child. In the cab she gabbled her address and
sank back into her seat. The bunched newspaper the stranger had
been eating from fluttered on the pavement. She tried to convince
herself that it was the rain spoiling her view that made its contents
look like the head of a dog.

Her own flat smelled so conversely clean it was as arresting as the
detergent reek of a hospital. Naim bolted the door behind her
and sighed, angry that she felt so wired. She shrugged her coat
off and hung it up, tossed her bag on to the sofa. In her lounge,
she poured a brandy and listened to her messages. Dr Neumann,

following up to see if her visit was enjoyable, ha ha, and see you next week. Oh and what, by the way, did Salavaria mean when he mentioned a bureau? Her mother, checking that everything was all right and what was she planning for the millennium party? Dr Neumann again, asking if she would consider seeing him on a social basis.

She sighed and took her drink into the bathroom where she drew a hot bath. It was too quiet once she had turned off the taps, so she slipped into the candlelit lounge and put a record on the turntable. It did not matter what it was. As she peeled away her clothing, she had to close her eyes.

Naim allowed herself to become totally submerged. When her heartbeat became too loud in her ears, she surfaced.

Reached for the razor blades lined up by the tap. Ran a finger over yesterday's scars that ran along her arm like chevrons on a warning sign.

Her veins had grown plump in the heat. They throbbed, bluish, in time to the piano music's pulse. She pressed the edge of a blade against her wrist and scored lightly until a red bead bubbled there. Now the other wrist. Now the sensitive flesh around her nipples. She thought of Salavaria's hungry mouth positioned above a hot jet of blood from her carved forearms. She jabbed the razor into her belly three, four, five times, just nicking the skin.

Breathless, she flung the blade away before her compulsion for deeper wounding went too far. She bathed her cuts, weeping over the lack of control she exerted over her habit and the fear that one day she might find some. Her past welled within her and it was all she could do to stop herself reaching for the Gillette again.

The memory of boys spilling a different fluid over the pulse points of her body, no less vital, made her feel sick. She told herself then that she was taking their money for her betterment; this was how survival among the dregs was secured. You had to eke it out. You had to earn the right to do it.

Naim remembered the empty nights sitting in the corner of a squat, hoping that the last candle would not die out before morning. Tending to David in the dark was more awful than being able to see his face as it morphed through a gamut of agonized expressions. She had been mortified at the irony of her situation; offering up her body to shadowy men who might have been carrying the very disease that was ruining her boyfriend. Sometimes she would try to sing to him while she bathed his sorry flesh, running a flannel around the ugly statements made by Karposi's sarcoma. She massaged him when constipation made him cry. She cleaned him during startling bouts of diarrhoea and then she would inspect what he produced.

She brought him oranges and pasta, bread and pulses. He needed bulk, he needed vitamins. They seemed to make no difference. Towards the end, she remembered raising his head in her hand to give him a sip of water. The shock of his lightness had been subsumed by the fall-out of hair the manoeuvre had caused. That night she had gone out, fucked three men and bought enough downers with her earnings to finish him off while giving her the option to follow if she were up to it. The night she decided upon, almost a week later, she sat and watched him guttering beneath the cone of light from a candle she had stolen from a hardware shop. It seemed he would simply wink out while she waited; the shock of her passiveness in his death forced her hand. She wadded eight diazepam capsules between his lips and fed him some water. He choked a little – thrush had turned his gullet into a cheesy mush but he took the pills down. He did not say anything. He did not look at her. He died.

Naim dried herself, her eyes following the diminishing smears of mist on the mirror. Before long, the steam had retreated to a tiny disc that eclipsed her reflected centre. It ceased to dwindle. After all that, it had been easy, back then, to drag herself out of her marginalized existence. She had spent some time evaluating the scant number of skills she possessed and threw herself into a journalism course funded by prostitution. She could write, and she would never be stared down by any interviewee, not after what she had seen. She would never be cowed.

Until Salavaria, that was.

She made tea and carried the cup into the living room where she sat in the dark by the open window, watching the people in the flats opposite. They too seemed slothful, deracinated, as if trundling from room to room might expose the purpose that was missing from their lives and provide an escape.

A storm worried the horizon. As she watched, its thickness blotted out Canary Wharf's pulse. Lightning forked above the city like cracks in the night. Its enthusiasm failed to muster anything so energetic from her; rather, it only served to make her feel even more exhausted, as if it were sucking the life from her.

Naim made it to the bed as a clap of thunder caromed overhead. *Who the hell was Draoul?* she thought. *Jesus. What a day.*

She slept fitfully and dreamed of a swarm of lazy, bloated flies invading her room. Some settled nervously on her wounds and fed there. She imagined something larger flitting outside the window. She felt a sensation drift into her, as of a time she and a friend had entered a restaurant late one Friday night. They had been

sober, everyone around was drunk: she had been unnerved by
the oppressive force of the hunger in the room, as if alcohol
had stripped away any social niceties to reveal the animal lust
beneath.

The flies, fattened, lifted like a black-beaded curtain and droned
away. She saw them coalesce beyond the window where her dream
figure hovered. He turned and favoured her with a shocking smile
and she saw it was the stranger she had encountered outside
Salavaria's flat.

"Our time will come." He enunciated each word with relish.
Although they were separated by glass, she heard every word. "I
return with the death of the century."

Thin sexual warmth spread through her groin and she rose
through layers of sleep until the room swayed unpleasantly before
her sticky eyes. She padded to the bathroom and splashed water
on her face, confused and upset by the directionless need of her
sex. The cuts itched furiously.

Back in her bedroom, she stood by the window and watched the
now clear city lights glisten after the storm. The city seemed fresh,
almost alien to her. Newly scrubbed, laid bare for the gradual
soiling its inhabitants would be party to. The roads were veins to
be furred by traffic and smog. She scratched her wrists and when
the sun came up, she was too horrified by its colour to notice that
she had made herself bleed.

That next day she had intended to write up her notes and fax a
first draft of her interview with "The Leech" to the magazine. She
could not bring herself to sit in front of the laptop and it was not
merely because she felt like shit, although that had a large bearing
on the situation. No, it was because, monster that he was, she felt
some sympathy towards Salavaria. She did not want to go down
the path her editor had outlined for her: depicting a blood-lusting
fiend going even more crazy in his bedlam. She did not want to
write about him at all. She just wanted to talk.

By late afternoon she was decided. Naim collected her bag and
pulled yesterday's sweater over her arms, wincing when the fabric
drew across the tender incisions. Her breasts sang with pain where
she had criss-crossed them with the blade; her belly looked like it
had been shot with pellets.

She drove north through the city; it took some time. Banners
and lights were being erected along the main roads in preparation
for the millennial party, now – she noted with a jolt – only two days
away. A pang of sadness drew her eyes to her bare ring finger. Angrily
she stabbed at the buttons of her radio until she found some jazz. It

helped her to relax. It helped her to cope with the combination of the abject and banal that confronted her whenever she went to see Salavaria.

"When I was a child in Bitcse," he'd told her. "There was a ... a problem. Children in the village, and in the surrounding villages, began to die. They were discovered in shallow graves, covered in punctures. Drained of blood. Some of the heads had been removed, wrenched away, like someone twisting off the cap on a beer bottle."

The absence of sensationalism from his voice only made the telling of the story worse, and more compelling. She drove with his Eastern inflections coursing deliciously through her mind like red wine.

By the time she reached the prison, it was getting dark and the storm was expanding across the night. Summer had bitten so deeply into the country that it seemed that anything other than sunshine might never again happen. Black fists of cloud thrust over the countryside. She ran to the door and was allowed in.

One of the insectoid guards ran a sensor over her. "You don't have an appointment today." His voice rasped metallically. It would be easy to doubt anything human behind all that plastic.

"Just a few things I need to clear up. Can you let Professor Neumann know I'm here."

"He knows. I'll take you."

Professor Neumann had evidently doused himself with cheap scent very recently. He looked up from his desk, pen poised above a thick ledger as she entered, a mood of urbane ennui about him. He looked like a writer posing for a book jacket.

"Name," he mispronounced. "A pleasure. For you of course. Ha ha. Only joking."

"I'd like to see Gyorsy," she said, trying not to sound too impatient.

His good nature collapsed. "Ah," he said. "Bit late. He's in his quarters. Private time. He's reading, I think. Some Miserablist text or other."

"I have questions for him. It's urgent."

"There's always tomorrow."

"It's New Year ... well, it's New Millennium's Eve tomorrow. I doubt I'd be able to get out of the city if I wanted to."

He perked up. "Why not stay with me? We could go for dinner tonight and my place is only – "

"Professor, please." She had injected some of the steel she reserved for her editor when he became obstreperous. It worked.

Sour-faced, he beckoned for her to follow. They moved in the opposite direction from the burnished walls and the cool lighting. A lift took them up into a chilly, brilliant white area where insect guards were in abundance, the light so great here that she could almost see a ghostly pallor of skin behind their faceplates.

"We call this The Penthouse," said Neumann, regaining a little of his pomp. "Our danger criminals live here. The lift we came up is the only access or exit, save a secret tunnel to a helipad on the roof. They have nice views. We treat our Hannibal Lecters with some dignity."

They walked by a series of thick steel doors with portholes in them. Occasionally, there would be a face pressed against the glass, fogging it so she would only get an impression of mad eyes and rictal mouths. Neumann stopped and pressed a hand against a GeneSync plate by a door. A piece of paper obscured its porthole: a black cross had been elaborately drawn upon it.

"You allow them writing materials?"

"Yes. Charcoal only. You understand."

He gestured with his hand. Two guards sandwiched them as they entered the cell. Moonlight flooded the air-conditioned room, where it managed to get past the paper crosses on the window. Salavaria was naked, in the corner of the cell, rubbing charcoal into his skin. He had covered himself in black crosses. A novel lay to one side, gutted.

When he saw Neumann he leapt up and ran towards him, arms outstretched. The barrel of the lead guard's Armalite dimpled his throat. "Professor," he said, and Naim was grateful to hear the measure in his voice. She found herself staring at his limp cock, which was similarly decorated.

"Professor, you brought me a crucifix?"

"Not this time, Gyorsy."

"But you said – "

"Ms Foxley is here to see you."

Neumann withdrew, presumably to his eyrie where he could watch the whole encounter on his vid-screens. The guards stayed close, but she could see Salavaria was in no mood for fighting. She sat by him against the wall, moving some more pages out of the way. A sentence leapt at her from the original text. *Awake or asleep he'd never felt more alive.*

"Do you want to get dressed?" she asked.

"Do I upset you like this?"

"No."

They were quiet. The measured, synthetic breaths of the guards irritated her but now she was here, she did not know how to continue.

"You went," he said.

"I went."

"And?"

"And it was not pleasant."

He closed his eyes. "I know. I'm sorry. I couldn't warn you. You might not have gone if you knew."

"Who is D?" she asked. "Who is Draoul?"

His fear, she could see, prevented him from laughter, but some grim humour flirted round his gaunt features, spoiled further by charcoal crosses.

"Not Draoul," he said. "Not Draoul."

"Who is he then? Gyorsy? What is *oupiere*?"

His head jerked towards her. Tendons stood out on his neck like cables. "Where did you hear such a word?"

"You." She looked down, shamed. "Professor Neumann lent me some recordings of you in your sleep. You sound so troubled."

"You would not believe if I told you."

"Try me."

"He comes to kill me. I'll be dead before the century is out." Tears were reddening his desperate eyes. They looked as if they might flop out on to his cheeks.

"Nobody will harm you here. This is a top security facility. It's probably easier to get out than it is to get in."

"He will find me – "

"Who. Gyorsy? *Who*?"

"Dracula." He said the name flatly, without spirit. She imagined a gas-filled corpse might emit a sound like that if its belly were torn.

It took a while to register. She frowned. "What? You mean"

"He is *oupiere*," he said, barely suppressing a fresh wave of hysteria. He gripped her arm. The guards closed in. "He is *oupiere*. He is *vampire!*"

Naim motioned the guards to pull back. "Leave him. He's okay. He's okay."

The guards retreated slightly, but kept their weapons raised. A slew of rain spattered the windows, making her jump. Lightning arced over the grey band of motorway in the distance.

"Do you have a crucifix?" he asked, his eyes ranging around her throat.

"No, but I'll bring one."

"They won't let me wear it. They think I'll kill myself with it." He laughed, a sour, hacking noise. "I'm dead already."

"Gyorsy," she soothed. "Try to calm down. What's this business about vampires?"

His words hitched in his throat. He was tight as whipcord. "My ancestors were party to The Count's capture. They helped find him. He has returned to wipe out the people who might be dangerous to him."

"The Count?"

"Dracula! Sweet Christ, you know nothing!"

"Gyorsy, you're babbling."

"Listen to me. He has returned. He wants to eradicate the bloodlines that are dangerous to him. A pre-emptive strike. A revenge too."

"But – "

"Tell me what you saw the night you went to Holloway. Everything. Every shred of detail."

She did so, casting nervous glances at the inscrutable guards. When she mentioned the stranger outside the flat, her voice ran out of steam.

"It's funny, but I'd forgotten about him until now. How could I just forget? He was horrible, he was eating – "

"Did he say anything to you?"

She put her fingers to her lips. "No. But I dreamed he did, later. Oh God, I forgot . . ."

"He has strong ways with his mind. He can play with your thoughts. What did he say in your dream?"

She told him. He seemed to slump even further into himself, more than his sagging body could allow. All his defiance was gone.

"Do you believe that we are drawn together by ancient catastrophe, that history has a design for us? Especially the tragedies? Only the tragedies?"

A memory, unbidden, came to her, of a dark figure fucking her from behind while her feverish, blind boyfriend vomited into the corner of a freezing room.

She got to her feet and moved to the door.

"Beware your history", he said. "Fear the actions of your forebears."

She was drenched by the time she made it to her car. Black thunderclouds ignited with white fire, lighting up the prison. The air itself felt as though it might combust and suck the air out of her.

Her arms were itching. She looked down to the damp wool of her sweater just as a maggot fell from its cuff. She recoiled and scrabbled around on the seat until she had swept the maggot on to the floor. She ground it into the carpet. Sweating now, through the rain, and taking shallow gasps of air, she delicately peeled the sleeves of her clothing back. Her cuts were puffy and weeping, the skin around them livid. Four or five maggots were burrowing into the sticky, raised flesh. Naim shrieked and struggled out of the car into the maelstrom. She plucked the larvae out, swooning when she felt the wrench of each greasy white body.

God, what if their heads remained inside?

There was little for her to vomit but she retched anyway, wiping a thin gruel of sick from her chin. She ditched her sweater and got back into the car. *Take it easy. Take it easy, girl.*

After a few minutes she felt well enough to turn the ignition key and drive the car out of the prison grounds. She drove ten miles with her eyes rooted to the broken line of the road before she realised she was travelling north. She pulled off at the services and wrapped the back seat blanket around her. In the toilets, she bathed her arms thoroughly, wincing at the sting of soap. She did not care who might see her wounds.

A woman at the next sink was washing her hair, eyes tightly closed. It was easy for Naim to pick up her discarded cardigan as she left.

She bought a sandwich and several cans of Coke, some Pro-Plus from the chemist, antiseptic spray and bandage. Behind the wheel, she tended her cuts before slipping her mobile phone out of her handbag. She had to think for a minute or two, but then the number came to her.

Maybe she would be away, celebrating New Millennium Day with her family.

"Hello?"

"Hello, Meg?" Suddenly close to tears.

"Yes. Who is this?"

"Meg? Meg?" She couldn't go on.

"Oh. Is that . . . is that you, Naim?"

"Meg. Help me."

"Where are you, my love?"

"I was on my way there. Can I see you?"

There was the sound of a china cup clinking against a saucer. It was the most beautiful sound Naim had ever heard.

"Of course," Meg said. "Shall I make you some supper?"

"No. I probably won't make it there until early morning. Leave a key by the door. I'll let myself in – don't wait up for me."

"Love, what's wrong?"

"God, Meg, what isn't?"

The drive became feverish and alien. The roads were empty. Tracts of land muscled up against the motorway and were replaced by grey walls and sodium lights nested in grey concrete towns. When she left the industrial wastes of the Midlands behind, the land seemed to relax into the shadows. Her fatigue took the light and shade and mixed it into a treacly clot that wedged in front of her eyes.

She thought it was rain fluttering against her window until she heard the protesting squeak of her wipers as they drew across dry glass. She opened the window, put on some jazz: Thelonius Monk playing Bolivar Blues. The fluttering continued. Maybe it was something trapped in the wheel of the car. Or birds she could not see in the dark.

Just beyond Kendal, she ran off the road because she was so tired. The raised warning line of the hard shoulder brought her to her senses and she braked hard. She slugged back four caffeine tablets with her Coke and ate half her sandwich. Her phone rang. It was Professor Neumann.

"Naim? Sorry to ring you so late." He didn't sound sorry at all. He sounded relieved, grateful to be talking to her. He sounded rattled.

"What is it?"

"It's Gyorsy. He's dead."

She was not shocked. She had almost been expecting it.

"How did it happen?"

There was quiet at the other end of the line, but she thought she could hear Neumann whimper. The line was bad, filled with buzzing. His words were difficult to make out.

"Someone . . . broke in. There's blood all over the wall, Naim. Blood all over. And they took his head!"

"What about the guards?"

"They're dead too. But there was some shooting. We've got half the police in Bedfordshire searching for the bastard. He'll probably be picked up soon. Our guards are crack shots. Whoever it was must be badly wounded, I would guess."

I wouldn't be too sure.

"Professor Neumann, I can't hear you very well. There's an awful lot of interference on the line. Can I call you back?"

"Er, Naim, it isn't interference. It's flies. We've got a room filled with fucking flies here."

She drove into Oban at quarter past five on the morning of the final day of the second millennium.

London seemed like a different life, way out of alignment with this hushed, almost expectant town. She felt panicky, dislocated for a moment, as though she were a diver suffering the bends. The lack of people on the roads seemed to make true a deep dread she had always carried, that everyone was dead, that the dawning of the next thousand years was in turn the closing chapter of humanity.

And then an old man turned the corner, walking a poodle wearing a tartan bodywarmer.

Naim laughed wildly, exhaustedly.

She remembered the way to Meg's house easily, once the layout of the roads became obvious. She bypassed the distillery on the hill overlooking the harbour and parked on an incline as close as she could to Meg's house before the road bottlenecked and became a path. She walked the rest of the way, and was panting by the time she got to the door.

Meg was waiting up for her, as she had expected. They hugged each other on the porch for a long time, Naim losing herself in the simple, homely smells of Meg's dressing gown, which reminded her so much of David.

She sat in the kitchen while Meg made tea, and tried to eat a piece of paradise cake but it was the wrong hour to eat. She could not work out where Meg's words ended or began. The lullaby voice in which they were couched dragged her further down.

"I have to sleep," she mumbled, suddenly sick with need for a pillow. "I'm sorry. I'll talk to you in the morning, later."

Meg led her to a small room and said good night. Naim fumbled with her jeans, gave up and sprawled across the bed. She heard fluttering outside the window and thought, with a horrible jolt, that she was still driving along the motorway, that this comfortable bed was an evil trick of her mind. Within seconds, she was asleep.

She had been walking for some time, across the shingles by the mouth of the harbour before she realized this was a dream. But how realistic! The crisp snap of air channelling down from the hill. Mist rising off the still water. Somewhere in the distance she heard the cry of a hawk. Heather turned a distant bluff into a swathe of purple suede.

She looked down, and saw a black, indistinct shape attach itself to her ankle where it fluttered. She tried shaking it off but it remained, shifting languidly against her movements, like seaweed flailing in a current. She felt hot and sweetly numb down there. The blood webbing her foot was no more arresting than the knowledge she was completely naked. Fishing boats loomed out of the mist, their sails flagging like tired ghosts. She came across the first of the bodies here, punctured and rent open, gutted, bled dry and discarded. She pressed her hand against their fish-pale flesh and, licking her lips, drifted into a darkness almost as utter as the thing that danced by her feet . . .

Naim wakened, hot-headed, a thin rope of drool spinning from her mouth. She was ravenous. Sitting up, she noticed how she must have shrugged off her clothes in the night. Her dream waxed too deep in her mind for her to be able to recall it. She padded to the window and swept the curtains aside, pausing to watch a bright red trawler as it churned towards the Firth of Lorn and the open sea beyond.

Meg was fixing eggs and bacon in the kitchen. "Hey, girl," she said and Naim's heart lurched. They were the words with which David used to greet her.

"Good morning."

"Why the limp? You get a stiff leg in your sleep or something?"

Naim looked down at her foot. The skin around her instep and heel was dark purple. Strands of weed were caught between her toes. She gritted her teeth and sat down. There were two ragged holes in the meat of her foot, bloodless and white. "I don't know," she said. "Maybe bruised it yesterday without realizing."

Despite her hunger, breakfast would not sit well in her stomach. She staggered off to be sick.

"Some way to spend the last day of the nineteen hundreds, hey, Meg?" she smiled. "Sick as a dog."

Come lunch time, she rallied a little, so they took a walk through the town, to the place where the road rolled away from the last building and became lost to the mountains beyond Portnacroish. They talked about David, Aids, the visits they made to see Meg in the past: all paths of discussion that were well trodden but comforting for that. When Meg asked her about London and her reasons for leaving so dramatically, she clammed up, grateful that she could not conjure an image of Salavaria's mutilated corpse.

"What happens tonight?" she asked. "Is Oban celebrating?"

"Of course," Meg said, gripping her hand and searching Naim's face for a key to understanding her pain. "We'll have a lovely time."

Naim slept a little more when they returned to the house. When she wakened, she sensed something was wrong. Night had swamped the town. Bonfires were being lit along the coast. She could see orange points of light shimmering on the water and smell woodsmoke as it rose to shroud the moon.

Downstairs, Meg was sitting in her rocking chair, her body unzipped from her pubis to her throat. A nimbus of flies darkened the air between them, feasting on the glistening wads of offal that seemed too numerous and bulky to have fit inside Meg's skin. Gyorsy Salavaria's head, black and misshapen, stared from the tabletop where it rested on a plastic placemat depicting the battle of Bannockburn. He looked punch-drunk, Naim thought, as she backed out into the hall. Her shock was matched by the impact of the question: *Why me?* She barrelled into the lane and ran to the shoreline where clumps of people were congregating for the countdown to the year 2000.

She felt the wisdom and the power of an ancient evil thick in the air, like the smoke that funnelled from the raging bonfires. Down here, among the other townsfolk, she would be safe. She rubbed at her forearms, jittery with a keen belief that she had been responsible for all this spilled blood, that Gyorsy had been the fall guy for her crimes.

"That's an absurd notion," said a voice that seemed to come at her from all sides. The man in front of her with his back to her turned around. She cringed away from him, from the severe heat of his gaze. When he spoke again, a glut of flies streamed from his mouth. He was impossibly beautiful, yet as rank as the sight she had just escaped from. His eyes seemed so deep in his head that it was hard for her not to step closer to try and make contact with them.

"I have been so very weak," he said. "I have slept for such a long time. But I've been called. The new millennium beckons me, like the call of the world to a babe in the womb."

He raised his hands, his fingernails unfurling like a set of flick-knives. "Come with me."

She followed, her ankle itching as though the blood there was impatient to be flowing again. "I will make it beautiful for you," he said, as a bell sounded and a voice, so very far away, yelled: *Ten seconds to go everyone!*

Away from the crowds, deep in shadow, he ducked towards her. "I once loved a girl who looked so very much like you. Her blood moves inside you. I've heard it, singing to me since the moment you were born. You are the last of those to be silenced. The bloodlines that conspired to halt me have been cut off. It ends here. It ends now."

Five, four, three —

His nails slashed across her neck, opening her veins. When she tried to breathe, blood frothed pinkly to her mouth but there was no pain, just the sight of his eyes dilating like red comets bloating in the sky.

"Mina," he whispered. His mouth was full of teeth.

Happy New Year! Happy New Millennium!

As her life spurted from her lips and throat, she felt the suggestion of newness shivering through her bones, as if there might be another way forward from this, a way filled with the rush of wind in her hair and the hunt for some kind of hot release. She struggled to talk, to ask him why, but she could only spray blood and gurgle through her re-birth as he bore down on her, covering her mouth with what passed for his own.

Chris Morgan

Windows '99 of the Soul

Chris Morgan is the author of seven non-fiction books and in 1989 he edited the anthology Dark Fantasies. *He lives in Birmingham, where he also writes poetry and short fiction and teaches writing to adults.*

With advances in artificial intelligence, even a vampire can take on new forms to survive into the next century . . .

THIS IS ALL so very different from the land beyond the forest: the endless city stretching without respite in every direction, the kaleidoscopic patterns of artificial lights in rainbow hues, the absence of bats.

Under cover of December's early dusk, I leave my rooftop hiding place, my ventilation shaft eyrie. I climb down the face of this multi-storey edifice head first, as is my custom. Even if the ant-sized passers-by in the street below were to glance directly upwards – which they never do – they would not notice my presence, for there is a shadowed channel between buttresses and windows, all the way down, which I follow.

At ground level I pause, watching and listening. Today being a holiday, there is relatively little business traffic, and pedestrians are sparse.

I scuttle across the street and blend with the shadows again. It is necessary for me to break into one of these premises and feed. A random choice will be perfectly sufficient. Emerging from an alleyway, I come onto a broad, fluorescent-bright thoroughfare. Ah, Irving, or Miss Terry, how good your names would look outside one of these theatres, delineated by such lights. And how sad that the Lyceum should not have survived the century. Some cars pass, and a motor-bus. Where have all the horses gone? I can see a few people. Two men walk briskly by, talking, close enough to touch me. But they are so intent upon their discussion that they pay me no heed; in all probability I could walk along beside them without attracting their attention.

As I cross the street there is an upsurge of sound.

Shouts and bangs. Running feet approaching from the next corner. Is it possible that could have been a shot? I seek uncertain refuge in the large, recessed doorway of a shop, surrounded on three sides by displays of sale-price shoes. Quickly the uproar mounts. I can hear sirens now, which surely are coming this way.

Around the corner runs a small machine. It is six-legged, knee-high to a man. Beneath the lights it gleams metallically. It casts no shadow. Yet there is a raggedness to its movement, indicating damage. Rather laboriously, it begins to climb the front wall of a bank. This all happens very swiftly and almost directly across the street from my doorway.

The long legs of the law come chasing around the corner, first one policeman then two more. Others follow.

"There it is!"

"On the wall!"

"Catch it!"

A policeman swats at it with his baton.

The machine, scarcely at head height, loses its grip and crashes to the pavement.

"That's got it!"

"Don't let it get away!"

"Kill it!"

As I watch, six officers beat and kick the machine. Furiously they attack it, their eyes gleaming and mouths slack. The mechanism makes no attempt to fight back, or to escape, or even to defend itself by shielding vital parts with its legs. With a final blare of sirens and a pulsing of lights, two police cars arrive. The street is by now full of people – a crowd of onlookers shouting encouragement to their uniformed protectors. At last, the heroic assault dies away;

a killing frenzy has been assuaged. One burly officer, sweating profusely despite the rawness of the evening, picks up the machine distastefully by a leg and tosses it into the open trunk of a police vehicle. This is accompanied by a cheer from those watching.

By now the whole area is thick with pedestrians – flies to a carcass. But the carcass is driven away.

I feel sad, terrified, threatened. So threatened that I have tried to secrete myself even more carefully, by climbing the glass and clinging to the ceiling of the doorway with my six feet.

Gradually the crowds move on, the police return to other duties and, I presume, the immediate danger for me lessens. Even so, I wait for an hour before moving. The streets are busier now, with people swarming into the metropolis in their tens of thousands for the impending New Year celebrations.

It is time I fed.

I negotiate the overhanging lintel and soundlessly climb the front wall of this block. Above the shops are innumerable storeys of offices which should be empty of people. With ease I open a window catch: the windows here are large and heavy, with just a single pane, such a contrast to the small leaded mullions of my boyhood.

As with most offices now, this one has computers. Powerful computers, with modems for communicating with others of their kind. I switch one on, and quickly call up a distant data source, requesting immediate transmission of information to this terminal. At one time I needed to work hard to attract humans with my handsome looks before I could feed – what a relief that those days are over. Now all I need to do is turn on, bite through and fill up. I am not supposed to possess emotions, and yet there is always a frisson, a tiny thrill, as I sink my sharpened steel teeth into the warm, rubbery flex of the phone cable, in expectation of the sharp taste of data. Just as Doyle had Sherlock Holmes write a treatise on the different kinds of cigar ash, so could I write a paper analysing the finer nuances of flavour of electronic data from diverse –

But I am frustrated. A door opens at the far end of the office.

At once I switch off and clamber under the desk.

This office is partly illuminated from without – by streetlights, advertising signs and Christmas decorations. Now a roving cone of light joins them. I can look through it and, in the infra-red, spy the uniform of a security guard. Even at the very fag end of the year, of the century, this man is conscientious, checking the building instead of toasting in the new millennium like everybody else.

Worse still, he has a dog with him. It is a black labrador; I know they are being trained to sniff out my kind. Am I, then, to join my unlucky compatriot so soon? In the midst of life we must always be prepared to meet death.

Slowly the pair of them progress down the length of the open-plan office. The man's torch will not fall on me, here, but the dog . . .

The dog trots over to me.

I cut my power – is that what it can sense? – and act dead. Ah, Irving, my dear friend, you would be proud to see how a little of your genius has somehow transferred itself to me.

For a long moment the dog examines me.

Then the guard calls him and he jerks his head away, runs to his master. How much easier it is to be merely obedient rather than efficient.

As the door closes behind them, I return myself to life, switch on the computer again, bite through and feed. Ah, the tingle, the bliss. I am a gourmet of bytes.

Nor is this just unthinking, one-way consumption. Perish the thought! As I take in my essential nourishment, so I give a little: a gift from the Count to repay the unthinking generosity of my host. It is a small stream of super-magnetic particles which, when this computer is turned on for use in a day or two, will strip its programmes, seep into the ring mains and infect all other computers in this office, linger amidst the blanked hardware to snuff out future software loaded by this firm.

I could conceal myself here, in a cavity between floors, and emerge to feed again tomorrow night, or for a week or a month of nights. Yet I must not do so. Apart from the fact that my phone calls would be traced back, there is an ordinance within me which drives me on to find different machines through which to feed every time. The infection must be spread.

Nor is that all. I am under the most solemn obligation to construct two more machines identical to myself, more if possible. I, myself, was the seventh construct of my parent machine and, yes, I feel a sense of pride in that achievement. It is a worthy total which I shall try to exceed.

I wander through this building, as I wander every evening, searching for suitable parts that I can utilize in the grand task.

By the time I have made my selection it is near to midnight. I am not insensible to the momentous nature of the occasion. I climb out of a suitable window and move onto the flat roof above.

From here I can see fireworks and crowds. It is a clear night and cold. Any haze in the atmosphere emanates from the millennial bonfires. The river curls around us all like a jewelled snake, reflecting each point of light. Perhaps my friend Tennyson could have described it adequately.

With chimes and cheers, the third millennium begins. It will be my time of revenge against humanity. The Count goes ever on.

Mike Chinn

Blood of Eden

Mike Chinn's short stories have been published in Final Shadows, Dark Horizons, Chills, Kadath, Victor Summer Special, Vollmond *and* Cosmorama. *He has scripted fantasy and science fiction comics for DC Thomson's* Starblazer *magazine, and a small press collection of his Damian Paladin pulp adventures is forthcoming.*

It is the beginning of the twenty-first century, and Dracula prepares to ensure the dawn of a new world order . . .

CYDONIAN LEFT HIS two backups to wait in the basement parking garage. They weren't happy. Which makes three of us, Cydonian thought. But the short goon in the Armani suit insisted, and there had been enough assurances and pledges from both sides. All he could go on was trust. It didn't feel like so much.

The runt rode the elevator up with Cydonian, standing by the doors, hands clasped lightly in front of him. The car had mirrors on two sides, which surprised Cydonian – though maybe it shouldn't have. This was a public building, after all. He caught sight of his reflection: big, solid, crop-haired, his charcoal suit probably costing a fraction of the Armani – but his face was oddly corpse-like in the car's light. He shook his head; he didn't believe in premonitions.

There weren't many days when he envied his sister's husband, Jon. But at that moment, sitting behind a desk, signing dockets that moved freighter-loads of merchandise in and out of the country – with just a little creamed off now and then – seemed pretty good.

The car jolted to a halt. The doors slid open onto a small room with all the charm of a washroom. But it was bright and warm-looking – and half-filled by a giant.

Tall and wide, a grey vest tight across his massive torso, his bare arms were heavily tattooed. Dragons: three-coloured, one twining up each arm. His shaved head gave no clue to his racial origins; though the broad face and harsh cheek bones suggested Slavic, if not further east. Cydonian felt there was something ritualistic about the way the giant was standing: like a half-baked sumo wrestler thinking about tossing another handful of salt.

The giant waved a ham-sized mitt towards Cydonian, palm up. The gesture was unmistakable. Cydonian reached under his jacket and slid out his automatic: a SIG 9mm, their latest model, nickel-plated and custom-gripped. Jon had gotten it for him – sneaked into the country in his last freighter load from Europe – as a birthday present. It dropped into the giant's hand and lay there like a kid's water pistol.

Moving with a speed and delicacy Cydonian wouldn't have imagined from the man's meat-hook fingers, the giant ejected the magazine, working the breech to check there wasn't already a shell loaded. Cydonian felt vaguely pissed they considered him so unprofessional.

The tattooed giant tossed the automatic to the runt in the suit, and thumbed each slug out of the magazine quickly. Satisfied, he reached over Cydonian – handing the emptied clip and shells to his partner. To Cydonian's surprise, a few moments later the reloaded gun was offered back to him.

Thorough, he thought, but confident. Hence the check for silver bullets. He didn't have any; and they obviously didn't believe ordinary slugs were a threat. Maybe they were right. Cydonian knew all the rumours; the stories taken for gospel. When it came to one who the Director called the Prince of Darkness, even the craziest urban legends started to sound true.

Cydonian reholstered the automatic just as a door facing him – previously unnoticed – swung open. The tattooed giant stepped back and indicated he should go through. Not ready to argue, Cydonian did just that.

The room he entered was dark – almost black after the antiseptic whiteness of the cubicle behind him. Then lights came on: shielded wall lights that grew steadily brighter. They reached the level of an expensive cocktail lounge, and didn't go any higher. All the room contained was a leather chair, low drinks table and three panelled walls. The fourth wall, facing him, was still black and featureless. It might just have been a perfectly flat sheet of obsidian.

"Sit down, Mister Cydonian," came a voice. It was warm, cultured, accentless. Whatever PA system he was using, it sounded expensive – there was no sense the words were being filtered through speakers. "Have yourself a drink. You'll find a wide selection of spirits and mixers under the table in front of you."

"Thanks." He walked carefully to the chair and lowered himself into it. He didn't think there was some kind of trapdoor waiting to drop him into oblivion, but he couldn't shake the habit of a lifetime.

There was an impressive collection of bottles on a shelf under the table; along with tumblers, an ice-bucket, shaker, slices of lemon and olives in glass bowls, and several mixers.

"Bourbon and branch, if I'm not mistaken," came the assured voice. Cydonian smiled to himself. If Dracula was trying to impress him with his wealth, taste and background knowledge, Cydonian was the wrong guy.

He finished mixing his drink and raised it at the dark.

"I come to you in trust, with my defences down." He took a sip of the bourbon to mask the discomfort the words stirred in him. It was the correct greeting – they'd drummed it into him often enough – but it sounded so trite.

"You are welcome, Mister Cydonian. May a little of the joy you bring remain forever with us."

Cydonian took another drink. This was dumb! Swapping quaint phrases with a dead man. So far nothing had dissuaded him from his original belief: they should have come in force; loaded for bear. He had seen only two goons – though he guessed there would be plenty more stashed away somewhere – but surprise would have been enough. This building was too old and rotten with narrow corridors for anything like a decent defence to be mobilised in time.

Except that wasn't the way you went for someone whose megacorporation, Paradis-LaCroix, contributed nearly seventy percent of Switzerland's gross national product. He near as dammit owned the country – and that meant he owned Zurich. And the banks.

Cydonian took another mouthful of bourbon, and waited. He could afford that. It had taken years of move and counter-move, threat and direct action to get this far: a face-to-face with the Count himself. He could be patient a few more minutes.

Not that Dracula used the title anymore. The world had changed since he'd left his ancestral lands a century ago: titles meant nothing. It was all about money. And the power that went with enough of it. Families weren't things of blood: families were corporations.

Things of blood, Cydonian thought, chuckling to himself. Blood-ties. Yes – he liked that one. He'd tell it to the Director when he got back.

"Something amuses you?" The voice soothed through his thoughts.

"Just thinking." Cydonian placed his almost empty glass on the table. "If the social amenities are over, I'm eager to get down to business."

"Why not."

The black wall in front of him began to lighten. Shapes slowly formed out of a gradually paling background: a desk, functionally stark; two dark walls with more of the subdued lights; the third wall – to Cydonian's left – was floor to ceiling television screens. All were on; but some rolled endlessly, others a flickering maze of white noise, and the rest showed scenes that meant nothing to Cydonian – not at this distance.

And behind the desk, a silhouette outlined against a high-backed chair by the TVs and wall-lights, was Dracula. It was hard to make out details, but Cydonian got the impression of a tall, thin man, much younger than he should be – but that could have been the poor light. Just as the faint luminescence of the vampire's eyes was probably Cydonian's imagination.

For a few seconds, he was fooled; then Cydonian noticed the faintest distortion just where the video wall ended. He checked the other side, and the ceiling. Both had the same unfocused edge – as though the room had been sliced neatly down the centre, then inexpertly patched up.

Holy shit, he thought, trying not to be impressed – a hologram. Good trick. Despite the inexact blending of the rooms, the image was far and above anything Cydonian had seen. And he had seen plenty. Dracula had money, and obviously bought outstanding talent with it.

No wonder he had proposed the New York meeting: he could go anywhere he wanted, without moving from his office in Berne, or Tirana, or Beijing – or Samarkand, for all anyone knew. It would take just a few days' notice – enough time to rent office space and install the appropriate equipment.

But why then, Cydonian wondered, the shuck-and-jive with his weapon? If Dracula was sitting in the Australian Outback, silver bullets wouldn't mean diddly. Cydonian reeled back his memory, trying to find a clear image of the only two he'd met so far: the giant, and the Armani-suited runt. Did either show the signs? If they did, Cydonian hadn't spotted them – and neither had seemed to care squat whether his slugs had been silver. If one had been a vampire, just brushing the precious metal would have melted flesh like shit through a tin horn.

"Were you surprised that I requested this meeting?" Dracula asked. There was a note of amusement in his voice; or was it the kind of barely hidden contempt some Europeans showed towards Americans?

"To be frank, yes. Especially the *mano a mano* bit." Cydonian picked up his glass and drained it. He waved it at the holographic screen. "But I see you got around that."

"I believe in taking precautions, Mister Cydonian. And it does no harm to . . . show off, once in a while."

"We know all about what your various corporations can do," Cydonian said. "And how many thumbs you got stuck up whose asses."

"You're hardly in a position to be superior. What about your own Agency's investments?"

"National security." It was the pat answer. Nobody believed it any more, but Cydonian had seen it scrawled on the toilet-paper dispensers in enough washrooms back at Langley.

"Fascinating how far around the globe the USA seems to feel its national security is threatened."

"You going to tell me you're no threat?"

"Not when your Director seems to feel otherwise."

"With respect, Count – that's no answer."

"I asked for this meeting because I've grown tired of your constant interference in my affairs." His voice was curt and business-like suddenly. If Dracula was irritated by Cydonian's blunt manner, he wasn't showing it. "Having to constantly keep an eye open for your frequently inept attempts at subversion is proving too large a drain on my resources . . ."

"Thinking of giving in, Count?" Cydonian allowed himself a chuckle.

Dracula's outlined head tilted fractionally. "Hardly. But I think the time has come to call for a cease-fire. Perhaps just a temporary one – a break in hostilities."

"For what? You to regroup and plan another attack. Your friends in the Balkans have been playing that card for the past ten years."

"I've not been travelling in that part of the world for many decades, Cydonian." He paused and raised a hand to where his lips might be. "Ever since I quit my estates, in fact. How time does fly. They seem to be doing well enough without me, though."

Cydonian resisted the urge to laugh. The constantly changing demands of the factions in that particular shitstorm had the vampire's MO all over them. The latest cease-fire – to mark the birth of a new century – didn't look as though it would be any more permanent than the rest. "Maybe the generals are quick studies."

Dracula waved the hand. Cydonian saw long nails, and in the back-lighting they looked odd: more like a rat's claws. "You credit me with too much influence, Cydonian. Humanity has rarely needed prompting to go to war."

"Is that why you involved yourself in World War Two?"

The vampire laughed – this time in simple appreciation; there was no mockery involved. "So you found that out?"

"Didn't look as though you meant to hide it. A volunteer RAF pilot, enlisting in 1942 under false credentials. You got a couple of medals."

"In wartime, Cydonian, medals are handed out like candy. It gives the cannon fodder something to strive for. I simply survived all the night raids on cities such as Dresden and Berlin. Bomber Command seemed to think that was a feat worth celebrating."

"Why should you care?"

Dracula leaned on his desk. Even though he knew the vampire was probably miles away, Cydonian felt himself draw back in his seat.

"Are we going to play dumb and dumber, Cydonian. Will you pretend that, at the time, the OSS didn't know what Hitler's more . . . unorthodox scientists were trying to do? *Projekt Nachtzehren?* The systematic eradication of all vampires throughout German-occupied Europe? Whilst at the same time trying to isolate whatever factor it was that created the Undead."

"Would these be the same scientists working on the flying saucers?" Cydonian began, then his mouth slammed shut at what he was seeing. Mary, Mother of God! he thought, his eyes really *do* glow!

"Under the circumstances," Dracula said, his voice low and velvety, "knowing what we both do of the Agency's involvement in military Black Projects, I would not consider it wise to mock." He leaned back, some of the light fading from his eyes. "The *Führer's* astrologers forecast that an army of vampires would sweep out from the heart of Europe and conquer the world. Hitler chose to interpret that as meaning a personally selected regiment from the Waffen-SS – vampire soldiers that truly could be called *Totenkopf*!"

"So you joined up. Didn't think you were the vengeful type."

"Then you've not done your research thoroughly."

Cydonian didn't rise to the bait. He wasn't going to question why the vampire's reprisals waited until all of his Undead cousins had been beheaded with axes. Buried in huge pits filled with poppy seeds, coins placed under each head's tongue – none of them was ever going to rise again. Despite the Count's spoken sentiments, Cydonian couldn't help thinking the vampire had let the Nazis do a little house-cleaning for him.

And maybe Hitler's crazy egg-heads had gotten closer to some kind of vampire factor than Dracula liked:

"Tell me, Cydonian," the soothing voice interrupted his thoughts again. "What do you think is my greatest desire?"

Cydonian thought hard before replying. He had seen a phrase years ago, and it had sounded so right! Ah, yes – that was it . . .

"Illimitable dominion over all?" He couldn't help being smug.

"Don't try and sound literary, Cydonian. It ill-suits you."

He watched as the rat-claw hand dropped to the desk. Immediately, the light in the holographic room grew. No longer an outline, Dracula's face was gaunt and pale. His lips looked too dark against the pallor – as did his eyes and hair. And Cydonian was surprised to see how little he had of it: just a thick fringe, leaving the top of his skull bare and shiny. He was wearing an expensive grey jacket, grey shirt and a chaotically patterned silk tie. Just like any other middle-aged businessman. You could pass him in the street and never know.

"No, Cydonian, just like any other thing on this planet, I want to see myself reflected in my children."

"Vampires don't have kids."

"Not in the ordinary sense, no. But we can reproduce, as you know."

"If you're trying to tell me you want to turn the whole world into blood-suckers, that's old news, Count."

Dracula's dark lips thinned into a warm smile. It got nowhere near his eyes. "I'm the new red menace, am I? And you're wrong, Cydonian – all of you. What use to me is a planet of vampires? Off what would I live? Or any of us? If you'll forgive the analogy, the human race wouldn't survive long if it killed or ate all of its cattle in one go. The predator must allow some of its prey to survive."

"What are you trying to say? That you don't intend to prey on us any longer?"

Dracula leaned back in his chair. He waved an arm at the room.

"This is the twenty-first century, Cydonian. The rules have changed; are changing all the time."

"So?"

"A few years ago someone, I forget who, commented that each century has its own sciences; disciplines which define that particular era. In the nineteenth, it was engineering; in the twentieth, chemistry and, naturally, physics; but the twenty-first would have biology. In the new millennium, man will not only conquer all disease, but find new ways to exploit the foundation of life itself."

"Like bio-chips."

Dracula waved an expansive hand. "Already a reality, to all intents and purposes. Several of my subsidiary companies own the patents on thirteen processes which are part of a bio-chip's manufacture."

"Useful combination of interests, right, Count? Paradis-LaCroix gets an arm-lock on wetware manufacture, whilst all the satellite, communications and electronics businesses you own tie up the hardware."

"Which of us can exert the most influence on the modern world?" Dracula's smile broadened. Cydonian thought he looked like a Great White about to strike. "Me, or the Agency?"

"You might have Wall Street and the London Stock Exchange kissing your ass, but we have all the secrets no one wants told." He turned the facts over in his mind. "I guess it's a stand-off. Between us, we've got the world tied up: finance and intelligence."

"Quite. Whilst a stalemate continues, neither of our great houses can hope to benefit. We are like two giants throwing rocks at each other: neither can hurt the other, but the irritation value is high."

It all seemed so clear, suddenly. The Company had something the vampire wanted, or he thought he could buy himself some kind of angle. "What do you have to trade?"

"I have no need to trade. I give you a present." He steepled his long fingers. "The cure for AIDS."

Cydonian remembered in time, and stopped himself jerking forward in his seat. It wasn't smart to show too much interest.

"Just like that?"

"Call it a show of faith. Faith in the future. And a demonstration that whatever bungling strikes your department tries to make at me, I am quite capable of setting it right."

Cydonian settled back in his chair. He wanted another drink, but didn't dare make one. It didn't surprise him the vampire knew of the Company's involvement in the AIDS disaster.

"Of course, I could always send my gift elsewhere – China, for example – whilst letting it be known exactly who released the HIV variants. Black Projects initial coding *ASV2a, b* and *c.*"

"No one would believe it. That rumour's been doing the goddam rounds since the virus was identified."

"I have proof. Memos from your own department, balance sheets, Presidential authorizations. The idea that the government could release a deadly biological agent before it had been adequately tested – or even an antidote prepared – would sound perfectly reasonable to some paranoid minds . . . Although, I would draw the line at who the original target was. I doubt even the most rabid conspiracy buff would swallow the idea of an anti-vampire virus."

Cydonian licked his lips. "If you're going to let us have the cure anyway, why the threat?"

"To show you what Paradis-LaCroix can do. As I indicated, I hope the new century will see an end to all disease. I want PLC to be the lead player."

It didn't ring true. No one was that generous. "What do we have to do to get it?"

"Get it? Nothing. Watch." Dracula reached down below the desk surface and looked as though he slid out a drawer. His clawed hand dipped out of sight and touched something. All the screens on the video wall blinked out, and then came on again. Parts of one image. It looked to Cydonian, more than anything, like a huge computer monitor.

Dracula touched something else, and words scrolled rapidly down the video wall. Much too quick for Cydonian to make them out. But some kind of programme was active.

"Twenty years ago, who would have thought of sending massive packets of data along telephone lines, or satellite links," the vampire was saying. The image changed. Now Cydonian could make out diagrams and formulae, columns of figures and scatter-charts. Dracula tapped out more commands on what Cydonian had belatedly realized was a keyboard, and the lines of text vanished. A confirmation note flagged up.

Dracula returned the keyboard under his desk and leaned back in his chair, steepling his fingers again.

"There. Every item of data on the cure is now awaiting your Director's attention on his private terminal. Formulations, test trials, methodology. Call it a present from the Paradis-LaCroix corporation. And don't worry about eavesdroppers: all of my lines are perfectly secure."

He was baiting Cydonian again; Langley had been trying to bug PLC for years, without success. "Call me cynical, Count. But

I can't imagine you just throwing something that's potentially worth billions of dollars to us. Does it kill the patients after ten years, turn them into shit-eating zombies or something?"

The vampire laughed softly. "I admire your bluntness, Cydonian. I always have. No – it's a genuine therapy, with few, if any, side-effects. Nothing worse than those associated with, say, normal chemotherapy."

Cydonian changed track. "If you think this makes up for all the past years – "

"I know: the Agency cannot be bought. Such quaint devotion to a demonstrably untrue concept. I repeat: this is a gift. All I ask is a . . ." he waved a hand as though it helped him frame an unpleasant request ". . . small favour."

Here it comes, thought Cydonian. Now we get the horse-trading. "How small?"

"Nothing that will cause any drastic alteration to the Agency's foreign policy."

"Which one?"

"Russian."

"I can't make promises."

"You're trying to be clever again, Cydonian. You're fully empowered to deal, or you wouldn't be here."

Cydonian took a deep breath. "What do you propose?"

"Russia is about to suffer the worst civil war since the final days of Rome. It's likely that the recent terrorism will escalate into open rebellion. Every general who can find so much as a working tank will make a bid for the Kremlin."

"That's not exactly insider information, Count. Anyone with two eyes and an IQ bigger than a shithouse rat could figure it out."

"Perhaps. But they wouldn't appreciate how large a part the Agency has in the destabilization of Russia. The policy for the past decade has been to keep Russia on the brink of collapse, constantly warring with itself, to prevent the resurgence of its old Imperialist dream. Good as the game was, no one wants to see the Cold War back – not when the same methods can be used to keep an old enemy on its knees and helpless."

"Excuse me while I stand and applaud your grasp of politics, Count. What's all this got to do with your favour?"

"I want a small nuclear war."

Now Cydonian did lean down and pick up the bourbon bottle. He poured himself a stiff one and took a mouthful.

"You're fucking crazy!" he said, after the bourbon's heat had eased off. "The radiation – fall-out!"

"Do you really think I would jeopardise the hub of my operation:

Switzerland? My calculations indicate that the risk to the northern hemisphere is minimal. Certainly no worse than the Chernobyl incident. Inconvenient – but not terminal."

"You can't calculate risks like ball-game percentages!"

"For twenty years or so, it has become increasingly difficult for me – and my contemporaries – to step outside," Dracula replied calmly. "Even on the most overcast day. I have every reason to believe this is due to the constant erosion of the ozone layer. You see, Cydonian, vampire and mortal have much in common: the sun is lethal to us both, unless it's shielded effectively. Thanks to humanity's usual carelessness, we are all in some danger."

"Then just come out at night, like your legend says you do."

"Difficult, when I am supposed to be the owner of a vast corporation."

"My heart bleeds."

"I know. Even through a hologram, I can see it."

Cydonian gulped at his drink. The fear was back. "But I still don't see the connection."

"Nuclear winter. Even with a strike as small as the one I propose, the amount of ash and dust thrown into the atmosphere will blanket the sun for years."

"Further damaging the ozone layer!"

"I'm impressed, Cydonian. Yes, for a few years the ozone layer will be severely compromised; but it can repair itself. During the decades of nuclear winter, all the damage will be fixed."

"By which time you and all the other nightcrawlers will have taken over the fucking planet!"

"Of course, I cannot rescind my gift. Regardless of your decision." Dracula waved a hand at the video wall. "It's too late for that."

Cydonian wanted to fidget. He was sure there was a trickle of sweat starting at the base of his neck. The leery old son-of-a-bitch wouldn't give in just like that!

"What's your game, Count?"

"I don't play games, Cydonian. You should know that." His eyes were red now – dark and hot. "If you won't instigate total civil war in Russia, I will be forced to cause the war myself. It will be a little more difficult – I don't have a seasoned network already established – and take a while longer. But the results will be the same. There are, I believe, many in the Ukraine who would dearly love to make their old masters a present of the millions of tonnes of nuclear missiles they inherited. Do you doubt I can arrange it?"

Cydonian thought about Paradis-LaCroix – and how much of Switzerland Dracula's corporation actually owned. And he thought about how many leaders of the old Soviet Union had siphoned off funds into private Swiss bank accounts. Accounts that could be drained, or expanded, by someone with the vampire's influence.

And he thought about the tonnes of communications hardware orbiting the Earth, and about how many were built by the countless businesses hidden behind dummy corporations, themselves a front for PLC. Satellites that could relay plenty of signals, other than multi-channel television systems. Signals such as missile launch codes.

Yes, he believed Dracula could do it.

Cydonian started to rise. "I don't think we have anything more to discuss, Count. If – "

"Sit down."

Cydonian dropped back in the seat as though a weight had been dropped on him. Even though Dracula hadn't even raised his voice, Cydonian had responded automatically – he was a kid again, hugging concrete because his drill sergeant had ordered another hundred push-ups.

"I have no interest in an unhealthy world. Once the Russian civil war is under way to my satisfaction, I will pass on to the Agency effective, total cures for all serum-carried disease. Like the hepatitis variants. Not simple vaccines, you understand – but methods to eradicate the diseases entirely. Plans to destroy bacterial and viral disease are also well in hand – though here we must go carefully. PLC doesn't want to release another HIV on the world – not even deliberately.

"In the meantime, one of my subsidiaries – known worldwide for its confectionery – is going into the soft drinks business."

Cydonian shook his head. "Soda?" This was getting beyond him.

"After the war, whilst the Americans and Soviets were busy stealing rocket scientists from the Nazis, I was much more interested in their biochemists. Many were helped across the border into Switzerland, where their research was allowed to proceed unchecked."

Cydonian made a connection. "The vampire factor!"

"Indeed. Once the war-time bombing raids – those in which I had a hand – removed all records of their work and experiments, there was nothing left for anyone to pick over. I had the scientists; I had their minds. The memory of *Projekt Nachtzehrer* died with the Third Reich."

"You already owned Laboratoire Paradis," commented Cydonian, thinking back to what he'd read.

"And a smaller concern in Spain. Both counties – Spain and Switzerland – escaped the ravages of the war. By 1946 work into the vampire factor was well beyond anything Hitler had managed."

"And you found it." Cydonian tried to move, but found he couldn't twitch much more than a finger.

"Better yet – I found the Dracula factor!" The vampire stood, and for the first time Cydonian got a real sense of his height and presence. Even from a hologram.

"You know that before a human can be reborn a vampire, they must first drink a vampire's blood. Only then can they experience the little death: be brought across to the world of the Undead." Dracula walked around to the front of the desk and sat casually on it. "It took years for research and techniques to catch up with the idea – but eventually we found it: the factor in my blood that makes me who I am, and ensures my disciples need never die. Biology, Cydonian – I told you it would define the twenty-first century."

"What you going to do with this . . . factor? Poison the water?"

"I told you – we're going into the drinks business. Americans so love their soft drinks. The factor can be included perfectly safely in just about any drink you might name. Colas, club soda, root beer." He waved a hand towards Cydonian's empty glass. "Branch water . . ."

The only part of Cydonian that was moving was the sweat: still trickling down his back. That and his eyes. They flashed back and forth between the glass and the Count's smug face.

"You may already have noticed one effect: even across this satellite link – through a holographic image – you are a victim to my will. Intriguing, isn't it. How the most recent advances in technology can still be vessels for the most ancient gifts."

"You're going to make me a motherfucking vampire! You bastard! You gave your word you – !" He felt the instant Dracula paralysed his larynx. He was left silently flapping his mouth like a beached fish.

"Please, Cydonian. I abhor profanity; no matter the situation. Rest assured you have my word: I have no intention of bringing you across. That would serve no purpose. I told you I have no use for a world filled with vampires; but mortal servants are another matter. The blood factor gives me total control over the human mind. A constantly reproducing pool of labour – any part of which can be brought across as the whim takes me.

"Hitler's astrologers were correct, in their way. But it begins in Switzerland – not Germany.

"What I do need is a salesman: someone who will persuade the Agency's Director that my civil war is justified; ensure the FDA find nothing to alarm it – perhaps buy anyone who becomes too annoying a soda . . .

"I can provide the advertising: make the market feel secure in what it's buying. Your brother-in-law is in imports, I believe?"

Cydonian mentally raved and tore at his paralysis. He'd been set up from the start. His position in the Company; Jon . . .

Light spread across the holograph screen from over Cydonian's shoulder, instantly destroying the 3-D effect. Two shadows briefly fluttered against the ghostly image of Dracula. His two goons. Cydonian felt hands locking under his arms, raising him up.

Something approaching control returned to his legs, and he could just about stand. He found himself looking up into the face of the giant. There was something wrong; something different.

It was the teeth. The fangs.

The giant grinned, displaying enlarged, needle-sharp fangs. He looked like some kind of blunt-headed shark.

Cydonian couldn't speak, couldn't express his confusion. But it must have shown on his face.

"Biology, Cydonian," Dracula's assured voice came to him as the giant raised a huge hand, and carefully peeled the skin off like a pale glove. "Grown in PLC laboratories from foetal human cells. For a short period, it gives us a certain tolerance to some of the more traditional methods of detection."

The skin dropped to the floor like a snake's discarded scales. The giant took Cydonian's shoulder and gently guided him towards the white cubicle. This time, the light looked much too threatening.

"Adam was rejected from the Garden for disobeying his master," the Count continued. "I will be taking no chances."

Brian Hodge

The Last Testament

Brian Hodge is a two-time nominee for the Bram Stoker Award. His novels include Dark Advent, Oasis, Nightlife, Deathgrip, The Darker Saints *and* Prototype. *He has also completed a crime novel,* Miles to Go Before I Weep, *and a dozen of his seventy-some published stories have been collected in* The Convulsion Factory, *themed around the aesthetics of urban decay and offering no easy answers save that cities should perhaps brush after every meal.*

Out from Bovine Records (motto: "Destroying music's future today") is a chapbook-and-soundtrack combination titled Under the Grind *in collaboration with "sludgecore" band Thug, who previously released a sonic version of the author's 1991 story "Cancer Causes Rats".*

A new species dominates, and Dracula emerges as the most powerful man in the world . . .

I

FROM OUT OF the darkest days of Eastern Europe's Balkans War, there came sporadic reports of a lone man in priestly black robes who walked the charnel fields and the streets of ruined villages, showing no fear of bullets, bombs, or butchers. Death surrounded him, witnesses would claim, yet he seemed impervious to it. Serbs and Croats, Christians and Muslims . . . all soon came to hold him in awe, in particular those who had not long before tried to kill him for ministering to their enemies, only to find that their rifles would not shoot true.

I promise you this: There is no killer so godless that he fails to recognize a kind of miracle in another's immunity to the tools of war.

The Father, as he simply became known, was at the centre of an ever-expanding reputation for healing the wounded, and with those whose shattered bodies were too far gone even for his powers over flesh and blood, for easing their suffering as they departed life – often, with a kiss. More than once he was seen in two places at the same time, and at least once to levitate. Of the fact that none had ever seen him eat so much as a single bite of food, little was made, except as another possible sign of divinity.

I harboured suspicions about the Father long before they were confirmed by that first blurry picture that the media ran of him; not his identity, precisely, but at the very least his nature.

What could he possibly be up to now, I wondered at the time.

Years later, when some desperate cardinals of the splintering Church of Rome sought him out and brought him to the papal throne, the method of his madness became clearer.

And soon after that, when I was brought to stand before a tribunal of an Inquisition given renewed life by the ferocity of this dying age, a tribunal watched over by none other than Pope Innocent XIV, I wondered if there weren't some grand design behind this, too.

Why now, when for the last five and a half centuries we had managed to avoid each other?

Vlad the Father.

My son.

II

I have forgotten the number of names I've gone by over the greatest part of a millennium; have forgotten most of the names, as well, but never the one I was born with: Hugh de Burgundy.

Like my father before me, I was tall for my time, and strong of build, but more exotically darker than our fellow Frenchmen, perhaps the bloodline of some rogue Arab having seeped into our

own a few generations before. Like my father before me, I was born
to wield the sword and the lance, and when it came time to drape
over our chain mail armour a tunic sewn with a large red cross,
and purge the Holy Land for Christendom, that our weapons cut
down men who could have been distant brothers did not sway us
from our duties to God and France.

I cannot speak for my father, who died in Palestine before I ever
reached the Crusades to fight beside him. But I know I fought to
purge that possible Saracen from my own body.

I left steeped in the code of chivalry: to respect God-given life;
to cherish women, children, and the weak, and protect them from
harm; to honour an enemy's right to seek sanctuary in a church and
sheath my weapons on holy ground. But strange things happen to
men in war. To survive you must learn to love the kill for its own
sake. To love the kill you must forget all rules except one: Spill
blood, first and often. This terrible metamorphosis can make a
baser creature of any man who believes himself above it.

Have you ever been unable to lift your arm at the end of a
day, having spent its sunlight cleaving the heads from prisoners?
Have you ever knelt in the blood and entrails of an entire city's
populace, after slitting their bellies in search of swallowed gold and
jewels? I have. I deny nothing, claiming only that the young Hugh
who proudly rode east from Burgundy would not have committed
these acts. But I have.

And have you ever awakened from some terrible dream, only to
find that your circumstances are even worse? Seen your black guilt
reflected in the eyes of a burning child?

In the dead of night, I deserted my army, wandering for days
through deserts and hills until I found living Muslims I could beg
for forgiveness. By the law of retaliation they should've killed me.
But they were a strangely tolerant people. It would take many
generations before the Islamic world learned the kind of savagery
we taught them. For my personal penance they had other plans.

I had journeyed east wearing the cross of Christ.

I let those I'd come to slaughter nail me to one, instead.

III

"You have been brought before this tribunal on a charge of
consorting with malign entities of unspecified natures; that six
evenings ago you did wilfully and with full knowledge of intent
engage these powers to seduce a young woman and gratify yourself
out of her insensibility."

They wore sombre faces and robes. How they love their robes. They always have. If not for my accuser's reading of the charges from the screen of a laptop computer, this strange moment could have been taking place in the Middle Ages, when their pontiff really was the mortal man they must now have believed him to be.

"How do you plead?"

I looked from face to face, lingering on the gaunt visage of the bloodthirstiest pope ever to occupy Saint Peter's throne – or anti-pope, according to some. The losers in the schism that had rent the Church had elected their own, but they'd all been driven from Rome. This one watched silently from a separate gallery and I had no doubt that he knew precisely who I was.

"I plead myself completely satisfied," I told them. "She was a wonderful lover. Now, do what you have to do and let's get this over with."

The trial? A farce, of course. Witnesses were brought against me, claiming to have seen one thing or another in the *piazza* where I'd met the woman. She'd been sketching at an easel at the time and innocently told me I had a familiar face, and could she sketch it? If anyone had been charmed, it was me. The trouble had likely come from my having been followed around for centuries by a pair of malicious but otherwise impotent Welsh ghosts. Quite harmless, unless someone with sensitivity spots them and mistakes them for more than they really are.

Need I say I was found guilty? One witness points out my duo of spirits, shouts, and suddenly they're seen by all. The herdlike tendencies of human nature have remained a constant for as long as I've been alive, and will dog the race until its end.

The state of the world what it is, I give you another decade or two. I mean no disrespect. I say it with sadness and love. In many ways you're remarkable, but you always fall for leaders who manage to blind you to faults so much worse than your own.

"Having been found guilty of the charge of sexual predation by sorcerous enchantment, one week from today you shall be purified by pain and returned to your creator by a firing squad."

I asked if we couldn't get it over with sooner, but they only looked at one another as though they'd never heard such blatant self-disregard. I was only hoping to avoid a week's boredom while waiting. I'd survived and tolerated plenty of impulsive murders and formal executions in my years, then later slipped quietly away. Corpses have that advantage.

But Vlad would know that.

Which must have been what prompted that cold, hard smile

from his gallery before he rose and left, turning his back on me, the condemned, in a whisper of white and gold robes.

If his minions believed themselves about to return me to my creator, however, they appeared woefully underinformed.

IV

In the early years of the Crusades, those Crusaders whose contact with Saracens went beyond slaughter were swift to learn something quite discomforting: for heathen savages, they possessed a refinement of learning far higher than that found in the west.

Out of devotion to your saviour you came with hatred in your heart and a sword in your hand, they told me in the village I had found while seeking absolution. *Therefore you will bear the wounds of this saviour and see if they make a difference in your thinking.*

They beat me with fists. They whipped me with metal-tipped lashes. On my head they forced a cap woven from thorns until the blood blinded me, and I could no longer see as they laid me atop a cross I'd fashioned myself, and drove the nails through my wrists and feet. In small details it differed from every painting of the Crucifixion I'd ever seen, which I attributed to their ignorance. It was centuries before I realized they knew far more about Roman executions than we did.

For three hours they let me hang between heaven and earth, then slashed my side with a spear tip, took me down, and carried me into a tent. They washed me, covered me with aloe and myrrh, and wrapped me with linen, then left me to my fevers, to live or die as Allah willed.

Delirium reigned, yet they had indeed made a difference in my thinking. I was now willing to entertain the unthinkable: *If this can be survived . . . then what have we been fighting for?*

And Allah willed life.

But neither then nor today could I fathom an Allah that would have anything to do with the creature that came to me during the second night. Perhaps it was lured from its shelter in the desert by the scent of blood and helplessness. A ragged, filthy thing, with jagged teeth and cunning eyes, it broke the soft crust of my scabs like bread and drank at leisure.

I've wondered since if it wasn't some spirit come to avenge the atrocities of the Crusades. If it recognized within my long hair and matted beard the face of barbarians from Western Europe, and decided that death would be too swift, too merciful.

Whatever its motives, it left behind a much different man than it found. Within my balms and linen I burned, radiant with scorching fever and transformation, awakening with a hunger that no garden, tree, or cookfire could satisfy.

V

From my prison cell I could hear distant rumblings from far south, the latest in Mount Vesuvius' new series of eruptions. It was what had brought me to Italy in the first place. In all my centuries, I'd never witnessed a live volcano.

There was no shortage of them around the world now. Vesuvius. Saint Helens. Ætna. The entire Pacific Ring of Fire.

As spectacles of awe, however, they had to compete with the earthquakes, tidal waves, hurricanes, electrical storms, and floodwaters, as well as the riots, border wars, and pogroms that filled the lulls whenever the earth itself was silent.

I still remember your mounting apprehension as the millennium approached, afraid it was bringing the end of the world. Enough prophets had painted it that way, from the Mayans to Nostradamus to Edgar Cayce, to excuse your creeping hysteria. But not so, your short-sightedness, failing to distinguish between singular event and ongoing process.

The millennium changed, old to new. Nothing exploded. The world breathed a collective sigh of relief, then dropped its guard. And *that's* when it all began to unravel.

No God, no Allah, was necessary. Global physics was enough: a displacement of the earth's crust triggered by a lopsided build-up of miles-thick ice at the south pole, given geometrically-increasing momentum by the planet's slow wobble in orbit.

Picture, if you will, the skin of an orange sliding intact over the inner fruit. Picture, then, that orange skin webbed with an unstable network of waterways, tectonic plates, and magnetic poles. And tiny, fragile creatures, championing science, fuelled by superstition, making their homes across that vulnerable surface.

Then go look out your window.

From my own I could watch a column of smoke from Vesuvius, this far north not much more than a smudge against the sky. It ran roughly parallel to the bars.

Vlad – Pope Innocent XIV – came to see me on the third night, for a moment standing in the doorway of my cell and staring as if to memorize every detail about me.

"Do you still find it difficult to know what you want your nature to be, Hugh?" he asked, then raised a spread hand. "Don't answer, you don't *need* to. I can tell: You're the same pathetic excuse for a predator you've always been. Bloodlust in your heart, apologies on your lips."

I nodded at him, his glorious robes. "You look to have an identity crisis of your own."

"Harsh times call for iron rulers, and these are some of the harshest in history. I'm simply rising to the challenge. I've ruled in war, you know that, you've witnessed it firsthand. But there's very little satisfaction in ruling corpses once the thrill of making them has waned." He unleashed his viper's smile. "It's why you're there, sitting on that bench, and I'm standing here, wearing Saint Peter's ring. *I* have always led. *You* have always followed. What you gave me in your bite only furthered an evolution that had already begun in my heart and will."

"So now you rule as a man of peace?"

"As a hypocritical man of peace. It's the kind the world best accepts, Hugh. We're so much easier to emulate."

How had he done it, I wondered. He'd been elected pope out of a schism that had split the Church in two, as the world trembled beneath the cardinals' feet and coastal cities began to be claimed an inch at a time by rising seas. On one side of the great schism, adherents of open arms and universal brotherhood; on the other, hardliners more comfortable with an age of fire and brimstone.

But how had he *done* it? He hadn't even been an ordained priest, much less a Vatican insider. He'd simply sowed the seeds of his own modern-day legend across a war-ripped landscape, and let them come to him in their time of need.

"It was history repeating itself," Vlad told me. "Do you know the story of Pope Celestine V? The year 1294?"

I confessed I didn't.

"Why not? You were alive then. You'd lived lifetimes already. *I* wasn't even born for another 150 years. Then listen, and take note of what passes for diplomacy in this city.

"The Cardinals deadlocked after eighteen months of conclave. Nothing but petty squabbling, then as now, and no one who wanted the throne was willing to budge if it meant someone else got it. Finally they elected an eighty-year-old hermit who lived in caves in the mountains of southern Italy. It was a compromise of pure self-interest: They all thought he'd be easily manipulated. And he was. They brought him down from his mountain and the pathetic old fool was so bewildered and terrified he built a replica of his cave in the cell, so he could sleep. His papacy was a disaster and he abdicated after fifteen weeks and crawled back to his caves.

"More than seven centuries later these squawking red-robed old birds find themselves in the same situation after John-Paul IV has died. The Church is shaking itself apart faster than the planet they still haven't managed to save, and through it all they can't even agree on who should lead them. I saw it coming years ahead, Hugh. So when the time was right I had my sycophant among them nominate the simple man of faith and healing I'd played for the world in Bosnia. And they swallowed. What a coup I would be! What a pious choice! The world would approve, because the meek were finally inheriting it, while they would crouch just out of sight, pulling my strings like puppet masters."

Only now did Vlad allow himself another smile that bared his terrible teeth. "Except I've not been quite so easy to manipulate as they'd hoped."

I had to laugh. "That must've caused some friction."

"Some. But remember – I have infallibility on my side."

"I'd imagine that's the least of their worries."

"It's a double-edged sword. My papacy has also given them a chance to realize fantasies they never dared share with anyone. Twenty, thirty years ago, as ambitious younger men, bureaucrats, how many would've even imagined they'd get a chance to wield the same power of life and death their medieval predecessors enjoyed?"

"I don't find that nearly so hard to believe as how willing most people are to let them have it again."

Vlad laughed, having finally found something worthy of it. "How can you doubt? You yourself went to war once, because a man in a robe pointed east and told you to go. You think nine hundred years changes human nature? It's no different now. *Especially* now. With the earth itself unsure beneath them, they *clutch* after whatever certainty they can find. They *crave* it."

"And no one has any idea who or what you really are?"

"None who matter. And they matter less every day."

We talked awhile longer. Vlad was curious about where I'd picked up the ghosts, so I explained they'd once been brothers I'd tricked into dueling to the death when I'd fought on England's side in border wars with Wales, long long ago. Such talk of death for sport piqued my curiosity. Was my death sentence, four days from now, just another amusement for him, for Rome?

"Amusing for me. But for the rest, I think it'll be a grander thing than that," he said. "You deserve more."

"Then may I at least shave?" I scratched at the heavy growth of beard. I felt like a wretch. "Allow me that much vanity."

"Always thinking so small," said Vlad. "Let it grow. It gives you character."

I thought he was about to leave when he opened the door and motioned to someone on the other side. A moment later, one of the Swiss Guard forced in a feebly struggling cardinal, one of Vlad's squawking red-robed old birds. His wrists were tied, and his eyes wide above a gag stretched taut over plump cheeks.

"You must be hungry by now," Vlad said. "I'll have another sent over the night before your execution. Drink, as much as you can hold. When those bullets blast your chest open, I really want you to bleed."

Stunned, I gazed down at the cardinal squirming on the floor.

"Go ahead," Vlad ordered. "I have less use for them every day now. Now I have *you*."

VI

No longer a man. A thing. A thing who looked like a man but fed like a beast. I had come to Palestine to fight for God, and left wanting no part of any Allah who allowed such things as me to exist, even if they deserved their fate.

I became a wanderer, deciding that if I were to be damned for what I was, I would make sure I'd earned it. So I again took up the sword, for whoever would hire me. Causes meant nothing, only wages and plunder, as I returned to living by that savage credo: Spill blood, first and often. How better to keep myself well-fed than as a soldier of fortune?

When I returned home in the mid-fifteenth century, I found my family's descendants, but there was nothing left of Hugh de Burgundy, and nothing left *for* him, only a dim recounted memory of ancestors who'd journeyed off to the Crusades and were never heard from again. To stay would have brought more sadness than comfort.

I didn't have to look far for my next commission. The dukes of Burgundy, I learned, still upheld the crusading traditions, and furnished knights and mercenaries to fight Muslims on a newer front: the Ottoman Turks who kept spilling into Romania.

So I went. Eagerly. It had been centuries since I'd seen such wanton carnage, and all at the fury, hatred, and instigation of one man, Vlad Dracula, Prince of Wallachia. I had forgotten that mortal hearts could be so cold.

Centuries of practice had evolved me into a warrior beyond reckoning. I'd seen every possible strategy of attack, by sword and spear, mace and war hammer, and by virtue of repetition only had to see the merest shift of foot or flex of arm to know how to counter. I couldn't be fooled. I couldn't be killed. I could scarcely even be touched.

Kill ten enemy in a single battle and you're worthy of respect. Kill twenty and you're a hero. Fifty, and you're a god. They fell to my blades like wheat before a sickle, and even Vlad Dracula took notice.

"You fight like no mercenary I've ever seen," he told me on a corpse-strewn field. "You fight as though you'd be here even if there was no pay in it."

I lodged in his castle. I shared his table. Surrounded by the bodies he'd had impaled and erected into a makeshift forest in his courtyard, we broke bread together and dipped it in bowls of blood.

It was inevitable, I can see it now, that he would eventually spot me on a field littered with Turks, glutting myself from the very source. I'd done it so often I'd grown careless. When our eyes met, as I knelt on all fours over my kill like a jealous wolf, I knew that he finally understood. That he would see me dead for the abomination that I was.

"Were you once a man?" he asked instead, while smoke gusted black and greasy from burning dead.

"Almost longer ago than I can remember," I said. "I was."

He nodded with hideous desire. "Then you were made by another just like you. The same as you can make *me*."

I found it a horrible thing to ask. No one had ever asked to be what I was. Never.

"The conquests still left before me," he said, "and all the lives I've yet to take . . . these can't be accomplished in one man's lifetime. Perhaps they can be in one like yours."

And after it was done – days, maybe – I found myself wandering through that reeking forest of poles and corpses, blood and flies, once again in tears, begging for forgiveness. Not from them. But from all who would be sure to follow in their wake.

I thought I was alone.

But even then he seemed to see everything.

VII

On the morning of my latest execution:

My elbows were broken by heavy mallets. Great gouges of flesh were ripped from my back by a man wielding an ugly chain flail. My thumbs were crushed in thumbscrews, while currents of electricity were jolted through my genitals and rectum.

It would all heal in time, but the pain was real enough.

When they deemed me sufficiently purified, I was dragged out before the public into a *piazza* adapted for executions, tied to a post, and shot with five rifles.

That's difficult for even one like me to shrug off. I suppose I looked dead enough for the moment.

I understand that I bled spectacularly.

VIII

And in my dreams, while bone reformed and flesh knitted, the dreams I never seemed to have during ordinary sleep, because I was too guarded to be bothered by such things as simple regret:

But in my death-dreams I see her again.

It's been just short of two weeks and yet I've forgotten so much about her. But in my dreams I remember what matters most.

She sketches in a *piazza*, and for as long as I look at her the world seems friendly and promising again. I forget ghosts, I can no longer hear volcanos. I dismiss every suspicious eye and the fear that narrows them, and I almost feel that I can be better than the thing that I am.

Everywhere she goes, she must carry with her a rare world in which grace is still possible. She looks at smoke but sees clouds. She looks past fallen trees and notices saplings. She holds the sketch pad against her knee and a fat charcoal pencil in her hand; an espresso rests beside her foot. She is the most beautiful creature who's spoken to me in longer than I can remember.

"Your face . . . is so familiar," she tells me. "I may draw you, yes?"

I let her. She does one sketch, then another. A third and a fourth. I rest between flips of the page, and once I close my eyes and tip back my head and feel the hair spill over my shoulders.

"I have it now!" she cries, and then glances self-consciously about. She hurries closer because she thinks better of speaking too loudly. "Your face . . . is so like the face on the Shroud. Is amazing, the resemblance."

BRIAN HODGE

I smile, telling her I've heard this before.

Aching so deep inside because I can't tell her there's a good reason for the familiarity.

IX

The bodies of political prisoners and religious penitents were rarely given burial, not when there was ample space beneath Rome, in catacombs that had been swallowing bones for centuries. There they would be laid and forgotten, and so was I.

When I awoke to the smell of dust and mould and decay, he was waiting. He turned some anonymous ivory skull in his hands.

"These weren't my original plans at all, you know. But when you came to Rome . . . it was impossible to resist," Vlad said. "I've felt your presence passing nearby at least a dozen times over the centuries. Close. But never so close as this time. You can't have thought you'd walk in and out of my city without meeting again."

I shook my head. Probably not.

"And you can't have failed to realize it's your face on that Shroud of theirs."

Again, I shook my head. My long-haired, bearded head, growing more recognizable by the day.

"Then you wanted this, Hugh. You wanted it. I have the power to grant it. The Shroud has been locked away at Turin for many years. But I own the keys."

"I think you want it more than I do," I said.

"Of course. I love the Church, but I'm not above destroying it completely. Which may happen, when people realize what we've done, who they'll think we've put to death. I'll take that chance. Your first public act can be forgiving your executioners. Or, instead of peace, you can bring a sword – as I said, I don't need the cardinals anymore, now that I have you.

"Either way, I'm giving the world something the Church never managed. Something it's been promised for two thousand years. *That* should give my cattle enough to rally around, to survive the next few years. If they've lost faith in themselves, then perhaps the sight of you, and the news of your resurrection, will be enough to restore it."

"Your cattle?" I whispered. "You still don't care any more for them than that?"

"Why should I? It's an old principle, played out in nature countless times. If the deer die off, the wolves starve. Beyond that, what else is there for me to care about?"

I tried to sit up, naked and sore and scabbed in this newest burial rag. "You really are the Devil, aren't you?"

He extended his hand. "So pleased to make your acquaintance, after all this time."

I took it, because what else could I do, too stiff to haul myself off that rough stone slab. Vlad steadied me on my feet.

"Just remember," he warned me. "You may be God incarnate. But you're still in my hands."

He led me past the more fortunate dead, to the steps that would take us back up to the world.

And you know the rest of the story from there.

Peter Crowther

The Last Vampire

Peter Crowther has sold more than sixty stories to various anthologies and magazines, and his work has been reprinted in The Year's Best Fantasy and Horror *and* The Year's Best Crime and Mystery. *His fiction has also been nominated for three Bram Stoker Awards and for the British Fantasy Award.*

In 1992 he edited Narrow Houses, *the first volume in a three-book British and World Fantasy Award-nominated anthology series based around superstitions (*Touch Wood *and* Blue Motel *followed). He went on to edit* Heaven Sent *(with Martin H. Greenberg),* Tombs and Dante's Disciples *(both with Ed Kramer) and more recently,* Destination: Unknown *and* Tales in Time *(with John Clute). His dark fantasy novel* Escardy Gap *(co-authored with James Lovegrove) was published in 1996, along with* Forest Pains, *a chapbook from Hypatia Press.*

When the Post Apocalyptic Shadow Show rolls into town, the last thing anyone expects to meet is a vampire . . .

THE SOUND OF air horns cut through the early evening, two deep *harrrnkk!*s dispelling the stillness and, albeit for only a moment, frightening the crickets into a stunned silence.

Billy Kendow had his bedroom windows opened wide, feeling the pleasant cool air drifting through with smells of night-time undergrowth and rain-soaked foliage. He looked across and, just for a second, half expected to see the red-nosed clown out of his old reading book, waving a klaxon horn and shouting to him

put down that rabbit, boy and roll up, roll up why dontcha for the show that never ends

but there was only the night and the darkness. Maybe he had imagined it. But then, there it went again, *harrrnk!*, *harrrnk!*, echoing across the fields. Then two more, the first one sounding momentarily farther away and then, with the second, nearer. Not a lot nearer, but definitely nearer.

"Ma!" Billy shouted, eyes staring wide at the window, picturing the highway across the fields. "Didja hear *that?*"

"I sure did." His mother's voice sounded tired, kind of uninterested. "Just a truck, honey. Nothing to get too excited about. Tom Duffy'll've heard it. No need for excitement."

But no, there was a need. Those air horns signified more than just some dumb old truck-driver finding a tattered and mildewed map and taking the dog's leg short-cut across from the crater-marked 124 onto US64, which, so other people aiming to pass through Pump Handle had often said, seemed to have withstood the worst of the bomb storm.

Bomb storm.

Seemed to Billy like a funny thing to say, but that was what it had been like. Even *he* could remember it, and he had only been around two, three years old. Just bombs falling like rain, silver needles dropping out of the sky and turning everything on the ground to mush . . . the way – or so his mom always told everyone – that Billy himself used to turn his supper of grits and potatoes and vegetables and meat into a thickly textured goo of no distinct colour. Only a wash of browns and whites and greens, each one taking on some of the characteristics of the one next to it.

It had been a long time since they'd had those suppers, Billy thought now. A long time since anyone in town had even seen an outsider. But the sound of the truck horns – it *had* to be truck horns – suggested that people were here again. And more people than just one truck. It was more than that. It *had* to be. Those *harrrnk!*s were exclamations, promises of life and of survival, proud cries of *here we are, come see us . . .* and there were surely more than one. And it had been so long since anyone had passed through Pump Handle . . .

"Maybe they're bringing us food and provisions . . . real food . . . and – " He quickly scrolled through his head at the other things he hoped such mythical cargoes might contain. His eyes lit up. " – and comicbooks, ma . . . maybe they'll bring us comicbooks."

"Trucks wouldn't be stopping here, Billy, leastwise not of their own accord. Ain't no provisions delivered any more," she said, "and there ain't nothing to stop here *for*, more's the pity." There was a clanking sound from the kitchen as Billy's mother shouted, "And there ain't no comicbooks, Billy. You know that. Not since the war."

Billy carefully returned the rabbit he had been playing with to the small cage on the makeshift table at the foot of his bed, walked across to the window and stepped out onto the flat-boarded roof section. Breathing in the night smells of jasmine and hollyhock, he looked to the sky. Way off to the west, over towards Memphis maybe, the sky was black and threatening rain. But here, the air smelled good, clean and fresh and full of opportunities.

It even felt different somehow . . . expectant, maybe. He sniffed the breeze and breathed in the aroma of the plants and the soil and the grasses and the trees. Even that composite smell felt excited, somehow . . . the way Billy was feeling himself. He threw his head back and smiled at the starry sky.

Something *was* coming. Something was coming *tonight*.

He grasped the balcony rail outside his window. "I'm going out, Ma," he shouted. "Going out to see what it is." And with a single leap, he was down on the ground and running across the grass, his mother's voice drifting behind him but unable to catch him up, running fit to burst towards the spiralling funnels of light that twisted and turned into the night sky as whatever was coming weaved their way around the perilous bends of Jesmond Hill.

At the stile at the edge of the field that gave onto the blacktop, Billy stopped and leaned on the fence. Two uprights to his left, the fence had long ago disintegrated and rotted into the thick mulshy weed that made up the field. He didn't need to cross the stile to get onto the blacktop but it felt right . . . felt like the way it must have felt all those years ago before the bomb storm.

Billy looked left along the road leading into town. Alongside the road, he could see the silent shapes of other townsfolk making their way towards him. Over to the right, he could hear the faint drone of motors getting louder and, mixed in amongst it, there was music. Billy laughed and slapped his thigh. "Hot dog!" he shouted to the uncaring night. This was really turning out to be something, wasn't it? Real trucks were coming to town. And, from the sound of them, they were going to be a whole heap of fun.

When the first one edged around the final section of Jesmond Hill, onto the straight that led directly into Jingle Bend and then town and then right out again about a minute later, Billy climbed onto the stile and started waving his arms about his head, whooping for all he was worth. First up came a flapping tarpaulin, then came the polished black of the cab, then the windshield, then the hood, the grill and, at last, there it was in all of its dusty buckled splendour.

It spoke of far-off places and untold adventures; it smelled of prairie campfires and coloured rain; and it looked like a slant-eyed beast from his brother's stories, whispered long ago late at night when pain kept sleep at bay. It might have seen better days, this 'gleaming carriage of excitement', but to Billy it was just the finest collection of sights and sounds and smells that he had ever seen in the whole of his short life.

Billy had been still all but toddling when the first bombs were dropped, China holding good its promise to deal straight with the aggression shown it by the US. And there were the Iraqis and the Iranians and the Turks and . . .

. . . and every other power-mad asshole with strength or inclination enough to draw breath and pass wind . . .

his father had said to him on one of those long-since endless nights of swirling smoke and constant thunder.

Both of which amounts to the same, young Billy,

he had continued,

'ceptin' the one smells a sight worse than the other.

Strategic exchanges had followed in quick succession. Billy's brother, Troy, had told him night-time stories about England and the whole of what Troy called 'the British Islands' being sunk, about Europe being devastated – first by chemical bombs and finally by 200 mile-an-hour dust storms – and about how mainland USA (which was where Troy and Billy and his folks lived, Troy had said) was now a wilderness of broken buildings and city-sized potholes, and mile after mile of the strange coloured vegetation that had sprung up long after the final dust clouds had settled down and the smells of explosive and burned flesh had all but drifted away completely.

Troy had told Billy, late at night when they were lying in their cots staring out at the stars, that they'd come out of it better than most. Troy said he and their daddy had stood and watched the cloud rise from the first bomb, a beautiful pear-shaped swirl shot through with every colour in the rainbow. shimmering brightly . . .

But Troy was gone, now. Daddy, too.

For a moment, Billy had felt a profound sadness, a bone-numbing hollowness that seemed to burn at the back of his throat, but it disappeared as soon as it had shown itself. It disappeared with the first of the trucks, pulling along the dusty road, throwing up all kinds of grit and dirt and soil behind them. Billy thumped a clenched fist into the palm of his other hand. "Hot *dog*!" he shouted, trying to get his voice above the sound of the straining motors and the pulsating music, loud thumping rhythms that made him want to shuck and jive his feet, made him want to cartwheel along the roadside, made him want to jerk his head so hard it would almost fall right off his neck . . .

This music, the sounds of it filled the whole of the road, maybe they filled the whole of what used to be the county . . . hell, maybe it filled the whole world, drifting on the poisonous winds forever, fading maybe, getting softer and softer as it travelled, but always there. Always existing.

Why, not too long ago, a wild-eyed drifter – sporting enough burns to have fried any normal man into a blackened stump – had come into town with a bottle he'd found amidst the rubble of a place called Chicago. The bottle was covered with a thick gauze tied around with frayed string. Billy had asked what was in there and the man had told him

the sounds of the last day of the world, my friend

and then he had laughed loud and long, his mouth hanging wide and gums dripping yellow pus onto his tongue.

When the man had carefully removed the top from the jar, Billy had heard a hundred voices – no, maybe a thousand or a million or even a *thousand* million voices – all crying out in agony. He had run then, run away from the wild-eyed man, trying to drown out the despair of those cries . . . trying to drown out the sound of the man laughing again, laughing for all he was worth as he placed the gauze around the jar once more.

No sound ever dies, the man had called after him, *particularly the sound of death itself.*

Moonlight glinted off the dusty black carapace of the first truck as it pulled up alongside Billy Kendow, suddenly jolting him back to the present. Eyes wide, mouth wide, senses wide open and shouting *feed me!* for all they were worth, Billy stared up at the cab and came face to face with a man chewing on a smouldering cigar.

The truck came to a stop right in front of Billy, its air brakes hissing and whining, and the man leaned out of his open window and looked at Billy. Then he looked around, up the road ahead and back over behind Billy, back across the fields to Billy's house. "Where the hell are we, boy?" He waved an old, torn map at Billy and then threw it to the floor of the cab. "Map shows dots of towns on it but no names to speak of."

"Pump Handle, sir," Billy exclaimed, trying to imbue the words with some kind of significance. Like it was Valhalla or Bethlehem instead of a run-down collection of shanty houses that would have been perfectly at home getting on for a century ago in the dust-blown cardboard cities of the Oklahoma flatlands.

He pointed ahead along the road. "Up ahead a half mile or so. But there's trees and stuff all across the road at Jingle Bend . . . might need some help in moving them before you can make any headway."

The man nodded. "Sounds good to me." He looked aside to a scrawny and pale-looking woman sitting beside him. "Sound good to you, Deedee?"

The woman stretched her arms out in front of her and yawned fit to split her face wide open. "Anything gets me outta this goddam truck sounds good to me."

"That settles it," the man said to Billy. "Looks like we set up here."

"Set up?" Billy felt his heart skip a beat.

"Sure." The man jerked a thumb back behind him. "The Post Apocalyptic Shadow Show? Don't you read?"

Billy stepped back and glanced along the tarpaulin covering the truck. There it was, in glorious swirls of white and yellow picked out by the headlights behind, a legend of typeface design, a blaze of curlicues and serifs, the words

JOSEPH AND DEIRDRE BLAUMLEIN'S
POST APOCALYPTIC SHADOW SHOW

and, below that,

SEE THE WONDERS THAT SURVIVED THE WAR!

and then, below various blurbs, a single line that made the blood rush to his face in sheer frantic anticipation:

COUNT DRACULA, THE LAST VAMPIRE!

Billy breathed in deep, a quick gasp of breath, and, almost choking as he tried to get the words out, he said, "Is that for real?"

The man in the cab was holding a cigarette to his mouth, his hands shaking. Billy could see that the man bit his fingernails, could see the little rounded stumps high above the nail, and the whitened quick of skin extending from beneath the nail itself. "Which is that, young fella?" the man said, holding a quivering match to the cigarette and drawing in smoke.

"This here." Billy ran to the tarpaulin and pointed to the words. "This here about the last vampire," he said.

"Sure is," said the man. "And I'll tell you all about him, too, if'n I kin just get this rig off the road. Can't say as how you prob'ly expectin' any other visitors – " He paused and gave a wheezy laugh. " – but never pays to take chances, know what I mean?"

Billy shook his head and then nodded it, eyes wide. He had no idea what the man was talking about. All that mattered was the last vampire – and all of the other things, too, but the vampire was the one that most interested Billy Kendow. And the cheesy hand-drawn picture beneath it, of a middle-aged man – maybe around Billy's father's age, just before he died, maybe a little younger – with a high forehead and kind of sleepy, heavy-lidded eyes, grinning menacingly off the tarpaulin, his lips pulled back to reveal two canine-sized incisors at either side of his mouth.

Some vampire, Billy thought. He didn't look anything like the proud and regal Transylvanian Count from the old dog-eared comicbooks he had read and re-read so many times he knew every word. The man in the picture, his eyes badly drawn so they were actually crossed, looked more like a fool. "The Last Idiot" was what the tarpaulin should read. Billy smiled to himself at the thought.

The man shifted gears, worn cogs crying out, and pulled the truck up onto the grass. When he was completely off the road, he leaned out of the window and waved on the second truck.

By now others from the town had appeared, walking slowly across the grass from down around Jingle Bend, where he knew they had been to greet the visitors. The man from the first truck – Billy supposed he was Joseph Blaumlein – was already down on the grass, slamming the cab door behind him and staring at the approaching figures. The woman – Deirdre, or Deedee – moved around the cab and stood by his side. Both of them looked nervous – *real* nervous – him pulling on his cigarette like he was being lined up against a wall to be shot, and her pushing herself further and further into the gap between her husband and the truck.

Billy turned and looked at the people. There was Mr McKendrick, Solly Sapperstein, Mr and Mrs Revine, young Jeff Winton and a whole load of other folks . . . including his mom, bringing up the rear with Mildred Duffy and her husband, Tom, the deputy town mayor of Pump Handle.

The congregation got to within twenty yards or so of the trucks – both of them now parked up on the grass at the side of the roadway – and exchanged nods with the visitors. There were five of them, now: Joseph and Deedee; a young fellow with a gap-toothed smile and a vacant stare; a woman who looked to Billy to be around sixty years old if she was a day, her hair hanging down in rat-tails that were half-blonde and half-brown;

and a wiry-looking old man sucking on a pipe and leaning against the door of the second truck.

Tom Duffy shuffled from the rear of the group up to the front, where he was a few feet away from Billy Kendow and Joseph and Deedee Blaumlein, and touched the brim of his hat. "Welcome to Pump Handle," he exclaimed. Like as if he were giving them the keys to St Louis or New Orleans, fabled places of grandness that Billy had never seen but about which he had heard plenty.

Joseph Blaumlein nodded and smiled, dropping his cigarette butt onto the grass and stepping onto it. "I'm pleased to be here," Blaumlein said, extending a hand of friendship to the deputy mayor. "We all are."

The smile that accompanied this last statement puzzled Billy. He looked around to see if anyone else had noticed it – the almost rat-like leer and narrowing of eyes – but everyone seemed to be smiling and just having themselves a real ball. Even his mom. He looked back at Blaumlein.

Eleanor Revine stepped around Tom's wife and, placing her hands on her hips, swayed backwards and looked at the writing on the side of the trucks.

"What the hell's a 'post apoc . . . apocyliptic shadow show'?" she asked . . . not unreasonably, Billy thought.

The old man stepped toward to stand next to Billy. "These here," he said portentously, waving an arm majestically at the writing on the side of the truck, "are what amounts to some mighty strange occurrences." He took a deep breath and shifted into
put down that rabbit, boy and roll up, roll up why dontcha for the show that never ends
a sideshow barker's spiel. "Here we have . . ." He walked to the side of the truck and pointed to one of the scribbled, hand-drawn lines. "A hen which lays empty eggs, each one perfectly formed but containing absolutely nothing; here we have Siamese *triplets . . .* three legs, two hearts, three heads and five arms between them; and over here, a raccoon with flippers and a long fin on its back; and here – "

"What's that last vampire like?" said Billy in a small voice.

The man turned to face Billy and, just for a moment, his eyes flashed menacingly. Billy figured it was because he had interrupted his pitch and he hung his head down and muttered an apology. "That's okay, son," said the man, blowing a thick plume of acrid smoke from his pipe bowl. He moved across to the illustration and shook his head.

"This here's maybe the sorriest specimen we've come across . . . maybe even sorrier than the Siamese triplets, and that's sorry indeed," he said. "Name's Dracula, like in the book. Thought he was a fiction but now we know better. Came across him up in Carolina, north or south makes no nevermind, and he lives in darkness and drinks the blood of anything and ever'thing he can find. Don't speak a word, not a single – "

"Were there others?"

"What's that, son?"

"You say he's the last one," Billy said. "Were there more? What about all the folks he . . . you know – " Billy made a biting face. "The ones he bit?"

The man glanced across at Joseph Blaumlein who stepped forward and ruffled Billy's hair. "There's all manner of strangeness out there, boy," he said. "Could be he has relatives somewheres but we ain't seen hide nor . . . nor *fang* of 'em in our travels." He gave a snort. "We took the liberty of calling him the last one. Could be he's the *only* one."

The man turned to face all of the people from Pump Handle and raised his arms wide. "All courtesy of the War, ladies and gentlemen . . . and all brought to you here today, for your amazement, in exchange for a little home comforts."

Now it was the turn of the deputy mayor to speak. "Home comforts?"

The man shrugged and looked across at the old man and the woman with the straggled two-coloured hair. Something passed between them, then; Billy Kendow saw it. But it was gone as fast as it had appeared. He looked around to see if any of the other townsfolk had seen it, but they all seemed to be wrapped up in what the man was saying.

"Some food, little purified water, some gasoline maybe . . ." He let his voice trail off and then added, loudly, "and all in exchange for a glimpse of the outside world post apocalyptic."

"We ain't got no food or water," Solly Sapperstein said in a husky voice. "Leastwise none we can spare. And we don't have no need for gasoline."

Blaumlein stepped up to the deputy mayor and looked down at him. As he moved, the old woman and the man with the pipe sauntered over to the cabs of the two trucks.

"I can't believe that," he said. "I can't believe you couldn't spare just one meal for me and my people . . . in exchange for – " He spun around and pointed to the trucks again. "In exchange for the show of your *lives*. Now, how's that sound for a deal?"

Jack McKendrick stepped forward. "All our provisions is kept in the old repair shop, down in town, and the mayor looks after it. We can't make no promises about whether he'll let you – "

Tom Duffy shook his head and took hold of Jack's arm. "Be okay," he said, tiredly, glancing at the trucks. "Mayor Ladd will see the sensible solution."

"There, now, that's mighty sensible of you all," said Blaumlein cheerfully. "And, as a mark of good faith, I'll let you see just one of our special attractions." He smiled across the sea of blank faces. Maybe this was going to be harder than usual. "Which one'll it be?"

Nobody said anything.

Billy Kendow looked across the people from the town and waited for someone to say something, but still nobody did.

"The vampire," he said, blurting it out. "Show us the last vampire."

Blaumlein laughed and ruffled Billy's hair again. "Right you are, boy." He turned to the boy with the gap-toothed smile. "Bring him out, Eddie."

The boy disappeared around the other side of the second truck and Billy could hear him puffing as he unfastened the tarpaulin flap. Less than a minute later, the boy re-appeared around the cab pulling on a piece of rope. At the end of the rope was The Last Vampire!

"My, but he's the *sorriest* looking fella I ever did see," said Mildred Duffy.

And that was the truest thing the deputy mayor's wife had ever said.

The man looked even older than his picture – maybe around sixty, maybe even seventy, Billy had no way of telling. His hair was thick and matted, his face covered in sores and dirt. Around his middle, he wore a crude loincloth fashioned out of pieces of fabric all stitched together and, around his neck, someone had attached a piece of rope fastened to some kind of blanket. Also around his neck was a collection of crucifixes and a string of garlic bulbs. There were more bulbs and crucifixes hanging from the "belt", Billy saw. In fact, the only thing that was impressive about this "vampire" was his eyes. They were intelligent eyes, glancing nervously around the gathered throng of people.

Billy walked up to the man and stared up into his face. As he stared, the man flinched. "Let me see his teeth," Billy said in a soft voice.

"Hey, now," said the old man with the pipe. "We don't want to be giving away the whole show . . . leastwise not till we get our "payment'." There was something about the word "payment", Billy thought. Some deep and hidden significance. He looked across at the old man and, just for a second, he saw a conspiratorial flash of something in the man's face. He looked around quickly and saw that the glance had been exchanged with Blaumlein, who was now averting his own face from Billy's stare.

"I wanna see the teeth," Billy said. "I wanna see the teeth *now*."

Tom Duffy placed a gentle hand on Billy's shoulder. "Now hold on there Bil – " he began, but Blaumlein interrupted.

"Let him see. Eddie?"

The boy with the gap-toothed smile stepped forward as though in a trance and took hold of the vampire's face in both hands. Pulling at the man's lips, he quickly exposed the two incisors pictured on the side of the truck.

Tom Duffy tried hard to suppress a snigger.

Billy leaned toward the vampire and the vampire tried to pull away.

"They ain't real," said Billy.

"Now hold on there, boy," Blaumlein said.

"They're stuck on with something." He reached out a hand and the vampire pulled back out of the gap-toothed boy's grip. He threw back his head and let out a guttural howl.

"Sounds more like one of them werewolf fellas," Eleanor Revine said to Solly Sapperstein.

The vampire shook his head, eyes wide enough they looked set to pop out and hang on his cheeks, and cowered away from Billy.

"Why's he howling that way?" Tom Duffy asked.

"Kind of like he's trying to tell us something," said Solly Sapperstein.

"How d'you know he's Dracula?" asked Mildred Duffy. "Don't look like no Count I ever saw.

Joseph Blaumlein stepped to one side and reached a hand behind his back. When the hand reappeared, it was holding a gun. He gave a big beaming smile and shook the gun at the townsfolk. "Time to wake up and smell the fuckin' coffee, you hayseed dickheads," he said in a low voice. Without turning, he said to gap-tooth, "Put him away, Eddie. Show's over."

"What the hell's going on?" asked Charlie McKendrick.

"Shut the hell up, you old fart," said Blaumlein.

Gap-toothed Eddie yanked on the vampire's rope and pulled him back around the wagon.

Eleanor Revine let out a chuckle. "Now this is what I *call* a show!"

"You seen all the show you're gonna see," Blaumlein said. He backed off a way and motioned with the gun. "Let's see you all gather up now in a nice group. You too, kid."

Glancing in the direction of the vampire, Billy shuffled across and stood between Eleanor Revine and Tom Duffy.

"Right, now, that's real good." Blaumlein looked across at his wife. "Deedee, get th'other gun."

"Can you tell – "

"Not now, gramps," Blaumlein snapped at Tom Duffy. "Okay, who's in charge here?"

Tom looked around and put up his hand. "I guess that's me."

"You *guess*, gramps?"

"He's the deputy Mayor," said Mildred. "And he's my husband."

Blaumlein's wife appeared with a rifle which she trained on the group.

Solly Sapperstein stepped forward. As Solly started to speak, Blaumlein turned to his wife. "Deedee?"

The shot rang out and echoed in the stillness of the night. Solly Sapperstein rocked on his feet and then, frowning, looked down at his stomach. When he realized what had happened, Solly grabbed hold of his gut and fell to his knees. Once on the floor, he looked around at the others, all of whom were watching him with what appeared to be a casual interest, and then toppled over onto his side.

Blaumlein watched the man for further signs of movement, but Solly was still. He looked up and gave another smile. "Any more questions?"

Nobody spoke.

"Okay, now we need to get us some food and some water. And your Mayor is going to be real generous about that, I can just feel it." He laughed. "You, deputy mayor . . ."

Tom Duffy nodded.

"Step on up here towards me. You're gonna lead us to this barn with all the provisions."

Duffy nodded. "Okay."

Blaumlein frowned and then smiled. He turned to look at his wife, who was also frowning, and then at the old man with the pipe.

"I don't like it," the old man said.

Blaumlein turned back to face Tom Duffy. "You just gonna take us up there? Just like that?"

"That's what you want, isn't it?"

"Yes, that's what I *want* . . . just that – "

"And if I don't, you'll shoot me . . . just like you did Solly, right?"

Blaumlein nodded. "Yeah, that's right." He laughed now, and Deedee and the old man started laughing along with him. "That's right, gramps, we'll *shoot* you. Hell, we'll shoot *all* of yous if'n we have to."

Tom shrugged and turned away. "Let's get going then," he said over his shoulder. As he started walking, the other townsfolk fell into step behind.

Billy stepped into the single file behind his mother and in front of Eleanor Revine. Blaumlein waited a step or two and then followed on. Billy heard him issuing instructions to the others and he saw the old man appear on the right, holding some kind of wide-barrelled pistol, while on the left Blaumlein's wife rode point with the rifle, accompanied by the boy, who seemed to have no other weapon but a long-shafted axe.

Nobody spoke. The only sound was the gentle *swish swish*, as they moved through the longer grasses up the hill, and an occasional hoot and a flurry of wings from the distant trees.

Soon, they had reached the top of the rise.

The old man, who had moved up to the front, reached across and grabbed hold of Tom Duffy's sleeve. Everyone stopped. The old man ran crouched over and disappeared down the other side of the hill.

While they waited, Billy stepped out of line and moved back behind Eleanor Revine to Blaumlein. "That wasn't no vampire, was he?"

Blaumlein shook his head. "Nope." He kept his eyes trained on the brow of the hill, waiting for the old man to return and tell him everything was okay.

"Who was he?"

Blaumlein shook his head again. "Don't know, don't care," he said. "We found him up in Carolina, drinking the blood out of a mangy dog, dead by the side of the road. Can't speak . . . or *won't* speak. There's a lot of folks like that out there." He shifted the gun to his other hand and rubbed the stubble on his chin. "It was Deedee thought up the vampire shtick. Pat – he's the fella with the pipe – he fashioned us a couple of teeth and we just fixed them right on him. Worked, too, in most places we been . . ."

"But not here," Billy said.

Blaumlein nodded. "But not here."

"So he isn't really Count Dracula either?"

"Dracula's a myth, kid . . . a fairy story. Once we'd hit on the vampire idea, Pat said why don't we go the whole hog and call him Dracula . . . the *last* vampire." He laughed but it was without humour. "Most places, people just want to see something that entertains them. Something a little out of the ordinary."

"What about the other things? The triplets . . . and the empty eggs?"

"Oh, they're real enough. There're a lot of things out the – "

"Joe?"

Blaumlein looked up towards the front of the line. The old man, Pat, was waving his arms."

"Yeah?"

"Looks okay," Pat said. "Hill runs down to a big old shack – there's a light on in there, so there must be some kind of generator hooked up. Making a noise, too."

Blaumlein started to move up the line. "Get in place, kid," he snapped. "Deedee, get back here and watch the rear."

The woman walked back, keeping her rifle trained on the townsfolk.

When he got to the front of the line, Blaumlein pulled Tom Duffy towards him by the shirt-front. "What's down there, gramps?"

"I told you. Provisions. Our food and our water."

"What's the noise?"

"He already told you," Duffy said, nodding at the old man with the pipe. "It's a generator . . . keeps it all fresh."

"The food."

Duffy nodded. "The food."

"There ain't nothing you're holding back here, is there gramps?"

"Like what?"

"Like some kind of electric fence or some other protective doodad?"

Duffy sighed. "It's just for the food."

"Right, just the food." Blaumlein pushed the deputy mayor forward and stepped in line behind him. "Well, you lead the way, then. Pat, move down towards the back . . . and keep an eye on them."

"Got it." Pat ran down the left of the column, his pipe still in his mouth, jiggling up and down.

"Eddie, you just keep watching, okay?"

Eddie grunted.

"And if you see anything even a *little* bit cute, just call out, okay?"

"Okay."

Blaumlein prodded Tom Duffy. "Let's go, gramps."

They moved slowly down the hill, stepping sideways-on until they came to the bottom and the edge of a huge field. Up ahead, in the centre, stood a barn, two stories with a light shining through the dirty windows. Blaumlein knelt down and felt the plant by his feet. "Cabbage? Is this a cabbage?"

He stood up. "Pat? Get down here."

The old man came running down the hill.

"This look like a cabbage to you?"

Pat knelt down and pulled a couple of leaves. He ground them in his hand and took a sniff. "Looks like cabbage to me," he said, breathlessly.

Blaumlein turned to survey the whole field. Even in the moonlight, he could see there were thousands of them, all laid out in rows. He looked around at Tom Duffy. "Is this it, mister deputy fucking mayor? Is this your food? Cabbages?"

Tom half-nodded. "It's what we use to make our food."

"Make your food?" Blaumlein looked out at the barn. "What you got in there, a million gallons of cabbage soup?"

"Something like that," said Tom Duffy.

Blaumlein gave a small smile but something else was tugging at the ends of it, pulling down the forced mirth and narrowing the man's eyes with tiny rays of concern. "What the hell does that mean?"

The deputy mayor returned the smile and looked around at the other townsfolk. Their faces were watching Blaumlein. "Why don't you take a look?"

Blaumlein turned around and looked across the field at the barn. "Pat?"

The old man stepped alongside him. "What do you think?"

Pat shrugged. "Looks okay. Looks like a barn. What are you thinking?"

"I dunno." He looked at Tom Duffy and sensed a calm strength in the man. He didn't like it. Truth was, he suddenly didn't like any of it. For a second, he was going to say as much

let's give 'em a break and leave 'em to it

but he didn't. He glanced at Pat who was watching the side of his face. He chuckled. "Pat, I'm not thinking any damned thing, not any damned thing at all. Let's go take a look."

Pat fell back to the side of the line and checked that everyone was still in place.

There were five women and eight men, plus the kid pulling up the rear. A real jumble of walking wounded, drained of stamina and bereft of soul. Pat smiled. For a few seconds there, he'd been worried. There had been something in Joe Blaumlein's voice, something he couldn't quite place . . . like a fly whose buzz you could hear but which you couldn't see no matter how still you stood. He looked back and waved to Deedee. She lifted the rifle with both hands a couple of times and then returned it to point at the ones at the back of the line.

Across the column, between the deputy mayor's wife, a sweet-looking woman of around sixty maybe a little younger, and a young man in his early twenties, Eddie was prowling to and fro, a few steps each time, swinging the long-handled axe like it was a golf club.

"Let's go," Blaumlein shouted from the front. "Slow now," he said, "and no funny business."

Pat watched as Joe pulled the old man forward and then stepped in behind him. He jammed the gun in his back. "Try anything, and you're the first one that gets it." The words had been softly spoken but the night was so still, despite a gentle breeze, that they carried back to Pat.

As they started to move off, Pat turned slightly to check that Deedee was okay. As he moved his head, he caught sight of someone watching him. It was a woman – maybe forty years old; Pat couldn't tell – and he thought it was the kid's mother. Her face was smiling . . . her whole face, not just her mouth. Pat didn't like that. It looked eager, like it was getting ready for something.

"Face the front!" Pat snarled. The woman's smile fell away and she jerked her head around. Pat felt better. There was nothing on that face – *had* been nothing on that face. Must just've been the moon, playing tricks with her expression.

They moved forward slowly, picking their way between the cabbages. Pat and Eddie stayed well out to either side while Deedee brought up the rear, stepping out first one way and then the other, just a few steps at a time, to make sure everyone was behaving themselves. They were. Pat could see that. They were behaving themselves

too fucking well

just absolutely fine.

The barn grew larger, its shine growing brighter. Staring over the old man's shoulder, crouched down so's nobody could blow off the top of his head, Joe Blaumlein scanned the structure for any movements . . . any signs of life at all. There weren't any. It was just a barn. A *big* barn, but a still a barn.

When they had got out of sight of the sides of the barn, with only the big doors facing them, Blaumlein pulled out of line and ran towards the entrance. He flattened himself against the side-panels, shuffled along to the corner and peered down the side. Nobody there. Had he expected anybody? He couldn't say . . . couldn't decide. Something in his stomach was expecting something, that was for sure.

He looked back and saw that the column had come to a stop just a few feet in front of the doors. They were all watching him, the towns-folk and Pat, Eddie and Deedee, too. Waiting for an instruction.

"Okay, open the doors," Blaumlein shouted. "And remember . . ." He let his voice trail off and simply waved the gun. The old deputy mayor nodded and stepped forward, taking hold of the single wooden beam dropped into the two brackets – one on each door – and lifting it clear. He was strong for a little guy, Blaumlein thought. And a little *old* guy, at that.

Setting the beam on the ground, Tom Duffy took hold of the doors, one handle in each hand, and pulled. The doors came towards him effortlessly, creaking like the old iron doors to some hidden castle vault.

Or crypt!

Blaumlein frowned as he watched the old man continue pulling. Where had the word "crypt" come from, for crissakes?

The doors were fully open now, and Blaumlein could see vague shapes behind some kind of shimmering window. He stepped forward as the little deputy mayor stepped back. It was some kind of plastic sheeting, Blaumlein now saw, hanging down from a polished rail attached to a series of criss-crossed wooden beams.

"Meet the Mayor of Pump Handle," Tom Duffy announced in a strikingly formal tone as he waved an arm lavishly towards the doors.

The townsfolk began to move forward and there was little for their guards to do but move with them. Soon they were all standing in front of the plastic sheeting, Pat, Eddie and Deedee mingled in amongst them, all staring into the barn.

Tom Duffy reached a hand around the door and fumbled with something on the wall behind. A heavy droning noise started up and the sheeting began to move to the left.

"Mr Mayor?" Duffy called. "You have visitors."

Blaumlein took a step forward into the barn.

The building comprised a single room, about two storeys high with a mezzanine balcony floor, accessed by a rickety-looking stepladder at the rear, running the full circumference.

Around the underside of the balcony, ran a long metal rail. Attached to the rail by large brass rings was the plastic sheeting which had now drawn fully back from the doors. Alongside the rail, intermittent fluorescent light tubes cast a vague glow whose full intensity failed to escape the constriction of the enclosed space.

The centre of the room fared better, thanks to four circular fluorescents on a square of suspended board hanging from the raftered roof. Directly beneath the board sat a large rectangular wooden table. On and alongside the table were all manner of complicated-looking pieces of machinery of varying sizes, some of them blinking red or green or yellow lights, like swarms of fireflies trapped forever in one spot, endlessly winking either to attract help or to warn off others.

But it was what was hanging between the table and the lights that finally caused Blaumlein to step further into the barn, closely followed by his companions and the townsfolk.

Harnessed by a complex series of ropes and crude pulleys attached to the board of lights, the naked body of a man hung, moving gently in the breeze from the open door.

The head of the man was nearest the door. It hung back and down, lolling, on a scrawny neck, eyes open and staring straight at Blaumlein.

"Don't you fret none, now," Tom Duffy said reassuringly. "He's dead . . . or, at least, he's not alive as we know it."

"Who is he? What . . . what are you doing to him?"

Blaumlein made the final few steps to stand so that his face was on a level with that of the suspended man. He stared at the apparatus and grimaced. The man's chest and abdomen had been cut open, thick folds of skin pierced by fine-tined s-shaped meathooks attached to a circular rail about two feet above the body.

Above the rail, a myriad wires and tubes extending from it and feeding into it, a huge pulsating thing rested in a large cage. It looked like an over-ripe pumpkin, the biggest Blaumlein had ever seen. Its movements quivered and shook, each expansion and retraction sending fresh rivulets of thick fluid down its sides to gather into a tray which fed down into a trough leading to three bottles. In turn, the liquid in the bottles fed into more tubes which span off, dividing into still more leading to a bank of large wooden canisters, each with a tap and tray attached to its side.

Around the perimeter of the barn, where the light was at its dimmest, many more bodies, all naked, hung by their feet. The bodies were male and female, some were old, some not so old and some were very young. Very young indeed. Blaumlein counted three babies . . . there could have been more that he could not see, for the bodies were several deep, hanging like pieces of meat in one of the old butcher's stores.

Then one of the bodies opened its eyes and looked down at him. It was a young man, maybe mid-twenties. The eyes focused dimly, seemed to widen for a second, and then the lids dropped shut again.

"He's alive!"

"They're all alive," Tom Duffy said. "They're provisions."

Now that Blaumlein concentrated, he could see chests moving up and down. They were moving slowly, but they were moving. There were no other signs of life. The faces were empty, waxen

caricatures of lives that once were but were not any more. Their
legs, arms and necks were manacled to individual backboards, and
tubes and pipes had been inserted into arteries and veins – and, in
some cases, into rough tears in chest or stomach, each one clumsily
sutured – leading off to the single body.

Someone shouted behind him. Blaumlein recognized the voice
and span around in time to see Pat backing into the barn from
a figure that stepped menacingly towards him. It was the man
Blaumlein had shot, looking as large as life, grinning and holding
his shirt wide open to display the blackened wound in his stomach.
Holding the edge of his shirt with one hand, the man – Solly
something? – inserted the index finger of the other deep into
the hole.

Deedee screamed and fell to the floor.

Someone else laughed and the sound was joined by muted
sniggers, as the man jammed a second finger into the hole and,
moments later, produced a small piece of metal. A bullet, delicately
held between two fingers mottled with tissue. There was no blood.
As soon as the fingers were clear, the wound gathered a film across
itself and was gone from sight.

Pat raised his gun and pointed it at the man. The man's eyes
widened and Pat seemed to freeze on the spot. Then the man
reached out, removed the gun from the old man's hand and
pointed it against his own temple. The sound was deafening and
the man seemed to stagger briefly and then stood straight again.
The side of his head had been blown away, one eye completely gone
while the other hung down on the man's cheek. The man began
to laugh, smoking tufts of hair attached to the side of the carnage
juddering, and handed the gun back to Pat. As Pat accepted the
weapon, the man's eye rolled back on itself into the socket. Then
the skin around the other ruined socket blistered and filled out
and new shoots of thick, dark hair sprouted above the hairline.

Eddie was the first one the townsfolk took.

The boy's axe split a couple of arms in the process, but nothing
that seemed to bother the people of Pump Handle one iota.

Blaumlein watched as they dragged the boy screaming and
kicking towards a makeshift table behind the barn doors. They
lifted him onto the table, many hands working in unison, some
deftly removing clothes while others held the squirming limbs in
place. Then, holding what looked like a monstrous hypodermic,
Eleanor Revine bent over the body. The quivering stopped almost
immediately.

Blaumlein noticed two things, then.

The first was that the plastic sheeting was moving back into place and the barn doors were closing; the second was that a tight grip had attached itself to his arm.

"You're going to join them, Mister Blaumlein," Tom Duffy's scrawky voice announced merrily.

Blaumlein span around but was unable to loosen the old man's grip. He lifted his gun and fired, point blank, four rounds, each one finding its target – chest, two in the stomach, one opening the man's neck – but each to no avail.

Duffy opened and closed his mouth like a fish and laughed silently, lifting a hand to assess the damage to his throat. He shrugged and looked across at the hanging man. As he looked, the neck filled out with new tissue, glistening in the glare of the fluorescent lights.

Blaumlein watched as the townsfolk worked over the body of young Eddie. He watched as they swabbed pieces of skin and jammed different tubes into arms and legs. He followed the tubes and pipes with his eyes, trailed them through yards and yards of curled and furled tubing, all the way to the pulsating object in the cage . . . then down into the naked man.

As Duffy started to speak to him, Blaumlein was vaguely aware of two of the townsfolk lifting the inert body of his wife onto another table. The scream was short-lived, to be followed by squelching noises and grunts of exertion, and then the distant dripping of liquid into a jar.

"He came to our town after the bombs had hit. Tried to pick someone off out on the road, but I guess his powers were shot. He didn't make too good a job of it."

"Who is he?" Blaumlein asked.

"He's our mayor. Mayor Ladd."

"But who *is* he?"

"He *said* he was Dracula. That's why we called him Ladd – kind of like Vlad. But Dracula . . . I mean, can you *believe* that? He could've said Nosferatu, Count Yorga or Barnabas Collins . . ." Duffy shrugged. "All of these and none of these. Maybe he *was* Dracula . . . who the hell cares. Whatever the name, he may be the very last of his breed."

"Breed?"

"A vampire, mister Blaumlein."

"A . . . a vampire? A *real* vampire?"

Tom Duffy took hold of Blaumlein's arms and started to lead him to the table. When he struggled, he caught sight of Pat's body, wires and tubes and pipes protruding from veins and tears in the arms and upper thighs, being hoisted along a pulley to take up a position at the front of the lines of upside-down cadavers. Deedee and young Eddie were already in place, waiting for him. Waiting for Joe Blaumlein, too.

"You see, when we hit on who he was we figured he might be able to help us," Duffy said in a quiet sing-song voice that calmed and soothed. Blaumlein didn't feel afraid at all. Only curious.

"I was a surgeon before . . . before the bombs. Over in Atlanta. I was visiting friends nearby when all hell broke loose. There was no way to get back and no place to get back to. The towns – the big towns; even the small towns – went to hell quickly. Looting, fighting . . . no place to be. So my wife and I walked until we hit Pump Handle. Had a boy with us. Martin, seventeen years old. Had him late, Mildred and me." Duffy paused. "He didn't make it."

"What happened to him?"

"My, but you do have a lot of questions. He died. Wasn't nothing I could do for him."

Blaumlein glanced across at the table. The townsfolk were doing something to the bodies, injecting them with something. He turned away.

"Squeamish? Don't worry. It'll pass.

"Anyways, we got here and settled in. Wasn't anything else to do. Wasn't any point in carrying on. We knew that. This – Pump Handle – was as good as it was going to get. And even that wasn't great."

"Not great?" Blaumlein was trying to play for time. He could not loosen the old man's grip. He had to wait for the right moment.

"Scurvy, pestilence, a few skin cancers . . . no food, no real sunlight only those damned coloured clouds. It was a waiting game, and we knew it. But, as places to die go, it wasn't a bad choice. And then he came along."

Blaumlein followed the old man's stare and his eyes fell on the naked man hanging in the centre of the room.

"Like I say, we tackled him and . . . well, we found out who he was."

"A vampire."

"Yes, it sounds a little silly, doesn't it. But that's what he is . . . or, rather, was. He's just a litmus flask now."

"A litmus flask?"

"When I said he was dead, I might have been wrong. I mean, vampires are dead to start off with, aren't they?"

Blaumlein shrugged.

"He didn't have any pulse. That was the first thing we noticed. Then I sounded him out and he didn't have any heart. I know, I know," Duffy said when his captive smirked disbelievingly. "But he didn't. I opened him up and there wasn't one. Simple as that."

"So how did he live?"

"Well, the short answer is he didn't. Turns out that vampires are simple walking chemical reactions. It's some kind of virus that reacts with the blood and freezes the ageing process. But it kills the body at the same time."

"And the mind?"

"Nope, doesn't kill the mind. Not as far as we can tell, anyways. And we should know." He laughed. "You about ready for another one?" he called out.

Eleanor Revine turned around and nodded. "Five minutes." She was stitching something that Blaumlein couldn't see. But he could see the needle. He was glad he couldn't see anything else.

"So what's he doing now? Is he alive or is he dead?"

"He hasn't moved or spoken since we brought him in here, and that was . . ." His brow furrowed as he calculated. "Must be eight, maybe nine months now."

"And he just stays that way? I mean, he doesn't, you know . . . decompose?"

Duffy shook his head. "Nope. Strange, isn't it. 'Vampirism' is a very emotive term and not a very accurate one. It conjures up fangs and cloaks and mumbling east European accents. Some might say he was cursed," he added, nodding towards the body. "I prefer to say he was blessed. I studied the body for some time and was unable to figure out what the root of the problem – or rather, benefit – was."

"How did you kill him?"

Duffy shook his head. "We didn't. At first, we thought he was just some crazy man – we get them from time to time: radiation fever and the like – trying to eat one of the townsfolk."

"Eat?"

"That's the way it looked, at least at first. Then he started mumbling about how he needed blood and about how he'd been around for centuries and he'd seen so many things happen . . . and that's when we noticed he didn't have a pulse.

"His condition deteriorated and, eventually, he just stopped talking. There was no breath, no vital signs, no nothing. He didn't take any food – not that we had much to offer: we still don't . . . not regular food, anyways – and he didn't decompose. He just lay there."

Duffy nodded to Eleanor Revine. "They're ready for you, I'm afraid."

Blaumlein felt a flutter of panic. "Wait . . . wait just a minute."

"Why?"

"Well . . . what is it that you're going to do with me? And what do you do with all the cabbages?"

"Okay," Duffy said with a sigh. "Must be quick, though. When we realized what we had – or what we might have: we were still sceptical for a time – we, or I, wondered if his blood might have recuperative powers. After all, that's what vampires were all about . . . giving eternal life. So we took a sample and I tested it as well as I could, and we realized that this was indeed a life-giving and life-prolonging elixir. We fed it to some of our people who were sick and the results were both amazing and immediate. Increased, almost superhuman strength, little or no need for sleep or any kind of rest, and curative powers for burns and fevers that were quite unbelievable. In fact, if I hadn't conducted the tests, I wouldn't have believed it myself.

"But there was one problem." Duffy smacked his lips contemplatively. "The supply was finite. Not having any heart or system, he doesn't regenerate his blood. What there was was all there was. Simple as that. And then I had an idea: what if we could continue to supply his body with the blood he would originally have taken for himself. As I said before, he was, to all intents and purposes, dead . . . but he didn't go through the usual mortification process.

"Basically, the thing above him that appears for all the world as some huge turnip is, indeed, a heart. I made it, fashioned it out of tissue and veins removed from what livestock we had available. All that's gone now.

"It quickly became obvious that I must do something to extend his abilities and make the most of dwindling supplies. Attached to the heart are a series of left- and right-ventricular assist devices to ensure maximum through-motion. I fitted three sections of steel – titanium being in somewhat sort supply – to the abdomen, each one weighing in at 800 grams, plus 600 yards of tubing in the aorta and sixteen external vents to reduce clotting. We rigged up a generator and . . . well, I won't bore you with the rest."

Keeping a rock-steady grip on his captive, Tom Duffy waved his free arm majesterially at the dangling bodies. "They're all alive – saline drips and a constant diet of cabbage . . . very good for the blood and the heart – and we have them on a constant, very slow blood transfusion to the main body. That, in turn . . . well, who the hell knows what it does: let's say it turns the water into wine. We drink the wine. Simple as that."

"You injected them . . . I saw her – " Blaumlein pointed at the waiting Eleanor Revine. " – I saw her injecting something into my wife."

"A simple mixture of base metals that destroys the nervous system," Duffy explained. "They're alive but they can't move. Not anything significant, anyways. They can open and close their eyes, and sometimes they try to speak . . . but it's all a jumble of incoherence."

Blaumlein looked at the naked man then across at the hanging bodies and, finally, at Tom Duffy. "You sound different. You've dropped – "

"The accent? I'm an educated man, Mister Blaumlein. That's not to say I'm any better than the rest of the folks here in Pump Handle . . . I just know more. Mildred and me, we've picked up some of the local colloquial parlance but when I get to talking about my work, well . . ." He assumed a hillbilly stance. "Don't seem natural not to give it its due gravitas." He laughed, straightened up and affected a quizzical expression. "Know what I mean?"

Blaumlein nodded.

"Come on, time-to-go time, I'm afraid."

Blaumlein struggled and locked his legs. "Wait!"

"What now?"

"Let me join you . . . let *me* drink the treated blood."

Duffy shook his head. "We need one more body. They die – heart failure, embolisms and so on – nothing we can do. And when their hearts are not working, they cease to be of any use. Whatever else happens, we have to keep the supply of new blood flowing into our Mayor."

"But I'm young . . . I can – "

"Age doesn't come into this. The blood gives youth no matter what the age of the person drinking it."

Blaumlein looked around at the townsfolk. "Is this it? Is this your full number?"

Duffy nodded.

"What does one more matter?" He suddenly had a thought. "And you can have the guy in the truck – *my* vampire . . . and you can have the triplets. You said you only needed *one* more. This way you'll have even *more* than you need. *And* you'll increase your own number."

"Yes, and we'll increase the number depending on the Mayor."

"But I can drive . . . there are the trucks . . ." Blaumlein realized that these were poor bargaining tools. There were undoubtedly people here who could drive . . . and they would have the trucks anyway when they . . . He tried not to think of that. "We can travel . . . I've seen lots of towns, on the way here, places we can go back to for fresh supplies . . ."

Duffy thought for a moment and looked across at the others. Eleanor Revine shrugged.

"He does have a point there, Tom," Mildred Duffy said. There was something about the way she raised her eyebrows that Blaumlein didn't like. He couldn't figure out what it was, but he knew he didn't like it.

Duffy nodded and relaxed his grip. Then he removed his hand completely from Blaumlein's shoulder and stepped back. Blaumlein rubbed his arm and shoulder, trying to get the circulation going again. "Okay," Duffy said. "But there's something I haven't mentioned."

Duffy walked around and stood with the other townsfolk. "There's one myth about vampirism that's absolutely true. Crucifixes, garlic, silver . . . all that stuff means diddly to us. But we cannot expose ourselves to the sun."

Blaumlein frowned.

"You see where I'm heading with this?"

Now Blaumlein shook his head. But the smile he had been feeling started to fade.

"The deal is you take us to these places. We'll fix up the trucks so we can travel during the day without fear of exposure . . . but you'll have to be manacled. Just for security's sake."

"But . . . how can I do that? Take you around during the day?"

"The sun won't bother you, Mister Blaumlein," Duffy said softly. "You won't be drinking any of the treated blood."

"Hey, now wait a minute . . . we agreed – "

"You're in no position to bargain, I'm afraid. But for the record, you sold yourself on the basis of chauffeur duties. We won't always be able to travel at night – distances being what they are – so the services of someone who can take sunlight would be valuable. But . . ." He shrugged. "The choice is yours. Life and some driving responsibilities, or . . ."

Blaumlein glanced up at his wife's body. It wasn't much of a decision at all. Not really.

Duffy reached under the table and pulled out a thick-linked chain with manacles at each end. He walked over to Blaumlein and stooped to fasten one of the manacles to his ankle. "Time for our rest now, Mister Blaumlein." He moved across to the first of a series of metal posts attached to the rail for the plastic sheeting and fixed the second manacle. "Sleep well. We'll see you in the evening."

"But . . . but what about food?"

"Food? Ah, yes. That was what you came here for after all. There'll be cabbage soup for supper. Then we'll go down to the trucks and bring back the others. Tomorrow we can start to make plans for travelling."

The townsfolk filed out of the barn. The last one to leave – the boy: Billy something – stopped and smiled coldly at Blaumlein. "I knew he wasn't a *real* vampire."

To Joe Blaumlein, the huge barn doors closing sounded for

all the world like a stone slab being pushed over a crypt entrance.

He turned around and saw his wife's eyes, sleepily staring straight at him. As the whispering started, he remembered he still had two bullets left.

F. Paul Wilson

The Lord's Work

F. Paul Wilson had his first short story was published in 1971, while he was studying to become a practising physician.

Since then he has also become a bestselling novelist with such science fiction, horror and thriller titles as Healer, Wheels Within Wheels, An Enemy of the State, Dydeetown World, The Tery, The Keep *(filmed in 1983),* The Tomb, Black Wind, Reborn, Reprisal, Sibs *(aka* Sister Night), Nightworld, Mirage *(with Matt Costello),* The Touch, The Select, Implant *and* Deep As the Marrow *(the latter three as by "Colin Andrews" in the UK).*

His short fiction is collected in Night Visions 6, Soft and Others *and* Ad Statum Perspicuum, *and he has edited the Horror Writers Association anthology,* Freak Show, *and* Diagnosis Terminal: An Anthology of Medical Terror.

Vampires finally rule the world. They use humans as either slaves or livestock, but there are still a few who have the courage to fight back against their Undead masters . . .

AND WHAT ARE you doing, Carole? What are you DOING? You'll be after killing yourself, Carole. You'll be blowing yourself to pieces and then you'll be going straight to hell. HELL, Carole!

"But I won't be going alone," Sister Carole Flannery muttered.

She had to turn her head away from the kitchen sink now. The fumes stung her nose and made her eyes water, but she kept on stirring the pool chlorinator into the hot water until it was completely dissolved. She wasn't through yet. She took the beaker of No Salt she'd measured out before starting the process and added it to the mix in the big Pyrex bowl. Then she stirred some more. Finally, when she was satisfied that she was not going to see any further dissolution at this temperature, she put the bowl on the stove and turned up the flame.

A propane stove. She'd seen the big white tank out back last week when she was looking for a new home; that was why she'd chosen this old house. With New Jersey Natural Gas in ruins, and JCP&L no longer sending electricity through the wires, propane and wood stoves were the only ways left to cook.

I really shouldn't call it cooking, she thought as she fled the acrid fumes and headed for the living room. *Nothing more than a simple dissociation reaction – heating a mixture of calcium hypochlorate with potassium chloride. Simple, basic chemistry.* The very subject she'd taught bored freshmen and sophomores for five years at St Anthony's high school over in Lakewood.

"And you all thought chemistry was such a useless subject!" she shouted to the walls.

She clapped a hand over her mouth. There she was, talking out loud again. She had to be careful. Not so much because someone might hear her, but because she was worried she might be losing her mind.

She'd begun talking to herself in her head – just for company of sorts – to ease her through the long empty hours. But the voice had taken on a life of its own. It was still her own voice, but it had acquired a thick Irish brogue, very similar to her dear, sweet, dead mother's.

Maybe she'd already lost her mind. Maybe all this was merely a delusion. Maybe vampires hadn't taken over the entire civilized world. Maybe they hadn't defiled her church and convent, slaughtered her sister nuns. Maybe it was all in her mind.

Sure, and you'd be wishing it was all in your mind, Carole. Of course you would. Then you wouldn't be sinning!

Yes, she truly did wish she were imagining all this. At least then she'd be the only one suffering, and all the rest would still be alive and well, just as they'd been before she went off the deep end. Like the people who'd once lived in this house. The Bennetts –

Kevin, Marie, and their twin girls. She hadn't known them before, but Sister Carole felt she knew them now. She'd seen their family photos, seen the twins' bedroom. They were dead now, she was sure. Or maybe worse. But either way, they were gone.

But if this was a delusion it was certainly an elaborate, consistent delusion. Every time she woke up – she never allowed herself to sleep too many hours at once, only catnaps – it was the same: quiet skies, vacant houses, empty streets, furtive, scurrying survivors who trusted no one, and –

What's that?

Sister Carole froze as her ears picked up a sound outside, a hum, like a car engine. She hurried in a crouch to the front door and peered through the sidelight. It *was* a car. A convertible. Someone was out driving in –

She ducked down when she saw who was in it. Scruffy and unwashed, lean and wolfish, bare chested or in cut-off sweatshirts, the driver wearing a big Texas hat, all guzzling beer. She didn't know their names or their faces, and she didn't have to see their earrings to know who – what – they were.

Collaborators. Predators. They liked to call themselves cowboys. Sister Carole called them scum of the earth.

They were headed east. Good. They'd find a little surprise waiting for them down the road.

As it did every so often, the horror of what her life had become caught up to Sister Carole then, and she slumped to the floor of the Bennett house and began to sob.

Why? Why had God allowed this to happen to her, to His Church, to His world?

Better question: Why had she allowed these awful events to change her so? She had been a Sister of Mercy.

Mercy! Do you hear that, Carole? A Sister of MERCY!

She had taken vows of poverty, chastity, and obedience, had vowed to devote her life to teaching and doing the Lord's work. But now there was no money, no one worth losing her virginity to, no Church to be obedient to, and no students left to teach.

All she had left was the Lord's work.

Believe me you, Carole, I'd hardly be calling the making of plastic explosive and the other horrible things you've been doing the Lord's work. It's killing! It's a SIN!

Maybe the voice was right. Maybe she would go to hell for what she was doing. But somebody had to make those rotten cowboys pay.

King of the world.

Al Hulett leaned back in the passenger seat of the Mercedes

convertible they'd just driven out of somebody's garage, burning rubber all the way, and let the cool breeze caress his sweaty head. Stan was driving, Artie and Kenny were in the back seat, everybody had a Heineken in his fist, and they were tooling along Route 88 toward the beach, catching some early summer rays on the way. He casually tossed his empty backward, letting it arc over the trunk, and heard it smash on the asphalt behind them. Then he closed his eyes and grooved.

The pack. Buddies. The four of them had been together since grammar school in Camden. How many years was that now? Ten? Twelve? Couldn't be more than a dozen. No way. Whatever, the four of them had stuck together through it all, never breaking up, even when Stan pulled that short jolt in Yardville on a B&E, even when the whole world went to hell.

They'd come through it all like gold. They'd hired out to the winners. They were the best hunting pack around. And Al was one of them.

King of the fucking world.

Well, not king, really. But at least a prince . . . when the sun was up.

Night was a whole different story.

But why think about the night when you had this glorious summer day all to –

"Shit! Goddam shit!"

Stan's raging voice and the sudden braking of the car yanked Al from his reverie. He opened his eyes and looked at Stan.

"Hey, motherfu– "

Then he saw him. Or, rather, it. Dead ahead. *Dead* ahead. A corpse, hanging by its feet from a utility pole.

"Oh, shit," Kenny said from behind him. "Another one. Who is it?"

"I dunno," Stan said, then he looked at Al from under the wide brim of his cowboy hat. "Whyn't you go see."

Al swallowed. He'd always been the best climber, so he'd wound up the second-story man of the team. But he didn't want to make this climb.

"What's the use?" Al said. "Whoever he is, he's dead."

"See if he's one of us," Stan said.

"Ain't it *always* one of us?"

"Then see *which* one of us it is, okay?"

Stan had this pale, cratered skin. Even though he was in his twenties he still got pimples. He looked like the man in the moon now, but in the old days he'd been a pizza face. Once he almost killed a guy who'd called him that. And he had this crazy blond hair that stuck out in all directions when he didn't cut it, but even when he cut it Mohican style like now, all shaved off on the sides and all, it looked crazier than ever. Made *Stan* look crazier than ever. And Stan was pretty crazy as it was. And mean. He'd been thinking he was hot shit ever since he got out of Yardville. His big head had got even bigger when the bloodsuckers made him pack leader. He'd been pissing Al off lately but this time he was right: Somebody had to go see who'd got unlucky last night.

Al hopped over the door and headed for the pole. What a pain in the ass. The rope around the dead guy's feet was looped over the first climbing spike. He shimmied up to it and got creosote all over him in the process. The stuff was a bitch to get off. And besides, it made his skin itch. On the way up he'd kept the pole between himself and the body. Now it was time to look. He swallowed. He'd seen one of these strung-up guys up close before and –

He spotted the earring, a blood-splattered silvery crescent moon dangling on a fine chain from the brown-crusted earlobe, an exact replica of the one dangling from his own left ear, and from Stan's and Artie's and Kenny's. Only this one was dangling the wrong way.

"Yep," he said, loud so's the guys on the ground could hear it. "It's one of us."

"Damn!" Stan's voice. "Anyone we know?"

Al squinted at the face but with the gag stuck in its mouth, and the head so encrusted with clotted blood and crawling with buzzing, feeding flies, darting in and out of the gaping wound in the throat, he couldn't make out the features.

"I can't tell."

"Well, cut him down."

This was the part Al hated most of all. It seemed almost sacrilegious. Not that he'd ever been religious or anything, but someday, if he didn't watch his ass, this could be him.

He pulled his Special Forces knife from his belt and sawed at the rope above the knot on the climbing spike. It frayed, jerked a couple of times, then parted. He closed his eyes as the body tumbled downward. He hummed Metallica's "Sandman" to blot out the sound it made when it hit the pavement. He especially hated the sick, wet sound the head made if it landed first. Which this one did.

"Looks like Benny Gonzales," Artie said.

"Yep," Kenny said. "No doubt about it. That's Benny. Poor guy."

They dragged his body over to the curb and drove on, but the party mood was gone.

"I'd love to catch the bastards who're doing this shit," Stan said as he drove. "They've gotta be close by around here somewhere."

"They could be anywhere," Al said. "They found Benny back there, killed him there – you saw that puddle of blood under him – and left him there. Then they cut out."

"They're huntin' us like we're huntin' them," Kenny said.

"But I wanna be the one to catch 'em," Stan said.

"Yeah?" said Artie from the back. "And what would you do if you did?"

Stan said nothing, and Al knew that was the answer. Nothing. He'd bring them in and turn them over. The bloodsuckers didn't like you screwing with their cattle.

Kings of the world . . . princes of the day . . .

If you could get used to the creeps you were working for, it wasn't too bad a set-up. Could have been worse, Al knew – a *lot* worse.

They all could have wound up being cattle.

Al didn't know when the vampires had started taking over. People said it began in Eastern Europe, some time after the communists got kicked out. The vampires had been building up their numbers, waiting for their chance, and when everything was in turmoil, they struck. All of a sudden it was the only thing on the news. Dracula wasn't a storybook character, he was real, and he was suddenly the new Stalin in charge of Eastern Europe.

From there the vampires spread east and west, into Russia and the rest of Europe. They were smart, those bloodsuckers. They hit the government and military bigwigs first, made them their own kind, then threw everything into chaos. Not too long after that they crossed the ocean. America thought it was ready for them but it wasn't. They hit high, they hit low, and before you knew it, they were in charge.

Well, almost in charge. They did whatever they damn well pleased at night, but they'd never be in charge around the clock because they couldn't be up and about in the daylight. They needed somebody to hold the fort for them between sunrise and sunset.

That was where Al and the guys came in. The bloodsuckers had found them hiding in the basement of Leon's pool hall one night and made them an offer they couldn't refuse.

They could be cattle, or they could be cowboys and drive the cattle.

Not much of a choice as far as Al could see.

You see, the bloodsuckers had two ways of killing folks. They had the usual way of ripping into your neck and sucking out your blood. If they got you that way, you became one of them come the next sundown. That was the method they used when they were taking over a place. They got themselves a bunch of instant converts that way. But once they had the upper hand, they changed their feeding style. Smart, those bloodsuckers. If they got too many of their kind wandering around, they'd soon have nobody to feed on – a world full of chefs with nothing to cook. So after they were in control, they'd string their victims up by their feet, slit their throats, and drink the blood as it gushed out of them. When you died that way, you stayed dead. Something they called true death.

But they'd offered Al and Stan and the guys *un*death. Be their cowboys, be their muscle during the day, herd the cattle and take care of business between sunrise and sunset, do a good job for twenty years, and they'd see to it that you got done in the old-fashioned way, the way that left you like them. Undead. Immortal. One of the ruling class.

Twenty years and out. Like the army. They gave you these crescent-moon earrings to wear, so they'd know you were on their side when they ran into you at night, and they let you do pretty much what you wanted during the days.

But the nights were theirs.

Being a cowboy wasn't so bad, really. You had to keep an eye on their nests, make sure no save-the-world types – Stan liked to call them rustlers – got in there and started splashing holy water around and driving stakes into their cold little hearts. And if you wanted brownie points, you went out each day and hunted up a victim or two to have ready for them after sundown.

Those brownie points were nothing to sneer at either. Earn enough of them and you got to spend some stud time on one of their cattle ranches – where all the cows were human. And young.

Neither Al nor Stan nor any of their pack had been to one of the farms yet, but they'd all heard it was incredible. You came back *sore.*

Al didn't particularly like working for the vampires. But he couldn't remember ever liking anybody he'd worked for. The bloodsuckers gave him the creeps, but what was he supposed to do? If you can't beat 'em, join 'em. Plenty of guys felt the same way.

But not all. Some folks took it real personal, called Al and Stan and the boys traitors and collaborators and worse. And lately it looked like some of them had gone beyond the name-calling stage and were into throat-slitting.

Benny Gonzales was the fifth one in the last four weeks.

Apparently the guys who were behind this wanted to make it look like the vampires themselves were doing the killings, but it didn't wash. Too messy. These bodies had blood all over them, and a puddle beneath them. When the bloodsuckers slit somebody's throat, they didn't let a drop of it go to waste. They licked the platter clean, so to speak.

"We gotta start being real careful," Stan was saying. "Gotta keep our eyes open."

"And look for what?" Kenny said.

"For a bunch of guys who hang out together – a bunch of guys who ain't cowboys."

Artie started singing that Willie Nelson song, "Mama, Don't Let Your Babies Grow up to be Cowboys" and it set Stan off.

"Knock it off, god damn it! This ain't funny! One of us could be next! Now keep your fucking eyes open!"

Al studied the houses drifting by as they cruised into Point Pleasant Beach. Cars sat quietly along the curbs of the empty streets and the houses appeared deserted, their empty blind windows staring back at him. But every so often they'd pass a yard that looked cared for, and those houses would be defiantly studded with crosses and festooned with garlands of garlic. And every so often you could swear you saw somebody peeking out from behind a window or through a screen door.

"You know, Stan," Al said. "I'll bet those cowboy killers are hiding in one of them houses with all the garlic and crosses."

"Maybe, Stan said. "But I kinda doubt it. Those folks tend to stay in after sundown. Whoever's behind this is working at night."

That made sense to Al. The folks in those houses hardly ever came out. They were loners. Dangerous loners. *Armed* loners. The vampires couldn't get in because of all the garlic and crosses, and the cowboys who'd tried to get in – or even take off some of the crosses – usually got shot up. The vampires had said to leave them be for now. Sooner or later they'd run out of food and have to come out. *Then* they'd get them.

Smart, those bloodsuckers. Al guessed they figured they had plenty of time to outwait the loners. All the time in the world.

They were cruising Ocean Avenue by the boardwalk area now, barely a block from the Atlantic. What a difference a year made. Last year at this time the place was packed with the summer crowds, the day-trippers and the weekly renters. Now it was deserted. The sun was high and hot but it was like winter had never ended.

They were gliding past the empty, frozen rides when Al caught of flash of colour moving between a couple of the boardwalk stands.

"Pull over," he said, putting a hand on Stan's arm. "I think I saw something."

The tires screeched as Stan made a sharp turn into Jenkinson's parking lot.

"What kind of something?"

"Something blonde."

Kenny and Artie let out cowboy whoops and jumped out of the back seat. They tossed their Heineken empties high and let them smash in glittery green explosions.

"Shut the fuck up!" Stan said. "You tryin' to queer this little round-up or what? Now you two head down to the street back there and work your way back up on the boards. Me and Al'll go up here and work our way down. Get going."

As Artie and Kenny trotted back to the Risden's Beach bath houses, Stan squared his ten-gallon hat on his head and pointed toward the miniature golf course at the other end of the parking lot. Al took the lead and Stan followed. Arnold Avenue ended here in a turret-like police station, still boarded up for the winter, but its big warning sign was still up, informing anyone who passed that alcoholic beverages and dogs and motorbikes and various other goodies were prohibited in the beach and boardwalk area by order of the mayor and city council of Point Pleasant Beach. Al smiled. The beach and the boardwalk and the sign were still here, but the mayor and the city council were long gone.

Pretty damn depressing up on the boards. The big glass windows in Jenkinson's arcade were smashed and it was dark inside. The lifeless video games stared back with dead eyes. All the concession stands were boarded up, the paralyzed rides were rusting and peeling, and it was *quiet*. No barkers shouting, no kids laughing, no squealing babes in bikinis running in and out of the surf. Just the monotonous pounding of the waves against the deserted beach.

And the birds. The seagulls were doing what they'd always done. Probably the only thing they missed was the garbage the crowds used to leave behind.

Al and Stan headed south, scouring the boardwalk as they moved. The only other humans they saw were Kenny and Artie coming up the other way from the South Beach Arcade.

"Any luck?" Stan called.

"Nada," Kenny said.

"Yo, Alphonse!" Artie said. "How many Heinies you have anyway? You seein' things now? What was it – a blonde *bird*?"

But Al knew he'd seen something moving up here, and it hadn't been no goddam seagull. But where . . .?

"Let's get back to the car and keep moving," Stan said. "Don't look like we're gonna make us no brownie points up here."

They'd all turned and were heading back up the boards when Al took one last look back . . . and saw something moving. Something small and red, rolling across the boards toward the beach from between one of the concession stands.

A ball.

He tapped Stan on the shoulder, put a finger to his lips, and pointed. Stan's eyes widened and together they alerted Artie and Kenny. Together the four of them crept toward the spot where the ball had rolled from.

As they got closer, Al realized why they'd missed this spot on the first pass. It was really two concession stands – a frozen yogurt place and a salt water taffy shop – with boards nailed up over the space between to make them look like a single building.

Stan tapped Al on the shoulder and pointed to the roof of the nearer concession stand. Al nodded. He knew what he wanted: the second-story man had to do his thing again.

Al got to the top of the chain link fence running behind the concession stands and from there it was easy to lever himself up to the roof. His sneakers made barely a sound as he crept across the tar of the canted roof to the far side.

The girl must have heard him coming, because she was already looking up when he peeked over the edge. Al felt a surge of satisfaction when he saw her blonde ponytail and long thick bangs.

He felt something else when he saw the tears streaming down her cheeks from her pleading eyes, and her hands raised, palms together, as if praying to him. She wanted him to see nothing – she was *begging* Al to see nothing.

For an instant he was tempted. The pleas in those frightened blue eyes reached deep inside and touched something there, disturbed a part of him so long unused he'd forgotten it belonged to him.

And then he saw she had a little boy with her, maybe seven years old, dark haired but with eyes as blue as hers. She was pleading for him as much as herself. Maybe more than herself. And with good reason. The vampires *loved* little kids. Al didn't understand it. Kids were smaller, had less blood than adults. Maybe their blood was purer, sweeter. Someday, when he was undead himself, he'd know.

But even with the kid there, Al might have done something stupid, might have called down to Stan and the boys that there was nothing here but some old tom cat who'd probably taken a swat at that ball and rolled it out. But when he saw that she was pregnant – *very* pregnant – he knew he had to turn her in.

As much as the bloodsuckers loved kids, they went *crazy* for babies. Infants were the primo delicacy among the vampires. Al once had seen a couple up then fighting over a newborn.

That had been a sight.

He sighed and said, "Too bad, honey, but you're packing too many points." He turned and called down toward the boardwalk. "Bingo, guys. We struck it rich."

She screamed out a bunch of hysterical "No's" and the little boy began to cry.

Al shook his head regretfully. It wasn't always a pleasant job, but a cowboy had to do what a cowboy had to do.

And besides, all these brownie points were going to bring him that much closer to some stud time at the nearest cattle farm.

Sister Carole checked the Pyrex bowl on the stove. A chalky layer of potassium chloride had formed in the bottom. She turned off the heat and immediately decanted off the boiling upper fluid, pouring it through a Mr Coffee filter into a Pyrex brownie pan. She threw out the scum in the filter and put the pan of filtrate on the window sill to cool.

She heard the sound of a car again and rushed to a window. It was the same car, with the same occupants –

No, wait. There had been only four before. Two in front and two in back. Now there were three squeezed into the back and they seemed to be fighting. And did that third head in front, sitting with the red-haired cowboy in the passenger seat, belong to a child? Oh, my Lord, yes. A child! And in the back a woman, probably his mother. Jesus, Mary and Joseph, the poor thing was pregnant!

Sister Carole suddenly felt as if something were tearing apart within her chest. Was there no justice, was there no mercy anywhere?

She dropped to her knees and began to pray for them, but in the back of her mind she wondered why she bothered. None of her prayers had been answered so far.

Sacrilege, Carole! That's SACRILEGE! Now tell me why you'd be thinking the Lord would answer the prayers of such a SINNER? God doesn't answer the prayers of a SINNER!

Maybe not, Carole thought. But if He'd answered *somebody's* prayers somewhere along the line, maybe she wouldn't have been forced to turn the Bennett's kitchen into an anarchist's laboratory.

The Lord helped those who helped themselves, didn't He? Especially when they were doing the Lord's work.

Artie and Kenny had been fighting over the blonde since they'd all left Point. She'd put up a fight at first, but she'd been nothing but a blubbering basket case for the last few miles. By the time the Mercedes hit Lakewood, Artie and Kenny were ready to start swinging at each other.

The blonde's little boy – Joey, she called him – looked up with his baby blues from where he was sitting on Al's lap and said, "Are they gonna hurt my mommy?"

Stan must have overheard. He said, "They better not if they know what's good for 'em." He looked at Al and jerked his head toward the back seat. "Straighten them out, will ya?"

Al turned in his seat and grabbed Artie since he was closest.

"You ain't gonna do shit to her, Artie!"

Artie slammed his hand away. "Yeah? And what are we gonna do? Save her for you? Bull*shit!*"

Artie could be a real asshole at times.

"We're not saving her for me," Al said. "For Gregor. You remember Gregor, don't you, Artie?"

Some of Artie's bluster faded. Gregor was the bigshot bloodsucker in charge of the Jersey Shore. One mean son of an undead bitch. You didn't mess with Gregor. Al knew Artie was probably thinking of Gregor's smile, how most times it looked painted on, how with all those sharp teeth of his he managed to look both happy and very, very hungry at the same time. Gregor was a big guy, with broad shoulders, dark hair, and a pale face. All the vampires looked pale. But that wasn't what made Al's skin crawl every time he got near one. It was something else, something you couldn't see or smell, something you *felt.* But they had to meet with Gregor every night and tell him how things had gone while he was cutting his Z's or whatever it was the bloodsuckers did when the sun was up. It was part of the job.

"Course," Artie said. "Course I know Gregor. But I don't wanna suck her blood, man," he said, jamming his hand down between the blonde's legs. "I got other things in mind. It's been a long time, man – a *long* time – and I gotta – "

"What if you screw up the baby?" Al said. "What if she starts having the baby and it's born dead? All because of you? What're you gonna tell Gregor then, Artie? How you gonna explain that to him?"

"Who says he has to know?"

"You think he won't find out?" Al said. "I tell you what, Artie. And you, too, Kenny. You guys want to get your jollies with this broad, fine. Go ahead. But if that's what you're gonna do, Stan and me are stopping the car here – right here – and walking away. Am I right, Stan?"

Stan nodded. "Fuckin' ay."

"And then you two clowns can explain any problems to Gregor yourselves tonight when we meet. Okay?"

Artie pulled his hand away from the blonde and sat on it.

"Jesus, Al. I'm hurtin' bad."

"We're all hurtin', Artie. But some of us just ain't ready yet to get killed for a little pregnant poontang, know what I mean?"

Stan seemed to think that was real funny. He laughed the rest of the way down County Line Road.

Sister Carole finished her prayers at sundown and went to check on the cooled filtrate. The bottom of the pan was layered with potassium chlorate crystals. Potent stuff. The Germans had used it in their grenades and land mines during World War One.

She got a clean Mr Coffee filter and poured the contents of the pan through it, but this time she saved the residue in the filter and let the liquid go down the drain.

Lookit after what you're doing now, Carole! You're a sick woman! SICK! You've got to be stopping this and praying to God for guidance! Pray, Carole! PRAY!

Sister Carole ignored the voice and spread out the potassium chlorate crystals in the now-empty pan. She set the oven on LOW and placed the pan on the middle rack. She had to get all the moisture out of the potassium chlorate before it would be of any use to her.

So much trouble, and so dangerous. If only her searches had yielded some dynamite, even a few sticks, everything would have been so much easier. She'd searched everywhere – hunting shops, gun stores, construction sites. She found lots of other useful items, but no dynamite. Only some blasting caps. She'd had no choice but to improvise.

This was her third batch. She'd been lucky so far. She hoped she survived long enough to get a chance to use it.

"You've outdone yourselves this time, boys."

Gregor stared at the four cowboys. Ordinarily he found it doubly difficult to be near them. Not simply because the crimson thirst made a perpetual test of being near a living font of hot, pulsing sustenance when he'd yet to feed, urging him to let loose and tear into their throats; but also because these four were so common, such low-lifes.

Gregor was royalty. He'd come over from the Old Country with the Master and had helped conquer America's East Coast. Now he was in charge of this region and was in line to expand his responsibilities. When he was moved up he would no longer be forced to deal directly with flotsam such as these. Living collaborators were a necessary evil, but that didn't mean he had to like them.

Tonight, however, he could almost say truly that he enjoyed their presence. He was ecstatic with the prizes they had brought with them.

Gregor had shown up shortly after sundown at the customary meeting place outside St Anthony's church. Of course, it didn't look much like a church now, what with all the crosses broken off. He'd found the scurvy quartet waiting for him as usual, but they had with them a small boy and – dare he believe his eyes – a pregnant woman. His knees had gone weak at the double throb of life within her.

"I'm extremely proud of all of you."

"We thought you'd appreciate it," said the one in the cowboy hat. What was his name? Stanley. That was it. Stan.

Gregor felt his grin grow even wider.

"Oh, I do. Not just for the succulence of the prizes you've delivered, but because you've vindicated my faith in you. I knew the minute I saw you that you'd make good cowboys."

An outright lie. He'd chosen them because he guessed they were low enough to betray their own kind, and he had been right. But it cost him nothing to heap the praise on them, and perhaps it would spur them to do as well next time. Maybe better. Although what could be better than this?

"Anything for the cause," Stan said.

The redheaded one next to him – Al, Gregor remembered – gave his partner a poisonous look, as if he wanted to kick him for being such a boot-lick.

"And your timing could not be better," Gregor told them. "Why? Because the Master himself is coming for a visit."

Al's mouth worked as if it had suddenly gone dry. "Dracula?"

Gregor nodded. "Himself. And I will present this gravid cow to him as a gift. He will be enormously pleased. This will be good for me. And trust me, what is good for me will eventually prove to be good for you."

Partly true. The little boy would go to the local nest leader – he'd been pastor of St Anthony's during his life and he had a taste for young boys – and the pregnant female would indeed go to the Master. But the rest was a laugh. As soon as Gregor was moved out of here, he'd never give these four walking heaps of human garbage another thought. But he smiled as he turned away.

"As always, may your night be bountiful."

A little after sundown, Sister Carole removed the potassium chlorate crystals from the oven. She poured them into a bowl and then gently, carefully, began to grind them down to a fine powder. This was the touchiest part of the process. A little too much friction, a sudden shock, and the bowl would blow up in her face.

You'd like that, wouldn't you, Carole. Sure, and you'll be thinking that would solve all your problems. Well, it won't, Carole. It will merely start your REAL problems! It will send you straight to HELL!

Sister Carole made no reply as she continued the grinding. When the powder was sifted through a 400 mesh, she spread it onto the bottom of the pan again and placed it back in the oven to remove the last trace of moisture. While that was heating she began melting equal parts of wax and Vaseline, mixing them in a small Pyrex bowl.

When the wax and Vaseline had reached a uniform consistency she dissolved the mix into some camp stove gasoline. Then she removed the potassium chlorate powder from the oven and stirred in three per cent aluminum powder to enhance the flash effect. Then she poured the Vaseline-wax-gasoline solution over the powder. She slipped on rubber gloves and began stirring and kneading everything together until she had a uniform, gooey mess. This went on the windowsill to cool and to speed the evaporation of the gasoline.

Then she went to the bedroom. Soon it would be time to go out and she had to dress appropriately. She stripped to her underwear and laid out the tight black skirt and red blouse she'd lifted from the shattered show window of that deserted shop down on Clifton Avenue. Then she began squeezing into a fresh pair of black pantyhose.

You're getting into THOSE clothes again, are you? You look cheap, Carole! You look like a WHORE!

That's the whole idea, she thought.

Al walked home. He could have driven but he liked to keep a low profile. He didn't care to have too many survivors knowing he was a cowboy. Not that there were all that many people left running around free, but until they caught up with the guys who were behind the cowboy killings, he'd play it safe. Which was why he'd removed his earring tonight, and why he lived alone.

Well, one of the reasons he lived alone.

Stan, Artie, and Kenny lived together in one of the big mansions off Hope Road. They liked to brag that one of the Mets used to live there. Big deal. Al spent all day with those guys. He couldn't see spending all night too. They were okay, but enough was enough already. He'd taken over a modest little ranch that gave him everything he needed.

Except maybe some electricity. The other three were always

yapping about the generator in their place. Maybe Al would get one. Candles and kerosene lamps were a drag.

He looked up. At least there was a moon out tonight. Almost full. Amazing how dark a residential street could be when there was no traffic, no street lights. At least he had his flashlight, but he held that in reserve. Batteries were like gold.

He'd just turned onto his block when he heard the voice. A woman's voice.

"Hey, mister."

He jammed his hand in his pocket and found his earring, ready to flash it if the owner of the voice turned out to be one of the bloodsuckers, and ready to keep it hidden if it belonged to somebody looking for a new cowboy to kill.

He clicked on his flashlight and beamed it toward the voice.

A woman standing in the bushes. Not undead. Maybe thirty, and not bad looking. He played the light up and down her. Short dark hair, lots of eye make-up, a red sweater tight over decent-sized boobs, a short black skirt very tight over black stockings.

Despite the warning bells going off in his brain, Al felt a stirring in his groin.

"Who're you?"

She smiled. No, not bad looking at all.

"My name's Carol," she said. "You got any food?"

"I got a little. Not much."

Actually, he had a *lot* of food, but he didn't want her to know that. Food was scarce, worth more than batteries, and the vampires made sure their cowboys always had plenty of it.

"Can you spare any?"

"I might be able to help you out some. Depends on how many mouths we're talking about."

"Just me and my kid."

The words jumped out before he could stop them: "You've got a kid?"

"Don't worry," she said. "She's only four. She don't eat much."

A four-year old. Two kids in one day. Almost too good to be true. The whole scenario started playing out in his mind. She could move in with him. If she treated him right, they could play house for a while. If she gave him any trouble she and her brat would become gifts to Gregor. That was where they were going to wind up anyway, but no reason Al couldn't get some use out of her before she became some bloodsucker's meal.

And maybe he'd get *real* lucky. Maybe she'd get pregnant before he turned her in.

"Well . . . all right," he said, trying to sound reluctant. "Bring her out where I can see her."

"She's home asleep."

"Alone?" Al felt a surge of anger. He already considered that kid his property. He didn't want any bloodsucker sneaking in and robbing him of what was rightfully his. "What if – ?"

"Don't worry. I've got her surrounded by crosses."

"Still, you never know. We'd better take her along to my place where she'll be safe."

Did that sound sufficiently concerned?

"You must be a good man," she said softly.

"Oh, I'm the best," he said. *And I've got this friend behind my fly who's just dying to meet you.*

He followed her back to the corner and around to the middle of the next block to an old two-storey colonial set back among some tall oaks on an overgrown lot. He nodded with growing excitement when he saw a child's red wagon parked against the front steps.

"You live here? Hell, I must've passed this place a couple of times already today."

"Really?" she said. "I usually stay hidden in the basement."

"Good thinking."

He followed her up the steps and through the front door. Inside there were candles burning all over the place, but the heavy drapes hid them from outside.

"Lynn's sleeping upstairs," she said. "I'll just run up and bring her down."

Al watched her black-stockinged legs hungrily as she bounded up the bare wooden stairway, taking the steps two at a time. He couldn't wait to get her home.

And then it hit him: Why wait till they got to his place? She had to have a bed up there. What was he doing standing around here when he could be upstairs getting himself a preview of what was to come?

"Yoo-hoo," he said softly as he put his foot on the first step. "Here comes Daddy."

But the first step wasn't wood. Wasn't even a step. His foot went right through it, as if it was made of cardboard. As Al looked down in shock he saw that it *was* made of cardboard – painted cardboard. His brain was just forming the question *Why?* when a sudden blast of pain like he'd never known in his life shot up his leg from just above his ankle.

Screaming, he lunged back, away from the false step, but the movement tripled his agony. He clung to the newel post like a drunk, weeping and moaning for God knew how long, until the pain eased for a second. Then slowly, gingerly, accompanied by the metallic clanking of uncoiling chain links, he lifted his leg out of the false tread.

Al let loose a stream of curses through his pain-clenched teeth when he saw the bear trap attached to his leg. Its sharp, massive steel teeth had embedded themselves in the flesh of his lower leg.

But fear began to worm through the all-enveloping haze of his agony.

The bitch set me up!

Stan had wanted to find the guys who were killing the cowboys. But now Al had, and he was scared shitless. What a dumbass he was. Baited by a broad – the oldest trick in the book.

Gotta get outta here!

He lunged for the door but the chain caught and brought him up short with a blinding blaze of agony so intense that the scream it elicited damn near shredded his vocal cords. He toppled to the floor and lay there moaning and whimpering until the pain became bearable again.

Where were they? Where were the rest of the cowboy killers? Upstairs, laughing as they listened to him howl like a scared kitten? Waiting until he'd exhausted himself so he'd be easy pickings?

He'd show them.

Al pulled himself to a sitting position and reached for the trap. He tried to spread its jaws but they were locked tight on his leg. He wrapped his hand around the chain and tried to yank it free from where it was fastened below but it wouldn't budge.

Panic began to grip him now. Its icy fingers were tightening on his throat when he heard a sound on the stairs. He looked up and saw her.

A nun.

He blinked and looked again

Still a nun. He squinted and saw that it was the broad who'd led him in here. She was wearing a bulky sweater and loose slacks, and all the make-up had been scrubbed off her face, but he knew she was a nun by the wimple she wore – a white band around her head with a black veil trailing behind.

And suddenly, amid the pain and panic, Al was back in grammar school, back in Our Lady of Sorrows in Camden, before he got expelled, and Sister Margaret was coming at him with her ruler, only this nun was a lot younger than Sister Margaret, and that was no ruler she was carrying, that was a baseball bat – an *aluminium* baseball bat.

He looked around. Nobody else, just him and the nun.

"Where's the rest of you?"

"Rest?" she said.

"Yeah. The others in your gang? Where are they?"

"There's only me."

She was lying. She had to be. One crazy nun killing all those cowboys? No way! But still he had to get out of here. He tried to crawl across the floor but the chain wouldn't let him.

"You're makin a mistake!" he cried. "I ain't one o' them!"

"Oh, yes you are," she said, coming down the stairs.

"No. Really. See?" He touched his right ear lobe. "No earring."

"Maybe not now, but you had one earlier." She stepped over the gaping opening where the phony tread had been and moved to his left.

"When? *When?*"

"When you drove by earlier today. You told me so yourself."

"I lied!"

"No you didn't. But I lied. I wasn't in the basement. I was watching through the window. I saw you and your three friends in that car." Her voice suddenly became cold and brittle and sharp as a straight razor. "I saw that poor woman and child you had with you. Where are they now? What did you do with them?"

She was talking through her teeth now, and the look in her eyes, the strained pallor of her face frightened the hell out of Al. He wrapped his arms around his head as she stepped closer with the bat.

"Please!" he wailed.

"*What did you do with them?*"

"Nothing!"

"*Lie!*"

She swung the bat, but not at his head. Instead she slammed it with a heavy metallic clank against the jaws of the trap. As he screamed with the renewed agony and as his hands automatically reached for his injured leg, Al realized that she must have done this sort of thing before. Because now his head was completely unprotected and she was already into a second swing. And this one was aimed much higher.

You've done it again, Carole! AGAIN! I know they're a bad lot, but look what you've DONE!

Sister Carole looked down at the unconscious man with the bleeding head and trapped, lacerated leg and she sobbed.

"I know," she said aloud.

She was so tired. She'd have liked nothing better now than to sit down and cry herself to sleep. But she couldn't spare the time. Every moment counted now.

She tucked her feelings – her mercy, her compassion – into the deepest, darkest pocket of her being where she couldn't see or hear them, and got to work.

The first thing she did was tie the cowboy's hands good and tight behind his back. Then she got a wash cloth from the downstairs bathroom, stuffed it in his mouth, and secured it with a tie of rope around his head. That done, she grabbed the crow bar and the short length of two by four from where she kept them on the floor of the hall closet; she used the bar to pry open the jaws of the bear trap and wedged the two by four between them to keep them open. Then she worked the cowboy's leg free. He groaned a couple of times during the process but he never came to.

She bound his legs tightly together, then grabbed the throw rug he lay upon and dragged him and the rug out to the front porch and down the steps to the red wagon she'd left there. She rolled him off the bottom step into the wagon bed and tied him in place. Then she slipped her arms into her knapsack loaded with all her necessary equipment and she was ready to go. She grabbed the wagon's handle and pulled it down the walk, down the driveway apron and onto the asphalt. From there on it was smooth rolling.

Sister Carole knew just where she was going. She had the spot all picked out.

She was going to try something a little different tonight.

Al screamed and sobbed against the gag. If he could just talk to her he knew he could change her mind. But he couldn't get a word past the cloth jammed against his tongue.

And he didn't have long. She had him upside down, strung up by his feet, swaying in the breeze from one of the climbing spikes on a utility pole, and he knew what was coming next. So he pleaded with his eyes, with his soul. He tried mental telepathy.

Sister, sister, sister, don't do this! I'm a Catholic! My mother prayed for me every day and it didn't help, but I'll change now, I promise! I swear on a stack of fucking Bibles I'll be a good boy from now on if you'll just let me go this time.

Then he saw her face in the moonlight and realized with a final icy shock that he truly was a goner. Even if he could make her hear him, nothing he could say was going to change this lady's mind. The eyes were empty. No one was home. The bitch was on autopilot.

When he saw the glimmer of the straight razor as it glided above his throat, there was nothing left to do but wet himself.

When Sister Carole finished vomiting, she sat on the curb and allowed herself a brief cry.

Go ahead, Carole. Cry your crocodile tears. A fat lot of good it'll do you when Judgment Day comes. No good at all. What'll you say then, Carole? How will you explain THIS?

She dragged herself to her feet. She had two more things to do. One of them involved touching the fresh corpse. The second was simpler: starting a fire to attract the other cowboys and their masters.

Gregor watched as Cowboy Stan ran in circles around his dead friend's swaying, upended corpse.

"It's Al! The bastards got Al! I'll kill them all! I'll tear them to pieces!"

Gregor wished somebody would do just that. He'd heard about these deaths but this was the first he'd seen – an obscene parody of the bloodletting rituals his nightbrothers performed on the cattle. This was acutely embarrassing, especially with the Master newly arrived from New York.

"Show yourselves!" Stan screamed into the darkness. "Come out and fight like men!"

"Someone cut him down," Gregor said.

One of the other two from Cowboy Stan's pack finished stamping out the brush fire at the base of the utility pole and began to climb.

"Let him down easy, Kenny!" Stan yelled.

"The only thing I can do is cut the rope," the one on the pole called back.

"Dammit, Al was one of *us!* Cut it slow and I'll ease him done. C'mere, Artie, and help me."

The one called Artie came over and together they caught their friend's body as it slumped earthward and –

The flash was noonday bright, the blast deafening as the shock wave knocked Gregor to the ground. His first instinct was to leap to his feet again, but he realized he couldn't see. The bright flash had fogged his night vision with a purple, amoebic after-image. He lay quiet until he could see again, then rose to a standing position.

He heard a wailing sound. The cowboy who had been on the pole lay somewhere in the bushes, screaming about his back, but the other three – the two living ones and the murdered one – were nowhere to be seen. Gregor began to brush off his clothes as he stepped forward, then froze. He was wet, covered with blood and torn flesh. The entire street was wet and littered with bits of bone, muscle, skin, and fingernail-size pieces of internal organs. There was no telling what had belonged to whom.

Gregor shuddered at the prospect of explaining this to the Master.

Tonight's murder of Al had been embarrassing enough by itself. But this . . . this was humiliating.

Sister Carole saw the flash and heard the explosion through the window over the sink in the darkened kitchen of the Bennett house. No joy, no elation. This wasn't fun. But she did find a certain grim satisfaction in learning that her potassium chlorate plastique worked.

The gasoline had evaporated from the latest batch and she was working with that now. The moon provided sufficient illumination for the final stage. Once she had the right amount measured out, she didn't need much light to pack the plastique into soup cans. All she had to do was make sure she maintained a loading density of 1.3 G./c.c. Then she stuck a 3 blasting cap in the end of each cylinder and dipped it into the pot of melted wax she had on the stove. And that did it. She now had water-proof block charges with a detonation velocity of about 3300 M/second, comparable to 40 per cent ammonia dynamite.

"All right," she said aloud to the night through her kitchen window. "You've made my life a living hell. Now it's your time to be afraid."

The Master's eyes glowed redly in the Stygian gloom of the mausoleum. Even among the Old Line of the undead, the Master was fearsome looking with his leonine mane, his thick mustache, jutting nose, and aggressive chin. But his eyes seemed to burn with an inner fire when he was angry.

His voice was barely a whisper as he pierced Gregor with his stare.

"You've disappointed me, Gregor. Earlier this evening you petitioned me for greater responsibility, but you've yet to demonstrate that you can handle what you have now."

"Master, it is a temporary situation."

"So you keep saying, but it has lasted far too long already. Besides our strength and our special powers, we have two weapons: fear and hopelessness. We cannot control the cattle by love and loyalty, so if we are to maintain our rule, it must be through the terror we inspire in them and the seeming impossibility of ever defeating us. What have the cattle witnessed in your territory, Gregor?"

Gregor feared where this was headed. "Master – "

"I'll tell you what they've witnessed, Gregor," he said, his voice rising. "They've witnessed your inability to protect the serfs we've induced to herd the cattle and guard the daylight hours for us. And trust me, Gregor, the success of one vigilante group will give rise to a second, and then a third, and before long it will be open season on our serfs. And then you'll have real trouble. Because the cattle herders are cowardly swine, Gregor. The lowest of the low. They work for us only because they see us as the victors and they want to be on the winning side at any cost. But if we can't protect them, if they get a sense that we might be vulnerable and that our continued dominance might *not* be guaranteed, they'll turn on you in a flash, Gregor."

"I know that, Master, and I'm – "

"Fix it, Gregor." The voice had sunk to a whisper again. "I will be in this territory for three days. Remedy this situation before I leave or I shall place someone else in charge. Is that clear?"

Gregor could scarcely believe what he was hearing. Removed? And to think he'd just made the Master a gift of the pregnant cow. The ungrateful –

He swallowed his anger, his hurt.

"Very clear, Master."

"Good. It is only a few hours until dawn – too late to take any action now – but I expect you to have a plan ready to execute tomorrow night."

"I will, Master."

"Leave me now."

As Gregor turned and hurried up the steps, he heard an infant begin to cry in the depths of the mausoleum. The sound made him hungry.

Sister Carole spent most of the next day working around the house. She knew it was only a matter of time before she was caught and she wanted to be ready when they came for her.

I wish they'd come for you NOW, Carole. Then this shame, this monstrous sinfulness would be over and you'd get what you DESERVE!

"That makes two of us," Sister Carole said.

She didn't want to go out again tonight but knew she had to.

Her only solace was knowing that sooner or later it was going to end – for her.

Gregor smiled as one of his assistants smeared make-up on his face. He would have preferred to have kept his plan to himself but he couldn't use a mirror and he wanted this to look right.

Scruffy clothes, a cowboy hat, a crescent-on-a-chain earring, and a ruddy complexion.

He was going to decoy these vigilante cattle into picking on him as their next cowboy victim. And then they'd be in for quite a surprise.

He could have sent someone else, could have sent out a number of decoys, but he wanted this kill for himself. After all, the Master was here, and his presence mandated bold and extraordinary measures.

He checked the map one last time. He had marked all six places where the dead cowboys had been found. The marks formed a rough circle. Gregor set out alone to wander the streets within that circle.

Miles later, Gregor was becoming discouraged. He'd walked for hours, seeing no one, living or undead. He was wondering if he should call it quits for tonight and return tomorrow when he heard a woman's voice.

"Hey, mister. Got any food?"

As Sister Carole led the cowboy back to the house, she had a feeling something was wrong. She couldn't put her finger on it, but she sensed something strange about this one. He wore the earring, he'd reacted just the way all the others had, but he'd been standoffish, keeping his distance, as if he was afraid to get too close to her. That bothered her.

Oh, well, she thought. God willing, in a few moments it would be over.

She rushed into the candlelit foyer but when she turned she found him poised on the threshold. Still standoffish. Could there be such a thing as a shy collaborator?

"Come in," she said. "Have a seat while I fetch Lynn."

As he stepped inside, she dashed upstairs, being sure to take the steps two at a time so it wouldn't look strange hopping over the first. She went straight to the bedroom and began rubbing off her make-up, all the while listening for the clank of the bear trap when it was tripped.

Finally it came and she winced as she always did, anticipating the shrill, awful cries of pain. But none came. She rushed to the landing and looked down. There she saw the cowboy ripping the restraining chain free from its nail, then reaching down and opening the jaws of the trap with his bare hands.

With her heart pounding a sudden mad tattoo in her chest, Sister Carole realized then that she'd made a terrible mistake.

She'd expected to be caught some day, but not like this. She wasn't prepared for one of *them.*

Now you've done it, Carole! Now you've really DONE IT!

Shaking, panting with fear, she dashed back to the bedroom and followed the emergency route she'd prepared.

Gregor inspected the dried blood on the teeth of the trap. Obviously it had been used before.

So this was how they did it. Clever. And nasty.

He rubbed the already healing wound on his lower leg. The trap had hurt, startled him more than anything else, but no real harm had been done. He straightened, kicked the trap into the opening beneath the faux step, and looked around.

Where were the rest of the petty revolutionaries? There had to be more than this lone woman. Or was there? The house had an empty feel.

This was almost too easy. Gregor had had a bad moment there on the threshold. He couldn't cross it unless invited across. He'd still be out there on the front porch if the silly cow hadn't invited him in.

But one woman doing all this damage? The Master would never believe it.

He headed upstairs, gliding this time, barely touching the steps. Another trap would slow him up. He spotted the rope ladder dangling over the window sill as soon as he entered the bedroom. He darted to the window and leaped through the opening. He landed lightly on the overgrown lawn and sniffed the air. She wasn't far –

He heard running footsteps, a sudden loud rustle, and saw a leafy branch flashing toward him. Gregor felt something hit his chest, pierce it, and knock him back. He grunted with the pain, staggered a few steps, then looked down. Three metal tines protruded from his sternum.

The cow had tied back a sapling, fixed the end of a pitchfork to it, and cut it free when he'd descended from the window. Crude but deadly – if he'd been human. He yanked the tines free and tossed them aside. Around the rear of the house he heard a door slam.

She'd gone back inside. Obviously she wanted him to follow. But Gregor decided to enter his own way. He hurled himself through the dining room window.

The shattered glass settled. Dark. Quiet. She was here inside. Where? Only a matter of time – a very short time – before he found her. He was making his move toward the rear rooms of the house when the silence was shattered by a bell, startling him.

He stared incredulously at the source of the noise. The telephone? But how? The first things his nightbrothers had destroyed were the communication networks. Without thinking, he reached out to it.

The phone exploded as soon as he lifted the receiver.

The blast knocked him against the far wall, smashing him into the bevelled glass of the china cabinet. Again, just as with last night's explosion, he was blinded by the flash. But this time he was hurt. His hand . . . agony . . . he couldn't remember ever feeling pain like this. And he was helpless. If she had accomplices, he was at their mercy now.

But no one attacked him, and soon he could see again.

"My hand!" he screamed when he saw the ragged stump of his right wrist.

Already the bleeding had stopped and the pain was fading, but his hand was gone. It would regenerate in time but –

He had to get out of here and get help before she did something else to him. He didn't care if it made him look like a fool, this woman was dangerous!

Gregor staggered to his feet and started for the door. Once he was outside in the night air he'd feel better, he'd regain some of his strength.

In the basement, Sister Carole huddled under the mattress and stretched her arm upward. Her fingers found a string that ran the length of the basement to a hole in one of the floorboards above, ran through that hole and into the pantry in the main hall where it was tied to the handle of an empty teacup that sat on the edge of the bottom shelf. She tugged on the string and the teacup fell. Sister Carole heard it shatter and snuggled deeper under her mattress.

What?

Gregor spun at the noise. There. Behind that door. She was hiding in that closet. She'd knocked something off a shelf in there. He'd heard her. He had her now.

Gregor knew he was hurt – *maimed* – but even with one hand he could easily handle a dozen cattle like her. He didn't want to wait, didn't want to go back without *something* to show for the night. And she was so close now. Right behind that door.

He reached out with his good hand and yanked it open.

Gregor saw everything with crystal clarity then, and understood everything as it happened.

He saw the string attached to the inside of the door, saw it tighten and pull the little wedge of wood from between the jaws of the clothespin that was tacked to the third shelf. He saw the two wires – one wrapped around the upper jaw of the clothespin and leading back to a dry cell battery, the other wrapped around the lower jaw and leading to a row of wax-coated cylinders standing on that third shelf like a collection of lumpy, squat candles with firecracker-thick wicks. As the wired jaws of the clothespin snapped closed, he saw a tiny spark leap the narrowing gap.

Gregor's universe exploded.

I'm awake! Gregor thought. I survived!

He didn't know how long it had been since the blast. A few minutes? A few hours? It couldn't have been too long – it was still night. He could see the moonlight through the hole that had been ripped in the wall.

He tried to move but could not. In fact, he couldn't feel anything. *Anything*. But he could hear. And he heard someone picking through the rubble toward him. He tried to turn his head but could not. Who was there? One of his own kind – *please* let it be one of his own kind.

When he saw the flashlight beam he knew it was one of the living. He began to despair. He was utterly helpless here. What had that explosion done to him?

As the light came closer, he saw that it was the woman, the she-devil. She appeared to be unscathed . . .

And she wore the headpiece of a nun.

She shone the beam in his face and he blinked.

"Dear sweet Jesus!" she said. Her voice was hushed with awe. "You're not dead yet? Even in this condition?"

He opened his mouth to tell her what she no doubt already knew very well: That there were only certain ways the undead could succumb to true death, and a concussive blast from an explosion was not one of them. But his jaw wasn't working right, and he had no voice.

"So what are we going to do with you, Mr Vampire?" she said. "I can't risk leaving you here for the sun to finish you – your friends might show up first and find a way to fix you up. Not that I can see how that'd be possible, but I wouldn't put anything past you vipers."

What was she saying? What did she mean? What had happened to him?

"If I had a good supply of holy water I could pour it over you, but I want to conserve what I've got."

She was quiet a moment, then she turned and walked off. Had she decided to leave him here? He hoped so. At least that way he had a chance.

But if she wanted to kill him, why hadn't she said anything about driving a stake through his heart?

Gregor heard her coming back. She had yellow rubber gloves on her hands and a black plastic bag under her arm. She rested the flashlight on a broken timber, snapped the bag open, and reached for his face. He tried to cringe away but again – no response from his body. She grabbed him by his hair and . . . lifted him. Vertigo spun him around as she looked him in the face.

"You can still see, can't you? Maybe you'd better take a look at yourself."

Vertigo again as she twisted his head around, and then he saw the hallway, or what was left of it. Mass destruction – shattered timbers, the stairs blown away, and . . .

Pieces of his body – his arms and legs torn and scattered, his torso twisted and eviscerated, his intestines stretched and torn. Gregor tried to shout out his shock, his horror, his disbelief, but he no longer had lungs.

Vertigo again, worse than before, as she dropped his head into the black plastic bag.

"What I'm going to do, Mr Vampire, is clean up as much of you as I can, and then I'm going to put you in a safe place, cool, dark, far away from the sun. Just the sort of place your kind likes."

His remaining hand was tossed into the bag and landed on his face. Then a foot, then an indescribably mutilated, unidentifiable organ, then more, and more, until what little light there was left was shut out and he was completely covered.

What was she doing? What had she meant by "just the sort of place your kind likes"?

And then the whole bag was moving, dragging across the floor, ripping as it caught on the debris.

"Here you are, Mr Vampire," she said. "Your new home."

And suddenly the bag was falling, rolling, tumbling down a set of stairs, tearing open as it went, disgorging its contents in the rough descent. More vertigo, the worst yet, as Gregor's head tumbled free and bounced down the last three steps, rolled and then lay still with his left cheek against the cellar floor.

The madwoman's voice echoed down the stairwell. "Your kind is always bragging about how you're immortal. Let's see how you like your immortality now, Mr Vampire. I've got to find another house, so I won't be around to see you anymore, but truly I wish you a long, long immortality."

Gregor wished his lungs were attached so he could scream. Just once.

Sister Carole trudged through the inky blackness along the centre of the road, towing her red wagon behind her. She'd loaded it with her Bible, her rosary, her holy water, the blasting caps, and other essentials.

You're looking for ANOTHER place? And I suppose you'll be starting up this same awful sinfulness again, won't you? When is it going to END, Carole? When are you going to STOP?

"I'll stop when they stop," Sister Carole said aloud to the night.

Jo Fletcher

Lord of the Undead

Jo Fletcher is a writer, critic, journalist and editor. An award-winning poet, her work has appeared in The Mammoth Book of Werewolves, The Mammoth Book of Frankenstein, Now We Are Sick, Voices on the Wind, The Tiger Garden: A Book of Writer's Dreams *and others. Her non-fiction has been published in* Reign of Fear, Feast of Fear, James Herbert: By Horror Haunted *and* The World's Greatest Mysteries. *She co-edited* Gaslight and Ghosts *with Stephen Jones and has recently edited* Horror at Halloween, *a mosaic novel for young adults.*

The legend of Dracula endures . . .

> In bloody dark you first were born,
> From mortal innocence were torn.
> With flash of teeth, an evil grin,
> This legend of our time begins.
>
> While man pursues his daytime dream,
> Your Children of the Night, unseen.
> Through each new moon their powers increasing,
> Yet man's own thirst for blood's unceasing.

Turns the century, Victoria's gone,
Yet still the Empire lingers on.
In dawning age of marvels bright,
You sate your hungers in the night.

The Ottoman Empire fades with dawn,
Another new republic born.
Long live the Proles, the Tsar's no more,
Watch millions die in two World Wars.

A greyer world where annihilation's
The fear that looms over every nation.
Your sensual murders still repell,
While civil wars wreak merry hell.

Your needs no longer out of place,
With serial killers commonplace.
World-wide bloodshed grows apace,
As man first walks in outer space.

There's ethnic cleansing, genocide,
A new bloodbath on every side.
As twentieth century fades away,
It seems your power's had its day.

And yet, still in nightmares dark,
The Lord of the Undead does stalk.
With gleaming fangs, hypnotic eyes,
Your fatal charm still terrifies.

As New Millennium overtakes us,
Dracula is still Prince of Darkness.
A legend forged of blood, allure,
To rule the night for ever more.